SARA PARETSKY

V. I. WARSHAWSKI

INDEMNITY ONLY

DEADLOCK

KILLING ORDERS

PENGUIN BOOKS

PENGUIN BOOKS

Published by the Penguin Group
Penguin Books Ltd, 27 Wrights Lane, London W8 5TZ, England
Penguin Books USA Inc., 375 Hudson Street, New York, New York 10014, USA
Penguin Books Australia Ltd, Ringwood, Victoria, Australia
Penguin Books Canada Ltd, 10 Alcorn Avenue, Toronto, Ontario, Canada M4V 3B2
Penguin Books (NZ) Ltd, 182–190 Wairau Road, Auckland 10, New Zealand

Penguin Books Ltd, Registered Offices: Harmondsworth, Middlesex, England

Indemnity Only first published in Great Britain by Victor Gollancz 1982
Published by Penguin Books 1987
Copyright © Sara Paretsky, 1982

Deadlock first published in Great Britain by Victor Gollancz 1984
Published by Penguin Books 1987
Copyright © Sara Paretsky, 1982

Killing Orders first published in Great Britain by Victor Gollancz 1986
Published by Penguin Books 1987
Copyright © Sara Paretsky, 1985

This collection first published by Penguin Books 1993
7 9 10 8

All rights reserved

Printed in England by Clays Ltd, St Ives plc

CONTENTS

INDEMNITY ONLY

For Stuart Kaminsky. Thanks.

CONTENTS

1
SUMMERTIME

The night air was thick and damp. As I drove south along Lake Michigan, I could smell rotting alewives like a faint perfume on the heavy air. Little fires shone here and there from late-night barbecues in the park. On the water a host of green and red running lights showed people seeking relief from the sultry air. On shore traffic was heavy, the city moving restlessly, trying to breathe. It was July in Chicago.

I got off Lake Shore Drive at Randolph Street and swung down Wabash under the iron arches of the elevated tracks. At Monroe I stopped the car and got out.

Away from the lake the city was quieter. The South Loop, with no entertainment beyond a few peepshows and the city lockup, was deserted – a drunk weaving uncertainly down the street was my only companion. I crossed Wabash and went into the Pulteney Building next to the Monroe Street Tobacco Store. At night it looked like a terrible place to have an office. The hall's mosaic-tiled walls were chipped and dirty. I wondered if anyone ever washed the scuffed linoleum floor. The lobby must create a reassuring impression on potential clients.

I pushed the elevator button. No response. I tried again. Again no response. I shoved open the heavy stairwell door, climbing slowly to the fourth floor. It was cool in the stairwell and I lingered there a few minutes before moving on down the badly lit hallway to the east end, the end where rents are cheaper because all the offices look out on the Wabash el. In the dim light I could read the inscription on the door: 'V. I. Warshawski. Private Investigator'.

I had called my answering service from a filling station on the North Side, just a routine check on my way home to a shower, air conditioning and a late supper. I was surprised when they told me I had a caller, and unhappy when they said he'd refused to give a name. Anonymous callers are a pain. They usually have something to hide, often something criminal, and they don't leave their names just so you can't find out what they're hiding ahead of time.

This guy was coming at 9.15, which didn't even give me time to eat. I'd spent a frustrating afternoon in the ozone-laden heat trying to track down a printer who owed me fifteen hundred dollars. I'd saved his firm from being muscled out by a national chain last spring and now I was sorry I'd done it. If my checking account hadn't been so damned anemic, I'd have ignored this phone call. As it was, I squared my shoulders and unlocked the door.

With the lights on my office looked spartan but not unpleasant and I cheered up slightly. Unlike my apartment, which is always in mild disarray, my office is usually tidy. I'd bought the big wooden desk at a police auction. The little Olivetti portable had been my mother's, as well as a reproduction of the Uffizi hanging over my green filing cabinet. That was supposed to make visitors realize that mine was a high-class operation. Two straight-backed chairs for clients completed the furniture. I didn't spend much time here and didn't need any other amenities.

I hadn't been in for several days and had a stack of bills and circulars to sort through. A computer firm wanted to arrange a demonstration of what computers could do to help my business. I wondered if a nice little desk-top IBM could find me paying customers.

The room was stuffy. I looked through the bills to see which ones were urgent. Car insurance – I'd better pay that. The others I threw out – most were first-time bills, a few second-time. I usually only pay the bills the third time they come around. If they want the money badly, they won't forget you. I stuffed the insurance into my shoulder bag, then turned to the window and switched the air conditioner onto high. The room went dark. I'd blown a fuse in the Pulteney's uncertain electrical system. Stupid. You can't turn an air conditioner right onto high in a building like this. I cursed myself and the building management equally and wondered whether the storeroom with the fuse boxes was open at night. During the years I'd spent in the building, I'd learned how to repair most of what could go wrong with it, including the bathroom on the seventh floor, whose toilet backed up about once a month.

I made my way back down the hall and down the stairs to the basement. A single naked bulb lit the bottom of the stairs. It showed a padlock on the supply-room door. Tom Czarnik, the building's crusty superintendent, didn't trust anyone. I can open some locks, but I didn't have time now for an American padlock. One of those days. I counted to ten in Italian, and started back upstairs with even less enthusiasm than before.

I could hear a heavy tread ahead of me and guessed it was my anonymous visitor. When I got to the top, I quietly opened the stairwell door and watched him in the dim light. He was knocking at my office door. I couldn't see him very well, but got the impression of a short stocky man. He held himself aggressively, and when he got no answer to his knocking, he opened the door without hesitation and went inside. I walked down the hallway and went in after him.

A five-foot-high sign from Arnie's Steak Joynt flashed red and yellow across the street, providing spasms of light to my office. I saw my visitor whirl as I opened the door. 'I'm looking for V. I. Warshawski,' he said, his voice husky but confident – the voice of a man used to having his own way.

'Yes,' I said, going past him to sit behind my desk.

'Yes, what?' he demanded.

'Yes, I'm V. I. Warshawski. You call my answering service for an appointment?'

'Yeah, but I didn't know it would mean walking up four flights

7

of stairs to a dark office. Why the hell doesn't the elevator work?'

'The tenants in this building are physical fitness nuts. We agreed to get rid of the elevator – climbing stairs is well known as a precaution against heart attacks.'

In one of the flashes from Arnie's I saw him make an angry gesture. 'I didn't come here to listen to a comedienne,' he said, his husky voice straining. 'When I ask questions I expect to hear them answered.'

'In that case, ask reasonable questions. Now, do you want to tell me why you need a private investigator?'

'I don't know. I need help all right, but this place – Jesus – and why is it so dark in here?'

'The lights are out,' I said, my temper riding me. 'You don't like my looks, leave. I don't like anonymous callers, either.'

'All right, all right,' he said placatingly. 'Simmer down. But do we have to sit in the dark?'

I laughed. 'A fuse blew a few minutes before you showed up. We can go over to Arnie's Steak Joynt if you want some light.' I wouldn't have minded getting a good look at him myself.

He shook his head. 'No, we can stay here.' He fidgeted around some, then sat in one of the visitors' chairs.

'You got a name?' I asked, to fill in the pause while he collected his thoughts.

'Oh, yeah, sorry,' he said, fumbling in his wallet. He pulled out a card and passed it across the desk. I held it up to read in a flash from Arnie's. 'John L. Thayer. Executive Vice-President, Trust, Ft. Dearborn Bank and Trust.' I pursed my lips. I didn't make it over to La Salle Street very often, but John Thayer was a very big name indeed at Chicago's biggest bank. Hot diggity, I thought. Play this fish right, Vic, I urged myself. Here come de rent!

I put the card in my jeans pocket. 'Yes, Mr Thayer. Now what seems to be the problem?'

'Well, it's about my son. That is, it's about his girlfriend. At least she's the one who –' He stopped. A lot of people, especially men, aren't used to sharing their problems, and it takes them a while to get going. 'You know, I don't mean any offense, but I'm not sure I should talk to you after all. Not unless you've got a partner or something.'

I didn't say anything.

'You got a partner?' he persisted.

'No, Mr Thayer,' I said evenly. 'I don't have a partner.'

'Well, this really isn't a job for a girl to take on alone.'

A pulse started throbbing in my right temple. 'I skipped dinner after a long day in the heat to meet you down here.' My voice was husky with anger. I cleared my throat and tried to steady myself. 'You wouldn't even identify yourself until I pushed you to it. You pick at my office, at me, but you can't come out and ask anything directly. Are you trying to find out whether I'm honest, rich, tough, or what? You want some references, ask for them. But don't waste my time like this. I don't need to argue you into hiring my services – it was you who insisted on making an appointment for the middle of the night.'

'I'm not questioning your honesty,' he said quickly. 'Look, I'm not trying to get your goat. But you are a girl, and things may get heavy.'

'I'm a woman, Mr Thayer, and I can look out for myself. If I couldn't, I wouldn't be in this kind of business. If things get heavy, I'll figure out a way to handle them – or go down trying. That's my problem, not yours. Now, you want to tell me about your son, or can I go home where I can turn on an air conditioner?'

He thought some more, and I took some deep breaths to calm myself, ease the tension in my throat.

'I don't know,' he finally said. 'I hate to, but I'm running out of options.' He looked up, but I couldn't see his face. 'Anything I tell you has to be strictly in confidence.'

'Righto, Mr Thayer,' I said wearily. 'Just you, me, and Arnie's Steak Joynt.'

He caught his breath but remembered he was trying to be conciliatory. 'It's really Anita, my son's girlfriend. Not that Pete – my son, that is – hasn't been a bit of a problem, too.'

Dope, I thought morosely. All these North Shore types think about is dope. If it was a pregnancy, they'd just pay for an abortion and be done with it. However, mine was not to pick and choose, so I grunted encouragingly.

'Well, this Anita is not really a very desirable type, and ever since Pete got mixed up with her he's been having some peculiar ideas.' The language sounded strangely formal in his husky voice.

'I'm afraid I only detect things, Mr Thayer. I can't do too much about what the boy thinks.'

'No, no, I know that. It's just that – they've been living together in some disgusting commune or other – did I tell you they're students at the University of Chicago? Anyway, he, Pete, he's taken to talking about becoming a union organizer and not going to business school, so I went down to talk to the girl. Make her see reason, kind of.'

'What's her last name, Mr Thayer?'

'Hill. Anita Hill. Well, as I said, I went down to try to make her see reason. And – right after that she disappeared.'

'It sounds to me like your problem's solved.'

'I wish it was. The thing is, now Pete's saying I bought her off, paid her to disappear. And he's threatening to change his name and drop out of sight unless she turns up again.'

Now I've heard everything, I thought. Hired to find a person so her boyfriend would go to business school.

'And were you responsible for her disappearance, Mr Thayer?'

'Me? If I was, I'd be able to get her back.'

'Not necessarily. She could have squeezed fifty grand out of you and gone off on her own so you couldn't get it back. Or you could have paid her to disappear completely. Or you may have killed her or caused her to be killed and want someone else to take the rap for you. A guy like you has a lot of resources.'

He seemed to laugh a little at that. 'Yeah, I suppose all that could be true. Anyway, I want you to find her – to find Anita.'

'Mr Thayer, I don't like to turn down work, but why not get

the police – they're much better equipped than I for this sort of thing.'

'The police and I –' he started, then broke off. 'I don't feel like advertising my family problems to the police,' he said heavily.

That had the ring of truth – but what had he started to say? 'And why were you so worried about things getting heavy?' I wondered aloud.

He shifted in his chair a bit. 'Some of those students can get pretty wild,' he muttered. I raised my eyebrows skeptically, but he couldn't see that in the dark.

'How did you get my name?' I asked. Like an advertising survey – did you hear about us in *Rolling Stone* or through a friend?

'I found your name in the Yellow Pages. And I wanted someone in the Loop and someone who didn't know – my business associates.'

'Mr Thayer. I charge a hundred and a quarter a day, plus expenses. And I need a five-hundred-dollar deposit. I make progress reports, but clients don't tell me how to do the job – any more than your widows and orphans tell you how to run the Fort Dearborn's Trust Department.'

'Then you will take the job?' he asked.

'Yes,' I said shortly. Unless the girl was dead, it shouldn't be too hard to find her. 'I'll need your son's address at the university,' I added. 'And a picture of the girl if you have one.'

He hesitated over that, seemed about to say something, but then gave it to me: 5462 South Harper. I hoped it was the right place. He also produced a picture of Anita Hill. I couldn't make it out in the spasmodic light, but it looked like a yearbook snap. My client asked me to call him at home to report progress, rather than at the office. I jotted his home number on the business card and put it back in my pocket.

'How soon do you think you'll know something?' he asked.

'I can't tell you until I've looked at it, Mr Thayer. But I'll get on the case first thing tomorrow.'

'Why can't you go down there tonight?' he persisted.

'Because I have other things to do,' I answered shortly. Like dinner and a drink.

He argued for a bit, not so much because he thought I'd change my mind as because he was used to getting his own way. He finally gave up on it and handed me five hundred-dollar bills.

I squinted at them in the light from Arnie's. 'I take checks, Mr Thayer.'

'I'm trying to keep people at the office from knowing I've been to a detective. And my secretary balances my checkbook.'

I was staggered, but not surprised. An amazing number of executives have their secretaries do that. My own feeling was that only God, the IRS, and my bank should have access to my financial transactions.

He got up to go and I walked out with him. By the time I'd locked the door, he had started down the stairs. I wanted to get a better look at him, and hurried after him. I didn't want to have to see every man in Chicago under a flashing neon sign to recognize my client again. The stairwell lighting wasn't that good, but under it his face appeared square and rugged. Irish-looking, I would have said, not what I would have thought of as second-in-commmand at the Fort Dearborn. His suit was expensive and well cut, but he looked more as if he'd stepped from an Edward G. Robinson movie than the nation's eighth largest bank. But then, did I look like a detective? Come to think of it, most people don't try to guess what women do for a living by the way they look – but they are usually astounded to find out what I do.

My client turned east, toward Michigan Avenue. I shrugged and crossed the street to Arnie's. The owner gave me a double Johnnie Walker Black and a sirloin from his private collection.

2

DROPPING OUT OF SCHOOL

I woke up early to a day that promised to be as hot and steamy as the one before. Four days out of seven, I try to force myself to get some kind of exercise. I'd missed the previous two days, hoping that the heat would break, but I knew I'd better get out this morning. When thirty is a fond memory, the more days that pass without exercise, the worse you feel going back to it. Then, too, I'm undisciplined in a way that makes it easier to exercise than to diet, and the running helps keep my weight down. It doesn't mean I love it, though, especially on mornings like this.

The five hundred dollars John Thayer had given me last night cheered me up considerably, and I felt good as I put on cutoffs and a T-shirt. The money helped take my mind off the thick air when I got outside. I did five easy miles – over to the lake and around Belmont Harbor and back to my large, cheap apartment on Halsted. It was only 8.30, but I was sweating freely from running in the heat. I drank a tall glass of orange juice and made coffee before taking a shower. I left my running clothes on a chair and didn't bother with the bed. After all, I was on a job and didn't have time – besides, who was going to see it?

Over coffee and some smoked herring I tried to decide how to approach Peter Thayer about his missing girlfriend. If his family disapproved of her, he would probably resent his father hiring a private detective to look into her disappearance. I'd have to be someone connected with the university – maybe in one of her classes wanting to borrow some notes? I looked pretty old for an undergraduate – and what if she wasn't registered for the summer quarter? Maybe I'd be from an underground journal, wanting her to do an article on something. Something on labor unions – Thayer had said she was trying to push Peter into being a union organizer.

I stacked my dishes by the sink and eyed them thoughtfully: one more day and I'd have to wash them. I took the garbage out, though – I'm messy but not a slob. Newspapers had been piling up for some time, so I took a few minutes to carry them out next to the garbage cans. The building super's son made extra money recycling paper.

I put on jeans and a yellow cotton top and surveyed myself in the mirror with critical approval. I look my best in the summer. I inherited my Italian mother's olive coloring, and tan beautifully. I grinned at myself. I could hear her saying, 'Yes, Vic, you are pretty – but pretty is no good. Any girl can be pretty – but to take care of yourself you must have brains. And you must have a job, a profession. You must work.' She had hoped I would be a singer and had trained me patiently; she certainly wouldn't have liked my being a detective. Nor would my father. He'd been a policeman himself, Polish in an Irish world. He'd never made it beyond sergeant, due partly to his lack of ambition, but also, I was sure, to his ancestry. But he'd expected great things of me . . . My grin went a little sour in the mirror and I turned away abruptly.

Before heading to the South Side, I walked over to my bank to deposit the five hundreds. First things first. The teller took them without a blink – I couldn't expect everyone to be as impressed with them as I was.

It was 10.30 when I eased my Chevy Monza onto the Belmont entrance to Lake Shore Drive. The sky was already bleached out, and the waves reflected back a coppery sheen. Housewives, children and detectives were the only people out at this time of day; I coasted to Hyde Park in twenty-three minutes and parked on the Midway.

I hadn't been on campus in ten years, but the place hadn't

changed much, not as much as I had. I'd read somewhere that the dirty, poverty-stricken collegiate appearance was giving way to the clean-cut look of the fifties. That movement had definitely passed Chicago by. Young people of indeterminate sex strolled by hand-in-hand or in groups, hair sticking out, sporting tattered cutoffs and torn work shirts – probably the closest contact any of them had with work. Supposedly a fifth of the student body came from homes with an annual income of fifty thousand dollars or more, but I'd hate to use looks to decide which fifth.

I walked out of the glare into cool stone halls and stopped at a campus phone to call the registrar. 'I'm trying to locate one of your students, a Miss Anita Hill.' The voice on the other end, old and creaky, told me to wait. Papers rustled in the background. 'Could you spell that name?' I obliged. More rustling. The creaky voice told me they had no student by that name. Did that mean she wasn't registered for the summer quarter? It meant they had no student by that name. I asked for Peter Thayer and was a little surprised when she gave me the Harper address – if Anita didn't exist, why should the boy?

'I'm sorry to be so much trouble, but I'm his aunt. Can you tell me what classes he might be in today? He's not home and I'm only in Hyde Park for the day.' I must have sounded benevolent, for Ms Creaky condescended to tell me that Peter was not registered this summer, but that the Political Science Department in the college might be able to help me find him. I thanked her benevolently and signed off.

I frowned at the phone and contemplated my next move. If there was no Anita Hill, how could I find her? And if there was no Anita Hill, how come someone was asking me to find her? And why had he told me the two were students at the university, when the registrar showed no record of the girl? Although maybe he was mistaken about her being at the University of Chicago – she might go to Roosevelt and live in Hyde Park. I thought I should go to the apartment and see if anyone was home.

I went back to my car. It was stifling inside and the steering wheel burned my fingers. Among the papers on the backseat was a towel I'd taken to the beach a few weeks ago. I rummaged for it and covered the steering wheel with it. It had been so long since I'd been in the neighborhood that I got confused in the one-way streets, but I eventually made it to Harper. Number 5462 was a three-story building that had once been yellow brick. The entryway smelled like an el station – musty, with a trace of urine in the air. A bag labeled Harold's Chicken Shack had been crumpled and thrown in a corner, and a few picked bones lay near it. The inner door hung loosely in its frame. It probably hadn't had a lock for some time. Its paint, once brown, had chipped and peeled badly. I wrinkled my nose. I couldn't blame the Thayers too much if they didn't like the place their son lived in.

The names on the bell panel had been hand-printed on index cards and taped to the wall. Thayer, Berne, Steiner, McGraw and Harata occupied a third-floor apartment. That must be the disgusting commune that had angered my client. No Hill. I wondered if he'd gotten Anita's last name wrong, or if she was using an assumed name. I rang the bell and waited. No response. I rang again. Still no answer.

It was noon now and I decided to take a break. The Wimpy's I remembered in the nearby shopping center had been replaced by a cool, attractive quasi-Greek restaurant. I had an excellent crabmeat salad and a glass of Chablis and walked back to the apartment. The kids probably had summer jobs and wouldn't be home until five, but I didn't have anything else to do that afternoon besides trying to find my welching printer.

There was still no answer, but a scruffy-looking young man came out as I was ringing. 'Do you know if anyone in the Thayer-Berne apartment is home?' I asked. He looked at me in a glazed way and mumbled that he hadn't seen any of them for several days. I pulled Anita's picture from my pocket and told him I was trying to track down my niece. 'She should be home right now, but I'm wondering if I have the right address,' I added.

He gave me a bored look. 'Yeah, I think she lives here. I don't know her name.'

'Anita,' I said, but he'd already shuffled outside. I leaned against the wall and thought for a few minutes. I could wait until tonight to see who showed up. On the other hand, if I went in now, I might find out more on my own than I could by asking questions.

I opened the inside door, whose lock I'd noticed that morning was missing, and climbed quickly to the third floor. Hammered on the Thayer-Berne apartment door. No answer. Put my ear to it and heard the faint hum of a window air conditioner. Pulled a collection of keys from my pocket and after a few false starts found one that turned the lock back.

I stepped inside and quietly shut the door. A small hallway opened directly onto a living room. It was sparsely furnished with some large denim-covered pillows on the bare floor and a stereo system. I went over and looked at it – Kenwood turntable and JBL speakers. Someone here had money. My client's son, no doubt.

The living room led to a hallway with rooms on either side of it, boxcar style. As I moved down it I could smell something rank, like stale garbage or a dead mouse. I poked my head into each of the rooms but didn't see anything. The hall ended in a kitchen. The smell was strongest there, but it took me a minute to see its source. A young man slumped over the kitchen table. I walked over to him. Despite the window air conditioner his body was in the early stages of decomposition.

The smell was strong, sweet and sickening. The crabmeat and Chablis began a protest march in my stomach, but I fought back my nausea and carefully lifted the boy's shoulders. A small hole had been put into his forehead. A trickle of blood had come out of it and dried across his face, but his face wasn't damaged. The back of his head was a mess.

I lowered him carefully to the table. Something, call it my woman's intuition, told me I was looking at the remains of Peter Thayer. I knew I ought to get out of the place and call the cops, but I might never have another chance to look over the apartment. The boy had clearly been dead for some time – the police could wait another few minutes for him.

I washed my hands at the sink and went back down the hall to explore the bedrooms. I wondered just how long the body had been there and why none of the inmates had called the police. The second question was partially answered by a list taped up next to the phone giving Berne's, Steiner's and Harata's summer addresses. Two of the bedrooms containing books and papers but no clothes must belong to some combination of those three.

The third room belonged to the dead boy and a girl named Anita McGraw. Her name was scrawled in a large, flowing hand across the flyleaves of numerous books. On the dilapidated wooden desk was an unframed photo of the dead boy and a girl out by the lake. The girl had wavy auburn hair and a vitality and intenseness that made the photo seem almost alive. It was a much better picture than the yearbook snap my client had given me last night. A boy might give up far more than business school for a girl like that. I wanted to meet Anita McGraw.

I looked through the papers, but they were impersonal – flyers urging people to boycott non-union-made sheets, some Marxist literature, and the massive number of notebooks and term papers to be expected in a student apartment. I found a couple of recent pay stubs made out to Peter Thayer from the Ajax Insurance Company stuffed in one drawer. Clearly the boy had had a summer job. I balanced them on my hand for a minute, then pushed them into my back jeans pocket. Wedged behind them were some other papers, including a voter registration card with a Winnetka address on it. I took that, too. You never know what may come in handy. I picked up the photograph and left the apartment.

Once outside I took some gulping breaths of the ozone-laden air. I never realized it could smell so good. I walked back to the shopping center and called the twenty-first police district. My dad had been dead for ten years, but I still knew the number by heart.

'Homicide, Drucker speaking,' growled a voice.

'There's a dead body at Fifty-four sixty-two South Harper, apartment three,' I said.

'Who are you?' he snapped.

'Fifty-four sixty-two South Harper, apartment three,' I repeated. 'Got that?' I hung up.

I went back to my car and left the scene. The cops might be all over me later for leaving, but right now I needed to sort some things out. I made it home in twenty-one minutes and took a long shower, trying to wash the sight of Peter Thayer's head from my mind. I put on white linen slacks and a black silk shirt – clean, elegant clothes to center me squarely in the world of the living. I pulled the assortment of stolen papers from my back jeans pocket and put them and the photograph into a big shoulder bag. I headed back downtown to my office, ensconced my evidence in my wall safe, then checked in with my answering service. There were no messages, so I tried the number Thayer had given me. It rang three times and a woman's voice answered: 'The number you have dialed – 674-9133 – is not in service at this time. Please check your number and dial again.' That monotonous voice destroyed whatever faith I still had in the identity of my last night's visitor. I was certain he was not John Thayer. Who was he, then, and why had he wanted me to find that body? And why had he brought the girl into it, then given her a phony name?

With an unidentified client and an identified corpse, I'd been wondering what my job was supposed to be – fall girl for finding the body, no doubt. Still . . . Ms McGraw had not been seen for several days. My client might just have wanted me to find the body, but I had a strong curiosity about the girl.

My job did not seem to include breaking the news of Peter's death to his father, if his father didn't already know. But before I completely wrote off last night's visitor as John Thayer, I should get his picture. 'Clear as you go' has ever been my motto. I pulled on my lower lip for a while in an agony of thought and finally realized where I could get a picture of the man with a

minimum of fuss and bother – and with no one knowing I was
getting it.

I locked the office and walked across the Loop to Monroe
and La Salle. The Fort Dearborn Trust occupied four massive
buildings, one on each corner of the intersection. I picked the
one with gold lettering over the door, and asked the guard for
the P R department.

'Thirty-second floor,' he mumbled. 'You got an appointment?'
I smiled seraphically and said I did and sailed up thirty-two
stories while he went back to chewing his cigar butt.

P R receptionists are always trim, well-lacquered and dressed
in the extreme of fashion. This one's form-fitting lavender
jumpsuit was probably the most outlandish costume in the bank.
She gave me a plastic smile and graciously tendered a copy of
the most recent annual report. I stuck on my own plastic smile
and went back to the elevator, nodded beneficently to the guard,
and sauntered out.

My stomach still felt a little jumpy, so I took the report over
to Rosie's Deli to read over ice cream and coffee. John L. Thayer,
Executive Vice-President, Trust Division, was pictured promi-
nently on the inside cover with some other bigwigs. He was
lean, tanned and dressed in banker's gray, and I did not have to
see him under a neon light to know that he bore no resemblance
to my last night's visitor.

I pulled some more on my lip. The police would be interviewing
all the neighbors. One clue I had that they didn't, because I had
taken it with me, was the boy's pay stubs. Ajax Insurance had
its national headquarters in the Loop, not far from where I
was now. It was three in the afternoon, not too late for business
calls.

Ajax occupied all sixty floors of a modern glass-and-steel
skyscraper. I'd always considered it one of the ugliest buildings
downtown from the outside. The lower lobby was drab, and
nothing about the interior made me want to reverse my first
impression. The guard here was more aggressive than the one
at the bank, and refused to let me in without a security pass. I

told him I had an appointment with Peter Thayer and asked what floor he was on.

'Not so fast, lady,' he snarled. 'We call up, and *if* the gentleman is here, he'll authorize you.'

'Authorize me? You mean he'll authorize my entry. He doesn't have any authority over my existence.'

The guard stomped over to his booth and called up. The news that Mr Thayer wasn't in today didn't surprise me. I demanded to talk to someone in his office. I was tired of being feminine and conciliatory, and made myself menacing enough that I was allowed to speak to a secretary.

'This is V. I. Warshawski,' I said crisply. 'Mr Thayer is expecting me.'

The soft female voice at the other end apologized, but 'Mr Thayer hasn't been in all week. We've even tried calling him at home, but no one answers.'

'Then I think I'd better talk to someone else in your office.' I kept my voice hard. She wanted to know what my business was.

'I'm a detective,' I said. 'Something rotten's going on which young Thayer wanted to talk to me about. If he's not in I'll talk to someone else who knows his job.' It sounded pretty thin to me, but she put me on hold and went off to consult someone. Five minutes later, the guard still glaring at me and fingering his gun, the soft-voiced female came back on the line, rather breathless. Mr Masters, the Claim Department vice-president, would talk to me.

The guard hated letting me go up – he even called back up to Ms Softy, in hopes I was lying. But I finally made it to the fortieth floor. Once off the elevator, my feet sank deep into green pile. I made my way through it to a reception area at the south end of the hall. A bored receptionist left her novel and shunted me to the soft-voiced young woman, seated at a teak desk with a typewriter to one side. She in turn ushered me in to see Masters.

Masters had an office big enough for the Bears to work out in, with a magnificent view of the lake. His face had the well-filled, faintly pink look a certain type of successful businessman takes on after forty-five, and he beamed at me above a well-cut gray summer suit. 'Hold my calls, Ellen,' he said to the secretary as she walked out.

I gave him my card as we exchanged firm handshakes.

'Now what was it you wanted, Miss – ah –?' He smiled patronizingly.

'Warshawski. I want to see Peter Thayer, Mr Masters. But as he's apparently not in and you've agreed to see me, I'd like to know why the boy felt he needed a private detective.'

'I really couldn't tell you that, Miss – ah – do you mind if I call you –' He looked at the card. 'What does the V stand for?'

'My first name, Mr Masters. Maybe you can tell me what Mr Thayer does here.'

'He's my assistant,' Masters obliged genially. 'Jack Thayer is a good friend of mine, and when his boy – who's a student at the University of Chicago – needed summer work, I was glad to help out.' He adjusted his features to look sorrowful. 'Certainly if the boy is in the kind of trouble that it takes a detective to solve, I think I should know about it.'

'What kinds of things does Mr Thayer do as your assistant? Settle claims?'

'Oh, no,' he beamed. 'That's all done at our field locations. No, we handle the business side of the business – budgets, that kind of thing. The boy adds up figures for me. And he does good staff work – reviews reports, et cetera. He's a good boy – I hope he's not in trouble with those hippies he runs around with down there.' He lowered his voice. 'Between you and me, Jack says they've given him a bad idea of the business world. The big point about this summer job was to give him a better picture of the business world from the inside.'

'And has it?' I asked.

'I'm hopeful. Miss – ah – I'm hopeful.' He rubbed his hands together. 'I certainly wish I could help you . . . If you could give me a clue about what was bothering the boy?'

I shook my head. 'He didn't say . . . Just called me and asked if I could stop by this afternoon. There wouldn't be anything going on here that he'd feel would require a detective, would there?'

'Well, a department head often doesn't know what's going on in his own department.' Masters frowned importantly. 'You're too remote – people don't confide in you.' He smiled again. 'But I'd be very surprised.'

'Why did you want to see me?' I asked.

'Oh, I promised Jack Thayer I'd keep an eye on his boy, you know. And when a private detective comes around, it sounds kind of serious. Still, I wouldn't worry about it too much, Miss – ah – although maybe we could hire you to find out where Peter's gone.' He chuckled at his joke. 'He hasn't been in all week, you know, and we can't reach him at home. I haven't told Jack yet – he's disappointed enough in the boy as it is.'

He ushered me down the hall and back to the elevator. I rode down to the thirty-second floor, got off, and rode back up. I strolled back down the hall.

'I'd like to see where young Thayer sits,' I told Ellen. She looked at Masters's door for guidance, but it was shut.

'I don't think –'

'Probably not,' I interrupted. 'But I'm going to look around his desk anyway. I can always get someone else to tell me where it is.'

She looked unhappy, but took me over to a partitioned cubicle. 'You know, I'm going to be in trouble if Mr Masters comes out and finds you here,' she said.

'I don't see why,' I told her. 'It's not your fault. I'll tell him you did your best to force me off the floor.'

Peter Thayer's desk was unlocked. Ellen stood watching me for a few minutes as I pulled open the drawers and sorted through the papers. 'You can search me on my way out to see if I've taken anything,' I told her without looking up. She sniffed, but walked back to her own desk.

These papers were as innocuous as those in the boy's apartment. Numerous ledger sheets with various aspects of the department's budget added up, a sheaf of computer printouts that dealt with Workers' Compensation case estimates, correspondence to Ajax claim handlers – 'Dear Mr So-and-So, please verify the case estimates for the following claimants.' Nothing you'd murder a boy for.

I was scratching my head over these slim pickings, wondering what to do next, when I realized someone was watching me. I looked up. It wasn't the secretary.

'You're certainly a lot more decorative than young Thayer,' my observer remarked. 'You taking his place?'

The speaker was in his shirt sleeves, a man in his thirties who didn't have to be told how good-looking he was. I appreciated his narrow waist and the way his Brooks Brothers trousers fit.

'Does anyone around here know Peter Thayer at all well?' I asked.

'Yardley's secretary is making herself sick over him, but I don't know whether she knows him.' He moved closer. 'Why the interest? Are you with the IRS? Has the kid omitted taxes on some of the vast family holdings deeded to him? Or absconded with Claim Department funds and made them over to the revolutionary committee?'

'You're in the right occupational ball park,' I conceded, 'and he has, apparently, disappeared. I've never talked to him,' I added carefully. 'Do you know him?'

'Better than most people around here.' He grinned cheerfully and seemed likeable despite his arrogance. 'He supposedly did legwork for Yardley – Yardley Masters – you were just seen talking to him. I'm Yardley's budget manager.'

'How about a drink?' I suggested.

He looked at his watch and grinned again.

'You've got a date, little lady.'

His name was Ralph Devereux. He was a suburbanite who had only recently moved to the city, following a divorce that left his wife in possession of their Downers Grove house, he informed in the elevator. The only Loop bar he knew was Billy's, where the Claim Department hung out. I suggested the Golden Glow a little farther west, to avoid the people he knew. As we walked down Adams Street I bought a *Sun-Times*.

The Golden Glow is an oddity in the South Loop. A tiny saloon dating back to the last century, it still has a mahogany horseshoe-shaped bar where serious drinkers sit. Eight or nine little tables and booths are crammed in along the walls, and a couple of real Tiffany lamps, installed when the place was built, provide a homey glow. Sal, the bartender, is a magnificent black woman, close to six feet tall. I've watched her break up a fight with just a word and a glance – no one messes with Sal. This afternoon she wore a silver pantsuit. Stunning.

She greeted me with a nod and brought a shot of Black Label to the booth. Ralph ordered a gin and tonic. Four o'clock is a little early, even for the Golden Glow's serious-drinking clientele, and the place was mostly deserted.

Devereux placed a five-dollar bill on the table for Sal. 'Now tell me why a gorgeous lady like yourself is interested in a young kid like Peter Thayer.'

I gave him back his money. 'Sal runs a tab for me,' I explained. I thumbed through the paper. The story hadn't come in soon enough for the front page, but they'd given it two quarter columns on page seven. RADICAL BANKING HEIR SHOT, the headline read. Thayer's father was briefly mentioned in the last paragraph; his four roommates and their radical activities were given the most play. The Ajax Insurance Company was not mentioned at all.

I folded the paper back and showed the column to Devereux. He glanced at it briefly, then did a double take and snatched the paper from me. I watched him read the story. It was short and he must have gone through it several times. Then he looked up at me, bewildered.

'Peter Thayer? Dead? What is this?'

'I don't know. I'd like to find out.'

'You knew when you bought the paper?'

I nodded. He glanced back down at the story, then at me. His mobile face looked angry.

'How did you know?'

'I found the body.'

'Why the hell didn't you tell me over at Ajax instead of putting me through this charade?' he demanded.

'Well, anyone could have killed him. You, Yardley Masters, his girlfriend . . . I wanted to get your reaction to the news.'

'Who the hell *are* you?'

'My name's V. I. Warshawski. I'm a private detective and I'm looking into Peter Thayer's death.' I handed him a business card.

'You? You're no more a detective than I am a ballet dancer,' he exclaimed.

'I'd like to see you in tights and a tutu,' I commented, pulling out the plastic-encased photostat of my private investigator's license. He studied it, then shrugged without speaking. I put it back in my wallet.

'Just to clear up the point, Mr Devereux, did you kill Peter Thayer?'

'No, I goddamn did not kill him.' His jaw worked angrily. He kept starting to talk, then stopping, unable to put his feelings into words.

I nodded at Sal and she brought us a couple more drinks. The bar was beginning to fill up with precommute drinkers. Devereux drank his second gin and relaxed somewhat. 'I'd like to have seen Yardley's face when you asked him if he killed Peter,' he commented dryly.

'I didn't ask him. I couldn't figure out why he wanted to talk to me, though. Was he really very protective of Thayer? That's what he intimated.'

'No.' He considered the question. 'He didn't pay much attention to him. But there was the family connection . . . If Peter was in trouble, Yardley'd feel he owed it to John Thayer to look after him . . . Dead . . . he was a hell of a nice boy, his radical ideas notwithstanding. Jesus, this is going to cut up Yardley. His old man, too. Thayer didn't like the kid living where he did – and now, shot by some junkie . . .'

'How do you know his father didn't like it?'

'Oh, it wasn't any secret. Shortly after Pete started with us, Jack Thayer came storming in showing his muscle and bellowing around like a vice-president in heat – how the kid was betraying the family with his labor-union talk, and why couldn't he live in a decent place – I guess they'd bought a condo for him down there, if you can believe that. I must say, the boy took it very well – didn't blow up back or anything.'

'Did he work with any – well, highly confidential – papers at Ajax?'

Devereux was surprised. 'You're not trying to link his death with Ajax, are you? I thought it was pretty clear that he was shot by one of those drug addicts who are always killing people in Hyde Park.'

'You make Hyde Park sound like the site of the Tong Wars, Mr Devereux. Of the thirty-two murders in the twenty-first police district last year, only six were in Hyde Park – one every two months. I don't think Peter Thayer is just the neighborhood's July–August statistic.'

'Well, what makes you think it's connected with Ajax, then?'

'I don't think so. I'm just trying to eliminate the possibilities . . . Have you ever seen a dead body – or at least a body that got that way because of a bullet?' He shook his head and moved defensively in his chair. 'Well, I have. And you can often tell from the way the body lies whether the victim was trying to fight off the attacker. Well, this boy was sitting at his kitchen table in a white shirt – probably ready to come down here Monday morning – and someone put a little hole smack in the middle of his head. Now a professional might have done that, but even so, he'd have to bring along someone whom the boy knew, to get his confidence. It could've been you, or Masters, or his father, or his girlfriend . . . I'm just trying to find out why it couldn't be you.'

He shook his head. 'I can't do anything to prove it. Except that I don't know how to handle a gun – but I'm not sure I could prove that to you.'

I laughed. 'You probably could . . . What about Masters?'

27

'Yardley? Come on! The guy's one of the most respected people you could hope to find at Ajax.'

'That doesn't preclude his being a murderer. Why don't you let me know more about what Peter did there?'

He protested some more, but he finally agreed to tell me about his work and what Peter Thayer had done for him. It just didn't seem to add up to murder. Masters was responsible for the financial side of the claim operation, reserving and so on, and Peter had added up numbers for him, checking office copies of issued drafts against known reserves for various claims, adding up overhead items in the field offices to see where they were going over budget, and all the dull day-to-day activities that businesses need in order to keep on going. And yet . . . and yet . . . Masters had agreed to see me, an unknown person, and a detective besides, on the spur of the moment. If he hadn't known Peter was in trouble – or even, maybe, known he was dead – I just couldn't believe his obligation to John Thayer would make him do that.

I contemplated Devereux. Was he just another pretty face, or did he know anything? His anger had seemed to me the result of genuine shock and bewilderment at finding out the boy was dead. But anger was a good cover for other emotions too . . . For the time being I decided to classify him as an innocent bystander.

Devereux's native Irish cockiness was starting to return – he began teasing me about my job. I felt I'd gotten all I could from him until I knew enough to ask better questions, so I let the matter drop and moved on to lighter subjects.

I signed the bar tab for Sal – she sends me a bill once a month – and went on to the Officers' Mess with Devereux for a protracted meal. It's Indian, and to my mind one of the most romantic restaurants in Chicago. They make a very nice Pimm's Cup, too. Coming on top of the Scotch, it left me with a muzzy impression of dancing at a succession of North Side discos. I might have had a few more drinks. It was after one when I returned, alone, to my apartment. I was glad just to fling my clothes onto a chair and fall into bed.

3
THAT PROFESSIONAL
TOUCH

Peter Thayer was protesting capitalist oppression by running wildly up and down the halls at Ajax, while Anita McGraw stood to one side carrying a picket sign and smiling. Ralph Devereux came out of his office and shot Thayer. The shot reverberated in the halls. It kept ringing and ringing and I tried seizing the gun from Devereux and throwing it away, but the sound continued and I jerked awake. The doorbell was shrilling furiously. I slid out of bed and pulled on jeans and a shirt as a loud knock sounded. The fuzziness in my mouth and eyes told me I'd had one or two Scotches too many too late in the evening before. I stumbled to the front room and looked through the peephole as heavy fists hammered the door again.

Two men were outside, both beefy, with jacket sleeves too short and hair crew-cut. I didn't know the younger one on the right, but the older one on the left was Bobby Mallory, Homicide lieutenant from the twenty-first district. I fumbled the lock open and tried to smile sunnily.

'Morning, Bobby. What a nice surprise.'

'Good morning, Vicki. Sorry to drag you out of bed,' Mallory said with heavy humor.

'Not at all, Bobby – I'm always glad to see you.' Bobby Mallory had been my dad's closest friend on the force. They'd started on the same beat together back in the thirties, and Bobby hadn't forgotten Tony even after promotions had moved him out of my dad's work life. I usually have Thanksgiving dinner with him and Eileen, his warmly maternal wife. And his six children and four grandchildren.

Most of the time Bobby tries to pretend I'm not working, or at least not working as an investigator. Now he was looking past me, not at me. 'This is Sergeant John McGonnigal,' he said heartily, waving his arm loosely in McGonnigal's direction. 'We'd like to come in and ask you a few questions.'

'Certainly,' I said politely, wishing my hair weren't sticking out in different directions all over my head. 'Nice to meet you, Sergeant. I'm V. I. Warshawski.'

McGonnigal and I shook hands and I stood back to let them into the small entryway. The hallway behind us leads straight back to the bathroom, with the bedroom and living rooms opening off to the right, and the dining room and kitchen to the left. This way in the mornings I can stumble straight from bedroom to bathroom to kitchen.

I took Bobby and McGonnigal to the kitchen and put on some coffee. I casually whisked some crumbs off the kitchen table and rummaged in the refrigerator for pumpernickel and cheddar cheese. Behind me, Bobby said, 'You ever clean up this dump?'

Eileen is a fanatical housekeeper. If she didn't love to watch people eat, you'd never see a dirty dish in their house. 'I've been working,' I said with what dignity I could muster, 'and I can't afford a housekeeper.'

Mallory looked around in disgust. 'You know, if Tony had turned you over his knee more often instead of spoiling you rotten, you'd be a happy housewife now, instead of playing at detective and making it harder for us to get our job done.'

'But I'm a happy detective, Bobby, and I made a lousy house-wife.' That was true. My brief foray into marriage eight years ago had ended in an acrimonious divorce after fourteen months: some men can only admire independent women at a distance.

'Being a detective is not a job for a girl like you, Vicki – it's not fun and games. I've told you this a million times. Now you've got yourself messed up in a murder. They were going to send Althans out to talk to you, but I pulled my rank to get the assignment. That still means you've got to talk. I want to know what you were doing messing around with the Thayer boy.'

'Thayer boy?' I echoed.

'Grow up, Vicki,' Mallory advised. 'We got a pretty good description of you from that doped-out specimen on the second floor you talked to on your way into the building. Drucker, who took the squeal, thought it might be your voice when he heard the description . . . And you left your thumbprint on the kitchen table.'

'I always said crime didn't pay, Bobby. You guys want some coffee or eggs or anything?'

'We already ate, clown. Working people can't stay in bed like sleeping beauty.'

It was only 8.10, I noticed, looking at the wooden clock next to the back door. No wonder my head felt so woolly. I methodically sliced cheese, green peppers and onions, put them on the pumpernickel, and put the open-faced sandwich under the broiler. I kept my back to Bobby and the sergeant while I waited for the cheese to melt, then transferred the whole thing to a plate and poured myself a cup of coffee. From his breathing I could tell Bobby's temper was mounting. His face was red by the time I put my food on the table and straddled a chair opposite him.

'I know very little about the Thayer boy, Bobby,' I apologized. 'I know he used to be a student at the University of Chicago, and that he's dead now. And I knew he's dead because I read it in the *Sun-Times*.'

'Don't be cute with me, Vicki; you know he's dead because you found the body.'

I swallowed a mouthful of toasted cheese and green pepper. 'Well, I assumed after reading the *Sun-Times* story that the boy was Thayer, but I certainly didn't know that when I saw the body. To me, he seemed to be just another corpse. Snuffed out in the springtime of life,' I added piously.

'Spare me his funeral oration and tell me what brought you down there,' Mallory demanded.

'You know me, Bobby – I have an instinct for crime. Where evil flourishes, there I will be, on my self-appointed mission to stamp it out.'

Mallory turned redder. McGonnigal coughed diffidently and changed the subject before his boss hemorrhaged. 'Do you have a client of some kind, Miss Warshawski?' he asked.

Of course I'd seen this one coming, but I still wasn't sure what I wanted to do. However, she who hesitates is lost in the detective biz, so I opted for partial disclosure.

'I was hired to get Peter Thayer to agree to go to business school.' Mallory choked. 'I'm not lying, Bobby,' I said earnestly. 'I went down there to meet the kid. And the door to his apartment was open, so I –'

'When you got there or after you'd picked the lock?' Mallory interrupted.

'So I went in,' I continued. 'Anyway, I guess I failed in my assignment, since I don't think Peter Thayer will ever go to business school. I'm not sure I still have a client.'

'Who hired you, Vicki?' Mallory was talking more quietly now. 'John Thayer?'

'Now why would John Thayer want to hire me, Bobby?'

'You tell me that, Vicki. Maybe he wanted some dirt to use as a lever to pry the kid off those potheads down there.'

I swallowed the rest of my coffee and looked at Mallory squarely. 'A guy came to me night before last and told me he was John Thayer. He wanted me to find his son's girlfriend, Anita. Anita Hill.'

'There's no Anita Hill in that setup,' McGonnigal volunteered. 'There's an Anita McGraw. It looks like he was sharing a room with a girl, but the whole setup is so unisex you can't tell who was with who.'

'Whom,' I said absently. McGonnigal looked blank. 'You can't tell who was with *whom*, Sergeant,' I explained. Mallory made explosive noises. 'Anyway,' I added hastily, 'I was beginning to suspect that the guy had sent me on a wildgoose chase when I found there was no Anita Hill at the university. Later I was sure of it.'

'Why?' Mallory demanded.

'I got a copy of Thayer's picture from the Fort Dearborn Bank and Trust. He wasn't my client.'

'Vicki,' Mallory said. 'I think you're a pain in the butt. I think Tony would turn in his grave if he knew what you were doing. But you're not a fool. Don't tell me you didn't ask for any identification.'

'He gave me his card and his home phone and a retainer. I figured I could get back to him.'

'Let me see the card,' Mallory demanded. Suspicious bastard.

'It's his card,' I said.

'Could I please see it anyway.' Tone of father barely restraining himself with recalcitrant child.

'It won't tell you anything it didn't tell me, Bobby.'

'I don't believe he gave you a card,' Mallory said. 'You knew the guy and you're covering for him.'

I shrugged and went to the bedroom and got the card out of my top drawer. I wiped it clean of prints with a scarf and brought it back to Mallory. The Fort Dearborn logo was in the lower left-hand corner. 'John L. Thayer. Executive Vice-President, Trust' was in the middle, with his phone number. On the bottom I had scribbled the alleged home number.

Mallory grunted with satisfaction and put it in a plastic bag. I didn't tell him the only prints on it at this point were mine. Why spoil one of his few pleasures?

Mallory leaned forward. 'What are you going to do next?'

'Well, I don't know. I got paid some money to find a girl and I feel like I ought to find her.'

'You going to ask for a revelation, Vicki?' Mallory said with heavy humor. 'Or do you have something to go on?'

'I might talk to some people.'

'Vicki, if you know anything that you're not telling me in connection with this murder –'

'You'll be the first to know, Bobby,' I promised. That wasn't exactly a lie, because I didn't know for sure that Ajax was involved in the murder – but we all have our own ideas on what's connected to what.

'Vicki, we're on the case. You don't have to prove anything to me about how cute or clever you are. But do me a favor – do a favor for Tony – let Sergeant McGonnigal and me find the murderer.'

I stared limpidly at Bobby. He leaned forward earnestly. 'Vicki, what did you notice about the body?'

'He'd been shot, Bobby. I didn't do a post mortem.'

'Vicki, for two cents I'd kick you in your cute little behind. You've made a career out of something which no nice girl would touch, but you're no dummy. I know when you – got yourself into that apartment – and we'll overlook just how you got in there right now – you didn't scream or throw up, the way any decent girl would. You looked the place over. And if something didn't strike you straight off about that corpus, you deserve to go out and get your head blown off.'

I sighed and slouched back in the chair. 'Okay, Bobby: the kid was set up. No dope-crazed radical fired that shot. Someone he knew, whom he would invite to sit down for a cup of coffee, had to be there. To my mind, a pro fired the shot, because it was perfectly done – just one bullet and right on the target – but someone he knew had to be along. Or it could have been an acquaintance who's a heck of a marksman . . . You looking into his family?'

Mallory ignored my question. 'I figured you'd work that out. It's because you're smart enough to see how dangerous this thing could be that I'm asking you to leave it alone.' I yawned. Mallory was determined not to lose his temper. 'Look, Vicki, stay out of that mess. I can smell organized crime, organized labor, a whole lot of organizations that you shouldn't mess with.'

'You figure because the boy's got radical friends and waves some posters he's glued into organized labor? Come on, Bobby!'

Mallory's struggle between the desire to get me out of the

Thayer case and the need to keep police secrets to himself showed on his face. Finally he said, 'We have evidence that the kids were getting some of their posters from a firm which does most of the printing for the Knifegrinders.'

I shook my head sorrowfully. 'Terrible.' The International Brotherhood of Knifegrinders was notorious for their underworld connections. They'd hired muscle in the rough-and-tumble days of the thirties and had never been able to get rid of them since. As a result most of their elections and a lot of their finances were corrupt and – and suddenly it dawned on me who my elusive client was, why Anita McGraw's name sounded familiar, and why the guy had picked me out of the Yellow Pages. I leaned farther back in my chair but said nothing.

Mallory's face turned red. 'Vicki, if I find you crossing my path on this case, I'm going to run you in for your own good!' He stood so violently that his chair turned over. He motioned to Sergeant McGonnigal and the two slammed the door behind them.

I poured myself another cup of coffee and took it into the bathroom with me where I dumped a generous dollop of Azuree mineral salts into the tub and ran myself a hot bath. As I sank into it, the after effects of my late-night drinking seeping out of my bones, I recalled a night more than twenty years ago. My mother was putting me to bed when the doorbell rang and the man who lived in the apartment below us staggered in. A burly man my dad's age, maybe younger – all big men seem old to little girls. I'd peeped around the door because everyone was making such a commotion and seen him covered with blood before my mother rounded on me and hustled me into the bedroom. She stayed there with me and together we heard snatches of conversation: The man had been shot, possibly by management-hired thugs, but he was afraid to go to the police officially because he'd hired thugs himself, and would my dad help him.

Tony did, fixing up the wound. But he ordered him – unusual in a man usually so gentle – to leave the neighborhood and never come around to us again. The man was Andrew McGraw.

I'd never seen him again, never even connected him with the McGraw who was now president of Local 108 and hence, in effect, of the whole union. But he'd obviously remembered my dad. I guessed he'd tried to reach Tony at the police and, when he'd learned my dad was dead, had pulled me out of the Yellow Pages, assuming I would be Tony's son. Well, I wasn't: I was his daughter, and not the easygoing type my dad had been. I have my Italian mother's drive, and I try to emulate her insistence on fighting battles to the finish. But regardless of what kind of person I am, McGraw might be finding himself now in trouble of the kind that not even easygoing Tony would have helped him out of.

I drank some more coffee and flexed my toes in the water. The bath shimmered turquoise, but clear. I peered through it at my feet, trying to figure out what I knew. McGraw had a daughter. She probably loved him, since she seemed dedicated to the labor movement. Children usually do not espouse causes or careers of parents they hate. Had she disappeared, or was he hiding her? Did he know who had killed young Peter and had she run away because of this? Or did he think she'd killed the boy? Most murders, I reminded myself, were committed between loved ones, which made her statistically the odds-on favorite. What were McGraw's connections with the hired muscle with whom the International Brotherhood lived so cozily? How easily could he have hired someone to fire that shot? He was someone the boy would let in and talk to, no matter what their feelings for each other were, because McGraw was his girlfriend's father.

The bathwater was warm, but I shivered as I finished my coffee.

4

YOU CAN'T SCARE ME (I'M STICKING TO THE UNION)

The headquarters of the International Brotherhood of Knife-grinders, Shear Edgers and Blade Sharpeners is located on Sheridan Road just south of Evanston. The ten-story building was put up about five years ago, and is sided with white Italian marble. The only other building in Chicago built with such opulence is the headquarters for Standard of Indiana; I figured that put the brotherhood's excess profits on a par with those of the oil industry.

Local 108 headquarters was on the ninth floor. I gave the floor receptionist my card. 'Mr McGraw is expecting me,' I told her. I was shunted down the north corridor. McGraw's secretary was guarding the entrance to a lakeside office in an antechamber that would have done Louis XIV proud. I wondered how the International Brothers felt when they saw what their dues had built for them. Or maybe there were some beaten-up offices lower down for entertaining the rank and file.

I gave my card to the secretary, a middle-aged woman with gray sausage curls and a red-and-white dress that revealed an unlovely sag in her upper arms. I keep thinking I should lift five-pound weights to firm up my triceps. Looking at her, I wondered if I would have time to stop at Stan's Sporting Goods on my way home to pick up some barbells.

'I have an appointment with Mr McGraw.'

'You're not in the book,' she said abruptly, not really looking at me. I had on my navy raw silk suit, with the blouson jacket. I look stunning in this outfit and thought I deserved a little more attention. Must be those sagging triceps.

I smiled. 'I'm sure you know as well as I do that Mr McGraw conducts some of his business on his own. He arranged to see me privately.'

'Mr McGraw may sometimes take up with whores,' she said, her face red, her eyes on her desk top, 'but this is the first time he's ever asked one up to his office.'

I restrained an impulse to brain her with her desk lamp. 'Good-looking lady like you in his front office, he doesn't need outside talent . . . Now will you please inform Mr McGraw that I'm here?'

Her shapeless face shook under the thick pancake. 'Mr McGraw is in conference and can't be disturbed.' Her voice trembled. I felt like a creep – I couldn't find a girl or a murderer, but I sure knew how to rough up middle-aged secretaries.

McGraw's office was soundproofed, but noise of the conference came into the antechamber. Quite a conference. I was about to announce my intention of sitting and waiting when one sentence rose above the din and penetrated the rosewood door.

'Goddamnit, you set my son up!'

How many people could possibly have sons who might have been set up in the last forty-eight hours and be connected with the Knifegrinders? Maybe more than one, but the odds were against it. With the sausage curls protesting loudly, I opened the door into the inner office.

Not as large as Masters's, but by no means shabby, it overlooked Lake Michigan and a nice little private beach. At the moment it was none too peaceful. Two men had been sitting at a round table in the corner, but one was on his feet, yelling to make his point. Even with his face distorted by anger I didn't have any trouble recognizing the original of the picture in the Fort Dearborn Trust's annual report. And rising to his feet and yelling back as I entered was surely my client. Short, squat without being fat, and wearing a shiny gray suit.

They both stopped cold as they saw me.

'What the hell are you doing in here!' my client roared. 'Mildred?'

Sausage curls waddled in, her eyes gleaming. 'I told her you wouldn't want to see her, but no, she has to come barging in like she's –'

'Mr McGraw, I am V. I. Warshawski.' I pitched my voice to penetrate the din. 'And you may not want to see me, but I look like an angel compared to a couple of homicide dicks who're going to be after you pretty soon . . . Hi, Mr Thayer,' I added, holding out a hand. 'I'm sorry about your son – I'm the person who found the body.'

'It's all right, Mildred,' McGraw said weakly. 'I know this lady and I do want to talk to her.' Mildred gave me a furious look, then turned and stalked out, shutting the door with what seemed unnecessary violence.

'Mr Thayer, what makes you think Mr McGraw set your son up?' I asked conversationally, seating myself in a leather armchair in a corner.

The banker had recovered himself. The anger had smoothed out of his face, leaving it dignified and blank. 'McGraw's daughter was going out with my son,' he said, smiling a little. 'When I learned my boy was dead, had been shot, I just stepped in to see if McGraw knew anything about it. I don't think he set Peter up.'

McGraw was too angry to play along with Thayer. 'The hell you say,' he yelled, his husky voice rising. 'Ever since Annie started hanging around with that whey-faced, North Shore pipsqueak, you've been coming around here, calling her names, calling me names. Now the kid is dead, you're trying to smear her! Well, by God you won't get away with it!'

'All right!' Thayer snapped. 'If that's the way you want to play ball, that's how we'll play it. Your daughter – I saw the kind of girl she was the first time I set eyes on her. Peter never had a chance – innocent young kid, high ideals, giving up everything his mother and I had planned for him for the sake of a girl who'd hop into bed with –'

'Watch what names you call my daughter,' McGraw growled.

'I practically begged McGraw here to leash his daughter,' Thayer continued. 'I might as well have saved my pride. This type of person doesn't respond to any human feeling. He and his daughter had earmarked Peter for some kind of setup because he came from a wealthy family. Then, when they couldn't get any money out of him, they killed him.'

McGraw was turning purple. 'Have you shared this theory with the police, Mr Thayer?' I asked.

'If you have, Thayer, I'll have your ass in court for slander,' McGraw put in.

'Don't threaten me, McGraw,' Thayer growled. John Wayne impersonation.

'Have you shared this theory with the police, Mr Thayer?' I repeated.

He flushed slightly under his careful tan. 'No, I didn't want it blurted all over the newspapers – I didn't want any of my neighbors to see what the boy was up to.'

I nodded. 'But you're really convinced that Mr McGraw here – and/or his daughter – set up Peter and had him shot.'

'Yes, I am, damnit!'

'And have you any evidence to support this allegation?' I asked.

'No, he doesn't, goddamnit!' McGraw yelled. 'No one could support such a goddamn asshole statement! Anita was in love with that North Shore snot. I told her that it was a colossal mistake. Get involved with the bosses and you get your ass burned. And now look what's happened.'

It seemed to me that the bosses had been the ones to get burned in this case, but I didn't think it would do any good to mention it.

'Did you give Mr McGraw one of your business cards when you were here before?' I asked Thayer.

'I don't know,' he said impatiently. 'I probably gave one to

40

his secretary when I arrived. Anyway, what business is it of yours?'

I smiled. 'I'm a private investigator, Mr Thayer, and I'm investigating a private matter for Mr McGraw here. He showed me one of your business cards the other night, and I wondered where he got it.'

McGraw shifted uncomfortably. Thayer stared at him with a look of disbelief. 'You showed her one of my cards? Why the hell did you do that? For that matter, why were you talking to a private investigator at all?'

'I had my reasons.' McGraw looked embarrassed, but he also looked mean.

'I bet you did,' Thayer said heavily. He turned to me. 'What are you doing for McGraw?'

I shook my head. 'My clients pay for privacy.'

'What kinds of things do you investigate?' Thayer asked. 'Divorces?'

'Most people think of divorce when they meet a private detective. Frankly divorce is pretty slimy. I do a lot of industrial cases . . . You know Edward Purcell, the man who used to be chairman of Transicon?'

Thayer nodded. 'I know of him anyway.'

'I did that investigation. He hired me because his board was pressuring him to find out where the disposable assets were going. Unfortunately he didn't cover his tracks well enough before he hired me.' Purcell's subsequent suicide and the reorganization of a badly damaged Transicon had been a ten-day wonder in Chicago.

Thayer leaned over me. 'In that case, what are you doing for McGraw?' He lacked McGraw's raw menace, but he, too, was a powerful man, used to intimidating others. The force of his personality was directed at me and I sat up straight to resist it.

'What business is it of yours, Mr Thayer?'

He gave me the frown that got obedience from his junior trust officers. 'If he gave you my card, it's my business.'

'It didn't have anything to do with you, Mr Thayer.'

'That's right, Thayer,' McGraw growled. 'Now get your ass out of my office.'

Thayer turned back to McGraw and I relaxed slightly. 'You're not trying to smear me with any of your dirty business are you, McGraw?'

'Watch it, Thayer. My name and my operation have been cleared in every court in this country. In Congress too. Don't give me that crap.'

'Yeah. Congress cleared you. Lucky, wasn't it, the way Derek Bernstein died right before the Senate hearings began.'

McGraw walked right up to the banker. 'You S O B. You get out of here now or I'll get some people to throw you out in a way that'll pop your high-and-mighty executive dignity for you.'

'I'm not afraid of your thugs, McGraw; don't threaten me.'

'Oh, come on,' I snapped. 'Both of you are tough as all get out, and you're both frightening me to pieces. So can you cut out this little-boy stuff? Why do you care so much about it, Mr Thayer? Mr McGraw here may have tossed a business card of yours around – but he hasn't tried to smear your name with his dirty business – if he's got dirty business. You got something on your conscience that's making you so upset? Or do you just have to prove you're the toughest guy in any crowd you're in?'

'Watch what you say to me, young lady. I've got a lot of powerful friends in this city, and they can –'

'That's what i mean,' I interrupted. 'Your powerful friends can take away my license. No doubt. But why do you care?'

He was silent for a minute. Finally he said, 'Just be careful what you get into with McGraw here. The courts may have cleared him, but he's into a lot of ugly business.'

'All right; I'll be careful.'

He gave me a sour look and left.

McGraw looked at me approvingly. 'You handled him just right, Warshawski.'

I ignored that. 'Why did you give me a fake name the other

night, McGraw? And why did you give your daughter a different phony one?'

'How'd you find me, anyway?'

'Once I saw the McGraw name, it began stirring in the back of my mind. I remembered you from the night you were shot – it came back to me when Lieutenant Mallory mentioned the Knifegrinders. Why'd you come to me to begin with? You think my dad might help you out the way he did back then?'

'What are you talking about?'

'Oh, can it, McGraw, I was there. You may not remember me – but I remember you. You came in absolutely covered with blood and my dad fixed up your shoulder and got you out of the building. Did you think he'd help you out of whatever trouble you're in this time, until you found out he was dead? Then what – you found my name in the Yellow Pages and thought maybe I was Tony's son? Now, why did you use Thayer's name?'

The fight died down in him a bit. 'I wasn't sure you'd do a job for me if you knew who I was.'

'But why Thayer? Why drag in the senior guy in Chicago's biggest bank? Why not just call yourself Joe Blow?'

'I don't know. It was just an impulse, I guess.'

'Impulse? You're not that dumb. He could sue you for slander or something, dragging his name in like that.'

'Then why the hell did you let him know I'd done it? You're on my payroll.'

'No, I'm not. You've hired me to do some independent professional work, but I'm not on your payroll. Which brings us to the original question: what'd you hire me for, anyway?'

'To find my daughter.'

'Then why did you give her a false name? How could I possibly look for her? No, I think you hired me to find the body.'

'Now, look here, Warshawski –'

'You look, McGraw. It's so obvious you knew the kid was dead. When did you find out? Or did you shoot him yourself?'

His eyes disappeared in his heavy face and he pushed close to me. 'Don't talk smart with me, Warshawski.'

43

My heart beat faster but I didn't back away. 'When did you find the body?'

He stared at me another minute, then half-smiled. 'You're no softie. I don't object to a lady with guts . . . I was worried about Anita. She usually calls me on Monday evening, and when she didn't, I thought I should go down and check up on her. You know what a dangerous neighborhood that is.'

'You know, Mr McGraw, it continues to astonish me the number of people who think the University of Chicago is in an unsafe neighborhood. Why parents ever send their children to school there at all amazes me. Now let's have a little more honesty. You knew Anita had disappeared when you came to see me, or you would never have given me her picture. You are worried about her, and you want her found. Do you think she killed the boy?'

That got an explosive reaction. 'No, I don't goddamnit. If you must know, she came home from work Tuesday night and found his dead body. She called me in a panic, and then she disappeared.'

'Did she accuse you of killing him?'

'Why should she do that?' He was bellicose but uncomfortable.

'I can think of lots of reasons. You hated young Thayer, thought your daughter was selling out to the bosses. So in a mistaken fit of paternal anxiety, you killed the kid, thinking it would restore your daughter to you. Instead —'

'You're crazy, Warshawski! No parent is that cuckoo.'

I've seen lots of kookier parents but decided not to argue that point. 'Well,' I said, 'you don't like that idea, try this one. Peter somehow got wind of some shady, possibly even criminal, activities that you and the Knifegrinders are involved in. He communicated his fears to Anita, but being in love he wouldn't welch on you to the cops. On the other hand, being young and idealistic, he had to confront you. And he couldn't be bought. You shot him — or had him shot — and Anita knew it had to be you. So she did a bunk.'

McGraw's nerves were acting up again, but he blustered and bellowed and called me names. Finally he said, 'Why in Sam

Hill would I want you to find my daughter if all she'd do is finger me?'

'I don't know. Maybe you were playing the odds – figuring you've been close and she wouldn't turn on you. Trouble is, the police are going to be making the connection between you and Anita before too long. They know the kids had some tie-in with the brotherhood because there was some literature around the house created by your printer. They're not dummies, and everyone knows you're head of the union and they know there was a McGraw in the apartment.

'When they come around, they're not going to care about your daughter, or your relationship with her. They've got a murder to solve, and they'll be happy to tag you with it – especially with a guy in Thayer's position pressuring them. Now if you tell me what you know, I may – no promises, but *may* – be able to salvage you and your daughter – if you're not guilty, of course.'

McGraw studied the floor for a while. I realized I'd been clutching the arms of the chair while I was talking and carefully relaxed my muscles. Finally he looked up at me and said, 'If I tell you something, will you promise not to take it to the police?'

I shook my head. 'Can't promise anything, Mr McGraw. I'd lose my license if I kept knowledge of a crime to myself.'

'Not that kind of knowledge, damnit! Goddamnit, Warshawski, you keep acting like I committed the goddamn murder or something.' He breathed heavily for a few minutes. Finally he said, 'I just want to tell you about – you're right. I did – I was – I did find the kid's body.' He choked that out, and the rest came easier. 'Annie – Anita – called me Tuesday night. She wasn't in the apartment, she wouldn't say where she was.' He shifted a bit in his chair. 'Anita's a good, levelheaded kid. She never got any special pampering as a child, and she grew up knowing how to be independent. She and I are, well, we're pretty close, and she's always been union all the way, but she's no clinging daddy's girl. And I never wanted her to be one.

'Tuesday night I hardly recognized her. She was pretty damn

45

near hysterical, yelling a lot of half-assed stuff which didn't make any sense at all. But she didn't mention the kid's murder.'

'What was she yelling?' I asked conversationally.

'Oh, just nonsense, I couldn't make anything out of it.'

'Same song, second verse,' I remarked.

'What?'

'Same as the first,' I explained. 'A little bit louder and a little bit worse.'

'Once and for all, she didn't accuse me of killing Peter Thayer!' he yelled at the top of his lungs.

We weren't moving too quickly.

'Okay, she didn't accuse you of murdering Peter. Did she tell you about his being dead?'

He stopped for a minute. If he said yes, the next question was, why had the girl done a bunk if she didn't think McGraw had committed the murder? 'No, like I said, she was just hysterical. She – Well, later, after I saw the body, I figured she was calling because of – of, well, that.' He stopped again, but this time it was to collect some memories. 'She hung up and I tried calling back, but there wasn't any answer, so I went down to see for myself. And I found the boy.'

'How'd you get in?' I asked curiously.

'I have a key. Annie gave it to me when she moved in, but I'd never used it before.' He fumbled in his pocket and pulled out a key. I looked at it and shrugged.

'That was Tuesday night?' He nodded. 'And you waited til Wednesday night to come to see me?'

'I waited all day hoping that someone else would find the body. When no report came out – you were right, you know.' He smiled ruefully, and his whole face became more attractive. 'I hoped that Tony was still alive. I hadn't talked to him for years, he'd warned me off good and proper over the Stellinek episode – didn't know old Tony had it in him – but he was the only guy I could think of who might help me.'

'Why didn't you call the cops yourself?' I asked.

His face closed up again. 'I didn't want to,' he said shortly.

I thought about it. 'You probably wanted your own source of information on the case and you didn't think your police contacts could help you.' He didn't disagree.

'Do the Knifegrinders have any pension money tied up with Fort Dearborn Trust?' I asked.

McGraw turned red again. 'Keep your goddamn mitts out of our pension fund, Warshawski. We have enough snoopers smelling around there to guarantee it grade A pure for the next century. I don't need you, too.'

'Do you have any financial dealings with the Fort Dearborn Trust?'

He was getting so angry I wondered what nerve I'd touched, but he denied it emphatically.

'What about the Ajax Insurance Company?'

'Well, what about them?' he demanded.

'I don't know, Mr McGraw – do you buy any insurance from them?'

'I don't know.' His face was set and he was eyeing me hard and cold, the way he no doubt had eyed young Timmy Wright of Kansas City Local 4318 when Timmy had tried to talk to him about running a clean election down there. (Timmy had shown up in the Missouri River two weeks later.) It was much more menacing than his red-faced bluster. I wondered.

'Well, what about your pensions? Ajax is big in the pension business.'

'Goddamnit, Warshawski, get out of the office. You were hired to find Anita, not to ask a lot of questions about something that isn't any of your goddamned business. Now get out and don't come back.'

'You want me to find Anita?' I asked.

McGraw suddenly deflated and put his head in his hands. 'Oh, jeez, I don't know what to do.'

I looked at him sympathetically. 'Someone got you in the squeeze?'

He just shook his head but wouldn't answer. We sat it out in silence for a while. Then he looked at me, and he looked gray.

'Warshawski, I don't know where Annie is. And I don't want to know. But I want you to find her. And when you do, just let me know if she's all right. Here's another five hundred dollars to keep you on for a whole week. Come to me when it runs out.' It wasn't a formal apology, but I accepted it and left.

I stopped at Barb's Bar-B-Q for some lunch and called my answering service. There was a message from Ralph Devereux at Ajax; would I meet him at the Cartwheel at 7.30 tonight. I called him and asked if he had discovered anything about Peter Thayer's work.

'Look,' he said, 'will you tell me your first name? How the hell can I keep on addressing someone as "V. I."?'

'The British do it all the time. What have you found out?'

'Nothing. I'm not looking – there's nothing to find. That kid wasn't working on sensitive stuff. And you know why – V. I.? Because insurance companies don't run to sensitive stuff. Our product, how we manufacture it, and what we charge for it are only regulated by about sixty-seven state and federal agencies.'

'Ralph, my first name is Victoria; my friends call me Vic. Never Vicki. I know insurance isn't your high-sensitivity business – but it offers a lot of luscious opportunities for embezzlement.'

A pregnant silence. 'No,' he finally said, 'at least – not here. We don't have any check-signing or authorizing responsibility.'

I thought that one over. 'Do you know if Ajax handles any of the Knifegrinders' pension money?'

'The Knifegrinders?' he echoed. 'What earthly connection does that set of hoodlums have with Peter Thayer?'

'I don't know. But do you have any of their pension money?'

'I doubt it. This is an insurance company, not a mob hangout.'

'Well, could you find out for me? And could you find out if they buy any insurance from you?'

'We sell all kinds of insurance, Vic – but not much that a union would buy.'

'Why not?'

'Look,' he said, 'it's a long story. Meet me at the Cartwheel at seven thirty and I'll give you chapter and verse on it.'

'Okay,' I agreed. 'But look into it for me, anyway. Please?'

'What's the *I* stand for?'

'None of your goddamn business.' I hung up. *I* stood for Iphigenia. My Italian mother had been devoted to Victor Emmanuel. This passion and her love of opera had led her to burden me with an insane name.

I drank a Fresca and ordered a chef's salad. I wanted ribs and fries, but the memory of Mildred's sagging arms stopped me. The salad didn't do much for me. I sternly put French fries out of my mind and pondered events.

Anita McGraw had called up and – at a minimum – told her father about the murder. My bet was she'd accused him of being involved. Ergo, Peter had found out something disreputable about the Knifegrinders and had told her. He probably found it out at Ajax, but possibly from the bank. I loved the idea of pensions. The Loyal Alliance Pension Fund got lots of publicity for their handling, or mishandling, of Knifegrinder pension money, but twenty million or so could easily have been laid off on a big bank or insurance company. And pension money gave one so much scope for fraudulent activity.

Why had McGraw gone down to the apartment? Well, in the first place, he knew whatever discreditable secret Thayer had uncovered. He was afraid that Anita was probably in on it – young lovers don't keep much to themselves. And if she called up because she'd found her boyfriend with a hole in his head, McGraw probably figured she'd be next, daughter or no daughter. So he went racing down to Hyde Park, terrified he'd find her dead body too. Instead she'd vanished. So far, so good.

Now, if I could find Anita, I'd know the secret. Or if I found the secret, I could publicize it, which would take the heat off the girl and maybe persuade her to return. It sounded good.

What about Thayer, though? Why had McGraw used his card,

and why had this upset him so much? Just the principle of the thing? I ought to talk to him alone.

I paid my bill and headed back to Hyde Park. The college Political Science Department was on the fourth floor of one of the older campus buildings. On a hot summer afternoon the hallways were empty. Through the windows along the stairwell I could see knots of students lying on the grass, some reading, some sleeping. A few energetic boys were playing Frisbee. An Irish setter loped around, trying to catch the disk.

A student was tending the desk in the department office. He looked about seventeen, his long blond hair hanging over his forehead, but no beard – he didn't appear ready to grow one yet. He was wearing a T-shirt with a hole under the left arm and was sitting hunched over a book. He looked up reluctantly when I said hello but kept the book open on his lap.

I smiled pleasantly and told him I was looking for Anita McGraw. He gave me a hostile look and turned back to his book without speaking.

'Come on. What's wrong with asking for her? She's a student in the department, right?' He refused to look up. I felt my temper rising, but I wondered if Mallory had been here before me. 'Have the police been around asking for her?'

'You ought to know,' he muttered, not looking up.

'You think just because I'm not wearing sloppy blue jeans I'm with the police?' I asked. 'How about digging out a departmental course list for me?'

He didn't move. I stepped around to his side of the desk and pulled open a drawer.

'Okay, okay,' he said huffily. He put the book spine up on the desk top. *Capitalism and Freedom*, by Marcuse. I might have guessed. He rummaged through the drawer and pulled out a nine-page list, typed and mimeographed, labeled 'College Time Schedule: Summer 1979'.

I flipped through it to the Political Science section. Their summer schedule filled a page. Class titles included such things as 'The Concept of Citizenship in Aristotle and Plato'; 'Idealism from Descartes Through Berkeley'; and 'Superpower Politics and the Idea of *Weltverschwinden*'. Fascinating. Finally I found one that sounded more promising: 'The Capitalist Standoff: Big Labor Versus Big Business'. Someone who taught a course like that would surely attract a young labor organizer like Anita McGraw. And might even know who some of her friends were. The instructor's name was Harold Weinstein.

I asked the youth where Weinstein's office was. He hunched further into Marcuse and pretended not to hear. I came around the desk again and sat on it facing him, grabbed his shirt collar and jerked his face up so that I could see his eyes. 'I know you think you're doing the revolution a great service by not revealing Anita's whereabouts to the pigs,' I said pleasantly. 'Perhaps when her body is found in a car trunk you will invite me to the party where you celebrate upholding your code of honor in the face of unendurable oppression.' I shook him a bit. 'Now tell me where to find Harold Weinstein's office.'

'You don't have to tell her anything, Howard,' someone said behind me. 'And you,' he said to me, 'don't be surprised when students equate police with fascism – I saw you roughing up that boy.'

The speaker was thin, with hot brown eyes and a mop of unruly hair. He was wearing a blue work shirt tucked neatly into a pair of khaki jeans.

'Mr Weinstein?' I said affably, letting go of Howard's shirt. Weinstein stared at me with his hands on his hips, brooding. It looked pretty noble. 'I'm not with the police – I'm a private detective. And when I ask anyone a civil question, I like to get a civil answer, not an arrogant shrug of the shoulders.

'Anita's father, Andrew McGraw, hired me to find her. I have a feeling, which he shares, that she may be in bad trouble. Shall we go somewhere and talk about it?'

'You have a feeling, do you,' he said heavily. 'Well, go feel about it somewhere else. We don't like police – public or private – on this campus.' He turned to stalk back down the corridor.

'Well executed,' I applauded. 'You've been studying Al Pacino.

51

Now that you've finished emoting, could we talk about Anita?'

The back of his neck turned red, and the color spread to his ears, but he stopped. 'What about her?'

'I'm sure you know she's disappeared, Mr Weinstein. You may also know that her boyfriend, Peter Thayer, is dead. I am trying to find her in the hopes of keeping her from sharing his fate.' I paused to let him absorb it. 'My guess is that she's hiding out someplace and she thinks she won't be found by whoever killed him. But I'm afraid she's crossed the path of an ugly type of killer. The kind that has a lot of money and can buy his way past most hideouts.'

He turned so that I could see his profile. 'Don't worry, Philip Marlowe – they won't bribe me into revealing her whereabouts.'

I wondered hopefully if he could be tortured into talking. Aloud, I said, 'Do you know where she is?'

'No comment.'

'Do you know any of her good friends around here?'

'No comment.'

'Gee, you're helpful. Mr Weinstein – you're my favorite prof. I wish you'd taught here when I went to school.' I pulled out my card and gave it to him. 'If you ever feel like commenting, call me at this number.'

Back outside in the heat I felt depressed. My navy silk suit was stunning, but too heavy for the weather; I was sweating, probably ruining the fabric under the arms. Besides, I seemed to be alienating everyone whose path I crossed. I wished I'd smashed in Howard's face.

A circular stone bench faced the college building. I walked over to it and sat down. Maybe I'd give up on this stupid case. Industrial espionage was more my speed, not a corrupt union and a bunch of snotty kids. Maybe I'd use the thousand dollars McGraw had given me to spend the summer on the Michigan peninsula. Maybe that would make him angry enough to send someone after me with cement leggings.

The Divinity School was just behind me. I sighed, pulled myself to my feet, and moved into its stone-walled coolness. A coffee shop used to serve overboiled coffee and tepid lemonade in the basement. I made my way downstairs and found the place still in operation. There was something reassuring in this continuity and in the sameness of the young faces behind the makeshift counter. Kindly and naïve, they preached a lot of violent dogma, believed that burglars had a right to the goods they took because of their social oppression, and yet would be rocked to their roots if someone ever required them to hold a machine gun themselves.

I took a Coke and retired to a dark corner with it. The chairs weren't comfortable, but I pulled my knees up to my chin and leaned against the wall. About a dozen students were seated around the wobbly tables, some of them trying to read in the dim light, most of them talking. Snatches of conversation reached me. 'Of course if you're going to look at it dialectically, the only thing they can do is –' 'I told her if she didn't put her foot down he'd –' 'Yeah, but Schopenhauer says –' I dozed off.

I was jerked awake a few seconds later by a loud voice saying, 'Did you *hear* about Peter Thayer?' I looked up. The speaker, a plump young woman with wild red hair, wearing an ill-fitting peasant blouse, had just come into the room. She dumped her book bag on the floor and joined a table of three in the middle of the room. 'I was just coming out of class when Ruth Yonkers told me.'

I got up and bought another Coke and sat down at a table behind the redhead.

A thin youth with equally wild but dark hair was saying, 'Oh, yeah, the cops were all over the Political Science Office this morning. You know, he was living with Anita McGraw, and she hasn't been seen since Sunday. Weinstein really told them off,' he added admiringly.

'Do they think she killed him?' the redhead asked.

A dark, somewhat older woman snorted. 'Anita McGraw? I've known her for two years. She might off a cop, but she wouldn't shoot her boyfriend.'

'Do you know him, Mary?' the redhead breathed.

'No,' Mary answered shortly. 'I never met him. Anita belongs to University Women United – that's how I know her. So does Geraldine Harata, her other roommate, but Geraldine's away for the summer. If she wasn't, the cops would probably suspect her. They always pick on women first.'

'I'm surprised you let her into UWU if she has a boyfriend,' a bearded young man put in. He was heavy and sloppy – his T-shirt gaped, revealing an unlovely expanse of stomach.

Mary looked at him haughtily and shrugged.

'Not everyone in UWU is a lesbian,' the redhead bristled.

'With so many men like Bob around, it's hard to understand why not,' Mary drawled. The fat youth flushed and muttered something, of which 'castrating' was the only word I caught.

'But I never met Anita,' the redhead continued. 'I only started going to UWU meetings in May. Has she really disappeared, Mary?'

Mary shrugged again. 'If the pigs are trying to put Peter Thayer's death off on her, I wouldn't be surprised.'

'Maybe she went home,' Bob suggested.

'No,' the thin youth said. 'If she'd done that, the police wouldn't have been around here looking for her.'

'Well,' Mary said, 'I, for one, hope they don't catch up with her.' She got up. 'I have to go listen to Bertram drone on about medieval culture. One more crack about witches as hysterical women and he'll find himself attacked by some, after class.'

She hoisted a knapsack over her left shoulder and ambled off. The others settled closer to the table and switched to an animated discussion of homo- versus heterosexual relationships. Poor Bob favored the latter, but didn't seem to get many opportunities for actively demonstrating it. The thin boy vigorously defended lesbianism. I listened in amusement. College students had enthusiastic opinions about so many topics. At four the boy behind the counter announced he was closing. People started gathering up their books. The three I was listening to continued their discussion for a few minutes until the counterman called over, 'Hey, folks, I want to get out of here.'

They reluctantly picked up their book bags and moved toward the stairs. I threw away my paper cup and slowly followed them out. At the top of the stairs I touched the redhead's arm. She stopped and looked at me, her face friendly and ingenuous.

'I heard you mention UWU,' I said. 'Can you tell me where they meet?'

'Are you new on campus?' she asked.

'I'm an old student, but I find I have to spend some time down here this summer,' I answered truthfully.

'Well, we have a room in a building at fifty-seven thirty-five University. It's one of those old homes the university has taken over. UWU meets there on Tuesday nights, and other women's activities go on during the rest of the week.'

I asked her about their women's center. It was clearly not large, but better than nothing at all, which was what we'd had in my college days when even women radicals treated women's liberation as a dirty phrase. They had a women's health counseling group and courses on self-defense, and they sponsored rap groups and the weekly University Women United meetings.

We had been moving across campus toward the Midway, where my car was parked. I offered her a ride home and she flung herself puppylike into the front seat, talking vigorously if ingenuously about women's oppression. She wanted to know what I did.

'Freelance work, mostly for corporations,' I said, expecting more probing, but she took that happily enough, asking if I would be taking photographs. I realized she assumed that I must be a freelance writer. I was afraid if I told her the truth, she would tell everyone at UWU and make it impossible for me to find any answers about Anita. Yet I didn't want to tell glaring lies, because if the truth did come out, these young radical women would be even more hostile. So I said 'no photographs' and asked her if she did any photography herself. She was still chattering cheerfully when we pulled up in front of her apartment.

'I'm Gail Sugarman,' she announced as she struggled clumsily out of the car.

'How do you do, Gail,' I replied politely. 'I'm V. I. Warshawski.'

'Veeyai!' she exclaimed. 'What an unusual name. Is it African?'

'No,' I answered gravely, 'it's Italian.' Driving off, I could see her in the rearview mirror, scrambling up the front steps of her apartment. She made me feel incredibly old. Even at twenty I had never possessed that naïve, bouncing friendliness; and now it made me feel cynical and remote. In fact, I felt a bit ashamed of deceiving her.

5
GOLD COAST BLUES

Lake Shore Drive, one long, large pothole, was being dug up and repaired. Only two northbound lanes were open and the traffic was backed up for miles. I decided to cut off onto the Stevenson Expressway going west, and then back north on the Kennedy, which went up the industrial North Side toward the airport. The rush-hour traffic was exacerbated by the load of people trying to get out of town on a stifling Friday night. It took me over an hour to fight my way to the Belmont exit, and then fifteen blocks east to my apartment. By the time I got there, all I could think of was a tall, cool drink and a long, soothing shower.

I hadn't noticed anyone coming up the stairs behind me, and was turning my key in the lock when I felt an arm on my shoulder. I'd been mugged once before in this hallway. Whirling reflexively, I snapped my knee and kicked in one motion, delivering directly onto my assailant's exposed shinbone. He grunted and backed off but came back with a solid punch aimed at my face. I ducked and took it on the left shoulder. A lot of the zip was gone, but it shook me a little and I drew away.

He was a short, stocky man, wearing an ill-fitting plaid jacket. He was panting a little, which pleased me: it meant he was out of shape, and a woman has better odds against an out-of-shape man. I waited for him to move or run away. Instead he drew a gun. I stood still.

'If this is a holdup, I only have thirteen dollars in my purse. Not worth killing for.'

'I'm not interested in your money. I want you to come with me.'

'Come with you where?' I asked.

'You'll find out when we get there.' He waved the gun at me and pointed down the stairs with his other arm.

'Beats me why well-paid hoods always dress so sloppily,' I commented. 'Your jacket doesn't fit, your shirt's untucked – you look like a mess. Now if you were a policeman, I could understand it; they –'

He cut me off with an enraged bellow. 'I don't need a goddamn broad to tell me how to dress!' He seized my arm with unnecessary force and started to hustle me down the stairs. He was holding me too close, though. I was able to turn slightly and bring my hand up with a short, strong chop under his gun wrist. He let go of me but didn't drop the gun. I followed through with a half-turn that brought my right elbow under his armpit and made a wedge of my right fist and forearm. I drove it into his ribs with my left hand, palm open, and heard a satisfying *pop* that told me I'd hit home between the fifth and sixth ribs and separated them. He yelled in pain and dropped the gun. I reached for it, but he had enough sense to step on my hand. I butted him in the stomach with my head and he let go, but I was off balance and sat down hard. Someone was clattering up the stairs behind me and I only had time to swing my foot and kick the gun away before turning to see who it was.

I thought it might be a neighbor, roused by the noise, but it seemed to be a partner, dressed nearly to match the first hood but bigger. He saw his buddy leaning against the wall, moaning, and hurled himself onto me. We rolled and I got both hands under his chin, forcing his neck back. He let go, but clobbered me on the right side of my head. It shook me all the way down my back, but I didn't give in to it. I kept rolling and leaped up with my back to the wall. I didn't want to give him time to draw a gun, so I grasped the paneling behind me for leverage and swung my feet at his chest, knocking him off balance but falling on top of him. He got another good punch in, to my shoulder,

58

just missing the jaw, before I wiggled away. He was stronger, but I was in better shape and more agile, and I was on my feet way in advance of him, kicking him hard over his left kidney. He collapsed at that, and I was hauling back to do it again when his partner recovered himself enough to pick up his gun and clip me under the left ear. My kick connected at the same time and then I was falling, falling, but remembering to fall rolling, and rolling off the edge of the world.

I wasn't out long but long enough for them to hustle me downstairs. Good work for two partially disabled men. I guessed any neighbors alerted by the sound had turned up their TVs to drown it out.

I regained a sickly sort of consciousness as they pushed me into the car, fought to hold it, threw up on one of them, and went under again. I came back more slowly the second time. We were still moving. The one with the separated ribs was driving; I'd thrown up on the other one, and the smell was rather strong. His face was very set and I thought he might be close to tears. It's not nice for two men to go after one woman and only get her after losing a rib and a kidney, and then to have her vomit down your jacket front and not be able to move or clean it off – I wouldn't have liked it, either. I fumbled in my jacket pocket for some Kleenex. I still felt sick, too sick to talk and not much like cleaning him up either, so I dropped the tissues on him and leaned back. He gave a little squeal of rage and knocked them to the floor.

When we stopped, we were close to North Michigan Avenue, just off Astor on Division, in the area where rich people live in beautiful old Victorian houses and apartments or enormous high-rise modern condominiums. My right-hand partner flung himself out the door, took off his jacket and dropped it in the street.

'Your gun's showing,' I told him. He looked down at it, then at his jacket. His face turned red. 'You goddamn bitch,' he said. He leaned into the car to take another poke at me, but the angle wasn't good and he couldn't get much leverage behind his arm.

Ribs spoke up. 'Come on, Joe – it's getting late and Earl don't like to be kept waiting.' This simple statement worked powerfully on Joe. He stopped swinging and yanked me out of the car, with Ribs pushing me from the side.

We went into one of the stately old houses that I always thought I'd like to own if I ever rescued an oil-tanker billionaire from international kidnappers and got set up for life as my reward. It was dull red brick, with elegant wrought-iron railings up the steps and around the front windows. Originally built as a single-family home, it was now a three-flat apartment. A cheerful black-and-white patterned wallpaper covered the entry hall and stairwell. The bannister was carved wood, probably walnut, and beautifully polished. The three of us made an ungainly journey up the carpeted stairs to the second floor. Ribs was having trouble moving his arms, and Joe seemed to be limping from his kidney kicks. I wasn't feeling very well myself.

The second-floor apartment door was opened by yet another gun-carrier. His clothes fit him better, but he didn't really look like the class of person that belonged in this neighborhood. He had a shock of black hair that stood up around his head in a wiry bush. On his right cheek was a deep red scar, cut roughly like a Z. It was so dark that it looked as though someone had painted him with lipstick.

'What kept you two so long? Earl's getting angry,' he demanded, ushering us into a wide hallway. Plush brown carpet on the floor, a nice little Louis Quinze side table, and a few pictures on the walls. Charming.

'Earl warned us this goddamn Warshawski bitch was a wise-ass, but he didn't say she was a goddamn karate expert.' That was Ribs. He pronounced my name 'Worchotsi'. I looked down at my hands modestly.

'Is that Joe and Freddie?' a nasal tenor squeaked from inside. 'What the hell took you guys so long?' Its owner appeared in the doorway. Short, pudgy and bald, he was familiar to me from my early days in Chicago law enforcement.

'Earl Smeissen. How absolutely delightful. But you know,

Earl, if you'd called me up and asked to see me, we could have gotten together with a lot less trouble.'

'Yeah, Warchoski, I just bet we would've,' he said heavily. Earl had carved himself a nice little niche on the North Side with classy prostitution setups for visiting conventioneers, and a little blackmail and extortion. He had a small piece of the drug business, and the rumor was that he would arrange a killing to oblige a friend if the price was right.

'Earl, this is quite a place you've got. Inflation must not be hurting business too much.'

He ignored me. 'Where the hell's your jacket, Joe? You been walking around Chicago showing your gun to every cop on the beat?'

Joe turned red again and started to mutter something. I intervened. 'I'm afraid that's my fault, Earl. Your friends here jumped me in my own hallway without introducing themselves or saying they had come from you. We had a bit of a fracas, and Freddie's ribs got separated – but he pulled himself together nicely and knocked me out. When I came to, I was sick on Joe's jacket. So don't blame the poor fellow for ditching it.'

Earl turned outraged to Freddie, who shrank back down the hall. 'You let a goddamn dame bust your ribs?' he yelled, his voice breaking to a squeak. 'The money I pay you and you can't do a simple little job like fetch a goddamn broad?'

One of the things I hate about my work is the cheap swearing indulged in by cheap crooks. I also hate the word *broad*. 'Earl, could you reserve your criticisms of your staff until I'm not here? I have an engagement this evening – I'd appreciate it if you told me why you wanted to see me so badly you sent two hoods to get me, so I can get there on time.'

Earl gave Freddie a vicious look and sent him off to see a doctor. He motioned the rest of us into the living room, and noticed Joe limping. 'You need a doctor, too? She break your leg?' he asked sarcastically.

'Kidneys,' I replied modestly. 'It all comes from knowing how.'

'Yeah, I know about you, Warchoski. I know what a wiseass you are, and I heard how you offed Joe Correl. If Freddie knocked you out, I'll give him a medal. I want you to understand you can't mess around with me.'

I sank down into a wide armchair. My head was throbbing and it hurt to focus on him. 'I'm not messing around with you, Earl,' I said earnestly. 'I'm not interested in prostitution or juice loans or –'

He hit me across the mouth. 'Shut up.' His voice rose to a squeak and his eyes got smaller in his pudgy face. In a detached way I felt some blood dribbling down my chin – he must have caught me with his ring.

'Is this a general warning, then? Are you hauling in all the private eyes in Chicago and saying, "Now hear this – don't mess around with Earl Smeissen!"?'

He swung at me again, but I blocked him with my left arm. He looked at his hand in surprise, as if he wondered what had happened to it.

'Don't clown with me, Warchoski – I can call in plenty of people to wipe that smirk off your face.'

'I don't think it would take very many,' I said, 'but I still don't have any idea what part of your turf I'm messing in.'

Earl signaled to the doorman, who came and held my shoulders against the chair. Joe was hovering in the background, a lascivious look on his face. My stomach turned slightly.

'Okay, Earl, I'm terrified,' I said.

He hit me again. I was going to look like absolute hell tomorrow, I thought. I hoped I wasn't shaking; my stomach was knotted with nervousness. I took several deep diaphragm breaths to try to relieve the tension.

The last slap seemed to satisfy Earl. He sat down on a dark couch close to my chair.

'Warchoski,' he squeaked, 'I called you down here to tell you to lay off the Thayer case.'

'You kill the boy, Earl?' I asked.

He was on his feet again. 'I can mark you good, so good that

62

no one will ever want to look at your face again,' he shouted. 'Now just do what I say and keep your mitts outta that.'

I decided not to argue with him – I didn't feel in any shape to take on both him and the doorman, who continued to hold my shoulders back. I wondered if his scar had turned redder with all the excitement but voted against asking him.

'Suppose you do scare me off? What about the police?' I objected. 'Bobby Mallory's hot on the trail, and whatever his faults, you can't buy Bobby.'

'I'm not worried about Mallory.' Earl's voice was back in its normal register, so I concluded the brainstorm was passing. 'And I'm not buying you – I'm telling you.'

'Who got you involved, Earl? College kids aren't part of your turf – unless young Thayer was cutting into your dope territory?'

'I thought I'd just told you not to pry into my affairs,' he said, getting up again. Earl was determined to pound me. Maybe it would be better to get it over with quickly and get out, rather than let him go on for hours. As he came at me, I pulled my foot back and kicked him squarely in the crotch. He howled in anguish and collapsed in a heap on the couch. 'Get her, Tony, get her,' he squealed.

I didn't have a chance against Tony, the doorman. He was trained in the art of working over loan defaulters without showing a mark. When he finished, Earl came hobbling over from the couch. 'This is just a taste, Warchoski,' he hissed. 'You lay off the Thayer case. Agreed?'

I looked at him without speaking. He really could kill me and get away with it – he'd done it to others. He had good connections with City Hall and probably in the police department too. I shrugged and winced. He seemed to accept that as agreement. 'Get her out, Tony.'

Tony dumped me unceremoniously outside the front door. I sat for a few minutes on the stairs, shivering in the heat and trying to pull myself together. I was violently ill over the railing, which cleared my headache a bit. A woman walking by with a man said, 'Disgusting so early in the evening. The police should keep people like that out of this neighborhood.' I agreed. I got to my feet, rather wobbly, but I could walk. I felt my arms. They were sore, but nothing was broken. I staggered over to the inner drive, parallel to Lake Shore Drive and only a block away, and hailed a taxi home. The first one pulled off after a look at me, but the second one took me. The driver clucked and fussed like a Jewish mother, wanting to know what I'd done to myself and offering to take me to a hospital or the police or both. I thanked him for his concern but assured him I was all right.

6

IN THE COOL OF THE NIGHT

I'd dropped my purse by my door when Freddie and I were scuffling, and asked the cabdriver to come upstairs with me to get paid off. Living at the top of the building, I was pretty confident that my bag would still be there. It was, and my keys were still in the door.

The driver tried one last protest. 'Thanks,' I said, 'but I just need a hot bath and a drink and I'll be all right.'

'Okay, lady.' He shrugged. 'It's your funeral.' He took his money, looked at me one last time, and went downstairs.

My apartment lacked the splendor of Earl's. My little hallway had a small rug, not wall-to-wall carpeting, and an umbrella stand rather than a Louis Quinze table. But it also wasn't filled with thugs.

I was surprised to find it was only seven. It had been only an hour and a half since I had come up the stairs the first time that evening. I felt as though I'd moved into a different time zone. I ran a bath for the second time that day and poured myself an inch of Scotch. I soaked in water as hot as I could bear it, lying in the dark with a wet towel wrapped around my head. Gradually my headache dissipated. I was very, very tired.

After thirty minutes of soaking and reheating the tub, I felt able to cope with some motion. Wrapping a large towel around me, I walked through the apartment, trying to keep my muscles from freezing on me. All I really wanted to do was sleep, but I knew if I did that now I wouldn't be able to walk for a week. I did some exercises, gingerly, fortifying myself with Black Label. Suddenly I caught sight of a clock and remembered my date with Devereux. I was already late and wondered if he was still there.

With an effort I found the restaurant's name in the phone book and dialed their number. The maître d'hôtel was very cooperative and offered to look for Mr Devereux in the bar. A few minutes passed, and I began to think he must have gone home when he came onto the line.

'Hello, Ralph.'

'This had better be good.'

'If I tried explaining it would take hours and you still wouldn't believe me,' I answered. 'Will you give me another half hour?'

He hesitated; I guessed he was looking for the pride to say no – good-looking guys aren't used to being stood up. 'Sure,' he said finally. 'But if you're not here by eight thirty, you can find your own way home.'

'Ralph,' I said, controlling my voice carefully, 'this has been one absolute zero of a day. I'd like to have a pleasant evening, learn a little bit about insurance, and try to forget what's gone before. Can we do that?'

He was embarrassed. 'Sure, Vicki – I mean Vic. See you in the bar.'

We hung up and I looked through my wardrobe for something elegant enough for the Cartwheel, but loose and flowing, and found a string-colored Mexican dress that I'd forgotten about. It was two-piece, with a long full skirt and a woven, square-necked top that tied at the waist and bloused out below. The long sleeves covered my puffy arms and I didn't have to wear pantyhose or a slip. Cork sandals completed the costume.

Surveying my face under the bathroom light made me want to reconsider going out in public. My lower lip was swollen where Earl's pinky ring had sliced it, and a purple smudge was showing on my left jaw, extending veinous red lines like a cracked egg along my cheek to the eye.

I tried some makeup; my base wasn't very heavy and didn't

conceal the worst of the purple but did cover the spidery red marks. Heavy shadow took the focus from an incipient black eye, and dark lipstick, applied more strongly than my usual style, made the swollen lip look pouty and sexy – or might if the lights were dim enough.

My legs were stiffening up, but my daily runs seemed to be paying off – I negotiated the stairs without more than minor tremors. A taxi was going by on Halsted; it dropped me in front of the Hanover House Hotel on Oak Street at 8.25.

This was my first visit to the Cartwheel. To me it typified the sterile places where bright, empty North Siders with more money than sense liked to eat. The bar, to the left of the entrance, was dark, with a piano amplified too loudly, playing songs that bring tears to the eyes of Yale graduates. The place was crowded, Friday night in Chicago. Ralph sat at the end of the bar with a drink. He looked up as I came in, smiled, sketched a wave, but didn't get up. I concentrated on walking smoothly, and made it to where he sat. He looked at his watch. 'You just made it.'

In more ways than one, I thought. 'Oh, you'd never have left without finishing your drink.' There weren't any empty stools. 'How about proving you're a more generous soul than I and letting me have that seat and a Scotch?'

He grinned and grabbed me, intending to pull me onto his lap. A spasm of pain shot through my ribs. 'Oh, Jesus, Ralph! Don't!'

He let go of me at once, got up stiffly and quietly, and offered me the barstool. I stood, feeling awkward. I don't like scenes, and I didn't feel like using the energy to calm Ralph down. He'd seemed like a guy made for sunshine; maybe his divorce had made him insecure with women. I saw I'd have to tell him the truth and put up with his sympathy. And I didn't want to reveal how badly Smeissen had shown me up that afternoon. It was no comfort that he would limp in pain for a day or two.

I dragged my attention back to Ralph. 'Would you like me to take you home?' he was asking.

'Ralph, I'd like a chance to explain some things to you. I know it must look as though I don't want to be here, showing up an hour late and all. Are you too upset for me to tell you about it?'

'Not at all,' he said politely.

'Well, could we go someplace and sit down? It's a little confusing and hard to do standing up.'

'I'll check on our table.' When he went off, I sank gratefully onto the barstool and ordered a Johnnie Walker Black. How many could I drink before they combined with my tired muscles and put me to sleep?

Ralph came back with the news that our table was a good ten-minute wait away. The ten stretched into twenty, while I sat with my uninjured cheek propped on my hand and he stood stiffly behind me. I sipped my Scotch. The bar was over-air-conditioned. Normally the heavy cotton of the dress would have kept me plenty warm, but now I started to shiver slightly.

'Cold?' Ralph asked.

'A little,' I admitted.

'I could put my arms around you,' he offered tentatively.

I looked up at him and smiled. 'That would be very nice,' I said. 'Just do it gently, please.'

He crossed his arms around my chest. I winced a little at first, but the warmth and the pressure felt good. I leaned back against him. He looked down at my face, and his eyes narrowed.

'Vic, what's wrong with your face?'

I raised an eyebrow. 'Nothing's wrong.'

'No, really,' he said, bending closer, 'you've gotten cut – and that looks like a bruise and swelling on your cheek.'

'Is it really bad?' I asked. 'I thought the makeup covered it pretty well.'

'Well, they're not going to put you on the cover of *Vogue* this week, but it's not too awful. It's just that as an old claims man I've seen lots of accident victims. And you look like one.'

'I feel like one too,' I agreed, 'but really, this wasn't –'

'Have you been to a doctor about this?' he interrupted.

'You sound just like the cabbie who took me home this afternoon. He wanted to rush me to Passavant – I practically expected him to come in with me and start making me chicken soup.'

'Was your car badly damaged?' he asked.

'My car is not damaged at all.' I was beginning to lose my temper – irrationally, I knew – but the probing made me feel defensive.

'Not damaged,' he echoed, 'then how –'

At that moment our table was announced in the bar. I got up and went over to the headwaiter, leaving Ralph to pay for drinks. The headwaiter led me off without waiting for Ralph, who caught up with us just as I was being seated. My spurt of temper had infected him; he said, 'I hate waiters who haul off ladies without waiting for their escorts.' He was just loud enough for the maître d' to hear. 'I'm sorry, sir – I didn't realize you were with madame,' he said with great dignity before moving off.

'Hey, Ralph, take it easy,' I said gently. 'A little too much ego-jockeying is going on – my fault as much as yours. Let's stop and get some facts and start over again.'

A waiter materialized. 'Would you care for a drink before dinner?'

Ralph looked up in irritation. 'Do you know how many hours we've spent in the bar waiting for this table? No, we don't want a drink – at least, I don't.' He turned to me. 'Do you?'

'No, thanks,' I agreed. 'Anymore and I'll fall asleep – which will probably ruin forever any chance I have of making you believe that I'm not trying to get out of an evening with you.'

Were we ready to order? the waiter persisted. Ralph told him roundly to go away for five minutes. My last remark had started to restore his native good humor, however. 'Okay, V. I. Warshawski – convince me that you really aren't trying to make this evening so awful that I'll never ask you out again.'

'Ralph,' I said, watching him carefully, 'do you know Earl Smeissen?'

'Who?' he asked uncomprehendingly. 'Is this some kind of detective guessing game?'

'Yeah, I guess so,' I answered. 'Between yesterday afternoon and this afternoon I've talked to a whole lot of different people who either knew Peter Thayer or his girlfriend – the gal who's vanished. You and your boss, among others.

'Well, when I got home late this afternoon, two hired thugs were waiting for me. We fought. I was able to hold them off for a while, but one of them knocked me out. They took me to Earl Smeissen's home. If you don't know Earl, don't try to meet him. He was just starting to muscle to the top of his racket – extortion, prostitution – when I was with the Public Defender ten years ago, and he seems to have kept right on trucking since then. He now has a stable of tough guys who all carry guns. He is not a nice person.'

I stopped to marshal my presentation. From the corner of my eye I saw the waiter shimmering up again, but Ralph waved him away. 'Anyway, he ordered me off the Thayer case, and set one of his tame goons on me to back it up.' I stopped. What had happened next in Earl's apartment was very raw in my mind. I had calculated it carefully at the time, decided that it was better to get everything over at once and convince Earl that I was scared than to sit there all evening while he took increasingly violent shots at me. None the less, the thought of being so helpless, the memory of Tony beating me, like a disloyal whore or a welching loan customer – to be so vulnerable was close to unbearable. Unconsciously, my left hand had clenched, and I realized I was slicing it against the tabletop. Ralph was watching me, an uncertain look on his face. His business and suburban life hadn't prepared him for this kind of emotion.

I shook my head and tried for a lighter touch. 'Anyway, my rib cage is a little sore – which is why I winced and yelled when you grabbed hold of me in the bar. The question that's exercising me, though, is who told Earl that I'd been around asking questions. Or more precisely, who cared so much that I'd been around that he asked – or paid – Earl to frighten me off.'

Ralph was still looking a little horrified. 'Have you been to the police about this?'

'No,' I said impatiently. 'I can't go to the police about this kind of thing. They know I'm interested in the case – they've asked me to get off, too, although more politely. If Bobby Mallory – the lieutenant in charge of the case – knew I'd been beaten up by Earl, Smeissen would deny the whole thing, and if I could prove it in court, he could say it was a million things other than this that made him do it. And Mallory wouldn't give me an earful of sympathy – he wants me out of there anyway.'

'Well, don't you think he's right? Murder really is a police matter. And this group seems pretty wild for you to be mixed up with.'

I felt a quick surge of anger, the anger I get when I feel someone is pushing me. I smiled with an effort. 'Ralph, I'm tired and I ache. I can't try explaining to you tonight why this is my job – but please believe that it is my job and that I can't give it to the police and run away. It's true I don't know specifically what's going on here, but I do know the temperament and reactions of a guy like Smeissen. I usually only deal with white-collar criminals – but when they're cornered, they're not much different from an extortion artist like Smeissen.'

'I see.' Ralph paused, thinking, then his attractive grin came. 'I have to admit that I don't know much about crooks of any kind – except the occasional swindlers who try to rip off insurance companies. But we fight them in the courts, not with hand-to-hand combat. I'll try to believe you know what you're up to, though.'

I laughed a little embarrassedly. 'Thanks. I'll try not to act too much like Joan of Arc – getting on a horse and charging around in all directions.'

The waiter was back, looking a little intimidated. Ralph ordered baked oysters and quail, but I opted for Senegalese soup and spinach salad. I was too exhausted to want a lot of food.

We talked about indifferent things for a while. I asked Ralph if he followed the Cubs. 'For my sins, I'm an ardent fan,' I explained. Ralph said he caught a game with his son every now and then. 'But I don't see how anyone can be an ardent Cub fan. They're doing pretty well right now – cleaned out the Reds –

but they'll fade the way they always do. No, give me the Yankees.'

'Yankees!' I expostulated. 'I don't see how anyone can root for them – it's like rooting for the Cosa Nostra. You know they've got the money to buy the muscle to win – but that doesn't make you cheer them on.'

'I like to see sports played well,' Ralph insisted. 'I can't stand the clowning around that Chicago teams do. Look at the mess Veeck's made of the White Sox this year.'

We were still arguing about it when the waiter brought the first course. The soup was excellent – light, creamy, with a hint of curry. I started feeling better and ate some bread and butter, too. When Ralph's quail arrived, I ordered another bowl of soup and some coffee.

'Now explain to me why a union wouldn't buy insurance from Ajax.'

'Oh, they could,' Ralph said, his mouth full. He chewed and swallowed. 'But it would only be for their headquarters – maybe fire coverage on the building, Workers' Compensation for the secretaries, things like that. There wouldn't be a whole lot of people to cover. And a union like the Knifegrinders – see, they get their insurance where they work. The big thing is Workers' Comp, and that's paid for by the company, not the union.'

'That covers disability payments, doesn't it?' I asked.

'Yes, or death if it's job-related. Medical bills even if there isn't lost time. I guess it's a funny kind of setup. Your rates depend on the kind of business you conduct – a factory pays more than an office, for instance. But the insurance company can be stuck with weekly payments for years if a guy is disabled on the job. We have some cases – not many, fortunately – that go back to 1927. But see, the insured doesn't pay more, or not that much more, if we get stuck with a whole lot of disability payments. Of course, we can cancel the insurance, but we're still required to cover any disabled workers who are already collecting.

'Well, this is getting off the subject. The thing is, there are lots of people who go on disability who shouldn't – it's pretty cushy and there are plenty of corrupt doctors – but it's hard to imagine a full-scale fraud connected with it that would do anyone else much good.' He ate some more quail. 'No, your real money is in pensions, as you suggested, or maybe life insurance. But it's easier for an insurance company to commit fraud with life insurance than for anyone else. Look at the Equity Funding case.'

'Well, could your boss be involved in something like that? Rigging phony policies with the Knifegrinders providing dummy policyholders?' I asked.

'Vic, why are you working so hard to prove that Yardley's a crook? He's really not a bad guy – I've worked for him for three years, and I've never heard anything against him.'

I laughed at that. 'It bugs me that he agreed to see me so easily. I don't know a lot about insurance, but I've been around big corporations before. He's a department head, and they're like gynecologists – their schedules are always booked for about twice as many appointments as they can realistically handle.'

Ralph clutched his head. 'You're making me dizzy, Vic, and you're doing it on purpose. How can a claim department head possibly be like a gynecologist!'

'Yeah, well, you get the idea. Why would he agree to see me? He'd never heard of me, he has wall-to-wall appointments – but he didn't even take phone calls while we were talking.'

'Yes, but you knew Peter was dead, and he didn't – so you were expecting him to behave in a certain guilty way and that's what you saw,' Ralph objected. 'He might have been worried about him, about Peter, because he'd promised Jack Thayer that he'd be responsible for the boy. I don't really see anything so surprising in Yardley's talking to you. If Peter had been just a stray kid, I might – but an old family friend's son? The kid hadn't been in for four days, he wasn't answering the phone – Yardley felt responsible as much as annoyed.'

I stopped, considering. What Ralph said made sense. I wondered if I had gotten carried away, whether my instinctive dislike

73

of over-hearty businessmen was making me see ghosts where there were none.

'Okay, you could be right. But why couldn't Masters be involved in a life-insurance fiddle?'

Ralph was finishing off his quail and ordering coffee and dessert. I asked for a large dish of ice cream. 'Oh, that's the way insurance companies are set up,' he said when the waiter had disappeared again. 'We're big – third largest in total premiums written, which is about eight point four billion dollars a year. That includes all lines, and all of the thirteen companies that make up the Ajax group. For legal reasons, life insurance can't be written by the same company that writes property and casualty. So the Ajax Assurance Company does all our life and pension products, while the Ajax Casualty and some of the smaller ones do property and casualty.'

The waiter returned with our desserts. Ralph was having some kind of gooey torte. I decided to get Kahlua for my ice cream.

'Well, with a company as big as ours,' Ralph continued, 'the guys involved in casualty – that's stuff like Workers' Comp, general liability, some of the auto – anyway, guys like Yardley and me don't know too much about the life side of the house. Sure, we know the people who run it, eat with them now and then, but they have a separate administrative structure, handle their own claims and so on. If we got close enough to the business to analyze it, let alone commit fraud with it, the political stink would be so high we'd be out on our butts within an hour. Guaranteed.'

I shook my head reluctantly and turned to my ice cream. Ajax did not sound promising, and I'd been pinning hopes to it. 'By the way,' I said, 'did you check on Ajax's pension money?'

Ralph laughed. 'You are persistent, Vic, I'll grant you that. Yeah, I called a friend of mine over there. Sorry, Vic. Nothing doing. He says he'll look into it, see whether we get any third-hand stuff laid off on us –' I looked a question. 'Like the Loyal Alliance people give some money to Dreyfus to manage and Dreyfus lays some of it off on us. Basically though, this guy says Ajax won't touch the Knifegrinders with a ten-foot pole. Which doesn't surprise me too much.'

I sighed and finished my ice cream, feeling suddenly tired again. If things came easily in this life, we would never feel pride in our achievements. My mother used to tell me that, standing over me while I practiced the piano. She'd probably disapprove of my work, if she were alive, but she would never let me slouch at the dinner table grumbling because it wasn't turning out right. Still, I was too tired tonight to try to grapple with the implications of everything I'd learned today.

'You look like your adventures are catching up with you,' Ralph said.

I felt a wave of fatigue sweep over me, almost carrying me off to sleep with it. 'Yeah, I'm fading,' I admitted. 'I think I'd better go to bed. Although in a way I hate to go to sleep, I'll be so sore in the morning. Maybe I could wake up enough to dance. If you keep moving, it's not so bad.'

'You look like you'd fall asleep on a disco floor right now, Vic, and I'd be arrested for beating you or something. Why does exercise help?'

'If you keep the blood circulating, it keeps the joints from stiffening so much.'

'Well, maybe we could do both – sleep and exercise, I mean.' The smile in his eyes was half embarrassed, half pleased.

I suddenly thought that after my evening with Earl and Tony, I'd like the comfort of someone in bed with me. 'Sure,' I said, smiling back.

Ralph called to the waiter for the bill and paid it promptly, his hands shaking slightly. I considered fighting him for it, especially since I could claim it as a business expense, but decided I'd done enough fighting for one day.

We waited outside for the doorman to fetch the car. Ralph stood close, not touching me, but tense. I realized he had been planning this ending all along and hadn't been sure he could carry it off, and I smiled a little to myself in the dark. When the car came, I sat close to him on the front seat. 'I live on Halsted,

75

just north of Belmont,' I said, and fell asleep on his shoulder.

He woke me up at the Belmont-Halsted intersection and asked for the address. My neighborhood is just north and west of a smarter part of town and there is usually good parking on the street; he found a place across from my front door.

It took a major effort to pull myself out of the car. The night air was warm and comforting and Ralph steadied me with shaking hands as we crossed the street and went into my front hallway. The three flights up looked very far away and I had a sudden mental flash of sitting on the front steps waiting for my dad to come home from work and carry me upstairs. If I asked Ralph to, he would carry me up. But it would alter the dependency balance in the relationship too much. I set my teeth and climbed the stairs. No one was lying in wait at the top.

I went into the kitchen and pulled a bottle of Martell from the liquor cupboard. I got two glasses down, two of my mother's Venetian glasses, part of the small dowry she had brought to her marriage. They were a beautiful clear red with twisted stems. It had been a long time since I had had anyone up to my apartment, and I suddenly felt shy and vulnerable. I'd been overexposed to men today and wasn't ready to do it again in bed.

When I brought the bottle and glasses back to the living room Ralph was sitting on the couch, leafing through *Fortune* without reading it. He got up and took the glasses from me, admiring them. I explained that my mother had left Italy right before the war broke out on a large scale. Her own mother was Jewish and they wanted her out of harm's way. The eight red glasses she wrapped carefully in her underwear to take in the one suitcase she had carried, and they had always held pride of place at any festive meal. I poured brandy.

Ralph told me that his family was Irish. 'That's why it's "Devereux" without an A — the As are French.' We sat for a while without talking, drinking our brandy. He was a bit nervous, too, and it helped me relax. Suddenly he grinned, his face lighting, and said, 'When I got divorced I moved into the city because I had a theory that that's where you meet the chicks —

sorry, women. But to tell you the truth, you're the first woman I've asked out in the six months I've been here – and you're not like any woman I ever met before.' He flushed a little. 'I just wanted you to know that I'm not hopping in and out of bed every night. But I would like to get into bed with you.'

I didn't answer him, but stood up and took his hand. Hand-in-hand, like five-year-olds, we walked into the bedroom. Ralph carefully helped me out of my dress and gently stroked my puffy arms. I unbuttoned his shirt. He took off his clothes and we climbed into the bed. I'd been afraid that I might have to help him along; recently-divorced men sometimes have problems because they feel very insecure. Fortunately he didn't, because I was too tired to help anyone. My last memory was of his breath expelling loudly, and then I was asleep.

7

A LITTLE HELP FROM A FRIEND

When I woke up, the room was full of the soft light of late morning, diffused through my heavy bedroom curtains. I was alone in the bed and lay still to collect my thoughts. Gradually the memory of yesterday's events returned, and I moved my head cautiously to look at the bedside clock. My neck was very stiff, and I had to turn my whole body to see the time – 11.30. I sat up. My stomach muscles were all right, but my thighs and calves were sore, and it was painful to stand upright. I did a slow shuffle to the bathroom, the kind you do the day after you run five miles when you haven't been out for a couple of months, and turned on the hot water in the tub full blast.

Ralph called to me from the living room. 'Good morning,' I called back. 'If you want to talk to me, you'll have to come here – I'm not walking any farther.' Ralph came into the bathroom, fully dressed, and joined me while I gloomily studied my face in the mirror over the sink. My incipient black eye had turned a deep blackish-purple, streaked with yellow and green. My uninjured left eye was bloodshot. My jaw had turned gray. The whole effect was unappealing.

Ralph seemed to share my feeling. I was watching his face in the mirror; he seemed a little disgusted. My bet was that Dorothy had never come home with a black eye – suburban life is so dull.

'Do you do this kind of thing often?' Ralph asked.

'You mean scrutinize my body, or what?' I asked.

He moved his hands vaguely. 'The fighting,' he said.

'Not as much as I did as a child. I grew up on the South Side. Ninetieth and Commercial, if you know the area – lots of Polish steelworkers who didn't welcome racial and ethnic newcomers – and the feeling was mutual. The law of the jungle ruled in my high school – if you couldn't swing a mean toe or fist, you might as well forget it.'

I turned from the mirror. Ralph was shaking his head, but he was trying to understand, trying not to back away. 'It's a different world,' he said slowly. 'I grew up in Libertyville, and I don't think I was ever in a real fight. And if my sister had come home with a black eye, my mother would have been hysterical for a month. Didn't your folks mind?'

'Oh, my mother hated it, but she died when I was fifteen, and my dad was thankful that I could take care of myself.' That was true – Gabriella had hated violence. But she was a fighter, and I got my scrappiness from her, not from my big, even-tempered father.

'Did all the girls in your school fight?' Ralph wanted to know.

I climbed into the hot water while I considered this. 'No, some of them just got scared off. And some got themselves boyfriends to protect them. The rest of us learned to protect ourselves. One girl I went to school with still loves to fight – she's a gorgeous redhead, and she loves going to bars and punching out guys who try to pick her up. Truly amazing.'

I sank back in the water and covered my face and neck with hot wet cloths. Ralph was quiet for a minute, then said, 'I'll make some coffee if you'll tell me the secret – I couldn't find any. And I didn't know whether you were saving those dishes for Christmas, so I washed them.'

I uncovered my mouth but kept the cloth over my eyes. I'd forgotten the goddamn dishes yesterday when I left the house. 'Thanks.' What else could I say? 'Coffee's in the freezer – whole beans. Use a tablespoon per cup. The grinder's by the stove – electric gadget. Filters are in the cupboard right over it, and the pot is still in the sink – unless you washed it.'

He leaned over to kiss me, then went out. I reheated the washcloth and flexed my legs in the steamy water. After a while they moved easily, so I was confident they would be fine in a few days. Before Ralph returned with the coffee I had soaked much of the stiffness out of my joints. I climbed out of the tub and enveloped myself in a large blue bath towel and walked – with much less difficulty – to the living room.

Ralph came in with the coffee. He admired my robe, but couldn't quite look me in the face. 'The weather's broken,' he remarked. 'I went out to get a paper and it's a beautiful day – clear and cool. Want to drive out to the Indiana Dunes?'

I started to shake my head, but the pain stopped me. 'No. It sounds lovely, but I've got some work to do.'

'Come on, Vic,' Ralph protested. 'Let the police handle this. You're in rotten shape – you need to take the day off.'

'You could be right,' I said, trying to keep down my anger. 'But I thought we went through all that last night. At any rate, I'm not taking the day off.'

'Well, how about some company. Need someone to drive you?'

I studied Ralph's face, but all I saw was friendly concern. Was he just having an attack of male protectiveness, or did he have some special reason for wanting me to stay off the job? As a companion he'd be able to keep tabs on my errands. And report them to Earl Smeissen?

'I'm going to Winnetka to talk to Peter Thayer's father. Since he's a neighbor of your boss, I'm not sure it would look too good for you to come along.'

'Probably not,' he agreed. 'Why do you have to see him?'

'It's like the man said about Annapurna, Ralph: because he's there.' There were a couple of other things I needed to do, too, things I'd just as soon be alone for.

'How about dinner tonight?' he suggested.

'Ralph, for heaven's sake, you're beginning to act like a Seeing Eye dog. No. No dinner tonight. You're sweet, I appreciate it, but I want some time to myself.'

'Okay, okay,' he grumbled. 'Just trying to be friendly.'

I stood up and walked painfully over to the couch where he was sitting. 'I know.' I put an arm around him and gave him a kiss. 'I'm just trying to be unfriendly.' He pulled me onto his lap. The dissatisfaction smoothed out of his face and he kissed me.

After a few minutes I pulled myself gently away and hobbled back to the bedroom to get dressed. The navy silk was lying over a chair, with a couple of rents in it and a fair amount of blood and dirt. My cleaner could probably fix it up, but I didn't think I'd ever care to wear it again. I threw it out and put on my green linen slacks with a pale-lemon shirt and a jacket. Perfect for suburbia. I decided not to worry about my face. It would look even more garish with makeup in sunlight than as it was.

I fixed myself Cream of Wheat while Ralph ate toast and jam. 'Well,' I said, 'time to head for suburbia.'

Ralph walked downstairs with me, trying to hold out a supporting hand. 'No, thanks,' I said. 'I'd better get used to doing this by myself.' At the bottom he won points by not lingering over his goodbyes. We kissed briefly; he sketched a cheerful wave and crossed the street to his car. I watched him out of sight, then hailed a passing cab.

The driver dropped me on Sheffield north of Addison, a neighborhood more decayed than mine, largely Puerto Rican. I rang Lotty Herschel's bell and was relieved when she answered it. 'Who's there?' she squawked through the intercom. 'It's me, Vic,' I said, and pushed the front door while the buzzer sounded.

Lotty lived on the second floor. She was waiting for me in the doorway when I made it to the top of the stairs. 'My dear Vic — what on earth is wrong with you?' she greeted me, her thick black eyebrows soaring to punctuate her astonishment.

I'd known Lotty for years. She was a doctor, about fifty, I thought, but with her vivid, clever face and trim, energetic body it was hard to tell. Sometime in her Viennese youth she had discovered the secret of perpetual motion. She held fierce opinions on a number of things, and put them to practice in medicine, often to the dismay of her colleagues. She'd been one of the physicians who performed abortions in connection with an underground referral service I'd belonged to at the University of Chicago in the days when abortion was illegal and a dirty word to most doctors. Now she ran a clinic in a shabby storefront down the street. She'd tried running it for nothing when she first opened it, but found the neighborhood people wouldn't trust medical care they didn't have to pay for. Still, it was one of the cheapest clinics in the city, and I often wondered what she lived on.

Now she shut the door behind me and ushered me into her living room. Like Lotty herself, it was sparely furnished, but glowed with strong colors – curtains in a vivid red and orange print, and an abstract painting like fire on the wall. Lotty sat me on a daybed and brought me a cup of the strong Viennese coffee she lived on.

'So now, Victoria, what have you been doing that makes you hobble upstairs like an old woman and turns your face black and blue? I am sure not a car accident, that's too tame for you – am I right?'

'Right as always, Lotty,' I answered, and gave her an abbreviated account of my adventures.

She pursed her lips at the tale of Smeissen but wasted no time arguing about whether I ought to go to the police or drop out of the case or spend the day in bed. She didn't always agree with me, but Lotty respected my decisions. She went into her bedroom and returned with a large, businesslike black bag. She pulled my face muscles and looked at my eyes with an ophthalmoscope. 'Nothing time won't cure,' she pronounced, and checked the reflexes in my legs and the muscles. 'Yes, I see, you are sore, and you will continue to be sore. But you are healthy, you take good care of yourself; it will pass off before too long.'

'Yes, I suspected as much,' I agreed. 'But I can't take the time to wait for these leg muscles to heal. And they're sore enough to slow me down quite a bit right now. I need something that will help me overlook the pain enough to do some errands and some thinking – not like codeine that knocks you out. Do you have anything?'

'Ah, yes, a miracle drug.' Lotty's face was amused. 'You shouldn't put so much faith in doctors and drugs, Vic. However, I'll give you a shot of phenylbutazone. That's what they give racehorses to keep them from aching when they run, and it seems to me you're galloping around like a horse.'

She disappeared for a few minutes, and I heard the refrigerator door open. She returned with a syringe and a small, rubber-stoppered bottle. 'Now, lie down; we'll do this in your behind so it goes quickly to the bloodstream. Pull your slacks down a bit, so; great stuff this, really, they call it "bute" for short, in half an hour you will be ready for the Derby, my dear.' As she talked, Lotty worked rapidly. I felt a small sting, and it was over. 'Now, sit. I'll tell you some stories about the clinic. I'm going to give you some nepenthe to take away with you. That's very strong, a painkiller; don't try to drive while you're taking it, and don't drink. I'll pack up some bute in tablets for you.'

I leaned back against a big pillow and tried not to relax too much. The temptation to lie down and sleep was very strong. I forced myself to follow Lotty's quick, clever talk, asking questions, but not debating her more outlandish statements. After a while I could feel the drug taking effect. My neck muscles eased considerably. I didn't feel like unarmed combat, but I was reasonably certain I could handle my car.

Lotty didn't try to stop my getting up. 'You've rested for close to an hour – you should do for a while.' She packed the bute tablets in a plastic bottle and gave me a bottle of nepenthe.

I thanked her. 'How much do I owe you?'

She shook her head. 'No, these are all samples. When you come for your long-overdue checkup, then I'll charge you what any good Michigan Avenue doctor would.'

She saw me to the door. 'Seriously, Vic, if you get worried about this Smeissen character you are always welcome in my spare room.' I thanked her – it was a good offer, and one that I might need.

Normally I would have walked back to my car; Lotty was only about eight blocks from me. But even with the shot I didn't feel quite up to par, so I walked slowly down to Addison and caught a cab. I rode it down to my office, where I picked up Peter Thayer's voter card with the Winnetka address on it, then flagged another cab back to my own car on the North Side. McGraw was going to have quite a bill for expenses – all these cabs, and then the navy suit had cost a hundred and sixty-seven dollars.

A lot of people were out enjoying the day, and the clean fresh air lifted my spirits too. By two I was on the Edens Expressway heading toward the North Shore. I started singing a snatch from Mozart's 'Ch'io mi scordi di te', but my rib cage protested and I had to settle for a Bartok concerto on WFMT.

For some reason the Edens ceases to be a beautiful expressway as it nears the homes of the rich. Close to Chicago it's lined with greensward and neat bungalows, but as you go farther out, shopping centers crop up and industrial parks and drive-ins take over. Once I turned right onto Willow Road, though, and headed toward the lake, the view became more impressive – large stately homes set well back on giant, carefully manicured lawns. I checked Thayer's address and turned south onto Sheridan Road, squinting at numbers on mailboxes. His house was on the east side, the side where lots face Lake Michigan, giving the children private beaches and boat moorings when they were home from Groton or Andover.

My Chevy felt embarrassed turning through twin stone pillars, especially when it saw a small Mercedes, an Alfa and an Audi Fox off to one side of the drive. The circular drive took me past some attractive flower gardens to the front door of a limestone mansion. Next to the door a small sign requested tradesmen to make deliveries in the rear. Was I a tradesman or -woman? I wasn't sure I had anything to deliver, but perhaps my host did.

I took a card from my wallet and wrote a short message on it: 'Let's talk about your relations with the Knifegrinders.' I rang the bell.

The expression on the face of the neatly uniformed woman

who answered the door reminded me of my black eye: the bute had put it out of my mind for a while. I gave her the card. 'I'd like to see Mr Thayer,' I said coolly.

She looked at me dubiously but took the card, shutting the door in my face. I could hear faint shouts from beaches farther up the road. As the minutes passed I left the porch to make a more detailed study of a flower bed on the other side of the drive. When the door opened I turned back. The maid frowned at me.

'I'm not stealing the flowers,' I assured her. 'But since you don't have magazines in the waiting area, I had to look at something.'

She sucked in her breath but only said, 'This way.' No 'please', no manners at all. Still, this was a house of mourning. I made allowances.

We moved at a fast clip through a large entry room graced by a dull-green statue, past a stairway and down a hall leading to the back of the house. John Thayer met us, coming from the other direction. He was wearing a white knit shirt and checked gray slacks – suburban attire but muted. His whole air was subdued, as if he were consciously trying to act like a mourning father.

'Thanks, Lucy. We'll go in here.' He took my arm and moved me into a room with comfortable armchairs and packed bookcases. The books were lined up neatly on the shelves. I wondered if he ever read any of them.

Thayer held out my card. 'What's this about, Warshawski?'

'Just what it says. I want to talk about your relations with the Knifegrinders.'

He gave a humorless smile. 'They are as minimal as possible. Now that Peter is – gone, I expect them to be non-existent.'

'I wonder if Mr McGraw would agree with that.'

He clenched his fist, crushing the card. 'Now we get to it. McGraw hired you to blackmail me, didn't he?'

'Then there is a connection between you and the Knifegrinders.'

'No!'

'Then how can Mr McGraw possibly blackmail you?'

'A man like that stops at nothing. I warned you yesterday to be careful around him.'

'Look, Mr Thayer. Yesterday you got terribly upset at learning that McGraw had brought your name into this. Today you're afraid he's blackmailing you. That's awfully suggestive.'

His face was set in harsh, strained lines. 'Of what?'

'Something was going on between you two that you don't want known. Your son found it out and you two had him killed to keep him quiet.'

'That's a lie, Warshawski, a goddamned lie,' he roared.

'Prove it.'

'The police arrested Peter's killer this morning.'

My head swam and I sat down suddenly in one of the leather chairs. 'What?' My voice squeaked.

'One of the commissioners called me. They found a drug addict who'd tried to rob the place. They say Peter caught him at it and was shot.'

'No,' I said.

'What do you mean, no? They arrested the guy.'

'No. Maybe they arrested him, but that wasn't the scene. No one robbed that place. Your son didn't catch anyone in the act. I tell you, Thayer, the boy was sitting at the kitchen table and someone shot him. That is not the work of a drug addict caught in a felony. Besides, nothing was taken.'

'What are you after, Warshawski? Maybe nothing was taken. Maybe he got scared and fled. I'd believe that before I'd believe your story – that I shot my own son.' His face was working with a strong emotion. Grief? Anger? Maybe horror?

'Mr Thayer, I'm sure you've noticed what a mess my face is. A couple of punks roughed me up last night to warn me off the investigation into your son's death. A drug addict doesn't have those kinds of resources. I saw several people who might have engineered that – and you and Andy McGraw were two of them.'

'People don't like busybodies, Warshawski. If someone beat you up, I'd take the hint.'

86

I was too tired to get angry. 'In other words, you are involved but you figure you've got your ass covered. So that means I'll have to figure out a way to saw the barrel off your tail. It'll be a pleasure.'

'Warshawski, I'm telling you for your own good: drop it.' He went over to his desk. 'I can see you're a conscientious girl – but McGraw is wasting your time. There's nothing to find.' He wrote a check and handed it to me. 'Here. You can give McGraw back whatever he's paid you and feel like you've done your duty.'

The check was for $5,000. 'You bastard. You accuse me of blackmail and then you try to buy me off?' A spurt of raw anger pushed my fatigue to one side. I ripped up the check and let the pieces fall to the floor.

Thayer turned white. Money was his raw nerve. 'The police made an arrest, Warshawski. I don't need to buy you off. But if you want to act stupid about it, there's nothing more to say. You'd better leave.'

The door opened and a girl came in. 'Oh, Dad, Mother wants you to –' She broke off. 'Sorry, didn't know you had company.' She was an attractive teenager. Her brown, straight hair was well brushed and hung down her back, framing a small oval face. She was wearing jeans and a striped man's shirt several sizes too big for her. Maybe her brother's. Normally she probably had the confident, healthy air that money can provide. Right now she drooped a bit.

'Miss Warshawski was just leaving, Jill. In fact, why don't you show her out and I'll go see what your mother wants.'

He got up and walked to the door, waiting until I followed him to say goodbye. I didn't offer to shake hands. Jill led me back the way I'd come earlier; her father walked briskly in the opposite direction.

'I'm very sorry about your brother,' I said as we got to the greenish statue.

'So am I,' she said, pulling her lips together. When we got to the front of the house, she followed me outside and stood staring up at my face, frowning a little. 'Did you know Peter?' she finally asked.

'No, I never met him,' I answered. 'I'm a private investigator, and I'm afraid I'm the person who found him the other morning.'

'They wouldn't let me look at him,' she said.

'His face was fine. Don't have nightmares about him – his face wasn't damaged.' She wanted more information. If he'd been shot in the head, how could his face look all right? I explained it to her in a toned-down, clinical way.

'Peter told me you could decide whether to trust people by their faces,' she said after a minute. 'But yours is pretty banged up so I can't tell. But you told me the truth about Peter and you're not talking to me as if I was a baby or something.' She paused. I waited. Finally she asked, 'Did Dad ask you to come out here?' When I replied, she asked, 'Why was he angry?'

'Well, he thinks the police have arrested your brother's murderer, but I think they've got the wrong person. And that made him angry.'

'Why?' she asked. 'I mean, not why is he mad, but why do you think they got the wrong person?'

'The reasons are pretty complicated. It's not because I know who did it, but because I saw your brother, and the apartment, and some other people who've been involved, and they've reacted to my seeing them. I've been in this business for a while, and I have a feel for when I'm hearing the truth. A drug addict wandering in off the streets just doesn't fit with what I've seen and heard.'

She stood on one foot, and her face was screwed up as if she were afraid she might start crying. I put an arm around her and pulled her to a sitting position on the shallow porch step.

'I'm okay,' she muttered. 'It's just – everything is so weird around here. You know, it's so terrible, Pete dying and everything. He – he – well –' She hiccuped back a sob. 'Never mind. It's Dad who's crazy. Probably he always was but I never noticed it before. He's been raving on and on about how Anita and her father shot Pete for his money and dumb stuff like that, and then he'll start saying how it served Pete right, like he's glad he's dead or something.' She gulped and ran her hand across her nose. 'Dad was always in such a stew about Peter disgracing the family name, you know, but he wouldn't have – even if he'd become a union organizer he would have been a successful one. He liked figuring things out, he was that kind of person, figuring things out and trying to do them the best way.' She hiccuped again. 'And I like Anita. Now I suppose I'll never see her again. I wasn't supposed to meet her, but she and Pete took me out to dinner sometimes, when Mom and Dad were out of town.'

'She's disappeared, you know,' I told her. 'You wouldn't know where she's gone, would you?'

She looked up at me with troubled eyes. 'Do you think something's happened to her?'

'No,' I said with a reassurance I didn't feel. 'I think she got scared and ran away.'

'Anita's really wonderful,' she said earnestly. 'But Dad and Mother just refused even to meet her. That was when Dad first started acting weird, when Pete and Anita began going together. Even today, when the police came, he wouldn't believe they'd arrested this man. He kept saying it was Mr McGraw. It was really awful.' She grimaced unconsciously. 'Oh, it's been just horrible here. Nobody cares about Pete. Mother just cares about the neighbors. Dad is freaked out. I'm the only one who cares he's dead.' Tears were streaming down her face now and she stopped trying to fight them. 'Sometimes I even get the crazy idea that Dad just freaked out totally, like he does, and killed Peter.'

This was the big fear. Once she'd said it, she started sobbing convulsively and shivering. I took off my jacket and wrapped it around her shoulders. I held her close for a few minutes and let her sob.

The door opened behind us. Lucy stood there, scowling. 'Your father wants to know where you've gone to – and he doesn't want you standing around gossiping with the detective.'

I stood up. 'Why don't you take her inside and wrap her up

in a blanket and get her something hot to drink: she's pretty upset with everything that's going on, and she needs some attention.'

Jill was still shivering, but she'd stopped sobbing. She gave me a watery little smile and handed me my jacket. 'I'm okay,' she whispered.

I dug a card out of my purse and handed it to her. 'Call me if you need me, Jill,' I said. 'Day or night.' Lucy hustled her inside at top speed and shut the door. I was really toning down the neighborhood – good thing they couldn't see me through the trees.

My shoulders and legs were beginning to hurt again and I walked slowly back to my car. The Chevy had a crease in the front right fender where someone had sideswiped it in last winter's heavy snow. The Alfa, the Fox and the Mercedes were all in mint condition. My car and I looked alike, whereas the Thayers seemed more like the sleek, scratchless Mercedes. There was a lesson in there someplace. Maybe too much urban living was bad for cars and people. Real profound, Vic.

I wanted to get back to Chicago and call Bobby and get the lowdown on this drug addict they'd arrested, but I needed to do something else while Lotty's painkiller was still holding me up. I drove back over to the Edens and went south to the Dempster exit. This road led through the predominantly Jewish suburb of Skokie, and I stopped at the Bagel Works delicatessen and bagel bakery there. I ordered a jumbo corned beef on rye and a Fresca, and sat in the car, eating while I tried to decide where to get a gun. I knew how to use them – my dad had seen too many shooting accidents in homes with guns. He'd decided the way to avoid one in our house was for my mother and me to learn how to use them. My mother had always refused: they gave her unhappy memories of the war and she would always say she'd use the time to pray for a world without weapons. But I used to go down to the police range with my dad on Saturday afternoons and practice target shooting. At one time I could clean and load and fire a .45 revolver in two minutes, but since my father had died ten years ago, I hadn't been out shooting. I'd given his gun to Bobby as a memento when he'd died, and I'd never needed one since then. I had killed a man once, but that had been an accident. Joe Correl had jumped me outside a warehouse when I was looking into some inventory losses for a company. I had broken his hold and smashed his jaw in, and when he fell, he'd hit his head on the edge of a forklift. I'd broken his jaw, but it was his skull against the forklift that killed him.

But Smeissen had a lot of hired muscle, and if he was really pissed off he could hire some more. A gun wouldn't completely protect me, but I thought it might narrow the odds.

The corned-beef sandwich was delicious. I hadn't had one for a long time, and decided to forget my weight-maintenance program for one afternoon and have another. There was a phone booth in the deli, and I let my fingers do the walking through the Yellow Pages. The phone book showed four columns of gun dealers. There was one not too far from where I was in the suburb of Lincolnwood. When I called and described what I wanted, they didn't have it. After $1.20 worth of calls I finally located a repeating, mediumweight Smith & Wesson on the far South Side of the city. My injuries were really throbbing by this time and I didn't feel like a forty-mile drive to the other end of the city. On the other hand, those injuries were why I needed the gun. I paid for the corned-beef sandwich and with my second Fresca swallowed four of the tablets Lotty had given me.

The drive south should have taken only an hour, but I was feeling light-headed, my head and body not connected too strongly. The last thing I wanted was for one of Chicago's finest to pull me over. I took it slowly, swallowed a couple more tablets of bute, and put all my effort into holding my concentration.

It was close to five when I exited from 1-57 to the south suburbs. By the time I got to Riley's they were ready to close. I insisted on coming in to make my purchase.

'I know what I want,' I said. 'I called a couple of hours ago — a Smith & Wesson thirty-eight.'

The clerk looked suspiciously at my face and took in the black eye. 'Why don't you come back on Monday, and if you still feel you want a gun, we can talk about a model more suited to a lady than a Smith & Wesson thirty-eight.'

'Despite what you may think I am not a wife-beating victim. I am not planning on buying a gun to go home and kill my husband. I'm a single woman living alone and I was attacked last night. I know how to use a gun, and I've decided I need one, and this is the kind I want.'

'Just a minute,' the clerk said. He hurried to the back of the store and began a whispered consultation with two men standing there. I went to the case and started inspecting guns and ammunition. The store was new, clean, and beautifully laid out. Their ad in the Yellow Pages proclaimed Riley's as Smith & Wesson specialists, but they had enough variety to please any kind of taste in shooting. One wall was devoted to rifles.

My clerk came over with one of the others, a pleasant-faced, middle-aged man. 'Ron Jaffrey,' he said. 'I'm the manager. What can we do for you?'

'I called up a couple of hours ago asking about a Smith & Wesson thirty-eight. I'd like to get one,' I repeated.

'Have you ever used one before?' the manager asked.

'No. I'm more used to the Colt forty-five,' I answered. 'But the S & W is lighter and better suited to my needs.'

The manager walked to one of the cases and unlocked it. My clerk went to the door to stop another last-minute customer from entering. I took the gun from the manager, balanced it in my hand, and tried the classic police firing stance: body turned to create as narrow a target as possible. The gun felt good. 'I'd like to try it before I buy it,' I told the manager. 'Do you have a target range?'

Jaffrey took a box of ammunition from the case. 'I have to say you look as though you know how to handle it. We have a range in the back – if you decide against the gun, we ask you to pay for the ammo. If you take the gun, we throw in a box free.'

'Fine,' I said. I followed him through a door in the back, which led to a small range.

'We give lessons back here on Sunday afternoons, and let people come in to practice on their own during the week. Need any help loading?'

'I may,' I told him. 'Time was when I could load and fire in thirty seconds, but it's been a while.' My hands were starting to shake a bit from fatigue and pain and it took me several minutes to insert eight rounds of cartridges. The manager showed me the safety and the action. I nodded, turned to the target, lifted the gun and fired. The action came as naturally as if ten days, not ten years, had passed, but my aim was way off. I emptied the gun but didn't get a bull's-eye, and only two in the inner ring. The gun was good, though, steady action and no noticeable distortion. 'Let me try another lot.'

I emptied the chambers and Jaffrey handed me some more cartridges. He gave me a couple of pointers. 'You obviously know what you're doing, but you're out of practice and you've picked up some bad habits. Your stance is good, but you're hunching your shoulder – keep it down and only raise the arm.'

I loaded and fired again, trying to keep my shoulder down. It was good advice – all but two shots got into the red and one grazed the bull's-eye. 'Okay,' I said. 'I'll take it. Give me a couple of boxes of ammo, and a complete cleaning kit.' I thought a minute. 'And a shoulder holster.'

We went back into the store. 'Larry!' Jaffrey called. My clerk came over. 'Clean and wrap this gun for the lady while I write up the bill.' Larry took the gun, and I went with Jaffrey to the cash register. A mirror was mounted behind it, and I saw myself in it without recognition for a few seconds. The left side of my face was now completely purple and badly swollen while my right eye stared with the dark anguish of a Paul Klee drawing. I almost turned to see who this battered woman was before realizing I was looking at myself. No wonder Larry hadn't wanted to let me in the store.

Jaffrey showed me the bill. 'Four hundred twenty-two dollars,' he said. 'Three-ten for the gun, ten for the second box of cartridges, fifty-four for the holster and belt, and twenty-eight for the cleaning kit. The rest is tax.' I wrote a check out, slowly and laboriously. 'I need a driver's license and two major credit cards or an interbank card,' he said, 'and I have to ask you to sign this register.' He looked at my driver's license. 'Monday you should go down to City Hall and register that gun. I send a list of all major purchases to the local police department, and they'll probably forward your name to the Chicago police.'

I nodded and quietly put my identification back in my billfold. The gun took a big chunk out of the thousand dollars I'd had from McGraw, and I didn't think I could legitimately charge it to him as an expense. Larry brought me the gun in a beautiful velvet case. I looked at it and asked them to put it in a bag for me. Ron Jaffrey ushered me urbanely to my car, magnificently ignoring my face. 'You live quite a ways from here, but if you want to come down and use the target just bring your bill with you – you get six months' free practice with the purchase.' He opened my car door for me. I thanked him, and he went back to the store.

The bute was still keeping the pain from crashing in on me completely, but I was absolutely exhausted. My last bit of energy had gone to buying the gun and using the target. I couldn't drive the thirty miles back to my apartment. I started the car and went slowly down the street, looking for a motel. I found a Best Western that had rooms backing onto a side street, away from the busy road I was on. The clerk looked cautiously at my face but made no comment. I paid cash and took the key.

The room was decent and quiet, the bed firm. I uncorked the bottle of nepenthe Lotty had given me and took a healthy swallow. I peeled off my clothes, wound my watch and put it on the bedside table, and crawled under the covers. I debated calling my answering service but decided I was too tired to handle anything even if it had come up. The air conditioner, set on high, drowned out any street noises and made the room cold enough to enjoy snuggling under the blankets. I lay down and was starting to think about John Thayer when I fell asleep.

8

SOME VISITORS DON'T KNOCK

I came to slowly, out of a sound sleep. I lay quietly, not sure at first where I was, and dozed again lightly. When I woke up the second time, I was refreshed and aware. The heavy drapes shut out any outside light; I switched on the bedside lamp and looked at my watch – 7.30. I had slept more than twelve hours.

I sat up and cautiously moved legs and neck. My muscles had stiffened again in my sleep, but not nearly as badly as the previous morning. I pulled myself from the bed and made it to the window with only minor twinges. Looking through a crack I pulled in the drapes, I saw bright morning sunlight.

I was puzzled by Thayer's account of a police arrest and wondered if there would be a story in the morning paper. I pulled on my slacks and shirt and went down to the lobby for a copy of the Sunday *Herald-Star*. Back upstairs I undressed again and ran a hot bath while I looked at the paper. DRUG ADDICT ARRESTED IN BANKING HEIR'S MURDER was on the lower right side of the front page.

Police have arrested Donald Mackenzie of 4302 S. Ellis in the murder of banking heir Peter Thayer last Monday. Asst. Police Commissioner Tim Sullivan praised the men working on the case and said an arrest was made early Saturday morning when one of the residents of the apartment where Peter Thayer lived identified Mackenzie as a man seen hanging around the building several times recently. It is believed that Mackenzie, allegedly addicted to cocaine, entered the Thayer apartment on Monday, July 16, believing no one to be at home. When he found Peter Thayer eating breakfast in the kitchen, he lost his nerve and shot him. Commissioner Sullivan says the Browning automatic that fired the fatal bullet has not yet been traced but that the police have every hope of recovering the weapon.

The story was continued on page sixty-three. Here, a full page had been devoted to the case. Pictures of the Thayer family with Jill, another sister, and a chic Mrs Thayer. A single shot of Peter in a baseball uniform for New Trier High School. A good candid picture of Anita McGraw. An accompanying story proclaimed LABOR LEADER'S DAUGHTER STILL MISSING. It suggested 'now that the police have made an arrest, there is hope that Miss McGraw will return to Chicago or call her family. Meanwhile, her picture has been circulated to state police in Wisconsin, Indiana and Michigan.'

That seemed to be that. I lay back in the water and closed my eyes. The police were supposedly hunting high and low for the Browning, questioning Mackenzie's friends, and searching his hangouts. But I didn't think they'd find it. I tried to remember what Earl's goons had been carrying. Fred had had a Colt, but I thought Tony might have had a Browning. Why was Thayer so willing to believe Mackenzie had killed his son? According to Jill, he'd been insisting at first it was McGraw. Something nagged at the back of my mind, but I couldn't put a finger on it. Could there possibly be any proof that Mackenzie had done it? On the other hand, what proof did I have that he hadn't? My stiff joints, the fact that nothing had been touched in the apartment . . . But what did it really add up to? I wondered if Bobby had made that arrest, whether he was among those diligent policemen whom Police Commissioner Sullivan unstintingly praised. I decided I needed to get back to Chicago and talk to him.

With this in mind I got dressed and left the motel. I realized I hadn't eaten since those two corned-beef sandwiches yesterday afternoon and stopped at a little coffee shop for a cheese omelette, juice and coffee. I was eating too much lately and not getting any exercise. I surreptitiously slid a finger around my waistband, but it didn't seem any tighter.

I took some more of Lotty's pills with my coffee and was feeling fine by the time I pulled off the Kennedy at Belmont. Sunday morning traffic was light and I made it to Halsted by a little after ten. There was a parking place across from my apartment, and a dark, unmarked car with a police antenna on it. I raised my eyebrows speculatively. Had the mountain come to Mohammed?

I crossed the street and looked into the car. Sergeant McGonnigal was sitting there alone with a newspaper. When he saw me he put the paper down and got out of the car. He was wearing a light sports jacket and gray slacks and his shoulder holster made a little bulge under his right armpit. A southpaw, I thought. 'Good morning, Sergeant,' I said. 'Beautiful day, isn't it?'

'Good morning, Miss Warshawski. Mind if I come up with you and ask you a few questions?'

'I don't know,' I answered. 'It depends on the questions. Bobby send you?'

'Yes. We got a couple of inquiries in and he thought I'd better come over to see if you're all right – that's quite a shiner you've picked up.'

'Yes, it is,' I agreed. I held the door to the building open for him and followed him in. 'How long have you been here?'

'I stopped by last night, but you weren't home. I called a couple of times. When I stopped by this morning I just thought I'd wait until noon to see if you showed up. Lieutenant Mallory was afraid the captain would order an APB on you if I reported you missing.'

'I see. I'm glad I decided to come home.'

We got to the top of the stairs. McGonnigal stopped. 'You usually leave your door open?'

'Never.' I moved past him. The door was cracked open, hanging a bit drunkenly. Someone had shot out the locks to get in – they don't respond to forcing. McGonnigal pulled out his gun, slammed the door open, and rolled into the room. I drew back against the hall wall, then followed him in.

My apartment was a mess. Someone had gone berserk in it. The sofa cushions had been cut open, pictures thrown on the floor, books opened and dropped so that they lay with open spines and crumpling pages. We walked through the apartment. My clothes were scattered around the bedroom, drawers dumped out. In the kitchen all the flour and sugar had been emptied onto the floor, while pans and plates were everywhere, some of them chipped from reckless handling. In the dining room the red Venetian glasses were lying crazily on the table. Two had fallen off. One rested safely on the carpet, but the other had shattered on the wood floor. I picked up the seven whole ones and stood them in the breakfront and sat to pick up the pieces of the other. My hands were shaking and I couldn't handle the tiny shards.

'Don't touch anything else, Miss Warshawski.' McGonnigal's voice was kind. 'I'm going to call Lieutenant Mallory and get some fingerprint experts over here. They probably won't find anything, but we've got to try. In the meantime, I'm afraid you'll have to leave things the way they are.'

I nodded. 'The phone is next to the couch – what used to be the couch,' I said, not looking up. Jesus, what next? Who the hell had been in here, and why? It just couldn't be a random burglar. A pro might take the place apart looking for valuables – but rip up the couch? Dump china onto the floor? My mother had carried those glasses from Italy in a suitcase and not a one had broken. Nineteen years married to a cop on the South Side of Chicago and not a one had broken. If I had become a singer, as she had wanted, this would never have happened. I sighed. My hands were calmer, so I picked up the little shards and put them in a dish on the table.

'Please don't touch anything,' McGonnigal said again, from the doorway.

'Goddamnit, McGonnigal, shut up!' I snapped. 'Even if you do find a fingerprint in here that doesn't belong to me or one of my friends, you think they're going to go all over these splinters of glass? And I'll bet you dinner at the Savoy that whoever came through here wore gloves and you won't find a damned thing anyway.' I stood up. 'I'd like to know what you were doing when the tornado came through — sitting out front reading your newspaper? Did you think the noise came from someone's television? Who came in and out of the building while you were here?'

He flushed. Mallory was going to ask him the same question. If he hadn't bothered to find out, he was in hot water.

'I don't think this was done while I was here, but I'll go ask your downstairs neighbors if they heard any noise. I know it must be very upsetting to come home and find your apartment destroyed, but please, Miss Warshawski — if we're going to have a prayer of finding these guys we've got to fingerprint the place.'

'Okay, okay,' I said. He went out to check downstairs. I went to the bedroom. My canvas suitcase was lying open but fortunately had not been cut. I didn't think canvas would take fingerprints, so I put it on the dismantled box springs and packed, going through the array of clothes and lingerie on the floor. I put the wrapped box from Riley's in, too, and then called Lotty on the bedside phone.

'Lotty, I can't talk right now, but my apartment has been ravaged. Can I come and stay a few nights?'

'Naturally, Vic. Do you need me to come get you?'

'No, I'm okay. I'll be over in a while — I need to talk to the police first.'

We hung up and I took the suitcase down to the car. McGonnigal was in the second-floor apartment; the door was half open and he was talking, with his back to the hallway. I put the suitcase in my trunk and was just unlocking the outer door to go back upstairs when Mallory came squealing up to the curb with a couple of squad cars hot behind him. They double-parked, lights flashing, and a group of kids gathered at the end of the street, staring. Police like to create public drama – no other need for all that show.

'Hello Bobby,' I said as cheerily as I could manage.

'What the hell is going on here, Vicki?' Bobby asked, so angry that he forgot his cardinal rule against swearing in front of women and children.

'Not nice, whatever it is: someone tore my place up. They smashed one of Gabriella's glasses.'

Mallory had been charging up the stairs, about to muscle me aside, but that stopped him – he'd drunk too many New Year's toasts out of those glasses. 'Christ, Vicki, I'm sorry, but what the hell were you doing poking your nose into this business anyway?'

'Why don't you send your boys upstairs and we'll sit here and talk. There's no place to sit down up there and frankly, I can't stand to look at it.'

He thought about it for a minute. 'Yeah, why don't we go sit in my car, and you answer a few questions. Finchley!' he bellowed. A young black cop stepped forward. 'Take the crew upstairs and fingerprint the place and search it if you can for any clues.' He turned to me. 'Anything valuable that might be missing?'

I shrugged. 'Who knows what's valuable to a ransacker? A couple of good pieces of jewelry – my mother's; I never wear them, too old-fashioned – a single diamond pendant set in a white gold filigree with matching earrings. A couple of rings. There's a little silver flatware. I don't know – a turntable. I haven't looked for anything – just looked and looked away.'

'Yeah, okay,' Bobby said. 'Go on.' He waved a hand and the four uniformed men started up the stairs. 'And send McGonnigal down to me,' he called after them.

We went to Bobby's car and sat together in the front seat. His full, red face was set – angry, but not, I thought, with me. 'I told you on Thursday to butt out of the Thayer case.'

'I heard the police made an arrest yesterday – Donald Mackenzie. Is there still a Thayer case?'

Bobby ignored that. 'What happened to your face?'

'I ran into a door.'

'Don't clown, Vicki. You know why I sent McGonnigal over to talk to you?'

'I give up. He fell in love with me and you were giving him an excuse to come by and see me?'

'I can't deal with you this morning!' Bobby yelled, top volume. 'A kid is dead, your place is a wreck, your face looks like hell, and all you can think of is getting my goat. Goddamnit, talk to me straight and pay attention to what I say.'

'Okay, okay,' I said pacifically. 'I give up: why did you send the sergeant over to see me?'

Bobby breathed heavily for a few minutes. He nodded, as if to affirm that he'd recovered his self-control. 'Because John Thayer told me last night that you'd been beaten up and you didn't believe that Mackenzie had committed the crime.'

'Thayer,' I echoed, incredulous. 'I talked to him yesterday and he threw me out of his house because I wouldn't accept his word that Mackenzie was the murderer. Now why's he turning around telling you that? How'd you come to be talking to him, anyway?'

Bobby smiled sourly. 'We had to go out to Winnetka to ask a few last questions. When it's the Thayer family, we wait on their convenience, and that was when it was convenient . . . He believes it was Mackenzie but he wants to be sure. Now tell me about your face.'

'There's nothing to tell. It looks worse than it is – you know how it is with black eyes.'

Bobby drummed on the steering wheel in exaggerated patience. 'Vicki, after I talked to Thayer I had McGonnigal go through our reports to see if anyone had turned in anything on a battered woman. And we found a cabbie had stopped at the Town Hall Station and mentioned picking up a woman at Astor and the Drive and dropping her at your address. Quite a coincidence, huh? The guy was worried because you looked in pretty bad shape, but there wasn't anything anyone could do about it – you weren't filing a complaint.'

101

'Right you are,' I said.

Mallory tightened his lips but didn't lose his temper. 'Now, Vicki,' he continued. 'McGonnigal wondered what you were doing down at Astor and the Drive looking so bloody. It's not really a mugger's spot. And he remembered how Earl Smeissen owns a condo down there on Astor, in from State Street – o Parkway they call it when it gets into the tony part of town. So now we want to know why Earl wanted to beat you up.'

'It's your story. You're saying he beat me up, you give me a reason why.'

'He probably had a bellyful of your clowning,' Bobby said, his voice rising again. 'For two cents I'd black your other goddamn eye for you.'

'Is that why you came over, to threaten me?'

'Vicki, I want to know why Earl beat you. The only reason I can think of is that he's tied to the Thayer boy – maybe had him shot when someone else fingered him.'

'Then you don't think that Mackenzie is responsible?' Mallory was silent. 'You make the arrest?'

'No,' Mallory said stiffly. I could see this hurt. 'Lieutenant Carlson did.'

'Carlson? I don't know him. Who's he work for?'

'Captain Vespucci,' Mallory said shortly.

I raised my eyebrows. 'Vespucci?' I was beginning to sound like a parrot. Vespucci had been a colleague my father was ashamed to talk about. He'd been implicated in a number of departmental scandals over the years, most of them having to do with police bought off by the mob, or turning the other cheek to mob activities in their territory. There'd never been enough evidence to justify throwing him off the force – but that, too, the rumors said, was because he had the kind of connections that made you keep quiet.

'Carlson and Vespucci pretty close?' I asked.

'Yes,' Bobby bit off.

I thought for a minute. 'Did someone – like Earl, say – bring pressure on Vespucci to make an arrest? Is Donald Mackenzie

102

another poor slob caught in a trap because he was wandering around the wrong part of town? Did he leave any prints in the apartment? Can you find the gun? Has he made a confession?'

'No, but he can't account for his time on Monday. And we're pretty sure he's been involved in some Hyde Park burglaries.'

'But you don't agree that he's the killer?'

'As far as the department is concerned, the case is closed. I talked to Mackenzie myself this morning.'

'And?'

'And nothing. My captain says it's a defensible arrest.'

'Your captain owe anything to Vespucci?' I asked.

Mallory made a violent motion with his torso. 'Don't talk like that to me, Vicki. We've got seventy-three unsolved homicides right now. If we wrap one up in a week, the captain has every right to be happy.'

'All right, Bobby.' I sighed. 'Sorry. Lieutenant Carlson arrested Mackenzie, and Vespucci told your captain, who told you to lay off, the case was closed . . . But you want to know why Earl beat me up.' Mallory turned red again. 'You can't have it both ways. If Mackenzie is the killer, why would Smeissen care about me and Peter Thayer? If he beat me up — and I mean *if* — it could have been for lots of reasons. He might've made a heavy pass I turned down. Earl doesn't like ladies who turn him down, you know — he's beaten a couple before. First time I ever saw Earl was when I was a starry-eyed rookie attorney on the Public Defender's roster. I was appearing for a lady whom Earl beat up. Nice young prostitute who didn't want to work for him. Sorry, I just committed slander: she alleged that Earl beat her up, but we couldn't make it stick.'

'You're not going to ask for charges, then,' Mallory said. 'Figures. Now tell me about your apartment. I haven't seen it, but I take it as read that it was torn apart — McGonnigal gave me a brief description. Someone was looking for something. What?'

I shook my head. 'Beats me. None of my clients has ever given me the secret to the neutron bomb or even a new brand

103

of toothpaste. I just don't deal with that kind of stuff. And anytime I do have volatile evidence, I leave it in a safe in my office . . .' My voice trailed off. Why hadn't I thought of that sooner? If someone had torn the apartment apart looking for something, they were probably down in my office now.

'Give me the address,' Bobby said. I gave it to him and he got on the car radio and ordered a patrol car to go up and check. 'Now, Vicki, I want you to be honest with me. This is off the record – no witnesses, no tapes. Tell me what you took out of that apartment that someone, call him Smeissen, wants back so badly.' He looked at me in a kindly, worried, fatherly, way. What did I have to lose by telling him about the picture and the pay stub?

'Bobby,' I said earnestly, 'I did look around the apartment but I didn't see anything that smacked remotely of Earl or any other person in particular. Not only that, the place didn't look as though anyone else had searched it.'

Sergeant McGonnigal came up to the car. 'Hi, Lieutenant – Finchley said you wanted me.'

'Yeah,' Bobby said. 'Who came in and out of the building while you were watching it?'

'Just one of the residents, sir.'

'You sure of that?'

'Yes, sir. She lives in the second-floor apartment. I was just talking to her – Mrs Alvarez – said she heard a lot of noise about three this morning, but didn't pay any attention to it – says Miss Warshawski often has strange guests and wouldn't thank her – Mrs Alvarez – for interfering.'

Thanks, Mrs Alvarez, I thought. The city needs more neighbors like you. Glad I wasn't home at the time. But what, I wondered, was whoever ransacked my place looking for so desperately? That pay stub linked Peter Thayer to Ajax, but that was no secret. And the picture of Anita? Even if the police hadn't connected her to Andrew McGraw, the picture didn't do that, either. I had put them both in my inner safe at my office, a small bomb- and fireproof box built into the wall at the back of the main safe. I had kept current case papers in there ever since the chairman of Transicon had hired someone to retrieve evidence from my safe two years ago. But I just didn't think that was it.

Bobby and I discussed the break-in for another half hour, touching occasionally on my battle wounds. Finally I said, 'Now you tell me something, Bobby: Why don't you believe it was Mackenzie?'

Mallory stared through the windshield. 'I'm not doubting it. I believe it. I'd be happier if we had a gun or a fingerprint, but I believe it.' I didn't say anything. 'I just wish I'd found him,' he said at last. 'My captain got a call from Commissioner Sullivan Friday afternoon saying he thought I was overworked and he was asking Vespucci to assign Carlson to help me out. I went home under orders – to get some sleep. Not off the case. Just to sleep. And next morning there was an arrest.' He turned to look at me. 'You didn't hear that,' he said.

I nodded agreement, and Bobby asked me a few more questions, but his heart wasn't in it. At last he gave up. 'If you won't talk, you won't. Just remember, Vicki: Earl Smeissen is a heavy. You know yourself the courts can't nail him. Don't try to play hardball with him – you're just not up to his weight at all.'

I nodded solemnly. 'Thanks, Bobby. I'll keep it in mind.' I opened the door.

'By the way,' Bobby said casually, 'we got a call last night from Riley's Gun Shop down in Hazelcrest. Said a V. I. Warshawski had bought a small handgun down there and he was worried – she looked rather wild. That wouldn't be anyone you'd know, would it, Vicki?'

I got out of the car, shut the door, and looked in through the open window. 'I'm the only one by that name in my family, Bobby – but there are some other Warshawskis in the city.'

For once Bobby didn't lose his temper. He looked at me very seriously. 'No one ever stopped you when you had your mind set on something, Vicki. But if you're planning on using that gun, get your ass down to City Hall first thing tomorrow morning and register it. Now tell Sergeant McGonnigal where you're going to be until your place is fixed up again.'

While I was giving McGonnigal my address, a squawk came in on Mallory's radio about my office: the place had been ransacked. I wondered if my business-interruption insurance would cover this. 'Remember, Vicki, you're playing hardball with a pro,' Bobby warned. 'Get in, McGonnigal.' They drove off.

9

FILING A CLAIM

When I got to Lotty's it was afternoon. I had stopped on the way to call my answering service – a Mr McGraw and a Mr Devereux had both phoned, and left numbers. I copied them into my pocket phone book but decided not to call until I got to Lotty's. She greeted me with a worried head shake. 'Not content with beating you, they beat your apartment. You run with a wild crowd, Vic.' But no censure, no horror – one of the things I liked in Lotty.

She examined my face and my eye with her ophthalmoscope. 'Coming along nicely. Much less swelling already. Headache? A bit? To be expected. Have you eaten? An empty stomach makes it worse. Come, a little boiled chicken – nice Eastern European Sunday dinner.' She had eaten, but drank coffee while I finished the chicken. I was surprised at how hungry I was.

'How long can I stay?' I asked.

'I'm expecting no one this month. As long as you like until August tenth.'

'I shouldn't be more than a week – probably less. But I'd like to ask the answering service to switch my home calls here.'

Lotty shrugged. 'In that case, I won't switch off the phone by the guest bed – mine rings at all hours – women having babies, boys being shot – they don't keep nine-to-five schedules. So you run the risk of answering my calls and if any come for you, I'll let you know.' She got up. 'Now I must leave you. My medical advice is for you to stay in, have a drink, relax – you're not in good shape and you've had a bad shock. But if you choose to disregard my professional advice, well, I'm not liable in a malpractice suit' – she chuckled slightly – 'and keys are in the basket by the sink. I have an answering machine by my bedroom phone – turn it on if you decide to go out.' She kissed the air near my face and left.

I wandered restlessly around the apartment for a few minutes. I knew I should go down to my office and assess the damage. I should call a guy I knew who ran a cleaning service to come and restore my apartment. I should call my answering service and get my calls transferred to Lotty's. And I needed to get back to Peter Thayer's apartment to see if there was something there that my apartment smashers believed I had.

Lotty was right: I was not in prime condition. The destruction of my apartment had been shocking. I was consumed with anger, the anger one has when victimized and unable to fight back. I opened my suitcase and got out the box with the gun in it. I unwrapped it and pulled out the Smith & Wesson. While I loaded it I had a fantasy of planting some kind of hint that would draw Smeissen – or whomever – back to my apartment while I stood in the hallway and pumped them full of bullets. The fantasy was very vivid and I played it through several times. The effect was cathartic – a lot of my anger drained away and I felt able to call my answering service. They took Lotty's number and agreed to transfer my calls.

Finally I sat down and called McGraw. 'Good afternoon, Mr McGraw,' I said when he answered. 'I hear you've been trying to get in touch with me.'

'Yes, about my daughter.' He sounded a little ill at ease.

'I haven't forgotten her, Mr McGraw. In fact, I have a lead – not on her directly, but on some people who may know where she's gone.'

'How far have you gone with them – these people?' he demanded sharply.

'As far as I could in the time I had. I don't drag cases on just to keep my expense bill mounting.'

'Yeah, no one's accusing you of that. I just don't want you to go any further.'

'What?' I said incredulously. 'You started this whole chain of events and now you don't want me to find Anita? Or did she turn up?'

'No, she hasn't turned up. But I think I flew off the handle a bit when she left her apartment. I thought she might be wrapped up in young Thayer's murder somehow. Now the police have arrested this drug addict, I see the two weren't connected.'

Some of my anger returned. 'You do? By divine inspiration, maybe? There were no signs of robbery in that apartment, and no sign that Mackenzie had been there. I don't believe he did it.'

'Look here, Warshawski, who are you to go around questioning the police? The goddamn punk has been held for two days now. If he hadn't done it, he'd have been let go by now. Now where the hell do you get off saying "I don't believe it"?' he mimicked me savagely.

'Since you and I last talked, McGraw, I have been beaten and my apartment and office decimated by Earl Smeissen in an effort to get me off the case. If Mackenzie is the murderer, why does Smeissen care so much?'

'What Earl does has no bearing on anything I do,' McGraw answered. 'I'm telling you to stop looking for my daughter. I hired you and I can fire you. Send me a bill for your expenses – throw in your apartment if you want to. But quit.'

'This is quite a change. You were worried sick about your daughter on Friday. What's happened since then?'

'Just get off the case, Warshawski,' McGraw bellowed. 'I've said I'll pay you – now stop fighting over it.'

'Very well,' I said in cold anger. 'I'm off the payroll. I'll send you a bill. But you're wrong about one thing, McGraw – and you can tell Earl from me – you can fire me, but you can't get rid of me.'

I hung up. Beautiful, Vic: beautiful rhetoric. It had just been possible that Smeissen believed he'd cowed me into quitting. So why be so full of female-chismo and yell challenges into the phone? I ought to write 'Think before acting' a hundred times on the blackboard.

At least McGraw had agreed to knowing Earl, or at least to knowing who he was. That had been a shot – not totally in the dark, however, since the Knifegrinders knew most of the hoods in Chicago. The fact that he knew Earl didn't mean he'd sikked him onto my apartment – or onto killing Peter Thayer – but it was sure a better connection than anything else I had.

I dialed Ralph's number. He wasn't home. I paced some more, but decided the time for action had arrived. I wasn't going to get any further thinking about the case, or worrying about intercepting a bullet from Tony's gun. I changed out of the green slacks into jeans and running shoes. I got out my collection of skeleton keys and put them in one pocket, car keys, driver's license, private investigator license and fifty dollars in the other. I fastened the shoulder holster over a loose, man-tailored shirt and practiced drawing the gun until it came out quickly and naturally.

Before leaving Lotty's I examined my face in the bathroom mirror. She was right – I did look better. The left side was still discolored – in fact it was showing some more yellow and green – but the swelling had gone down considerably. My left eye was completely open and not inflamed, even though the purple had spread farther. It cheered me up a bit; I switched on Lotty's telephone answering machine, slipped on a jean jacket and left, carefully locking the doors behind me.

The Cubs were playing a doubleheader with St Louis, and Addison was filled with people leaving the first game and those arriving for the second. I turned on CBS radio just in time to hear DeJesus lead off the bottom of the first inning with a hard drive to the shortstop. He was cut down easily at first, but at least he hadn't hit into a double play.

Once clear of Wrigley Field traffic it was a quick twenty-minute drive downtown. It being Sunday, I was able to park on the street outside my office. The police had left the area, but a patrolman came over as I entered the building.

'What's your business here, miss?' he asked sharply but not unpleasantly.

'I'm V. I. Warshawski,' I told him. 'I have an office here which was broken into earlier today and I've come to inspect the damage.'

'I'd like to see some identification, please.'

I pulled out my driver's license and my private investigator photo-ID. He examined them, nodded, and gave them back to me. 'Okay, you can go on up. Lieutenant Mallory told me to keep an eye out and not let anyone but tenants into the building. He told me you'd probably stop by.'

I thanked him and went inside. For once the elevator was working and I took it rather than the stairs – I could keep fit someday when I wasn't feeling quite so terrible. The office door was closed, but its upper glass half had been shattered. When I went inside, though, the damage wasn't as severe as to my apartment. True, all my files had been dumped onto the floor, but the furniture had been left intact. No safe is totally entry-proof: someone had been into the little one in back of the big one. But it must have taken five hours at least. No wonder they'd been so angry by the time they got to my apartment – all that effort for nothing. Fortunately I hadn't had any money or sensitive papers in the place at the time.

I decided to leave the papers where they were: tomorrow I'd get a Kelly Girl to come in and file them all for me again. But I'd better call a boarding service for the door, or the place would be ransacked by thieves. I'd lost one of Gabriella's glasses; I didn't want the Olivetti to go as well. I got a twenty-four-hour place to agree to send someone over, and went downstairs. The patrolman wasn't too happy when I explained what I'd done, but he finally agreed to check it with the lieutenant. I left him at the phone and continued on my way to the South Side.

The bright, cool weather was continuing, and I had a pleasant drive south. The lake was dotted with sailboats along the horizon.

Nearer the shore were a few swimmers. The game was in the bottom of the third, and Kingman struck out: 2-0, St Louis. The Cubs had bad days, too – in fact, more than I did, probably.

I parked in the shopping center lot behind the Thayer apartment and re-entered the building. The chicken bones had disappeared, but the smell of urine remained. No one came out to question my right to be in the building, and I had no trouble finding a key to open the third-floor apartment.

I should have been prepared for the shambles, but it took me by surprise. When I'd been here before there had just been the typical disorder of a student apartment. Now, the same hand or hands that had been to my place had done a similar job here. I shook my head to clear it. Of course. They were missing something, and they had been here first. It was only after they hadn't found it that they had come to me. I whistled a bit between my teeth – the opening bars to the third act of *Simon Boccanegra* – and tried to decide what to do. I wondered what was missing and thought it most likely to be a piece of paper of some kind. It might be evidence of fraud or a picture, but I didn't think it would be an actual object.

It didn't seem too likely that it was still in the apartment. Young Thayer might have given it to Anita. If she had it, she was in worse danger than she seemed to be already. I scratched my head. It looked as though Smeissen's boys had covered all the possibilities – sofa cushions ripped, papers and books dumped on the floor. I decided to believe that they had gone through everything page by page – only if my search didn't turn up anything would I take that job on. In a student apartment with several hundred books it would take a sizable chunk of time to examine each one in detail. The only things that were still intact were appliances and floors. I made a methodical search of all the rooms for loose boards or tiles. I found a few and pried them up, using a hammer I found under the kitchen sink, but didn't turn up anything more interesting than some old termite damage. Then I went through the bathroom fixture by fixture, taking down the shower rod and looking into it, and the toilet and sink pipes. That was quite a job; I had to go to my car for tools and break into the basement to turn off the water. It took me more than an hour to get the rusted fittings loose enough to open them. I wasn't surprised to find nothing but water in them – if anyone had been into them, they would have opened more easily.

It was 6.30 and the sun was going down when I returned to the kitchen. The chair where Peter Thayer had been sitting had had its back to the stove. It was possible, of course, that the missing thing had not been hidden deliberately, but had dropped. A piece of paper might float unnoticed under the stove. I lay on my stomach and shone a flashlight under it. I couldn't see anything, and the opening was pretty small. How thorough did I want to be? My muscles were aching and I had left my phenylbutazone at Lotty's. But I went to the living room and got some bricks from a brick-and-board bookcase. Using the jack from my trunk as a lever and the bricks as a wedge, I slowly pried the stove off the floor. It was an impossible task; the jack would catch and raise the thing, and just as I was kicking a brick under the side, down it would slip again. Finally, by dint of pulling the table over and wedging the jack underneath it, I was able to get one brick under the right side. After that the left came up more easily. I checked the gas line to make sure it wasn't straining, and carefully raised the stove by another brick. I then got down on my stomach again and looked underneath. There it was, a piece of paper stuck by grease to the bottom of the stove. I peeled it slowly off in order not to tear it, and took it over to the window to examine.

It was a carbon copy about eight inches square. The top left corner had the Ajax logo on it. In the center it read, 'Draft only: not negotiable', and it was made out to Joseph Gielczowski, of 13227 South Ingleside in Matteson, Illinois. He could take this to a bank and have it certified, at which point Ajax would pay the sum of $250 to the bank as a Workers' Compensation indemnity payment. The name meant nothing to me and the transaction sounded perfectly straightforward. What was so important about it? Ralph would know, but I didn't want to call

113

him from here – better get the stove down and leave while the leaving was good.

I levered up the stove, using the table again as a wedge, and pulled the bricks out. The stove made a dull thud as it dropped – I hoped the downstairs neighbors weren't home or were too self-engrossed to call the police. I gathered up my tools, folded the claim draft and put it in my shirt pocket, and left. A second-floor apartment door opened a crack as I went by. 'Plumber,' I called. 'There won't be any water on the third floor tonight.' The door closed again and I left the building quickly.

When I got back to my car the game was long over and I had to wait for the eight o'clock news to come on to get the score. The Cubs had pulled it out in the eighth inning. Good old Jerry Martin had hit a double; Ontiveros had singled, and wonderful Dave Kingman had gotten all three of them home with his thirty-second homer of the season. And all this with two out. I knew how the Cubs were feeling tonight, and sang a little *Figaro* on the way home to show it.

10
BEAUTIFUL PEOPLE

Lotty lifted her thick eyebrows as I came into the living room. 'Ah,' she said, 'success shows in your walk. The office was all right?'

'No, but I found what they were looking for.' I took out the draft and showed it to her. 'Make anything of it?'

She put on a pair of glasses and looked at it intently, pursing her lips. 'I see these from time to time, you understand, when I get paid for administering to industrial accident victims. It looks totally in order, as far as I can tell – of course, I don't read them for their content, just glance at them and send them to the bank. And the name Gielczowski means nothing to me, except that it is Polish: should it?'

I shrugged. 'I don't know. Doesn't mean anything to me either. I'd better make a copy of it and get it stowed away, though. Have you eaten?'

'I was waiting for you, my dear,' she answered.

'Then let me take you out to dinner. I need it – it took a lot of work finding this, physical I mean, although the mental process helped – nothing like a university education to teach you logic.'

Lotty agreed. I showered and changed into a respectable pair of slacks. A dressy shirt and a loose jacket completed the outfit, and the shoulder holster fitted neatly under my left arm. I put the claim draft in my jacket pocket.

Lotty scrutinized me when I came back into the living room. 'You hide it well, Vic.' I looked puzzled and she laughed. 'My dear, you left the empty box in the kitchen garbage, and I knew I had brought no Smith & Wesson into the house. Shall we go?'

I laughed but said nothing. Lotty drove us down to Belmont and Sheridan and we had a pleasant, simple dinner in the wine cellar at the Chesterton Hotel. An Austrian wine store, it had expanded to include a tiny restaurant. Lotty approved of their coffee and ate two of the rich Viennese pastries.

When we got home I insisted on checking front and back entrances, but no one had been around. Inside, I called Larry Anderson, my cleaning friend, and arranged for him to right my apartment. Not tomorrow – he had a big job on, but he'd go over with his best crew personally on Tuesday. Not at all, he'd be delighted. I got hold of Ralph and agreed to meet him for dinner the next night at Ahab's. 'How's your face?' he asked.

'Much better, thanks. I should look almost presentable for you tomorrow night.'

At eleven I bade Lotty a very sleepy good night and fell into bed. I was instantly asleep, falling down a black hole into total oblivion. Much later I began dreaming. The red Venetian glasses were lined up on my mother's dining-room table. 'Now you must hit high C, Vicki, and hold it,' my mother said. I made a tremendous effort and sustained the note. Under my horrified eyes the row of glasses dissolved into a red pool. It was my mother's blood. With a tremendous effort I pulled myself awake. The phone was ringing.

Lofty had answered it on her extension by the time I oriented myself in the strange bed. When I lifted the receiver, I could hear her crisp, soothing voice saying, 'Yes, this is Dr Herschel.' I hung up and squinted at the little illuminated face of the bedside clock: 5.13. Poor Lotty, I thought, what a life, and rolled back over to sleep.

The ringing phone dragged me back to life again several hours later. I dimly remembered the earlier call and, wondering if Lotty were back yet, reached for the phone. 'Hello?' I said, and heard Lotty on the other extension. I was about to hang up again when a tremulous little voice said, 'Is Miss Warshawski there?'

'Yes, speaking. What can I do for you?' I heard the click as Lotty hung up again.

'This is Jill Thayer,' the little voice quavered, trying to speak calmly. 'Can you come out to my house, please?'

'You mean right now?' I asked.

'Yes,' she breathed.

'Sure thing, honey. Be right out. Can you tell me the trouble now?' I had shoved the receiver between my right shoulder and my ear and was pulling on some clothes. It was 7.30 and Lotty's burlap curtains let in enough light to dress by without my having to fumble for the lamp switch.

'It's – I can't talk right now. My mother wants me. Just come, *please.*'

'Okay, Jill. Hold the fort. I'll be there in forty minutes.' I hung up and hurriedly finished dressing in the clothes I'd worn last night, not omitting the gun under my left shoulder. I stopped in the kitchen where Lotty was eating toast and drinking the inevitable thick Viennese coffee.

'So,' she said, 'the second emergency of the day? Mine was a silly hemorrhaging child who had a bad abortion because she was afraid to come to me in the first place.' She grimaced. 'And the mother was not to know, of course. And you?'

'Off to Winnetka. Another child, but pleasant, not silly.' Lotty had the *Sun-Times* open in front of her. 'Anything new about the Thayers? She sounded quite panicked.'

Lotty poured me a cup of coffee, which I swallowed in scalding gulps while scanning the paper, but I found nothing. I shrugged, took a piece of buttered toast from Lotty, kissed her cheek, and was gone.

Native caution made me check the stairwells and the front walk carefully before going to the street. I even examined the backseat and the engine for untoward activity before getting into the car. Smeissen really had me spooked.

Traffic on the Kennedy was heavy with the Monday morning rush hour and people staggering home at the last minute from weekends in the country. Once I hit the outbound Edens, however, I had the road chiefly to myself. I had given Jill Thayer my card more to let her feel someone cared than because I expected an SOS, and with the half of my mind that wasn't looking for speed traps I wondered what had caused the cry for help. A suburban teenager who had never seen death might find anything connected with it upsetting, yet she had struck me as essentially levelheaded. I wondered if her father had gone off the deep end in a big way.

I had left Lotty's at 7.42, and turned onto Willow Road at 8.03. Pretty good time for fifteen miles, considering that three had been in the heavy city traffic on Addison. At 8.09 I pulled up to the gates of the Thayer house. That was as far as I got. Whatever had happened, it was excitement in a big way. The entrance was blocked by a Winnetka police car, lights flashing, and as far as I could see into the yard it was filled with more cars and many policemen. I backed the Chevy down the road a bit and parked it on the gravel verge. It wasn't until I turned the motor off and got out that I noticed the sleek black Mercedes that had been in the yard on Saturday. Only it wasn't in the yard, it was tilted at a strange angle off the road. And it was no longer sleek. The front tires were flat, and the front windshield was a series of glass shards, fragments left from radiating circles. My guess was that bullets, and many of them, had caused the damage.

In my neighborhood a noisy crowd would have gathered to gape over the sight. This being the North Shore, a crowd had gathered, but a smaller and quieter one than Halsted and Belmont would have attracted. They were being held at bay by a lean young policeman with a mustache.

'Gee, they really got Mr Thayer's car,' I said to the young man, strolling over.

When disaster strikes, the police like to keep all the news to themselves. They never tell you what happened and they never answer leading questions. Winnetka's finest were no exception. 'What do you want?' the young man said suspiciously.

I was about to tell him the candid truth when it occurred to me that it would never get me past the herd in the driveway. 'My name is V. I. Warshawski,' I said smiling in what I hoped was a saintly way. 'I used to be Miss Jill Thayer's governess. When all the trouble started this morning, she called me and asked me to come out to be with her.'

The young cop frowned. 'Do you have any identification?' he demanded.

'Certainly,' I said righteously. I wondered what use a driver's license would be in proving my story, but I obligingly dug it out and handed it to him.

'All right,' he said after studying it long enough to memorize the number, 'you can talk to the sergeant.'

He left his post long enough to walk me to the gate. 'Sarge!' he yelled. One of the men by the door looked up. 'This is the Thayer girl's governess!' he called, cupping his hands.

'Thank you, Officer,' I said, imitating Miss Jean Brodie's manner. I walked up the drive to the doorway and repeated my story to the sergeant.

He frowned in turn. 'We didn't have any word about a governess showing up. I'm afraid no one is allowed in right now. You're not with a newspaper, are you?'

'Certainly not!' I snapped. 'Look, Sergeant,' I said, smiling a bit to show I could be conciliatory, 'how about just asking Miss Thayer to come to the door. She can tell you if she wants me here or not. If she doesn't, I can leave again. But since she did ask for me, she's likely to be upset if I'm not allowed inside.'

The upsetness of a Thayer, even one as young as Jill, seemed to concern the sergeant. I was afraid he might ring for Lucy, but instead he asked one of his men to fetch Miss Thayer.

Minutes went by without her appearance, and I began to wonder whether Lucy had seen me after all and set the police straight on my governess story. Eventually Jill arrived, however. Her oval face was pinched and anxious and her brown hair had not been brushed. Her face cleared a little when she saw me. 'Oh, it's you!' she said. 'They told me my governess was here and I thought it was old Mrs Wilkens.'

'Isn't this your governess?' the patrolman demanded.

Jill gave me an anguished look. I moved into the house. 'Just tell the man you sent for me,' I said.

'Oh, yes, yes, I did. I called Miss Warshawski an hour ago and begged her to come up here.'

The patrolman was looking at me suspiciously, but I was in the house and one of the powerful Thayers wanted me to be there. He compromised by having me spell out my name, letter by laborious letter, for his notebook. Jill tugged on my arm while I was doing this, and as soon as we were through spelling, before he could ask more questions, I gave her a little pat and propelled her toward the hall. She led me to a little room near the big green statue and shut the door.

'Did you say you were my governess?' She was still trying to figure that one out.

'I was afraid they wouldn't let me inside if I told them the truth,' I explained. 'Police don't like private detectives on their turf. Now suppose you tell me what's going on.'

The bleak look reappeared. She screwed up her face. 'Did you see the car outside?' I nodded. 'My father – that was him, they shot him.'

'Did you see them do it?' I asked.

She shook her head and wiped her hand across her nose and forehead. Tears were suddenly streaming down her face. 'I heard them,' she wailed.

The little room had a settee and a table with some magazines on it. Two heavy-armed chairs stood on either side of a window overlooking the south lawn. I pulled them up to the table and sat Jill in one of them. I sat in the other, facing her. 'I'm sorry to put you through it, but I'm going to have to ask you to tell me how it happened. Just take your time, though, and don't mind crying.'

The story came out in little sobs. 'My dad always leaves –

leaves for work between seven and seven thirty,' she said. 'Sometimes he goes earlier. If something special – special is – going on at the bank. I'm usually asleep when he goes. Lucy makes – made him breakfast, then I get up and she makes another breakfast. Mother has toast and coffee in her room. She's – she's always on a – a diet.'

I nodded to explain not only that I understood these details but why she was reporting them. 'But today you weren't asleep.'

'No,' she agreed. 'All this stuff about Pete – his funeral was yesterday, you know, and it shook me up so I couldn't – couldn't sleep very well.' She'd stopped crying and was trying to control her voice. 'I heard Daddy get up, but I didn't go down to eat with him. He'd been so strange, you know, and I didn't want to hear him say anything terrible about Pete.' Suddenly she was sobbing, 'I wouldn't eat with him, and now he's dead, and now I'll never have another chance.' The words came out in great heaving bursts between sobs; she kept repeating them.

I took her hands. 'Yes, I know, it's tough, Jill. But you didn't kill him by not eating with him, you know.' I patted her hands but didn't say anything else for a while. Finally, though, as the sobs quieted a bit, I said, 'Tell me what did happen, honey, and then we can try to figure out an answer to it.'

She worked hard to pull herself together, and then said, 'There's not much else to tell. My bedroom is above here and I can see the side of the house. I sort of – of wandered to the window and watched him – watched him drive his car down to the road.' She stopped to swallow but she had herself in hand. 'You can't see the road because of all the bushes in front of it, and anyway, you can't see all the way down to the bottom from my room, but I knew from the sound that he'd gotten down and turned onto Sheridan.' I nodded encouragingly, still holding her hands tightly. 'Well, I was sort of going back to my bed, I thought I might get dressed, when I heard all these shots. Only I didn't know – know what they were.' She carefully wiped two new tears away. 'It sounded horrid. I heard glass shattering, and then this squeal, you know, the way a car sounds when it's turning a corner too fast or something, and I thought, maybe Daddy had an accident. You know, he was acting so crazy, he could have gone charging down Sheridan Road and hit someone.

'So I ran downstairs without taking off my nightgown and Lucy came running from the back of the house. She was yelling something, and trying to get me to go back upstairs and get some clothes on, but I went outside anyway and ran down to the drive and found the car.' She screwed up her face, shutting her eyes and fighting against her tears again. 'It was terrible. Daddy – Daddy was bleeding and lying all spread out on the steering wheel.' She shook her head. 'I still thought he'd been in an accident, but I couldn't see the other car. I thought maybe they'd driven off, you know, the ones with the squealing tires, but Lucy seemed to guess about the shooting. Anyway, she kept me from going over to the car – I didn't have any shoes on, and by then a whole lot of cars had stopped to stare at it and she – Lucy – made one of them call the police on his CB. She wanted me to come back to the house but I wouldn't, not until the police came.' She sniffed. 'I didn't like to leave him there all by himself, you know.'

'Yeah, sure, honey. You did real well. Did your mother come out?'

'No, we went back to the house when the police came, and I came upstairs to get dressed and then I remembered you and called you. But you know when I hung up?' I nodded. 'Well, Lucy went to wake up Mother and tell her, and she – she started crying and made Lucy get me, and she came in just then so I had to hang up.'

'So you didn't get a glimpse of the people who killed your dad?' She shook her head. 'Do the police believe he was in the car you heard taking off?'

'Yes, it's something to do with shells. I think there weren't any shells or something, so they think they must be in the car.'

I nodded. 'That makes sense. Now for the big question, Jill: Did you want me to come out for comfort and support –

which I'm happy to provide – or to take some kind of action?'

She stared at me through gray eyes that had seen and heard too much for her age lately. 'What can you do?' she asked.

'You can hire me to find out who killed your dad and your brother,' I said matter-of-factly.

'I don't have any money, only my allowance. When I'm twenty-one I get some of my trust money, but I'm only fourteen now.'

I laughed. 'Not to worry. If you want to hire me, give me a dollar and I'll give you a receipt, and that will mean you've hired me. You'll have to talk to your mother about it, though.'

'My money's upstairs,' she said, getting up. 'Do you think the same person killed Daddy who killed Pete?'

'It seems probable, although I don't really have any facts to go on.'

'Do you think it's someone who might – well, is someone trying to wipe out my family?'

I considered that. It wasn't completely out of the question, but it was an awfully dramatic way to do it, and rather slow. 'I doubt it,' I said finally. 'Not completely impossible – but if they wanted to do that, why not just get you all when you were in the car together yesterday?'

'I'll go get my money,' Jill said, going to the door. She opened it and Lucy appeared, crossing the hall. 'So that's where you are,' she said sharply. 'How can you disappear like that and your mother wanting you?' She looked into the room. 'Now don't tell me that detective woman got in here! Come on, you,' she said to me. 'Out you go! We've got trouble enough around here without you stirring it up.'

'If you please, Lucy,' Jill said in a very grown-up way, 'Miss Warshawski came up here because I invited her, and she will leave when I ask her to.'

'Well, your mother will have something to say about that,' Lucy snapped.

'I'll talk to her myself,' Jill snapped back. 'Can you wait here, please, while I get my money,' she added to me, 'and then would you mind coming to see my mother with me? I don't think I can explain it to her by myself.'

'Not at all,' I said politely, giving her an encouraging smile.

After Jill had gone, Lucy said, 'All I can say is that Mr Thayer didn't want you here, and what he would say if he could see you –'

'Well, we both know he can't,' I interrupted. 'However, if he had been able to explain – to me or to anyone else – what was on his mind, he would very likely be alive this morning.

'Look. I like Jill and I'd like to help her out. She called me this morning not because she has the faintest idea of what I can do for her as a private detective, but because she feels I'm supporting her. Don't you think she gets left out around here?'

Lucy looked at me sourly. 'Maybe so, Miss Detective, maybe so. But if Jill had any consideration for her mother, maybe she'd get a little consideration back.'

'I see,' I said dryly. Jill came back downstairs.

'Your mother is waiting for you,' Lucy reminded her sharply.

'I know!' Jill yelled. 'I'm coming.' She handed me a dollar, and I gravely wrote out a receipt on a scrap of paper from my handbag. Lucy watched the whole thing angrily, her lips shut in a thin line. We then retraced the route I'd taken Saturday through the long hall. We passed the library door and went clear to the back of the house.

Lucy opened the door to a room on the left, saying, 'Here she is, Mrs Thayer. She's got some terrible detective with her who's trying to take money from her. Mr Thayer threw her out of the house on Saturday, but now she's back.'

A patrolman standing beside the door gave me a startled look.

'Lucy!' Jill stormed. 'That's a lie!' She pushed her way past the disapproving figure into the room. I stood behind Lucy, looking over her shoulder. It was a delightful room, completely windows on three sides. It overlooked the lake on the east side, and a beautiful lawn, complete with a grass tennis court, on the north. It was furnished with white bamboo furniture with cheerful color accents in reds and yellows in the cushions, lamp bases and floor covering. A profusion of plants gave it a greenhouse effect.

In the middle of this charming setting was Mrs Thayer. Even with no makeup and a few tearstains, she was very handsome, easily recognizable as the original of the picture in yesterday's *Herald-Star*. A very pretty young woman, an older edition of Jill, sat solicitously on one side of her, and a handsome young man in a polo shirt and checked trousers sat across from her, looking a little ill at ease.

'Please, Jill, I don't understand a word you or Lucy are saying, but don't shout, darling, my nerves absolutely won't stand it.'

I moved past Lucy into the room and went over to Mrs Thayer's couch. 'Mrs Thayer, I'm very sorry about your husband and your son,' I said. 'My name is V. I. Warshawski. I'm a private detective. Your daughter asked me to come up here this morning to see if I could help out.'

The young man answered, sticking his jaw out. 'I'm Mrs Thayer's son-in-law, and I think I can safely say that if my father-in-law threw you out of the house on Saturday, you're probably not wanted here.'

'Jill, did you call her?' the young woman asked, shocked.

'Yes, I did,' Jill answered, setting her jaw mulishly. 'And you can't throw her out, Jack: it's not your house. I asked her to come up, and I've hired her to find out who killed Daddy and Pete. She thinks the same person did it both times.'

'Really, Jill,' the other woman said, 'I think we can leave this to the police without upsetting Mother by bringing in hired detectives.'

'Just what I tried telling her, Mrs Thorndale, but of course she wouldn't listen.' That was Lucy, triumphant.

Jill's face was screwed up again, as if she were going to cry. 'Take it easy, honey,' I said. 'Let's not get everyone more worked up than they are already. Why don't you tell me who's who?'

'Sorry,' she gulped. 'This is my mother, my sister, Susan Thorndale, and her husband, Jack. And Jack thinks because he can boss Susan around he can do that to me, but –'

'Steady, Jill,' I said, putting a hand on her shoulder.

Susan's face was pink. 'Jill, if you hadn't been spoiled rotten all these years you would show a little respect to someone like Jack who has a lot more experience than you do. Do you have any idea what people are going to be saying about Daddy, the way he was killed and all? Why, why it looks like a gang killing, and it makes Daddy look as if he was involved with the gang.' Her voice rose to a high pitch on the last sentence.

'Mob,' I said. Susan looked at me blankly. 'It looks like a mob killing. Some gangs may go in for that style of execution, but usually they don't have the resources.'

'Now look here,' Jack said angrily. 'We've already asked you to leave. Why don't you go, instead of showing off your smart mouth! Like Susan said, it's going to be hard enough explaining away the way Mr Thayer died, without having to explain why we got a private detective involved as well.'

'Is that all you care about?' Jill cried. 'What people will say? With Pete dead, and Daddy dead?'

'No one is sorrier than me that Peter was shot,' Jack said, 'but if he had done what your father wanted and lived in a proper apartment, instead of that slummy dump with that slut of a girl, he would never have been shot in the first place.'

'Oh!' Jill screamed. 'How can you talk about Peter that way! He was trying to do something warm and real instead of – You're such a fake. All you and Susan care about is how much money you make and what the neighbors will say! I hate you!' She ended on another flood of tears and flung herself into my arms. I gave her a hug and wrapped my right arm around her while I fished in my bag for some tissues with the left.

'Jill,' her mother said in a soft, complaining voice, 'Jill, honey, please don't shout like that in here. My nerves just absolutely cannot take it. I'm just as sorry as you are that Petey is dead, but Jack is right, honey: if he'd listened to your father all this wouldn't have happened, and your father wouldn't be – be . . .' Her voice broke off and she started weeping quietly.

Susan put an arm around her mother and patted her shoulder.

'Now, see what you've done,' she said venomously, whether to me or to her sister I wasn't sure.

'Now you've caused enough disturbance, you polack detective, whatever your name is,' Lucy began.

'Don't you dare talk to her like that,' Jill cried, her voice partly muffled by my shoulder. 'Her name is Miss Warshawski, and you should call her Miss Warshawski!'

'Well, Mother Thayer,' Jack said with a rueful laugh, 'sorry to drag you into this, but since Jill won't listen to her sister or me, will you tell her that she has to get this woman out of the house?'

'Oh, please, Jack,' his mother-in-law said, leaning on Susan. She stretched out a hand to him without looking at him, and I was interested to note that her eyes didn't turn red with crying. 'I just don't have the strength to deal with Jill in one of her moods.' However, she pulled herself into a sitting position, still holding on to Jack's hand, and looked at Jill earnestly. 'Jill, I just cannot stand for you to have one of your temper tantrums right now. You and Peter never listen to what anyone has to say to you. If Petey had, he wouldn't be dead now. With Petey dead, and John, I just can't take anything else. So don't talk to this private detective any longer. She's taking advantage of you to get her name in the paper, and I can't bear another scandal about this family.'

Before I could say anything Jill tore herself away from me, her little face crimson. 'Don't talk like that to me!' she screamed. 'I care about Pete and Daddy and you don't! You're the one who's bringing scandals into the house. Everybody knows you didn't love Daddy! Everybody knows what you and Dr Mulgrave were up to! Daddy was probably —'

Susan leaped up from the couch and slapped her sister hard on the face. 'You goddamn brat, be quiet!' Mrs Thayer started weeping in earnest. Jill, overcome by assorted strong and uncontrollable feelings, began sobbing again.

At that moment a worried-looking man in a business suit came into the room, escorted by one of the patrolmen. He crossed to Mrs Thayer and clasped her hands. 'Margaret! I came as soon as I heard the news. How are you?'

Susan blushed. Jill's sobs died away. Jack looked as though he had been stuffed. Mrs Thayer turned large tragic eyes to the newcomer's face. 'Ted. How kind of you,' she said in a brave voice, barely above a whisper.

'Dr Mulgrave, I presume,' I said.

He dropped Mrs Thayer's wrists and stood up straight. 'Yes, I'm Dr Mulgrave.' He looked at Jack. 'Is this a policewoman?'

'No,' I said. 'I'm a private investigator. Miss Thayer has hired me to find out who killed her father and brother.'

'Margaret?' he asked incredulously.

'No. *Miss* Thayer. Jill,' I said.

Jack said, 'Mrs Thayer just ordered you to leave her house and leave her daughter alone. I'd think even an ambulance chaser like you would know how to take a hint like that.'

'Oh, cool it, Thorndale,' I said. 'What's eating you? Jill asked me to come up here because she's scared silly – as any normal person would be with all this going on. But you guys are so defensive you make me wonder what you're hiding.'

'What do you mean?' he scowled.

'Well, why don't you want me looking into your father-in-law's death? What are you afraid I'll find out – that he and Peter caught you with your fingers in the till and you had them shot to shut them up?'

I ignored his outraged gasp. 'What about you, Doctor? Did Mr Thayer learn about your relations with his wife and threaten divorce – but you decided a wealthy widow was a better bet than a woman who couldn't make a very good case for alimony?'

'Now look here, whatever your name is. I don't have to listen to that kind of crap,' Mulgrave started.

'Then leave,' I said. 'Maybe Lucy is using this house as a center for burglarizing wealthy homes on the North Shore – after all, as a maid she probably hears a lot about where jewelry, documents and so on are kept. When Mr Thayer and his son got too hot on her trail, she hired a murderer.' I smiled enthusiasti-

128

cally at Susan, who was starting to babble – I was getting carried away by my own fantasies. 'I could probably think of a motive for you too, Mrs Thorndale. All I'm trying to say is, you people are so hostile that it starts me wondering. The less you want me to undertake a murder investigation, the more I start thinking there might be something to my ideas.'

When I stopped talking, they were silent for a minute. Mulgrave was clasping Mrs Thayer's hands again, sitting next to her now. Susan looked like a kitten getting ready to spit at a dog. My client was sitting on one of the bamboo side chairs, her hands clenched in her lap, her face intent. Then Mulgrave said, 'Are you trying to threaten us – threaten the Thayer family?'

'If you mean, am I threatening to find out the truth, the answer is yes; if that means turning up a lot of sordid junk along the way, tough.'

'Just a minute, Ted,' Jack said, waving an arm at the older man. 'I know how to deal with her.' He nodded at me. 'Come on, name your price,' he said, pulling out his checkbook.

My fingers itched to bring out the Smith & Wesson and pistol-whip him. 'Grow up, Thorndale,' I snapped. 'There are things in this life that money can't buy. Regardless of what you, or your mother-in-law, or the mayor of Winnetka says, I am investigating this murder – these murders.' I laughed a little, mirthlessly. 'Two days ago, John Thayer tried to give me $5,000 to buy me out of this case. You guys up here on the North Shore live in some kind of dream world. You think you can buy a cover-up for anything that goes wrong in your lives, just like you hire the garbage men to take away your filth, or Lucy here to clean it up and carry it outside for you. It doesn't work that way. John Thayer is dead. He couldn't pay enough to get whatever filth he was involved in away from him, nor away from his son. Now whatever it was that caused their deaths isn't private anymore. It doesn't belong to you. Anyone who wants to can find out about it. I intend to.'

Mrs Thayer was moaning softly. Jack looked uncomfortable. With an effort to save his dignity he said, 'Naturally, if you choose to poke around in something that's none of your business we can't stop you. It's just that we think matters are better left to the police.'

'Yeah, well, they're not batting a thousand right now,' I said. 'They thought they had a guy behind bars for the crime, but while he was eating his prison breakfast this morning John Thayer got killed.'

Susan turned to Jill. 'This is all your fault! You brought this person up here. Now we've been insulted and embarrassed – I've never been more ashamed in my life. Daddy's been killed and all you can think about is bringing in some outsider to call us names.'

Mulgrave turned back to Mrs Thorndale, and Jack and Susan both started talking to him at once. While this was going on, I walked over to Jill and knelt down to look her in the face. She was looking as though she might collapse or go into shock. 'Look, I think you need to get away from all this. Is there any friend or relative you can visit until the worst of the fuss is over?'

She thought for a minute, then shook her head. 'Not really. I've got lots of friends, you know, but I don't think any of their mothers would like having me around right now.' She gave a wobbly smile. 'The scandal, you know, like Jack said. I wish Anita were here.'

I hesitated a minute. 'Would you like to come back to Chicago with me? My apartment's been torn up, and I'm staying with a friend, but she'll be glad to have you, too, for a few days.' Lotty would never mind another stray. I needed Jill where I could ask her some questions, and I wanted her away from her family. She was tough and could fight back, but she didn't need to do that kind of fighting on top of the shock of her father's death.

Her face lightened. 'Do you really mean that?'

I nodded. 'Why don't you run upstairs now and pack an overnight bag while everyone is still arguing here.'

When she had left the room, I explained what I was doing to Mrs Thayer. This, predictably, started a fresh uproar from the family. Finally, though, Mulgrave said, 'It's important that

Margaret – Mrs Thayer – be kept absolutely quiet. If Jill really is worrying her, perhaps it would be better if she did leave for a few days. I can make some inquiries about this person, and if she's not reliable, we can always bring Jill back home.'

Mrs Thayer gave a martyred smile. 'Thank you, Ted. If you say it's all right, I'm sure it will be. As long as you live in a safe neighborhood, Miss –'

'Warshawski,' I said dryly. 'Well, no one's been machine-gunned there this week.'

Mulgrave and Jack decided I ought to give them some references to call. I saw that as a face-saving effort and gave them the name of one of my old law professors. He would be startled but supportive if he got an inquiry into my character.

When Jill came back she'd brushed her hair and washed her face. She went over to her mother, who was still sitting on the couch. 'I'm sorry, Mother,' she muttered. 'I didn't mean to be rude to you.'

Mrs Thayer smiled wanly. 'It's all right, dear. I don't expect you to understand how I feel.' She looked at me. 'Take good care of her for me.'

'Sure,' I answered.

'I don't want any trouble,' Jack warned me.

'I'll keep that in mind, Mr Thorndale.' I picked up Jill's suitcase and she followed me out the door.

She stopped in the doorway to look at her family. 'Well, goodbye,' she said. They all looked at her but no one said anything.

When we got to the front door I explained to the sergeant that Miss Thayer was coming home with me for a few days to get a little rest and attention; had the police taken all the statements they needed from her? After some talk with his lieutenant over the walkie-talkie, he agreed that she could leave, as long as I gave him my address. I gave it to him and we walked down the drive.

Jill didn't say anything on the way over to the Edens. She looked straight ahead and didn't pay much attention to the

131

countryside. As we joined the stop-and-go traffic on the southbound Kennedy, though, she turned to look at me. 'Do you think I was wrong, leaving my mother like that?'

I braked to let a fifty-ton semi merge in front of me. 'Well, Jill, it seemed to me that everyone there was trying to play on your guilt feelings. Now you're feeling guilty, so maybe they got what they wanted out of you.'

She digested that for a few minutes. 'Is that a scandal, the way my father was killed?'

'People are probably talking about it, and that will make Jack and Susan very uncomfortable. The real question, though, is why he was killed – and even the answer to that question doesn't have to be a scandal to you.' I threaded my way around a *Herald-Star* delivery van. 'Thing is, you have to have your own sense of what's right built inside you. If your father ran afoul of the type of people who do machine-gun-style executions, it may be because they tried to violate his sense of what's right. No scandal to that. And even if he happened to be involved in some kind of shady activity, it doesn't have to affect you unless you want it to.' I changed lanes. 'I don't believe in the visitation of the sins of the fathers, and I don't believe in people brooding over vengeance for twenty years.'

Jill turned a puzzled face toward me. 'Oh, it can happen. It's just that you've got to want to make it happen. Like your mother – unhappy woman – right?' Jill nodded. 'And probably unhappy because of things that happened thirty years ago. That's her choice. You've got the same choice. Suppose your father did something criminal and we find that out? It's going to be rough, but it only has to be a scandal and make your life miserable if you let it. Lots of things in this life happen to you no matter what you do, or through no fault of your own – like your father and brother getting killed. But how you make those events part of your life is under your control. You can get bitter, although I don't think you have that kind of character, or you can learn and grow from it.'

I realized that I'd passed the Addison exit and turned onto the

Belmont off-ramp. 'Sorry – that answer turned into a sermon, and I got so carried away I missed my exit. Does it help any?'

Jill nodded and was quiet again as I drove north along Pulaski and then turned east on Addison. 'It's lonely now, with Peter gone,' she said finally. 'He was the only one in the family who – who cared about me.'

'Yeah, it's going to be rough, sweetie,' I said gently, and squeezed her hand.

'Thank you for coming up, Miss Warshawski,' she whispered. I had to lean over to hear her. 'My friends call me Vic,' I said.

11
FRIENDLY PERSUASION

I stopped at the clinic before going to the apartment to let Lotty know I'd made free with her hospitality and to see if she thought Jill needed anything for shock. A small group of women, most of them with young children, were waiting in the little anteroom. Jill looked around her curiously. I poked my head into the inner door, where Lotty's nurse, a young Puerto Rican woman, saw me. 'Hello, Vic,' she said. 'Lotty's with a patient. Do you need something?'

'Hi, Carol. Tell her that I'd like to bring my young friend back to her apartment – the one I went out this morning to see. She'll know whom you mean. And ask her if she can take a quick look at her – healthy kid, but she's had a lot of stress lately.'

Carol went into the tiny examining room where she spoke for a few minutes. 'Bring her into the office. Lotty will take a quick look at her after Mrs Segi has left. And of course, take her to the apartment.'

I took Jill into Lotty's office, among disapproving frowns from those who had been waiting longer. While we waited I told her a little bit about Lotty, Austrian war refugee, brilliant London University medical student, maverick doctor, warm friend. Lotty herself came bustling in.

'So, this is Miss Thayer,' she said briskly. 'Vic has brought you down for a little rest? That's good.' She lifted Jill's chin with her hand, looked at her pupils, made her do some simple tests, talking all the while.

'What was the trouble?' she asked.

'Her father was shot,' I explained.

Lotty clicked her tongue and shook her head, then turned to Jill. 'Now, open your mouth. No, I know you haven't got a sore throat, but it's free, I'm a doctor, and I have to look. Good. Nothing wrong with you, but you need some rest and something to eat. Vic, when you get her home, a little brandy. Don't talk too much, let her get some rest. Are you going out?'

'Yes, I've got a lot to do.'

She pursed her lips and thought a minute. 'I'll send Carol over in about an hour. She can stay with Jill until one of us gets home.'

At that moment I realized how much I liked Lotty. I'd been a little uneasy about leaving Jill alone, in case Earl was close on my trail. Whether Lotty knew that, or simply felt a scared young girl should not be left alone, it was a worry I now did not have to speak aloud.

'Great. I'll wait until she gets there.'

We left the clinic among more baleful stares while Carol summoned the next patient. 'She's nice, isn't she?' Jill said as we got into the car.

'Lotty or Carol?'

'Both, but Lotty, I meant. She really doesn't mind me showing up like this, does she?'

'No,' I agreed. 'All of Lotty's instincts are directed at helping people. She's just not sentimental about it.'

When we got back to the apartment I made Jill stay in the car while I checked the street and the entrance way. I didn't want to add to her fears, but I didn't want anyone getting a shot at her, either. The coast was still clear. Maybe Earl really did believe he'd scared me off. Or maybe with the police arresting poor Donald Mackenzie, he was resting easy.

When we got inside I told Jill to take a hot bath. I was going to prepare some breakfast, and I would have to ask her a few questions, but then she was to sleep. 'I can tell by your eyes that you haven't been doing that for a while,' I said.

Jill agreed shyly. I helped her unpack her small suitcase in the room I'd been sleeping in; I could sleep on the daybed in the living room. I got out one of Lotty's enormous white bath sheets and showed her the bathroom.

I realized that I was quite hungry; it was ten and I hadn't eaten the toast Lotty had thrust at me. I foraged in the refrigerator; no juice – Lotty never drank anything out of cans. I found a drawer full of oranges and squeezed a small pitcher of juice, and then took some of Lotty's thick light Viennese bread and turned it into French toast, whistling under my breath. I realized I felt good, despite Thayer's death and all the unexplained dangling pieces to the case. Some instinct told me that things were finally starting to happen.

When Jill emerged pink and sleepy from the bath I set her to eating, holding my questions and telling her a little bit about myself in answer to her inquiries. She wanted to know if I always caught the killer.

'This is the first time I've ever really dealt directly with a killer,' I answered. 'But generally, yes, I do get to the root of the problems I'm asked to look into.'

'Are you scared?' Jill asked. 'I mean, you've been beaten up and your apartment got torn up, and they – they shot Daddy and Pete.'

'Yes, of course I'm scared,' I said calmly. 'Only a fool would look at a mess like this and not be. It's just that it doesn't panic me – it makes me careful, being scared does, but it doesn't override my judgement.

'Now, I want you to tell me everything you can remember about whom your father talked to in the last few days, and what they said. We'll go sit on the bed, and you'll drink some hot milk with brandy as Lotty ordered, so that when I'm done you'll go to sleep.'

She followed me into the bedroom and got into bed, obediently sipping at the milk. I had put in brown sugar and nutmeg and laced it heavily. She made a face but continued sipping it while we talked.

'When I came out on Saturday, you said your father at first didn't believe this Mackenzie they've arrested killed your brother, but the neighbors talked him out of it. What neighbors?'

'Well, a lot of people came by, and they all more or less said the same thing. Do you want all their names?'

'If you can remember them and remember what they said.'

We went through a list of about a dozen people, which included Yardley Masters and his wife, the only name I recognized. I got some long histories of relations among the families, and Jill contorted her face in the effort of trying to remember exactly what they'd all said.

'You said they "all more or less said the same thing",' I repeated after a while. 'Was anyone more emphatic about it than the others?'

She nodded at that. 'Mr Masters. Daddy kept raving that he was sure that Anita's father had done it, and Mr Masters said something like, "Look, John, you don't want to keep going around saying things like that. A lot of things could come out that you don't want to hear." Then Daddy got mad and started yelling, "What do you mean? Are you threatening me?" And Mr Masters said, "No, of course not, John. We're friends. Just giving you some advice," or something like that.'

'I see,' I said. Very illuminating. 'Was that all?'

'Yes, but it was after Mr and Mrs Masters left that Daddy said he guessed he was wrong, which made me glad at the time, because of course Anita wouldn't try to kill Peter. But then he started saying terrible things about Peter.'

'Yeah, let's not talk about that now. I want you to calm down so you can sleep. Did anything happen yesterday?'

'Well, he got into a fight with someone on the phone, but I don't know who, or what it was about. I think it was some deal going on at the bank, because he said, "I won't be a party to it" – that's all I heard. He'd been so – strange.' She gulped and swallowed some more milk. 'At the funeral, you know, I sort of was staying out of his way. And when I heard him start yelling

137

on the phone, I just went outside. Susan was after me anyway to put on a dress and sit in the living room entertaining all these gruesome people who came over after the funeral, so I just sort of left and went down to the beach.'

I laughed a little. 'Good for you. This fight on the telephone – did your father get a call or make a call?'

'I'm pretty sure he made it. At least, I don't remember hearing the phone ring.'

'Okay, all that's a help. Now try to put it out of your mind. You finish your milk while I brush your hair, and then you sleep.'

She was really very tired; between the hairbrushing and the brandy she relaxed and lay down. 'Stay with me,' she asked drowsily. I pulled the shades behind the burlap curtains and sat down beside Jill, holding her hand. Something about her pierced my heart, made me long for the child I'd never had, and I watched her carefully until she was in a deep sleep.

While I waited for Carol I made some phone calls, first to Ralph. I had to wait a few minutes while a secretary hunted him down on the floor, but he was as cheerful as ever when he came on the line. 'How's it going, Sherlock?' he asked breezily.

'Pretty well,' I answered.

'You're not calling to cancel dinner tonight, are you?'

'No, no,' I assured him. 'I'd just like you to do something that you can find out more easily than I can.'

'What's that?'

'Just find out if your boss has had any calls from a guy named Andrew McGraw. And do it without letting him know you're asking.'

'Are you still flogging that dead horse?' he asked, a little exasperated.

'I haven't written anyone off, Ralph, not even you.'

'But the police made an arrest.'

'Well, in that case, your boss is innocent. Just look on it as a a favor to a lady who's had a rough week.'

'All right,' he agreed, not too happily. 'But I wish you could believe the police know as much about catching murderers as you do.'

I laughed. 'You're not the only one . . . By the way, did you know young Peter's father was killed this morning?'

'What!' he exclaimed. 'How did that happen?'

'Well, he was shot. Too bad Donald Mackenzie is already in jail, but there must be some dope dealers on the North Shore to take the blame for this one.'

'You think Peter's death is connected to this?'

'Well, it staggers the imagination if two members of the same family are killed within a week of each other and those events are only randomly associated.'

'All right, all right,' Ralph said. 'You've made your point — no need to be sarcastic . . . I'll ask Yardley's secretary.'

'Thanks, Ralph, see you tonight.'

The claim draft, Masters's remarks to Thayer, which might or might not have been vague threats. It didn't add up to much, but it was worth pursuing. The other piece to the puzzle was McGraw and the fact that McGraw knew Smeissen. Now, if I could connect McGraw and Masters, or Masters and Smeissen . . . I should have asked Ralph to check on Earl too. Well, I could do that tonight. Say McGraw and Masters were doing an unspecified something together. If they were smart, they wouldn't leave names when they called each other. Even McGraw's enchanting secretary might give him away to the police if the evidence was hot enough. But they might get together, meet for a drink. I might make a trip to bars in the Loop and near Knifegrinder headquarters to see if the two had ever been seen together. Or Thayer with McGraw, for that matter. I needed some photographs, and I had no idea where to find them.

Carol arrived as I was looking up a number in the directory. 'Jill's asleep,' I told her. 'I hope she'll sleep through the afternoon.'

'Good,' she answered. 'I've brought all the old medical records

139

over: we're always too busy at the clinic to get them updated, but this is a good opportunity.'

We chatted for a few minutes about her mother, who had emphysema, and the prospects for finding the arsonists who were plaguing the neighborhood, before I went back to the phone.

Murray Ryerson was the crime reporter for the *Herald-Star* who interviewed me after the Transicon case broke. He'd had a by-line, and a lot of his stuff was good. It was getting close to lunch, and I wasn't sure he'd be in when I called the city desk, but my luck seemed to be turning.

'Ryerson,' he rumbled into the phone.

'This is V. I. Warshawski.'

'Oh, hi,' he said, mind turning over competently and remembering me without trouble. 'Got any good stories for me today?'

'Not today. But I might have later in the week. I need some help, though. A couple of pictures.'

'Whose?'

'Look, if I tell you, will you promise not to put two and two together in the paper until I have some evidence?'

'Maybe. Depends on how close you're coming to a story that we know is happening anyway.'

'Andrew McGraw on any of your hot lists?'

'Oh, he's a perennial favorite but we don't have anything breaking on him right now. Who's the other?'

'Guy named Yardley Masters. He's a vice-president over at Ajax, and you probably have something in your file from Crusade of Mercy publicity or something like that.'

'You tying McGraw to Ajax?'

'Stop slobbering in the phone, Murray; Ajax doesn't do any business with the Knifegrinders.'

'Well, are you tying McGraw to Masters?' he persisted.

'What is this, twenty questions?' I said irritably. 'I need two pictures. If a story breaks, you can have it – you did all right from me on Transicon, didn't you?'

'Tell you what – you eaten yet? Good, I'll meet you at Fiorella's

140

in an hour with the pictures, if any, and try to pick your brains over a beer.'

'Great, Murray, thanks.' I hung up and looked at my watch. An hour would give me some time to stop and register the Smith & Wesson. I started humming 'Ch'io mi scordi di te', again. 'Tell Lotty I'll be back around six but I'll be eating dinner out,' I called to Carol on my way out.

12
PUB CRAWL

The eager bureaucrats at City Hall took longer than I expected
with forms, fees, incomprehensible directions, and anger at being
asked to repeat them. I was already running late, but I decided
to stop at my lawyer's office to drop off a Xerox of the claim
draft I'd found in Peter Thayer's apartment. He was a dry,
imperturbable man, and accepted without a blink my instructions
to give the draft to Murray Ryerson should anything happen to
me in the next few days.

By the time I got to Fiorella's, a pleasant restaurant whose
outdoor tables overlooked the Chicago River, Murray was already
finishing his second beer. He was a big man who looked like a
red-haired Elliott Gould, and he waved a hand at me lazily when
he saw me coming.

A high-masted sailboat was floating past. 'You know, they're
going to raise every drawbridge along here for that one boat.
Hell of a system, isn't it,' he said as I came up.

'Oh, there's something appealing about a little boat being able to stop all the traffic on Michigan Avenue. Unless, of
course, the bridge gets stuck up just when you need to cross
the river.' This was an all-too-frequent happening: motorists
had no choice but to sit and boil quietly while they waited.
'Has there ever been a murder when one of these bridges is
stuck – someone getting too angry and shooting the bridge
tender or something?'

'Not yet,' Murray said. 'If it happens, I'll be on the spot to
interview you . . . What are you drinking?'

I don't like beer that well; I ordered a white wine.

'Got your pix for you.' Murray tossed a folder over to me. 'We had a lot of choice on McGraw, but only dug one up for Masters – he's receiving some civic award out in Winnetka – they never ran the shot but it's a pretty good three-quarter view. I got you a couple of copies.'

'Thanks,' I said, opening the folder. The one of Masters was good. He was shaking hands with the Illinois president of the Boy Scouts of America. At his right was a solemn-faced youth in uniform who apparently was his son. The picture was two years old.

Murray had brought me several of McGraw, one outside a federal courtroom where he was walking pugnaciously in front of a trio of Treasury men. Another, taken under happier circumstances, showed him at the gala celebration when he was first elected president of the Knifegrinders nine years ago. The best for my purposes, though, was a close-up, taken apparently without his knowledge. His face was relaxed, but concentrating.

I held it out toward Murray. 'This is great. Where was it taken?'

Murray smiled. 'Senate hearings on racketeering and the unions.'

No wonder he looked so thoughtful.

A waiter came by for our order. I asked for mostaccioli; Murray chose spaghetti with meatballs. I was going to have to start running again, sore muscles or not, with all the starch I was eating lately.

'Now, V. I. Warshawski, most beautiful detective in Chicago, what gives with these pictures?' Murray said, clasping his hands together on the table and leaning over them toward me. 'I recall seeing that dead young Peter Thayer worked for Ajax, in fact for Mr Masters, an old family friend. Also, somewhere in the thousands of lines that have been churned out since he died, I recall reading that his girlfriend, the lovely and dedicated Anita McGraw, was the daughter of well-known union leader Andrew

143

McGraw. Now you want pictures of both of them. Is it possible that you are suggesting they colluded in the death of young Thayer, and possibly his father as well?'

I looked at him seriously. 'It was like this, Murray: McGraw has what amounts to a psychopathic hatred of capitalist bosses. When he realized that his pure young daughter, who had always been protected from any contact with management, was seriously considering marrying not just a boss, but the son of one of Chicago's wealthiest businessmen, he decided the only thing to do was to have the young man put six feet underground. His psychosis is such that he decided to have John Thayer eliminated as well, just for –'

'Spare me the rest,' Murray said. 'I can spell it out for myself. Is either McGraw or Masters your client?'

'You'd better be buying this lunch, Murray – it is definitely a business expense.'

The waiter brought our food, slapping it down in the hurried, careless way that is the hallmark of business restaurants at lunch. I snatched the pictures back just in time to save them from spaghetti sauce and started sprinkling cheese on my pasta: I love it really cheesy.

'Do you have a client?' he asked, spearing a meatball.

'Yes, I do.'

'But you won't tell me who it is?' I smiled and nodded agreement.

'You buy Mackenzie as Thayer Junior's murderer?' Murray asked.

'I haven't talked to the man. But one does have to wonder who killed Thayer Senior if Mackenzie killed the son. I don't like the thought of two people in the same family killed in the same week for totally unconnected reasons by unconnected people: laws of chance are against that,' I answered. 'What about you?'

He gave a big Elliott Gould smile. 'You know, I talked to Lieutenant Mallory after the case first broke, and he didn't say anything about robbery, either of the boy or of the apartment.

144

Now, you found the body, didn't you? Well, did the apartment look ransacked?'

'I couldn't really tell if anything had been taken – I didn't know what was supposed to be there.'

'By the way, what took you down there in the first place?' he asked casually.

'Nostalgia, Murray – I used to go to school down there and I got an itch to see what the old place looked like.'

Murray laughed. 'Okay, Vic, you win – can't fault me for trying though, can you?'

I laughed too. I didn't mind. I finished my pasta – no child had ever died in India because of my inhumane failure to clean my plate.

'If I find out anything you might be interested in, I'll let you know,' I said.

Murray asked me when I thought the Cubs would break this year. They were looking scrappy right now – two and a half games out.

'You know, Murray, I am a person with very few illusions about life. I like to have the Cubs as one of them.' I stirred my coffee. 'But I'd guess the second week in August. What about you?'

'Well, this is the third week in July. I give them ten more games. Martin and Buckner can't carry that team.'

I agreed sadly. We finished lunch on baseball and split the check when it came.

'There is one thing, Murray.'

He looked at me intently. I almost laughed, the change in his whole posture had been so complete – he really looked like a bloodhound on the trail, now.

'I have what I think is a clue. I don't know what it means, or why it is a clue. But I've left a copy of it with my attorney. If I should be bumped off, or put out of action for any length of time, he has instructions to give it to you.'

'What is it?' Murray asked.

'You ought to be a detective, Murray – you ask as many

questions and you're just as hot when you're on the trail. One thing I will say – Earl Smeissen's hovering around this case. He gave me this beautiful black eye which you've been too gentlemanly to mention. It wouldn't be totally out of the question for my body to come floating down the Chicago River – you might look out your office window every hour or so to see.'

Murray didn't look surprised. 'You already knew that?' I asked.

He grinned. 'You know who arrested Donald Mackenzie?'

'Yes, Frank Carlson.'

'And whose boy is Carlson?' he asked.

'Henry Vespucci's.'

'And do you know who's been covering Vespucci's back all these years?'

I thought about it. 'Tim Sullivan?' I guessed.

'The lady wins a Kewpie doll,' Murray said. 'Since you know that much, I'll tell you who Sullivan spent Christmas in Florida with last year.'

'Oh, Christ! Not Earl.'

Murray laughed. 'Yes. Earl Smeissen himself. If you're playing around with that crowd, you'd better be very, very careful.'

I got up and stuck the folder in my shoulder bag. 'Thanks, Murray, you're not the first one to tell me so. Thanks for the pictures. I'll let you know if anything turns up.'

As I climbed over the barrier separating the restaurant from the sidewalk I could hear Murray yelling a question behind me. He came pounding up to me just as I reached the top of the stairs leading from the river level to Michigan Avenue. 'I want to know what it was you gave your lawyer,' he panted.

I grinned. 'So long, Murray,' I said, and boarded a Michigan Avenue bus.

I had a plan that was really a stab in the dark more than anything else. I was assuming that McGraw and Masters worked together. And I was hoping they met at some point. They could handle everything over the phone or by mail. But McGraw might be wary of federal wiretaps and mail interception. He might prefer to do business in person. So say they met from time to time. Why not in a bar? And if in a bar, why not one near to one or the other of their offices? Of course, it was possible that they met as far from any place connected to either of them as they could. But my whole plan was based on a series of shots in the dark. I didn't have the resources to comb the whole city, so I'd just have to add one more assumption to my agenda, and hope that if they met, and if they met in a bar, they did so near where they worked. My plan might not net me anything, but it was all I could think of. I was pinning more hope on what I might learn about Anita from the radical women's group tomorrow night; in the meantime I needed to keep busy.

Ajax's glass-and-steel high-rise was on Michigan Avenue at Adams. In the Loop, Michigan is the easternmost street. The Art Institute is across the street, and then Grant Park goes down to the lake in a series of pleasant fountains and gardens. I decided to take the Fort Dearborn Trust on La Salle Street as my western border, and to work from Van Buren, two blocks south of Ajax, up to Washington, three blocks north. A purely arbitrary decision, but the bars in that area would keep me busy for some time; I could expand it in desperation if that was necessary.

I rode my bus south past the Art Institute to Van Buren and got off. I felt very small walking between the high-rises when I thought of the vast territory I had to cover. I wondered how much I might have to drink to get responses from the myriad bartenders. There probably is a better way to do this, I thought, but this was the only way that occurred to me. I had to work with what I could come up with – no Peter Wimsey at home thinking of the perfect logical answer for me.

I squared my shoulders and walked half a block along Van Buren and went into the Spot, the first bar I came to. I'd debated about an elaborate cover story, and finally decided that something approximating the truth was best.

The Spot was a dark, narrow bar built like a railway caboose. Booths lined the west wall and a long bar ran the length of the east, leaving just enough room for the stout, bleached waitress who had to tend to orders in the booths.

I sat up at the bar. The bartender was cleaning glasses. Most of the luncheon trade had left; only a few diehard drinkers were sitting farther down from me. A couple of women were finishing hamburgers and daiquiris in one of the booths. The bartender continued his work methodically until the last glass was rinsed before coming down to take my order. I stared ahead with the air of a woman in no particular hurry.

Beer is not my usual drink, but it was probably the best thing to order on an all-day pub crawl. It wouldn't make me drunk. Or at least not as quickly as wine or liquor.

'I'd like a draft,' I said.

He went to his spigots and filled a glass with pale yellow and foam. When he brought it back to me, I pulled out my folder. 'You ever see these two guys come in here?' I asked.

He gave me a sour look. 'What are you, a cop or something?'

'Yes,' I said. 'Have you ever seen these two guys in here together?'

'I'd better get the boss on this one,' he said. Raising his voice, he called 'Herman!' and a heavy man in a polyester suit got up from the booth at the far end of the room. I hadn't noticed him when I came in, but now I saw that another waitress was sitting in the booth. The two were sharing a late lunch after the hectic noon-hour rush.

The heavy man joined the bartender behind the bar.

'What's up, Luke?'

Luke jerked his head toward me. 'Lady's got a question.' He went back to his glasses, stacking them in careful pyramids on either side of the cash register. Herman came down toward me. His heavyset face looked tough but not mean. 'What do you want, ma'am?'

I pulled my photos out again. 'I'm trying to find out if these two men have ever been in here together.' I said in a neutral voice.

'You got a legal reason for asking?'

I pulled my PI license from my handbag. 'I'm a private investigator. There's a grand jury investigation and there's some question of collusion between a witness and a juror.' I showed him the ID.

He looked at the ID briefly, grunted, and tossed it back to me. 'Yeah, I see you're a private investigator, all right. But I don't know about this grand jury story. I know this guy.' He tapped Masters's picture. 'He works up at Ajax. Doesn't come in here often, maybe three times a year, but he's been doing it as long as I've owned the place.'

I didn't say anything, but took a swallow of beer. Anything tastes good when your throat is dry from embarrassment.

'Tell you for free, though, this other fellow's never been in here. At least not when I've been here.' He gave a shout of laughter and reached across the bar to pat my cheek. 'That's okay, cookie, I won't spoil your story for you.'

'Thanks,' I said dryly. 'What do I owe you for the beer?'

'On the house.' He gave another snort of laughter and rolled back down the aisle to his unfinished lunch. I took another swallow of the thin beer. Then I put a dollar on the counter for Luke and walked slowly out of the bar.

I walked on down Van Buren past Sears's main Chicago store. A lot of short-order food places were on the other side, but I had to go another block to find another bar. The bartender looked blankly at the photos and called the waitress over. She looked at both of them doubtfully, and then picked up McGraw's. 'He looks kind of familiar,' she said. 'Is he on TV or something?' I said no, but had she ever seen him in the bar. She didn't think so, but she couldn't swear to it. What about Masters? She didn't think so, but a lot of businessmen came in there, and all men with gray hair and business suits ran together in her mind after a while. I put two singles on the counter, one for her and one for the bartender, and went on down the street.

Her TV question gave me an idea for a better cover story. The next place I went to I said I was a market researcher looking for viewer recognition. Did anyone remember ever seeing these two people together? This approach got more interest, but drew another blank.

The game was on TV in this bar, bottom of the fourth with Cincinnati leading 4–0. I watched Büttner hit a single and then die on second after a hair-raising steal before I moved on. In all, I went to thirty-two bars that afternoon, catching most of the game in between. The Cubs lost, 6–2. I'd covered my territory pretty thoroughly. A couple of places recognized McGraw vaguely, but I put that down to the number of times his picture had been in the paper over the years. Most people probably had a vague recognition of Jimmy Hoffa, too. One other bar knew Masters by sight as one of the men from Ajax, and Billy's knew him by name and title as well. But neither place remembered seeing McGraw with him. Some places were hostile and took a combination of bribes and threats to get an answer. Some were indifferent. Others, like the Spot, had to have the manager make the decision. But none of them had seen my pair together.

It was after six by the time I got to Washington and State, two blocks west of Michigan. After my fifth bar I'd stopped drinking any of the beer I ordered, but I was feeling slightly bloated, as well as sweaty and depressed. I'd agreed to meet Ralph at Ahab's at eight. I decided to call it an afternoon and go home to wash up first.

Marshall Field occupies the whole north side of the street between State and Wabash. It seemed to me there might be one other bar on Washington, close to Michigan, if my memory of the layout was correct. That could wait until another day. I went down the stairs to the State Street subway and boarded a B train to Addison.

Evening rush hour was still in full force. I couldn't get a seat and had to stand all the way to Fullerton.

At Lotty's I headed straight for the bathroom and a cold shower. When I came out, I looked into the guest room; Jill was up, so I dumped my clothes in a drawer and put on a caftan. Jill was sitting on the living-room floor playing with two rosy-cheeked, dark-haired children who looked to be three or four.

'Hi, honey. You get a good rest?'

She looked up at me and smiled. A lot of color had returned to her face and she seemed much more relaxed. 'Hi,' she said. 'Yes, I only woke up an hour ago. These are Carol's nieces. She was supposed to baby-sit tonight, but Lotty talked her into coming over here and making homemade enchiladas, yum-yum.'

'Yum-yum,' the two little girls chorused.

'That sounds great. I'm afraid I have to go back out tonight, so I'll have to give it a miss.'

Jill nodded. 'Lotty told me. Are you doing some more detecting?'

'Well, I hope so.'

Lotty called out from the kitchen and I went in to say hi. Carol was working busily at the stove and turned briefly to flash me a bright smile. Lotty was sitting at the table reading the paper, drinking her everlasting coffee. She looked at me through narrowed eyes. 'The detective work wasn't so agreeable this afternoon, eh?'

I laughed. 'No. I learned nothing and had to drink too much beer doing so. This stuff smells great; wish I could cancel this evening out.'

'Then do so.'

I shook my head. 'I feel as though I don't have much time – maybe this second murder. Even though I feel a little rocky – too long a day, too much heat, I can't stop. I just hope I don't get sick at dinner – my date is getting fed up with me as it is. Although maybe if I fainted or something it would make him feel stronger, more protective.' I shrugged. 'Jill looks a lot better, don't you think?'

'Oh yes. The sleep did her good. That was well thought of, to get her out of that house for a while. I talked to her a bit when I came in; she's very well behaved, doesn't whine and complain, but it's obvious the mother has no emotions to spare for her. As for the sister –' Lotty made an expressive gesture.

'Yeah, I agree. We can't keep her down here forever, though. Besides, what on earth can she do during the day? I've got to be gone again tomorrow, and not on the kind of errand that she can go along with.'

'Well, I've been thinking about that. Carol and I had a bit of an idea, watching her with Rosa and Tracy – the two nieces. Jill is good with these children – took them on, we didn't ask her to look after them. Babies are good when you're depressed – something soft and unquestioning to cuddle. What would you think of her coming over to the clinic and minding children there for a day? As you saw this morning, they're always tumbling around the place – mothers who are sick can't leave them alone; or if one baby is sick, who looks after the other when Mama brings him in?'

I thought it over for a minute, but couldn't see anything wrong with it. 'Ask her,' I said. 'I'm sure the best thing for her right now would be to have something to do.'

Lotty got up and went to the living room. I followed. We stood for a minute, watching the three girls on the floor. They were terribly busy about something, although it wasn't clear what. Lotty squatted down next to them, moving easily. I moved into the background. Lotty spoke perfect Spanish, and she talked to the little girls in that language for a minute. Jill watched her respectfully.

Then Lotty turned to Jill, still balancing easily on her haunches. 'You're very good with these little ones. Have you worked with young children before?'

'I was a counselor at a little neighborhood day camp in June,' Jill said, flushing a bit. 'But that's all. I never baby-sit or anything like that.'

'Well, I had a bit of a plan. See what you think. Vic must be gone all the time, trying to find out why your father and brother were killed. Now while you are visiting down here, you could be of great help to me at the clinic.' She outlined her idea.

Jill's face lit up. 'But you know,' she said seriously, 'I don't have any training. I might not know what to do if they all started to cry or something.'

'Well, if that happens, that will be the test of your knack and

152

patience,' Lotty said. 'I will provide you a little assistance by way of a drawerful of lollipops. Bad for the teeth, perhaps, but great for tears.'

I went into the bedroom to change for dinner. Jill hadn't made the bed. The sheets were crumpled. I straightened them out, then thought I might just lie down for a minute to recover my equilibrium.

The next thing I knew Lotty was shaking me awake. 'It's seven thirty, Vic: don't you have to be going?'

'Oh hell!' I swore. My head was thick with sleep. 'Thanks, Lotty.' I swung out of bed and hurriedly put on a bright orange sundress. I stuck the Smith & Wesson in my handbag, grabbed a sweater, and ran out the door, calling goodbye to Jill as I went. Poor Ralph, I thought. I really am abusing him, keeping him waiting in restaurants just so that I can pick his brains about Ajax.

It was 7.50 when I turned south on Lake Shore Drive and just 8.00 when I got onto Rush Street, where the restaurant lay. One of my prejudices is against paying to park the car, but tonight I didn't waste time looking for street parking. I turned the car over to a parking attendant across from Ahab's. I looked at my watch as I went in the door: 8.08. Damned good, I thought. My head still felt woolly from my hour of sleep, but I was glad I'd gotten it.

Ralph was waiting by the entrance. He kissed me lightly in greeting, then stood back to examine my face. 'Definitely improving,' he agreed. 'And I see you can walk again.'

The headwaiter came over. Monday was a light night and he took us directly to our table. 'Tim will be your waiter,' he said. 'Would you like a drink?'

Ralph ordered a gin and tonic; I settled for a glass of club soda – Scotch on top of beer didn't sound too appetizing.

'One of the things about being divorced and moving into the city is all the great restaurants,' Ralph remarked. 'I've come to this place a couple of times, but there are a lot in my neighborhood.'

'Where do you live?' I asked.

'Over on Elm Street, not too far from here, actually. It's a furnished place with a housekeeping service.'

'Convenient.' That must cost a fair amount, I thought. I wondered what his income was. 'That's quite a lot of money with your alimony, too.'

'Don't tell me.' He grinned. 'I didn't know anything about the city when I moved in here, barring the area right around Ajax, and I didn't want to get into a long lease in a place I'd hate. Eventually I expect I'll buy a condominium.'

'By the way, did you find out whether McGraw had ever called Masters?'

'Yes, I did you that little favor, Vic. And it's just what I told you. He's never had a call from the guy.'

'You didn't ask him, did you?'

'No.' Ralph's cheerful face clouded with resentment. 'I kept your wishes in mind and only talked to his secretary. Of course, I don't have any guarantee that she won't mention the matter to him. Do you think you could let this drop now?'

I was feeling a little angry too, but I kept it under control: I still wanted Ralph to look at the claim draft.

Tim arrived to take our orders. I asked for poached salmon and Ralph took the scampi. We both went to the salad bar while I cast about for a neutral topic to keep us going until after dinner. I didn't want to produce the draft until we'd eaten.

'I've talked so much about my divorce I've never asked whether you were ever married,' Ralph remarked.

'Yes, I was.'

'What happened?'

'It was a long time ago. I don't think either of us was ready for it. He's a successful attorney now living in Hinsdale with a wife and three young children.'

'Do you still see him?' Ralph wanted to know.

'No, and I really don't think about him. But his name is in the papers a fair amount. He sent me a card at Christmas, that's how I know about the children and Hinsdale – one of those gooey

154

things with the children smiling sentimentally in front of a fireplace. I'm not sure whether he sent it to prove his virility or to let me know what I'm missing.'

'Do you miss it?'

I was getting angry. 'Are you trying to ask in a subtle way about whether I wish I had a husband and a family? I certainly do not miss Dick, nor am I sorry that I don't have three kids getting under my feet.'

Ralph looked astonished. 'Take it easy, Vic. Can't you miss having a family without confusing that with Dick's family? I don't miss Dorothy – but that doesn't mean I'm giving up on marriage. And I wouldn't be much of a man if I didn't miss my children.'

Tim brought our dinners. The salmon had a very good pimento sauce, but my emotions were still riding me and I couldn't enjoy it properly. I forced a smile. 'Sorry. Guess I'm overreacting to people who think a woman without a child is like Welch's without grapes.'

'Well, please don't take it out on me. Just because I've been acting like a protective man, trying to stop you from running after gangsters, doesn't mean I think you ought to be sitting home watching soaps and doing laundry.'

I ate some salmon and thought about Dick and our short, unhappy marriage. Ralph was looking at me, and his mobile face showed concern and a little anxiety.

'The reason my first marriage fell apart was because I'm too independent. Also, I'm not into housekeeping, as you noticed the other night. But the real problem is my independence. I guess you could call it a strong sense of turf. It's – it's hard for me –' I smiled. 'It's hard for me to talk about it.' I swallowed and concentrated on my plate for a few minutes. I bit my lower lip and continued. 'I have some close women friends, because I don't feel they're trying to take over my turf. But with men, it always seems, or often seems, as though I'm having to fight to maintain who I am.'

Ralph nodded. I wasn't sure he understood, but he seemed

interested. I ate a little more fish and swallowed some wine.

'With Dick, it was worse. I'm not sure why I married him – sometimes I think it's because he represented the white Anglo-Saxon establishment, and part of me wanted to belong to that. But Dick was a terrible husband for someone like me. He was an attorney with Crawford, Meade – they're a very big, high-prestige corporate firm, if you don't know them – and I was an eager young lawyer on the Public Defender's roster. We met at a bar association meeting. Dick thought he'd fallen in love with me because I'm so independent; afterwards it seemed to me that it was because he saw my independence as a challenge, and when he couldn't break it down, he got angry.

'Then I got disillusioned with working for the Public Defender. The setup is pretty corrupt – you're never arguing for justice, always on points of law. I wanted to get out of it, but I still wanted to do something that would make me feel that I was working on my concept of justice, not legal point-scoring. I resigned from the Public Defender's office, and was wondering what to do next, when a girl came to me and asked me to clear her brother of a robbery charge. He looked hopelessly guilty – it was a charge of stealing video equipment from a big corporate studio, and he had access, opportunity, and so on, but I took the case on and I discovered he was innocent by finding out who the guilty person really was.'

I drank some more wine and poked at my salmon. Ralph's plate was clean, but he was waving off Tim – 'Wait until the lady's finished.'

'Well, all this time, Dick was waiting for me to settle down to being a housewife. He was very supportive when I was worrying through leaving the Public Defender, but it turned out that that was because he was hoping I'd quit to stay home on the sidelines applauding him while he clawed his way up the ladder in the legal world. When I took on that case – although it didn't seem like a case at the time, just a favor to the woman who had sent the girl to me –' (That had been Lotty.) It had been a while since I'd thought about all this and I started to laugh. Ralph looked a question. 'Well, I take my obligations very seriously, and I ended up spending a night on a loading dock, which was really the turning point in the case. It was the same night that Crawford, Meade were having a big cocktail party, wives invited. I had on a cocktail dress, because I thought I'd just slip down to the dock and then go to the party, but the time slipped away, and Dick couldn't forgive me for not showing up. So we split up. At the time it was horrible, but when I look back on it, the evening was so ludicrous it makes me laugh.'

I pushed my plate away. I'd only eaten half the fish, but I didn't have much of an appetite. 'The trouble is, I guess I'm a bit gun-shy now. There really are times when I wish I did have a couple of children and was doing the middle-class family thing. But that's a myth, you know: very few people live like an advertisement, with golden harmony, and enough money, and so on. And I know I'm feeling a longing for a myth, not the reality. It's just – I get scared that I've made the wrong choice, or – I don't quite know how to say it. Maybe I should be home watching the soaps, maybe I'm not doing the best thing with my life. So if people try to suggest it, I bite their heads off.'

Ralph reached across the table and squeezed my hand. 'I think you're remarkable, Vic. I like your style. Dick sounds like an ass. Don't give up on us men just because of him.'

I smiled and squeezed his hand in return. 'I know. But – I'm a good detective, and I've got an established name now. And it's not a job that's easy to combine with marriage. It's only intermittently demanding, but when I'm hot after something, I don't want to be distracted by the thought of someone at home stewing because he doesn't know what to do about dinner. Or fussing at me because Earl Smeissen beat me up.'

Ralph looked down at his empty plate, nodding thoughtfully. 'I see.' He grinned. 'Of course, you might find a guy who'd already done the children-and-suburbia number who would stand on the sidelines cheering your successes.'

Tim came back to take dessert orders. I chose Ahab's spectacular ice-cream-and-cordial dessert. I hadn't eaten all my fish, and

I was sick of being virtuous anyway. Ralph decided to have some too.

'But I think this Earl Smeissen business would take a lot of getting used to,' he added after Tim had disappeared again.

'Aren't there any dangers to claim handling?' I asked. 'I would imagine you'd come across fraudulent claimants from time to time who aren't too happy to have their frauds uncovered.'

'That's true,' he agreed. 'But it's harder to prove a fraudulent claim than you might think. Especially if it's an accident case. There are lots of corrupt doctors out there who will happily testify to nonprovable injuries – something like a strained back, which doesn't show up on an X ray – for a cut of the award.

'I've never been in any danger. Usually what happens if you know it's a blown-up claim, and they know you know, but no one can prove it either way, you give them a cash settlement considerably below what it would be if it came to court. That gets them off your back – litigation is very expensive for an insurance company, because juries almost always favor the claimant, so it's really not as shocking as it sounds.'

'How much of there is that?' I asked.

'Well, everyone thinks the insurance company is there to give them a free ride – they don't understand that it all comes out in higher rates in the end. But how often do we really get taken to the cleaners? I couldn't say. When I was working in the field, my gut sense was that maybe one in every twenty or thirty cases was a phony. You handle so many, though, that it's hard to evaluate each one of them properly – you just concentrate on the big ones.'

Tim had brought the ice cream, which was sinfully delicious. I scraped the last drops out of the bottom of my dish. 'I found a claim draft lying around an apartment the other day. It was an Ajax draft, a carbon of one. I wondered if it was a real one.'

'You did?' Ralph was surprised. 'Where did you find it? In your apartment?'

'No. Actually, in young Thayer's place.'

'Do you have it? I'd like to see it.'

158

I picked my bag up from the floor and got the paper out of the zippered side compartment and handed it to Ralph. He studied it intently. Finally he said, 'This looks like one of ours all right. I wonder what the boy was doing with that on him. No claim files are supposed to go home with you.'

He folded it and put it in his wallet. 'This should go back to the office.'

I wasn't surprised, just pleased I'd had the forethought to make Xeroxes of it. 'Do you know the claimant?' I asked.

He pulled out the paper again and looked at the name. 'No, I can't even pronounce it. But it's the maximum indemnity payment for this state, so he must be on a total disability case – either temporary or permanent. That means there should be a pretty comprehensive file on him. How did it get so greasy?'

'Oh, it was lying on the floor,' I said vaguely.

When Tim brought the check, I insisted on splitting it with Ralph. 'Too many dinners like this and you'll have to give up either your alimony or your apartment.'

He finally let me pay my part of the bill. 'By the way, before they kick me out for not paying the rent, would you like to see my place?'

I laughed. 'Sure, Ralph. I'd love to.'

13

THE MARK OF ZAV

Ralph's alarm went off at 6.30; I cracked my eyes briefly to look at the clock and then buried my head under the pillows. Ralph tried burrowing in after me, but I kept the covers pulled around my ears and fought him off successfully. The skirmish woke me up more thoroughly. I sat up. 'Why so early? Do you have to be at the office at seven thirty?'

'This isn't early to me, baby: when I lived in Downers Grove I had to get up at five forty-five every day – this is luxury. Besides, I like morning – best time of day.'

I groaned and lay down again. 'Yeah. I've often said God must have loved mornings, he made so many of them. How about bringing me some coffee?'

He got out of bed and flexed his muscles. 'Sure thing, Miss Warshawski, ma'am. Service with a smile.'

I had to laugh. 'If you're going to be so full of pep this early in the day, I think I'll head back north for breakfast.' I swung my legs out of bed. It was now the fourth morning since my encounter with Earl and his boys, and I scarcely felt a twinge. Clearly, exercising paid off. I'd better get at it again – it would be easy to get out of the habit on the excuse that I was an invalid.

'I can feed you,' Ralph said. 'Not lavishly, but I've got toast.'

'Tell you the truth, I want to go running this morning before I eat. I haven't been out for five days, and it's easy to go downhill if you don't keep it up. Besides, I have a teenage guest at Lotty's and I ought to go see how she's doing.'

'Just as long as you aren't importing teenage boys for some weird orgy or other, I don't mind. How about coming back here tonight?'

'Mmm, maybe not. I've got to go to a meeting tonight, and I want to spend some time with Lotty and my friend.' I was still bothered by Ralph's persistence. Did he want to keep tabs on me, or was he a lonely guy going after the first woman he'd met who turned him on? If Masters were involved in the deaths of John and Peter Thayer, it wasn't impossible that his assistant, who had worked for him for three years, was involved as well.

'You get to work early every morning?' I asked.

'Unless I'm sick.'

'Last Monday morning too?' I asked.

He looked at me, puzzled. 'I suppose. Why do you ask – oh. When Peter was shot. No, I forgot: I wasn't in early that morning. I went down to Thayer's apartment and held him down while Yardley shot him.'

'Yardley get in on time that morning?' I persisted.

'I'm not his goddamn secretary!' Ralph snapped. 'He doesn't always show up at the same time – he has breakfast meetings and crap – and I don't sit with a stopwatch waiting for him to arrive.'

'Okay, okay. Take it easy. I know you think Masters is purity personified. But if he were doing something illegal, wouldn't he call on you, his trusty henchman, for help? You wouldn't want him relying on someone else, someone less able than you, would you?'

His face relaxed and he gave a snort of laughter. 'You're outrageous. If you were a man, you couldn't get away with crap like that.'

'If I were a man, I wouldn't be lying here,' I pointed out. I held out an arm and pulled him back down into the bed, but I still wondered what he'd been doing Monday morning.

Ralph went off to shower, whistling slightly. I pulled the curtains back to look outside. The air had a faint yellow tinge.

Even this early in the morning the city looked slightly baked. The break in the weather was over; we were in for another hot, polluted spell.

I showered and dressed and joined Ralph at the table for a cup of coffee. His apartment included one large room with a half wall making a partially private eating area. The kitchen must have once been a closet: stove, sink and refrigerator were stacked neatly, allowing room to stand and work, but not enough space even for a chair. It wasn't a bad-looking place. A large couch faced the front entrance, and a heavy armchair stood pulled back from the windows at right angles to it. I'd read somewhere that people who lived in rooms with floor-to-ceiling windows keep the furniture pulled back away from them – some illusion of falling if you're right up against the glass. A good two feet lay between the chair back and the lightly curtained windows. All the upholstery and the curtains were in the same light floral pattern. Nice for a prefurnished place.

At 7.30 Ralph stood up. 'I hear those claims calling me,' he explained. 'I'll get in touch with you tomorrow, Vic.'

'Fine,' I said. We rode down in the elevator in amiable silence. Ralph walked me to my car, which I'd had to park near Lake Shore Drive. 'Want a ride downtown?' I asked. He declined, saying he got his exercise walking the mile and a half to Ajax each day.

As I drove off I could see him moving down the street in my rearview mirror, a jaunty figure despite the close air.

It was only eight when I got back to Lotty's. She was having toast and coffee in the kitchen. Jill, her oval face alive and expressive, was talking animatedly, a half-drunk glass of milk in front of her. Her innocent good spirits made me feel old and decadent. I made a face at myself.

'Good morning, ladies. It's a stinker outside.'

'Good morning, Vic,' said Lotty, her face amused. 'What a pity you had to work all night.'

I gave her a playful punch on the shoulder. Jill asked, 'Were you really working all night?' in a serious, worried voice.

'No, and Lotty knows it. I spent the night at a friend's place after doing a little work. You have a pleasant evening? How were the enchiladas?'

'Oh, they were great!' Jill said enthusiastically. 'Did you know that Carol has been cooking since she was seven?' She giggled. 'I don't know how to do one useful thing, like ironing or even making scrambled eggs. Carol says I'd better marry someone with lots of money.'

'Oh, just marry someone who likes to cook and iron,' I said.

'Well, maybe you can practice on some scrambled eggs tonight,' Lotty suggested. 'Are you going to be here tonight?' she asked me.

'Can you make it an early dinner? I've got a seven thirty meeting down at the University of Chicago – someone who may be able to help me find Anita.'

'How about it, Jill?' Lotty asked.

Jill made a face. 'I think I'll plan on marrying someone rich.' Lotty and I laughed. 'How about peanut butter sandwiches?' she suggested. 'I already know how to make those.'

'I'll make you a fritata, Lotty,' I promised, 'if you and Jill will pick up some spinach and onions on your way home.'

Lotty made a face. 'Vic is a good cook, but a messy one,' she told Jill. 'She'll make a simple dinner for four in half an hour, but you and I will spend the night cleaning the kitchen.'

'Lotty!' I expostulated. 'From a fritata? I promise you' – I thought a minute, then laughed. 'No promises. I don't want to be late for my meeting. Jill, you can clean up.'

Jill looked at me uncertainly: Was I angry because she didn't want to make dinner? 'Look,' I said, 'you don't have to be perfect: Lotty and I will like you even if you have temper tantrums, don't make your bed, and refuse to cook dinner. Okay?'

'Certainly,' Lotty agreed, amused. 'I've been Vic's friend these last fifteen years, and I've yet to see her make a bed.'

Jill smiled at that. 'Are you going detecting today?'

'Yes, up to the North Side. Looking for a needle in a haystack.

I'd like to have lunch with you, but I don't know what my timetable is going to be like. I'll call down to the clinic around noon, though.'

I went into the guest room and changed into shorts, T-shirt and running shoes. Jill came in as I was halfway through my warm-up stretches. My muscles had tightened up in response to their abuse, and I was having to go more slowly and carefully than normal. When Jill came in, I was sweating a little, not from exertion, but from the residual pain. She stood watching me for a minute. 'Mind if I get dressed while you're in here?' she asked finally.

'No,' I grunted. 'Unless – you'd feel more – comfortable – alone.' I pulled myself upright. 'You thought about calling your mother?'

She made a face. 'Lotty had the same idea. I've decided to be a runaway and stay down here.' She put on her jeans and one of her man-sized shirts. 'I like it here.'

'It's just the novelty. You'll get lonesome for your private beach after a while.' I gave her a quick hug. 'But I invite you to stay at Lotty's for as long as you like.'

She laughed at that. 'Okay, I'll call my mom.'

'Atta girl. 'Bye, Lotty,' I called, and started out the door. Sheffield Avenue is about a mile from the lake. I figured if I ran over to the lake, eight blocks down to Diversey and back again, that would give me close to four miles. I went slowly, partly to ease my muscles and partly because of the stifling weather. I usually run seven-and-a-half-minute miles, but I tried to pace it at about nine minutes this morning. I was sweating freely by the time I got to Diversey, and my legs felt wobbly, I cut the pace going north, but I was so tired I wasn't paying too much attention to the traffic around me. As I left the lake path, a squad car pulled out in front of me. Sergeant McGonnigal was sitting in the passenger seat.

'Good morning, Miss Warshawski.'

'Morning, Sergeant,' I said, trying to breathe evenly.

'Lieutenant Mallory asked me to find you,' he said, getting

out of the car. 'He got a call yesterday from the Winnetka police. Seems you fast-talked your way past them to get into the Thayer house.'

'Oh, yeah?' I said. 'Nice to see so much cooperation between the suburban and the city forces.' I did a few toe touches to keep my leg muscles from stiffening.

'They're concerned about the Thayer girl. They think she should be home with her mother.'

'That's thoughtful of them. They can call her at Dr Herschel's and suggest that to her. Is that why you tracked me down?'

'Not entirely. The Winnetka police finally turned up a witness to the shooter's car, though not to the shooting.' He paused.

'Oh, yeah? Enough of an ID to make an arrest?'

'Unfortunately the witness is only five years old. He's scared silly and his parents have roped him around with lawyers and guards. Seems he'd been playing in the ditch alongside Sheridan Road, which was a no-no, but his folks were asleep, so he sneaked out. That's apparently why he went – because it's off limits. He was playing some crazy game, you know how kids are, thought he was stalking Darth Vader or something, when he saw the car. Big black car, he says, sitting outside the Thayer house. He decided to stalk it when he saw a guy in the passenger seat who scared the daylights out of him.'

McGonnigal stopped again to make sure I was following. He emphasized his next words carefully. 'He finally said – after hours of talk, and many promises to the parents that we wouldn't subpoena him or publish the news – that what scared him about the guy was that Zorro had got him. Why Zorro? It seems this guy had some kind of mark on his face. That's all he knows: He saw it, panicked, and ran for his life. Doesn't know if the guy saw him or not.'

'Sounds like a good lead,' I commented politely. 'All you have to do is find a big black car and a man with a mark on his face, and ask him if he knows Zorro.'

McGonnigal looked sharply at me. 'We police are not total idiots, Miss Warshawski. It's not something we can take to court, because of promising the parents and the lawyers. Anyway, the testimony isn't very good. But Zorro – you know, Zorro's mark is a big Z, and the lieutenant and I wondered if you knew anyone with a big Z on his face?'

I felt my face twitch. Earl's gofer, Tony, had had such a scar. I·shook my head. 'Should I?'

'Not too many guys with that kind of mark. We thought it might be Tony Bronsky. He got cut like that by a guy named Zav who objected to Tony taking away his girlfriend seven – eight years ago. He hangs around Earl Smeissen these days.'

'Oh?' I said. 'Earl and I aren't exactly social friends, Sergeant – I don't know all his companions.'

'Well, the lieutenant thought you'd like to know about it. He said he knew you'd sure hate for anything to happen to the little Thayer girl while you were looking after her.' He got back into his car.

'The lieutenant has a fine sense of drama,' I called after him. 'He's been watching too many *Kojak* reruns late at night. Tell him that from me.'

McGonnigal drove off and I walked the rest of the way home. I'd completely lost interest in exercise. Lotty and Jill had already left. I took a long, hot shower, easing my leg muscles and thinking over McGonnigal's message. It didn't surprise me that Earl was involved in John Thayer's death. I wondered if Jill really was in any danger, though. And if she was, was she worse off with Lotty and me? I toweled dry and weighed myself. I was down two pounds, surprising with all the starch I'd been eating lately.

I went into the kitchen to squeeze some orange juice. There was one way in which Jill was worse off with me, I realized. If Earl decided I needed to be blown away completely, she'd make a perfect hostage for him. I suddenly felt very cold.

Nothing I was doing was getting me any place – unless Thayer's execution could be called a destination. I couldn't tie McGraw to Masters or Thayer. I didn't have a clue about

Anita. The one person who might supply me with anything was McGraw, and he wouldn't. Why the hell had he come to me in the first place?

On impulse I looked up the Knifegrinders' number in the white pages and dialed. The receptionist transferred me to Mildred. I didn't identify myself but asked for McGraw. He was in a meeting and couldn't be disturbed.

'It's important,' I said. 'Tell him it concerns Earl Smeissen and John Thayer.'

Mildred put me on hold. I studied my fingernails. They needed filing. At last the phone clicked and McGraw's husky voice came on the line.

'Yes? What is it?' he asked.

'This is V. I. Warshawski. Did you finger Thayer for Earl?'

'What the hell are you talking about? I told you to stay out of my business.'

'You dragged me in in the first place, McGraw. You made it my business. Now I want to know, did you finger Thayer for Earl?'

He was quiet.

'One of Earl's men shot Thayer. You brought Thayer's name into this to begin with. You've hedged about why. Did you want to be sure he got dragged into the case from the beginning? You were afraid the police might jump on Anita, and you wanted to make sure his name got in the pot? Then what – he threatened to squeal, and you asked Earl to kill him just in case?'

'Warshawski, I got a tape running. You make any more accusations like this and I could see you in court.'

'Don't try it, McGraw: They might subpoena the rest of your tapes.'

He slammed the phone down. I didn't feel any better.

I dressed in a hurry but checked the Smith & Wesson carefully before putting it in my shoulder holster. My continuing hope was that Earl thought he'd rendered me negligible, and that he'd continue thinking so until I'd unraveled enough of the truth to make it too late for any other action he might take. But I took no chances, leaving the apartment from the rear and circling the block to come to my car. The coast was still clear.

I decided to abandon Loop bars and go to the Knifegrinders' neighborhood. I could return to the Loop tomorrow if necessary. On my way north I stopped at the clinic. Although it was early in the day the waiting room was already full. I again walked past the baleful glares from those who had been sitting for an hour.

'I need to talk to Lotty,' I said abruptly to Carol. She took one look at my face and got Lotty out of the examining room. I quickly explained to her what had happened. 'I don't want to get Jill upset,' I said, 'but I don't want to feel like we're sitting on a land mine here.'

Lotty nodded. 'Yes, but what's to stop them from taking her out of the Thayer house?' she asked. 'If they decide she would be a good hostage, I'm afraid they could get her wherever she was. It is not your peace of mind, but Jill's we need to think of. And I think she's better down here for another couple of days. Until her father's funeral, anyway; she called the mother – the funeral won't be until Friday.'

'Yes, but, Lotty, I'm running against the clock here. I've got to keep going, I can't sit guarding Jill.'

'No.' She frowned, then her face cleared. 'Carol's brother. Big, bruising, good-natured guy. He's an architecture student at Circle – maybe he can come and watch out for thugs.' She called to Carol, who listened eagerly to the problem, threw up her hands at the thought of Jill in danger, but agreed that Paul would be glad to come and help. 'He looks mean and stupid,' she said. 'A perfect disguise, since he is really friendly and brilliant.'

I had to be satisfied with that, but I wasn't happy: I'd have liked to ship Jill up to Wisconsin until everything was over.

I went on north and drove around the Knifegrinder territory, staking out my route for the day. There weren't nearly as many bars here as there were in the Loop. I picked a twenty-block square and decided to keep the car. This morning, no matter what sort of ill will it raised in the bars, I was not going to drink. I cannot face beer before noon. Or even Scotch.

I started at the west end of my territory, along the Howard el tracks. The first place, Clara's, looked so down-at-the-heels, I wasn't sure I wanted to go into it. Surely someone as fastidious as Masters looked would not go to a dump like that. On the other hand, maybe that's the kind of place he'd want – something that no one would associate with him. I braced my shoulders and pushed into the gloom out of the sticky air.

By noon I'd drawn nine blanks and was beginning to think I'd come up with a truly rotten idea, one that was wasting a lot of valuable time as well. I would finish my present stint, but not go back for a second crack at the Loop. I called the clinic. Carol's brother was in residence, enchanted by Jill and helping entertain some seven toddlers. I told Lotty I was going to stay where I was and to give my apologies to Jill.

By now the humid, polluted heat was stifling. I felt as though I were being pushed to the earth by it every time I walked back outside. The smell of stale beer in the bars began to nauseate me. Everyplace I went into had a few pathetic souls riveted to their stools, sipping down one drink after another, even though it was only morning. I was meeting with the same variety of hostility, indifference and cooperation that I'd found downtown, and the same lack of recognition of my photos.

After calling Lotty, I decided to get lunch. I wasn't far from Sheridan Road; I walked over and found a decent-looking steak house at the end of the block. I opted against lunch in a bar, and walked in thankfully out of the heat. The High Corral, as the place called itself, was small, clean and full of good food smells, a welcome contrast to sour beer. About two-thirds of the tables were filled. A plump, middle-aged woman came up with a menu and a cheerful smile and led me to a corner table. I began to feel better.

I ordered a small butt steak, an undressed salad, and a tall gin fizz and took my time over the food when it arrived. No one would ever write it up for *Chicago* magazine, but it was a simple, well-prepared meal and mellowed my spirits considerably. I ordered coffee, and lingered over that too. At 1.45 I realized I was procrastinating. '"When duty beckons, 'Lo thou must,' Youth replies to Age, 'I can,'"' I muttered encouragingly to myself. I put two dollars on the table and carried my bill over to the cash register. The plump hostess bustled up from the back of the restaurant to take my money.

'Very pleasant lunch,' I said.

'I'm glad you enjoyed it. Are you new to this neighborhood?'

I shook my head. 'I was just passing by and your sign looked inviting.' On impulse I pulled out my folder, now grimy and wilted around the edges. 'I wonder if these two men have ever come in here together?'

She picked up the pictures and looked at them. 'Oh, yes.'

I couldn't believe it. 'Are you sure?'

'I couldn't be mistaken. Not unless it's something I'd have to go to court for.' Her friendly face clouded a bit. 'If it's a legal matter you're talking about —' She shoved the pictures back at me.

'Not at all,' I said hastily. 'Or at least, not one that you'll have to be involved in.' I couldn't think of a plausible story on the spur of the moment.

'If anyone sends me a summons, I never saw either of them,' she reiterated.

'But off the record, just for my ears, how long have they been coming here?' I said, in what I hoped was a sincere, persuasive voice.

'What's the problem?' She was still suspicious.

'Paternity suit,' I said promptly, the first thing that came into my mind. It sounded ridiculous, even to me, but she relaxed.

'Well, that doesn't sound too dreadful. I guess it's been about five years. This is my husband's restaurant, and we've been working it together for eighteen years now. I remember most of my regular customers.'

'Do they come in often?' I asked.

'Oh, maybe three times a year. But over a period of time, you get to recognize your regulars. Besides, this man' — she tapped

170

McGraw's picture – 'comes in a lot. I think he's with that big union down the road.'

'Oh, really?' I said politely. I pulled Thayer's picture out. 'What about him?' I asked.

She studied it. 'It looks familiar,' she said, 'but he's never been in here.'

'Well, I certainly won't spread your name any further. And thanks for a very nice lunch.'

I felt dizzy walking out into the blinding heat. I couldn't believe my luck. Every now and then you get a break like that as a detective, and you start to think maybe you're on the side of right and good after all and a benevolent Providence is guiding your steps. Hot damn! I thought. I've got Masters tied to McGraw. And McGraw knows Smeissen. And the twig is on the branch, the branch is on the tree, the tree is on the hill. Vic, you are a genius, I told myself. The only question is, what is tying these two guys together? It must be that beautiful claim draft I found in Peter Thayer's apartment, but how?

I found a pay phone and called Ralph to see if he had tracked down the Gielczowski file. He was in a meeting. No, I wouldn't leave a message, I'd call later.

There was another question too. What was the connection among Thayer, McGraw and Masters? Still, that shouldn't be too difficult to find out. The whole thing probably revolved around some way to make money, maybe nontaxable money. If that were so, then Thayer came in naturally as Masters's neighbor and good friend and vice-president of a bank. He could probably launder money in a dozen different ways that I couldn't begin to imagine. Say he laundered the money and Peter found out. McGraw got Smeissen to kill Peter. Then Thayer was overcome with remorse. 'I won't be a party to it,' he said – to Masters? to McGraw? and they got Earl to blow him away too.

Steady, Vic, I told myself, getting into the car. So far you only have one fact: McGraw and Masters know each other. But what a beautiful, highly suggestive fact.

It was the bottom of the fifth inning at Wrigley Field, and the

Cubs were rolling over Philadelphia. For some reason, smoggy, wilting air acted on them like a tonic; everyone else was dying, but the Cubs were leading 8–1. Kingman hit his thirty-fourth homer. I thought maybe I'd earned a trip to the park to see the rest of the game, but sternly squashed the idea.

I got back to the clinic at 2.30. The outer room was even more crowded than it had been in the morning. A small window air conditioner fought against the heat and the combined bodies and lost. As I walked into the room the inner door opened and a face looked around. 'Mean and stupid' summed it up exactly. I went on across the room. 'You must be Paul,' I said, holding out a hand. 'I'm Vic.'

He smiled. The transformation was incredible. I could see the bright intelligence in his eyes, and he looked handsome rather than brutish. I wondered fleetingly if Jill was old enough to fall in love.

'Everything's quiet here,' he said. 'Everything but the babies, of course. Do you want to come out and see how Jill is doing?'

I followed him to the back. Lotty had moved the steel table out of her second examining room. In this tiny space Jill sat playing with five children between the ages of two and seven. She had the self-important look of someone coping with a major crisis. I grinned to myself. A baby was asleep in a basket in the corner. Jill looked up when I came in, and said hello, but her smile was for Paul. Was that an unnecessary complication or a help? I wondered.

'How's it going?' I asked.

'Great. Whenever things get too hectic, Paul makes a quick trip to the Good Humor man. I'm just afraid they'll catch on and squawk all the time.'

'Do you think you could leave them for a few minutes? I'd like to ask you a few questions.'

She looked at the group doubtfully. 'Go ahead,' Paul said cheerfully. 'I'll fill in for you – you've been at it too long, anyway.'

She got up. One of the children, a little boy, protested. 'You can't go,' he said in a loud, bossy voice.

'Sure, she can,' Paul said, squatting easily in her place. 'Now where were you?'

I took Jill into Lotty's office. 'Looks like you're a natural,' I said. 'Lotty will probably try to talk you into spending the rest of the summer down here.'

She flushed. 'I'd like to. I wonder if I really could.'

'No reason not, once we get this other business cleared up. Have you ever met Anita's father?'

She shook her head. I pulled out my package of pictures and took out the ones of McGraw. 'This is he. Have you ever seen him either with your dad, or maybe in the neighborhood?'

She studied them for a while. 'I don't think I've ever seen him before. He doesn't look at all like Anita.'

I stopped for a minute, not sure of the least hurting way to say what I wanted. 'I think Mr McGraw and Mr Masters are partners in some scheme or other – I don't know what. I believe your father must have been involved in some way, maybe without realizing what it was he was involved in.' In fact, I suddenly thought, if Thayer had been obviously a party to it, wouldn't Peter have confronted him first? 'Do you remember Peter and your father fighting in the last week or two before Peter's death?'

'No. In fact, Peter hadn't been home for seven weeks. If he and Daddy had a fight, it had to be over the telephone. Maybe at the office, but not out at the house.'

'That's good. Now, going back to this other business, I've got to know what it is your father knew about their deal. Can you think of anything that might help me? Did he and Mr Masters lock themselves up in the study for long talks?'

'Yes, but lots of men do that – did that. Daddy did business with lots of people, and they would often come over to the house to talk about it.'

'Well, what about money?' I asked. 'Did Mr Masters ever give your father a lot of money? Or the other way around?'

She laughed embarrassedly and shrugged her shoulders. 'I just don't know about any of that kind of stuff. I know Daddy worked for the bank and was an officer and all, but I don't know what he did exactly, and I don't know anything about the money. I guess I should. I know my family is well off, we've all got these big trusts from my grandparents, but I don't know anything about Daddy's money.'

That wasn't too surprising. 'Suppose I asked you to go back to Winnetka and look through his study to see if he had any papers that mention McGraw or Masters or both. Would that make you feel dishonest and slimy?'

She shook her head. 'If it would help I'll do it. But I don't want to leave here.'

'That is a problem,' I agreed. I looked at my watch and calculated times. 'I don't think we could fit it in before dinner this evening, anyway. But how about first thing tomorrow morning? Then we could come back here to the clinic in time for the baby rush hour.'

'Sure,' she agreed. 'Would you want to come along? I mean, I don't have a car or anything, and I would like to come back, and they might try to talk me into staying up there once I got there.'

'I wouldn't miss it.' By tomorrow morning the house probably wouldn't be filled with police anymore, either.

Jill got up and went back to the nursery. I could hear her saying in a maternal voice, 'Well, whose turn is it?' I grinned, popped my head in Lotty's door, and told her I was going home to sleep.

14

IN THE HEAT OF THE NIGHT

I set off for the University Women United meeting at seven. I'd slept for three hours and felt on top of the world. The fritata had turned out well – an old recipe of my mother's, accompanied by lots of toast, a salad constructed by Paul, and Paul's warm appreciation. He'd decided his bodyguarding included spending the night, and had brought a sleeping bag. The dining room was the only place with space for him, Lotty warned him. 'And I want you to stay in it,' she added. Jill was delighted. I could just imagine her sister's reaction if she came back with Paul as a boyfriend.

It was an easy drive south, a lazy evening with a lot of people out cooling off. This was my favorite time of day in the summer. There was something about the smell and feel of it that evoked the magic of childhood.

I didn't have any trouble parking on campus, and got into the meeting room just before things began. About a dozen women were there, wearing work pants and oversized T-shirts, or denim skirts made out of blue jeans with the legs cut apart and restitched, seams facing out. I was wearing jeans and a big loose shirt to cover the gun, but I was still dressed more elegantly than anyone else in the room.

Gail Sugarman was there. She recognized me when I came in, and said, 'Hi, I'm glad you remembered the meeting.' The others stopped to look at me. 'This is –' Gail stopped, embarrassed.

'I've forgotten your name – it's Italian, I remember you told me that. Anyway, I met her at the Swift coffee shop last week and told her about the meetings and here she is.'

'You're not a reporter, are you?' one woman asked.

'No, I'm not,' I said neutrally. ' I have a B A from here, pretty old degree at this point. I was down here the other day talking to Harold Weinstein and ran into Gail.'

'Weinstein,' another one snorted. 'Thinks he's a radical because he wears work shirts and curses capitalism.'

'Yeah,' another agreed. 'I was in his class on "Big Business and Big Labor". He felt the major battle against oppression had been won when Ford lost the battle with the U A W in the forties. If you tried to talk about how women have been excluded not just from big business but from the unions as well, he said that didn't indicate oppression, merely a reflection of the current social mores.'

'That argument justifies all oppression,' a plump woman with short curling hair put in. 'Hell, the Stalin labor camps reflected Soviet mores of the thirties. Not to mention Scharansky's exile with hard labor.'

Thin, dark Mary, the older woman who'd been with Gail at the coffee shop on Friday, tried to call the group to order. 'We don't have a program tonight,' she said. 'In the summer our attendance is too low to justify a speaker. But why don't we get in a circle on the floor so that we can have a group discussion.' She was smoking, sucking in her cheeks with her intense inhaling. I had a feeling she was eyeing me suspiciously, but that may have just been my own nerves.

I obediently took a spot on the floor, drawing my legs up in front of me. My calf muscles were sensitive. The other women straggled over, getting cups of evil-looking coffee as they came. I'd taken one look at the overboiled brew on my way in and decided it wasn't necessary to drink it to prove I was one of the group.

When all but two were seated, Mary suggested we go around the circle and introduce ourselves. 'There are a couple of new people here tonight,' she said. 'I'm Mary Annasdaughter.' She turned to the woman on her right, the one who'd protested women's exclusion from big unions. When they got to me, I said, 'I'm V. I. Warshawski. Most people call me Vic.'

When they'd finished, one said curiously, 'Do you go by your initials or is Vic your real name?'

'It's a nickname,' I said. 'I usually use my initials. I started out my working life as a lawyer, and I found it was harder for male colleagues and opponents to patronize me if they didn't know my first name.'

'Good point,' Mary said, taking the meeting back. 'Tonight I'd like to see what we can do to support the ERA booth at the Illinois State Fair. The state NOW group usually has a booth where they distribute literature. This year they want to do something more elaborate, have a slide show, and they need more people. Someone who can go down to Springfield for one or more days the week of August fourth to tenth to staff the booth and the slide show.'

'Are they sending a car down?' the plump, curly-haired one asked.

'I expect the transportation will depend on how many people volunteer. I thought I might go. If some of the rest of you want to, we could all take the bus together – it's not that long a ride.'

'Where would we stay?' someone wanted to know.

'I plan to camp out,' Mary said. 'But you can probably find some NOW people to share a hotel room with. I can check back at the headquarters.'

'I kind of hate doing anything with NOW,' a rosy-cheeked woman with waist-long hair said. She was wearing a T-shirt and bib overalls; she had the face of a peaceful Victorian matron.

'Why, Annette?' Gail asked.

'They ignore the real issues – women's social position, inequities of marriage, divorce, child care – and go screwing around supporting establishment politicians. They'll support a candidate who does one measly little thing for child care, and overlook the fact that he doesn't have any women on his staff, and that his wife is a plastic mannequin sitting at home supporting his career.'

'Well, you're never going to have social justice until you get some basic political and economic inequalities solved,' a stocky woman, whose name I thought was Ruth, said. 'And political problems can be grappled with. You can't go around trying to uproot the fundamental oppression between men and women without some tool to dig with: laws represent that tool.'

This was an old argument; it went back to the start of radical feminism in the late sixties: Do you concentrate on equal pay and equal legal rights, or do you go off and try to convert the whole society to a new set of sexual values? Mary let the tide roll in for ten minutes. Then she rapped the floor with her knuckles.

'I'm not asking for a consensus on NOW, or even on the ERA,' she said. 'I just want a head count of those who'd like to go to Springfield.'

Gail volunteered first, predictably, and Ruth. The two who'd been dissecting Weinstein's politics also agreed to go.

'What about you, Vic?' Mary said.

'Thanks, but no,' I said.

'Why don't you tell us why you're really here,' Mary said in a steely voice. 'You may be an old UC student, but no one stops by a rap group on Tuesday night just to check out politics on the old campus.'

'They don't change that much, but you're right: I came here because I'm trying to find Anita McGraw. I don't know anyone here well, but I know this is a group she was close to, and I'm hoping that someone here can tell me where she is.'

'In that case, you can get out,' Mary said angrily. The group silently closed against me; I could feel their hostility like a physical force. 'We've all had the police on us – now I guess they thought a woman pig could infiltrate this meeting and worm Anita's address out of one of us – assuming we had it to worm. I don't know it myself – I don't know if anyone in here knows it – but you pigs just can't give up, can you?'

I didn't move. 'I'm not with the police, and I'm not a reporter.

Do you think the police want to find Anita so that they can lay Peter Thayer's death on her?'

'Of course,' Mary snorted. 'They've been poking around trying to find if Peter slept around and Anita was jealous or if he'd made a will leaving her money. Well, I'm sorry – you can go back and tell them that they just cannot get away with that.'

'I'd like to present an alternative scenario,' I said.

'Screw yourself,' Mary said. 'We're not interested. Now get out.'

'Not until you've listened to me.'

'Do you want me to throw her out, Mary?' Annette asked.

'You can try,' I said. 'But it'll just make you madder if I hurt one of you, and I'm still not going to leave until you've listened to what I have to say.'

'All right,' Mary said angrily. She took out her watch. 'You can have five minutes. Then Annette throws you out.'

'Thank you. My tale is short: I can embellish it later if you have questions.

'Yesterday morning, John Thayer, Peter's father, was gunned down in front of his home. The police presume, but cannot prove, that this was the work of a hired killer known to them. It is my belief, not shared by the police, that this same killer shot Peter Thayer last Monday.

'Now, why was Peter shot? The answer is that he knew something that was potentially damaging to a very powerful and very corrupt labor leader. I don't know what he knew, but I assume it had something to do with illegal financial transactions. It is further possible that his father was a party to these trans-actions, as was the man Peter worked for.'

I stretched my legs out and leaned back on my hands. No one spoke. 'These are all assumptions. I have no proof at the moment that could be used in court, but I have the proof that comes from watching human relationships and reactions. If I am correct in my assumptions, then I believe Anita McGraw's life is in serious danger. The overwhelming probability is that Peter Thayer shared with her the secret that got him killed, and that when she came home last Monday evening to find his dead body, she panicked and ran. But as long as she is alive, and in lonely possession of this secret – whatever it is – then the men who have killed twice to protect it will not care about killing her as well.'

'You know a lot about it,' Ruth said. 'How do you happen to be involved if you're not a reporter and not a cop?'

'I'm a private investigator,' I said levelly. 'At the moment my client is a fourteen-year-old girl who saw her father murdered and is very frightened.'

Mary was still angry. 'You're still a cop, then. It doesn't make any difference who is paying your salary.'

'You're wrong,' I said. 'It makes an enormous difference. I'm the only person I take orders from, not a hierarchy of officers, aldermen, and commissioners.'

'What kind of proof do you have?' Ruth asked.

'I was beaten up last Friday night by the man who employs the killer who probably killed the two Thayers. He warned me away from the case. I have a presumption, not provable, of who hired him: a man who got his name from an associate on speaking terms with many prominent criminals. This man is the person Peter Thayer was working for this summer. And I know the other guy, the one with the criminal contacts, has been seen with Peter's boss. Ex-boss. I don't know about the money, that's just a guess. No one in that crowd would be hurt by sex scandals, and spying is very unlikely.'

'What about dope?' Gail asked.

'I don't think so,' I said. 'But anyway, that is certainly an illegal source of income for which you might kill to cover up.'

'Frankly, V.I., or Vic, or whatever your real name is, you haven't convinced me. I don't believe Anita's life could be in danger. But if anyone disagrees with me and knows where Anita is, go ahead and betray her.'

'I have another question,' Ruth said. 'Assuming we did know where she is and told you, what good would that do her – if everything you're saying is true?'

'If I can find out what the transaction is, I can probably get some definite proof of who the murderer is,' I said. 'The more quickly that happens, the less likely it is that this hired killer can get to her.'

No one said anything else. I waited a few minutes. I kind of hoped Annette would try to throw me out: I felt like breaking someone's arm. Radicals are so goddamn paranoid. And radical students combine that with isolation and pomposity. Maybe I'd break all their arms, just for fun. But Annette didn't move. And no one chirped up with Anita's address.

'Satisfied?' Mary asked triumphantly, her thin cheeks pulled back in a smirk.

'Thanks for the time, sisters,' I said. 'If any of you changes her mind, I'm leaving some business cards with my phone number by the coffee.' I put them down and left.

I felt very depressed driving home. Peter Wimsey would have gone in and charmed all those uncouth radicals into slobbering all over him. He would never have revealed he was a private detective – he would have started some clever conversation that would have told him everything he wanted to know and then given two hundred pounds to the Lesbian Freedom Fund.

I turned left onto Lake Shore Drive, going much too fast and getting a reckless pleasure from feeling the car careening, almost out of control. I didn't even care at this point if someone stopped me. I did the four miles between Fifty-seventh Street and McCormick Place in three minutes. It was at that point that I realized someone was following me.

The speed limit in that area is forty-five and I was doing eighty, yet I was holding the same pair of headlights in my rearview mirror that had been behind me in the other lane when I got on the Drive. I braked quickly, and changed to the outside lane. The other car didn't change lanes, but slowed down also.

How long had I been carrying a tail, and why? If Earl wanted to blow me away, he had unlimited opportunities, no need to waste manpower and money on a tail. He might not know where I'd gone after leaving my apartment, but I didn't think so. My answering service had Lotty's phone number, and it's a simple matter to get an address from the phone company if you have the number.

Maybe they wanted Jill and didn't realize I'd taken her to Lotty's. I drove slowly and normally, not trying to change lanes or make an unexpected exit. My companion stayed with me, in the center lane, letting a few cars get between us. As we moved downtown, the lights got brighter and I could see the car better – a mid-sized gray sedan, it looked like.

If they got Jill, they would have a potent weapon to force me off the case. I couldn't believe that Earl thought I had a case. He'd given me the big scare, he'd torn my apartment apart, and he'd gotten the police to make an arrest. As far as I could tell, despite John Thayer's death, Donald Mackenzie was still in jail. Perhaps they thought I could lead them to the document they had overlooked at Peter Thayer's, and not found in my apartment.

The phrase 'lead them to' clicked in my brain. Of course. They weren't interested in me, or in Jill, or even in that claim draft. They wanted Anita McGraw, just as I did, and they thought I could lead them to her. How had they known I was going to the campus tonight? They hadn't: they'd followed me there. I'd told McGraw I had a lead on a lead to Anita and he had told – Smeissen? – Masters? I didn't like the thought of McGraw fingering his daughter. He must have told someone he thought he could trust. Surely not Masters, though.

If my deduction was correct, I ought to keep them guessing. As long as they thought I knew something, my life was probably safe. I got off the Drive downtown, going past Buckingham Fountain as it shot up jets of colored water high into the night. A large crowd had gathered to see the nightly show. I wondered if I could lose myself in it, but didn't think much of my chances. I went on over to Michigan Avenue, and parked across the street from the Conrad Hilton Hotel. I locked the car door and leisurely crossed the street. I stopped inside the glass doors for a glance outside, and was pleased to see the gray sedan pull up next to my car. I didn't wait to see what the occupants would do, but moved quickly down the hotel's long corridor to the side entrance on Eighth Street.

This part of the hotel had airline ticket offices, and as I walked past them, a doorman was calling. 'Last call for the airport bus. Nonstop to O'Hare Field.' Without thinking or stopping to look behind me, I pushed in front of a small crew of laughing flight attendants and got on the bus. They followed me more slowly; the conductor checked his load and got off, and the bus started moving. As we turned the corner onto Michigan, I could see a man looking up and down the street. I thought it might be Freddie.

The bus moved ponderously across the Loop to Ontario Street, some twelve blocks north, and I kept an anxious lookout through the rear window, but it seemed as though Freddie's slow wits had not considered the possibility of my being on the bus.

It was 9.30 when we got to O'Hare. I moved from the bus to stand in the shadow of one of the giant pillars supporting the terminal, but saw no gray sedan. I was about to step out when I thought perhaps they had a second car, so I looked to see if any vehicle repeated its circuit more than once, and scanned the occupants to see if I recognized any of Smeissen's crew. By ten I decided I was clear and caught a cab back to Lotty's.

I had the driver drop me at the top of her street. Then I went down the alley behind her building, keeping a hand close to my gun. I didn't see anyone but a group of three teenage boys, drinking beer and talking lazily.

I had to pound on the back door for several minutes before Lotty heard and came to let me in. Her thick black eyebrows went up in surprise. 'Trouble?' she said.

'A little, downtown. I'm not sure whether anyone is watching the front.'

'Jill?' she asked.

'I don't think so. I think they're hoping I'll lead them to Anita McGraw. Unless I do, or unless they find her first, I think we're all pretty safe.' I shook my head in dissatisfaction. 'I don't like it, though. They could snatch Jill and hold her to ransom if they thought I knew where Anita was. I didn't find out tonight. I'm sure one of those goddamned radical women knows where she is, but they think they're being noble and winning a great war against the pigs, and they won't tell me. It's so frustrating.'

'Yes, I see,' Lotty said seriously. 'Maybe it's not so good for the child to be here. She and Paul are watching the movie on television,' she added, jerking her head toward the living room.

'I left my car downtown,' I said. 'Someone was following me back from the university and I shook them off in the Loop – took the bus out to O'Hare – long and expensive way to shake a tail, but it worked.

'Tomorrow, Jill's taking me out to Winnetka to go through her father's papers. Maybe she should just stay there.'

'We'll sleep on it,' Lotty suggested. 'Paul is loving his guard duty, but he couldn't do much against men with machine guns. Besides, he is an architecture student and should not miss too many of his classes.'

We went back into the living room. Jill was curled up on the daybed, watching the movie. Paul was lying on his stomach, looking up at her every few minutes. Jill didn't seem aware of the impression she was creating – this seemed to be her first conquest – but she glowed with contentment.

I went into the guest room to make some phone calls. Larry Anderson said they'd finished my apartment. 'I didn't think you'd want that couch, so I let one of the guys take it home. And about the door – I've got a friend who does some carpentry. He has a beautiful oak door, out of some mansion or other. He could fix it up for you and put some dead bolts in it, if you'd like.'

'Larry. I can't begin to thank you,' I said, much moved. 'That sounds like a beautiful idea. How did you close the place up today?'

'Oh, we nailed it shut,' he said cheerfully. Larry and I had gone to school together years ago, but he'd dropped out earlier and further than I had. We chatted for a few minutes, then I hung up to call Ralph.

184

'It's me, Sherlock Holmes,' I said. 'How did your claim files go?'

'Oh, fine. Summer is a busy time for accidents with so many people on the road. They should stay home, but then they'd cut off their legs with lawnmowers or something and we'd be paying just the same.'

'Did you refile that draft without any trouble?' I asked.

'Actually not, I couldn't find the file. I looked up the guy's account, though: he must have been in a doozy of an accident – we've been sending him weekly checks for four years now.' He chuckled a little. 'I was going to inspect Yardley's face today to see if he looked guilty of multiple homicide, but he's taking the rest of the week off – apparently cut up about Thayer's death.'

'I see.' I wasn't going to bother telling him about the link I'd found between Masters and McGraw; I was tired of arguing with him over whether I had a case or not.

'Dinner tomorrow night?' he asked.

'Make it Thursday,' I suggested. 'Tomorrow's going to be pretty open-ended.'

As soon as I put the phone down, it rang. 'Dr Herschel's residence,' I said. It was my favorite reporter, Murray Ryerson.

'Just got a squeal that Tony Bronsky may have killed John Thayer,' he said.

'Oh, really? Are you going to publish that?'

'Oh, I think we'll paint a murky picture of gangland involvement. It's just a whiff, no proof, he wasn't caught at the scene, and our legal people have decided mentioning his name would be actionable.'

'Thanks for sharing the news,' I said politely.

'I wasn't calling out of charity,' Murray responded. 'But in my lumbering Swedish way it dawned on me that Bronsky works for Smeissen. We agreed yesterday that his name has been cropping up here and there around the place. What's his angle, Vic – why would he kill a respectable banker and his son?'

'Beats the hell out of me, Murray,' I said, and hung up.

I went back and watched the rest of the movie, *The Guns of*

Navarone, with Lotty, Jill and Paul. I felt restless and on edge. Lotty didn't keep Scotch. She didn't have any liquor at all except brandy. I went into the kitchen and poured myself a healthy slug. Lotty looked questioningly at me, but said nothing.

Around midnight, as the movie was ending, the phone rang. Lotty answered it in her bedroom and came back, her face troubled. She gave me a quiet signal to follow her to the kitchen. 'A man,' she said in a low voice. 'He asked if you were here; when I said yes, he hung up.'

'Oh, hell,' I muttered. 'Well, nothing to be done about it now . . . My apartment will be ready tomorrow night – I'll go back and remove this powder keg from your home.'

Lotty shook her head and gave her twisted smile. 'Not to worry, Vic – I'm counting on you fixing the AMA for me someday.'

Lotty sent Jill unceremoniously off to bed. Paul got out his sleeping bag. I helped him move the heavy walnut dining-room table against the wall, and Lotty brought him a pillow from her bed, then went to sleep, herself.

The night was muggy; Lotty's brick, thick-walled building kept out the worst of the weather, and exhaust fans in the kitchen and dining room moved the air enough to make sleep possible. But the air felt close, to me anyway. I lay on the daybed in a T-shirt, and sweated, dozed a bit, woke, tossed, and dozed again. At last I sat up angrily. I wanted to do something, but there was nothing for me to do. I turned on the light. It was 3.30.

I pulled on a pair of jeans and tiptoed out to the kitchen to make some coffee. While water dripped through the white porcelain filter I looked through a bookcase in the living room for something to read. All books look equally boring in the middle of the night. I finally selected *Vienna in the Seventeenth Century* by Dorfman, fetched a cup of coffee, and flipped the pages, reading about the devastating plague following the Thirty Years' War, and the street now called Graben – 'the grave' – because so many dead had been buried there. The terrible story fit my jangled mood.

Above the hum of the fans I could hear the phone ring faintly in Lotty's room. We'd turned it off next to the spare bed where Jill was sleeping. I told myself it had to be for Lotty – some mother in labor, or some bleeding teenager – but I sat tensely anyway and was somehow not surprised when Lotty came out of her room, wrapped in a thin, striped cotton robe.

'For you. A Ruth Yonkers.'

I shrugged my shoulders; the name meant nothing to me. 'Sorry to get you up,' I said, and went down the short hallway to Lotty's room. I felt as if all the night's tension had had its focus in waiting for this unexpected phone call from an unknown woman. The instrument was on a small Indonesian table next to Lotty's bed. I sat on the bed and spoke into it.

'This is Ruth Yonkers,' a husky voice responded. 'I talked to you at the UWU meeting tonight.'

'Oh yes,' I said calmly. 'I remember you.' She'd been the stocky, square young woman who'd asked me all the questions at the end.

'I talked to Anita after the meeting. I didn't know how seriously to take you, but I thought she ought to know about it.' I held my breath and said nothing. 'She called me last week, told me about finding Peter's – finding Peter. She made me promise not to tell anyone where she was without checking with her first. Not even her father, or the police. It was all rather – bizarre.'

'I see,' I said.

'Do you?' she asked doubtfully.

'You thought she'd killed Peter, didn't you?' I said in a comfortable tone. 'And you felt caught by her choosing you to confide in. You didn't want to betray her, but you didn't want to be involved in a murder. So you were relieved to have a promise to fall back on.'

Ruth gave a little sigh, half laugh, that came ghostily over the line. 'Yes, that was it exactly. You're smarter than I thought you were. I hadn't realized Anita might be in danger herself – that was why she sounded so scared. Anyway, I called her.

We've been talking for several hours. She's never heard of you and we've been debating whether we can trust you.' She paused and I was quiet. 'I think we have to. That's what it boils down to. If it's true, if there really are some mob people after her – it all sounds surreal, but she says you're right.'

'Where is she?' I asked gently.

'Up in Wisconsin. I'll take you to her.'

'No. Tell me where she is, and I'll find her. I'm being followed, and it'll just double the danger to try to meet up with you.'

'Then I won't tell you where she is,' Ruth said. 'My agreement with her was that I would bring you to her.'

'You've been a good friend, Ruth, and you've carried a heavy load. But if the people who are after Anita find out you know where she is, and suspect you're in her confidence, your own life is in danger. Let me run the risk – it's my job, after all.'

We argued for several more minutes, but Ruth let herself be persuaded. She'd been under a tremendous strain for the five days since Anita had first called her, and she was glad to let someone else take it over. Anita was in Hartford, a little town northwest of Milwaukee. She was working as a waitress in a café. She'd cut her red hair short and dyed it black, and she was calling herself Jody Hill. If I left now, I could catch her just as the café opened for breakfast in the morning.

It was after four when I hung up. I felt refreshed and alert, as if I'd slept soundly for eight hours instead of tossing miserably for three.

Lotty was sitting in the kitchen, drinking coffee and reading. 'Lotty, I do apologize. You get little enough sleep as it is. But I think this is the beginning of the end.'

'Ah, good,' she said, putting a marker in her book and shutting it. 'The missing girl?'

'Yes. That was a friend who gave me the address. All I have to do now is get away from here without being seen.'

'Where is she?' I hesitated. 'My dear, I've been questioned by tougher experts than these Smeissen hoodlums. And perhaps someone else should know.'

I grinned. 'You're right,' I told her, then added, 'The question is, what about Jill? We were going to go up to Winnetka tomorrow – today, that is – to see if her father had any papers that might explain his connection with Masters and McGraw. Now maybe Anita can make that tie-in for me. But I'd still be happier to get Jill back up there. This whole arrangement – Paul under the dining-room table, Jill and the babies – makes me uncomfortable. If she wants to come back for the rest of the summer, sure – she can stay with me once this mess is cleared up. But for now – let's get her back home.'

Lotty pursed her lips and stared into her coffee cup for several minutes. Finally she said, 'Yes. I believe you're right. She's much better – two good nights of sleep, with calm people who like her – she can probably go back to her family. I agree. The whole thing with Paul is too volatile. Very sweet, but too volatile in such a cramped space.'

'My car is across from the Conrad Hilton downtown. I can't take it – it's being watched. Maybe Paul can pick it up tomorrow, take Jill home. I'll be back here tomorrow night, say goodbye, and give you a little privacy.'

'Do you want to take my car?' Lotty suggested.

I thought it over. 'Where are you parked?'

'Out front. Across the street.'

'Thanks, but I've got to get away from here without being seen. I don't know that your place is being watched – but these guys want Anita McGraw very badly. And they did call earlier to make sure I was here.'

Lotty got up and turned out the kitchen light. She looked out the window, concealed partly by a hanging geranium and thin gauze curtains. 'I don't see anyone . . . Why not wake up Paul? He can take my car, drive it around the block a few times. Then, if no one follows him, he can pick you up in the alley. You drop him down the street.'

'I don't like it. You'll be without a car, and when he comes back on foot, if there is someone out there, they'll be suspicious.'

'Vic, my dear, it's not like you to be so full of quibbles. We

189

won't be without a car – we'll have yours. As for the second –'
She thought a minute. 'Ah! Drop Paul at the clinic. He can finish
his sleep there. We have a bed, for nights when Carol or I have
to stay over.'

I laughed. 'Can't think of any more quibbles, Lotty. Let's
wake up Paul and give it a try.'

Paul woke up quickly and cheerfully. When the plan was
explained to him he accepted it enthusiastically. 'Want me to
beat up anyone hanging around outside?'

'Unnecessary, my dear,' said Lotty, amused. 'Let's try not to
attract too much attention to ourselves. There's an all-night
restaurant on Sheffield off Addison – give us a call from there.'

We left Paul to dress in privacy. He came out to the kitchen
a few minutes later, pushing his black hair back from his square
face with his left hand and buttoning a blue work shirt with the
right. Lotty gave him her car keys. We watched the street from
Lotty's dark bedroom. No one attacked Paul as he got into the
car and started it; we couldn't see anyone follow him down the
street.

I went back to the living room and dressed properly. Lotty
watched me without speaking while I loaded the Smith & Wesson
and stuck it into the shoulder holster. I was wearing well-cut
jeans and a blouson jacket over a ribbed knit shirt.

About ten minutes later Lotty's phone rang. 'All clear,' Paul
said. 'There is someone out front, though. I think I'd better not
drive down the alley – it might bring him around to the rear.
I'll be at the mouth of the alley at the north end of the street.'

I relayed this to Lotty. She nodded. 'Why don't you leave
from the basement? You can go down there from inside, and
outside the door is hidden by stairs and garbage cans.' She led
me downstairs. I felt very alert, very keyed up. Through a
window on the stairwell we could see the night clearing into a
predawn gray. It was 4.40 and the apartment was very quiet. A
siren sounded in the distance, but no traffic was going down
Lotty's street.

Lotty had brought a flashlight with her, rather than turn on a light that might show through the street-side window. She pointed it down the stairs so I could see the way, then turned it off. I padded down after her. At the bottom she seized my wrist, led me around bicycles and a washing machine, and very slowly and quietly drew back the dead bolts in the outside door. There was a little *click* as they snapped open. She waited several minutes before pulling the door open. It moved into the basement quietly, on oiled hinges. I slipped out up the stairs in crepe-soled shoes.

From behind the screen of garbage cans I peered into the alley. Freddie sat propped against the back of the wall at the south end of the alley two buildings down. As far as I could tell, he was asleep.

I moved quietly back down the stairs. 'Give me ten minutes,' I mouthed into Lotty's ear. 'I may need a quick escape route.' Lotty nodded without speaking.

At the top of the stairs I checked Freddie again. Did he have the subtlety to fake sleep? I moved from behind the garbage cans into the shadow of the next building, my right hand on the revolver's handle. Freddie didn't stir. Keeping close to the walls, I moved quickly down the alley. As soon as I was halfway down, I broke into a quiet sprint.

15
THE UNION MAID

Paul was waiting as promised. He had a good head – the car was out of sight of the alley. I slid into the front seat and drew the door closed. 'Any trouble?' he said, starting the engine and pulling away from the curb.

'No, but I recognized a guy asleep in the alley. You'd better call Lotty from the clinic. Tell her not to leave Jill alone in the apartment. Maybe she can get a police escort to the clinic. Tell her to call a Lieutenant Mallory to request it.'

'Sure thing.' He was very likeable. We drove the short way to the clinic in silence. I handed him my car keys, and reiterated where the car was. 'It's a dark blue Monza.'

'Good luck,' he said in his rich voice. 'Don't worry about Jill and Lotty – I'll take care of them.'

'I never worry about Lotty,' I said, sliding into the driver's seat. 'She's a force unto herself.' I adjusted the side mirror and the rearview mirror, and let in the clutch: Lotty drove a small Datsun, as practical and unadorned as she was.

I kept checking the road behind me as I drove across Addison to the Kennedy, but it seemed to be clear. The air was clammy, the damp of a muggy night before the sun would rise and turn it into smog again. The eastern sky was light now, and I was moving quickly through the empty streets. Traffic was light on the expressway, and I cleared the suburbs to the northbound Milwaukee toll road in forty-five minutes.

Lotty's Datsun handled well, although I was out of practice with a standard shift and ground the gears a bit changing down.

She had an FM radio, and I listened to WFMT well past the Illinois border. After that the reception grew fuzzy so I switched it off.

It was six in clear daylight when I reached the Milwaukee bypass. I'd never been to Hartford, but I'd been to Port Washington, thirty miles to the east of it on Lake Michigan, many times. As far as I could tell, the route was the same, except for turning west onto route 60 instead of east when you get twenty miles north of Milwaukee.

At 6.50 I eased the Datsun to a halt on Hartford's main street, across from Ronna's Café – Homemade Food, and in front of the First National Bank of Hartford. My heart was beating fast. I unbuckled the seat belt and got out, stretching my legs. The trip had been just under 140 miles; I'd done it in two hours and ten minutes. Not bad.

Hartford is in the beautiful moraine country, the heart of Wisconsin dairy farming. There's a small Chrysler plant there that makes outboard motors, and up the hill I could see a Libby's cannery. But most of the money in the town comes from farming, and people were up early. Ronna's opened at 5.30, according to the legend on the door, and at seven most of the tables were full. I bought the *Milwaukee Sentinel* from a coin box by the door, and sat down at an empty table near the back.

One waitress was taking care of the crowd at the counter. Another covered all the tables. She was rushing through the swinging doors at the back, her arms loaded up with plates. Her short, curly hair had been dyed black. It was Anita McGraw.

She unloaded pancakes, fried eggs, toast, hash browns, at a table where three heavyset men in bib overalls were drinking coffee, and brought a fried egg to a good-looking young guy in a dark blue boiler suit at the table next to me. She looked at me with the harassment common to all overworked waitresses in coffee shops. 'I'll be right with you. Coffee?'

I nodded. 'Take your time,' I said, opening the paper. The men in the bib overalls were kidding the good-looking guy – he was a veterinarian, apparently, and they were farmers who'd used his services. 'You grow that beard to make everyone think you're grown up, Doc?' one of them said.

'Naw, just to hide from the FBI,' the vet said. Anita was carrying a cup of coffee to me; her hand shook and she spilled it on the veterinarian. She flushed and started apologizing. I got up and took the cup from her before any more spilled, and the young man said good-naturedly, 'Oh, it just wakes you up faster if you pour it all over yourself – especially if it's still hot. Believe me, Jody,' he added as she dabbed ineffectually at the wet spot on his arm with a napkin, 'this is the nicest stuff that's likely to spill on this outfit today.'

The farmers laughed at that, and Anita came over to take my order. I asked for a Denver omelette, no potatoes, wholewheat toast and juice. When in farm country, eat like a farmer. The vet finished his egg and coffee. 'Well, I hear those cows calling me,' he said, put some some money on the table, and left. Other people began drifting out too. It was 7.15 – time for the day to be under way. For the farmers this was a short break between morning milking and some business in town. They lingered over a second cup of coffee. By the time Anita brought back my omelette, though, only three tables had people still eating, and just a handful were left at the counter.

I ate half the omelette, slowly, and read every word in the paper. People kept drifting in and out; I had a fourth cup of coffee. When Anita brought my bill, I put a five on it and, on top of that, one of my cards. I'd written on it: 'Ruth sent me. I'm in the green Datsun across the street.'

I went out and put some money in the meter, then got back in the car. I sat for another half hour, working the crossword puzzle, before Anita appeared. She opened the passenger door and sat down without speaking. I folded up the paper and put it in the backseat and looked at her gravely. The picture I'd found in her apartment had shown a laughing young woman, not precisely beautiful, but full of the vitality that is better than beauty in a young woman. Now her face was strained and gaunt.

The police would never have found her from a photograph – she looked closer to thirty than twenty – lack of sleep, fear and tension cutting unnatural lines in her young face. The black hair did not go with her skin, the delicate creamy skin of a true redhead.

'What made you choose Hartford?' I asked.

She looked surprised – possibly the last question she'd expected. 'Peter and I came up here last summer to the Washington County Fair – just for fun. We had a sandwich in that café, and I remembered it.' Her voice was husky with fatigue. She turned to look at me and said rapidly, 'I hope I can trust you – I've got to trust someone. Ruth doesn't know – doesn't know the kind of people who – who might shoot someone. I don't either, really, but I think I have a better idea than she does.' She gave a bleak smile. 'I'm going to lose my mind if I stay here alone any longer. But I can't go back to Chicago. I need help. If you can't do it, if you blow it and I get shot – or if you're some clever female hit man who fooled Ruth into giving you my address – I don't know. I have to take the chance.' She was holding her hands together so tightly that the knuckles were white.

'I'm a private investigator,' I said. 'Your father hired me last week to find you, and I found Peter Thayer's body instead. Over the weekend, he told me to stop looking. I have my own guesses as to what all that was about. That's how I got involved. I agree that you're in a pretty tough spot. And if I blow it, neither of us will be in very good shape. You can't hide here forever, though, and I think that I'm tough enough, quick enough, and smart enough to get things settled so that you can come out of hiding. I can't cure the pain, and there's more to come, but I can get you back to Chicago – or wherever else you want so that you can live openly and with dignity.'

She thought about that, nodding her head. People were walking up and down the sidewalk; I felt as if we were in a fishbowl. 'Is there somewhere we can go to talk – somewhere with a little more room?'

'There's a park.'

'That'd be fine.' It was back along route 60 toward Milwaukee. I parked the Datsun out of sight of the road and we walked down to sit on the bank of a little stream that ran through the park, dividing it from the back wall of the Chrysler plant on the other side. The day was hot but here in the country the air was clear and sweet.

'You said something about living with dignity,' she said, looking at the water, her mouth twisted in a harsh smile. 'I don't think I'll ever do that again. I know what happened to Peter, you see. In a way, I guess you could say I killed him.'

'Why do you say that?' I asked gently.

'You say you found his body. Well, so did I. I came home at four and found him. I knew then what had happened. I lost my head and ran. I didn't know where to go – I didn't come here until the next day. I spent the night at Mary's house, and then I came up here. I couldn't figure out why they weren't waiting for me, but I knew if I went back they'd get me.' She was starting to sob, great dry sobs that heaved her shoulders and chest. 'Dignity!' she said in a hoarse voice. 'Oh, Christ! I'd settle for a night's sleep.' I didn't say anything, but sat watching her. After a few minutes she calmed down a bit. 'How much do you know?' she asked.

'I don't know much for certain – that I can prove, I mean. But I've got some guesses. What I know for certain is that your father and Yardley Masters have a deal going. I don't know what it is, but I found a claim draft from Ajax in your apartment. I presume that Peter brought it home, so one of my guesses is that the deal has to do with claim drafts. I know that your father knows Earl Smeissen, and I know that someone wanted something very badly that they thought was in your apartment and then thought that I had taken it and put in mine. They wanted it badly enough to ransack both places. My guess is that they were looking for the claim draft, and that it was Smeissen, or one of his people, who did the ransacking.'

'Is Smeissen a killer?' she asked in her harsh, strained voice.

196

'Well, he's doing pretty well these days: he doesn't kill, himself, but he's got muscle to do it for him.'

'So my father had him kill Peter, didn't he?' She stared at me challengingly, her eyes hard and dry, her mouth twisted. This was the nightmare she'd been lying down with every night. No wonder she wasn't sleeping.

'I don't know. This is one of my guesses. Your father loves you, you know, and he's going nuts right now. He would never knowingly have put your life in danger. And he would never knowingly have let Peter be shot. I think what happened was that Peter confronted Masters, and Masters panicked and called your dad.' I stopped. 'This isn't pretty and it's hard to say to you. But your dad knows the kind of people who will put someone away for a price. He's made it to the top of a rough union in a rough industry, and he's had to know those kinds of people.'

She nodded wearily, not looking at me. 'I know. I never wanted to know it in the past, but I know it now. So my – my father, gave him this Smeissen's name. Is that what you're getting at?'

'Yes. I'm sure Masters didn't tell him who it was who'd crossed his path – just that someone had tumbled to the secret, and had to be eliminated. It's the only thing that explains your father's behavior.'

'What do you mean?' she asked, not very interested.

'Your father came to me last Wednesday, gave me a fake name and a phony story, but he wanted me to find you. He knew about Peter's death at that point, and he was upset because you'd run away. You called and accused him of killing Peter, didn't you?'

She nodded again. 'It was too stupid for words. I was off my head, with anger, and fear and – and grief. Not just for Peter, you know, but for my father, and the union and everything I'd grown up thinking was fine and – and worth fighting for.'

'Yes, that was tough.' She didn't say anything else, so I went on. 'Your father didn't know at first what had happened. It was only a few days later that he connected Peter with Masters. Then he knew that Masters had had Peter killed. Then he knew that you were in trouble, too. And that's when he fired me. He didn't want me to find you because he didn't want anyone else to find you, either.'

She looked at me again. 'I hear you,' she said in that same weary voice. 'I hear you, but it doesn't make it any better. My father is the kind of man who gets people killed, and he got Peter killed.'

We sat looking at the stream for a few minutes without talking. Then she said, 'I grew up on the union. My mother died when I was three. I didn't have any brothers or sisters, and my dad and I – we were very close. He was a hero, I knew he was in a lot of fights, but he was a hero. I grew up knowing he had to fight because of the bosses, and that if he could lick them, America would be a better place for working men and women everywhere.' She smiled mirthlessly again. 'It sounds like a child's history book, doesn't it? It was child's history. As my dad moved up in the union, we had more money. The University of Chicago – that was something I'd always wanted. Seven thousand dollars a year? No problem. He bought it for me. My own car, you name it. Part of me knew that a working-class hero didn't have that kind of money, but I pushed it aside. "He's entitled," I'd say. And when I met Peter, I thought, why not? The Thayers have more money than my father ever dreamed of, and they never worked for it.' She paused again. 'That was my rationalization, you see. And guys like Smeissen. They're around the house – not much, but some. I just wouldn't believe any of it. You read about some mobster in the paper, and he's been over drinking with your father? No way.' She shook her head.

'Peter came home from the office, you see. He'd been working for Masters as a favor to his dad. He was sick of the whole money thing – that was before we fell in love, even, although I know his father blamed me for it. He wanted to do something really fine with his life – he didn't know what. But just to be nice, he agreed to work at Ajax. I don't think my father knew. I didn't tell him. I didn't talk to him about Peter much – he didn't like me going around with the son of such an important banker. And he is kind of a puritan – he hated my living with Peter like that. So like I said, I didn't talk to him about Peter.

'Anyway, Peter knew who some of the big shots in the union are. You know, when you're in love, you learn that kind of thing about each other. I knew who the chairman of the Fort Dearborn Trust is, and that's not the kind of thing I know as a rule.'

The story was starting to come easily now. I didn't say anything, just made myself part of the landscape that Anita was talking to.

'Well, Peter did rather boring things for Masters. It was a kind of make-work job in the budget department. He worked for the budget director, a guy he liked, and one of the things they asked him to do was check records of claim drafts against claim files – see if they matched, you know. Did Joe Blow get fifteen thousand dollars when his file shows he should only have gotten twelve thousand dollars? That kind of thing. They had a computer program that did it, but they thought there was something wrong with the program, so they wanted Peter to do a manual check.' She laughed, a laugh that was really a sob. 'You know, if Ajax had a good computer system, Peter would still be alive. I think of that sometimes, too, and it makes me want to shoot all their programers. Oh, well. He started with the biggest ones – there were thousands and thousands – they have three hundred thousand Workers' Compensation claims every year, but he was only going to do a spot check. So he started with some of the really big ones – total disability claims that had been going on for a while. At first it was fun, you know, to see what kind of things had happened to people. Then one day he found a claim set up for Carl O'Malley. Total disability, lost his right arm and been crippled by a freak accident with a conveyor belt. That happens, you know – someone gets caught on a belt and pulled into a machine. It's really terrible.'

I nodded agreement.

She looked at me and started talking to me, rather than just in front of me. 'Only it hadn't happened, you see. Carl is one of the senior vice-presidents, my dad's right-hand man – he's been part of my life since before I can remember. I call him Uncle Carl. Peter knew that, so he brought home the address, and it was Carl's address. Carl is as well as you or me – he's never been in an accident, and he's been away from the assembly line for twenty-three years.'

'I see. You didn't know what to think, but you didn't ask your father about it?'

'No, I didn't know what to ask. I couldn't figure it out. I guess I thought Uncle Carl had put in for a fake accident, and we kind of treated it like a joke, Peter and I did. But he got to thinking about it; he was like that, you know, he really thought things through. And he looked up the other guys on the executive board. And they all had indemnity claims. Not all of them for total disability, and not all of them permanent, but all of them good-sized sums. And that was the terrible thing. You see, my dad had one, too. Then I got scared, and I didn't want to say anything to him.'

'Is Joseph Gielczowski on the executive board?' I asked.

'Yes, he's one of the vice-presidents, and president of Local 3051, a very powerful local in Calumet City. Do you know him?'

'That was the name of the claim draft I found.' I could see why they didn't want that innocent little stick of dynamite in my hands. No wonder they'd torn my place apart looking for it. 'So Peter decided to talk to Masters? You didn't know Masters was involved did you?'

'No, and Peter thought he owed it to him, to talk to him first, you know. We weren't sure what we would do next – talk to my dad, we had to. But we thought Masters should know.' Her blue eyes were dark pools of fear in her face. 'What happened was, he told Masters, and Masters told him it sounded really serious, and that he'd like to talk it over with Peter in private, because it might have to go to the State Insurance Commission. So Peter said sure, and Masters said he would come down Monday morning before work.' She looked at me. 'That was strange, wasn't it? We should have known it was strange, we should have known a vice-president doesn't do that, he talks to you in his office. I guess we just assumed it was Peter being a friend of the family.' She looked back at the stream. 'I wanted to be there, but I had a job, you see, I was doing some research for one of the guys in the Political Science Department.'

'Harold Weinstein?' I guessed.

'Yeah. You really have been detecting me, haven't you? Well, I had to be there at eight thirty, and Masters was coming by around nine, so I left Peter to it. I really left him to it, didn't I? Oh, God, why did I think that job was so goddamn important? Why didn't I stay there with him?' Now she was crying, real tears, not the dry heaves. She hid her face in her hands and sobbed. She kept repeating that she'd left Peter alone to be killed, and she should have been the one that died; her father was the one with all the criminal friends, not his. I let her go on for several minutes.

'Listen, Anita,' I said in a clear sharp voice, 'you can blame yourself for this for the rest of your life. But you didn't kill Peter. You didn't abandon him. You didn't set him up. If you had been there, you'd be dead too, and the truth of what happened might never come out.'

'I don't care about the truth,' she sobbed. 'I know it. It doesn't matter whether the rest of the world knows it or not.'

'If the rest of the world doesn't know it, then you're as good as dead,' I said brutally. 'And the next nice young boy or girl who goes through those files and learns what you and Peter learned is dead too. I know this is rotten. I know you've been through hell and more besides, and you've got worse ahead. But the quicker we get going and finish off this business, the quicker you can get that part over with. It will only get more unbearable, the longer you have to anticipate it.'

She sat with her head in her hands, but her sobs died down. After a while she sat up and looked at me again. Her face was tear-streaked and her eyes red, but some of the strain had gone out of it, and she looked younger, less like a death mask of herself. 'You're right. I was brought up not to be afraid of dealing with people. But I don't want to go through this with my dad.'

'I know,' I said gently. 'My father died ten years ago. I was his only child, and we were very close. I know what you must be feeling.'

She was wearing a ridiculous waitress costume, black rayon with a white apron. She blew her nose into the apron.

'Who cashed the drafts?' I asked. 'The people they were made out to?'

She shook her head. 'There's no way of telling. You don't cash drafts, you see: you present them to the bank and the bank verifies you have an account there and tells the insurance company to send a check to that account. You'd have to know what bank the drafts were presented to, and that information wasn't in the files – only carbons of the drafts were there. I don't know if they kept the originals or if they went to the controller's department, or what. And Peter – Peter didn't like to probe too far without Masters knowing.'

'How was Peter's father involved?' I asked.

Her eyes opened at that. 'Peter's father? He wasn't.'

'He had to be: he was killed the other day – Monday.'

Her head started moving back and forth and she looked ill. 'I'm sorry,' I said. 'That was thoughtless, to spring it on you like that.' I put an arm around her shoulders. I didn't say anything more. But I bet Thayer had helped Masters and McGraw cash in on the drafts. Maybe some of the other Knife-grinders were involved, but they wouldn't share a kitty like that with the whole executive board. Besides, that was the kind of secret that everyone would know if that many people knew. Masters and McGraw, maybe a doctor, to put a bonafide report in the files. Thayer sets up an account for them. Doesn't know what it is, doesn't ask any questions. But they give him a present every year, maybe, and when he threatens to push the investigation into his son's death, they stick in the knife: he's been involved, and he can be prosecuted. It looked good to me. I wondered if Paul and Jill would find anything in Thayer's study. Or if Lucy would let either of them into the house. Meanwhile there was Anita to think of.

We sat quietly for a while. Anita was off in her own thoughts, sorting out our conversation. Presently she said, 'It makes it better, telling someone else about it. Not quite so horrible.'

I grunted agreement. She looked down at her absurd outfit. 'Me, dressed up like this! If Peter could see me, he'd –' The sentence trailed off into a sniff. 'I'd like to leave here, stop doing the Jody Hill thing. Do you think I can go back to Chicago?'

I considered this. 'Where were you planning to go?'

She thought for a few minutes. 'That's a problem, I guess. I can't involve Ruth and Mary any more.'

'You're right. Not just because of Ruth and Mary, but also because I was followed to the UWU meeting last night, so chances are Earl will keep an eye on some of the members for a while. And you know you can't go home until this whole business is cleared up.'

'Okay,' she agreed. 'It's just – it's so hard – it was smart in a way, coming up here, but I'm always looking over my shoulder, you know, and I can't talk to anyone about what's going on in my mind. They're always teasing me about boyfriends, like that nice Dr Dan, the one I spilled coffee on this morning, and I can't tell them about Peter, so they think I'm unfriendly.'

'I could probably get you back to Chicago,' I said slowly. 'But you'd have to hole up for a few days – until I get matters straightened out . . . We could publish an account of the insurance scheme, but that would get your dad in trouble without necessarily getting Masters. And I want him implicated in a way he can't slide out of before I let everything else out. Do you understand?' She nodded. 'Okay, in that case, I can see that you get put up in a Chicago hotel. I think I can fix it so that no one will know you are there. You wouldn't be able to go out. But someone trustworthy would stop by every now and then to talk to you so you won't go completely stir crazy. That sound all right?'

She made a face. 'I guess I don't have any choice, do I? At

least I'd be back in Chicago, closer to the things I know . . . Thanks,' she added belatedly. 'I didn't mean to sound so grudging – I really appreciate everything you're doing for me.'

'Don't worry about your party manners right now; I'm not doing it for the thanks, anyway.'

We walked slowly back to the Datsun together. Little insects hummed and jumped in the grass and birds kept up an unending medley. A woman with two young children had come into the park. The children were rooting industriously in the dirt. The woman was reading a book, looking up at them every few minutes. They had a picnic basket propped under a tree. As we walked by, the woman called, 'Matt! Eve! How about a snack?' The children came running up. I felt a small stirring of envy. On a beautiful summer day it might be nice to be having a picnic with my children instead of hiding a fugitive from the police and the mob.

'Is there anything you want to collect in Hartford?' I asked.

She shook her head. 'I should stop at Ronna's and tell them I'm leaving.'

I parked in front of the restaurant and she went in while I used a phone on the corner to call the *Herald-Star*. It was almost ten and Ryerson was at his desk.

'Murray, I've got the story of a lifetime for you if you can keep a key witness on ice for a few days.'

'Where are you?' he asked. 'You sound like you're calling from the North Pole. Who's the witness? The McGraw girl?'

'Murray, your mind works like a steel trap. I want a promise and I need some help.'

'I've already helped you,' he protested. 'Lots. First by giving you those photos, and then by not running a story that you were dead so I could collect your document from your lawyer.'

'Murray, if there was another soul on earth I could turn to right now, I would. But you are absolutely incorruptible if faced with the promise of a good story.'

'All right,' he agreed. 'I'll do what I can for you.'

'Good. I'm in Hartford, Wisconsin, with Anita McGraw. I

want to get her back to Chicago and keep her under close wraps until this case blows over. That means no one must have a whiff of where she is, because if they do, you'll be covering her obituary. I can't bring her down myself because I'm a hot property now. What I want to do is take her to Milwaukee and put her on a train and have you meet her at Union Station. When you do, get her into a hotel. Some place far enough from the Loop that some smart bellhop on Smeissen's payroll won't put two and two together when she comes in. Can do?'

'Jesus, Vic, you don't do anything in a small way, do you? Sure. What's the story? Why is she in danger? Smeissen knock off her boyfriend?'

'Murray, I'm telling you, you put any of this in print before the whole story is finished, and they're going to be fishing *your* body out of the Chicago River: I guarantee I'll put it there.'

'You have my word of honor as a gent who is waiting to scoop the City of Chicago. What time is the train coming in?'

'I don't know. I'll call you again from Milwaukee.'

When I hung up, Anita had come back out and was waiting by the car. 'They weren't real happy about me quitting,' she said.

I laughed. 'Well, worry about that on the way down. It'll keep your mind off your troubles.'

16
PRICE OF A CLAIM

We had to wait in Milwaukee until 1.30 for a Chicago train. I left Anita at the station and went to buy her some jeans and a shirt. When she had washed up in the station rest room and changed, she looked younger and healthier. As soon as she got that terrible black dye out of her hair, she'd be in good shape. She thought her life was ruined, and it certainly didn't look great at the moment. But she was only twenty; she'd recover.

Murray agreed to meet the train and get her to a hotel. He'd decided on the Ritz. 'If she's going to be holed up for a few days, it might as well be some place where she'll be comfortable,' he explained. 'The *Star* will share the bill with you.'

'Thanks, Murray,' I said dryly. He was to call my answering service and leave a message: yes or no – no name. 'No,' meant something had gone wrong with pickup or delivery and I would get back to him. I wasn't going to go near the hotel. He'd stop by a couple of times a day with food and chat – we didn't want Anita calling room service.

As soon as the train pulled out I headed back to the tollway and Chicago. I had almost all the threads in my hands now. The problem was, I couldn't prove that Masters had killed Peter Thayer. Caused him to be killed. Of course, Anita's story confirmed it: Masters had had an appointment with Peter. But there was no proof, nothing that would make Bobby swear out a warrant and bring handcuffs to a senior vice-president of an influential Chicago corporation. Somehow I had to stir around in the nest enough to make the king hornet come out and get me.

As I left the toll road for the Edens Expressway, I made a detour to Winnetka to see if Jill had gone home, and if she had turned up anything among her father's papers. I stopped at a service station on Willow Road and called the Thayer house.

Jack answered the phone. Yes, Jill had come home, but she wasn't talking to reporters. 'I'm not a reporter,' I said. 'This is V. I. Warshawski.'

'She certainly isn't talking to you. You've caused Mother Thayer enough pain already.'

'Thorndale, you are the stupidest SOB I have ever met. If you don't put Jill on the phone, I will be at the house in five minutes. I will make a lot of noise, and I will go and bother all the neighbors until I find one who will put a phone call through to Jill for me.'

He banged the receiver down hard, on a tabletop I guessed, since the connection still held. A few minutes later Jill's clear, high voice came onto the line. 'What did you say to Jack?' she giggled. 'I've never seen him so angry.'

'Oh, I just threatened to get all your neighbors involved in what's going on,' I answered. 'Not that they aren't anyway – the police have probably been visiting all of them, asking questions . . . You get out to Winnetka all right?'

'Oh, yes. It was very exciting. Paul got a police escort for us to the clinic. Lotty didn't want to do it, but he insisted. Then he went and got your car and we got a blast-off with sirens from the clinic. Sergeant McGonnigal was really, really super.'

'Sounds good. How are things on the home front?'

'Oh, they're okay. Mother has decided to forgive me, but Jack is acting like the stupid phony he is. He keeps telling me I've made Mother very, very unhappy. I asked Paul to stay to lunch, and Jack kept treating him as if he were the garbage collector or something. I got really mad, but Paul told me he was used to it. I hate Jack,' she concluded.

I laughed at this outburst. 'Good girl! Paul's a neat guy – worth standing up for. Did you have a chance to look through your father's papers?'

'Oh, yes. Of course, Lucy had a fit. But I just pretended I was Lotty and didn't pay any attention to her. I didn't really know what I was looking for,' she said, 'but I found some kind of document that had both Mr Masters's and Mr McGraw's names on it.'

I suddenly felt completely at peace, as though I'd been through a major crisis and come out whole on the other side. I found myself grinning into the telephone. 'Did you now,' I said. 'What was it?'

'I don't know,' Jill said doubtfully. 'Do you want me to get it and read it to you?'

'That's probably the best thing,' I agreed. She put the phone down. I started singing under my breath. What will you be, O document? What kind of laundry ticket?

'It's a Xerox,' Jill announced, back at the phone. 'My dad wrote the date in ink at the top – March eighteenth, 1974. Then it says: "Agreement of Trust. The Undersigned, Yardley Leland Masters and Andrew Solomon McGraw, are herein granted fiduciary responsibility for any and all monies submitted to this account under their authority for the following."' She stumbled over *fiduciary*. 'Then it gives a list of names – Andrew McGraw, Carl O'Malley, Joseph Giel – I can't pronounce it. There are about – let's see –' I could hear her counting under her breath; '– twenty-three names. Then it adds, "and any other names as shall be added at their discretion under my countersignature". Then Daddy's name, and a place for him to sign it. Is that what you were looking for?'

'That's what I was looking for, Jill.' My voice was as calm and steady as if I were announcing that the Cubs had won the World Series.

'What does it mean?' she asked. She was sobering up from her glee at triumphing over Jack and Lucy. 'Does it mean Daddy killed Peter?'

'No, Jill, it does not. Your father did not kill your brother. What it means is that your father knew about a dirty scheme that your brother found out about. Your brother was killed because he found out about it.'

'I see.' She was quiet for a few minutes. 'Do you know who killed him?' she asked presently.

'I think so. You hang loose, Jill. Stay close to the house and don't go out with anyone but Paul. I'll come up to see you tomorrow or the next day – everything should be over by then.' I started to hang up, then thought I should warn her to hide the paper. 'Oh, Jill,' I said, but she had hung up. Oh, well, I thought. If anyone suspected it was there, they would have been around looking by now.

What that document meant was that Masters could set up fake claims for anyone; then he and McGraw could cash the drafts, or whatever one did with them. Put them into the trust account, which Thayer ostensibly oversaw. In fact, I wondered why they even bothered to use real names. Why not just made-up people – easier to disguise. If they'd done that, Peter Thayer and his father would still be alive. Maybe they'd gotten to that later. I'd have to see a complete list of the names on the account and check them against the Knifegrinders' roster.

It was almost four. Anita should have made it to Chicago by now. I called my answering service, but no one had rung up with the message of yes or no. I got back in the car and returned to the Edens. Inbound traffic moved at a crawl. Repairs on two of the lanes turned rush hour into a nightmare. I oozed slowly onto the Kennedy, irate and impatient, although I didn't have an agenda. Just an impatience. I didn't know what to do next. I could certainly expose the fake claim drafts. But as I'd pointed out to Anita, Masters would certainly disclaim all knowledge: the Knifegrinders might well have set them up, with complete doctors' reports. Did claim handlers actually physically look at accident victims? I wondered. I'd better talk to Ralph, explain what I'd learned today, and see if there was some legal angle that would link Masters irretrievably with the fraud. Even that wasn't good enough though, I had to link him with the killing. And I couldn't think of a way.

It was 5.30 by the time I exited at Addison, and then I had to fight my way across town. I finally swung off onto a small side street, full of potholes, but not much traffic. I was about to turn up Sheffield to Lotty's, when I thought that might mean walking open-armed into a setup. I found the all-night restaurant on the corner of Addison and gave her a call.

'My dear Vic,' she greeted me. 'Can you believe, those Gestapo actually had the effrontery to break into this apartment? Whether they were looking for you, Jill or the McGraw girl, I couldn't say, but they have been here.'

'Oh, my God, Lotty,' I said, my stomach sinking. 'I am so sorry. How bad is the damage?'

'Oh, it's nothing – just the locks, and Paul is here now replacing them; it's just the wantonness of it that makes me so angry.'

'I know,' I said remorsefully. 'I'll certainly repair whatever damage has been done. I'll come by to get my stuff right now, and be gone.'

I hung up and decided to take my chances on a trap. It would be just as well if Smeissen knew I had gone back home – I didn't want Lotty put in any more danger, or to suffer any more invasions. I raced up the street to her building, and only gave cursory attention to potential marksmen in the street. I didn't see anyone I knew, and no one opened fire as I dashed up the stairs.

Paul was in the doorway, screwing a dead-bolt lock into the door. His square face looked very mean. 'This is pretty bad, Vic – you think Jill is in any danger?'

'Not too likely,' I said.

'Well, I think I should go up there and see.'

I grinned. 'Sounds like a good idea to me. Be careful though, you hear?'

'Don't worry.' His breathtaking smile came. 'But I'm not sure whether I'm protecting her from that brother-in-law or from a gunman.'

'Well, do both.' I went on into the apartment. Lotty was at the back, trying to reattach a screen to the back door. For a woman with such skillful medical fingers she was remarkably inept. I took the hammer from her and quickly finished the job. Her thin face was set and hard, her mouth in a fine line.

'I am glad you gave the warning to Paul and had that Sergeant Mc-Whatever take us to the clinic. At the time, I was annoyed, with you and with Paul, but clearly it saved the child's life.' Her Viennese accent was very heavy in her anger. I thought she was exaggerating about the danger to Jill but didn't want to argue the point. I went through the apartment with her but had to agree that there really had been no damage. Not even the medical samples, some of which had great street value, had been removed.

During the inspection Lotty kept up a stream of invective which became heavily laden with German, a language I don't speak. I gave up trying to calm her down and merely nodded and grunted agreement. Paul finally brought it to a halt by coming in to say that the front door was now secure, and did she want him to do anything else?

'No, my dear, thank you. Go out and visit Jill, and take very good care of her. We don't want her harmed.'

Paul agreed fervently. He gave me my car keys and told me the Chevy was over on Seminary off Irving Park Road. I'd thought about leaving him the car, but felt I'd better hang on to it: I didn't know what the evening would bring in the way of action.

I called Larry to see if my apartment was ready for occupation. It was; he'd left the keys to the new locks with the first-floor tenants; they'd seemed a bit friendlier than Mrs Alvarez on the second floor.

'Well, everything is all set, Lotty: I can go home. Sorry I didn't yesterday, and sleep with the place nailed shut – it would have spared you this invasion.'

Her mouth twisted in her sardonic smile. 'Ah, forget it, Vic, my anger storm has passed, blown over. Now I am feeling a little melancholy at being alone – I shall miss those two children.

They are very sweet together . . . I forgot to ask: Did you find Miss McGraw?'

'I forgot to tell you – I did. And I should check to see whether she is safely ensconced in her new hiding place.' I put in a call to my answering service; yes, that long-suffering outfit reported, someone had called up and left a message: 'yes'. They had not left a name, but said I would know what it meant. I told them they could switch my office calls to my own home number. In the activity of the last few days I'd forgotten to get a Kelly Girl to tidy my office, but at least it was boarded shut. I'd wait until tomorrow to go down there.

I tried Ralph, but there was no answer. He wasn't at the office, either. Out for dinner? Was I jealous? 'Well, Lotty, this is it. Thanks for letting me disrupt your life for a few days. You've made a major impression on Jill – she told me the maid up there was trying to hassle her but she "pretended she was Lotty" and didn't pay her any mind.'

'I'm not sure that's such a good idea – to model herself on me, that is. A very attractive girl – amazing that she's avoided all that suburban insularity.' She sat on the daybed to watch me pack. 'What now? Can you expose the killer?'

'I've got to find a lever,' I said. 'I know who did it – not who fired the actual shot, that's probably a guy named Tony Bronsky, but it could have been any one of several of Smeissen's crew. But who desired that shot to be fired – that I know but can't prove. I know what the crime was, though, and I know how it was worked.' I zipped the canvas bag shut. 'What I need is a lever, or maybe a wedge.' I was talking to myself more than to Lotty. 'A wedge to pry this guy apart a bit. If I can find out that the fiddle couldn't be worked without his involvement, then maybe I can force him into the open.'

I was standing with one foot on the bed, absentmindedly tapping the suitcase with my fingers while I thought. Lotty said, 'If I were a sculptor, I would make a statue of you – Nemesis come to life. You will think of a way – I see it in your face.' She stood on tiptoe and gave me a kiss. 'I'll walk you to the street –

if anyone shoots at you, then I can patch you up quickly, before too much blood is lost.'

I laughed. 'Lotty, you're wonderful. By all means, cover my back for me.'

She walked me to the corner of Seminary, but the street was clear. 'That's because of that Sergeant Mc-Something,' she said. 'I think he's been driving around here from time to time. Still, Vic, be careful: you have no mother, but you are a daughter of my spirit. I should not like anything to happen to you.'

'Lotty, that's melodrama,' I protested. 'Don't start getting old, for God's sake.' She shrugged her thin shoulders in a way wholly European and gave me a sardonic smile, but her eyes were serious as I walked up the street to my car.

17

SHOOT-OUT ON ELM STREET

Larry and his friend the carpenter had done a beautiful job on my apartment. The door was a masterpiece, with carved flowers on the panels. The carpenter had installed two dead bolts, and the action on them was clean and quiet. Inside, the place shone as it had not for months. Not a trace of the weekend ravage remained. Although Larry had sent the shredded couch away, he had moved chairs and an occasional table around to fill the empty space. He had left a bill in the middle of the kitchen table. Two people for two days at $8.00 an hour, $256.00. The door, locks and installation, $315. New supplies of flour, sugar, beans and spices; new pillows for the bed: $97.00. It seemed like a pretty reasonable bill to me. I wondered who was going to pay me, though. Maybe Jill could borrow from her mother until her trust fund matured.

I went to look through my jewelry box. By some miracle the vandals had not taken my mother's few valuable pieces but I thought I'd better lock them in a bank vault and not leave them around for the next invader. Larry seemed to have thrown out the shards of the broken Venetian glass. I should have told him to save them, but that couldn't be helped; it was beyond restoration, anyway. The other seven held pride of place in the built-in china cupboard, but I couldn't look at them without a thud in my stomach.

I tried Ralph again. This time he answered on the fourth ring.

'What's up, Miss Marple?' he asked. 'I thought you were out after Professor Moriarty until tomorrow.'

'I found him earlier than I expected. In fact, I found out the secret that Peter Thayer died to protect. Only he didn't want to protect it. You know that claim draft I gave you? Did you ever find the file?'

'No. I told you I put it on the missing-file search, but it hasn't turned up.'

'Well, it may never. Do you know who Joseph Gielczowski is?'

'What is this? Twenty questions? I've got someone coming over in twenty minutes, Vic.'

'Joseph Gielczowski is a senior vice-president of the Knife-grinders' union. He has not been on an assembly line for twenty-three years. If you went to visit him in his home, you would find he was as healthy as you are. Or you could go see him at Knifegrinders' headquarters where he is able to work and draw a salary without needing any indemnity payments.'

There was a pause. 'Are you trying to tell me that that guy is fraudulently drawing Workers' Compensation payments?'

'No,' I said.

'Goddamnit, Vic, if he's healthy and is getting indemnity drafts, then he's drawing them fraudulently.'

'No,' I reiterated. 'Sure, they're fraudulent, but he's not drawing them.'

'Well, who is, then?'

'Your boss.'

Ralph exploded into the phone. 'You've got this damned bee in your bonnet about Masters, Vic, and I'm sick of it! He's one of the most respected members of a highly respected company in a very respectable industry. To suggest that he's involved in something like that –'

'I'm not suggesting it, I know it,' I said coldly. 'I know that he and Andrew McGraw, head of the Knifegrinders' union, set

215

up a fund with themselves as joint trustees, enabling them to cash drafts, or whatever it is you do to get payments on drafts, drawn to Gielczowski and at least twenty-two other healthy people.'

'How can you possibly know something like that?' Ralph said, furious.

'Because, I just listened to someone read a copy of the agreement to me over the phone. I've also found someone who has seen Masters with McGraw on numerous occasions up near Knifegrinder headquarters. And I know that Masters had an appointment with Peter Thayer – at his apartment – at nine on the morning he was killed.'

'I don't believe it. I have worked for Yardley for three years, and been in his organization for ten years before that, and I'm sure there's a different explanation for everything you've found out – if you've found it out. You haven't seen this trust agreement. And Yardley may have eaten with McGraw, or drunk with him or something – maybe he was checking out some coverage or claims, or something. We do do that from time to time.'

I felt like screaming with frustration. 'Just let me know ten minutes before you go to Masters to check the story with him, will you? So I can get there in time to save your ass.'

'If you think I'm going to jeopardize my career by telling my boss that I've been listening to that kind of rumor about him, you're nuts,' Ralph roared. 'As a matter of fact, he's coming over here in a few minutes, and I promise you, without any difficulty, that I am not such an ass as to tell him about it. Of course, if that Gielczowski claim is fraudulent, that explains a lot. I'll tell him that.'

My hair seemed to stand straight up on my head. 'What? Ralph, you are so goddamn naïve it's unbelievable. Why the hell is he coming over?'

'You really don't have any right to ask me that,' he snapped, 'but I'll tell you anyway, since you started the whole uproar by finding that draft. Claims that big are handled out of the home

216

office, not by a field adjustor. I went around to the guys today and asked who'd handled the file. No one remembered it. If anyone had been handling such a big file for so many years, there's no way they would forget it. This puzzled me, so when I called Yardley this afternoon – he hasn't been in the office this week – I call him at home once a day – I mentioned it to him.'

'Oh, Christ! That is the absolute end. So he told you it sounded like a serious problem, didn't he? And that since he had to come down to the city tonight for some other reason, he'd just drop by and talk it over with you? Is that right?' I said savagely.

'Why, yes, it is,' he shouted. 'Now go find someone's missing poodle and stop screwing around in the Claim Department.'

'Ralph, I'm coming over. Tell Yardley *that* when he walks in the door, as soon as he walks in, and maybe it will save your goddamn ass for a few minutes.' I slammed down the phone without waiting for his answer.

I looked at my watch: 7.12. Masters was due there in twenty minutes. Roughly. Say he got there around 7.30, maybe a few minutes earlier. I put my driver's license, my gun permit and my PI license in my hip pocket with some money – I didn't want a purse in my way at this point. Checked the gun. Put extra rounds in my jacket pocket. Wasted forty-five seconds changing to running shoes. Locked the new, oiled dead bolts behind me and sprinted down the stairs three at a time. Ran the half-block to my car in fifteen seconds. Put it in gear and headed for Lake Shore Drive.

Why was every goddamn person in Chicago out tonight, and why were so many of them on Belmont Avenue? I wondered savagely. And why were the lights timed so that every time you hit a corner they turned and some asshole grandfather wouldn't clear the intersection in front of you on the yellow? I pounded the steering wheel in impatience, but it didn't make the traffic flow faster. No point in sitting on the horn, either. I took some deep diaphragm breaths to steady myself. Ralph, you stupid jerk. Making a present of your life to a man who's had two people killed in the last two weeks. Because Masters wears the old-boy-network tie and you're on his team he couldn't possibly do something criminal. Naturally not. I swooped around a bus and got a clear run to Sheridan Road and the mouth of the Drive. It was 7.24. I prayed to the patron saint who protects speeders from speed traps and floored the Monza. At 7.26 I slid off the Drive onto La Salle Street, and down the inner parallel road to Elm Street. At 7.29 I left the car at a fire plug next to Ralph's building and sprinted inside.

The building didn't have a doorman. I pushed twenty buttons in quick succession. Several people squawked 'Who is it?' through the intercom, but someone buzzed me in. No matter how many break-ins are executed this way, there is always some stupid idiot who will buzz you into an apartment building without knowing who you are. The elevator took a century or two to arrive. Once it came, though, it carried me quickly to the seventeenth floor. I ran down the hall to Ralph's apartment and pounded on the door, my Smith & Wesson in my hand.

I flattened myself against the wall as the door opened, then dove into the apartment, gun out. Ralph was staring at me in amazement. 'What the hell do you think you're doing?' he said. No one else was in the room.

'Good question,' I said, standing up.

The bell rang and Ralph went to push the buzzer. 'I wouldn't mind if you left,' he remarked. I didn't move. 'At least put that goddamn gun away.' I put it in my jacket pocket but kept my hand on it.

'Do me one favor,' I said. 'When you open the door, stand behind it, don't frame yourself in the doorway.'

'You are the craziest goddamn —'

'If you call me a crazy broad I will shoot you in the back. Block your damned body with the door when you open it.'

Ralph glared at me. When the knocking came a few minutes later, he went straight to the door and deliberately opened it so that it would frame his body squarely. I moved to the side of the room parallel with the door and braced myself. No shots sounded.

'Hello, Yardley, what's all this?' Ralph was saying.

'This is my young neighbor, Jill Thayer, and these are some associates who've come along with me.'

I was stunned and moved toward the door to look. 'Jill?' I said.

'Are you here, Vic?' the clear little voice quavered a bit. 'I'm sorry. Paul called to say he was coming up on the train and I started to walk into town to meet him at the station. And Mr – Mr Masters passed me in his car and stopped to give me a lift – and – and I asked him about that paper and he made me come along with him. I'm sorry, Vic, I know I shouldn't have said anything.'

'That's okay, honey –' I started to say, but Masters interrupted with. 'Ah, you're here, are you? We thought we'd come visit you and that Viennese doctor Jill admires so much a little later, but you've saved us a trip.' He looked at my gun, which I'd pulled out, and smiled offensively. 'I would put that away if I were you. Tony here is pretty trigger-happy and I know you'd hate to watch anything happen to Jill.'

Tony Bronsky had come into the room behind Masters. With him was Earl. Ralph was shaking his head, like a man trying to wake up from a dream. I put the gun back into my pocket.

'Don't blame the girl,' Masters said to me. 'But you really shouldn't have gotten her involved, you know. As soon as Margaret Thayer told me she had come back home, I tried finding a way of talking to her without anyone in the house knowing about it. Sheer luck, really, that she walked down Sheridan just at that time. But we got her to explain quite a bit, didn't we, Jill?'

I could see now that there was an ugly bruise on the side of her face. 'Cute, Masters,' I said. 'You're at your best when you're beating up little girls. I'd like to see you with a grandmother.' He was right: I'd been stupid to bring her down to Lotty's and get her involved in things that Masters and Smeissen didn't want anyone to know about. I'd save my self-reproach for later, though – I didn't have time for it now.

'Want me to put her away?' Tony breathed, his eyes glistening with happiness, his Z-shaped scar vivid as a wound.

'Not yet, Tony,' Masters said. 'We want to find out how much she knows and who she's told it to . . . You, too, Ralph. It's really a shame you got this Polish gal over here – we weren't going to shoot you unless it was absolutely necessary, but now I'm afraid we'll have to.' He turned to Smeissen. 'Earl, you've had more experience at this kind of thing than I have. What's the best way to set them up?'

'Get the Warchoski broad's gun away from her,' Earl said in his squeaky voice. 'Then have her and the guy sit together on the couch so that Tony can cover them both.'

'You heard him,' Masters said. He started toward me.

'No,' Earl squeaked. 'Don't go close to her. Make her drop it. Tony, cover the kid.'

Tony pointed his Browning at Jill. I dropped the S & W on the floor. Earl came and kicked it into the corner. Jill's little face was white and pinched.

'Over to the couch,' Masters said. Tony continued to cover Jill. I went and sat down. The couch was firm, one good thing – one didn't sink into it. I kept my weight distributed forward onto my legs and feet. 'Move,' Earl squeaked at Ralph. Ralph was looking dazed. Little drops of sweat covered his face. He stumbled a bit on the thick carpet as he came to sit next to me.

'You know, Masters, this cesspool you've built is stinking so high you're going to have to kill everyone in Chicago to cover it up,' I said.

'You think so, do you? Who knows about it besides you?' He was still smiling unpleasantly. My hand itched to break his lower jaw.

'Oh, the *Star* has a pretty good idea. My attorney. A few others. Even little Earl over here isn't going to be able to buy off the cops if you shoot down an entire newspaper crew.'

'Is this true, Yardley?' Ralph asked. His voice came out in a hoarse whisper and he cleared his throat. 'I don't believe it. I wouldn't believe Vic when she tried to tell me. You didn't shoot Peter, did you?'

Masters gave a superior little laugh. 'Of course not. Tony here shot him. I had to go along, though, just as I did tonight – to get Tony into the building. And Earl came along as an accessory. Earl doesn't usually get involved, do you, Earl? But we don't want any blackmail after this.'

'That's good, Masters,' I praised him. 'The reason Earl's ass is so fat is because he's been protecting it all these years.'

Earl turned red. 'You two-cent bitch, just for that, I'm going to let Tony work you over again before he shoots you!' he squeaked.

'Attaboy, Earl.' I looked at Masters. 'Earl never beats anyone up himself,' I explained. 'I used to think it was because he didn't have any balls, but last week I found out that wasn't true, right, Earl?'

Earl started for me, as I hoped he would, but Masters held him back. 'Calm down, Earl, she's just trying to ride you. You can do whatever you want to her – after I find out how much she knows and where Anita McGraw is.'

'I don't know, Yardley,' I said brightly.

'Don't give me that,' he said, leaning forward to hit me on the mouth. 'You disappeared early this morning. That heap of shit Smeissen had watching the back alley went to sleep and you got away. But we questioned some of the girls you talked to at the UWU meeting last night and Tony here – persuaded – one of them to tell him where Anita had gone. But when we got to Hartford, Wisconsin, at noon, she'd disappeared. And the woman at the restaurant described you pretty well. An older sister, she thought, who'd come to take Jody Hill away with her. Now where is she?'

I uttered a silent prayer of thanks for the urge that had prompted Anita to want to leave Hartford. 'There's got to be more to this racket than just those twenty-three names on the original deed of trust Jill found,' I said. 'Even at two hundred fifty dollars a week apiece, that isn't paying for the services of a guy like Smeissen. Round-the-clock surveillance on me? That must have cost you a bundle, Masters.'

'Tony,' Masters said conversationally, 'hit the girl. Hard.'

Jill gave a gasp, a scream held back. Good girl. Lots of guts. 'You kill the girl, Masters, you got nothing to stop me,' I said. 'You're in a little ol' jam. The minute Tony takes that gun off her, she's going to roll on the floor and get behind that big chair, and I'm going to jump Tony and break his neck. And if he kills her, the same thing will happen. So sure, I don't want to watch you rough up Jill, but you're using up your weapon doing it.'

'Go ahead and kill Warchoski,' Earl squeaked. 'You're going to sooner or later anyway.'

Masters shook his head. 'Not until we know where the McGraw girl is.'

'Tell you what, Yardley,' I offered. 'I'll trade you Jill for Anita. You send the kid outside, let her go home, and I'll tell you where Anita is.'

Masters actually wasted a minute thinking about it. 'You do think I'm dumb, don't you? If I let her go, all she'll do is call the police.'

'Of course I think you're dumb. As Dick Tracy once put it so well, all crooks are dumb. How many fake claimants do you have pulling indemnity payments into that dummy account?'

He laughed, his fake-hearty laugh again. 'Oh, close to three hundred now, set up in different parts of the country. That deed of trust is quite outdated, and I see John never bothered to go back and check the original to see how it was growing.'

'What was his cut for overseeing the account?'

'I really didn't come here to answer a smart-mouthed broad's questions,' Yardley said, still good-natured, still in control. 'I want to know how much you know.'

'Oh, I know quite a bit,' I said. 'I know that you called McGraw and got Earl's name from him when Peter Thayer came to you with those incriminating files. I know you didn't tell McGraw who you were having put away, and when he found out, he panicked. You've got him in a cleft stick, haven't you: he knows you're gunning for his kid, but he can't turn state's evidence, or he hasn't got the guts to, anyway, because then he'll be an accessory before the fact, sending a professional killer to you. Let's see. I also know that you talked Thayer out of continuing the investigation into his son's death by telling him he'd been a party to the crime for which Peter died. And that if he pushed the investigation, the Thayer name would be mud and he'd lose his position at the bank. And I know he wrestled with that grim news for two days, then decided he couldn't live with himself and called you and told you he wouldn't be a party to his son's death. So you got cute little Tony here to gun him down the next morning before he could get to the state's attorney.' I turned to Tony. 'You aren't as good as you used to be, Tony, my boy: someone saw you waiting outside the Thayer place. That witness is on ice now – you didn't get him when you had the opportunity.'

Earl's face turned red again. 'You had a witness and you didn't see him?' he screeched, as much of a shout as his high voice could manage. 'Goddamnit, what do I pay you for? I want amateurs, I pull one off the street. And what about Freddie? He's paid to watch – he doesn't see anyone? Goddamn dumb bastards, all of you!' He was pumping his fat little arms up and down in his rage. I glanced at Ralph; his face was gray. He was in shock. I couldn't do anything about that now. Jill gave me a little smile. She'd caught the message. As soon as Tony lifted the gun, she'd roll behind the chair.

'See,' I said disgustedly, 'you guys have made so many mistakes that piling up three more corpses isn't going to help you one bit. I told you before, Earl: Bobby Mallory's no dummy. You can't knock off four people in his territory and get away with it forever.'

Earl smirked. 'They never hung one on me yet, Warchoski, you know that.'

'It's Warshawski, you goddamn kraut. You know why Polish jokes are so short?' I asked Masters. 'So the Germans can remember them.'

'This is enough. Warchoski or whatever your name is,'

Masters said. He used a stern voice, the kind that got him heard with his junior staff. 'You tell me where the McGraw girl is. You're right – Jill is as good as dead. I hate to do it, I've known that girl since she was born, but I just can't take the risk. But you've got a choice. I can have Tony kill her, one clean shot and it's done, or I can have him rape her while you watch, and then kill her. You tell me where the McGraw girl is, and you'll save her a lot of grief.'

Jill was very white; her gray eyes looked huge and black in her face. 'Oh, jeez, Yardley,' I said. 'You big he-men really impress the shit out of me. Are you telling me Tony's going to rape that girl on your command? Why do you think the boy carries a gun? He can't get it up, never could, so he has a big old penis he carries around in his hand.'

I braced my hands on the couch at my sides as I spoke. Tony turned crimson and gave a primitive shriek in the back of his throat. He turned to look at me.

'Now!' I yelled, and jumped. Jill dived behind the armchair. Tony's bullet went wide and I reached him in one spring and chopped his gun arm hard enough to break the bone. He screamed in pain and dropped the Browning. As I spun away, Masters lunged over for it. I made a diving slide, but he got there first, sitting down hard. He brandished the Browning at me while he got up and I backed away a few paces.

The report from Tony's shot had brought Ralph back to life. Out of the corner of my eye I saw him move over on the couch toward the phone and lift the receiver. Masters saw it, too, and turned and shot him. In the second he turned, I made a rolling fall into the corner of the room and got the Smith & Wesson. As Masters turned to fire at me, I shot him in the knee. He wasn't used to pain: he fell with a great cry of surprised agony and dropped the gun. Earl, who'd been dancing in the background, pretending he was part of the fight, moved forward to get it. I shot at his hand. I was out of practice and missed, but he jumped back anyway.

I pointed the Smith & Wesson at Tony. 'Onto the couch.

Move.' Tears were running down his cheeks. His right arm hung in a funny way: I'd broken the ulna. 'You guys are worse than trash and I'd love to shoot the three of you dead. Save the state a lot of money. If any of you goes for that gun, I'll kill you. Earl, get your fat little body over on the couch next to Tony.' He looked like a two-year-old whose mother has unexpectedly spanked him; his whole face was squashed up as if he, too, were about to burst into tears. But he moved over next to Tony. I picked up the Browning continuing to cover the two on the couch. Masters was bleeding into the carpet. He wasn't in any shape to move. 'The police are going to love this gun,' I said. 'I bet it fired the bullet that shot Peter Thayer, didn't it, Tony?'

I called to Jill. 'You still alive back there, honey?'

'Yes, Vic,' she said in a little voice.

'Good. You come on out now and call the number I'm going to give you. We're going to call the police and have them collect this garbage. Then maybe you'd better call Lotty, get her over here to look at Ralph.' I hoped there was something left of him for Lotty to work on. He wasn't moving, but I couldn't go to him – he'd fallen on the far side of the room, and the couch and phone table would block me if I went over to where he lay.

Jill came out from behind the big armchair where she'd been crouching. The little oval face was still very white, and she was shaking a bit. 'Walk behind me, honey,' I told her. 'And take a couple of deep breaths. In a few minutes you can relax and let it all out, but right now you've got to keep on going.'

She turned her head away from the floor where Masters lay bleeding and walked over to the phone. I gave her Mallory's office number and told her to ask for him. He'd gone home for the day, she reported. I gave her the home number. 'Is Lieutenant Mallory there, please?' she asked in her clear, polite voice. When he came on the line, I told her to bring the phone over to me, but not to get in front of me at all.

'Bobby? Vic. I'm at two-oh-three East Elm with Earl Smeissen,

Tony Bronsky and a guy from Ajax named Yardley Masters. Masters has a shattered knee, and Bronsky a broken ulna. I also have the gun that was used to shoot Peter Thayer.'

Mallory made an explosive noise into the phone 'Is this some kind of joke, Vicki?'

'Bobby. I'm a cop's daughter. I never make that kind of joke. Two-oh-three East Elm. Apartment seventeen-oh-eight. I'll try not to kill the three of them before you get here.'

18

BLOOD IS THICKER THAN GOLD

It was ten, and the short black nurse said, 'You shouldn't be here at all, but he won't go to sleep until you stop by.' I followed her into the room where Ralph lay, his face very white, but his gray eyes alive. Lotty had made a good job of bandaging him up and the surgeon at Passavant had only changed the dressing without disturbing her work. As Lotty said, she'd done a lot of bullet wounds.

Paul had come with Lotty to Ralph's apartment, frantic. He'd gotten to Winnetka and forced his way past Lucy about twenty minutes after Masters had picked up Jill. He went straight from there to Lotty's. The two of them had called me, called the police to report Jill missing, but fortunately had stayed at Lotty's close to the phone.

Jill ran sobbing into Paul's arms when they arrived and Lotty had given a characteristic shake of the head. 'Good idea. Get her out of here, get her some brandy,' then turned her attention to Ralph, who lay unconscious and bleeding in the corner. The bullet had gone through his right shoulder, tearing up a lot of bone and muscle, but coming out clean on the other side.

Now I looked down at him on the hospital bed. He took hold of my right hand with his left and squeezed it weakly; he was pretty drugged. I sat on the bed.

'Get off the bed,' the little nurse said.

I was exhausted. I wanted to tell her to go to hell, but I didn't feel like fighting the hospital on top of everything else. I stood up.

'I'm sorry,' Ralph said, his words slightly slurred.

'Don't worry about it. As it turned out, that was probably the best thing that could have happened. I couldn't figure out how to get Masters to show his hand.'

'No, but I should have listened to you. I couldn't believe you knew what you were talking about. I guess deep down I didn't take your detecting seriously. I thought it was a hobby, like Dorothy's painting.'

I didn't say anything.

'Yardley shot me. I worked for him for three years and didn't see that about him. You met him once and knew he was that kind of guy.' His words were slurred but his eyes were hurt and angry.

'Don't keep hitting yourself with that,' I said gently. 'I know what it means to be a team player. You don't expect your teammates, your quarterback, to do that kind of thing. I came at it from the outside, so I was able to see things differently.'

He was quiet again, but the hold on my fingers tightened, so I knew he wasn't sleeping. Presently he said, 'I've been falling in love with you, Vic, but you don't need me.' His mouth twisted and he turned his head to one side to hide some tears.

My throat was tight and I couldn't get any words out. 'That's not true,' I tried to say, but I didn't know if it was or not. I swallowed and cleared my throat. 'I wasn't just using you to get Masters.' My words came out in a harsh squawk. 'I liked you, Ralph.'

He shook his head slightly; the movement made him wince. 'It's not the same thing. It just wouldn't work out.'

I squeezed his hand painfully. 'No. It would never work out.' I wished I didn't feel so much like crying.

Gradually the hold on my fingers relaxed. He was asleep. The little nurse pulled me away from the bed; I didn't look around before leaving the room.

I wanted to go home and get drunk and go to bed or pass out or something but I owed Murray his story, and Anita should be let out of captivity. I called Murray from the Passavant lobby.

'I was beginning to wonder about you, Vic,' he said. 'The news about Smeissen's arrest just came in, and my gofer at the police station says Bronsky and an Ajax executive are both in the police ward at Cook County.'

'Yeah.' I was bone tired. 'Things are mostly over. Anita can come out of hiding. I'd like to pick her up and take her down to see her dad. That's something that's got to be done sooner or later, and it might as well be now.' Masters was sure to squeal on McGraw as soon as he started talking, and I wanted to see him before Mallory did.

'Tell you what,' Murray said. 'I'll meet you in the lobby at the Ritz, and you can tell me about it on the way down. Then I can get a few heartrending shots of the crusty old union guy being reunited with his daughter.'

'Bad idea, Murray. I'll meet you in the lobby and fill you in on the broad outline. If Anita wants you to come along, you can, but don't bet on it. Don't worry about your story, though: you'll still scoop the town.'

I hung up and walked out of the hospital. I was going to have to talk to Bobby myself. I'd gone with Lotty and Ralph when the ambulance came, and Mallory had been too busy to do more than shout, 'I need to talk to you!' at me as I went out the door. I didn't feel like doing it tonight. Jill was going to be okay, that was one good thing. But poor Anita – Still, I owed it to her to get her down to her father before the police got to him.

It was only four blocks from the hospital to the Ritz. The night was clear and warm and caressing. I needed a mother just now, and mother night felt like a good companion, folding dark arms around me.

The lobby of the Ritz, plush and discreet, hovered twelve stories above the street. The rich atmosphere jarred on my mood. I didn't fit in too well with it, either. In the mirrored walls of the elevator riding up, I'd seen myself disheveled, with blood on my jacket and jeans, my hair uncombed. As I waited for Murray, I half expected the house detective. Murray and he arrived at the same time.

'Excuse me, madam,' he said urbanely, 'I wonder if you'd mind coming with me.'

Murray laughed. 'Sorry, Vic, but you earned that.' He turned to the house detective. 'I'm Murray Ryerson, with the *Star*. This is V. I. Warshawski, a private investigator. We've come to pick up a guest of yours, and then we'll be gone.'

The detective frowned over Murray's press card, then nodded. 'Very well, sir. Madam, I wonder if you would mind waiting near the desk.'

'Not at all,' I said politely. 'I understand that most of your guests never see any more blood than is contained by the average steak tartare . . . Actually, maybe I could wash up while Mr Ryerson waits for Miss McGraw?'

The detective ushered me happily to a private washroom in the manager's office. I scrubbed off the worst of the mess and washed my face. I found a brush in the cabinet over the sink and got my hair shaped up. On the whole I looked a lot better. Maybe not material for the Ritz, but not someone to be thrown out on sight.

Anita was waiting with Murray in the lobby when I got back. She looked at me doubtfully. 'Murray says I'm out of danger?'

'Yes. Smeissen, Masters and Smeissen's gunman have been arrested. Do you want to talk to your dad before he's arrested, too?' Murray's mouth dropped open. I put a hand on his arm to keep him from talking.

Anita thought for a minute. 'Yes,' she finally said. 'I've been thinking it over today. You're right – the longer I put it off the worse it will be.'

'I'm coming along,' Murray announced.

'No,' Anita said. 'No, I'm not showing all that to the news-

230

papers. Vic will give you the story later. But I'm not having reporters hanging around for this.'

'You got it, Murray,' I said. 'Catch up with me later on tonight. I'll be – I don't know. I'll be at my bar downtown.'

Anita and I started for the elevator. 'Where's that?' he demanded, catching up with us.

'The Golden Glow on Federal and Adams.'

I called a cab to take us back to my car. A zealous officer, possibly one who'd been left guarding the lobby, had put a parking ticket on the windshield. Twenty dollars for blocking a fire hydrant. They serve and protect.

I was so tired I didn't think I could drive and talk at the same time. I realized that this was the same day that I'd made the three-hundred-mile round trip to Hartford, and that I hadn't slept the night before. It was all catching up with me now.

Anita was preoccupied with her private worries. After giving me directions on how to get to her father's Elmwood Park house, she sat quietly, staring out the window. I liked her, I felt a lot of empathy with her, but I was too drained to reach out and give her anything at the moment.

We were on the Eisenhower Expressway, the road that runs from the Loop to the western suburbs, and had gone about five miles before Anita spoke. 'What happened to Masters?'

'He showed up with his hired help to try to blow me and Ralph Devereux away. They had Jill Thayer with them – they were using her as a hostage. I managed to jump the gunman and break his arm, and disable Masters. Jill is all right.'

'Is she? She's such a good kid. I'd hate like hell for anything to happen to her. Have you met her at all?'

'Yes, she spent a few days with me. She's a great kid, you're right.'

'She's a lot like Peter. The mother is very self-centered, into clothes and the body beautiful, and the sister is incredible, you'd think someone made her up for a book. But Jill and Peter both are – are . . .' She groped for words ' . . . Self-assured, but completely turned out on the world. Everything always is – was

231

– so interesting to Peter – what makes it work, how to solve the problem. Every person was someone he might want to be best friends with. Jill's a lot the same.'

'I think she's falling in love with a Puerto Rican boy. That should keep things stirred up in Winnetka.'

Anita gave a little chuckle. 'For sure. That'll be worse than me – I was a labor leader's daughter, but at least I wasn't black or Spanish.' She was quiet for a while. Then she said, 'You know, this week has changed my life. Or made it seem upside-down. My whole life was directed to the union. I was going to go to law school and be a union lawyer. Now – it doesn't seem worth a lifetime. But there's a big empty hole. I don't know what to put there instead. And with Peter gone – I lost the union and Peter all at the same time. I was so busy last week being terrified that I didn't notice it. Now I do.'

'Oh, yes. That's going to take a while. All mourning takes a long time, and you can't rush it along. My dad's been dead ten years now, and every now and then, something comes up that lets me know that the mourning is still going on, and another piece of it is in place. The hard part doesn't last so long. While it is going on, though, don't fight it – the more you poke away the grief and anger, the longer it takes to sort it out.'

She wanted to know more about my dad and our life together. The rest of the way out I spent telling her about Tony. Funny that he should have the same name as that stupid gunman of Earl's. My father, my Tony, had been a bit of a dreamer, an idealist, a man who had never shot another human being in all his years on the force – warning shots in the air, but no one killed because of Tony Warshawski. Mallory couldn't believe it – I remember that, as Tony was dying. They were talking one evening, Bobby came over a lot at night those days, and Bobby asked him how many people he'd killed in his years on the force. Tony replied he'd never even wounded a man.

After a few minutes of silence, I thought of a small point that had been bothering me. 'What's with this fake-name business? When your father first came to me he called you Anita Hill. Up

232

in Wisconsin you were Jody Hill. I can see he gave you a false name in a not-too-bright effort to keep you out of things – but why'd you both use Hill?'

'Oh, not collusion. But Joe Hill has always been a big hero of ours. Jody Hill just came to me subconsciously. He probably picked it for the same reason.'

We had reached our exit, and Anita started giving me detailed directions. When we pulled up in front of the house, she sat for a bit without speaking. Finally she said, 'I couldn't decide whether to ask you to come in with me or not. But I think you should. This whole thing got started – or your involvement got started – because he came to you. Now I don't know whether he'll believe it's over without your story.'

'Okay.' We walked up to the house together. A man was sitting outside the front door.

'Bodyguard,' Anita murmured to me. 'Daddy's had one as long as I can remember.' Aloud she said, 'Hi, Chuck. It's me, Anita – I've dyed my hair.'

The man was taken aback. 'I heard you ran off, that someone was gunning for you. You okay?'

'Oh, yes, I'm fine. My dad home?'

'Yup, he's in there alone.'

We went into the house, a small ranch house on a large plot. Anita led me through the living room to a sunken family room. Andrew McGraw was watching television. He turned as he heard us coming. For a second he didn't recognize Anita with her short black hair. Then he jumped up.

'Annie?'

'Yes, it's me,' she said quietly. 'Miss Warshawski here found me, as you asked her to. She shot Yardley Masters, and broke the arm of Earl Smeissen's hired gunman. They're all three in jail now. So we can talk.'

'Is that true?' he demanded. 'You disabled Bronsky and shot Masters?'

'Yes,' I said. 'But your troubles aren't over, you know: as soon as Masters has recovered somewhat, he's going to talk.'

He looked from me to Anita, the heavy square face uncertain. 'How much do you know?' he finally said.

'I know a lot,' Anita said. Her voice wasn't hostile, but it was cold, the voice of someone who didn't know the person she was talking to very well and wasn't sure she'd want to. 'I know you've been using the union as a front for collecting money on illegal insurance claims. I know that Peter found that out and went to Yardley Masters about it. And Masters called you and got the name of a hit man.'

'Listen, Annie,' he said in a low urgent tone, much different from the angry bluster I'd heard before. 'You've got to believe I didn't know it was Peter when Yardley called.'

She stayed in the doorway to the room, looking down at him as he stood in his shirt-sleeves. I moved over to one side. 'Don't you see,' she said, her voice breaking a little, 'it doesn't matter. It doesn't matter whether you knew who it was or not. What matters is that you were using the union for fraud, and that you knew a killer when Masters needed one. I know you wouldn't have had Peter shot in cold blood. But it's because you knew how to get people shot that it happened at all.'

He was silent, thinking. 'Yes, I see,' he said finally, in that same low voice. 'Do you think I haven't seen it, sitting here for ten days wondering if I'd see you dead, too, and know that I had killed you?' She said nothing. 'Look, Annie. You and the union – that's been my whole life for twenty years. I thought for ten days that I'd lost both of you. Now you're back. I'm going to have to give up the union – are you going to make me do without you as well?'

Behind us an insanely grinning woman on TV was urging the room to buy some kind of shampoo. Anita stared at her father. 'It can never be the same, you know. Our life, you know, the foundation's broken.'

'Look at me, Annie,' he said hoarsely. 'I haven't slept for ten days, I haven't eaten. I keep watching television, expecting to hear that they've found your dead body someplace . . . I asked Warshawski here to find you when I thought I could keep a step ahead of Masters. But when they made it clear you'd be dead if you showed up, I had to call her off.'

He looked at me. 'You were right – about almost everything. I used Thayer's card because I wanted to plant the idea of him in your mind. It was stupid. Everything I've done this last week's been stupid. Once I realized Annie was in trouble, I just lost my head and acted on crazy impulses. I wasn't mad at you, you know. I was just hoping to God you'd stop before you found Annie. I knew if Earl was watching you you'd lead him straight to her.'

I nodded.

'Maybe I should never have known any gangsters,' he said to Anita. 'But that started so long ago. Before you were born. Once you get in bed with those boys, you don't get out again. The Knifegrinders were a pretty rough bunch in those days – you think we're tough now, you should have seen us then. And the big manufacturers, they all hired hooligans to kill us and keep the union out. We hired muscle to get the union in. Only once we were in, we couldn't get rid of the muscle. If I'd wanted to get away, the only way I could have done it was to leave the Knifegrinders. And I couldn't do that. I was a shop steward when I was fifteen. I met your mother when I was picketing Western Springs Cutlery and she was a kid herself screwing scissors together. The union was my life. And guys like Smeissen were the dirty part that came along with it.'

'But you betrayed the union. You betrayed it when you started dealing with Masters on those phony claims.' Anita was close to tears.

'Yeah, you're right.' He ran a hand through his hair. 'Probably the dumbest thing I ever did. He came up to me at Comiskey Park one day. Someone pointed me out to him. He'd been looking for years, I guess – he'd figured out the deal, you see, but he needed someone on the outside to send the claims into him.

'All I saw was the money. I just didn't want to look down that road. If I had . . . It's like some story I heard once. Some guy,

Greek I think, was so greedy he begged the gods to give him a gift – everything he touched would turn to gold. Only thing is, these gods, they zap you: they always give you what you ask for but it turns out not to be what you want. Well, this guy was like me: he had a daughter that he loved more than life. But he forgot to look down the road. And when he touched her, she turned to gold, too. That's what I've done, haven't I?'

'King Midas,' I said. 'But he repented, and the gods forgave him and brought his daughter back to life.'

Anita looked uncertainly at her father; he looked back, his harsh face stripped and pleading. Murray was waiting for his story. I didn't say goodbye.

DEADLOCK

For Lucella Wieser,
a lady who sailed these seas
with wit and great courage
for over a hundred and six years

ACKNOWLEDGEMENTS

The Canada Steamship Line very generously allowed me to get a first-hand look at a Great Lakes freighter in operation during the fall of 1980. Captain Bowman, master of their 720-foot self-unloading vessel the *J. W. McGiffin*, invited me to sail with him from Thunder Bay through the Soo locks to the Welland Canal. He gave me run of the ship, from the bridge to the holds. Chief Engineer Thomas Taylor took me through the engine room and explained the intricacies of the self-unloader. I wish I could have put his humor and his love of machines into this story. However, no resemblance is intended between any of the officers or crew of the *McGiffin* and those of the ships in this novel. Nor are the operations of Grafalk Steamship or the Pole Star Line meant to resemble Canada Steamship in any way.

A former naval person who advised me on ships and maritime law and customs also has my heartfelt thanks.

CONTENTS

CONTENTS

1
A HERO'S DEATH

More than a thousand people attended Boom Boom's funeral. Many of them were children, fans from the suburbs and the Gold Coast. A handful came from Chicago's depressed South Side where Boom Boom had learned to fight and skate. He was a wing with the Black Hawks until he shattered his left ankle hang-gliding three years earlier. And before Wayne Gretzky came along, he'd been the game's biggest hero since Bobby Hull.

He underwent surgery for the ankle three times, refusing to admit he couldn't skate any more. His doctors hadn't even wanted to attempt the third operation, but Boom Boom bowed to reality only when he could find no one to perform a fourth. After that he drifted through a series of jobs. A lot of people were willing to pay him to generate customers and goodwill, but Boom Boom was the kind of person who had to be doing, had to sink his teeth into – whatever it was.

He finally ended up with the Eudora Grain Company, where his father had been a stevedore during the thirties and forties. It was their regional vice-president, Clayton Phillips, who found Boom Boom's body floating close to the wharf last Tuesday. Phillips tried calling me since Boom Boom's employment forms listed me as his nearest relative. However, I was out of town on a case that took me to Peoria for three weeks. By the time the police located me one of Boom Boom's mother's numerous sisters had identified the body and begun arranging a big Polish funeral.

Boom Boom's father and mine were brothers, and we'd grown up together in South Chicago. We were both only children and were closer than many brothers and sisters. My Aunt Marie, a good Polish Catholic, had produced endless babies, dying in her twelfth attempt. Boom Boom was the fourth, and the only one who lived more than three days.

He grew up playing hockey. I don't know where he got the craze or the skill but, despite Marie's frenzy over the danger, he spent most of his childhood thinking up ways to play without her knowing. A lot of them involved me – I lived six blocks away, and a visit to Cousin Vic was often a cover for a few precious hours with the puck. In those days all the hockey-mad kids adulated Boom-Boom Geoffrion. My cousin copied his slap shot slavishly; to please him the other boys took to calling him 'Boom Boom' and the nickname stuck. In fact when the Chicago police found me at my Peoria hotel and asked if I was Bernard Warshawski's cousin it took me a few seconds to realize who they meant.

Now I sat in the front pew at St Wenceslas Church with Boom Boom's moist, indistinguishable aunts and cousins. All in black, they were offended by my navy wool suit. Several took the trouble to tell me so in loud whispers during the prelude.

I fixed my eyes on the imitation Tiffany windows, depicting in garish colors highlights in the life of St Wenceslas, as well as the Crucifixion and the wedding at Cana. Whoever designed the windows had combined Chinese perspective with a kind of pseudo-cubism. As a result, jugs of water spouted from people's heads and long arms stretched menacingly from behind the cross. Attaching people to their own limbs and sorting out who was doing what to whom kept me fully occupied during the service and gave me – I hope – a convincing air of pious absorption.

Neither of my parents had been religious. My Italian mother was half Jewish, my father Polish, from a long line of skeptics. They'd decided not to inflict any faith on me, although my mother always baked me little *orecchi d'Aman* at Purim. The violent religiosity of Boom Boom's mother and the cheap plaster icons in her house always terrified me as a child.

My own taste would have been for a quiet service at a non-denominational chapel, with a chance for Boom Boom's old teammates to make a short speech – they'd asked to, but the aunts had turned them down. I certainly would not have picked this vulgar church in the old neighborhood, presided over by a priest who had never met my cousin and talked about him now with hypocritical fulsomeness.

However, I left the funeral arrangements to his aunts. My cousin named me his executor, a duty that was bound to absorb a lot of energy. I knew he would not care how he was buried, whereas the little excitement in his aunts' lives came from weddings and funerals. They made sure we spent several hours over a full-blown mass for the dead, followed by an interminable procession to the Sacred Heart cemetery on the far South Side.

After the interment Bobby Mallory fought through the crowd to me in his lieutenant's dress uniform. I was on my way to Boom Boom's Aunt Helen, or maybe his Aunt Sarah, for an afternoon of piroshkis and meatballs. I was glad Bobby had come: he was an old friend of my father's from the Chicago Police Department, and the first person from the old neighborhood I really wanted to see.

'I was real sorry about Boom Boom, Vicki. I know how close you two were.'

Bobby's the only person I allow to call me Vicki. 'Thanks, Bobby. It's been tough. I appreciate your coming.'

A chilly April wind ruffled my hair and made me shiver in my wool suit. I wished I'd worn a coat. Mallory walked with me toward the limousines carrying the fifty-three members of the immediate family. The funeral would probably eat fifteen thousand out of the estate, but I didn't care.

'Are you going to the party? May I ride with you? They'll never miss me in that crowd.'

Mallory agreed good-naturedly and helped me into the back seat of the police limo he'd commandeered. He introduced me to the driver. 'Vicki, Officer Cuthbert was one of Boom Boom's many fans.'

'Yes, miss. I was real sorry when Boom . . . sorry, when your cousin had to stop playing. I figure he could've beat Gretzky's record easy.'

'Go ahead and call him Boom Boom,' I said. 'He loved the name and everyone used it . . . Bobby, I couldn't get any information out of the guy at the grain company when I phoned him. How did Boom Boom die?'

He looked at me sternly. 'Do you really need to know that, Vicki? I know you think you're tough, but you'll be happier remembering Boom Boom the way he was on the ice.'

I pressed my lips together; I wasn't going to lose my temper at Boom Boom's funeral. 'I'm not indulging an appetite for gore, Bobby. I want to know what happened to my cousin. He was an athlete; it's hard for me to picture him slipping and falling like that.'

Bobby's expression softened a bit. 'You're not thinking he drowned himself, are you?'

I moved my hands indecisively. 'He left an urgent message for me with my answering service – I've been out of town, you know. I wondered if he might've been feeling desperate.'

Bobby shook his head. 'Your cousin wasn't the kind of man to throw himself under a ship. You should know that as well as I do.'

I didn't want a lecture on the cowardice of suicide. 'Is that what happened?'

'If the grain company didn't let you know, they had a reason. But you can't accept that, can you?' He sighed. 'You'll probably just go butting your head in down there if I don't tell you. A ship was tied up at the dock and Boom Boom went under the screw as she pulled away. He was chewed up pretty badly.'

'I see.' I turned my head to look at the Eisenhower Expressway and the unpainted homes lining it.

'It was a wet day, Vicki. That's an old wooden dock – they get very slippery in the rain. I read the M E's report myself. I think he slipped and fell in. I don't think he jumped.'

I nodded and patted his hand. Hockey had been Boom Boom's life and he hadn't taken easily to forced retirement. I agreed with Bobby that my cousin wasn't a quitter, but he'd been apathetic the last year or so. Apathetic enough to fall under the propeller of a ship?

I tried to push the thought out of my mind as we pulled up in front of the tidy brick ranch house where Boom Boom's Aunt Helen lived. She had followed a flock of other South Chicago Poles to Elmwood

Park. I believe she had a husband around someplace, a retired steelworker, but, like all the Wojcik men, he stayed far in the background.

Cuthbert let us out in front of the house, then went off to park the limo behind a long string of Cadillacs. Bobby accompanied me to the door, but I quickly lost sight of him in the crowd.

The next two hours put a formidable strain on my frayed temper. Various relatives said it was a pity Bernard insisted on playing hockey when poor dear Marie hated it so much. Others said it was a pity I had divorced Dick and didn't have a family to keep me busy – just look at Cheryl's and Martha's and Betty's babies. The house was swarming with children: all the Wojciks were appallingly prolific.

It was a pity Boom Boom's marriage had only lasted three weeks – but then, he shouldn't have been playing hockey. Why was he working at Eudora Grain, though? Breathing grain dust all his life had killed his father. Still, those Warshawskis never had much stamina anyway.

The small house filled with cigarette smoke, with the heavy smell of Polish cooking, with the squeals of children. I edged my way past one aunt who said she expected me to help wash up since I hadn't handled any of the preparation. I had vowed that I would not say anything over the baked meats beyond 'Yes,' 'No,' and 'I don't know,' but it was getting harder.

Then Grandma Wojcik, eighty-two, fat, dressed in shiny black, grabbed my arm in a policeman's grip. She looked at me with a rheumy blue eye. Breathing onions, she said, 'The girls are talking about Bernard.'

The girls were the aunts, of course.

'They're saying he was in trouble down at the elevator. They're saying he threw himself under the ship so he wouldn't be arrested.'

'Who's telling you that?' I demanded.

'Helen. And Sarah. Cheryl says Pete says he just jumped in the water when no one was looking. No Wojcik ever killed himself. But the Warshawskis . . . Those Jews. I warned Marie over and over.'

I pried her fingers from my arm. The smoke and noise and the sour cabbage smell were filling my brain. I put my head down to look her in the eyes, started to say something rude, then thought better of it. I fought my way through the smog, tripping over babies, and found the men hovering around a table filled with sausages and sauerkraut in one corner. If their minds had been as full as their stomachs they could have saved America.

'Who are you telling that Boom Boom jumped off the wharf? And how the hell do you know, anyway?'

Cheryl's husband Pete looked at me with stupid blue eyes. 'Hey, don't lose your pants, Vic. I heard it down at the dock.'

'What trouble was he in at the elevator? Grandma Wojcik says you're telling everyone he was in trouble down there.'

Pete shifted a glass of beer from one hand to the other. 'It's just talk, Vic. He didn't get along with his boss. Someone said he stole some papers. I don't believe it. Boom Boom didn't need to steal.'

My eyes fogged and I felt my head buzzing. 'It's not true, goddamn you! Boom Boom never did anything cheap in his life, even when he was poor.'

The others stared at me uneasily. 'Take it easy, Vic,' one said. 'We all liked Boom Boom. Pete said he didn't believe it. Don't get so wild over it.'

He was right. What was I doing, anyway, starting a scene at the funeral? I shook my head, like a dog coming out of water, and pushed back through the crowd to the living room. I made my way past a Bleeding Heart of Mary tastefully adorning the front door and went out into the chilly spring air.

I opened my jacket to let the cool air flow through me and cleanse me. I wanted to go home, but my car was at my apartment on Chicago's North Side. I scanned the street: as I'd feared, Cuthbert and Mallory had long since disappeared. While I looked doubtfully around me, wondering whether I could find a cab or possibly walk to a train station in high heels, a young woman joined me. She was small and tidy, with dark hair falling straight just below her ears, and honey-colored eyes. She wore a pale gray silk shantung suit with a full skirt and a bolero jacket fastened by large mother-of-pearl buttons. She looked elegant, perfect, and vaguely familiar.

'Wherever Boom Boom is, I'm sure he'd rather be there than

here.' She jerked her head toward the house and gave a quick, sardonic smile.

'Me too.'

'You're his cousin, aren't you? . . . I'm Paige Carrington.'

'I thought I recognized you. I've seen you a few times, but only on stage.' Carrington was a dancer who had created a comic one-woman show with the Windy City Balletworks.

She gave the triangular smile audiences loved. 'I've been seeing a lot of your cousin the last few months. We kept it quiet because we didn't want Herguth or Greta splashing it around the gossip columns – your cousin was news even when he stopped skating.'

She was right. I was always seeing my cousin's name in print. It's funny being close to someone famous. You read a lot about them, but the person in print's never the one you know.

'I think Boom Boom cared more for you than anyone.' She frowned, thinking about the statement. Even her frown was perfect, giving her an absorbed, considering look. Then she smiled, a bit wistfully. 'I think we were in love, but I don't know. I'll never be sure now.'

I mumbled something soothing.

'I wanted to meet you. Boom Boom talked about you all the time. He loved you very much. I'm sorry he never introduced us.'

'Yes. I hadn't seen him for several months . . . Are you driving back to the city? Can I beg a ride? I had to come out with the procession and my car is on the North Side.'

She pushed back the white silk cuff emerging from her jacket sleeve and looked at her watch. 'I have to be at a rehearsal in an hour. Okay if I drop you downtown?'

'That'd be great. I feel like Br'er Rabbit out here in suburbia – I need to get back to my brier patch.'

She laughed at that. 'I know what you mean. I grew up in Lake Bluff myself. But now when I go out there to visit I feel like my oxygen's been cut off.'

I looked at the house, wondering if I should make a formal farewell. Good manners certainly dictated it, but I didn't want a fifteen-minute lecture on why I should clean up both the dishes and

249

my life. I shrugged and followed Paige Carrington down the street.

She drove a silver Audi 5000. Either the Windy City Balletworks paid better than the average struggling theater or the Lake Bluff connection supplied money for shantung suits and foreign sports cars.

Paige drove with the quick, precise grace that characterized her dancing. Since neither of us knew the area, she made a few wrong turns in the rows of identical houses before finding an access ramp to the Eisenhower.

She didn't say much on the ride back to town. I was quiet too, thinking about my cousin and feeling melancholy – and guilty. That was why I'd had a temper tantrum with those stupid, hulking cousins, I realized. I hadn't kept up with Boom Boom. I knew he was depressed but I hadn't kept in touch. If only I'd left my Peoria number with my answering service. Was he sick with despair? Maybe he'd thought love would cure him and it hadn't. Or maybe it was the talk on the docks that he'd stolen some papers – he thought I could help him combat it, like the thousand other battles we'd fought together. Only I wasn't there.

With his death, I'd lost my whole family. It's true my mother had an aunt in Melrose Park. But I'd rarely met her, and neither she nor her fat, self-important son seemed like real relations to me. But Boom Boom and I had played, fought, protected each other. If we hadn't spent much time together in the last ten years, we'd always counted on the other being around to help out. And I hadn't helped him out.

As we neared in I-90/94 interchange rain started spattering the windshield, breaking into my fruitless reverie. I realized Paige was glancing at me speculatively. I turned to face her, eyebrows raised.

'You're Boom Boom's executor, aren't you?'

I assented. She drummed her fingers on the steering wheel. 'Boom Boom and I – never got to the stage of exchanging keys.' She gave a quick, embarrassed smile. 'I'd like to go to his place and get some things I left there.'

'Sure. I was planning on being there tomorrow afternoon for a preliminary look at his papers. Want to meet me there at two?'

'Thanks. You're sweet . . . Do you mind if I call you Vic? Boom Boom talked about you so much I feel as though I know you.'

We were going under the post office, where six lanes had been carved out of the building's foundations. Paige gave a satisfied nod. 'And you must call me Paige.' She changed lanes, nosed the Audi around a garbage truck, and turned left on Wabash. She dropped me at my office – the Pulteney Building on the corner of Wabash and Monroe.

Overhead an el train thundered. 'Good-bye,' I yelled above the din. 'See you tomorrow at two.'

2
LOVE'S LABORS LOST

The Hawks had paid Boom Boom a lot of money to play hockey. He'd spent a fair amount of it on a condo in a slick glass building on Lake Shore Drive north of Chestnut Street. Since he bought it five years ago I'd been there a number of times, often with a crowd of drunken friendly hockey players.

Gerald Simonds, Boom Boom's lawyer, gave me the building keys, along with those to my cousin's Jaguar. We spent the morning going over Boom Boom's will, a document likely to raise more uproar with the aunts – my cousin left the bulk of his estate to various charities and to the Hockey Widows Pension Fund; no aunts were mentioned. He left me some money with a request not to spend it all on Black Label. Simonds frowned disapprovingly as I laughed. He explained that he had tried to keep his client from inserting that particular clause, but Mr Warshawski had been adamant.

It was about noon when we finished. There were a couple of things I could have done in the financial district for one of my clients but I just didn't feel like working. I didn't have any interesting cases going at the moment – just a couple of processes to serve. I was also trying to track down a man who had disappeared with half the assets in a partnership, including a forty-foot cabin cruiser. They could all wait. I retrieved my car, a green Mercury Lynx, from the Fort Dearborn Trust's parking lot and headed over to the Gold Coast.

Like most posh places, Boom Boom's building had a doorman. A pudgy, middle-aged white man, he was helping an old lady out of her Seville when I got there, and didn't pay much attention to me. I fumbled with the keys, trying to find the one that opened the inner door.

Inside the lobby, a woman got off the elevator with a tiny poodle, its fluffy white hair tied in blue ribbons. She opened the outer door, and I went inside, giving the dog a commiserating look. The dog lurched at its rhinestone-studded leash to smell my leg. 'Now, Fifi,' the woman said, pulling the poodle back to her side. Dogs like that aren't supposed to sniff at things or do anything else to remind their owners they're animals.

The inner lobby wasn't big. It held a few potted trees, two off-white couches where residents could chat, and a large hanging. You see these hangings all over the place, at least in this kind of building: they're woven usually with large knots of wool sticking out here and there and a few long strands trailing down the middle. While I waited for an elevator I studied this one without enthusiasm. It covered the west wall and was made from different shades of green and mustard. I was just as glad I lived in a tired three-flat with no neighbors like Fifi's owner to decide what should hang in the lobby.

The elevator opened quietly behind me. A woman my age came out dressed for running, followed by two older women on their way to Saks, debating whether to eat lunch at Water Tower on the way over. I looked at my watch: twelve forty-five. Why weren't they at work on a Tuesday? Perhaps like me they were all private investigators taking time off to handle a relative's estate. I pressed 22 and the elevator carried me up swiftly and noiselessly.

Each floor of the thirty-storey condo had four units. Boom Boom had paid over a quarter of a million to get one in the northeast corner. It contained just about fifteen hundred square feet – three bedrooms, three baths, including one with a sunken tub off the master bedroom – and a magnificent view of the lake from the north and east sides.

I opened the door to 22C and went through the hallway to the living room, my feet soundless in the deep pile of the wall-to-wall carpeting. Blue print drapes were pulled away from the glass forming the room's east wall. The panoramic view drew me – lake and sky forming one giant gray-green ball. I let the vastness absorb me until I felt a sense of peace. I stood so a long moment, then realized with a start of resentment that I wasn't alone in the apartment. I wasn't sure what alerted me; I concentrated hard for several minutes, then heard a slight rasping noise. Paper rustling.

I moved back to the entryway. This led to a hall on the right where the three bedrooms and the master bath were. The dining room and kitchen were off a second, smaller hallway to the left. The rustling had come from the right, the bedroom side.

I'd worn a suit and heels to see Simonds, clothing totally unsuitable for handling an intruder. I quietly opened the outside door to provide an escape route, slipped off my shoes, and left the handbag next to a magazine rack in the entryway.

I went back into the living room, listening hard, looking for a potential weapon. A bronze trophy on the mantelpiece, a tribute to Boom Boom as most valuable player in a Stanley Cup victory. I picked it up quietly and moved cautiously down the hallway toward the bedrooms.

All the doors were open. I tiptoed to the nearest room, which Boom Boom had used as a study. Flattening myself against the wall, bracing my right arm with the heavy trophy, I stuck my head slowly into the open doorway.

Her back to me, Paige Carrington sat at Boom Boom's desk sorting through some papers. I felt both foolish and angry. I retreated up the hall, put the trophy down on the magazine table, and slipped into my shoes. I walked back to the study.

'Early, aren't you? How did you get in?'

She jumped in the chair and dropped the papers she was holding. Crimson suffused her face from the neck of her open shirt to the roots of her dark hair. 'Oh! I wasn't expecting you until two.'

'Me either. I thought you didn't have a key.'

'Please don't get so angry, Vic. We had an extra rehearsal called for two o'clock, and I really wanted to find my letters. So I persuaded Hinckley – he's the doorman – I persuaded him to come up and let me in.' For a minute I thought I saw tears in the honey-colored eyes, but she flicked the back of her hand across them and smiled guiltily. 'I hoped I'd be gone before you showed up. These letters are terribly,

terribly personal and I couldn't bear for anyone, even you, to see them.' She held out her right hand beseechingly.

I narrowed my eyes at her. 'Find anything?'

She shrugged. 'He may just not have kept them.' She bent over to pick up the papers she'd scattered at my entrance. I knelt to help her. It looked like a stack of business letters – I caught Myron Fackley's name a couple of times. He'd been Boom Boom's agent.

'I've only been through two drawers, and there are six others with papers in them. He saved everything, I think – one drawer is stuffed full of fan letters.'

I looked at the room with jaundiced eyes. Eight drawers full of papers. Sorting and cleaning have always been my worst skills on aptitude tests.

I sat on the desk and patted Paige's shoulder. 'Look. This is going to be totally boring to sort through. I'm going to have to examine even the stuff you've looked at because I have to see anything that might affect the estate. So why don't you leave me to it? I promise you if I see any personal letters to Boom Boom I won't read them – I'll put them in an envelope for you.'

She smiled up at me, but the smile wobbled. 'Maybe I'm just being vain, but if he saved a bunch of letters from kids he never met I thought he'd keep what I wrote him.' She looked away.

I gripped her shoulder for a minute. 'Don't worry, Paige. I'm sure they'll turn up.'

She sniffed a tiny, elegant sniff. 'I think I'm just fixating on them because they keep me from thinking, "Yes, he's really . . . gone."'

'Yeah. That's why I'm cursing him for being such a damned pack rat. And I can't even get back at him by making him *my* executor.'

She laughed a little at that. 'I brought a suitcase with me. I might as well pack up the clothes and makeup I left over here and get going.'

She went to the master bedroom to pull out her things. I puttered around aimlessly, trying to take stock of my task. Paige was right: Boom Boom had saved everything. Every inch of wall space was covered with hockey photographs, starting with the peewee team my cousin belonged to in second grade. There were group photos of him with the Black Hawks, locker-room pictures filled with champagne after Stanley Cup triumphs, solo shots of Boom Boom making difficult plays, signed pictures from Esposito, Howe, Hull – even one from Boom-Boom Geoffrion inscribed, 'To the little cannon'.

In the middle of the collection, incongruous, was a picture of me in my maroon robes getting my law degree from the University of Chicago. The sun was shining behind me and I was grinning at the camera. My cousin had never gone to college and he set inordinate store by my education. I frowned at this younger, happy V. I. Warshawski and went into the master bedroom to see if Paige needed any help.

The case sat open on the bed, clothes folded neatly. As I came in she was rummaging through a dresser drawer, pulling out a bright red pullover.

'Are you going through all his clothes and everything? I think I've got all my stuff, but let me know if you find anything – size sixes are probably mine, not his.' She went into the bathroom where I heard her opening cabinets.

The bedroom was masculine but homey. A king-size bed dominated the middle of the floor, covered with a black and white quilt. Floor-length drapes in a heavy off-white cloth were pulled back, showing the lake. Boom Boom's hockey stick was mounted over the severe walnut bureau. A purple and red painting provided a splash of color and a couple of rugs picked it up again in the same red. He'd avoided the mirrors that so many bachelors think make the complete singles apartment.

A bedside table held a few magazines. I sat on the bed to see what my cousin had read before going to sleep – *Sports Illustrated, Hockey World*, and a densely printed paper called *Grain News*. I looked at this with interest. Published in Kansas City, it was filled with information about grain – the size of various crops, prices on different options exchanges, rates for shipping by rail and boat, contracts awarded to different transporters. It was pretty interesting if grain was important to you.

'Is that something special?'

I'd gotten so absorbed I hadn't noticed Paige come out of the bathroom to finish her packing. I hesitated, then said, 'I've been worried about whether Boom Boom went under that propeller – deliberately. This thing' – I waved the paper at her – 'tells you everything you'd ever want to know about grains and shipping them. It apparently comes out twice a month, weekly during the harvest. If Boom Boom was involved enough at Eudora Grain to study something like this, it gives me some reassurance.'

Paige looked at me intently. She took *Grain News* and flipped through it. Looking at the pages, she said, 'I know losing hockey upset him – I can imagine how I'd feel if I couldn't dance, and I'm not nearly as good a ballerina as he was a hockey player. But I think his involvement with me – kept him from being too depressed. I hope that doesn't offend you.'

'Not at all. If it's true, I'm pleased.'

Her thin, penciled brows rose. '*If* it's true? Do you mind explaining that?'

'Nothing to explain, Paige. I hadn't seen Boom Boom since January. He was still fighting the blues then. If knowing you helped him out of the depths, I'm glad . . . There was some talk at the funeral about his being in trouble down at Eudora Grain – I guess there's a rumor going around that he stole some papers. Did he say anything about that to you?'

The honey-colored eyes widened. 'No. Not a word. If people were talking about it, it must not have bothered him enough to mention it; we had dinner the day before he died. I wouldn't believe it, anyway.'

'Do you know what he wanted to talk to me about?'

She looked startled. 'Was he trying to get in touch with you?'

'He left an urgent message for me with my answering service, but he didn't say what it was about. I wondered: if there was some story going around the docks maybe he wanted my professional help.'

She shook her head, fiddling with the zipper on her purse. 'I don't know. He seemed fine Monday night. Look – I've got to get going. I'm sorry if I upset you earlier, but I have to run now.'

I walked back to the front door with her and shut it behind her – I'd forgotten to close it when I came back for my shoes earlier. I also fastened the deadbolt. I was damned if the doorman was going to let in anyone else without telling me – at least not while I was in the apartment.

Before getting down to the dispiriting task of sorting my cousin's papers I took a quick look around. Unlike me, he was – had been – phenomenally tidy. If I'd been dead for a week and someone came into my place, they'd find some nasty surprises in the sink and a good layer of dust, not to mention an array of clothes and papers in the bedroom.

Boom Boom's kitchen was spotless. The refrigerator was clean inside as well as out. I went through it and got rid of vegetables which were going bad. Two gallons of milk went down the sink – I guess he never got out of the habit of drinking it, even when he wasn't training any longer. Tidy, tidy. I'd often said the same thing to Boom Boom, teasing him. Remembering those words made my stomach turn over, as if the air had been sucked out from underneath it. It's like that when someone you love dies. I'd been through it with my parents, too. Little things keep reminding you and it takes a while before the physical pain goes out of the memory.

I went back to the study and made an organized attack on the drawers. Left to right, top to bottom. If it has to be done, do it thoroughly so there's no need to take extra time backtracking. Fortunately, my cousin was not only a pack rat, he was also organized. The eight drawers all had neatly labeled file folders.

The top left held fan mail. Given the size of the turnout at the funeral, I shouldn't have been surprised to see how many letters people sent him. He still got three or four a week in labored boyish handwriting.

Dear Boom Boom Warshawski,

I think you're the greatest hockey player in the universe. Please send me your picture.

Your friend,
Alan Palmerlee

P.S. Here is a picture of me playing wing for the Algonquin Maple Leafs.

Across each letter was a neatly written note indicating the date and the reply – 'March 26, sent signed picture' or 'Called Myron. Asked him to arrange speaking date.' A lot of high schools wanted him to speak at graduation or at sports banquets.

The next drawer contained material relating to Boom Boom's endorsement contracts. I'd have to go over these with Fackley and Simonds. My cousin had done some TV spots for the American Dairy Association. Maybe that explained his milk – if you advertise it, you have to drink it. There was also the Warshawski hockey stick, a warmup jersey, and an ice-skate endorsement.

At five o'clock I rummaged through the spotless kitchen and found a can of coffee and an electric percolator. I made a pot and carried it back into the study with me. At eight-thirty I located Boom Boom's liquor supply in a carved Chinese chest in the dining room and poured myself a Chivas – not my first choice in Scotch but an adequate substitute for Black Label.

By ten o'clock I was surrounded by stacks of papers – a pile for Fackley, the agent. One for the attorney, Simonds. Quite a few for the garbage. A few things of sentimental value to me. One or two that might interest Paige. Some memorabilia for the Hockey Hall of Fame in Eveleth, Minnesota, and some other items for the Black Hawks.

I was tired. My olive silk blouse had a smear of greasy dust across the front. My nylons were full of runs. I was hungry. I hadn't found Paige's letters. Maybe I'd feel better after some food. At any rate, I'd been through all the drawers, including the ones in the desk. What had I really expected to find?

Abruptly I stood and skirted the mounds of paper to get to the telephone. I dialed a number I knew by heart and was relieved to hear it answered on the third ring.

'This is Dr Herschel.'

'Lotty: it's Vic. I've been sorting through my cousin's papers and gotten myself thoroughly depressed. Have you eaten?'

She had had dinner several hours ago but agreed to meet me at the Chesterton Hotel for coffee while I got something to eat.

I washed up in the master bathroom, looking enviously at the sunken tub with its whirlpool attachment. Relief for my cousin's shattered ankle. I wondered if he'd bought the condo for the whirlpool. It would be like Boom Boom, tidy in details but not very practical.

On my way out I stopped to talk to the doorman, Hinckley. He was long gone for the day. The man on duty now was more of a security guard. He sat behind a desk with T V consoles on it – he could see the street or the garage or look at any of the thirty floors. A tired old black man with tiny wrinkles that showed only when I got close to him, he looked at me impassively as I explained who I was. I showed him my power of attorney from Simonds and told him I would be coming around until my cousin's affairs were straightened out and the unit was sold.

He didn't say anything. He didn't blink or move his head, just looked at me through expressionless brown eyes whose irises were stained yellow with age.

I could feel my voice rising and checked it. 'The man on duty this afternoon let someone into the apartment. Can you please see that no one goes in unless I accompany him or her?'

He continued to stare at me with unblinking eyes. I felt anger flush my face. I turned and left him sitting under the mustard-colored weaving.

3

REFLECTIONS

'What were you looking for?' Lotty sat drinking coffee, her sharp black eyes probing me, but with affection.

I took a bite of my sandwich. 'I don't know. I guess I've been a detective too long – I keep expecting to find secrets in people's desks.'

We were sitting in the Dortmunder Restaurant in the basement of the Chesterton Hotel. I had picked a half bottle of Pomerol from the wine bins that lined the walls and was drinking it with a sandwich – Emmenthaler on thin, homemade rye bread. Service is slow at Dortmunder's – they're used to the old ladies who live in the hotel whiling away an afternoon over a cup of coffee and a single pastry.

'My dear, I don't want to press you if you don't want to think about it. But you never sort papers. Even for your cousin you would give them to the attorney unless you were looking for something. So what you were looking for was very important to you, right?'

Lotty is Austrian. She learned English in London where she spent her adolescence, and a trace of a Viennese accent underlies the English inflection of her sharp, crisp words. We've been friends for a long time.

I finished my sandwich and drank some more wine, then held the glass, turning it to catch the light. I stared into the ruby glow and thought. Finally I put the glass down.

'Boom Boom left an urgent message with my answering service. I don't know if he was just terribly depressed or in some trouble at Eudora Grain, but he never left that kind of message for me before.' I stared again at the wine. 'Lotty, I was looking for a letter that said, "Dear Vic, I've been accused of stealing some papers. Between that and losing my ankle I'm so blue I can't take it any more." Or "Dear Vic – I'm in love with Paige Carrington and life is great." She says he was and maybe so – but she's so – so, oh, sophisticated, maybe. Or perfect – it's hard for me to picture him in love with her. He liked women who were more human.'

Lotty set down her coffee cup and put her square, strong fingers over mine. 'Could you be jealous?'

'Oh, a little. But not so much that it would distort my judgement. Maybe it's egocentrism, though. I hadn't called him for two months. I keep going over it in my head – we'd often let months go by without being in touch. But I can't help feeling I let him down.'

The hold on my fingers tightened. 'Boom Boom knew he could count on you, Vic. You have too many times to remember when that was so. He called you. And he knew you'd come through, even if he had to wait a few days.'

I disengaged my left hand and picked up my wineglass. I swallowed and the tightness in my throat eased. I looked at Lotty. She gave an impish smile.

'You are a detective, Vic. If you really want to be totally sure about Boom Boom, you could try investigating what happened.'

4

ON THE WATERFRONT

The Eudora Grain Company elevator lay in the labyrinth that makes up the Port of Chicago. The Port lines six miles of the Calumet River as it snakes south and west from its mouth near 95th Street. Each elevator or plant along the river has its own access road, and none of them is clearly marked.

I covered the twenty miles from my North Side apartment to 130th Street in good time, reaching the exit by eight o'clock. After that I got lost trying to make my way past the Calumet River, some steel mills, and a Ford assembly plant. It was nine-thirty before I found Eudora Grain's regional office.

Their regional headquarters, a modern, single-story block, lay next to a giant elevator on the river. The elevator loomed behind the building at right angles, two sections of massive tubes, each containing perhaps a hundred ten-story-high cylinders. The sections were split by a slip where a boat could tie up. On the right side, railway tracks ran into a shed. A few hopper cars were there now and a small group of hard-hatted men were fixing one onto a hoist. I watched, fascinated: the car disappeared up inside the elevator. On the far left side I could see the tip of a ship poking out – someone was apparently taking on a load of grain.

The building had a modern lobby with wide windows opening onto the river. Pictures of grain harvests – combines sweeping through thousands of acres of golden wheat, smaller versions of the mammoth elevator outside, trains taking on their golden hoard, boats unloading – covered the walls. I took a quick glance around, then approached a receptionist behind a marble counter set in the middle of the room. She was young and eager to help. After a spirited interchange with his secretary, she located the regional vice-president, Clayton Phillips. He came out to the foyer to meet me.

Phillips was a wooden man, perhaps in his early forties, with straw-colored hair and pale brown eyes. I took an immediate dislike to him, perhaps because he failed to offer me any condolences for Boom Boom, even when I introduced myself as his closest relative.

Phillips dithered around at the thought of my asking questions at the elevator. He couldn't bring himself to say no, however, and I didn't give him any help. He had an irritating habit of darting his eyes around the room when I asked him a question, instead of looking at me. I wondered if he found inspiration from the photographs lining the foyer.

'I don't need to take any more of your time, Mr Phillips,' I finally said. 'I can find my way around the elevator and ask the questions I want on my own.'

'Oh, I'll come with you, uh – uh –' He looked at my business card, frowning.

'Miss Warshawski,' I said helpfully.

'Miss Warshawski. The foreman won't like it if you come without an introduction.' His voice was deep but tight, the voice of a tense man speaking from the vocal cords rather than through the nasal passages.

Pete Margolis, the elevator foreman, didn't seem happy to see us. However, I quickly realized his annoyance was directed more at Phillips than at me. Phillips merely introduced me as 'a young lady interested in the elevator.' When I gave Margolis my name and told him I was Boom Boom's cousin, his manner changed abruptly. He wiped a dirty paw on the side of his overalls and shook hands with me, told me how sorry he was about my cousin's accident, how much the men liked him, and how badly the company would miss him. He dug out a hard hat for me from under a pile of papers in his minuscule office.

Paying little attention to Phillips, he gave me a long and detailed tour, showing me where the hopper cars came in to dump their loads and how to operate the automatic hoist that lifted them into the heart

264

of the elevator. Phillips trailed along, making ineffectual comments. He had his own hard hat, his name neatly lettered across the top, but his gray silk summer suit was totally out of place in the dirty plant.

Margolis took us up a long flight of narrow stairs that led into the interior of the elevator, perhaps three stories up. He opened a fire door at the top, and noise shattered my eardrums.

Dust covered everything. It swirled through the air, landing in layers on the high steel beams, creating a squeaky film on the metal floor. My toes quickly felt greasy inside their thick cotton socks. My running shoes skidded on the dusty floor. Under the ill-fitting, heavy hard hat, my hair became matted and sticky.

We stood on a catwalk looking down on the concrete floor of the elevator. Only a narrow waist-high handrail stood between me and an unpleasant crash onto the conveyor belts below. If I fell, they'd have to change the sign posted in the doorway: 9,640 man-hours without an accident.

Pete Margolis stood at my right side. He grabbed my arm and gesticulated with his free hand. I shook my head. He leaned over next to my right ear. 'This is where it comes in,' he bellowed. 'They bring the boxcars up here and dump them. Then it goes by conveyor belt.'

I nodded. A series of conveyor belts caused much of the clanking, shattering noise, but the hoist that lifted boxcars ninety feet in the air as though they were toys also contributed to the din. The belts ferried grain from the towers where boxcars dumped it over to chutes that spilled it into cargo holds of ships moored outside. A lot of grain dust escaped in the process. Most of the men on the floor wore respirators, but few seemed to have any ear protection.

'Wheat?' I screamed into Margolis's ear.

'Barley. About thirty-five bushels to the ton.'

He shouted something at Phillips and we went on across the gangway outside, to a narrow ledge overlooking the water. I gulped in the cold April air and let my ears adjust to the relative quiet.

Below us sat a dirty old ship tied to the dock by a series of cables. She was riding above her normal waterline, where the black paint on the hull gave way abruptly to a peeling greenish color. On her deck, more men in hard hats and dirty boiler suits were guiding three massive grain chutes with ropes, filling the holds through some twelve or fourteen openings in the deck. Next to each opening lay its lid – 'hatch cover,' Phillips told me. A mass of coiled ropes lay near the back end, our end, where the pilothouse stood. I felt slightly dizzy. I grew up in South Chicago where steel mills dot the lake, so I've seen plenty of Great Lakes freighters close up, but they always give me the same feeling – stomach contractions and shivers up the spine. Something about the hull thrusting invisibly into black water.

A cold wind whipped around the river. The water was too sheltered here for whitecaps, but grain dust blew up at us, mixed with cigarette wrappers and potato chip bags. I coughed and turned my head aside.

'Your cousin was standing at the stern.' I followed Phillips's pointing finger. 'Even if someone were leaning forward they wouldn't have been able to see him from up here.'

I tried, but the angle of the elevator cut off the view part way along the pilothouse. 'What about all those people on deck? And there're a couple down there on the ground.'

Phillips swallowed a superior smile. 'The *O. R. Daley*'s tied up now and loading. When the ship is casting off all the elevator people are gone and everyone connected with the ship has an assignment. They wouldn't pay much attention to a guy on the wharf.'

'Someone must have seen him,' I said stubbornly. 'What about it, Mr Margolis? Any problem with you if I talk to the men on the elevator?'

Margolis shrugged. 'Everyone liked your cousin, Miss Warshawski. If they'd seen anything they'd have come forward with it by now . . . But if you think it'll do some good I don't mind. They'll break for lunch in two shifts starting in twenty-five minutes.'

I scanned the wharf. 'Maybe you could show me exactly where my cousin went in.'

'We don't really know,' Phillips responded, his deep voice trying to hide impatience. 'But if it will make you feel better in some way . . . Pete, maybe you could take Miss Warshawski down.'

Margolis looked back at the elevator, hesitated, then reluctantly agreed.

'This isn't the ship that was here then, is it?'

'No, of course not,' Phillips said.

'Know which one was?' I asked.

'There's no way of knowing that,' Phillips said, just as Margolis said, 'The *Bertha Krupnik*.'

'Well, maybe you're right.' Phillips gave a strained smile. 'I keep forgetting that Pete here has the day-to-day details of this operation at his fingertips.'

'Yup. It was supposed to be the *Lucella Wieser*. Then she had that accident – water in the holds or something – and they brought up three old tubs to take her load. The *Bertha* was the last of 'em. Pilot's an old friend of mine. He like to've lost his lunch when he heard about Boom Boom . . . your cousin, I mean. He was a hockey fan himself.'

'Where's the *Bertha Krupnik* now?'

Margolis shook his head. 'No way of knowing that. She's one of Grafalk's, though. You could ask them. Their dispatcher would know.' He hesitated a minute. 'You might want to check with the *Lucella*. She was tied up over there.' He pointed across the old boat at our feet to another pier about two hundred yards away. 'They moved her over out of the way while they cleaned out her holds. She moved out yesterday or the day before.' He shook his head. 'Don't think anyone's going to be able to tell you anything, though. You know what people are like. If they'd seen your cousin go in they'd have said something fast enough at the time.'

Unless they were embarrassed at not doing anything to help, I thought. 'Where's Grafalk's office?'

'Do you really want to go there, Miss Warshawski?' Phillips asked. 'It's not the kind of place you should just go into without some sort of credential or justification.'

'I have a credential.' I fished my private investigator's licence out of my wallet. 'I've asked a lot of people a lot of questions based on this.'

His wooden expression didn't change, but he turned red to the roots of his pale blond hair. 'I think I should go over with you and introduce you to the right person.'

'You want to swing by the *Lucella* with her, too, Mr Phillips?' Margolis asked.

'Not particularly. I'm running late as it is. I'll have to go back to your office, Pete, and call Rodriguez from there.'

'Look, Mr Phillips,' I put in, 'I can take care of myself perfectly well. I don't need you to interrupt your schedule to ferry me around.'

He assured me it was no problem, he really wanted to do it if I thought it was necessary. It occurred to me he might be worrying that I would turn up some witness suggesting that Eudora Grain had been negligent. In any case, he could smooth my path at Grafalk's, so I didn't mind his tagging along.

While he went back through the elevator to use the phone, Margolis took me down a narrow iron ladder to the wharf. Close up, the ship looked even dirtier. Heavy cables extended from the deck and tied her fast to large knobs sticking out of the concrete wharf. Like the ship, the cables were old, frayed, and none too clean. As Margolis led me to the rear of the *O. R. Daley*, I noticed how badly the paint had cracked above the waterline. '*O. R. Daley*. Grafalk Steamship Line. Chicago.' was painted in chipped white letters near the back.

'Your cousin was probably standing here.' The concrete had ended, replaced by faded wood planks. 'It was a sloppy day. We had to stop loading every few hours, cover the hatches, and wait for the rain to end. Very long job. Anyway, wood like this – real old, you know – gets very slippery when it's wet. If Boom Boom – your cousin, I mean – was leaning over to see something, he might've just slipped and fallen right in. He did have that bad leg.'

'What would he be leaning over to look at, though?'

'Anything. He was an inquisitive guy. Very interested in everything and anything about the ships and the business. Between you and me, he got on Phillips's nerves a bit.' He spat expertly into the water. 'But, what I hear, Argus got him this job and Phillips didn't like to stand up to him.'

David Argus was chairman of Eudora Grain. He'd flown in from Eudora, Kansas, to attend Boom Boom's funeral and had made a hundred-dollar donation to a children's home in Boom Boom's name. He hadn't gone to the postfuneral party, lucky devil, but he'd shaken my hand briefly after the ceremony, a short, stocky guy in his sixties who exuded a blast-furnace personality. If he had been my cousin's patron, Boom Boom was well protected in the organization. But I couldn't believe Boom Boom would abuse the relationship, and said so.

'Naw, nothing like that. But Phillips didn't like having a young guy around that he had to look after. Nope, Boom Boom worked real hard, didn't ask for any special favors the way he might've, being a star and all. I'd say the fellows liked him pretty well.'

'Someone was telling me there was a lot of talk down here about my cousin – that he might have committed suicide.' I looked at the foreman steadily.

He gave a surprised grimace. 'Not so far as I know. I haven't heard anything. You could talk to the men. But, like I say, I haven't heard anything.'

Phillips walked toward us dusting his hands. Margolis jerked his head toward Phillips. 'You going with him? Want to come back later to talk to the men?'

We settled on ten the next morning, break time for the morning shift. Margolis said he would talk to them in the meantime, but he really thought if anyone had seen anything he would have volunteered it. 'An accident always gets a lot of talk. And Warshawski, being a celebrity and all, everyone who knew anything was mouthing off. I don't think you'll find out anything.'

Phillips came up to us. 'Are you ready? I've talked to the dispatcher at Grafalk's. They're very reluctant to let you know where the *Bertha Krupnik* is, but they'll talk to you if I bring you over.' He looked self-consciously at his watch.

I shook hands with Margolis, told him I'd see him in the morning, and followed Phillips on down the pier and around the back of the elevator. We picked our way across the deeply pocked yard, stepping over strips of rusted metal, to where Phillips's green Alfa sat, sleek and incongruous between an old Impala and a rusty pickup. He put his hard hat carefully on the back seat and made a great show of starting the car, reversing it between ruts and sliding to the yard entrance. Once we'd turned onto 130th Street and were moving with the traffic I said, 'You're clearly annoyed about chauffeuring me around the Port. It doesn't bother me to barge in on people without an escort – just as I did on you this morning. Why do you feel you have to come with me?'

He shot a quick glance at me. I noticed his hands gripping the wheel so tightly that the knuckles showed white. He didn't say anything for a few minutes and I thought perhaps he was going to ignore me altogether. Finally he said in his deep, tight voice, 'Who asked you to come down to the Port?'

'No one: I came on my own. Boom Boom Warshawski was my cousin and I feel an obligation to find out the circumstances surrounding his death.'

'Argus came to the funeral. Did he suggest there was anything wrong?'

'What are you trying to tell me, Phillips? Is there some reason to think that my cousin's death was not an accident?'

'No. No,' he repeated quickly. He smiled and suddenly looked more human. 'He came down here on Thursday – Argus did – and put us through the wringer on safety at the elevators. He took a personal interest in your cousin and he was very upset when he died. I just wondered if he'd asked you to investigate this as part of your professional function rather than as Warshawski's cousin.'

'I see . . . Well, Mr Argus didn't hire me. I guess I hired myself.' I thought about explaining my personal concern but my detective training made me cautious. Rule number something or other – never tell anybody anything unless you're going to get something better in return. Maybe someday I'd write up a *Manual for the Neophyte Detective*.

We were driving past the elevators lining the Calumet River and the entrance to the main Port. Large ships loomed everywhere, poking black smokestacks between gray columns of grain and cement elevators. Little trees struggled for life in patches of earth between railroad tracks, slag heaps, and pitted roadbeds. We passed a dead steel mill, a massive complex of rust-red buildings and railway junctions. The cyclone fence was padlocked shut at the entrance: the recession having its impact – the plant was closed.

The headquarters for the Port of Chicago were completely rebuilt a few years ago. With new buildings, modern docks, and a well-paved road the place looked modern and efficient. Phillips stopped at a guard station where a city cop looked up from his paper and nodded him in. The Alfa purred across smooth tarmac and we stopped in a slot labeled EUDORA GRAIN. We locked the doors and I followed Phillips toward a row of modern buildings.

Everything here was built on a giant scale. A series of cranes towered over the slips for the ships. Giant teeth hovered over one huge vessel and easily lifted the back of a fifty-ton semi from a stack and lowered it onto a waiting truck bed. Some ten ships were docked here at the main facility, flying the flags of many nations.

All the Port buildings are constructed from the same tan brick, two stories high. The Grafalk Steamship Line offices occupied all of one of the larger blocks halfway along the wharf. A receptionist, middle-aged and pleasant, recognized Phillips by sight and sent us on back to see Percy MacKelvy, the dispatcher.

Phillips was clearly a frequent visitor. Greeting various people by name, he led me through a narrow hall which crossed a couple of small rooms. We found the dispatcher in an office crammed with paper. Charts covered every wall and stacks of paper hid the desk, three chairs, and a good deal of the floor. A rumpled man in his mid-forties, wearing a white shirt long since wrinkled for the day, MacKelvy was on the phone when we came in. He took a cigar out of his mouth long enough to say hello.

He grunted into the phone, moved a red tack on a chart of the lakes at his right hand, punched a query into a computer terminal next to the phone, and grunted again. Finally he said, 'Six eighty-three a ton. Take it or leave it . . . Pick up on the fourth, six eighty-two . . . Can't bring it any lower than that . . . No deal? Maybe next time.' He hung up, added a few numbers to the terminal, and snatched up a second phone which had started to ring. 'This is a zoo,' he said to me, loosening his tie further. 'MacKelvy . . . Yeah, yeah.' I watched as he followed a similar sequence with chart, tacks, and computer.

When he hung up he said, 'Hi, Clayton. This the lady you mentioned?'

'Hi,' I said. 'I'm V. I. Warshawski. My cousin Bernard Warshawski was killed last Monday when he fell under the *Bertha Krupnik*'s propeller.'

The phone was ringing again. 'Yeah? MacKelvy here. Yeah, hold on just a second . . . You figuring the *Bertha* was at fault somehow?'

'No. I have some personal concerns as my cousin's executor. I'd like to know if anyone saw the accident. Phillips here says you can tell me when the *Bertha* might be expected, either back here, or at some port where I could go talk to the crew.'

'Hi, Duff,' he spoke into the phone. 'Sulphur from Buffalo? Three eighty-eight a ton, pick up on the sixth, deliver to Chicago on the eighth. You got it.' He hung up. 'What's the scoop, Clayton? She likely to sue?'

Phillips was standing as far from the desk as possible in the crowded room. He stood very still as if to make himself psychologically as well as physically remote. He shrugged. 'David has expressed some interest.'

'What about Niels?'

'I haven't discussed it with him.'

I put my hands on the mass of papers and leaned across the desk as the phone rang again.

'MacKelvy here . . . Hi, Gumboldt. Hold on a sec, will you?'

'Mr MacKelvy, I'm not a hysterical widow trying to get financial restitution from the easiest possible source. I'm trying to find anyone who might have seen my cousin in the last minutes of his life. We're talking about an open dock at ten in the morning. I can't believe not a living soul saw him. I want to talk with the crew on the *Bertha* just to make sure.'

'Yeah, Gum? Yeah . . . yeah . . . Toledo on the sixteenth? How about the seventeenth? Can't help ya, fella. Night of the sixteenth? Say two-three in the morning? . . . Okay, fella, some other time.' He shook his head worriedly. 'Business is rotten. The steel slump's killing us and so are the thousand-footers. Thank God, Eudora's still shipping with us.'

The constant interruptions were getting on my nerves. 'I'm sure I can find the *Bertha Krupnik*, Mr MacKelvy. I'm a private investigator and I'm used to tracking things down. An active ship on the Great Lakes can't be that difficult to locate. I'm just asking you to make it easier.'

MacKelvy shrugged. 'I'll have to talk to Niels. He's coming down here for lunch, Miss – who'd you say? – and I'll check with him then. Stop back here around two. Right, Clayton?'

The phone rang again. 'Who's Niels?' I asked Phillips as we walked out of the office.

'Niels Grafalk. He owns Grafalk Steamship.'

'Want to give me a lift back to your office? I can pick up my car there and leave you to your meetings.'

His pale eyes were darting around the hall, as if looking for someone or trying to get help from someplace. 'Uh, sure.'

We were in the front office, Phillips saying good-bye to the receptionist, when we heard a tremendous crash. I felt a shudder through the concrete floor and then the sound of glass breaking and metal screaming. The receptionist got out of her chair, startled.

'What was that?'

A couple of people came into the reception room from inside the building. 'An earthquake?' 'Sounds like a car crash.' 'Was the building hit?' 'Is the building falling over?'

I went to the outer door. Car crash? Maybe, but a damned big car. Maybe one of those semis they'd been loading?

Outside a large crowd was gathering. A siren in the distance grew louder. And at the north end of the pier a freighter stood, nose plowed into the side of the dock. Large chunks of concrete had broken in front of it like a metal road divider before a speeding car. Glass fragments broke loose from the sides of the ship as I moved with the crowd to gawk. A tall crane at the edge of the wharf twisted and slowly fell, crumpling on itself like a dying swan.

Two police cars, blue lights flashing, squealed to a stop as close to the disaster as possible. I jumped to one side to avoid an ambulance wailing and honking behind me. The crowd in front of me parted to let it through. I followed quickly in its wake and made it close to the wreck.

A crane and a couple of forklift trucks had been waiting at dockside. All three were thoroughly chewed up by the oncoming freighter. The police helped the ambulance driver pry one of the forklift drivers out of the mess of crumpled steel. An ugly sight. The crowd – stevedores, drivers, crew members – watched avidly. Disasters are good bowling-league conversation pieces.

I turned away and found a man in a dirty white boiler suit looking at me. His face was sunburned dark red-brown and his eyes were a deep bright blue. 'What happened?' I asked.

He shrugged. 'Ship rammed the dock. My guess is they were bringing it in from the engine room and someone went full ahead instead of full astern.'

'Sorry, I'm a stranger here. Can you translate?'

'Know anything about how to steer a ship?'

I shook my head.

'Oh. Well, it's hard to explain without showing you the controls. But basically you have two levers, one for each screw. Now if you're out at sea you steer by turning the wheel. But coming into the dock, you use the levers. Putting one full ahead and one full astern – toward the back, that is – will swing you to the right or the left, depending on which one you move which way. Putting both of them full astern is like putting your car in reverse. Slows the ship way down and brings you gently up against the wharf. It looks like some poor bastard thought that was what he was doing but went full ahead instead.'

'I see. It seems strange that a little thing like that could cause so much damage.'

'Well, if you drove your car at the pier – assuming you could get down in the water and do it – you'd be chewed up and the concrete walls would laugh at you. But your car – what kind do you drive? – about a ton and two hundred horsepower? Now that thing has twelve thousand horsepower and weighs around ten thousand tons. They did the equivalent of flooring her accelerator and that's the result.'

Someone had rigged a ladder up to the front of the ship. A couple

274

of crew members, rather shaky, came down onto the pier. I felt a hand on my shoulder and jerked around. A tall man with a sunburned face and a magnificent shock of white hair shouldered past me. 'Excuse me. Out of the way, please.'

The police, who were keeping everyone else back from the forklift trucks and the ladder, let the white-haired man through without a question.

'Who's that?' I asked my informative acquaintance. 'He looks like a Viking.'

'He is a Viking. That's Niels Grafalk. He owns this sorry hunk of steel . . . Poor devil!'

Niels Grafalk. I didn't think the timing was too hot to go swarming up the ladder after him in search of the *Bertha Krupnik*. Unless . . .

'Is this the *Bertha Krupnik*?'

'No,' my friend answered. 'It's the *Leif Ericsson*. You got some special interest in the *Bertha*?'

'Yeah, I'm trying to find out where she is. I can't get MacKelvy – d'you know him? – to let the information loose without Grafalk's say-so. You wouldn't know, would you?'

When my acquaintance wanted to know the reason, I felt an impulse to shut up and go home. I couldn't think of anything much stupider than my obsession about Boom Boom and his accident. Obviously, from the crowd converging here, disaster brought a lot of people to the scene. Margolis had been right: if the men at the elevator knew anything about Boom Boom's death, they would have been talking about it. It was probably high time to return to Chicago and serve some processes to their reluctant recipients.

My companion saw my hesitation. 'Look – it's time for lunch. Why don't you let me take you over to the Salle de la Mer – it's the private club for owners and officers here. I just need to shed this boiler suit and get a jacket.'

I looked at my jeans and running shoes. 'I'm hardly dressed for a private club.'

He assured me they didn't care about what women wore – only men have to observe clothing rules in the modern restaurant. He left me to watch the débâcle at the pier for a few minutes while he went to change. I was wondering vaguely what had happened to Phillips when I saw him picking his way tentatively through the crowd to the *Leif Ericsson*. Something in his hesitant manner irritated me profoundly.

5

A GLASS IN THE HAND

'I'm Mike Sheridan, chief engineer on the *Lucella Wieser*.'

'And I'm V. I. Warshawski, a private investigator.'

The waiter brought our drinks, white wine for me and vodka and tonic for Sheridan.

'You're related to Boom Boom Warshawski, aren't you?'

'I'm his cousin . . . You connected with the *Lucella Wieser* that was across from the *Bertha Krupnik* when he fell under the propeller last week?'

He agreed, and I commented enthusiastically on what a small world it was. 'I've been trying to find someone who might have seen my cousin die. To tell you the truth, I think it's pretty hopeless — judging by the crowd that wreck out there drew.' I explained my search and why the *Lucella* was included in it.

Sheridan drank some vodka. 'I have to admit I knew who you were when you were standing on the wharf. Someone pointed you out to me and I wanted to talk to you.' He smiled apologetically. 'People gossip a lot in a place like this . . . Your cousin was coming over to talk to John Bemis, the *Lucella*'s captain, that afternoon. He claimed to know something about an act of vandalism that kept us from loading for a week. In fact that's why we were tied up across the way: we were supposed to be taking on grain at that Eudora elevator, but we ended up with water in our holds. We had to dry them out and get Board of Health clearance again before we could load.'

'You mean someone deliberately put water in your holds? That was the vandalism?'

He nodded. 'We assumed it was done by a disgruntled crewman.

We asked him to leave the ship. He didn't raise a fuss about it so I think we were right. But your cousin sounded serious, and of course Bemis wanted to talk to him. You wouldn't know anything about what was on his mind, would you?'

I shook my head. 'That's part of my problem. I hadn't seen Boom Boom for two or three months before he died. To tell you the truth, I was mostly worried that he might have – well, let himself fall because he was terribly depressed about not being able to skate or play hockey any more. But, from what you're saying and what Pete Margolis at the elevator said, he'd gotten pretty involved in what was going on down here, not depressed at all. I'd sure like to know, though, if anyone on the *Bertha* or the *Lucella* saw the accident firsthand.'

Sheridan shook his head. 'It's true we were tied up across the way, but the *Bertha Krupnik* lay between us and the wharf. I don't think anyone on the *Lucella* could have seen anything.'

The waiter came back to take our orders; we told him we needed a few minutes to study the menu. He was back again within thirty seconds, coughing apologetically.

'Mr Grafalk wants to know if you and the lady would join him and Mr Phillips at his table.'

Sheridan and I looked at each other in surprise. I hadn't noticed either of them come in. We followed the waiter across the rose and purple carpet to a table in the corner on the other side. Grafalk stood up to shake hands with Sheridan.

'Thanks for interrupting your lunch to join us, Mike.' To me he added, 'I'm Niels Grafalk.'

'How do you do, Mr Grafalk. I'm V. I. Warshawski.'

Grafalk wore a soft tweed jacket, tailored to fit his body, and an open-necked white shirt. I didn't have to know he was born with money to feel that he was a man used to controlling things around him. He exuded a seafaring atmosphere, his hair bleached white, his face red with wind and sunburn.

'Phillips here told me you were asking some questions of Percy MacKelvy. Since I'm on the spot, maybe you can tell me why you're interested in Grafalk Steamship.'

I embarked on a story which by now seemed very threadbare. 'Mr

278

PENGUIN BOOKS

V. I. WARSHAWSKI

Sara Paretsky was brought up in rural Kansas. After a variety of jobs ranging from dishwashing to marketing she now writes full time. She is a founder and past President of Sisters in Crime, an advocacy group for women in the thriller field. She lives in Chicago with a University of Chicago physicist and their golden retriever.

She is the author of several V. I. Warshawski stories, of which Penguin publish *Indemnity Only*; *Deadlock*; *Killing Orders* (also published together in one volume under the title *V. I. Warshawski*); *Bitter Medicine*; *Toxic Shock*, winner of the 1988 Crime Writers' Association Silver Dagger Award; *Blood Shot*; *Burn Marks*; *Guardian Angel*; *Tunnel Vision*, which was shortlisted for the 1994 Crime Writers' Association Gold Dagger Award; and her short-story collection, *Windy City Blues*, based on V. I. Warshawski, starring Kathleen Turner,

MacKelvy thought he ought to check with you before he told me where the *Bertha Krupnik* is,' I finished.

'I see.' Grafalk looked at me sharply. 'Phillips told me you were a private investigator. I thought maybe you'd decided to do some snooping around my company.'

'When people meet a policeman unexpectedly they often feel guilty: nameless crimes rise up to confront them. When they meet a private investigator they usually feel defensive: don't come snooping around me. I'm used to it,' I said.

Grafalk threw his head back and let out a loud crack of laughter. Sheridan gave me a sardonic smile but Phillips looked as strained as ever.

'If you have a minute after lunch, walk back with me to the office – I'll get Percy to cough up the *Bertha*'s whereabouts for you.'

The waiter came to take our order. I asked for a whole artichoke stuffed with shrimp. Grafalk chose grilled lake trout, as did Phillips. Sheridan ordered a steak. 'When you spend nine months of your life on the water, beef has a solid, earthy appeal.'

'So tell me, how does a young woman like you get involved in a career as a detective? You work for a firm or for yourself?'

'I've been in business for myself for about six years. Before that I was an attorney with the Public Defender in Cook County. I got tired of seeing poor innocent chumps go off to Stateville because the police wouldn't follow up our investigations and find the real culprits. And I got even more tired of watching clever guilty rascals get off scot-free because they could afford attorneys who know how to tap-dance around the law. So I thought – *à la* Doña Quixote perhaps – that I'd see what I could do on my own about the situation.'

Grafalk smiled with amusement over a glass of Niersteiner gutes Domthal. 'Who usually hires you?'

'I do a certain amount of financial crime – that's my specialty. The Transicon Company; that business last year with Ajax Insurance and the Knifegrinders . . . I just finished a job involving computer fraud in wire transfers at a small bank in Peoria. I fill in the gaps tracking down missing witnesses and serving subpoenas on people anxious to avoid a day in court.'

Grafalk was watching me with the same amused smile – wealthy man enjoying the foibles of the middle class: what do the simple folk do if they don't own a steamship company? The smile grew rigid. He was looking at someone behind me whom he apparently didn't want to see. I turned as a stocky man in a gray business suit walked up to the table.

'Hello, Martin.'

'Hello, Niels . . . Hi, Sheridan. Niels trying to enlist your help with the *Ericsson*?'

'Hi, Martin. This is V. I. Warshawski. She's Boom Boom Warshawski's cousin – down here asking us all a few questions about his death,' Sheridan said.

'How do you do, Miss Warshawski. I was very sorry about the accident to your cousin. None of us knew him well, but we all admired him as a hockey player.'

'Thanks,' I said.

He was introduced as Martin Bledsoe, owner of the Pole Star Line, which included the *Lucella Wieser*. He took a vacant chair between Sheridan and Phillips, asking Grafalk after he sat down if it was okay to join us.

'Glad to have you, Martin,' the Viking said warmly. I must have imagined the strain in his smile a few minutes before.

'Sorry about the *Ericsson*, Niels. Hell of a mess out there. You figure out what happened?'

'Looked to me like she ran into the dock, Martin. But we'll know for sure after we've made a complete investigation.'

I suddenly wondered what Grafalk was doing eating a leisurely lunch when he had several hundred thousand dollars' worth of damage sitting outside.

'What happens in a case like this?' I asked. 'Do you have insurance to cover your hull damage?'

'Yes.' Grafalk grimaced. 'We have coverage for everything. But it'll boost my premium by a good deal . . . I'd rather not think about it right now, if you don't mind.'

I changed the subject by asking him some general questions about shipping. His family owned the oldest company still operating on the

Great Lakes. It was also the biggest. An early ancestor from Norway had started it in 1838 with a clipper that carried fur and ore from Chicago to Buffalo. Grafalk became quite enthusiastic, recounting some of the great ships and shipwrecks of the family fleet, then caught himself up apologetically. 'Sorry – I'm a fanatic on shipping history . . . My family's been involved in it for so long . . . Anyway, my private yacht is called the *Brynulf Nordemark* in memory of the captain who went down so gallantly in the disaster of 1857.'

'Grafalk's a fantastic sailor in his own right,' Phillips put in. 'He keeps two sailboats – his grandfather's old yacht and a racing boat. You sail in the Mackinac race every year, don't you, Niels?'

'I've only missed two since graduating from college – that probably happened before you were born, Miss Warshawski.'

He'd been to Northwestern, another family tradition. I vaguely remembered a Grafalk Hall on the Northwestern campus and the Grafalk Maritime Museum next to Shedd Aquarium.

'What about the Pole Star Line?' I asked Bledsoe. 'That an old family company?'

'Martin's a Johnny-come-lately,' Grafalk said lightly. 'How old's P S L now? Eight years?'

'I used to have Percy MacKelvy's job,' Bledsoe said. 'So Niels remembers every day since my desertion.'

'Well, Martin, you were the best dispatcher in the industry. Of course I felt deserted when you wanted to go into competition against me . . . By the way, I heard about the sabotage on the *Lucella*. That sounded like an ugly incident. It was one of your crew members?'

Waiters were bringing our entrées. Even though they slid the plates in front of us, barely moving the airwaves, it was enough of a distraction that I missed Bledsoe's facial reaction.

'Well, the damage was minor, after all,' he said. 'I was furious at the time, but at least the ship is intact: it'd be a pain in the ass to have to spend the main part of the season patching the *Lucella*'s hull.'

'True enough,' Grafalk agreed. 'You do have two smaller ships, though, don't you?' He smiled at me blandly. 'We have sixty-three other vessels to pick up any slack the *Ericsson*'s incapacitation has caused.'

I wondered what the hell was going on here. Phillips was sitting stiffly, not making any pretense of eating, while Sheridan seemed to be casting about for something to say. Grafalk ate some minced vegetables and Bledsoe attacked his broiled swordfish with gusto.

'And even though my engineer really screwed up down there, I'm convinced that the guy just got overexcited and made a mistake. It's not like having deliberate vandalism among the crew.'

'You're right,' Bledsoe said. 'I did wonder if this was part of your program to junk your 360-footers.'

Grafalk dropped his fork. A waiter moved forward and wafted a new one to the table. 'We're satisfied with what we've got out there,' Grafalk said. 'I do hope you've isolated *your* trouble, though, Martin.'

'I hope so too,' Bledsoe said politely, picking up his wineglass.

'It's so distressing when someone in your organization turns out to be unreliable,' Grafalk persisted.

'I wouldn't go that far,' Bledsoe responded, 'but then I've never shared the Hobbesian view of the social contract with you.'

Grafalk smiled. 'You'll have to explain that one to me, Martin.' He turned to me again. 'At Martin's school they went in for a lot of memorizing. I had an easier time, being a gentleman: we weren't expected to know anything.'

I was starting to laugh when I heard glass shatter. I turned with the rest to stare at Bledsoe. He had crushed his wineglass in his hand and the clear shards sticking out of his palm were rapidly engulfed in red. As I leaped to my feet to send for a doctor I wondered what all that had been about. Of all the remarks exchanged, Grafalk's last one had been the least offensive. Why had it produced such an extraordinary reaction?

I sent a very concerned maître d'hôtel to call an ambulance. He confided in a moment of unprofessional panic that he knew he should never have allowed Mr Bledsoe to join Mr Grafalk. But then – Mr Bledsoe was not a gentleman, he had no sensitivity, one could not keep him from barging in where he did not belong.

Quiet panic prevailed at our table. The men stared helplessly at the pool of red growing on the tablecloth, on Bledsoe's cuff, on his lap. I told them an ambulance was coming and meanwhile we should probably try to get as much glass as possible out of his hand. I sent the waiters for another ice bucket and began packing Bledsoe's hand with ice and some extra napkins.

Bledsoe was in pain but not in danger of fainting. Instead he was cursing himself steadily for his stupidity.

'You're right,' I said. 'It was damned stupid. In fact I don't know when I've ever seen anything to compare with it. But fretting over it won't alter the past, so why don't you concentrate on the present instead?' He smiled a bit at that and thanked me for my help.

I glanced briefly at Grafalk. He was watching us with a strange expression. It wasn't pity and it wasn't satisfaction. Speculative. But what about?

6

A CAPITAL SHIP

After the ambulance carted Bledsoe away, everyone returned to lunch a little furtively, as though eating were in bad taste. The headwaiter cleared Bledsoe's place with palpable relief and brought Grafalk a fresh bottle of Niersteiner gutes Domthal – 'with our compliments, sir.'

'They don't like your boss here,' I said to Sheridan.

The chief engineer shrugged. 'The maître d' is a snob. Martin's a self-made man and that offends him. Niels here brings class to his joint. Martin slashes his hand open and Niels gets a free bottle of wine so he won't be offended and drop his membership.'

Grafalk laughed. 'You're right. The most insufferable snobs are the hangers-on to the rich. If we lose our glamor, they lose the basis for their existence.'

While we talked Phillips kept darting glances at his watch and muttering. 'Uh, Niels,' in his tight voice. He reminded me of a child tugging at its mother's skirts while she's absorbed in conversation – Grafalk gave him about the same amount of attention. Finally Phillips stood up. 'Uh, Niels, I'd better leave now. I have a meeting with, uh, Rodriguez.'

Grafalk looked at his watch. 'We'd all better be going, I guess. Miss Warshawski, let me take you over to Percy MacKelvy and get the *Bertha Krupnik*'s location for you.' He got a bill from the waiter and signed it without looking at the amount, politely waiting for me to finish. I dug the heart out of my artichoke and cut it into four pieces, savoring each one, before putting my napkin to one side and getting up.

Phillips lingered with us in the doorway, despite his meeting. He seemed to be waiting for some sign from Grafalk, a recognition of who he was, perhaps, that would enable him to leave in peace. The power of the rich to bestow meaning on people seemed as though it might work with Phillips.

'Don't you have a meeting, Clayton?' Grafalk asked.

'Uh, yes. Yes.' Phillips turned at that and walked back across the tarmac to his Alfa.

Sheridan accompanied me over to Grafalk's office. 'I want you to come back to the *Lucella* and talk to Captain Bemis when you're finished here,' he said. 'We need to know if you can tell us anything about what your cousin wanted to say.'

I couldn't, of course, but I wanted to know what they could tell me about Boom Boom, so I agreed.

Our visit to Grafalk's office was interrupted by reporters, a television crew, and an anxious phone call from the chairman of Ajax Insurance, which covered Grafalk Steamship.

Grafalk handled all of these with genial urbanity. Treating me like a treasured guest, he asked the NBC television crew to wait while he answered a question for me. He took the call from Ajax chairman Gordon Firth in MacKelvy's office.

'Just a minute, Gordon. I have an attractive young lady here who needs some information.' He put Firth on hold and asked MacKelvy to dig up the *Bertha*'s location. She was making a tour of the Great Lakes, picking up coal in Pittsburgh to drop in Detroit, then steaming up to Thunder Bay. She'd be back in Chicago in two weeks. MacKelvy was to instruct the captain to place himself and the crew at my disposal. Grafalk brushed my thanks aside: Boom Boom had been an impressive young man, just the kind of person the shipping industry needed to attract. Whatever they could do to help, just let him know. He returned to Firth and I found my way out alone.

Sheridan had waited for me outside, away from the reporters and television crews. As I came out the cameraman thrust a microphone under my nose. Had I seen the disaster, what did I think of it – all the inane questions television reporters ask in the wake of a disaster. 'Unparalleled tragedy,' I said. 'Mr Grafalk will give you the details.'

Sheridan grinned as I ducked away from the mike. 'You're quicker on your feet than I am – I couldn't think of a snappy remark on the spur of the moment.'

We walked down the pier to the parking lot where his Capri sat. As he backed it out of the lot he asked if Grafalk had told me what I wanted to know.

'Yeah. He was pretty gracious about it.' Overwhelmingly gracious. I wondered if he were bent on erasing any unfavorable ideas I might have picked up as a result of his interchange with Bledsoe. 'Why did Grafalk's remark about where Bledsoe went to school upset him so much?' I asked abruptly.

'Was that what set him off? I couldn't remember.'

'Grafalk said: "At Martin's school they went in for a lot of memorizing." Then something about *his* being a gentleman and not needing to know anything. Even if Bledsoe went to some tacky place like West Schaumburg Tech, that's scarcely a reason to shatter a wineglass in your fist.'

Sheridan braked at a light at 103rd and Torrence. A Howard Johnson's on our left struggled ineffectually with prairie grass and a junk-yard. Sheridan turned right. 'I don't think Martin went to school at all. He grew up in Cleveland and started sailing when he was sixteen by lying about his age. Maybe he doesn't like a North-western man reminding him he's self-educated.'

That didn't make sense – self-educated people are usually proud of the fact. 'Well, why is there so much animosity between him and Grafalk?'

'Oh, that's easy to explain. Niels looks on Grafalk Steamship as a fiefdom. He's filthy rich, has lots of other holdings, but the shipping company's the only thing he cares about. If you work for him, he thinks it's a lifelong contract, just like a baron swearing loyalty to William the Conqueror or something.

'I know: I started my career at Grafalk. He was sore as hell when I left. John Bemis too – the captain of the *Lucella*. But our going never bugged him when we left the way it did with Martin. He regarded that as the ultimate betrayal, maybe because Martin was the best dispatcher on the lakes. Which is why Pole Star's done as well as it has. Martin has that sixth sense that tells him what fraction of a dollar he can offer to be the low bidder and still make a profit.'

We were pulling into the yard of another elevator. Sheridan bumped the car across the ruts and parked behind a weather-beaten shed. Four hopper cars were being maneuvered on the tracks in front of us onto the elevator hoist. We picked our way around them, through the ground floor of the giant building, and out to the wharf.

The *Lucella* loomed high above us. Her red paint was smooth and unchipped. She made the other ships I'd seen that day look like puny tubs. A thousand feet long, her giant hull filled the near horizon. I felt the familiar churning in my stomach and shut my eyes briefly before following Sheridan up a steel ladder attached to her side.

He climbed briskly. I followed quickly, putting from my mind the thought of the black depths below, of the hull thrusting invisibly into murky water, of the sea, alive and menacing.

We met Captain Bemis in the mahogany-paneled bridge perched on top of the pilothouse. Through glass windows encircling the bridge we could see the deck stretching away beneath us. Men in yellow slickers were washing out the holds with high-pressure hoses.

Captain Bemis was a sturdy, short man, barely my height. He had steady gray eyes and a calm manner – useful, no doubt, in a high sea. He called down to the deck on a walkie-talkie to his first mate, asking him to join us. A yellow-slickered figure detached itself from the group on deck and disappeared into the pilothouse.

'We're very concerned about this vandalism to the *Lucella*,' Bemis told me. 'We were sorry when young Warshawski died. But we'd also like to know what it was he had to say.'

I shook my head. 'I don't know. I hadn't talked to Boom Boom for several months . . . I was hoping he might have said something to you that would give me a clue about his state of mind.'

Bemis gave a frustrated sign. 'He wanted to talk to us about this business with the holds. Sheridan told you about that? Well, Warshawski asked if we'd found the culprit. I told him yes. He said he thought there might be more to it than just a dissatisfied seaman. He had some additional checking to do, but he wanted to talk to me the next day.'

The first mate came onto the bridge and Bemis stopped talking to introduce me. The mate's name was Keith Winstein. He was a wiry young man, perhaps thirty years old, with a shock of curly black hair.

'I'm telling her about the business with young Warshawski,' Bemis explained to the mate. 'Anyway, Keith here and I waited on the bridge until five on Tuesday, hoping to talk to him. Then we got the news that he'd died.'

'So no one here saw him fall!' I exclaimed.

The first mate shook his head regretfully. 'I'm sorry, but we didn't even realize there'd been an accident. We were tied up across the way, but none of our men was on deck when the ambulance came.'

I felt a sharp twist of disappointment. It seemed so – so unfair that Boom Boom could slide out of life without one person to see him do it. I tried to concentrate on the captain and his problem, but none of it seemed important to me. I felt stupid, as though I'd wasted a day. What had I expected to find out, anyway? Rushing around the wharf, playing detective, just to avoid admitting that my cousin was dead.

I suggested to Bemis and Winstein that they find the man they'd fired and question him more thoroughly, then pleaded a meeting in the Loop and asked the chief engineer to drive me back to the Eudora Grain parking lot. I picked up my Lynx there and headed north.

7
WATCHMAN, TELL US
OF THE NIGHT

My apartment is the large, inexpensive top of a three-flat on Halsted, north of Belmont. Every year the hip young professionals in Lincoln Park move a little closer, threatening to chase me farther north with their condominium conversions, their wine bars, and their designer running clothes. So far Diversey, two blocks south, has held firm as the dividing line, but it could go any day.

I got home around seven, exhausted and confused. On the long drive back, snarled in commuter traffic for two hours, I'd wrestled with my depression. By the time I parked in front of my gray stone building the gloom had lifted a bit. I began wondering about some of the strange behavior down at the Port.

I poured myself a solid two fingers of Black Label and ran a bath. When you thought about it, it was very odd that Boom Boom had called the captain, made an appointment to discuss vandalism, and then died. It hadn't even occurred to me to ask Bemis or Winstein about the papers Boom Boom might have stolen.

It sounded as though Boom Boom might have been playing detective. Maybe that was why he was calling me – not out of despair but for a professional consultation. What had he discovered? Something worth my finding out too? Was I still looking for some deeper importance to his death than an accident, or was there something to know?

I sipped my whisky. I couldn't sort my feelings out enough to tell. It was incredible to me that someone might kill Boom Boom to keep him from talking to Bemis. Still. What about the tension between Grafalk and Bledsoe? Boom Boom's death following so quickly after his phone call to Bemis? The accident today at the wharf?

I got out of the tub and wrapped myself in a red bath sheet and poured another slug of Scotch. There were enough odd actions down at the Port that it would be worth my asking a few more questions. Anyway, I thought, tossing off the whisky, so what if I work out my grief by carrying out an investigation? Is that any stupider than getting drunk or whatever else people do when someone they love dies?

I put on a pair of clean jeans and a T-shirt and wandered out to the kitchen. A depressing sight – pans stacked around the sink, crumbs on the table, an old piece of aluminum foil, cheese congealed on the stove from a pasta primavera I'd made a few nights ago. I set about washing up – there are days when the mess hits you so squarely that you can't add to it.

The refrigerator didn't have much of interest in it. The wooden clock by the back door said nine – too late to go out for dinner, as tired as I was, so I settled for a bowl of canned pea soup and some toast.

Over another Scotch I watched the tail end of a depressing Cubs defeat in New York – their eighth in a row. The New Tradition takes hold, I thought gloomily, and went to bed.

I woke up around six to another cold cloudy day. The first week in May and the weather was like November. I put on my long running pants and conscientiously did five miles around Belmont Harbor and back. I'd been using Boom Boom's death as an excuse for indolence and the run left me panting more than it should have.

I drank orange juice, showered, and had some fresh-ground coffee with a hard roll and cheese. It was seven-thirty. I was due at Eudora Grain in three hours to talk to the men. In the interim I could go back for a quick scan of Boom Boom's belongings. I'd been looking for something personal on my previous visit, something that might indicate his state of mind. This time I'd concentrate on something that indicated a crime.

A small trickle of beautifully suited lawyers and doctors oozed from the 210 East Chestnut building. They had the unhealthy faces of people who eat and drink too much most of the time but keep their weight down through strenuous diets and racquetball in between. One of them held the door without really noticing me.

Up in Boom Boom's condo I stopped again for a few minutes to look at the lake. The wind whipped whitecaps up on the green water. A tiny red sliver moved on the horizon, a freighter on its journey to the other side of the lakes. I stared for a long time before bracing my shoulders and heading to the study.

An appalling sight met me. The papers I had left in eight discrete piles were thrown pell-mell around the room. Drawers were open-ended, pictures pulled from the wall, pillows torn from a daybed in the corner and the bedding strewn about.

The wreckage was so confused and so violent that the worst abomination didn't hit me for a few seconds. A body lay crumpled in the corner on the far side of the desk.

I walked gingerly past the mess of papers, trying not to disturb the chaos lest it contain any evidence. The man was dead. He held a gun in his hand, a Smith & Wesson .358, but he'd never used it. His neck had been broken, as nearly as I could tell without moving the body – I couldn't see any wounds.

I lifted the head gently. The face stared at me impassively, the same expressionless face that had looked at me two nights ago in the lobby. It was the old black man who'd been on night duty. I lowered his head carefully and sprinted to Boom Boom's lavish bathroom.

I drank a glass of water from the bathroom tap and the heaving subsided in my stomach. Using the phone next to the king-size bed to call the police, I noticed that the bedroom had come in for some minor disruption. The red and purple painting on the wall had been taken down and the magazines thrown to the floor. Drawers stood open in the polished walnut dresser and socks and underwear were on the floor.

I went through the rest of the apartment. Someone had clearly been looking for something. But what?

The night guard's name had been Henry Kelvin. Mrs Kelvin came with the police to identify the body, a dark, dignified woman whose grief was more impressive for the restraint with which she contained it.

The cops who showed up insisted on treating this as an ordinary break-in. Boom Boom's death had been widely publicized. Some enterprising burglar no doubt took advantage of the situation; it was unfortunate that Kelvin had surprised him in the act. I kept pointing out that nothing of value had been taken but they insisted that Kelvin's death had frightened off the intruders. In the end I gave up on it.

I called Margolis, the elevator foreman, to explain that I would be delayed, perhaps until the following day. At noon the police finished with me and took the body away on a stretcher. They were going to seal the apartment until they finished fingerprinting and analyzing everything.

I took a last look around. Either the intruders had found what they came for, or my cousin had hidden what they were looking for elsewhere, or there was nothing to find but they were running scared. My mind flicked to Paige Carrington. Love letters? How close had she been to Boom Boom, really? I needed to talk to her again. Maybe to some of my cousin's friends as well.

Mrs Kelvin was sitting stiffly on the edge of one of the nubby white sofas in the lobby. When I got off the elevator she came over to me.

'I need to talk to you.' Her voice was harsh, the voice of someone who wanted to cry and was becoming angry instead.

'All right. I have an office downtown. Will that do?'

She looked around the exposed lobby, at the residents staring at her on their way to and from the elevator, and agreed. She followed me silently outside and over to Delaware, where I'd found a place to squeeze my little Mercury. Someday I'd have enough money for something really wonderful, like an Audi Quarto. But in the meantime I buy American.

Mrs Kelvin didn't say anything on the way downtown. I parked the car in a garage across from the Pulteney Building. She didn't spare a glance for the dirty mosaic floors and the pitted marble walls. Fortunately the tired elevator was functioning. It creaked down to the ground floor and saved me the embarrassment of asking her to climb the four flights to my office.

We walked to the east end of the hall where my office overlooks the Wabash Avenue el, the side where cheap rents are even lower because of the noise. A train was squeaking and rattling its way past as I unlocked the door and ushered her to the armchair I keep for visitors.

I took the seat behind my desk, a big wooden model I picked up at a police auction. My desk faces the wall so that open space lies between me and my clients. I've never liked using furniture for hiding or intimidating.

Mrs Kelvin sat stiffly in the armchair, her black handbag upright in her lap. Her black hair was straightened and shaped away from her long face in severely regimented waves. She wore no make-up except for a dark orange lipstick.

'You talked to my husband Tuesday night, didn't you?' she finally said.

'Yes, I did.' I kept my voice neutral. People talk more when you make yourself part of their scenery.

She nodded to herself. 'He came home and told me about it. This job was pretty boring for him, so anything out of the way happened, he told me about it.' She nodded again. 'You young Warshawski's executor or something, that right?'

'I'm his cousin and his executor. My name is V. I. Warshawski.'

'My husband wasn't a hockey fan, but he liked young Warshawski. Anyway, he came home Tuesday night – yesterday morning that would be – and told me some uppity white girl was telling him to look after the boy's apartment. That was you.' She nodded again. I didn't say anything.

'Now Henry did not need anybody telling him how to do his job.' She gave an angry half sob and controlled herself again. 'But you told him special not to let anyone into your cousin's apartment. So you must have known something was going on. Is that right?'

I looked at her steadily and shook my head. 'The day man, Hinckley, had let someone into the apartment without my knowing about it ahead of time. There were things there that some crazy fan would find valuable – his hockey stick, stuff like that – and legal documents I didn't want anyone else going through.'

'You didn't know someone was going to break in like that?'

'No, Mrs Kelvin. If I'd had any suspicion of such a thing I would have taken greater precautions.'

She compressed her lips. 'You say you had no suspicion. Yet you took it upon yourself to tell my husband how to do his job.'

'I didn't know your husband, Mrs Kelvin. I'd never met him. So I couldn't see whether he was the kind of person who took his work seriously. I wasn't trying to tell him how to do his job, just trying to safeguard the interests my cousin left to my charge.'

'Well, he told me, he said, "I don't know who that girl" – that's you – "thinks is going to try to get into that place. But I got my eye on it." So he plays the hero, and he gets killed. But you say you weren't expecting anything special.'

'I'm sorry,' I said.

'Sorry doesn't bring the dead back to life.'

After she left I sat for a long time without doing anything. I did feel in a way as though I had sent the old man to his death. He got my goat Tuesday, acting like I was a talking elevator door or something. But he'd taken what I said seriously – more seriously than I had. He must have kept a close watch on the twenty-second floor from his T V console and seen someone go into my cousin's place. Then he'd gone up after him. The rest was unpleasantly clear.

It was true I'd had no reason to think anyone would be going into Boom Boom's apartment, let alone be so desperate to find something he'd kill for it. Yet it had happened, and I felt responsible. It seemed to me I had a murdered man's death to investigate.

Paige Carrington's answering service took my phone call. I didn't leave a message but looked up the address for the Windy City Balletworks: 5400 N. Clark. I stopped on the way for a sandwich and a Coke.

The Balletworks occupied an old warehouse between a Korean restaurant and a package goods store. The warehouse was dingy on the outside but had been refinished within. An empty hallway with a clapboard box office was lined with pictures of the Windy City ballerinas in various roles. The company did some standard pieces, including a lot of Balanchine, but it also experimented with its own choreography. Paige was on the wall as a cowgirl in *Rodeo*, as Bianca in *Taming of the Shrew*, and in her own light comic role in *Clark Street Fantasy*. I'd seen that piece twice.

The auditorium was to the left. A little sign outside it announced that a rehearsal was in progress. I slipped in quietly and joined a handful of people seated in the house. Onstage someone was clapping her hands and calling for quiet.

'We'll take it from the scherzo entrance again. Karl, you're coming in a second behind the beat. And, Paige, you want to stay downstage until the *grand jeté*. Places, please.'

The dancers wore a motley collection of garments, their legs covered with heavy warmers to prevent muscle cramps. Paige had on a bronze leotard with matching leg warmers. Her dark hair was pulled back from her face in a pony tail. She looked about sixteen from where I sat.

Someone operated a fancy tape deck in front of the stage. The music began. The piece was a jarring modern one and the choreography matched it, a dance on the depravity of modern urban life. Karl, entering on time in what was apparently the scherzo movement – hard to tell amidst all the wailing and jangling – seemed to be dying of a heroin overdose. Paige arrived on the scene seconds ahead of the narc squad, watched him die, and departed. I didn't pick all that up right away, but I got to see the thing six times before the director was satisfied with it.

A little after five the director dismissed the troupe, reminding them that they had a rehearsal at ten in the morning and a performance at eight the next night. I moved up front with the other members of the audience. We followed the dancers backstage; no one questioned our right to be there.

Following the sound of voices, I stuck my head into a dressing room. A young woman pulling a leotard from her freckled body asked me what I wanted. I told her I was looking for Paige.

'Oh, Paige . . . She's in the soloists' dressing-room – three doors down on your left.'

The soloists' dressing-room door was shut. I knocked and entered. Two women were there. One of them told me Paige was taking a shower and asked me to wait in the hall – there wasn't an inch of extra room in the place.

Presently Paige herself came down the hall from the shower, muffled in a white terry-cloth robe with a large white towel wrapped around her head.

'Vic! What are you doing here?'

'Hi, Paige. I came to talk to you. When you're dressed I'll take you out for coffee or gin or whatever you drink this time of day.'

The honey-colored eyes widened slightly: she wasn't used to being on the receiving end of orders, even when given in a subtle way. 'I'm not sure I have time.'

'Then I'll talk to you while you get dressed.'

'Is it that important?'

'It's extremely important.'

She shrugged. 'Wait for me here. I'll only be a few minutes.'

The few minutes stretched into forty before she reappeared. The other two women came out together, carrying on a vigorous conversation about someone named Larry. They glanced at me and one of them broke off to say, 'She's about halfway through her makeup,' as they passed.

Paige presently emerged in a gold silk shirt and white full skirt. She wore a couple of thin gold chains at her throat with little diamond chips in them. Her makeup was perfect – rusty tones that looked like the delicate flush of Mother Nature – and her hair framed her face in a smooth pageboy.

'Sorry to keep you waiting – it always takes longer than I think it will – and the more I try to hurry the longer it seems to take.'

'You people work up a good sweat. What was that you were rehearsing this afternoon? It looked pretty grim.'

'It's one of Ann's flights – Ann Bidermyer, the director, you know. *Pavane for a Dope Dealer*. Not in the best taste but it's a good role. For Karl too. Gives us both a great chance to show off. We open with it tomorrow. Want to see it? I'll get them to leave a ticket for you at the box office.'

'Thanks . . . Any place around here to talk, or do we need to head farther south?'

She considered. 'There's a little coffee shop around the corner on Victoria. It's a hole in the wall but they have good cappuccino.'

We went out into the brisk spring evening. The coffee shop seated only six people at tiny round tables on spindly cast-iron chairs. They sold fresh coffee beans, a vast assortment of tea, and a few homemade pastries. I ordered espresso and Paige had English Breakfast tea. Both came in heavy porcelain mugs.

'What were you looking for in my cousin's apartment?'

Paige drew herself up in her chair. 'My letters, Vic. I told you that.'

'You're not the kind of person who embarrasses easily – I just can't picture you getting that worked up about some letters, even if they are personal . . . Come to think of it, why would two people in the same city write each other anyway?'

She flushed below the rouge. 'We were on tour.'

'How did you meet Boom Boom?'

'At a party. A man I know was thinking about buying a share in the Black Hawks and Guy Odinflute invited some of the players. Boom Boom came.' Her voice was cold.

Odinflute was a North Shore tycoon with a flair for business matchmaking. He'd be the ideal person to bring together buyers and sellers of the Black Hawks.

'When was that?'

'At Christmas, Vic, if you must know.'

I'd seen Boom Boom a couple of times during the winter and he'd never mentioned Paige. But was that so strange? I never told him who I was dating either. When he got married, at twenty-four, I first met his wife a few weeks before the wedding. That was a little different – he's been slightly ashamed to introduce me to Connie. When she left him three weeks later and received an annulment, he'd gotten gloriously drunk with me, but still hadn't really talked about it. He kept his private life emphatically private.

'What are you thinking, Vic? You look very hostile, and I resent it.'

'Do you? Henry Kelvin was killed last night when some people broke into Boom Boom's place. They tore it apart. I want to know if they were looking for the same thing you were. And if so, what?'

'Henry? The night watchman? Oh, I'm so sorry, Vic. Sorry to get mad at you, too. If you'd only told me, instead of playing games with me . . . Was anything stolen? Could it have been a robbery?'

'Nothing was taken, but the place was sure chewed up pretty thoroughly. I think I saw everything Boom Boom had in his files and I can't imagine what value any of it would have to anyone besides a hockey memorabilia collector.'

She shook her head, her eyes troubled. 'I don't know either. Unless it was a robbery. I know he kept some share certificates there, even though I kept telling him to put them in a safe deposit box. He just couldn't be bothered with stuff like that. Were those gone?'

'I didn't see them when I was there on Tuesday. Maybe he did take them to a bank.' Another point to check with the lawyer Simonds.

'They were probably the most valuable things in the place, barring that antique chest in the dining room. Why don't you try to locate them?' She put her hand on my arm. 'I know it sounds crazy about the letters. But it's true. In fact I'll show you the one your cousin wrote me while we were away, if that's what it will take to convince you.' She rummaged in her large handbag and unzipped a side compartment. She pulled out a letter, still in its typed envelope, addressed to her at the Royal York Hotel in Toronto. Paige unfolded the letter. I recognized my cousin's tiny, careful handwriting at once. It began, 'Beautiful Paige'. I didn't think I should read the rest.

'I see,' I said. 'I'm sorry.'

The honey-colored eyes looked at me reproachfully and with a hint of coldness. 'I'm sorry, too. Sorry that you couldn't trust what I said to you.'

I didn't say anything. I didn't doubt Boom Boom had sent the letter – his handwriting was unmistakable – but why was she carrying it around in her handbag ready to show to anyone?

'I hope you're not jealous of me for being Boom Boom's lover.'

I grinned. 'I hope not too, Paige.' Of course, that might explain my suspicions. Maybe to Paige at any rate.

We took off shortly after that, Paige to an unknown destination and I for home. What a thoroughly dispiriting day. Kelvin dead, the encounter with Mrs Kelvin, and an unsatisfactory meeting with Paige. Maybe I was just a tiny bit jealous. If you were going to fall in love, Cousin, did it have to be with someone that perfect?

I couldn't figure out where Boom Boom would have kept his most private papers. He didn't have a safe deposit box. Simonds, his attorney, didn't have any secret documents. Myron Fackley, his agent, didn't have any. I didn't. If Paige was right about the stock certificates, where were they? Whom had Boom Boom trusted besides me? Perhaps his old teammates. I'd call Fackley tomorrow and see if he could put me in touch with Pierre Bouchard, the guy Boom Boom was closest to.

I took myself out to dinner at the Gypsy, a pleasant, quiet restaurant farther south on Clark. After the frustrating day I'd had I was due some peace and quiet. Over calf's liver with mustard sauce and a half bottle of Barolo I made a list of things to do. Find out something about Paige Carrington's background. Get Pierre Bouchard's phone number from Fackley. And get back down to the Port of Chicago. If Henry Kelvin's death and Boom Boom's were connected, the link lay in something my cousin had learned down there.

This was one of the rare occasions when I wished I had a partner, someone who could dig into Paige's background while I disguised myself as a load of wheat and infiltrated Eudora Grain.

I paid the bill and headed for home and a free phone. Relatively free. Murray Ryerson, crime reporter for the *Herald-Star*, had left for the night. They took a message from me at the city desk. I also left my name and number on Fackley's phone machine. There was nothing more I could do tonight, so I went to bed. A life of non-stop thrills.

8
LEARNING THE BUSINESS

I tried Murray again in the morning after my run. I was getting up too early these days – the star reporter hadn't arrived for work yet. I left another message and got dressed: navy linen slacks, a white shirt, and a navy Chanel jacket. A crimson scarf and low-heeled navy loafers completed the ensemble. Tough but elegant, the image I wanted to get across at Eudora Grain. I tossed an outsize shirt and my running shoes into the back seat to wear at the elevator – I wasn't going to ruin any good clothes down there.

Margolis was waiting for me. As the men came off shift for their morning break I talked to them informally in the yard. Most were pretty cooperative: seeing a detective, even a lady detective, relieved the monotony of the day. None of them had seen anything of my cousin's death, however. One of them suggested that I talk to the men on the *Lucella*. Another said I ought to speak to Phillips.

'He hanging around here? I don't remember that,' a short fellow with enormous forearms said.

'Yup. He was here. He come through with Warshawski and told Dubcek here to put on his earmuffs.'

They debated the matter and finally agreed that the speaker was right. 'He stuck pretty close to Warshawski. Don't know how he missed him out there on the wharf. Guess he was in with Margolis.'

I asked about the papers Boom Boom was supposed to have stolen. They were reticent but I finally pried out the information that Phillips and Boom Boom had had a terrible argument about some papers. That Phillips had accused my cousin of stealing? I asked. No, someone else said – it was the other way around. Warshawski had

300

accused Phillips. None of them had actually heard the argument – it was just a rumor.

That seemed to be that. I checked back with Margolis. Phillips had been with him at what might have been the critical time. After the *Bertha Krupnik* pulled away he had asked impatiently for Warshawski and had gone out to the wharf to get him and found him floating off the pier. They'd hauled Boom Boom up right away and given first aid, but he had been dead for twenty minutes or more.

'You know anything about the water in the holds of the *Lucella*?'

Margolis shrugged. 'Guess they found the guy who did it. She was tied up here, waitin' to load, when it happened. They pulled off the hatch covers and started to pour into the central hold when someone saw there was water in the thing. So they had to move her off and clean 'em out. Quite a mess, by the time they got twenty thousand bushels in there.'

'My cousin didn't discuss it with you?'

Margolis shook his head. 'Course, we didn't talk too much. He'd ask me about the load and we'd chat about the Hawks's chances but that'd be about it.'

He kept looking at the elevator as we were talking and I realized I was keeping him from his job. I couldn't think of anything else to ask. I thanked him for his time and took off for Eudora Grain's regional headquarters.

The receptionist vaguely remembered me from the other day and smiled at me. I reminded her who I was and told her that I had come to go through my cousin's papers to see if he'd left anything personal down there.

She spoke to me between phone calls. 'Why, certainly. We all liked Mr Warshawski very much. It was a terrible thing that happened to him. I'll just get his secretary to come out and get you . . . I hope you weren't planning to see Mr Phillips, because he's out of the office right now . . . Janet, Mr Warshawski's cousin is here. She wants to look at his papers. Will you come out for her? . . . Good morning, Eudora Grain. One moment, please . . . Good morning, Eudora Grain . . . Won't you sit down, Miss Warshawski? Janet will be right here.' She went back to her waiting calls and I flipped through the *Wall Street Journal* lying on the table in the waiting area.

Janet proved to be a woman at least twenty years my senior. She was quiet and well put together in a simple shirtwaist dress and canvas wedgies. She didn't wear makeup or stockings – no one down in the Port dressed up as much as they do in the Loop. She told me she had come to the funeral and she was sorry she hadn't talked to me then, but she knew what funerals were like – you had enough to do with your own relations without a lot of strangers bothering you.

She took me back to Boom Boom's office, a cubbyhole, really, whose walls were glass from waist-height up. Like the Grafalk dispatcher MacKelvy's, it had charts of the lakes covering all the walls. Unlike MacKelvy's, it was extremely tidy.

I flipped through some reports lying on his desk top. 'Can you tell me what Boom Boom was doing?'

She stood in the doorway. I gestured to one of the vinyl-covered chairs. After a minute's hesitation she turned to a woman in the outer area behind us. 'Can you take my calls, Effie?' She sat down.

'Mr Argus brought him in here just out of sympathy at first. But after a few months everyone could see your cousin was really smart. So Mr Argus was having Mr Phillips train him. The idea was he would be able to take over one of the regional offices in another year or so – probably Toledo, where old Mr Cagney is getting ready to retire.'

Secretaries always know what is going on in an office. 'Did Phillips know Boom Boom was being groomed? How did he feel about it?'

She looked at me consideringly. 'You don't look much like your cousin, if you don't mind my saying so.'

'No. Our fathers were brothers, but Boom Boom and I both took after our mothers in appearance.'

'But you're very like him around the eyes . . . It's hard to tell how Mr Phillips feels about anything. But I'd say he was glad your cousin was going to be off his hands before long.'

'Did they fight?'

'Oh no. At least not so that anyone here would know about it. But

302

your cousin was an impatient person in a lot of ways. Maybe playing hockey made him want to do everything faster than Mr Phillips is used to – he's more the deliberate type.' She hesitated and my stomach muscles tightened: she was about to say something important if she didn't think it would be indiscreet. I tried to make my eyes look like Boom Boom's.

'The thing is, Mr Phillips didn't want him so involved in the shipping contracts. Each regional vice-president sort of owns his own contracts, and Mr Phillips seemed to think if Mr Warshawski got too involved with the customers he might be able to shift some of them to Toledo with him.'

'So did they argue about the contracts? Or the customers?'

'Now if I tell you this, I don't want you getting me in trouble with Mr Phillips.'

I promised her her secret was safe.

'You see, Lois – Mr Phillips's secretary – doesn't like anyone touching the contract files.' She looked over her shoulder, as though Lois might be standing there listening. 'It's silly, really, because all the sales reps have to use them. We all have to be in and out of them all day long. But she acts like they're – they're diamonds or something. So if you take them you're supposed to write a note on her desk saying which ones you've taken and then let her know when you bring them back.'

The boss's secretary has a lot of control in an office and often exercises it through petty tyrannies like these. I murmured something encouraging.

'Mr Warshawski thought rules like that were pretty stupid. So he'd just ignore them. Lois couldn't stand him because he didn't pay any attention to anything she said.' She smiled briefly, a tender, amused smile, not spiteful. Boom Boom must have livened up the place quite a bit. Stanley Cup winners don't get there by too scrupulous attention to rules. Lois's petty ways must have struck him as some kind of decrepit penalty box.

'Anyway, the week before he died, Mr Warshawski pulled several months of contracts – all last summer's, I think – and took them home with him. If Lois found out she'd really get me in trouble, because he's gone and I was his secretary and she'd have to blame someone.'

'Don't worry: I won't tell anyone you told me. What did he do with them?'

'I don't know. But I do know he took a couple of them in with him to see Mr Phillips late Monday night.'

'Did they have any kind of argument?'

She shrugged helplessly. 'I don't know. We were all on our way out the door when he went in. Even Lois. Not that she'd say if she knew.'

I scratched my head. That was probably the origin of the rumors about Boom Boom stealing papers and fighting with Phillips. Maybe my cousin thought Phillips was enticing customers from the ancient Mr Cagney in Toledo. Or that Phillips hadn't been telling him everything he needed to know. I wondered if I'd be able to understand a shipping contract if I saw one.

'Any chance I could look at the files my cousin took home with him?'

She wanted to know why. I looked at her kind, middle-aged face. She had been fond of Boom Boom, her young boss. 'I'm not satisfied with the accounts I've heard of my cousin's death. He was an athlete, you know, despite his bad ankle. It would take more than a slippery wharf to get him into the lake. If he'd had a fight with Phillips over something important, he might have been mad enough to get careless. He had quite a temper, but he couldn't fight Phillips with fists and sticks the way he could the Islanders.'

She pursed her mouth up, thinking it over. 'I don't think he was angry the morning he died. He came here before going over to the elevator, you know, and I'd say his mood was – excited. He reminded me of my little boy when he's just pulled off some big stunt on his dirt bike.'

'The other thing I'm wondering is if someone might have pushed him in.'

She gulped once or twice at that. Why would someone push a nice young man like Mr Warshawski to his death? I didn't know, I told her, but it was possible those files might give me some kind of clue. I explained to her that I was a private investigator by profession. That seemed to satisfy her: she promised to hunt them up for me while Lois was at lunch.

I asked her if there were anyone else in the office with whom Boom Boom might have quarreled. Or, failing that, whom he might have been close to.

'The people he worked with most were the sales reps. They do all the buying and selling. And of course Mr Quinchley, who handles the Board of Trade on his computer.'

She gave me names of some of the likelier prospects and went back to her desk. I went out to the pit to see if I could find Brimford or Ashton, two of the reps Boom Boom had usually worked with. They were both on the phone, so I wandered around a bit, getting covert stares. There were some half dozen typists handling correspondence, bills, contracts, invoices, who knows what else. A few cubbyholes like Boom Boom's were stuck along the windows here and there. One of them held a man sitting at a computer terminal – Quinchley, hard at work with the Board of Trade.

Phillips's office was in the far corner. His secretary, a woman about my age with a bouffant hairdo I'd last seen in seventh grade, was over interrogating Janet. What does that cousin of Warshawski's want now? I grinned to myself.

Ashton hung up his phone. I stopped him as he started dialing again and asked if he'd mind talking to me for a few minutes. He was a heavyset guy in his middle or late forties; he followed me good-naturedly into Boom Boom's cubicle. I explained again who I was and that I was trying to find out more about Boom Boom's job and whether he had tangled with anyone in the organization.

Ashton was friendly, but he didn't want to commit himself to anything. Not with a strange woman, anyway. He agreed with Janet's description of my cousin's job. He liked Boom Boom – he livened the place up quite a bit, and he was smart, too. Didn't try to trade on his relations with Argus. But as to whether he quarreled with anyone – he didn't think so, but I'd have to talk to Phillips about that. How had Boom Boom and Phillips gotten along? Again, I'd have to ask Phillips, and that was that.

By the time we finished, the other guy, Brimford, had taken off. I shrugged. I didn't think talking to him would help me any. Going through Boom Boom's tidy, well-sorted drawers, I quickly realized he could have had a dozen dangerous documents connected with the shipping industry and I wouldn't know it. He had lists of farmers supplying Eudora Grain, lists of Great Lakes carriers, lists of rail carriers and their jobbers, bills of lading, reports of loads, by date, back copies of *Grain News*, weather forecasts . . . I flipped through three drawers with neatly labeled files. They were all organized topic by topic but none of it meant anything to me. Other than that Boom Boom had gotten totally immersed in a very complicated business.

I shut the file drawers and rummaged through the top of the desk, where I found pads of paper covered with Boom Boom's meticulous handwriting. The sight of it suddenly made me want to cry. Little notes he had written to himself to remind him of what he'd learned or what he had to do. Boom Boom planned everything very carefully. Maybe that was what gave him the energy to be so wild on the ice – he knew he had his life in shape behind him.

His desk diary was filled in with appointments. I copied the names he'd entered in the last few weeks of his life. He'd seen Paige on Saturday and again on Monday night. For Tuesday, April 27, he had written in John Bemis's name and Argus with a question mark. He wanted to talk to Bemis on the *Lucella* and then – depending on what was said – he would call Argus? That was interesting.

Flipping through the pages, I noticed that he'd taken to circling some of the dates. I sat up in my chair and started through the diary page by page. Nothing in January, February, or March, but three dates in April – the twenty-third, the sixteenth, and the fifth. I turned back to the front cover, which displayed a 1981 and 1983 calendar along with 1982 at a glance. He had circled twenty-three days in 1981 and three in 1982. In 1981 he'd started with March 28 and ended with November 13. I put the diary in my handbag and looked through the rest of the office.

I'd covered about everything there was – unless I looked at each sheet of paper – when Janet reappeared. 'Mr Phillips has come in and he'd like to see you.' She paused. 'I'll leave those files in here for you before you go . . . You won't say anything to him, will you?'

I reassured her and went over to the corner office. It was a real office – the heart of the castle, guarded by a frosty turnkey. Lois looked up briefly from her typing. Efficiency personified. 'He's expecting you. Go on in.'

Phillips was on the phone when I went in. He covered the mouth piece long enough to ask me to sit down, then went on with his conversation. His office contrasted with the utilitarian furnishings elsewhere in the building. Not that they were remarkably ornate, but they were of good quality. The furniture was made out of real wood, perhaps walnut, rather than pressed board coated with vinyl. Thick gray carpeting covered the floor and an antique clock adorned the wall facing the desk. A view of the parking lot was mercifully shrouded by heavy drapes.

Phillips himself was looking handsome, if a trifle heavy and stiff, in a pale blue woolen suit. A darker blue shirt with his initials on the pocket set off the suit and his fair hair to perfection. He must make a good packet: the way he dressed, that Alfa – a fourteen-thousand-dollar car, and it was a new one – the antique clock.

Phillips disengaged himself from the phone call. He smiled woodenly and said, 'I was a little surprised to see you down here this morning. I thought we'd taken care of your questions the other day.'

'I'm afraid not. My questions are like Hydra's heads – the more you lop off the more I have to ask.'

'Well, uh, I hear you've been going around bothering the folks here. Girls like Janet have their jobs to do. If you have questions, could you bring them to me? I'd sure appreciate that, and we wouldn't have to interrupt the other folks' work out there.'

I felt he was trying too hard for a casual approach. It didn't fit his perfect tailoring or his deep, tight voice.

'Okay. Why was my cousin discussing last summer's shipping contracts with you?'

A tide of crimson washed through his face and receded abruptly, leaving a row of freckles standing out on his cheekbones. I hadn't noticed those before.

'Contracts? We weren't!'

I crossed my legs. 'Boom Boom made a note of it in his desk diary,' I lied. 'He was very meticulous, you know: he wrote down everything he did.'

'Maybe he did discuss them with me at some point. I don't remember everything we talked about – we were together a great deal. I was training him, you know.'

'Maybe you can remember what he discussed with you the night before he died if it wasn't the contracts. I understand he stayed late to meet with you.' He didn't say anything. 'That was last Monday night, if you've forgotten. April 26.'

'I haven't forgotten when your cousin died. But the only reason we stayed late was to go over some routine items we didn't have time for during the day. In my position I'm often tied up for hours at a time. Lois tries to help me keep on top of my calendar but it isn't always possible. So Warshawski and I would stay late to go over questions that we couldn't get to earlier.'

'I see.' I had promised Janet I wouldn't get her in trouble, so I couldn't tell him I had a witness who'd seen Boom Boom with the files. She was the only person who could have told me – Lois wouldn't have any trouble figuring that out.

Phillips was looking more relaxed. He stuck a cautious finger behind his collar and eased his tie a bit. 'Anything else?'

'Are your sales reps paid on commission?'

'Sure. That's the best way to keep them active.'

'What about you?'

'Well, we officers don't have access to direct sales, so it wouldn't be a very fair system.'

'But the pay is good.'

He looked at me with something approaching shock: well-behaved Americans don't discuss their salaries.

'Well, you've got a nice car, nice clothes, nice clock. I just wondered.'

'It's none of your damned business. If you don't have anything further to say, I have a lot of work to do and I need to get to it.'

308

I got up. 'I'll just be taking my cousin's personal items home with me.'

He started dialing. 'He didn't leave any, so I expect you not to take anything away with you.'

'You went through his desk, Phillips? Or did the all-efficient Lois?'

He stopped mid-dial and turned very red again. He didn't say anything for a second, his pale brown eyes darting around the room. Then he said with an assumption of naturalness, 'Of course we went through his papers. We didn't know if he was in the middle of anything critical that someone else would have to take over.'

'I see.' I went back toward Boom Boom's cubbyhole. No one was on the floor. A black and white institutional clock above the far entrance said twelve-thirty. They must all be at lunch. Janet had left a neatly wrapped package on the desk with my name on it, or rather, as she had forgotten my name, 'Mr Warshawski's cousin'. Beneath it she'd written: 'Please (heavily underscored) return as early as possible.' I scooped it up and walked out the door. Phillips didn't try to stop me.

9

JUST ANOTHER DEAD
BLACK

Interstate 94 back to the city was clear that time of day. I made it to
my office around one-thirty and checked in with my answering service. Murray had returned my call. I got back to him immediately.

'What's up, Vic? You got something on the Kelvin death for
me?'

'Not a sniffle. But I'm hoping you might oblige a lady and get one
of your society people to do a little digging for me.'

'Vic, any time you want something like that, it's usually a
cover-up for some big story you don't let us in on until after it's
over.'

'Murray! What a remark. How about Anita McGraw? How
about Edward Purcell? And John Cotton? Weren't those good
stories?'

'Yeah, they were. But you led me around in circles first. You got
something hot on Kelvin?'

'Well, maybe, in a way. I want some background on Paige
Carrington.'

'Who's she?'

'She's a dancer. And she was hanging out with my cousin before
he died. She was looking for some love letters in his condo the other
day. Then Kelvin got knocked off. Whoever did it searched the place
pretty thoroughly. It makes me nervous – I'd like to find out
something about her background, and I also wondered if any of your
gossip people – Greta Simon, for example – had sniffed out the
relationship between her and Boom Boom.'

'Oh yeah. Boom Boom Warshawski was your cousin. I should

have guessed. You're the only two Warshawskis I ever heard of. I was sorry to hear he died: I was quite a fan of his . . . Nothing fishy about his death, is there?'

'Not as far as I know, Murray. He seems to have slipped on some wet planks and gone under the screw of a lakes freighter.'

'Ouch. Jesus! Hard to imagine someone as agile as Boom Boom doing something like that . . . Look, as an old fan of his, I'll be glad to help you out. But I've got dibs if anything turns up. Paige Carrington . . . What's her father's name?'

'I don't know. She did mention something about growing up in Lake Bluff.'

'Okay, Vic. I'll call you in two-three days.'

I unwrapped Janet's tidy package and pulled out the papers. Three big accordion files marked June, July, and August were filled with hundreds of flimsies, each a carbon of a computer printout. Before going through them I went downstairs to Johnnie's Steak Joynt, where I had a Fresca and a gyros sandwich. Thumbing through the *Herald-Star*, I saw a notice about Kelvin's wake. It was today, starting at four, in a funeral home on the South Side. Maybe I should go.

Back in my office I cleared off the desk top by putting everything into the bottom drawer and spread the files out in front of me. They were computer reports, all arranged in the same way. Each showed a transaction date, a point of origin, a destination, a carrier, volume, weight, type, cost per bushel, and date of arrival. They reflected Eudora Grain's shipments of grain over a three-month period. They weren't legal documents but records of legal transactions. Each report was actually titled 'Contract Verification Form'.

I scratched my head but started reading through them. Some showed more than one carrier, many three or four. Thus, I'd find Thunder Bay to St Catharines on June 15 via G S L, canceled, via P S L, canceled, and finally picked up by a third carrier at a different rate. I should have brought my cousin's list of the Great Lakes steamship lines. I frowned. P S L might be Bledsoe's outfit, the Pole Star Line. G S L was perhaps Grafalk Steamship. But there were dozens of initials. I'd need a guide.

I looked at Boom Boom's diary and pulled the forms that matched the dates he'd marked for last summer. There were fourteen for those three days. Since the forms were all in date order it was easy to pick out the ones I wanted, although frequently there was more than one report for each date. There were thirty-two records altogether. Twenty-one were multiple-contract shipments, eight of which ended up with GSL. Of the other eleven, five were with GSL. What did that mean? If GSL was Grafalk's line, Eudora did a lot of business with him. But he had told me he had the biggest fleet on the lakes, so that wasn't too surprising. PSL had lost seven shipments to GSL but had gotten two of its own in August. Their August rates were lower than the June rates; that might be the reason.

I looked at my watch. It was almost three o'clock. If I was going to Kelvin's wake I'd have to go home and put on a dress. I gathered up all the files and took them to an office service shop on the building's fifth floor where they do clerical jobs for one-person offices like mine. I asked them to make me a copy of each of the forms and refile them in date order. The man behind the counter was pleased but someone in the background groaned.

I drove home and changed quickly into the navy suit I'd worn to Boom Boom's funeral. I made good time going back south – it was only four-thirty when I got to the funeral home. A tan brick bungalow at 71st and Damen with a tiny lawn manicured within an inch of the ground had been converted to a funeral parlor. A vacant lot on its south side was packed with cars. I found a place for the Lynx on 71st Place and went into the home. I was the only white person there.

Kelvin's body was displayed in an open casket surrounded with waxy lilies and candles. I made the obligatory stop to look. He was laid out in his best suit; his face in repose had the same unresponsive stare I'd encountered Tuesday night.

I turned to condole with the family. Mrs Kelvin was standing in quiet dignity, wearing a black wool dress and surrounded by her children. I shook hands with a woman my own age in a black suit and pearls, two younger men, and with Mrs Kelvin.

'Thank you for coming down, Miss Warshawski,' the widow said in her deep voice. 'These are my children and my grandchildren.' She gave me their names and I told them how sorry I was.

The little room was crowded with friends and relations, heavy-bosomed women clutching handkerchiefs, dark-suited men, and preternaturally quiet children. They moved a little closer to the grieving family as I stood there – protection against the white woman who drove Kelvin to his death.

'I was a little hasty in how I spoke to you yesterday,' Mrs Kelvin said. 'I believed you must have known something was going to happen in that apartment.'

There was a little murmur of assent from the group behind me.

'I still think you must have known something was going on. But blaming people won't bring my husband back to life.' She gave the ghost of a smile. 'He was a very stubborn man. He could have called for help if he knew someone was going into that place – he should have called for help, called the police.' Again the murmur of assent from the people around her. 'But once he knew someone was breaking in, he wanted to handle it by himself. And that's not your fault.'

'Do the police have any leads?' I asked.

The young woman in the black suit gave a bitter smile. Daughter or daughter-in-law – I couldn't remember. 'They aren't going to do anything. They have the pictures, the film from the TV consoles Daddy watched, but the killers had their faces and hands covered. So the police say if no one can recognize them there's nothing they can do.'

Mrs Kelvin spoke sadly. 'We keep telling them there was some-thing going on in that apartment – we keep telling them that you knew about it. But they aren't going to do anything. They're just treating it like another black killing and they aren't going to do a thing.'

I looked around at the group. People were watching me steadily. Not exactly with hostility – more as though I was some unpredictable species, perhaps an ibex.

'You know my cousin died last week, Mrs Kelvin. He fell from a wharf under the screw of a freighter. There were no witnesses. I'm trying to find out whether he fell or was pushed. Your husband's death makes me think he was pushed. If I can find out for sure and find out who did it, they'll probably be the same people who killed Mr Kelvin. I know catching the murderer is a small consolation in the midst of great grief, but it's the best I can offer – for myself as well as you.'

'Little white girl going to succeed where the police failed.' The person behind me spoke softly but audibly and a few people laughed.

'Amelia!' Mrs Kelvin spoke sharply. 'No need to be rude. She's trying to be kind.'

I looked around coolly. 'I'm a detective and I have a pretty good record.' I turned back to Mrs Kelvin. 'I'll let you know what I find out.'

I shook her hand and left, heading back to the Dan Ryan and the Loop. It was after five and traffic scarcely moved. Fourteen lanes and all of it bumper-to-bumper within high concrete walls. Truck exhaust mingled with the damp still air. I shut the windows and wriggled out of my jacket. It was chilly on the lakefront but muggy in the expressway's canyon.

I inched my way downtown and oozed off the expressway at Roosevelt Road. Main police headquarters are at State and Roosevelt, a good location, close to a lot of crime. I wanted to see if anyone there would give me any information about Kelvin.

My dad had been a sergeant, working mostly out of the Twenty-First District on the South Side. The brick building on 12th Street brought on a twinge of nostalgia – it had the same linoleum, the same cinder-block walls with yellow paint peeling away. A few harassed, overweight men behind the desk were processing everyone from drivers putting up bond for their licenses to women trying to see men brought in on assault charges. I waited my turn in line.

The desk officer I finally spoke to called inside on a microphone. 'Sergeant McGonnigal, lady here to see you on the Kelvin case.'

McGonnigal came out a few minutes later, big, muscular, wearing a rumpled white shirt and brown slacks. We'd met a couple of years back when he was on the South Side and he remembered me immediately.

'Miss Warshawski. Nice to see you.' He ushered me back through the linoleum corridors to a tiny room he shared with three other men.

'Nice to see you, Sergeant. When were you transferred downtown?'

'Six, seven months ago. I got assigned to the Kelvin case last night.'

I explained that the murder had taken place in my cousin's apartment and that I wanted to know when I could get back in and straighten out his papers. McGonnigal expressed the usual regrets at Boom Boom's death – he'd been a fan, et cetera, and said they were almost finished with the apartment.

'Did you turn up anything? I understand the T V films showed two men going in. Any fingerprints?'

He grimaced. 'They were too smart for that. We did find a footprint on the papers. One of them wears size twelve Arroyo hiking boots. But that doesn't tell us much.'

'What killed Kelvin? He wasn't shot, was he?'

He shook his head. 'Someone gave him an almighty hard blow to the jaw and broke his neck. May only have meant to knock him out. Jesus! What a fist. Doesn't tie in to any of our known B & E men.'

'You think this is a straight break and entry job?'

'What else would it be, Miss Warshawski?'

'Nothing of value was taken. Boom Boom had a stereo, some fancy cuff links and stuff, and it was all there.'

'Well, figure the guys are surprised by Kelvin. Then they see they've killed him rather than just stunning him like they intended. So they get nervous and leave. They don't know whether someone else is going to come up looking for the guy if he doesn't come back in so many minutes.'

I could see his point. Maybe I was making a mountain out of a molehill. Maybe I was upset by my cousin's death and I wanted to blow it up into something bigger than an accident.

'You're not trying to get involved in this, are you?'

'I am involved, Sergeant: it happened in my cousin's apartment.'

315

'The lieutenant is not going to be happy if he hears you're trying to stir up this case. You know that.'

I knew that. The lieutenant was Bobby Mallory and he did not like me to get involved in police work, especially murder cases.

I smiled. 'If I stumble across anything looking through my cousin's affairs, I don't think that'll upset him too much.'

'Just give us a chance to do our job, Miss Warshawski.'

'I spoke with the Kelvin family this afternoon. They're not too sure you guys are really trying your hardest.'

He slammed his palm on his desk top. The three other men in the room tried to pretend they were still working. 'Now why the hell did you go talk to them? One of the sons came around here and gave me a snootful. We're doing our best. But, Christ, we haven't got a damned thing to start from other than two pictures no one can identify and a size twelve boot!'

He pulled a file savagely from a stack on his desk and yanked a photograph from it to toss at me. I picked it up. It was a still made from the TV film of the men going into Boom Boom's place. Two men, one in jeans and the other in chinos. They both wore corduroy sports jackets and had those Irish caps held up over their faces. McGonnigal handed me a couple of other stills. One showed them getting off the elevator – backward. Another showed them walking down the hall, crouched over to disguise their height. You could see their hands pretty clearly – they were wearing surgical gloves.

I gave the pictures back to McGonnigal. 'Good luck, Sergeant. I'll let you know if I come across anything . . . When can I get the keys to the place back?'

He said Friday morning and warned me to be very, very careful. The police are always telling me that.

10
DOWN THE HATCHES

From my apartment I tried Boom Boom's agent again, even though it was after six. Like me, Fackley worked unusual hours. He was in and answered the phone himself. I told him I wanted to get in touch with Pierre Bouchard, star forward for the Hawks and another of his clients. Fackley told me Bouchard was in his hometown, Quebec, playing in the Coeur d'Argent, a demonstration hockey tournament. Fackley gave me his Chicago phone number and agreed to see me the following Wednesday to go through Boom Boom's papers.

I tried phoning the Pole Star Line but no one answered. There wasn't much else I could do tonight. I called Lotty and we went out for dinner together and then to see *Chariots of Fire*.

The photocopies of Eudora Grain's shipping records were ready for me at ten the next morning. I stuck them in a large canvas shoulder bag. The originals I wrapped in heavy brown paper, taped securely. Starting to write Janet's name on top, I realized I didn't know her last name. Women exist in a world of first names in business. Lois, Janet, Mr Phillips, Mr Warshawski. That's why I use my initials.

I reached the Port before lunch and dropped the packet off with the receptionist at Eudora Grain, then swung around to the main entrance, where Grafalk and Bledsoe had their offices. The guard at the gate gave me some static about going in without a pass but I finally convinced him I needed to talk to someone at Pole Star and he let me have a two-hour permit.

The Pole Star Line occupied only two rooms in one of the large sand-colored buildings at the far end of the pier. Although much smaller than Grafalk's operation, their offices included the same organized chaos of computers, charts, and telephones. All were manipulated in an electronic symphony by one harassed but friendly young woman. She unplugged herself from the phone long enough to tell me that Bledsoe was at Elevator 9 with the *Lucella*. She sketched rough directions for me – it was back along the Calumet River several miles – and returned to a madly ringing phone.

Phillips came out of the Grafalk building as I passed it on the way to my car. He wasn't sure whether to recognize me or not, so I solved the problem by saying hello to him.

'What are you doing here?' he demanded.

'Signing up for a water ballet class. How about you?'

He turned red again. 'I assume you're still asking questions about your cousin. More Hydra heads?'

I was surprised to find he could be whimsical. 'I just want to clear all the bases – I still have to talk to the crew on the *Lucella* before she sails.'

'Well, I think you'll find you've put a lot of energy into something not worth the effort. It's to be hoped you find that out soon.'

'I'm moving as fast as I can. I figure water ballet can only help.' He snorted and strode over to the green Alfa. As I was climbing into the Lynx I heard him roar past, spitting a little gravel.

Elevator 9 was not one of Eudora Grain's but belonged to the Tri-State Grain Co-op. A chain fence separated the elevator yard from the road. Train tracks ran through a gap in it and a small guardhouse with a heavy, red-faced man reading the *Sun-Times* stood at the entrance. The Lynx bounced along the ruts to the guardhouse, where Redface reluctantly put down his paper and asked me what I wanted.

'I need to talk to Martin Bledsoe or John Bemis.'

He waved me in. It didn't seem like much of a security system to me. I drove on around the potholes and pulled up into a gravel yard. A couple of boxcars were slowly moving along the rail siding and I stood for a minute to watch the hoist carry them up inside the elevator and dump their loads. Amazing process, really. I could understand why my cousin had gotten so intrigued by it.

I skirted around the elevator to the wharf where the *Lucella* lay.

She was enormous and a sense of mystery and dread filled me. The giant lay momentarily still, held down by steel cables three inches thick – a huge amphibious spider immobile in the coils of its own web. But when she started to move, what things would stir in the depths beneath that gigantic keel? I looked at the black water absorbing the hull and felt sick and slightly dizzy.

Little flecks of grain dust swirled through the air and reached me where I stood behind her. No one knew I was here. I began to see how Boom Boom could have fallen in unnoticed. I shivered and moved forward to the scene of the action.

An extension ladder was attached high up on the ship, with feet reaching the dock. It was sturdy and I forgot about the dark water underneath as I climbed up.

Except for a faint sound from the elevator and the chaff blowing in my eyes, I hadn't noticed any activity down on the wharf. On deck was another story. It only takes twenty people or so to load a freighter but they were extremely busy.

Five giant chutes were poised over openings in the deck. Guided by three men pulling them around with ropes, they spilled grain into the holds in a series of vast waterfalls. I couldn't see all the way down the thousand-foot deck – a cloud of grain dust billowed up and obscured the bow from view.

I stood at the edge of a giant machine which seemed to be a long conveyor belt on a swivel, rather like a tank turret, and watched. The area beyond was posted HARD HATS ONLY.

No one noticed me for a few minutes. Then a whitened figure in a blue boiler suit came over to me. He took off his hard hat and I recognized the first mate, Keith Winstein. His curly black hair was powdered white below a line made by his hat.

'Hi, Mr Winstein. I'm V. I. Warshawski – we met the other day. I'm looking for Mr Bledsoe.'

'Sure, I remember you. Bledsoe's up on the bridge with the captain. Want me to take you up? Or you want to watch some of this first?'

He dug out a battered hard hat for me from the supply room behind the tank turret – 'self-unloader,' he explained. It was attached to a series of conveyor belts in the holds and could unload the entire ship in under twenty-four hours.

Winstein led me along the port side away from the main activity with the chutes. The holds were about half full, he said; they'd be through in another twelve hours or so.

'We'll take this cargo to the entrance of the Welland Canal and unload it onto oceangoing ships there. We're too big for the Welland – the longest ships through there are the 740-footers.'

The *Lucella* had five cargo holds underneath with some thirty-five hatches opening into them. The chutes moved among the hatches, distributing the load evenly. In addition to the men guiding the chutes, another man watched the flow of grain at each hold and directed those at the ropes among the various openings. Winstein went around and checked their work, then escorted me onto the bridge.

Bledsoe and the captain were standing at the front of the glass-enclosed room looking down at the deck. Bemis was leaning against the wheel, a piece of mahogany as tall as I am. Neither of them turned around until Winstein announced to the captain that he'd brought a visitor.

'Hello, Miss Warshawski.' The captain came over to me in a leisurely way. 'Come to see what a freighter looks like in action?'

'It's most impressive . . . I have a couple of questions for you, Mr Bledsoe, if you have some time.'

Bledsoe's right hand was swathed in bandages. I asked how it was doing. He assured me that it was healing well. 'No tendons cut . . . What have you got for me?'

Bemis took Winstein off to one corner to inquire about progress below. Bledsoe and I sat at a couple of high wooden stools behind a large drafting table covered with navigation charts. I pulled the photocopies of the contract verification forms from my canvas bag, flicking off some pieces of chaff which had settled on them. Putting the papers on the drafting table, I leafed through them to find July 17, one of Boom Boom's circled dates.

Bledsoe took the stack from me and fanned it. 'These are Eudora

Grain's shipping contract records. How'd you come to have them?'

'One of the secretaries lent them to me. Captain Bemis told me you were the most knowledgeable person around on these sorts of deals. I can't follow them – I was hoping you'd explain them to me.'

'Why not get Phillips to?'

'Oh, I wanted to go to the expert.'

The gray eyes were intelligent. He smiled ironically. 'Well, there's no great secret to them. You start off with a load at point A and you want to move it to point B. We shippers move any cargo, but Eudora Grain is concerned chiefly with grain – although they may have a bit of lumber and coal now. So we're talking about grain. Now, on this one, the order was first placed on July 17, so that's the initial transaction date.'

He studied the documents for a few minutes. 'We have three million bushels of soybeans in Peoria and we want to move them to Buffalo. Hansel Baltic is buying the shipment there and that's where our responsibility ends. So Phillips's sales reps start scurrying around trying to find someone to carry the load. G L S L. They start there – Great Lakes Shipping Line. They're charging four dollars and thirty-two cents a ton to carry it from Chicago to Buffalo and they need five vessels. With that big a load you'd normally bid it out among several carriers – I guess the rep was just being a little lazy on this one. Phillips has to bring it from Peoria by rail by the twenty-fourth of July and they'll get it to Buffalo on the thirty-first or earlier.

'Now, in our business, contracts are set up and canceled routinely. That's what makes it so confusing – and why the difference of a few cents is so important. See, here, later on the seventeenth, we offer to carry the load for four twenty-nine a ton. That was before we had the *Lucella* – we can go way under our old prices now because these thousand-footers are so much cheaper to operate.

'Anyway, then Grafalk came in on the eighteenth at $4.30 a ton but a promise to get it there by the twenty-ninth. Cutting it pretty close, really – wonder if they made it.'

'So there's nothing out of the ordinary about this?'

Bledsoe studied it intently. 'Not as far as I can tell. What made you think there would be?'

The chief engineer came in at that point. 'Oh, hi there. What do you have?'

'Hi, Sheridan. Miss Warshawski's been going over Eudora's shipping orders. She thought something might be wrong with them.'

'No, not that. I just needed help understanding them. I've been trying to figure out what my cousin might have known that he wanted to tell Captain Bemis. So I went through his papers yesterday over at Eudora Grain, and I learned he'd been particularly interested in these documents right before he died. I wondered if the fact that all these Pole Star contracts ended up with Grafalk was important.'

Bledsoe looked at the documents again. 'Not especially. Either they underbid us or they were promising an earlier delivery date.'

'The other question I had was why Boom Boom was interested in certain dates this spring.'

'What dates this spring?' Bledsoe asked.

'One was the twenty-third of April. I don't remember the others offhand.' I had the diary in my canvas bag but I didn't want to show it to them.

Bledsoe and Sheridan looked at each other thoughtfully. Finally Bledsoe said, 'The twenty-third was the date we were supposed to load up the *Lucella*.'

'You mean the day you found water in the holds?'

Sheridan nodded.

'Maybe the other dates also were connected with shipping accidents. Is there a record of such things?'

Bledsoe's face twisted in thought. He shook his head. 'That's a pretty tall order. There are so many steamship lines and so many ports. The *Great Lakes Underwriter* discusses them if they've got anything to do with hull or cargo damage. That'd be the best place to start. Recent dates, one of us might be able to help you out.'

I was getting tired of all the legwork that didn't lead in any real direction. I supposed I could track down the *Great Lakes Underwriter* and look for accidents to ships, but what would that tell me? Had Boom Boom uncovered some criminal ring vandalizing freighters? Just knowing that accidents had occurred wouldn't tell me that.

Winstein had gone back down to the deck and Captain Bemis wandered over to join our group. 'No further accidents are going to strike this ship. I've arranged for a security patrol on deck when they finish loading for the day.'

Bledsoe nodded. 'I've been thinking maybe I'll sail out with you.' He grinned. 'No aspersion on your management of the ship, John, but the *Lucella*'s precious to all of us. I want to see her get this load to St Catharines.'

'No problem, Martin. I'll have the head cook get the stateroom ready.'

'We don't run to people like stewards on freighters,' Bledsoe explained to me. 'The head cook takes responsibility for the captain's and the guest quarters. Everyone else fends for himself . . . What time do you figure to sail, John?'

The captain looked at his watch. 'We've got about eleven more hours of loading, and Tri-State doesn't want to pay overtime unless it's just an hour or two. So any time after nineteen hundred hours tomorrow.'

Bledsoe offered to give me a tour of the ship, if Bemis didn't object. The captain gave his permission with a tolerant smile. Sheridan followed us down the narrow wooden stairs. 'I get to show off the engine room,' he explained.

The bridge was perched on top of the pilothouse. There were four levels above deck, each smaller than the one below it. The captain and the chief engineer had their quarters on the third story, directly below the bridge. Sheridan opened his door so I could take a quick look inside.

I was surprised. 'I thought everyone slept in narrow bunk beds with a tiny sink.' The chief engineer had a three-room suite, with an outsize bed in the bedroom, and an office cluttered with paper and tools.

Bledsoe laughed. 'That was true in Dana's day, but times have changed. The crew sleep six to a room but they have a big recreational lounge. They even have a ping-pong table, which provides its amusing moments in a high sea.'

The other officers and the head cook shared the second floor with the stateroom. The galley and the dining rooms – the captain's dining room and crew's mess – were on the deck floor and the crew's quarters on the first floor below deck.

'We should have put the officers' quarters over the stem,' Sheridan told Bledsoe as we went down below the water level to the engine room. 'Even up where John and I are the engines throb horribly all night long. I can't think why we let them build the whole caboodle into the pilothouse.'

We climbed narrow steel rungs set into the wall down to the belly of the ship where the engines lay. Bledsoe disappeared for this part of the tour. 'Once the chief gets started on engines he keeps going for a month or two. I'll see you on deck before you leave.'

'Engine room' was really a misnomer. The engines themselves were in the bottom of the ship, each the size of a small building, say a garage. Moving parts were installed around them on three floors – drive shafts two feet in diameter, foot-wide piston heads, giant valves. Everything was controlled from a small room at the entrance to the holds. A panel some six feet wide and three feet deep was covered with switches and buttons. Transformers, sewage disposal, ballast, as well as the engines themselves, were all operated from there.

Sheridan showed me the controls that could be used for moving the ship. 'Remember when the *Leif Ericsson* ran into the dock the other day? I was telling you about the controls in the engine room. This one is for the port engine, this for the starboard.' They were large metal sticks, easy to move, with clearly marked grooves – 'Full ahead, Half ahead, Half astern, Full astern'.

He looked at his watch and laughed. It was after five. 'Martin's right – I'd stay down here all day. I keep forgetting not everyone shares my love of moving parts.'

I assured him I'd found it fascinating. It was hard to figure out on one visit, but interesting. The engines were laid out sort of like a giant car engine, with every piece exposed so it could be cared for quickly. If you were a Lilliputian you would climb up and down a car engine just this way. Every piece would be laid out neatly, easy to get at, just impossible to move.

I went back up to the bridge to pick up my papers. While we'd been down with the engines, the loading had stopped for the day. I watched while a couple of small deck cranes lifted covers over the hatches.

'We won't bolt 'em down,' Bemis said. 'It's supposed to be clear tonight, for a miracle. I just don't want to take any chances with four million dollars' worth of barley.'

Bledsoe came up to us. 'Oh, there you are . . . Look – I feel I owe you an apology for ruining lunch the other day. I wondered if I could persuade you to eat dinner with me. There's a good French restaurant about twenty minutes from here in Crown Point, Indiana.'

I'd worn a black corduroy pantsuit that day and it was covered with fine particles of barley. Bledsoe saw me eye it doubtfully.

'It's not that formal a place – and there's some kind of clothesbrush in the stateroom if you want to brush your suit. You look great, though.'

11

GROUNDED

Dinner at Louis Retaillou's Bon Appétit was delightful. The restaurant took up the ground floor of an old Victorian house. The family, who all played a role in preparing and presenting the meal, lived upstairs. It was Thursday, a quiet night with only a few of the inlaid wooden tables filled, and Louis came out to talk to Bledsoe, who was a frequent guest. I had the best duckling I've ever eaten and we shared a respectable St Estephe.

Bledsoe turned out to be an entertaining companion. Over champagne cocktails we became 'Martin' and 'Vic'. He regaled me with shipping stories, while I tried to pry discreetly into his past. I told him a bit about my childhood on Chicago's South Side and some of Boom Boom's and my adventures. He countered with stories of life on Cleveland's waterfront. I talked about being an undergraduate during the turbulent Vietnam years and asked him about his education. He'd gone straight to work out of high school. With Grafalk Steamship? Yes, with Grafalk Steamship – which reminded him of the first time he'd been on a laker when a big storm came up. And so on.

It was ten-thirty when Bledsoe dropped me back at the *Lucella* to pick up my car. The guard nodded to Bledsoe without taking his eyes from a television set perched on a shelf above him.

'Good thing you have a patrol on the boat – anyone could get past this fellow,' I commented.

Bledsoe nodded in agreement, his square face in shadow. 'Ship,' he said absently. 'A boat is something you haul aboard a ship.'

He walked over with me to my car – he was going back on board the

326

Lucella for one last look around. The elevator and the boat – ship – beyond loomed as giant black shapes in the dimly lit yard. I shivered a bit in my corduroy jacket.

'Thanks for introducing me to a great new restaurant, Martin. I enjoyed it. Next time I'll take you to an out-of-the-way Italian place on the West Side.'

'Thanks, Vic. I'd like to do that.' He squeezed my hand in the dark, started toward the ship, then leaned back into the car and kissed me. It was a good kiss, firm and not sloppy, and I gave it the attention it deserved. He mumbled something about calling when he got back to town and left.

I backed the Lynx out of the yard and onto 130th Street. Few cars were out and I had an easy time back to I-94. The traffic there was heavier but flowing smoothly – trailer trucks moving their loads at seventy miles an hour under cover of darkness, and the restless flow of people always out on nameless errands in a great city.

The night was clear, as the forecast had promised Bemis, but the air was unseasonably cool. I kept the car windows rolled up as I drove north, passing slag heaps and mobile homes huddled together under the shadow of expressway and steel mills. At 103rd Street the highway merged with the Dan Ryan. I was back in the city now, the Dan Ryan el on my left and a steep grassy bank on my right. Perched on top were tiny bungalows and liquor stores. A peaceful urban sight, but not a place to stop in the middle of the night. A lot of unwary tourists have been mugged close to the Dan Ryan.

I was nearing the University of Chicago exit when I heard a tearing in the engine, a noise like a giant can opener peeling a strip off the engine block. I slammed on the brakes. The car didn't slow. The brakes didn't respond. I pushed again. Still nothing. The brakes had failed. I turned the wheel to move toward the exit. It spun loose in my hand. No steering. No brakes. In the rearview mirror I could see the lights of a semi bearing down on me. Another truck was boxing me in on the right.

Sweat came out on my forehead and the bottom fell out of my stomach. I pumped gently on the brakes and felt a little response. Gently, gently. Switched on the hazard indicator, put the car in neutral, leaned on the horn. The Lynx was veering to the right and I couldn't stop it. I held my breath. The truck to my right pulled out of my way but the one behind me was moving fast and blaring on his horn.

'Goddamn you, move!' I screamed at him. My speedometer needle had inched down to thirty; he was going at least seventy. I was still sliding towards the right lane.

At the last second the semi behind me swerved to the left. I heard a horrible shattering of glass and metal on metal. A car spun into the lane in front of me.

I pumped the brakes but there was nothing left in them. I couldn't stop. I couldn't do anything. In the last seconds as the car in front of me flipped over I hunched down and crossed my hands in front of my face.

Metal on metal. Wrenching jolts. Glass shattering on the street. A violent blow on my shoulder, a pool of wet warmth on my arm. Light and noise shattered inside my head and then quiet.

My head ached. My eyes would hurt terribly if I opened them. I had the measles. That was what Mama said. I would be well soon. I tried calling her name; a gurgling sound came out and her hand was on my wrist, dry and cool.

'She's stirring.'

Not Gabriella's voice. Of course, she was dead. If she was dead I couldn't be eight and sick with the measles. It hurt my head to think.

'The steering,' I croaked, and forced my eyes open.

A blur of white figures hovered over me. The light stabbed my eyes. I shut them.

'Turn off the overhead lights.' That was a woman's voice. I knew it and struggled to open my eyes again.

'Lotty?'

She leaned over me. 'So, *Liebchen.* You gave us a few bad hours but you're all right now.'

'What happened?' I could hardly talk; the words choked in my throat.

328

'Soon I'll tell you. Now I want you to sleep. You are in Billings Hospital.'

The University of Chicago. I felt a small sting in my side and slept.

When I woke up again the room was empty. The pain in my head was still there but small and manageable. I tried to sit up. As I moved, the pain swept over me full force. I felt vilely ill and lay back down, panting. After an interval I opened my eyes again. My left arm was attached to the ceiling by a pulley. I stared at it dreamily. I moved my right fingers up the arm, encountering thick tape, then a cast. I poked the shoulder around the edges of the cast and gave a cry of unanticipated pain. My shoulder was either dislocated or broken.

What had I done to my shoulder? I frowned in concentration, making my headache worse. But I remembered. My car. The brakes failing. A sedan turning over in front of me? Yes. I couldn't remember the rest. I must have plowed right into it, though. Lucky to have my shoulder belt on. Could anyone in the sedan have lived through that?

I started feeling very angry. I needed to see the police. I needed to talk to everyone. Phillips, Bledsoe, Bemis, the guard at the Tri-State elevator.

A nurse came crisply into the room. 'Oh, you're awake now. That's good. We'll take your temperature.'

'I don't want my temperature taken. I want to see the police.'

She smiled brightly and ignored me. 'Just stick this under your tongue.' She was poking a plastic-wrapped thermometer into my mouth.

My fury was mounting, fueled by the helplessness of lying there attached to the ceiling while being ignored.

'I can tell you what my temperature is: it's rising by the second. Will you kindly get someone to call the police for me?'

'Now let's calm down. You don't want to get excited: you've had some concussion.' She forced the thermometer into my mouth and started counting my pulse. 'Dr Herschel will be by later and if she feels it's wise for you to start talking to people she'll let us know.'

329

'Were there any other survivors?' I asked over the thermometer.

'Dr Herschel will tell you what you need to know.'

I shut my eyes while she solemnly wrote my vital statistics into the chart. Patient continues to breathe. Heart operates. 'What's my temperature?'

She ignored me.

I opened my eyes.

'What's my pulse?' No answer. 'Come on, damn-it, it's my body – tell me what it's doing.'

She left to spread the good news that the patient was alive and disagreeable. I shut my eyes and fumed. My body was still weak. I went back to sleep.

When I woke up the third time my mind had cleared. I sat up in bed, slowly and still painfully, and surveyed my body. One problem shoulder. Knees covered with gauze – doubtless badly scraped. Bruises on the right arm. There was a table at the bedside with a mirror on it. Also a telephone. If I'd been thinking instead of yapping earlier I would have realized that. I looked at my face in the mirror. An impressive bandage covered my hair. Scalp wound: that accounted for the headache, though I didn't remember hitting my head. My eyes were bloodshot but my face wasn't damaged, thank the Lord – I'd still be beautiful at forty.

I picked up the telephone and stuck it under my chin. I had to raise the bed to use it, since I couldn't prop the phone against my right shoulder while lying down as long as the left one was attached to the ceiling. Pain shot through my left shoulder as I moved but I ignored it. I dialed Mallory's office number. I had no idea what time it was, but my luck was in: the lieutenant was there.

'Vicki, you'd better not be calling to sweet-talk me. McGonnigal told me about you horning in on the Kelvin investigation. I want you out. O-U-T. It's just my bad luck it happened in Boom Boom's apartment.'

Ah, Bobby. It did me good to hear him ranting. 'Bobby, you'll never believe this, but I'm in the hospital.'

There was silence on the other end as Mallory collected his thoughts.

'Yup. Down at Billings . . . Someone else wanted me out of this case, too, and they took out my brakes and steering while I was at the Port yesterday. If it was yesterday. What day is today?'

Bobby ignored the question. 'Come on, Vicki – don't fool around with me. What happened?'

'That's why I'm calling you – I hope you can find out. I was coming home around ten-thirty, eleven, when the steering went and then the brakes, and I ended up running into a sedan. I think a Mack truck had hit it and knocked it into my lane.'

'Oh, nuts, Vicki. Why can't you stay home and raise a family and just stay the heck out of this kind of mess?' Bobby doesn't believe in using bad language in front of women and children. And even though I refuse to do woman's work I count as a woman with him.

'I can't help it, Bobby; trouble follows me.'

There was a snort at the other end.

'I'm lying here with a dislocated shoulder and a concussion,' I said plaintively. 'I can't do anything – get involved in a mess or raise a family – for a while, anyway. But I would like to know what happened to my car. Can you find out who scooped me off the Dan Ryan and see if they examined my car?'

Bobby breathed heavily for a few minutes. 'Yeah, I guess I could do that. Billings, you say? What's the number?'

I looked at the phone and read him the number. I asked him again for the day. It was Friday, 6.00 pm.

Lotty must have gone back to her clinic on the North Side. She's the person I list to call in case of emergencies and I guess she's my doctor, too. I wondered if I could persuade her to release me – I needed to get going.

A middle-aged nurse popped her head through the door. 'How are we doing?'

'Some of us are doing better than others. Do you know when Dr Herschel is coming back?'

'Probably around seven.' The nurse came in to feel my pulse. If there isn't anything else to do, make sure the patient's heart is still beating. Gray eyes twinkled with meaningless jollity in her red face.

'Well, we're certainly a lot stronger than we were a few hours ago. Is the shoulder giving us any pain?'

I looked at her sourly. 'Well, it isn't giving me any – I don't know about you.' I don't want anyone throwing codeine or Darvon at me. Actually it was throbbing rather badly.

When she left I used the phone again to call Pole Star and ask for Bledsoe. The helpful woman in his office told me he was over at the *Lucella*, which had a ship-to-shore line. She gave me the number and told me how to get an operator to connect me. This was going to be complicated – I'd have to bill it to my office phone.

I was in the middle of giving the operator the dialing and billing instructions when my middle-aged nurse came back. 'Now, we're not to do anything like this until Doctor says we're up to it.'

I ignored her.

'I'm sorry, Miss Warshawski: we can't have you doing anything to excite yourself.' She pulled the phone from my outraged grasp. 'Hello? This is Billings Hospital. Your party is not going to be able to complete the call at this time.'

'How dare you? How dare you decide for me whether I can talk on the phone or not? I'm a person, not a sack of hospital clothes lying here.'

She looked at me sternly. 'The hospital has certain rules. One of them is to keep concussion and accident victims quiet. Dr Herschel will let us know if you're ready to start phoning people yet.'

I was wild with rage. I started to get out of bed to wrestle the phone from her, but the damned pulley kept me attached. 'Quiet!' I shouted. 'Who's getting me excited? You are, pulling that phone away!'

She unplugged it from the wall and walked away with it. I lay in bed panting with exhaustion and fury. One thing was clear – I couldn't wait for Lotty. After my breathing returned to normal I raised myself up again and inspected the pulley. It was holding my shoulder steady. Again I explored it with my right fingers, this time gingerly. The plaster was hard. Even if my shoulder was broken, the cast would keep it in place without traction. No reason I couldn't go home as long as I was careful.

I undid the wires with my right hand. My left shoulder relaxed against the bed with a spasm of pain so strong tears ran down my cheeks. After much ungainly fumbling with the bedclothes I managed to pull the left arm forward again. But helplessness compounded my frustration and I felt momentarily like abandoning the struggle. I shut my eyes and rested for ten minutes. A sling would solve my problems. I looked around doubtfully and finally found a white cloth on the bottom shelf on the bedside table. It took a lot of effort to move around and I was panting and red in the face by the time I managed to turn on my side, reach the cloth, and pull it up to bed level.

After a short rest I put one corner of the cloth in my mouth and slung it around my neck. Using teeth and my right hand, I rigged up a decent sling.

I staggered out of bed, trying not to move the left shoulder more than I had to, and opened the narrow lockers by the entrance. My clothes were in the second. The black pants were torn at the knees and the jacket was stiff with dried blood. One of my favorite outfits. I pulled the pants on with one hand, ignoring underwear, and was trying to figure out what to do about the top when Lotty came in.

'Glad to see you're feeling better, my dear,' she said dryly.

'The nurse said I shouldn't be excited. Since she was agitating me so much I thought I'd better get home where I can rest.'

Lotty's mouth twisted in an ironic smile. She took my right elbow and shepherded me back to the bed. 'Vic, you must stay here another day or two. You dislocated your shoulder. You must keep it still to minimize the tear on the muscles. That's the point of the traction. And you hit your head against the door as your car turned over. It's badly cut and you were unconscious for six hours. I'm not letting you take chances with your health.'

I sat on the bed. 'But, Lotty, I've got so many people to talk to. And the *Lucella* sails at seven – I'll miss them if I don't get through soon.'

'I'm afraid it's after seven now . . . I'll get the phone back in and you can make your calls. But really, Vic, even with your constitution, you must keep this shoulder in a stationary position for two more days. Come.'

333

Tears of frustration pricked my eyes. My head was throbbing. I lay back on the bed and let Lotty undress me and reattach my arm to the pulley. I hated to admit it, but I was glad to be lying down.

She went out to the nurses' station and returned with the phone. When she saw me fumbling with the receiver she took it from me and placed the call herself. But the *Lucella* had already sailed.

12
BEDSIDE STORIES

The next day I entertained a stream of visitors. Charles McCormick, a sergeant from the Traffic Division, came to report to me on the accident and to find out my version of what had happened. I told him as much as I could remember. As I suspected, the semi that was bearing down on me had hit a car when it moved into the left lane. The sedan's driver had been thrown into the windshield and killed. Two passengers were on the critical list, one with spinal cord injuries. I must have looked as horrified and guilty as I felt, for he tried to reassure me.

'They weren't wearing seat belts. I'm not saying it would have saved them, but it might have helped. It certainly saved your life when your car went over on its side. We arrested the truck driver – not a scratch on him, of course – reckless driving and involuntary manslaughter.'

'Did you inspect my car?'

He looked at me curiously. 'Someone had emptied all the brake fluid for you. And cut through the power steering cables. You had enough left to get you going, but moving the wheel would have worked through the last bit of the cables for you.'

'How come I could stop at the lights down on 130th?'

'If you were braking gently, there was probably enough fluid left in the lines to hold you. But if you slammed on the brakes you wouldn't get anything . . . Now who would do a thing like that? Where had you parked your car?'

I told him. He shook his head. 'Lot of vandals down in the Port. You're lucky you got out of this alive.'

'There's a feeble excuse for a guard down at the Tri-State yard. You might have somebody talk to him and see if he noticed anything.'

McCormick said he'd think about it. He asked a few more questions and took off.

Someone brought in an enormous bouquet of spring flowers. The note read:

Vic:

So sorry to read about your accident. Speedy recovery.

Paige

That was kind. Bobby Mallory's wife sent a plant. Murray Ryerson came in person, carrying a cactus. His idea of a joke. 'Vic! You must have cat blood. Nobody ever gets hit by a semi and lives to tell it.'

Murray is a big guy with curly reddish hair. He looks sort of like a Swedish Elliott Gould. His hearty voice and forty-six-inch shoulders contracted the hospital room into half its size.

'Hi, Murray. You read too many sensational newspapers. I wasn't hit by a semi – it got off my tail and ran into some other poor bastard.'

He pulled a vinyl-covered chair over to the bedside and straddled it backward. 'What happened?'

'Is this an interview or a sick visit?' I asked crossly.

'How about an interview in exchange for the story on Paige? Or are you up to that sort of thing?'

I brightened up considerably. 'What'd you find out?'

'Ms Carrington's a hardworking girl – excuse me, young woman. She has one older sister, no brothers. She had a scholarship at the American Ballet Theater when she was fifteen but wasn't good enough for them in the long haul. She lives in a condo on Astor Place. Father's dead. Mother lives in Park Forest South. Her family doesn't have a lot of money. She may have a rich friend helping her out, or the ballet people may pay her a lot – you'd have to sic a detective on her to find out for sure. Anyway, she's lived at the same place for several years now.'

I wrinkled my face. 'Park Forest South? She told me she grew up in Lake Bluff.'

'Maybe she did. That's just where her mother lives . . . Anyway, about her and your cousin. There was some talk about her and Boom Boom the last month or so before he died. They didn't go to any of the celebrity hot spots, so it took Greta a while to catch on – someone spotted her with him at the Stadium back in March. If it was serious they kept it mighty quiet. We talked to some of the other hockey players. They seemed to think she was pursuing him – he wasn't so involved.'

I felt an ignoble twitch of pleasure at that.

'Your turn.' Murray's blue eyes were bright with amusement. I told him everything I knew about the accident.

'Who emptied your brake fluid?'

'Police say it's vandals down at the Port.'

'And you say?'

'I say it was whoever pushed my cousin under the *Bertha Krupnik*.' But that I said to myself. 'Not a glimmer, Murray. I can't figure it out.'

'Vic, with anyone else I'd believe it. But not with you. You got someone mad and they cut your power steering. Now, who?'

I shut my eyes. 'Could have been Lieutenant Mallory – he wants me to keep my nose out of the Kelvin case.'

'Someone at the Port.'

'I'm an invalid, Murray.'

'Someone connected with Kelvin.'

'No comment.'

'I'm going to follow you around, Vic. I want to see this thing happening before it happens.'

'Murray, if you don't get out of here I'm going to sic the nurses on you. They're a very mean lot in this hospital.'

He laughed and ruffled my hair. 'Get well soon, Vic. I'd miss you if you got to your ninth life . . . Just for laughs, I'm going to talk to your red-faced guard over at Tri-State Grain.'

I opened my eyes. 'If you find anything, you'd better let me know.'

'Read about it in the *Star*, Vic.' He laughed and was gone before I could think of a snappy comeback.

After he left, quiet descended for a while. I raised the head of the bed and struggled to fix up the side table so that I could write. I'd never mangled an arm before and hadn't realized how hard it is to do things with one hand. Thank goodness for power steering, I thought, then remembered I didn't have a car, either. I called my insurance agent to report the loss. I hoped my policy covered vandalism.

I doodled around on a sheet of cheap hospital paper – a freighter bouncing through a high sea, a few crocodiles. Anyone down at the Port could have sabotaged my car. Phillips knew I was there – he'd seen me outside the Pole Star offices. He could have told Grafalk or anyone at Grafalk's – the dispatcher, for example.

I added a shark with rows of wild teeth, jaws big enough to swallow the freighter, and a few panicky fishes. Everyone at the *Lucella* knew I was there. That included Bledsoe. Trouble was, Bledsoe kissed well. Could anyone who kissed that well be evil enough to put my car out of commission? Still, the *Lucella* had a complete machine shop in the engine room. Sheridan or Winstein – even Bemis – could have taken care of my car while Bledsoe fed me dinner.

Then, take Phillips. He acted strange whenever I talked to him. Maybe he had fallen in love with me and couldn't articulate it, but I didn't think so. Also, Boom Boom and he argued over the contracts the day before my cousin's accident.

I drew a round ball and added a thatch of hair. That was supposed to be Phillips. I labeled it in case one of the nurses wanted to save the picture for her grandchildren. I should really talk to all of them – Grafalk, Phillips, Bemis, Sheridan, Bledsoe – and soon.

I looked balefully at my left shoulder. I couldn't do much while I lay here attached to my pulley. Still, what about those Eudora shipping contracts? Someone had rescued my canvas bag from the wreckage of the Lynx. It lay now on the lower shelf of the bedside table.

I lowered the bed, stuck my head over the side to fish the diary out of the bag, raised the bed again, and stared fixedly at the dates circled in the front of the book. I keep track of my period by circling the dates

338

when I get it in my desk calendar, but that wouldn't be true in my cousin's case. I grinned to myself, picturing Boom Boom's reaction if I'd suggested that to him.

The dates might not track Boom Boom's menstrual cycle, but maybe they indicated some other periodic occurrence. I copied all of them down on a single sheet of paper. Some were two days apart, some seventeen, eleven, five – all prime numbers – nope, six, three, four, two again. They started at the end of March and ended in November, then started in April again.

That meant the Great Lakes shipping season. Elementary, my dear Warshawski. It began in late March or early April and ended around New Year's when ice built up too heavily on the upper lakes for anyone to want to go crashing around in them.

Eudora Grain operated all year round, of course, but they could only ship by water nine months of the year. So the case against Phillips had something to do with his shipping contracts. But what?

My head was starting to feel worse; I drank some water and lowered the bed to rest. I slept for a while. When I woke up a young man was sitting in the visitor's chair watching me with nervous concern. His smooth, round face with its broken nose and doggy brown eyes looked vaguely familiar. I collected myself.

'Pierre Bouchard! How nice to see you. Myron told me you were out of town.'

He smiled and looked much more familiar – I had never seen him around Boom Boom without a smile. 'Yes, well, I got back last night. And Anna pointed out the story of your accident in the paper.' He shook his head woefully. 'I am so sorry, Vic. First Boom Boom and now this.'

I smiled awkwardly. 'My shoulder will heal. And I know you won't give me sympathy for a mere dislocated shoulder when you've had your leg tied up for weeks, and your nose broken three times –'

'Four,' he corrected with a twinkle.

'So did Myron tell you I wanted to see you?'

'Myron? No. How could he when I have only just returned to Chicago? No, Vic. I came for your sake.' He pulled a package from the floor and handed it to me.

I opened it up. Inside was a seal carved from the soapstone used by Eskimos. I was very touched and told him so.

'Well, in a hospital one gets tired of flowers all day long. I know. This little fellow was carved by Eskimos two-three hundred years ago. I hope he will bring you luck.'

'Thank you, Pierre. I hope he will too. And he will always help me think of you.'

He beamed. 'Good, good – only don't let Anna hear you say that!' He paused a minute. 'I came, too, on an errand of Boom Boom's. I have been in Quebec for two weeks – I flew down for the funeral, you know – then went right back there.

'Well, I got home last night and there was a letter waiting from him! He had mailed it the day before he died.' He fumbled in the breast pocket of his tweedy brown jacket and pulled out the letter, which he handed to me.

Boom Boom was haunting me from the grave with his letters. Everyone was bringing me personal correspondence from him – why didn't he ever write me? I pulled the single white sheet from its envelope and read the small, neat handwriting.

Pierre

Anna tells me you're playing in the Coeur d'Argent. Break their heads for me, my friend. I thought I saw Howard the other day in very odd circumstances. I tried calling him but Elsie said he was in Quebec with you. Give me a ring when you get back and let me know.

Boom Boom

'Who's Howard? Howard Mattingly?'

Pierre nodded. Mattingly was a second-string wing. 'Elsie's his wife. Poor girl. If he told her he was going to the Coeur d'Argent she would believe him – just in order not to find out where he really was.'

'So he wasn't in Quebec with you?'

He shook his head. 'Always a new girl, Mattingly. Boom Boom never cared for him – he can't even play hockey. And he brags, you know.'

340

The unforgivable male sin – bragging about your success with girls and on the ice – especially when neither was very admirable.

I looked at the letter again, dubiously. It seemed totally unrelated to the mess I was trying to sort out. But it had been important enough that my cousin called, then wrote Bouchard. It must mean something. I'd at least have to try to find out where Boom Boom had been the last few days before he died. The letter was dated the twenty-sixth. He'd died on the twenty-seventh. That meant going back maybe to the twenty-third – when the *Lucella* had taken water on in her holds. Could Mattingly have been involved in that? I started feeling overwhelmed by the enormous amount of work I had to do, and looked despairingly at my arm attached to the ceiling.

'Do you have a good photo of Mattingly?'

Bouchard fingered his chin. 'Publicity picture. Myron could give me one.'

'Could you get me half a dozen copies? I want to see if I can find anyone who can ID him in some out-of-the-way places that occur to me.'

'Sure. Right away.' He got up enthusiastically. Action. That's what hockey players thrive on. 'Maybe you want me to take it around while you're lying here?'

'Let me think about it . . . I know who I need to talk to and you might not be able to get to them.'

He took off in a cloud of antiseptic. I looked at my cousin's calendar again. On the twenty-third he'd seen Margolis. Must have been over at the elevator. On the twenty-fourth, a Saturday, he'd been with Paige. He hadn't written in any other appointments. On Monday he talked to MacKelvy, the dispatcher at Grafalk, and to two people whose names I didn't recognize. I'd show Mattingly's picture to Margolis. Maybe get Pierre to do that.

I looked at my watch, strapped awkwardly on my right wrist. Four-thirty – Paige was probably at the theater. I called, got her answering service, and left a message.

Lotty came in around five, noting the disarray of papers and bedclothes with her thick black eyebrows raised. 'You're a terrible patient, my dear. They tell me you're rejecting all medication . . .

Now I do not mind if you don't want the pain pills – that's your choice. But you must take the antibiotics. I don't want any secondary infection in the arm.'

She straightened the mess around the bed with a few efficient motions. I like watching Lotty – she's so compact and tidy. She sat down on the bed. A nurse, bringing in a supper tray, pursed her lips in disapproval. No sitting on beds, but doctors are sacrosanct.

Lotty looked at the food. 'Everything's boiled to death. Good – no digestive problems for you.' She grinned wickedly.

'Pizza,' I groaned. 'Pasta. Wine.'

She laughed. 'Everything's coming along nicely. If you can stand it for one more day I'll take you home on Monday. Maybe spend a few days with me while you recover, okay?'

I looked at her through narrowed eyes. 'I've got work to do, Lotty. I'm not going to lie in bed for two weeks waiting for these shoulder muscles to heal.'

'Don't threaten me, Vic: I'm not one of these silly nurses. When have I ever tried to stop you from doing your job, even when you were being a pit dog?'

I struggled up. 'Pit dog, Lotty? Pit dog! What the hell do you mean?'

'A dog that has to get down in the pit – the ring – and fight every damn person, even its friends.'

I lay down again. 'You're right, Lotty. Sorry. It's very kind of you to invite me home. I would appreciate that.'

She brushed a kiss on my cheek and disappeared for a while, coming back with a deep-dish onion and anchovy pizza. My favorite. 'No wine while you're on antibiotics.'

We ate the pizza and played gin. Lotty won. She whiled away a lot of World War II in London bomb shelters playing gin with the family who had taken her in. She almost always beats me.

Sunday morning I tried Paige again but she still wasn't home. Around noon, however, she showed up in person, looking beautiful in a green ruffled blouse and black and green Guatemalan skirt. She moved buoyantly into the room, smelling faintly of spring, and kissed me on the forehead.

'Paige! How nice to see you. Thanks so much for the flowers – they brighten the place up, as you can see.'

'Vic, I was so sorry about the accident. But I'm glad you weren't hurt more seriously. My answering service said you were trying to get in touch with me – I thought I'd come in person and see how you're doing.'

I asked how *Pavane for a Dope Dealer* was doing and she laughed and told me about the performance. We chatted for a few minutes, then I explained that I was trying to follow up on my cousin's movements the last few days before he died.

Her arched brows snapped together in momentary annoyance. 'Are you still trailing him around? Don't you think it's time you let the dead bury the dead, Vic?'

I smiled with what calmness I could, feeling at a disadvantage with my hair unwashed and wearing a hospital gown. 'I'm doing a favor for an old friend of Boom Boom's – Pierre Bouchard.'

Yes, she'd met Pierre. He was a sweetheart. What did he want to know?

'If you'd seen Howard Mattingly recently.'

An indefinable expression crossed her face. 'I don't know who that is.'

'He's one of the second-string players. Boom Boom didn't like him, so he might never have introduced you to him . . . Where did you two go on that last Saturday? Any place that he might have seen the guy?'

She shrugged and gave me a disdainful look, designed to make me feel like a ghoul. I waited. 'You're being extremely vulgar, Vic. That was my last private day with Boom Boom. I want to keep it to myself.'

'You didn't see him Monday night?'

She turned red. 'Vic! I know you're a detective, but this is excessive. You have a morbid interest in your cousin that's very unhealthy. I believe you can't stand the thought that he might have been close to any other woman but you!'

'Paige, I'm not asking you to tell me what kind of a lover Boom Boom was or to describe any intimate passages of your lives together.

I just want to know what you did on Saturday and whether you saw him on Monday . . . Look, I don't want to turn this into a big, hostile ordeal. I like you. I don't want to start calling Ann Bidermyer and your mother and everyone you know to get a bead on you. I'm just asking you.'

The honey-colored eyes filled with tears. 'I liked you too, Vic. You reminded me of Boom Boom. But he was never so aggressive, even though he was a hockey player.

'We were sailing on Saturday. We got back at four so I could get to rehearsal. He may have stayed in Lake Bluff with the boat. I don't know. Monday night we had dinner at the Gypsy. I never saw him after that. Are you satisfied? Does that tell you what you have to find out? Or will you still be calling my mother and everyone else I know?'

She turned and left. My head was aching again.

13
SHERRY AT VALHALLA

Monday morning, Lotty removed the cast, pronounced the swelling down and healing well underway, and had me released from bondage. We went north to her tidy apartment.

Lotty drives her green Datsun recklessly, believing that all other cars will move out of the way. A dent in the right fender and a long scrape along the passenger door are testimony to the success of her approach. I opened my eyes on Addison – a mistake, since it was in time to see her swerve in front of a CTA bus to turn right onto Sheffield.

'Lotty, if you're going to drive like this, get a semi – the guy who's responsible for putting my shoulder in this sling walked away from the accident unscratched.'

Lotty turned off the ignition and hopped out of the car. 'Firmness is necessary, Vic. Firmness or the others will drive one from the streets.'

It was hopeless; I gave up an unequal struggle.

We had stopped by my apartment to pick up clothes and a bottle of Black Label – Lotty doesn't keep whisky in the house. I'd also taken my Smith & Wesson from a locked cupboard in the bedroom closet. Someone had tried to smash me to bits on the Dan Ryan. I didn't feel like roving the streets unprotected.

Lotty went to the clinic she operates nearby. I settled down in her living room with a telephone. I was going to talk to everyone who'd had a chance to take a crack at me. My rage had disappeared as my head wound healed, but my sense of purpose was strengthened.

I reached the helpful young office manager at the Pole Star Line on the third ring. The news she gave me was not encouraging. The *Lucella Wieser* had delivered her load in Buffalo and was steaming to Erie to pick up coal bound for Detroit. After that she was booked on the upper lakes for some time – they didn't expect her in Chicago until the middle of June. They could help me set up a radio conversation if it was urgent. I couldn't see going over the issues I needed to cover by radio – I'd have to speak to the Pole Star contingent face to face.

Baffled there, I called down to Eudora Grain's office and asked for Janet. She came to the phone and told me she was sorry about my accident and glad I was feeling better. I asked her if she knew where Phillips lived – I might pay a surprise visit to his wife to find out what time her husband had come home the night of my accident.

Janet didn't know. It was up north someplace. If it was important, she could ask around and find out. It was important, I said, and gave her Lotty's number.

While I was waiting I got Howard Mattingly's number from Myron Fackley. Boom Boom told Pierre he'd seen Mattingly in a strange place. I was betting Mattingly was hanging around Lake Bluff when Boom Boom went sailing there with Paige the Saturday before he died. I wanted to find out.

Mattingly wasn't home, but his wife Elsie the Breathless, was. I reminded her we'd met at a number of hockey functions. Oh yes, she gasped, she remembered me.

'Boom Boom told me he'd seen your husband sailing on the twenty-third. Did you go with him?'

She hadn't gone out with Howard that day – she was pregnant and she got tired so easily. She didn't know if he'd been sailing or not – he certainly hadn't said anything about it. Yes, she'd tell Howard to call me. She hung up without asking why I wanted to know.

Lotty came home for lunch. I fixed sardines on toast with cucumber and tomato and Lotty made a pot of the thick Viennese coffee she survives on. If I drank as much of it as she does they'd have to pull me off the chandeliers. I had orange juice and half a sandwich. My head still bothered me and I didn't have much appetite.

Janet called from Eudora Grain after lunch. She'd pilfered the

346

personnel files while everyone was eating and gotten Phillips's address: on Harbor Road in Lake Bluff. I thanked her absently – a lot seemed to go on in Lake Bluff. Grafalk. Paige had grown up there. Phillips lived there. And Paige and Boom Boom had gone sailing there on the twenty-third of April. I realized Janet had hung up and that I was still holding the receiver.

I put it down and went into the guest room to dress for a trip to the northern suburbs. We were in the second week in May and the air was still cold. My dad used to say Chicago had two seasons: winter and August. It was still winter.

I put on the blue Chanel jacket with a white shirt and white wool slacks. The effect was elegant and professional. Lotty had given me a canvas sling to keep as much pressure off the shoulder as possible – I'd wear it up in the car and take it off when I got to Phillips's house.

Lotty's spare room doubles as her study and I rummaged in the desk for a pad of paper and some pens. I also found a small leather briefcase. I put the Smith & Wesson in there along with the writing equipment. Ready for any occurrence.

Until they processed my claim check, the Ajax Insurance Company provided me a Chevette with the stiffest steering I've ever encountered. I'd considered using Boom Boom's Jaguar but didn't think I could operate a stick shift one-handed. I was trying to get Ajax to exchange the Chevette for something easier to handle. In the meantime it was going to make getting around difficult.

Driving up the Edens to Lake Bluff was a major undertaking. Every turn of the wheel wrenched my healing shoulder and strained the muscles in my neck, also weak from the accident. By the time I pulled off the Tri-State Tollway onto Route 137, my entire upper back was aching and my professionally crisp white blouse was wet under the armpits.

At two-thirty on a weekday Lake Bluff was still. Just south of the Great Lakes Naval Training Station on Lake Michigan, the town is a tiny pocket of wealth. To be sure, there are small lots and eight-room ranch houses, but imposing mansions predominate. A weak spring sun shone on nascent lawns and the trees sporting their first pale green frills.

I turned south on Green Bay Road and meandered around until I found Harbor Road. As I suspected, it overlooked the lake. I passed an outsize red brick dwelling sprawled on a huge lot, perhaps ten acres, with tennis courts visible through the budding shrubs – they'd be hidden by midsummer when the plants were in full foliage. Three lots later I came to the Phillipses.

Theirs was not an imposing mansion, but the setting was beautiful. As I wrenched the Chevette up the drive I could see Lake Michigan unfold behind the house. It was a two-story frame structure, topped with those rough shingles people think imitate thatching. Painted white, with a silvery trim around the windows, it looked as if it might have ten rooms or so – a big place to keep up, but an energetic person could do it without help if she (or he) didn't work outside the home.

A dark blue Olds 88 sedan, new model, rested outside the attached three-car garage. It looked as if the lady of the house might be in.

I rang the front bell. After a wait the door opened. A woman in her early forties, dark hair cut expensively to fall around her ears, stood there in a simple shirtwaist – Massandrea, it looked like. A good two hundred fifty dollars at Charles A. Stevens. Even though it was Monday afternoon at home, her makeup was perfect, ready for any unexpected visitors. Diamond drops hung from gold filigree attached to her ears.

She looked at me coldly. 'Yes?'

'Good afternoon, Mrs Phillips. I'm Ellen Edwards with Tri-State Research. We're doing a survey of the wives of important corporate executives and I wanted to talk to you. Do you have a few minutes this afternoon, or could we set a time when it would be convenient?'

She looked at me unblinkingly for a few minutes. 'Who sent you?'

'Tri-State did. Oh, you mean how did we get your name? By surveying the biggest companies in the Chicago area – or divisions of big companies like Eudora Grain – and getting the names of their top men.'

'Is this going to be published someplace?'

'We won't use your name, Mrs Phillips. We're talking to five hundred women and we'll just do some composite profiles.'

She thought about it and finally decided, grudgingly, that she would talk to me. She took me into the house, into a back room that gave a good view of Lake Michigan. Through the window I watched a tanned, well-muscled young man struggling with an eighteen-foot sailboat tied to a mooring about twenty yards from the shore.

We sat in wing chairs covered with needlepointed scenes in orange, blue, and green. Mrs Phillips lighted a Kent. She didn't offer me one – not that I smoke, it just would have been good manners.

'Do you sail, Mrs Phillips?'

'No. I never cared to learn. That's my son Paul. He just got home from Claremont for the summer.'

'Do you have any other children?'

They had two daughters, both in high school. What were her own hobbies? Needlepointing, of course – the ugly chair covers were examples of her handiwork. And tennis, she adored tennis. Now that they belonged to the Maritime Country Club she could play year round with good professionals.

Had she lived in Lake Bluff long? The last five years. Before that they'd been in Park Forest South. Much closer to the Port, of course – but Lake Bluff was such a wonderful place to live. Such a good home for the girls, and, of course, for her.

I told her the main things we were interested in were the advantages and disadvantages of being a corporate spouse. So the advantages had to include life-style – right? Unless she or he had independent means to support it?

She gave a rather self-conscious laugh. 'No, we're not like the – like some of the families around here. Every penny we spend Clayton earns. Not that some of these people aren't finding out what it's like to have to struggle a bit.' She seemed about to expand on the statement but thought better of it.

'Most of the women we talk to find their husbands' schedules one of the biggest disadvantages – raising families alone, spending too much time alone. I imagine an executive like your husband puts in pretty long hours – and of course it's quite a drive from here down to the Port.' The Tri-State Tollway to I-94 would be a smooth run, but he'd be doing it with the traffic as far as the Loop going in and starting at the Loop going home. Maybe ninety minutes if everything went well.

'What time does he usually get home?'

That varied, but generally by seven o'clock.

Paul had gotten the sails up and was untying the boat. It looked pretty big for one person to handle alone, but Mrs Phillips didn't seem worried. She didn't even watch as the boat bobbed off into the lake. Maybe she had total confidence in her son's ability to handle the boat. Maybe she didn't care what he did.

I told her we'd just take a typical day in their lives together and go through it – say last Thursday. What time they had gotten up, what they had for breakfast, what she did with herself. What time her husband got home from work. I heard all the dreary details of a life without focus, the hours at the tennis club, at the beauty parlor, at the Edens Plaza Shopping Center, before I got the information I'd come for. Clayton hadn't gotten home that night until after nine. She remembered because she'd cooked a roast and finally she and the girls ate it without waiting for him. She couldn't remember if he seemed upset or tired or if his clothes were covered with grease.

'Covered with grease?' she echoed, astonished. 'Why would your research firm want to know a thing like that?'

I'd forgotten who I was supposed to be for a minute. 'I wondered if you do your own laundry, or send it out, or have a maid do it.'

'We send it out. We can't afford a maid.' She gave a sour smile. 'Not yet, anyway. Maybe next year.'

'Well, thank you for your time, Mrs Phillips. We'll mail you a copy of the report when we complete it. We'll be bringing it out later this summer.'

She took me back through the house. The furniture was expensive but not very attractive. Someone with more money than taste had picked it out – she, or Phillips, or the two of them together. As I said good-bye I idly asked who lived in the big brick place up the road, the one with the tennis courts.

An expression combining awe and envy crossed her well-made-up face. 'That's the Grafalks. You ought to talk to her. Her husband owns one of the biggest firms in town, ships. They have maids and a chauffeur – the works.'

'Do you spend much time with them?'

'Oh well, they lead their lives, we lead ours. They sponsored us in the Maritime Club and Niels takes Paul and Clayton sailing with him sometimes. But *she's* pretty standoffish. If you don't belong to the Symphony Board you aren't worth much to her.' She seemed to feel she might have said too much, for she hastily changed the subject and said good-bye.

I backed the Chevette on to Harbor Road and drove past the Grafalks'. So that was where the Viking lived. A pretty nice spread. I stopped the car and looked at it, half tempted to go in and try my pitch on Mrs Grafalk. As I sat, a Bentley nosed its way through the gates and turned onto the road. A thin, middle-aged woman with graying black hair was at the wheel. She didn't look at me as she came out – maybe they were used to gawkers. Or perhaps she wasn't the owner but just a visitor – a sister member of the Symphony Board.

Harbor Road turned west toward Sheridan a hundred yards beyond the Grafalk estate. The Bentley disappeared around the corner at a good clip. I put the Chevette into gear and was getting ready to follow when a dark blue sports car came around the bend. Going fifty or so, the driver turned left across my path. I braked hard and avoided a collision by inches. The car, a Ferrari, went on through the brick pillars lining the drive, stopping with a great squeal just clear of the road.

Niels Grafalk came up to the Chevette before I had time to disappear. I couldn't fool him with some tale about opinion polls. He was wearing a brown tweed jacket and an open-necked white shirt and his face was alive with anger.

'What the hell did you think you were doing?' he exploded at the Chevette.

'I'd like to ask you the same question. Do you ever signal before you turn?'

'What were you doing in front of my house anyway?' Anger had obscured his attention and he hadn't noticed who I was at first; now recognition mixed with the anger. 'Oh, it's you – the lady detective. What were you doing – trying to catch my wife or me in an indiscreet position?'

'Just admiring the view. I didn't realize I needed life insurance to travel to the northern suburbs.' I started once more to move the car up Harbor Road, but he stuck a hand through the open window and seized my left arm. It was attached at the top to my dislocated shoulder and his grasp sent a shudder of pain through both arm and shoulder. I stopped the car once more.

'That's right, you don't do divorces, do you?' His dark blue eyes were flooded with emotion – anger, excitement, it was hard to tell. He released my arm and I turned off the ignition. My fingers strayed to my left shoulder to rub it. I let them fall – I wasn't going to let him see he'd hurt me. I got out of the car, almost against my will, pulled by the force of his energy. That's what it means to have a magnetic personality.

'You missed your wife.'

'I know – I passed her on the road. Now I want to know why you were spying on my property.'

'Honest Injun, Mr Grafalk – I wasn't spying. If I were, I wouldn't do it right outside your front door like that. I'd conceal myself and you'd never know I was here.'

The blaze died down a bit in the blue eyes and he laughed. 'What were you doing here, then?'

'Just passing through. Someone told me you lived here and I was gawking at it – it's quite a place.'

'You didn't find Clayton at home, did you?'

'Clayton? Oh, Clayton Phillips. No, I expect he'd be at work on a Monday afternoon, wouldn't he?' It wouldn't do to deny I'd been at the Phillipses – even though I'd used a fake name, Grafalk could check that pretty easily.

'You talked to Jeannine, then. What did you think of her?'

'Are you interviewing her for a job?'

'What?' He looked puzzled, then secretly amused. 'How about a drink? Or don't private eyes drink on duty?'

I looked at my watch – it was almost four-thirty. 'Let me just move

352

the Chevette out of the way of any further Lake Bluff menaces. It isn't mine and I'd hate for something to happen to it.'

Grafalk was through being angry, or at least he had buried his anger below the civilized urbanity I'd seen down at the Port last week. He leaned against one of the brick pillars while I hauled at the stiff steering and maneuvered the car onto the grass verge. Inside the gates he put an arm around me to guide me up the drive. I gently disengaged it.

The house, made from the same brick as the pillars, lay about two hundred yards back from the road. Trees lined the front on both sides, so that you had no clue to how big the place really was as you approached it.

The lawn was almost completely green – another week and they'd have to give it the season's first mowing. The trees were coming into leaf. Tulips and jonquils provided bursts of color at the corners of the house. Birds twittered with the business of springtime. They were nesting on some of the most expensive real estate in Chicago but they probably didn't feel snobbish toward the sparrows in my neighborhood. I complimented Grafalk on the grounds.

'My father built the place back in the twenties. It's a little more ornate than we care for today – but my wife likes it, so I've never done anything to change it.'

We went in through a side door and back to a glassed-in porch overlooking Lake Michigan. The lawn sloped down steeply to a sandy beach with a little cabana and a couple of beach umbrellas. A raft was anchored about thirty yards offshore but I didn't see a boat.

'Don't you keep your boat out back here?'

Grafalk gave his rich man's chuckle. He didn't share his birds' social indifference. 'The beaches here have a very gradual slope – you can't keep anything with more than a four-foot draw close to the shore.'

'Is there a harbor in Lake Bluff, then?'

'The closest public harbor's in Waukegan. It's extremely polluted, however. No, the commandant at Great Lakes Naval Station, Rear Admiral Jergensen, is a personal friend. I tie my sailboat up there.'

That was handy. The Great Lakes Naval Training Station lay on Lake Bluff's northern border. Where would Grafalk keep his yacht

353

when Jergensen retired? The problems the very rich face are different from yours and mine.

I sat in a bamboo chaise-longue. Grafalk opened a window. He busied himself with ice and glasses in a bar built into the room's teak panels. I opted for sherry – Mike Hammer is the only detective I know who can think and move while drinking whisky. Or at least move. Maybe Mike's secret is he doesn't try to think.

With his back still turned to me Grafalk spoke. 'If you weren't spying on me, you must have been spying on Clayton. What'd you find out?'

I put my feet on the red-flowered cushion sewn to the bamboo. 'Let's see. You want to know what I think about Jeannine and what I found out about Clayton. If I did divorces I'd suspect you of sleeping with Jeannine and wondering how much Phillips knew about it. Except you don't strike me as the type who cares very much what men think about your cavorting with their wives.'

Grafalk threw back his sun-bleached head and gave a great shout of laughter. He brought me a fluted tulip-shaped glass filled with straw-colored liquid. I sipped it. The sherry was as smooth as liquid gold. I wished now I'd asked for Scotch. A millionaire's whisky might be something unique.

Grafalk sat facing me in a chintz-covered armchair. 'I guess I'm being too subtle, Miss Warshawski. I know you've been asking questions around the Port. When I find you up here it makes me think you've found something out about Phillips. We carry a lot of grain for Eudora. I'd like to know if there's something going on with their Chicago operation I should know about.'

I took another sip of sherry and put the glass on a tiled table at my right hand. The floor was covered with hand-painted Italian tiles in bright reds and greens and yellows and the table top matched them.

'If there are problems with Eudora Grain that you should know about, ask David Argus. My main concern is who tried to kill me last Thursday night.'

'Kill you?' Grafalk's bushy eyebrows arched. 'You don't strike me as the hysterical type, but that's a pretty wild accusation.'

'Someone took out my brakes and steering last Thursday. It was

354

only luck that kept me from careening into a semi on the Dan Ryan.'

Grafalk finished whatever he was drinking – it looked like a martini. Good old-fashioned businessman – no Perrier or white wine for him. 'Do you have a good reason for thinking Clayton might have done it?'

'Well, he certainly had opportunity. But motive – no. No more than you or Martin Bledsoe or Mike Sheridan.'

Grafalk stopped on his way back to the bar and looked at me. 'You suspect them as well? You're sure the – uh – damage took place at the Port? Could it have been vandals?'

I swallowed some more sherry. 'Yes, yes, and possibly, although I don't believe it. It's true anyone could empty brake fluid with a little ingenuity – but what vandals carry around a ratchet wrench and a cutting torch just on the off chance that they'll find a car to mutilate? They're much more likely to slash tires, steal hubcaps, or smash in windows. Or all three.'

Grafalk brought over the sherry bottle and topped off my glass. I tried to pretend I drank the stuff every day and didn't attempt to read the label. I'd never be able to afford this sherry anyway; what did I care what it was called?

He sat back down with a fresh martini and looked at me intently. He was turning something over in his mind. 'How much do you know about Martin Bledsoe?'

I stiffened. 'I've met him a few times. Why?'

'He didn't tell you anything about his background at dinner on Thursday?'

I put the expensive glass down with a snap on the tiled table. 'Now who is spying on whom, Mr Grafalk?'

He laughed again. 'The Port is a small community, Miss Warshawski, and gossip about shipowners travels fast. Martin hasn't asked a woman out to dinner since his wife died six years ago. Everyone was talking about it. Likewise your accident. I knew you were in the hospital but I didn't know someone had deliberately tampered with your car.'

'The *Herald-Star* gave me a front-page story – picture of my poor

355

Lynx with its front missing and everything . . . Gossip about Bledsoe must be buried pretty deep. No one gave me a whiff about his background that sounded as troublesome as you're seeming to imply.'

'It is buried deep. I've never told anyone about it, even when Martin left me and I was mad enough to want to hurt him badly. But if there has been a crime committed, if there's been an attempt on your life, you should know about it.'

I didn't say anything. Outside, the house cast a lengthening shadow on the beach.

'Martin grew up in Cleveland. Bledsoe is his mother's maiden name. He never knew who his father was. It could have been any of a series of drunken sailors on Cleveland's waterfront.'

'That's not a crime, Mr Grafalk. And scarcely his fault.'

'True. That's just to give you a flavor of his home life. He left when he was fifteen, lied about his age, and signed on to sail the Great Lakes. In those days you didn't need the training you do now, and of course there was a lot more shipping – no waiting around union halls hoping to get called up for a job. Any warm body that could haul ropes and lift two hundred pounds would do. And Martin was strong for his age.' He paused to swallow his drink.

'Well, he was a smart fellow and he came to the attention of one of my mates. A man who liked to help the young men in his charge, not stand on their heads. When he was nineteen Martin ended up in our Toledo office. He obviously had far too many brains to waste just doing muscle work that any stupid Polack could handle.'

'I see,' I murmured. 'Maybe you could find an opening for me on one of your boats if detective work palls.'

He stared at me for a minute. 'Oh. Warshawski. I see. Don't show your hackles – it's not worth it. The waterfront is filled with Poles strong as oxen but not much brainpower.'

I thought of Boom Boom's cousins and declined arguing the point.

'Anyway, to make a long story very short, Martin was operating in an environment he could understand intellectually but not socially. He'd never had much formal education and he never learned any sense of ethics or morality. He was handling too much money

356

and he siphoned some of it off. I lost a tough argument with my father about prosecuting Martin. I had found him, I had pushed him – I was only thirty myself at the time. I wanted to give him a second chance. Dad refused and Martin spent two years in a Cantonville prison. My father died the month before he was released and I hired him back immediately. He never did anything else criminal that I'm aware of – but if there's some trouble between Pole Star and Eudora Grain or at Eudora Grain itself that involves money, you should know about Martin's background. I'm relying on your discretion to keep it to yourself – I wouldn't want Argus, or even Clayton, for that matter, to know about it if it turns out nothing's wrong.'

I finished my sherry. 'So that was what you meant that day at lunch. Bledsoe educated himself in prison and you were hinting you could tell people about it if you wanted to.'

'I didn't think you'd caught that.'

'Even a boneheaded Polack couldn't miss that one . . . Last week you were threatening him, today you're protecting him – sort of. Which is it?'

Anger flashed across Grafalk's face and was quickly erased. 'Martin and I have – a tacit understanding. He doesn't attack my fleet, I don't tell people about his disreputable past. He was making fun of the Grafalk Line. I was backing him off.'

'What do *you* think is going on at Eudora Grain?'

'What do you mean?'

'You've leaped to a couple of conclusions, based on my investigations down at the Port. You think there might be some kind of a financial problem down there. You're concerned enough to reveal a well-concealed truth about Bledsoe. Not even his ship's officers know it – or if they do, they're too loyal to betray it. You must think something pretty serious is wrong.'

Grafalk shook his head and gave a slightly condescending smile. 'Now *you're* leaping to conclusions, Miss Warshawski. Everyone knows you've been looking into your cousin's death. And they know you and Phillips have had a few words together – you just can't keep secrets in a closed community like that. If there is something wrong at Eudora Grain, it would have to involve money. Nothing else important could be wrong there.' He swirled the olive in his glass. 'It's none of my business – but I do periodically wonder where Clayton Phillips get his money.'

I looked at him steadily. 'Argus pays him well. He inherited it. His wife did. Any reason why one of those possibilities wouldn't be good enough?'

He shrugged. 'I'm a very wealthy man, Miss Warshawski. I grew up with a lot of money and I'm used to living with it. There are plenty of people without money who are at ease with and around it – Martin's one and Admiral Jergensen another. But Clayton and Jeannine aren't. If they inherited it, it was an unexpected windfall late in life.'

'Still possible. They don't have to measure it in your class to afford that house and their other amenities. Maybe a crabby old grand-mother hoarded it so that it would give everyone the least possible pleasure – that happens at least as often as embezzlement.'

'Embezzlement?'

'You're suggesting that, aren't you?'

'I'm not suggesting anything – just asking.'

'Well, you sponsored them at the Maritime Club. That's impos-sible for the *nouveaux riches* to crack, from everything I read. Not enough to have a quarter million a year for that place – you have to trace yourself back to the Palmers and the McCormicks. But you got them in. You must have known something about them.'

'That was my wife. She undertakes odd charities – Jeannine was one that she's since come to regret.'

A phone rang somewhere in the house, followed shortly by a buzz on an instrument I hadn't noticed earlier, set in an alcove by the bar. Grafalk answered it. 'Yes? Yes, I'll take the call . . . Will you excuse me, Miss Warshawski?'

I got up politely and moved into the hallway, going the opposite direction from which we'd come in. I wandered into a dining room where a thickset middle-aged woman in a white blouse and blue skirt was laying the table for ten. She was putting four forks and three spoons at each place. I was impressed – imagine having seventy matching forks and spoons. There were a couple of knives apiece, too.

'I bet they've got more besides that.'

'Are you talking to me, miss?'

'No. I was thinking aloud. You remember what time Mr Grafalk got home Thursday night?'

She looked up at that. 'If you're not feeling quite well, miss, there's a powder room down the hall to your left.'

I wondered if it was the sherry. Maybe Grafalk had put something into it, or maybe it was just too smooth for my Scotch-raddled palate. 'I feel fine, thanks. I just wanted to know if Mr Grafalk got home late Thursday night.'

'I'm afraid I couldn't say.' She went back to the silver. I was wondering if I could beat her into talking with my good arm but it didn't seem worth the effort. Grafalk came up behind me.

'Oh, there you are. Everything under control, Karen?'

'Yes, sir. Mrs Grafalk left word she'll be back by seven.'

'I'm afraid I'm going to have to ask you to leave now, Miss Warshawski. We're expecting company and I've got to do a couple of things before they arrive.'

He showed me to the front door and stood watching until I went through the brick pillars and got into the Chevette. It was six o'clock. The sherry left a nice light glow in my head. Not anything like drunk, not even mildly sloshed. Just glowing enough to take my mind off my aching shoulder, not enough to impair my consummate handling of the stiff steering.

14
POTLUCK

As I headed back toward the Edens and poverty, I felt as though someone were spinning me around in a swivel chair. Grafalk's sherry and Grafalk's story had clearly been provided for a reason. But what? By the time I got back to Lotty's the sherry had worn off and my shoulder ached.

Lotty's street is even more decrepit than the stretch of Halsted I inhabit. Bottles mingled with crumpled paper cups in the gutter. A '72 Impala drooped on the near front side where someone had removed the wheel. An overweight woman bustled along with five small children, each staggering under a heavy bag of groceries. She yelled at them in shrill Spanish. I don't speak it, but it's close enough to Italian for me to know it was good-natured chivvying, not angry bullying.

Someone had left a beer can on Lotty's front steps. I picked it up and carried it in with me. Lotty creates a small island of sanity and sanitation on the street and I wanted to help maintain that.

I smelled *pot-au-feu* as I opened the door; I suddenly felt good about being here to eat a hearty meal rather than at a seven-course affair in Lake Bluff. Lotty was sitting in the spotless kitchen reading when I came in. She put a marker in her book, took off her black-rimmed glasses, and placed both on a corner of the butcher block.

'It smells great. Anything for me to do? . . . Lotty, did you ever own seventy matching forks and spoons?'

Her dark eyes gleamed with amusement. 'No, my dear, but my grandmother did. At least that many. I had to polish them every

Friday afternoon when I was eight. Where have you been that they have seventy matching forks and spoons?'

I told her about my afternoon's inquiries while she finished the stew and served it. We ate it with thick-crusted Viennese bread. 'The trouble is, I'm going in too many different directions. I need to find out about Bledsoe. I need to find out about my car. I need to find out about Phillips's money. I need to know who broke into Boom Boom's apartment and killed Henry Kelvin. What were they looking for, anyway? I'd been through all his papers and he didn't have anything that looked like a hot secret to me.' I pushed an onion around my plate, brooding. 'And of course, top of the list, who pushed Boom Boom into Lake Michigan?'

'Well, what tasks can you turn over to someone else – the police, or perhaps Pierre Bouchard? He wants to help.'

'Yeah, the police. According to the Kelvin family, they're doing sweet nothing about locating his murderers. I can see Sergeant McGonnigal's point, of course: they haven't got a clue *qua* clue. Trouble is, they refuse to connect Kelvin with Boom Boom. If they did that, they might be able to muscle in and get some real information out of the Port. But they think Boom Boom died accidentally. Same thing with my crash. They want that to be vandals.' I fiddled with my spoon. It was stainless steel and matched my knife and fork. Lotty had style.

'I have a kind of crazy idea. I want to go meet the *Lucella* at the next port she calls in and have it out with Bledsoe – find out what he's been up to and whether Grafalk's telling the truth and whether the chief engineer or the captain could've monkeyed with my car. I know there's stuff I can do down here. But it'll wait three or four days. I want to talk to those guys *now*.'

Lotty pursed her lips, dark eyes alert. 'Why not, after all? They won't be back here for – what did you say? Seven weeks? You can't wait that long, anyway – their memories will have gone stale.'

'The way to do it is to track them down through *Grain News*. It lists contracts and when and where they're to be picked up. That way, Bledsoe's office won't be able to warn him that I'm coming: I like to catch people *au naturel*.'

I got up and stacked the plates in the sink, running hot water from the tap.

'What is this?' Lotty demanded. 'Your head wound must have been worse than I thought.'

I looked at her suspiciously.

'When did you ever clean up dishes within two days of using them?'

I swatted her with a dish towel and pursued my idea. It sounded good. I could get my corporate spy, Janet, to find out how much Phillips earned. Maybe she could even snatch a look at his bankbook, although Lois probably guarded that with her fiery dragon breath. If Bouchard was in town he could find out who this guy was who was interested in buying a share of the Black Hawks. That was the person who'd introduced Paige to Boom Boom last Christmas.

Lotty rubbed Myoflex into my shoulder before I went to bed and fixed me up with a sling to keep me from twisting the joint in my sleep. Nonetheless I woke the next morning barely able to use my left arm. I wasn't going to be able to drive that damned car any place, and I'd planned on taking it down to my cousin's apartment to look at his copies of *Grain News*. The police were through there; as soon as I collected the keys I could go back to it.

Lotty offered me her car, but I couldn't see one-handedly driving a stick shift. I stomped around the apartment, enjoying a first-rate tantrum.

As she left for the clinic, Lotty said dryly, 'I hesitate to interfere, but what problems will your rage solve? Can't you do some of your business by phone?'

I stiffened momentarily, then relaxed. 'Right, Lotty. Pit-dog Warshawski will be called off.'

She blew me a kiss and left, and I phoned Janet at Eudora Grain to see if she could find out how much Phillips earned.

'I don't think I could do that, Miss Warshawski. Payroll information is confidential.'

'Janet, wouldn't you like Boom Boom's murderer caught?'

'Well, I've been thinking that over. I don't see how he could have been murdered. Who would want to do it, anyway?'

362

I counted to ten in Italian. 'Someone on your case about the information you've been getting me?'

Not exactly, she explained, but Lois had started asking her what she was doing in the office while everyone else was at lunch. Yesterday she'd come in just seconds after Janet closed the drawer where Mr Phillips's home address was filed. 'If I stay late today, she's sure to hang around to spy on me.'

I tapped my teeth with a pencil, trying to figure out some way she could get Phillips's salary without getting into trouble. Nothing occurred to me.

'How often do you get paid?'

'Every other week. Our next paycheck is due Friday.'

'Is there any chance you could look in his wastebasket at the end of the day? A lot of people just toss their pay stubs; maybe he does too.'

'I'll try,' she said dubiously.

'That's the spirit,' I said heartily. 'One other thing. Could you call over to the Pole Star Line and find out where the *Lucella Wieser* will be in the next couple of days?'

She sounded more reluctant than ever but copied the information down and said she would get back to me.

Bouchard was out; I left a message with his wife. After that I didn't have anything to do but pace. I didn't want to leave the apartment and risk missing Janet's call. In the end, to pass the time, I worked on some vocal exercises. My mother had been a singer and she had trained me as a musician, hoping I would have the operatic career Hitler and Mussolini deprived her of. That never worked out, but I know a lot of breathing exercises and can sing all the main arias from *Iphigénie en Tauride*, the only opera my mother sang in professionally before she left Italy in 1938.

I was halfway through Iphigenia's second-act entrance, creaking like a windy parlor organ, when Janet phoned back. The *Lucella* would be in Thunder Bay Thursday and Friday. They were unloading coal in Detroit today and would leave there this evening.

'And really, Miss Warshawski, I can't help you any more. I'm calling you now from a pay phone at the 7-11 but Lois was all over me about calling Pole Star. Now that Mr Warshawski's gone, I'm just back in the typing pool and there isn't any reason for me to do things like that, you see.'

'I see. Well, Janet, you've done a great deal and I appreciate it very much.' I hesitated a second. 'Do me one favor, though – if you hear anything suspicious, call me from home. Could you do that much?'

'I suppose,' she said doubtfully. 'Although I don't really know what I would hear.'

'Probably nothing. Just on the chance that you do,' I said patiently. We hung up and I massaged my sore left shoulder. Somewhere among the hundreds of books that lined Lotty's walls must be an atlas. I started in the living room and worked my way along. I found a pre-World War II map of Austria, a 1941 Guide to the London Underground, and an old US atlas. None of them showed any place along the Great Lakes called Thunder Bay. That was a big help.

Finally I called a travel agent and asked if there were any flights between Chicago and Thunder Bay. Air Canada had one flight a day, leaving Toronto at 6.20, arriving at 10.12 p.m. I'd have to take a 3.15 flight to Toronto.

'How far away is that, anyway?' I demanded. That was seven hours of travel. The travel agent didn't know. Where was Thunder Bay? In Ontario. The agent didn't know any more than that but agreed to make a reservation on the next day's flight for me. Two hundred fifteen dollars to spend seven hours in an airplane – they ought to pay me. I charged it to my American Express account, tickets to be picked up tomorrow at O'Hare.

I looked for Thunder Bay on the Canadian side of the Great Lakes but still couldn't find it. I guessed I'd know when I got there.

The rest of the day I spent in a whirlpool at the Irving Park Y, the poor person's health club. I pay ninety dollars a year to use the pool and the Nautilus room. The only other people who go there are earnest youths intent on building perfect biceps or catching a game of basketball – no racquet ball courts, no bars, no disco lights, and no hot pink warm-up outfits with designer labels.

15

THE FROZEN NORTH

The ticket agent at Air Canada told me Thunder Bay was Canada's westernmost port on Lake Superior. I asked him why it hadn't shown up on my map and he shrugged indifferently. One of the flight attendants was more helpful. On the way to Toronto she explained that the town used to be called Port Arthur; the name had been changed about ten years ago. I made a mental note to buy Lotty a modern atlas as a hostess present.

I checked my small canvas bag through in Chicago, since it contained the Smith & Wesson (disassembled in accordance with federal firearms regulations). I'd packed lightly, not intending to be gone beyond a day or two, just jeans, shirts, a heavy sweater, and underwear. I didn't even carry a purse – just stuck my wallet in my jeans pocket.

After an hour's layover in Toronto's bright modern airport, I boarded Air Canada's Ontario puddle jumper. We stopped five times on the way to Thunder Bay on tiny airstrips which loomed out of open country to receive us. As people got on and off they exchanged greetings and light conversation. It reminded me of a bus ride through rural Louisiana in the freedom-march days; I got just as many covert stares.

At Thunder Bay, the fifteen of us who'd made the final leg of the trip climbed down rollaway stairs into a clear, cold night. We were perhaps six hundred miles north of Chicago, a difference in latitude sufficient for winter to have barely ended.

Most of my fellow passengers were wrapped in winter coats. I shivered across the tarmac in a cotton shirt and corduroy jacket, wishing I had carried my sweater instead of packing it. A husky young fellow with red, wind-whipped cheeks and a shock of black hair followed close behind with the luggage. I picked up my canvas bag and set off in search of a night's lodgings. Thunder Bay boasted a Holiday Inn. That sounded good enough to me. They had plenty of vacancies. I booked a room for two nights.

They told me they would send a car along for me – their regular van was broken. I waited forty-five minutes inside the tiny terminal, drinking a cup of bitter coffee from a vending machine to entertain myself. When the limo finally came, it was a beat-up station wagon which I almost missed until it was rolling away. Then I could read THUNDER BAY HOLIDAY INN painted on its side. I went racing after it, yelling frantically, my canvas bag bumping me in the leg. I longed for the gigantic, impersonal efficiency of O'Hare with its ranks of surly, illiterate cab drivers.

The car stopped fifty feet ahead of me and waited while I came panting up to it. The driver was a heavyset man dressed in a graying white pullover. When he turned to look at me, a pungent draft of stale beer swept over me. The forty-five minutes I'd been waiting he must have spent in a bar. However, if I tried to get a cab I might be there all night. I told him to take me to the Holiday Inn and I leaned back in the seat with my eyes shut, grasping the side strap. It couldn't be any worse than riding with Lotty sober but the memory of my own accident was too fresh for me not to be nervous. We moved along at a good clip, ignoring honking horns.

It was well past eleven when my driver deposited me, intact, and I couldn't find any place in walking distance still open for dinner. The motel restaurant was closed and so was a little Mandarin place across the street. I finally took an apple from a basket in the lobby and went to bed hungry. My shoulder was sore and the long flight had worn me out. I slept soundly and woke up again after nine.

My shoulder had recovered in the night – most of the stiffness was gone. I dressed more easily than I had for days, only feeling a twinge when I pulled the heavy wool sweater over my head. Before going down to breakfast I reassembled the Smith & Wesson and loaded it. I didn't expect Bledsoe to jump me in front of the entire crew of the

Lucella Wieser, but if he did the gun wasn't going to do me much good with the barrel unattached to the hammer.

I hadn't had much appetite while my shoulder was in pain and I'd dropped five or six pounds. This morning I felt better and sat down to pecan waffles, sausages, strawberries, and coffee.

I was a latecomer in the little restaurant and the middle-aged waitress had time to talk. As she poured my second cup of coffee I asked her where I could rent a car. There was an Avis place in town, she said, but one of her sons had a couple of old cars he rented out if I didn't need anything too fancy. I told her that would be fine as long as they had automatic transmissions, and she trotted off to call her son.

Roland Graham his name was, and he spoke with a Canadian accent, a lilting drawl that sounds as if it has a trace of Scots buried in it. His car was a '75 Ford Fairmont, old but perfectly clean and respectable. I told him I'd only need it until the next morning. The fee, payable in advance in cash, was thirty dollars.

The Holiday Inn was in the heart of town. Across the street was the largest Presbyterian church I've ever seen. A modern city hall faced the motel, but the street behind us had a lot of run-down stores and premises to let. As I got down to the waterfront the stores gave way rapidly to bars and girlie joints. I've often wondered whether seamen really have the primitive appetites port towns attribute to them, or whether they go to sleazy joints because that's the only thing the locals offer.

Finding the *Lucella* turned out to be a larger problem than I'd anticipated. Thunder Bay is an enormous port, even though the town itself doesn't have more than a hundred thousand people in it. But much of the grain shipped by water in North America passes through that port heading east and south, and the lakefront includes mile upon mile of towering elevators.

My first thought had been to stop in at each elevator to see if the *Lucella* was docked there, but the miles of towers made that seem like a waste of time. I did go into the yard of the first one I came to. After bumping around the mud-filled ruts, I found a tiny, green-sided office. But a harassed man inside handling the phone assured me that he didn't have the foggiest idea of where the *Lucella* was; he only knew she wasn't there.

I went back into the town and found the local newspaper. As I'd hoped, it listed the ships that were in port and where they were. The *Lucella* was docked at Elevator 67, the Manitoba Grain Co-op.

There didn't seem to be any logical order to the yard numbers. I was near number 11, but I went past yard 90 without seeing the Manitoba Grain Co-op and wasted time backtracking. I finally found it another two miles down the road, well past the town.

I turned the Ford into the gravel yard, my heart pounding with nervous anticipation. The Manitoba elevator was enormous, some two hundred giant paper towel tubes banked together. Huge though it was, it didn't dwarf the ship tied up on its eastern end. The *Lucella*'s red hulk gleamed sleekly in the late morning sun. Above her, like clouds covering and revealing Mount Everest, hovered a mass of white smoke. Grain dust. The *Lucella* was loading.

The yard was a mess of gravelly mud. In the corners of the elevator, out of the sun's reach, a gray-white residue of winter was still melting. I parked clear of the more obvious holes and picked my way through the mud, the metal shards, pasteboard, and grain clumps making up the now familiar elevator scene.

The Smith & Wesson dug uncomfortably into my side as I climbed the *Lucella*'s ladder to the main deck. I stopped for a minute at the edge of the hardhat area to survey the busy scene and ran a surreptitious finger under the leather holster digging into my diaphragm. Squinting at the whitened figures, I couldn't be sure if any of my quarry were present. I thought I might recognize Bledsoe's stocky body, but it was hard to say.

I went into the pilothouse and climbed the four flights to the mahogany-paneled bridge. Only the first mate, Keith Winstein, was there. He looked up in surprise when I came in. He recognized me at once.

'Miss Warshawski! What – is Captain Bemis expecting you?'

'I don't think so. Is he around? And what about the chief engineer and Martin Bledsoe?' It would be really annoying if Bledsoe had returned to Chicago.

'They're all in Thunder Bay this morning. Going to the bank, doing that kind of business. They won't be back until late afternoon. Not until right before we sail, I'm afraid.'

'You're sailing today?' I sat down on one of the mahogany stools. 'Your office said you'd be here through tomorrow.'

'No, we made good time up from Detroit. Got here a day early. Time is money in this business, so we started loading last night at midnight. We'll finish around four and sail at five.'

'Any idea where I can find Bledsoe or Sheridan?'

He shook his head regretfully. 'Everyone keeps bank accounts in Thunder Bay because we're here so often. This is a good chance to catch up on personal affairs – I'll be taking off myself for a few hours as soon as the second mate gets back.'

I rubbed my forehead in exasperation. 'Where do you go from here?'

Winstein was getting a little irritated. 'We take this load to St Catharines, at the other side of the lakes. Why do you ask?'

'What's your route, I mean – do you stop any place along the way where I could get off?'

The first mate looked at me strangely. 'If you're thinking of sailing with us, you'll have to clear that with the captain, Miss Warshawski.'

'Yes, well, let's assume he's going to give his permission. Where's the nearest place I could get off?'

He shook his head. 'There isn't any place on board for you to sleep – Mr Bledsoe's in the stateroom.'

I started to feel my temper rising. 'I'm not asking for a place to sleep. That's why I want to get off at the nearest place possible.'

'I guess that would be Sault Ste Marie,' he said dubiously. 'You could get off when we're at the bottom of the lock. But we won't reach there until three tomorrow afternoon, at the earliest. You'd still have to find someplace to spend the night.'

'Oh, never mind that,' I said impatiently. 'I'll lie down on the couch here in the bridge if I need to. But I've got to talk to the captain and Bledsoe. To Sheridan, too. And I'm damned if I'm going to fly around the country on the off chance of meeting up with them someplace.'

369

'It isn't really my decision,' Winstein said pacifically. 'You'll have to talk to Captain Bemis.' He returned to his papers and I left the bridge.

16
STOWAWAY

I took the Fairmont back to the Holiday Inn, singing 'A capital ship
for an ocean trip' and 'The Barbary Pirates'. I repacked the little
canvas bag and checked out, leaving a note for Roland Graham with
the Ford's keys at the counter. It was one o'clock. If the *Lucella*
wasn't sailing until five, I might as well get some lunch.

By the time I'd eaten and found a taxi to take me out to Elevator
67 it was after three-thirty. The midday sun made the air hot
enough for me to take off my sweater and stuff it into my canvas
bag before once more climbing the ladder to the *Lucella*'s main
deck.

They had just finished loading. The heavy grain chutes were being
hauled into the elevator from above. Under the second mate's
direction, men began operating two little deck gantries to put the
hatch covers back onto the hold openings. One man worked each
crane, using controls in front of a small seat on the starboard side. He
lifted the hatch cover while two seamen steadied it at either end –
they are very large, unstable steel lids. Then he lowered the cover
while the other two fitted it onto some twenty or thirty protruding
bolts. The three would move along to the next cover while a fourth
seaman followed behind with an enormous wrench, screwing all the
bolts into place.

As I stood watching, I felt the ship begin to vibrate. The engines
had been turned on. Soon the air was filled with their urgent racket.
A trail of black diesel smoke drifted upward from the giant funnel. I
had no idea how long the engines ran before the ship moved out, but I
noticed a couple of seamen at the guy ropes on shore, ready to loose

them as soon as the signal was given. I hadn't come back a minute too early.

I felt very keyed up. I knew I was wasting time on deck when I should have been on the bridge confronting anyone who had returned, but I was very nervous and didn't know what to say once I got up there. In my heightened state I thought I saw someone swimming away from the port side of the ship. I moved as quickly as I could past the clutter around the self-unloader but didn't see anything. I stood straining my eyes against the reflecting water and finally saw a figure break the surface twenty yards away, close to the shore.

When I turned back, Bledsoe was just coming on board. He stopped to talk to the second mate, then headed for the bridge without seeing me. I was about to follow when it occurred to me I might be better off just stowing away and presenting myself after castoff. Accordingly, I moved to the back of the pilothouse where a stack of giant oil drums served as both garbage cans and an effective shield from the bridge. I sat down on a metal box, placed my bag against a coil of rope, and leaned back to enjoy the view.

I had momentarily forgotten the figure I'd seen, but now I noticed him – or her – walk out of the water some fifty yards away, on the other side of the elevator yard. A clump of trees soon hid the person from my sight. After that nothing happened for about forty-five minutes. Then the *Lucella* gave two deep hoots and slowly pulled away from the wharf.

Two gray-green troughs appeared at my feet, the wake of the giant screws, and the distance between the ship and the wharf widened quickly. Actually, the ship didn't seem to move; rather, the shore appeared to back away from us. I waited another ten minutes, until we were a good mile or two from land and no one would be disposed to turn around to send me back.

Leaving my bag amidst the coiled rope, I made my way up to the bridge. I loosened the gun in its holster and released the safety catch. For all I knew, I was going up to face one or more killers. A few crew members passed me on my way up. They gave me curious stares but didn't question my right to be there. My heart pounding, I opened the door to the bridge.

Up the flight of narrow wooden stairs. A murmur of voices at the top. I emerged into a busy scene – Winstein was going over charts at the drafting table. A burly, red-haired man with two inches of cigar in his mouth stood at the wheel taking directions from Captain Bemis. 'Off the second port island,' Bemis said. 'Off the second port island,' the helmsman repeated, turning the wheel slightly to his left.

Bledsoe stood behind, looking on. Neither he nor the captain turned when I came in, but Winstein looked up from the charts and saw me. 'There she is,' he said quietly.

The captain turned at that. 'Ah, Miss Warshawski. The first mate said you'd turn up.'

'Technically you're a stowaway, Vic.' Bledsoe gave the glimmer of a smile. 'We could lock you in the holds until we get to Sault Ste Marie.'

I sat down at the round table. Now that I was here my nervous tension receded; I felt calm and in charge. 'I only have a rudimentary knowledge of maritime law. I gather the captain is complete master of the ship – that he evaluates any crimes committed under his jurisdiction and dispenses judgment, if any?'

Bemis looked at me seriously. 'Technically, yes, as long as the ship is at sea. If some crime was committed on board, though, I'd probably just hang onto the person and turn him over to the regular judiciary at our next port of call.'

He turned to Winstein and told him to take over the bridge for a few minutes. The first mate finished drawing a line on the chart and then got up to stand by the helmsman. We were going through a channel with a lot of little islands planted in it – humps of earth with one or two trees or a scraggly bush clinging to them. The sun glinted off the gray-green water. Behind us, Thunder Bay was still visible with its line of elevators.

Bledsoe and Bemis joined me at the table. 'You're not supposed to come on board without the captain's permission.' Bemis was serious but not angry. 'You don't strike me as a frivolous person and I doubt you did it frivolously, but it's still a major breach of maritime custom. It's not a crime, per se, but I don't think that's what you were referring to, was it?'

'No. What I really wanted to know was this: suppose you have someone on board who committed a crime while he was on shore. You find out about it while you're at sea. What do you do with that person?'

'It would depend in part on what the crime was.'

'Attempted murder.'

Bledsoe's eyes narrowed. 'I assume that isn't hypothetical, Vic. Do you think one of this crew tried killing someone? Who and why?'

I looked at him steadily. 'I was the intended victim. I'm trying to find out for sure that someone here wasn't after me.'

For a count of ten there was no sound in the small room but the faint throb of the engines. The helmsman kept his eyes in front of him, but his back twitched. Bemis's jaw set in an angry line.

'You'd better explain that one, Miss Warshawski.'

'Gladly. Last Thursday night Martin Bledsoe here took me out for dinner. I left my car in the elevator yard. While we were gone someone cut through the steering controls with a cutting torch and emptied the brake fluid. It was a miracle that when my car crashed on the Dan Ryan I escaped with minor injuries. An innocent driver was killed, though, and one of his passengers is now paralyzed for life. That's murder, assault, and a lot of other ugly stuff.'

Bledsoe gave an exclamation. 'My God, Vic!' He fished around for something else to say but made several false starts before he could get a coherent thought out. I watched him carefully. Surprise is such an easy feeling to counterfeit. It looked genuine, but . . .

The captain looked at me with narrowed eyes. 'You seem pretty cool about it.'

'Would it be more believable if I lay down on the floor and screamed?'

Bemis made a gesture of annoyance. 'I assume I could radio the Chicago police and get some verification of this.'

I pointed to the radio on the port wall. 'By all means. A Lieutenant Robert Mallory can tell you anything you want to know.'

'Can you give us some more detail on what happened?' That was Bledsoe, finding his voice and his authoritative manner.

I obliged with as much of the accident as I could recall.

374

'Now what makes you think someone on the *Lucella* might be involved?'

'There's a limited universe of who could have done it,' I explained. 'Only a few people knew I was down there. Only a few could identify my car.'

'How do you figure that?' That was the captain again. 'There are a lot of vandals down at the Port and this frankly sounds like vandalism.'

'Captain, I don't know what your exposure to vandals is, but I see a lot of them. I don't know of any vandal who goes around with a cutting torch and a ratchet wrench to disable cars. It's a lengthy procedure with a very high risk of getting caught, and there's no point to it. Especially in a place like a grain elevator, which is hard to get to.'

Bemis's brow creased. 'You think just because the *Lucella* was tied up there we're implicated somehow?'

'You people and Clayton Phillips are the only ones who knew I was down there . . . Captain, I'm certain that my cousin was pushed overboard last month – or underboard, to be literal about it. And I know someone else was killed in connection with my cousin's affairs. The way I see it, the killer is either connected with this ship or with Eudora Grain. Now you've got a big machine shop here. I'm sure you have a couple of cutting torches lying around –'

'No!' Bemis exploded. 'No way in hell is Mike Sheridan involved in this.'

'How long have you known him?'

'Twenty years. At least twenty years. We've been sailing together a long time. I know that man better than I know – my wife. I see more of him.'

'Besides,' Bledsoe put in, 'there's no reason for Mike – or any of us – to want to kill you.'

I rubbed my forehead tiredly. 'Ah, yes. The reason. That's the real stumper. If I knew what my cousin had found out I'd know who did the murders. I thought it had something to do with those grain shipment orders, Martin, but you assured me they were perfectly legitimate. But what if it had something to do with the vandalism to your cargo holds? You told me that was what Boom Boom called you about.'

'Yes but, Vic, we all need this ship operating to make a living. Why would we put it out of commission?'

'Yes, well, something occurred to me about that, too.' I looked at my hands, then at Bledsoe. 'What if someone were blackmailing you – something along the lines of "I'll tell your secret history if you don't give up that load".'

Bledsoe's face turned white under his windburn. 'How dare you!'

'How dare I what? Suggest such a thing – or bring up your past?'

'Either.' He smashed the table with his fist. 'If I had such a past, such a secret, who told it to you?'

Bemis turned to Bledsoe in surprise. 'Martin – what are you talking about? Do you have a mad wife stashed away in Cleveland that I never heard of?'

Bledsoe recovered himself. 'You'll have to ask Warshawski here. She's telling the story.'

Up to that point I hadn't been sure whether Grafalk had told the truth. But he must have to get that reaction. I shook my head.

'It's just a hypothesis, Captain. And if there is something in Bledsoe's past – why, he's kept it to himself long enough. I don't think it would be very interesting to anyone else these days.'

'You don't?' Bledsoe pounced on that. 'Then why would anyone blackmail me to keep it quiet?'

'Oh, I don't think it's very interesting. But you clearly do. Your reaction just now clinches it. What set me wondering was why you smashed a wineglass just because Grafalk made a crack that day about where you went to school.'

'I see.' Bledsoe gave a short laugh. 'You're not so dumb, are you?'

'I get by . . . I'd like to ask you one question in private, however.'

Bemis stood up politely. 'I ought to look at the course, anyway . . . By the way, Martin's occupying our only guest room. We'll put a cot up for you in my dining room.'

I thanked him. Bledsoe looked at me speculatively. I leaned forward and said in a low voice, 'I want to know that you didn't get Sheridan to doctor my car while we were at dinner that night.' I saw a pulse start to move in his jaw. 'Believe me, I hate to ask it. I hate even to think it. But that was a pretty horrifying experience – it shook my trust in human nature.'

Bledsoe pushed back his chair with enough force to knock it over. 'Go ask him yourself! I'm fucked if I'll put up with any more of this.'

He stormed down the stairs and the bridge echoed with the vibration of the slammed door. Bemis looked at me coldly. 'I'm running a ship, Miss Warshawski, not a soap opera.'

I felt a violent surge of anger. 'Are you, now? I've had a cousin killed and someone's tried to kill me. Until I'm sure your ship and crew didn't do it, you'll damned well live in my soap opera and like it.'

Bemis left the helm and came over to lean across the table into my face. 'I don't blame you for being upset. You lost a cousin. You've been badly hurt. But I think you're blowing up a couple of very sad accidents into a conspiracy and I won't have you disrupting my ship while you do it.'

My temples pounded. I kept just enough control not to offer any grandiose threats. 'Very well,' I said tightly, my vocal cords straining, 'I won't disrupt your ship. I would like to talk to the chief engineer while I am on board, however.'

Bemis jerked his head at Winstein. 'Get the lady a hard hat, Mate.' He turned back to me. 'You may question the chief. However, I don't want you talking to the crew unless either the first mate or I am present. He'll instruct the second mate to make sure that happens.'

'Thanks,' I said stiffly. While I waited for Winstein to bring me a hard hat, I stared moodily out the rear of the bridge. The sun was setting now and the shoreline showed as a distant wedge of purple in front of it. To the port side I could see a few chunks of ice. Winter lasted a long time in these parts.

I was doing a really swell job. So far I didn't know a damned thing I hadn't known three weeks ago, except how to load a Great Lakes freighter full of grain. In my mind's ear I could hear my mother chewing me out for self-pity. 'Anything but that, Victoria. Better for you to break the dishes than lie about feeling sorry for yourself.' She was right. I was just worn out from the aftermath of my accident. But

377

that, in Gabriella's eyes, was the reason, not the excuse – there was no excuse for sitting around sulking.

I pulled myself together. The first mate was waiting to escort me from the bridge. We walked down the narrow staircase, me following on his heels. He gave me a hard hat with his name on the front in faded black type; he explained that it was his spare and I was welcome to it as long as I was on board.

'If you're thinking of going down to talk to the chief now, why not wait until dinner? The chief eats dinner in the captain's dining room and you can talk to him there. You won't be able to hear each other over the engines, anyway.'

I looked at him grudgingly, wondering if he was deflecting me from Sheridan long enough to let Bledsoe tell him his version of the story.

'Where's the captain's dining room?' I asked.

Winstein took me there, a small, formal room on the starboard side of the main deck. Flowered curtains hung at the portholes and an enormous photo of the *Lucella*'s launching decorated the forward wall. The crew's mess was next door to it. The same galley served both, but the captain was waited on at table by the cooks whereas the crew served themselves cafeteria style. The cooks would serve dinner between five-thirty and seven-thirty, Winstein told me. I could get breakfast there between six and eight in the morning.

Winstein left me to go back to the bridge. I waited until he was out of sight and then descended into the engine room. I vaguely remembered my way from the previous visit, going through a utility room with a washer and dryer in it, then climbing down a flight of linoleum-covered stairs to the engine-room entrance.

Winstein was right about the noise. It was appalling. It filled every inch of my body and left my teeth shaking. A young man in greasy overalls was in the control booth that made up the entrance to the engines. I roared at him over the noise; after several tries he understood my query and told me I would find the chief engineer on level two inspecting the port journal bearings. Apparently only an idiot would not know about port journal bearings. Declining further assistance, I swung myself down a metal ladder to the level below.

The engines take up a good amount of space and I wandered around quite a bit before I saw anyone. I finally spotted a couple of hard-hatted figures behind a mass of pipes and made my way over to them. One was the chief engineer, Sheridan. The other was a young fellow whom I hadn't seen before. I didn't know whether to be pleased or disappointed not to find Bledsoe with Sheridan – it would have given a more solid direction to my inchoate searching to see them in cahoots.

The chief and the other man were totally absorbed in their inspection of a valve in a pipe running at eye level in front of them. They didn't turn when I came up but continued their work.

The younger man unscrewed the bottom part of a pipe which came up from the floor at right angles to the overhead valve and then joined it. He stuck a stainless steel tube into the opening, checked his watch, and pulled the tube out again. It was covered with oil, which seemed to satisfy both of them. They tightened up the pipes again and wiped their hands on their grimy boiler suits.

At that point they realized I was there, or perhaps just realized I wasn't a regular member of the team. Sheridan put his hands to my head to bellow an inquiry at me. I bellowed back at him. It was obvious that no one could conduct a conversation over the roar of the engines. I yelled in his ear that I would talk to him at dinner; I wasn't sure he heard me but I turned and climbed back up onto the main deck.

Once outside I breathed in the late afternoon air thankfully. We were well away from the shore and it was quite cold. I remembered my bag resting among the coils of the rope behind the pilothouse and went back there to take out my heavy sweater and put it on. I dug out a tam and pulled it down over my ears.

The engines clattered at my feet, less loudly but still noticeably. Turbulent water lifted the stern periodically, giving the *Lucella* a choppy, lurching ride.

In search of quiet I walked down to the bow. No one else was outside. As I walked the length of the ship, nearly a quarter mile, the noise gradually abated. By the time I reached the stem, the frontmost tip of the vessel, I couldn't hear a sound except the water breaking

379

against the bow. The sun setting behind us cast a long shadow of the bridge onto the deck.

No guardrail separated the deck from the water. Two thick parallel cables, about two feet apart, were strung around the edge of the ship, attached to poles protruding every six feet or so. It would be quite easy to slip between them into the water.

A little bench had been screwed into the stem. You could sit on it and lean against a small toolshed and look into the water. The surface was greeny black, but where the ship cut through it the water turned over in a sheen of colors from lavender-white to blue-green to green to black – like dropping black ink onto wet paper and watching it separate into its individual hues.

A change in the light behind me made me brace myself. I reached for the Smith & Wesson as Bledsoe came up beside me.

'It would be easy to push you in, you know, and claim that you fell.'

'Is that a threat or an observation?' I pulled the gun out and released the safety.

He looked startled. 'Put that damned thing away. I came out here to talk to you.'

I put the safety on and returned the gun to its holster. It wouldn't do me much good at close quarters, anyway – I'd brought it out mainly for show.

Bledsoe was wearing a thick tweed jacket over a pale blue cashmere sweater. He looked nautical and comfortable. I was feeling the chill in my left shoulder – it had started to ache as I sat staring into the water.

'I blow up too fast,' he said abruptly. 'But you don't need a gun to keep me at bay, for Christ's sake.'

'Fine.' I kept my feet braced, ready to spring to one side.

'Don't make things so fucking difficult,' he snapped.

I didn't move, but I didn't relax either. He debated some point with himself – to stomp off offended or say what was on his mind. The second party won.

'It was Grafalk who told you about my youthful misadventure?'

'Yes.'

He nodded to himself. 'I don't think there's another person who knows – or still cares . . . I was eighteen years old. I'd grown up in a waterfront slum. When he pulled me into the Cleveland office I ended up handling a lot of cash transactions. His mistake – he should never have put anyone that age in front of so much money. I didn't steal it. That is, of course I stole it. What I mean is, I wasn't thinking of stashing away loot and escaping to Argentina. I just wanted to live in a grand style. I bought myself a car.' He smiled reminiscently. 'A red Packard roadster. Cars were hard to get in those days, right after the war, and I thought I was the slickest thing on the waterfront.'

The smile left his face. 'Anyway, I was young and foolish and I spent the stuff blatantly, begging to be caught, really. Niels saw me through it, rehired me right out of Cantonville. He never mentioned it in twenty years. But he took it very personally when I set up Pole Star back in '74. And he started throwing it in my face – that he knew I was a criminal at heart, that I'd stayed with him just to learn the secrets of his organization and then left.'

'Why did you leave?'

'I'd wanted to run my own show for years. My wife was sick, had Hodgkin's disease, and we never had any children. I guess I turned all my energy to shipping. Besides, after Niels refused to build any thousand-footers, I wanted to have a ship like this one.' He patted the guy ropes affectionately. 'This is a beautiful ship. It took four years to build. Took me three years to put the financing together. But it's worth it. These things run at about a third the cost of the old five-hundred-footers. The cargo space goes up almost as the square of the length – I can carry seven times the load of a five-hundred-foot vessel . . . Anyway, I wanted one very badly and I had to start my own company to get it.'

How badly? I wondered to myself. Badly enough to run a more sophisticated scam than he'd thought of thirty years ago and come up with the necessary capital? 'What does a ship like this cost to build?'

'The *Lucella* ran just a hair under fifty million.'

'You float stock or bonds or what?'

'We did some of everything. Sheridan and Bemis coughed up their savings. I put mine in. The Fort Dearborn Trust owns the biggest chunk of this and we finally got them to arrange a series of loans with about ten other banks. Other people put in personal money. It's a tremendous investment, and I want to make sure it carries a cargo every day between March 28 and January 1 so we can pay off the debt.'

He sat down next to me on the small bench and looked at me, his gray eyes probing. 'But that isn't what I came out here to say to you. I want to know why Niels brought up the story of my past. Not even Bemis and Sheridan know it, and if the tale had gotten around three years ago, I could never have built this beauty. If Niels wanted to hurt me, he could have done it then. So why did he tell you now?'

It was a good question. I stared into the churning water, trying to recall my conversation with Grafalk. Maybe he wanted to ventilate some of his pent-up bitterness against Bledsoe. It couldn't have been from a desire to protect Phillips – he'd raised questions about Phillips too.

'What do you know about the relationship between Grafalk and Clayton Phillips?'

'Phillips? Not much. Niels took him up as a protégé about the time I started Pole Star – a year or two later, maybe. Since he and I didn't part too amicably, I didn't see much of him. I don't know what the deal was. Niels likes to patronize young men – I was probably the first one and he took up a number of others over the years.' He wrinkled his forehead. 'Usually they seemed to have better abilities than Phillips. I don't know how he manages to keep that office in the black.'

I looked at him intently. 'What do you mean?'

Bledsoe shrugged. 'He's too – too finicky. Not the right word. He's got brains but he gets in their way all the time. He has sales reps who are supposed to handle all the shipping contracts but he can't leave 'em to it. He's always getting involved in the negotiations. Since he doesn't have day-to-day knowledge of the markets, he often screws up good deals and saddles Eudora with expensive contracts. I noticed that when I was Niels's dispatcher ten years ago and I see it now with my own business.'

That didn't sound criminal, just stupid. I said as much and Bledsoe laughed. 'You looking for a crime just to drum up business or what?'

'I don't need to drum up business. I've plenty in Chicago to occupy me if I ever get this mess unsnarled.' I got up. Stowing away on the *Lucella* had been one of my stupider ideas. None of them would tell me anything and I didn't know how to sort out natural loyalty to the ship and each other from concealing a crime. 'But I'll find out.' I spoke aloud without realizing it.

'Vic, don't be so angry. No one on this ship tried to kill you. I'm not convinced anyone tried to kill you.' He held up a hand as I started to talk. 'I know your car was vandalized. But it was probably done by a couple of punks who never saw you in their life.'

I shook my head, tired. 'There are too many coincidences, Martin. I just can't believe that Boom Boom and the watchman in his building died and I was almost killed through a series of unrelated events. I can't believe it. And I start wondering why you and the captain want me to believe it so badly.'

He stuck his hands in his pockets and whistled silently. 'Why don't you step me through your logic? I'm not saying I'll buy it. But give me a chance.'

I drew a breath. If he was responsible, he knew all about it anyway. If he wasn't, there wasn't any harm in his knowing. I explained about Boom Boom's death, the quarrel with Phillips, the search through my cousin's apartment, Henry Kelvin's death.

'There's got to be a reason for it and the reason is at the Port. It has to be. You told me those shipping orders I showed you last week seemed perfectly legitimate. So I don't know where else to look. If Phillips was deliberately fudging the contracts and running Eudora Grain's Chicago office at a loss, that'd be a reason. Although I think Argus would have been on his tail for that a long time ago, especially if he's been doing it for ten years.' I pushed back the tam and rubbed my forehead. 'I was hoping it would be those shipping orders, since that's what Boom Boom was arguing over with Phillips two days before he died.'

Bledsoe looked at me seriously. 'If you really want to be certain, you'll have to look at the invoices. The contracts themselves appear fine, but you want to see what Phillips actually paid for the orders. How much do you know about the way an office like that operates?'

I shook my head. 'Not much.'

'Well, Phillips's main job is to act as the controller. He should leave the sales to his salesmen but doesn't. He handles all the financial stuff. Now it's his job, too, to know prices and what the market is doing so that when he pays bills he can check on his reps to make sure they're getting the best prices. But he's supposed to stay out of the selling end. He handles the money.'

I narrowed my eyes. A man who handled all the money bore further investigation. Trouble was, everything in this damned case bore further investigation and I wasn't getting anywhere. I massaged my stiffening shoulder, trying to push my frustration away.

Bledsoe was still speaking; I'd missed some of it.

'You getting off in Sault Ste Marie? I'll fly you down to Chicago – my plane is there and I'm planning on going back to the office this week.'

We got up together and started back down the long deck. The sun had set and the sky was turning from purple to gray-black. Overhead, the first stars were coming out, pricks of light in the dusky curtain. I'd have to come back out when it was completely dark. In the city one doesn't see too many stars.

17
DEADLOCK

Bledsoe and I joined the chief engineer in the captain's dining room, where he was eating roast beef and mashed potatoes. Bemis was still up on the bridge – Bledsoe explained that the captain would stay up there until the ship was out of a tricky channel and well into the middle of Lake Superior. We three were the only ones in the dining room – the other officers ate with the crew. Handwritten menus at our plates offered a choice of two entrees, vegetables, and dessert. Over baked chicken and broccoli I talked to Sheridan about my accident.

The chief agreed that he had cutting torches of different sizes on board, as well as every possible variety of wrench. 'But if you're asking me to tell you if any of them were used last Thursday, I couldn't. We don't keep the tools under lock and key – it'd be too time-consuming to get at them.' He buttered a roll and ate a chunk of it. 'We have eight people on engine-room duty when the ship's at sea and all of them need to get at the tools. We've never had any problems and as long as we don't I plan to keep free access to them.'

No liquor was allowed on the ship, so I was drinking coffee with dinner. The coffee was thin and I poured a lot of cream into it to give it some flavor.

'Could someone have come onto the ship, taken some tools, and brought them back without anyone noticing?'

Sheridan thought about it. 'I suppose so,' he said reluctantly. 'This isn't like the navy where someone is always on watch. No one has to stay on board when we're in port, and people come and go without anyone paying attention. Theoretically someone could go to the engine room without being caught, assuming he knew where the tools were. He'd have to be lucky, too, and not have anyone come on him by surprise . . . At any rate, I'd rather believe that than that one of my own men was involved.'

'Could one of your own men have done it?'

Again, it was possible, but why? I suggested that someone – perhaps Phillips, for example, – had hired one of the crew to do his dirty work. Bledsoe and Sheridan discussed that energetically. They were both convinced that they'd gotten rid of their lone bad apple when they fired the man who put water in the holds last month.

Sheridan felt great confidence in the men under him. 'I know my judgment could be wrong, but I can't imagine any one of those guys deliberately sabotaging somebody's car.'

We went on talking long after one of the junior cooks had cleared away the table and cleaned up the galley. Finally the chief engineer excused himself to go back to the engine room. He said I could question the other engineers and the four boilermen, but he didn't think it would do me any good.

As he walked through the doorway, I said casually, 'Were you in the engine room that night?'

He turned and looked me straight in the eye. 'Yes, I was. And Yalmouth – my first engineer – was with me. We were going over the hydraulics preparatory to starting up the engines the next day.'

'Not out of each other's sight all evening?'

'Not long enough to monkey with a car.'

He went on out the door. Bledsoe said, 'Satisfied, Vic? Is Pole Star clean in your eyes?'

I shrugged in irritation. 'I suppose so. Short of launching a full-scale investigation into everyone's movements last Thursday night there's not much else I can do to check up on you guys.' Something occurred to me. 'You had a security force on board that night, didn't you? Maybe Bemis can give me their names – they'd know if anyone had been climbing around with tools.' My villain might have persuaded a guard that he belonged on board: that probably wouldn't be too difficult. But a guard would surely remember someone leaving the ship with a blowtorch and a ratchet wrench. Of course, if Bledsoe was behind the whole business, he might have paid off the guards, anyway.

I drank some cold coffee, looking at Bledsoe over the rim of the cup. 'The whole thing turns on money, lots of money. It's in the Eudora Grain contracts, but that's not the only place.'

'True,' Bledsoe agreed. 'There's also a great deal in the freighter business itself, and there's the amount I had to raise to pay for the *Lucella*. Maybe I embezzled it from Niels to pay for my flagship just before I left Grafalk Steamship.'

'Yes, and if he suspected that but couldn't prove it, he might want to alert me to the possibility.'

Bledsoe smiled genially. 'I can see that. You should definitely look into my finances as well as Phillips's. I'll tell my secretary to give you access to my files when we get back to Chicago.'

I thanked him politely. All that offer meant was, if he had something to hide, he had it concealed someplace other than in Pole Star's books.

We spent the rest of the evening talking about opera. They'd had a collection of librettos in the Cantonville prison library and he'd read all of them. After he got out of prison he started attending the Cleveland Opera.

'Now I fly to New York five, six times a year for the Met and get season tickets to the Lyric . . . It gives me a queer feeling to talk about Cantonville with someone. My wife was the only person who knew about it – except Niels, of course. And neither of them ever mentioned it. It makes me feel almost guilty when I bring it up now.'

Around ten-thirty, two of the crew members came in with a cot and some blankets. They set the narrow bed up under the portholes in the starboard wall, bracing it to the side so it wouldn't slide around with the rocking of the ship.

After they left, Bledsoe stood fiddling the change in his pockets with the awkwardness of a man who wants to make a pass but isn't sure how it will be received. I didn't try to help him out. I liked the way he kissed. But I'm not the kind of detective who hops nonchalantly from bed to bed: if someone's been trying to kill me, it cools my enthusiasm. And I still didn't have total trust in Bledsoe's purity.

'Time for me to turn in,' I said briskly. 'I'll see you in the morning.'

He hesitated for a few seconds longer, scanning my face for encouragement, then turned and went upstairs to the stateroom. I put the Smith & Wesson under the little pillow and climbed under the blankets in my jeans and shirt. Despite the noise of the engines and the lurching of the ship, I went to sleep almost immediately and slept soundly through the night.

The cooks woke me the next morning before six as they started clattering around in the galley next to the captain's dining room. I tried pulling the bedding up over my ears but the disturbance was too persistent. Finally I got up and stumbled up to the next floor where the bathroom was. I changed my underwear and shirt and brushed my teeth.

It was too early for me to feel like eating, even though breakfast was ready, so I went out on deck to look at the day. The sun had just come up, a ball of liquid orange low in the eastern sky. A purple shoreline lay a mile or so to our left. We were going past some more of the small clumps of islands which had dotted the channel as we left Thunder Bay.

At breakfast Captain Bemis, the chief engineer, and Bledsoe were all in affable moods. Perhaps the fact I was leaving soon cheered them up. At any rate, even the captain was gracious, explaining our course to me. We were coming down the southeast coast of Lake Superior leading into the St Mary's Channel. 'This is where the *Edmund Fitzgerald* went down in 1975,' he said. 'It's the best approach to the St Mary's, but it's still a very shallow route, only thirty feet deep in places.'

'What happend to the *Edmund Fitzgerald*?'

'Everyone has his own theory. I don't suppose they'll ever know for certain. When they dove down to look at her, they found she'd been cut neatly in three pieces. Sank immediately. I've always blamed the Coast Guard for not keeping the channel markings in proper order. The waves were thirty feet high out here that night – one of them must have pushed the *Fitzgerald* into a trough and caused her to scrape against the bottom and snap. If they'd marked the channel properly, Captain McSorley would have avoided the shallowest spots.'

'The thing is,' the chief engineer added, 'these lakers don't have much support through the middle. They're floating cargo holds. If they put a lot of beams through the holds they'd take up too much valuable cargo space. So you get these twenty- or thirty-foot waves out here, and they pick up a ship like this one on either end. The middle doesn't have any support and it just snaps. You go down very quickly.'

The head cook, a thick Polish woman in her mid-fifties, was pouring the captain's coffee. As the chief spoke, she dropped the cup on the floor. 'You should not talk like that, Chief Engineer. It is very bad luck.' She called to her underlings to come in and clean up the mess.

Sheridan shrugged. 'It's all the men do talk about when there's a storm brewing. Ship disasters are like cancer – the other guy is always the one who's going to get it, anyway.' All the same, he apologized to the cook and changed the subject.

Bemis told me we'd be getting into the Soo locks around three o'clock. He suggested that I watch from the bridge so I could see the approach and the way the ship was steered into the channel. After lunch I packed up my little canvas bag for a quick departure: Bledsoe told me we'd have about two minutes to climb over the side of the *Lucella* onto shore before they opened the lock gates and she went on through to Lake Huron.

I checked that my credit cards and cash were in my front jeans pocket and put the Smith & Wesson into the bag. There didn't seem much point in lugging it around in the shoulder holster while I was on board. I stowed the bag next to the pilothouse while I went up on the bridge to watch the *Lucella* slide into the lock. We were now well into the channel of the St Mary's River, following a slow-moving procession.

'Your position into the locks is determined by your position when you arrive at the mouth of the channel,' Bemis explained. 'So there's a lot of racing to get into the channel first. We passed a couple of five-hundred-footers earlier this morning. I can't stand tying up here – enforced boredom and everyone gets restless.'

'It's expensive to tie up,' Bledsoe said sharply. 'This ship costs ten thousand dollars a day to operate. She has to make every second count.'

I raised my eyebrows, trying to calculate costs in my head. Bledsoe looked at me angrily. 'Yes, it's another financial motive, Vic.'

I shrugged and walked over to where the helmsman, Red, was turning the wheel. Two inches of cigar stuck out of his pudgy face. He steered off various landmarks without glancing at the tiller. The huge ship moved easily under his hands.

As we drew nearer to the locks, the U S Coast Guard started talking to Bemis on the radio. The captain gave them his ship's name, length, and weight. Of the four locks closing the twenty-four-foot drop between Lake Superior and Lake Huron, only the Poe was big enough to handle the thousand-foot freighters. We would be the second ship into the Poe, following an upbound vessel.

Bemis slowed the diesels to their lowest possible speed. He called down to the engine room and ordered them to put the engines into neutral. Behind us I could see three or four other freighters sitting in the channel. Those farther back tied up at the bank while they waited.

Below us the deck stretched magnificently away. We watched the first mate, Winstein, talking with a group of seamen who would climb down ladders to the sides of the lock and tie up the ship. Theirs was a demanding job physically – they had to keep up tension on the cables as the ship sank and the ropes became slack. Then, just before the gates opened into Lake Huron they would untie the ropes and leap back on board.

We waited about half a mile from the locks themselves. The sun glinted off the water and dressed up the dingy skylines of the twin cities. Canada's Sault Ste Marie lay to our left, dominated by the giant Algoma Steelworks on the shoreline. In fact, coming up to our current resting place, the captain had steered using different parts of the Algoma plant – off the second smokestack, off the first coal heap, and so on.

After a forty-minute wait the Coast Guard told Bemis he could proceed. As the engines increased their revolutions slightly, a giant freighter passed us upbound, giving one long hoot on its whistle. Bemis pushed a button and the *Lucella* responded with an equally long blast and began to move forward. A few minutes later we were nosing into the lock.

The Poe Lock is only 110 feet wide; the *Lucella*, 105. That gave Red two and a half feet on either side – not much room for error. Slowly we glided forward, bisecting the distance and coming to a halt about twenty feet from the southern gate. Red never once looked at the wheel.

The gates were mammoth wooden structures reinforced with thick steel struts. I turned to watch them swing shut behind us, guided electrically from the bank.

As soon as the gates closed, our crew lowered ladders and scrambled down to the bank. I thanked Bemis for the use of his ship and the chance to talk to some of his crew and turned to go with Bledsoe down to the deck.

Most of the crew came on deck for the passage through the Soo. I shook hands with the head cook, Anna, thanking her in my few words of stumbling Polish for her cooking. Delighted, she unleashed a torrent of smiling Polish on me, which I ducked from as gracefully as I could.

It only takes about fifteen minutes for the lock to empty its two million-plus gallons of water into Lake Huron. We sank rapidly while the men alongside us tightened the cables. As soon as the *Lucella* was level with the lock, Bledsoe and I would hop across the two-foot gap to land. We'd have about thirty seconds before the forward gates opened.

An observation tower on the American side allows tourists to watch the ships as they rise and fall between the two lakes. The May day was still quite chilly and few people were out. I looked at them idly across the intervening MacArthur Lock and then squinted a second time at a man on the lower level. He had a thatch of bright red hair unusual for an adult. The hair reminded me of someone, but I couldn't place him, especially not at a distance of thirty or forty yards. As I peered across the water, he picked up an outsize set of binoculars and focused on us. I shrugged and looked down through the gap between the side of the *Lucella* and the side of the lock where the fetid water was rushing away. The deck was almost level now with the top of the lock. Bledsoe touched me on the arm and I walked back toward the pilot-house to pick up my bag.

I was almost there when I was thrown to the ground. I landed with a thud on the deck, the wind knocked out of me. I thought at first I'd been hit and looked around defensively as I gasped for breath. But when I tried to stand up, I realized the deck was shuddering underneath me. Almost everyone else had been flung from their feet as well by some gigantic shock.

The head cook was teetering at the edge of the rocking ship, groping for the steel cables. I wanted to go to her to help, but the deck was too unstable; I tried to move to her and was thrown to the ground again. I watched in horror as she lost her balance and fell over the side. Her screams were drowned in a roaring that blocked out all other sound.

We were rising again. We didn't have the buoyancy of a ship in water, but rocked as if balanced on the air itself. Sheridan's comment at breakfast came back to me: the *Fitzgerald* being held in the air and snapped in two. I didn't understand what was happening, why we were rising, why there was no water pushing us up, but I felt vilely sick.

Bledsoe was standing near me, his face gray. I clung to the self-unloader for support and pulled myself up for the second time. The crew were crawling away from the open sides of the ship toward the pilot house, but we could not help one another. The ship was too unstable.

As we rose, sheets of water rushed up like giant geysers between the sides of the ship and the lock. They towered skyward in a thick curtain cutting us off from the land, and then from the sky. A hundred feet above us the water rushed before falling in a pounding torrent onto the deck, knocking me over again, knocking everyone over. I could hear some of the men near me screaming.

I peered stupidly at the curtain of water, trying to see through it to the men at the sides with their cables. They couldn't be holding them, couldn't be restraining the ship as she rose lurchingly upward, lashing forward and backward in her concrete confines.

Holding the self-unloader, I struggled to my knees. A wall of water was pounding the forward gate, ripping panels from it. Great logs spewed into the air and disappeared through the sheets of water which still rose on either side of the ship.

I wanted to shut my eyes, shut out the disaster, but I couldn't stop staring, horror-stricken. It was like watching through a marijuana high. Pieces of the lock broke off in slow motion. I could see each one, each separate fragment, each drop of water spraying loose, knowing all the time that the scene was moving very quickly.

Just when it seemed that nothing could keep us from diving forward and smashing against the rocks in the rapids below us, a great cry sounded above the roaring, the cry of a million women weeping in anguish, an unearthly screaming. The deck cracked in front of me.

People were trying to shout at each other to hold on, but no one could be heard over those screams as the beams wrenched and tore and the ship broke in two. The geysers of water rising above us shut off abruptly. We fell again into the lock, falling forward and down at a great jolting speed, ramming the forward gates and the bottom with a bone-jarring impact. A hatch cover popped free and knocked over one of the crewmen. Wet barley poured out, covering everyone in the middle of the ship with pale gold mud. The deck slanted sharply down toward the crack and I grabbed the self-unloader to keep from being hurled into the center. The broken giant lay still.

18

THE LONG JOURNEY
HOME

The air was blessedly quiet following the roar of the explosion and the screams of the ship; all other sounds carried through it. People were yelling, both on the *Lucella* and on land. In the distance we could hear sirens beginning to wail. Every few seconds another piece of the deck broke and clattered down the inclined plane toward the gash in the middle.

My legs were shaking. I let go of the self-unloader's side and massaged the aching muscles in my left shoulder. Bledsoe still stood next to me, his eyes glassy, his face gray. I wanted to say something to him, but no words came. An explosion. Someone blew up a sixty-thousand-ton ship. Sixty thousand tons. Sixty thousand tons. The words beat meaninglessly in my brain.

The deck swam up and down in front of me; I thought it was starting to rise again. My trembling legs buckled and I collapsed. I fainted for a few seconds only, but lay on the deck until the swimming in my head passed, then forced myself to my feet. Bledsoe was still standing near me.

I saw Captain Bemis stagger from the entrance to the pilothouse. Red, the helmsman, followed, the two-inch cigar stub still poking out of his face. He walked heavily to the port side of the ship. I could hear him retching behind me.

'Martin. Our ship. Our ship. What happened?' That was Bemis.

'Someone planted explosives on your hull, Captain.' The words came from far away. Bemis was looking at me strangely: I realized it was I who was talking.

He shook his head, a jack-in-the-box on a spring; he couldn't stop shaking it. 'No. Not my ship. It must have been in the lock.'

'Couldn't have been.' I started to argue with him but my brain felt flaccid. I wanted to sleep. Disjointed images floated in the gray mist of my mind. The geysers of water towering over the ship. The water changing color as the *Lucella* cut through it. The troughs of water dug by the screws as we left Thunder Bay. A dark figure in a wet suit climbing out of the water.

The figure in the wet suit. That meant something. I forced myself to focus on it. That was the person who planted the charges. It was done yesterday. In Thunder Bay.

I opened my mouth to blurt it out, then swallowed the words. No one was in any state to deal with such news.

Keith Winstein made his way over to us. His face was streaked with tears and mud. 'Karpansky and Bittenberg. They're both – both dead, sir. They were down on the bank with the cables. They must've – must've been – smashed into the side.' He gulped and shuddered.

'Who else?' Bemis demanded.

'Anna. She fell over the side. She – she was crushed. She never had a chance. Vergil fell into the hold. Oh, Jesus! He fell into the hold and suffocated in the barley.' He started laughing and crying wildly. 'Drowned in barley. Oh, Christ!' he screamed. 'Drowned in barley.'

Focus and energy returned to the captain's face. He straightened and took Winstein by the shoulders, shaking him hard. 'Listen, Mate. The ones left are still your responsibility. Get them together. See who needs medical care. Radio the Coast Guard for a helicopter.'

The first mate nodded. He stopped sobbing, gave a few last shuddering breaths, and turned to the dazed crew.

'Martin needs some help too,' I said. 'Can you get him to sit down?' I needed to get away from the crowd on the deck. Somewhere, just out of reach in my mind, important information hovered. If I could just get away, stay awake, force myself into focus . . . I started back toward the pilothouse.

On my way I passed the chief engineer. He was covered with mud and oil. He looked like a miner emerging from three weeks in the pit. His blue eyes stared with horror through his mask of black.

'Where's the captain?' he asked me hoarsely.

'On deck. How are things below?'

'We've got a man with a broken leg. That's the only injury, thank God. But there's water everywhere. Port engine is gone . . . It was a bomb, you know. Depth charges. Must have been planted right on the center beam. Set off by radio signal. But why?'

I shook my head, helplessly, but his words jarred my mind loose. If it was set off by remote signal, it was done by someone along the bank. In the observation deck. The man with bright red hair and a pair of binoculars. Howard Mattingly, the second-string hockey player had hair like that. Boom Boom saw him someplace he shouldn't be three weeks ago. Now here he was at the observation deck with binoculars when the *Lucella* blew up.

I forgot the ache in my left shoulder. I needed to find Mattingly. Now. Before he got away. I turned abruptly in front of Sheridan and moved back out on deck. My gun. I wasn't going to tackle Mattingly without the Smith & Wesson. I went back to where I'd left it, to where Bledsoe and the captain were standing.

The bag was gone. I hunted for a few minutes, but I knew it was useless. Two shirts, a sweater, a pair of jeans, and a three-hundred-dollar Smith & Wesson were all lying with Vergil in fifty thousand tons of barley.

'I'm going,' I said to the captain. 'I've got an idea I need to follow up. Better get one of your junior cooks to get him some hot tea with lots of sugar. He's not doing too well.' I cocked my thumb in Bledsoe's direction. I didn't wait for Bemis's response but turned to go.

It wasn't difficult getting off the *Lucella*. She was resting at the bottom of the lock, her deck even with the bank. Clinging to the cables around the side, I swung easily across the two feet between her upraised stern and the side of the lock. As I picked my way up the narrow strip of land separating me from the MacArthur Lock, I passed an emergency crew coming from the Coast Guard and the Army Corps of Engineers. Men in green fatigues, medics, a stretcher crew – a solemn procession befitting a major disaster. Bringing up the rear, of course, was a television news team. They were the only ones who took any notice of me. One of them stuck a microphone under my nose and asked whether I was coming from the ship and what I knew about it.

I shrugged my shoulders in embarrassment and said in Italian that I didn't know any English. Disappointed, the cameramen continued in the wake of the Coast Guard.

The crossway stretched on in front of me, two concrete strips sandwiching a wedge of grass. The wind chilled my sore shoulder. I wanted to run but I couldn't. My legs were leaden posts and would not race for me. I staggered up to the gates closed in front of the MacArthur Lock and made my way across the narrow path on top of them. Beyond me lay the rocks lining the channel into Lake Huron. We were lucky the gates had held.

A tremendous crowd had gathered at the observation deck. It took time and energy to force my way through the crush of people. Mattingly was no longer there.

Before elbowing my way out again, I looked for a minute at the *Lucella*. She was an appalling sight. Bow and stern both stuck up from the lock at jagged angles. A number of cables had snapped from the self-unloader and swung meaninglessly above the remains of the deck. Wet barley oozed from the open cargo holds into a yellow smear across the visible parts of the gaping decks. I strained my eyes at the figures on board and decided that Bledsoe must finally have gone inside. A helicopter had landed near the bow, deploying men with stretchers.

The crowd was enjoying the show. Live disasters are wonderful attractions when you're safe on the other side of them. As we watched, the Coast Guard fished the dead bodies out of the water and a delighted shudder fluttered throughout the observation deck. I turned and shouldered my way down the stairs and across the street to a little coffee shop.

I ordered a cup of hot chocolate. Like Bledsoe and the crew, I'd had a shock and I needed hot liquid and sugar. The chocolate was pretty dismal, made from a powdered mix and water, but it was sweet and the warmth gradually made itself felt inside my numbed fingers and frozen toes.

I ordered another and a hamburger and french fries. Some instinct told me that calories under these circumstances would do me nothing but good. I pressed the plastic mug against my tired forehead. So Mattingly had left already. On his way back to Chicago by car, unless he'd had a private plane waiting for him at Sault Ste Marie's little airport.

I ate the hamburger, a greasy, hardened black slab, greedily in a few bites. The best thing for me to do was call Bobby and tell him to look out for Mattingly when he got back to Chicago. After all, I couldn't chase him.

As soon as I finished the french fries, I went in search of a pay phone. There was one outside the observation booth, but eight people were lined up waiting to use it. I finally found another three blocks down, in front of a burnt-out hotel. I called the Sault Ste Marie airport. The one daily flight for Chicago left in two hours. I booked a seat and found a Sault Ste Marie taxi company which sent a cab over to take me to the airport.

Sault Ste Marie is even smaller than Thunder Bay. The airport was a hangar and a hut, both very weather-beaten. A few private planes, Cessnas and the like, stood at the edge of the field. I didn't see anything that looked like a commercial plane. I didn't even see any people. Finally, after ten minutes of walking around, peering in corners, I found a man lying on his back under a tiny plane.

He slid out reluctantly in response to my shouts.

'I'm looking for the plane to Chicago.'

He wiped a greasy hand across an already grimy face. 'No planes to Chicago here. Just a few private planes use this place.'

'I just called. I just made a reservation.'

He shook his head. 'Commercial airport's twenty miles down the interstate. You'd better get down there.'

My shoulders sagged. I didn't know where to find the energy to go another twenty miles. I sighed. 'You have a phone I could use to call a cab?'

He gestured toward the far end of the dusty building and turned to crawl back under the plane.

398

A thought occurred to me. 'Martin Bledsoe keep his plane here or down at the other place?'

The man glanced back up at me. 'It was here. Cappy flew it out about twenty minutes ago.'

'Cappy?'

'His pilot. Some guy came along, said Bledsoe wanted Cappy to fly him to Chicago.'

I was too tired to feel anything – surprise, shock, anger – my emotions were pushed somewhere far away. 'Guy have bright red hair? Scar on the left side of his face?'

The mechanic shrugged. 'Don't know about the scar. He had red hair all right.' Cappy was expecting the guy – Bledsoe had phoned and told him the night before. All the mechanic knew was he'd given Cappy a course to Chicago. Weather still looked clear across Lake Michigan. They should make it in by six or so. He crawled back under the plane.

I staggered across the floor and found a phone, an old black clunker in the style GTE is ashamed to sell nowadays. The cab company agreed to send someone out to meet me.

I crouched on the sidewalk in front of the hangar while I waited, too weary to stand, fighting sleep. I wondered dreamily what I'd do if the taxi couldn't get me to the other airport on time.

I had a long wait. The cab's honking horn roused me from a doze and I got stiffly to my feet. I fell asleep again on the drive south. We made it to the Chippewa County International Airport with ten minutes to spare. Another tiny terminal, where a friendly fat man sold me a ticket and helped me and two other passengers board the propeller plane.

I thought I would sleep out the flight, but I kept churning thoughts around uselessly during the interminable journey. The plane stopped at three little Michigan towns. I endured the flight with the passivity born of too much emotion. Why would Bledsoe have blown up his own ship? What else was Mattingly doing for him? Bledsoe had blandly offered to let me look at his financial papers. And that meant the real documents were hidden someplace else with fake books available for bankers and detectives. But he had really been in shock when the *Lucella* blew up. That gray face wasn't faked. Well, maybe he just wanted to incapacitate her slightly, to collect enough insurance to meet his financial obligations. He didn't want his pride and joy blown to bits, but Mattingly had gotten hold of the wrong kind of explosive. Or too powerful an explosive. Anyway, he'd way exceeded his instructions.

Why had Bledsoe offered me a ride in his plane if he was turning it over to Mattingly, anyway? Maybe he knew he wouldn't have to make good on the offer. Or, if he expected the *Lucella* to be damaged only slightly, he could have taken off. But then how would he have explained Mattingly to me?

Round and round I went on these useless speculations, giving myself nothing but a headache. At the root of it all, I felt very bitter. It looked as though Bledsoe, who talked to me charmingly last night about *Peter Grimes*, had fooled me. Maybe he thought I'd be an impartial witness to his surprise at the wreck. I didn't like the wound to my ego. At least I hadn't gone to bed with him.

At O'Hare I looked Mattingly up in the phone book. He lived near Logan Square. Late as it was, exhausted, my head pounding and my clothes in ruins, I took a cab straight down there from the airport. It was nine-thirty when I rang the bell of a tidy bungalow in the 3600 North block of Pulaski.

It was opened almost immediately by Howard's young, helpless wife, Elsie. She was struggling with the latter stages of pregnancy and she gasped when she saw me. I realized I must present a shocking sight.

'Hello, Elsie,' I said, walking past her into a tiny vestibule. 'I'm V. I. Warshawski – Boom Boom's cousin. We met a couple of times at hockey parties – remember? I need to talk to Howard.'

'I – Yes, I remember you. Howard – Howard's not here.'

'No? You're sure he's not upstairs in bed asleep or something?'

Tears started rolling down her round, girlish cheeks. 'He's not here. He isn't. Pierre – Pierre has called three times, and the last time he left a threat. But really, I don't know where he is. I haven't seen him for four days. I thought – I thought he was at – at the Coeur d'Argent with Pierre. But he wasn't and I don't know where he is and the baby may come any day and I'm so scared.' She was really sobbing now.

I coaxed her into the living room and sat her down on a bright blue sofa covered with plastic. A stack of knitting lay folded neatly on the veneer coffee table – she had obviously filled her lonely, frightened days making baby clothes. I rubbed her hands and talked soothingly to her. When she seemed a little calmer I made my way to the kitchen and fixed her a mug of steaming milk. Hunting around, I found some gin under the sink. I poured myself a healthy slug of that with a little orange juice and carried the two drinks back to the living room. My left arm protested even this insubstantial load.

'Here: drink this. It'll make you feel a little better . . . Now. When was the last time you saw Howard?'

He had left Monday with a small overnight bag, saying he would be back on Wednesday. Here it was Friday and where was he? No, he hadn't said where he was going. Did Thunder Bay sound familiar? She shrugged helplessly, tears swimming in her round blue eyes. Sault Ste Marie? She just shook her head, crying gently, not saying anything.

'Has Howard said anything about the people he's been running around with?'

'No,' she hiccoughed. 'And when I told him you'd asked, he – he got really mad at me. He – he hit me and told me to keep our business to our – ourselves. And then he packed up and left and said he'd better not tell me where – where he was going, because I – I would just – just blab it around to people.'

I grimaced, silently thanking Boom Boom for the times he and Pierre had beaten up Howard.

'What about money? Howard had enough money lately?'

She brightened at that. Yes, he'd made a lot of money this spring and he'd given her two hundred dollars to buy a really nice crib and everything for the baby. She was quite proud of that and rambled on about it for a while – the only thing she could brag about.

I asked her if she had a mother or a sister or anyone she could stay with. She shrugged helplessly again and said all her family lived in Oklahoma. I looked at her impatiently. She wasn't the kind of stray I wanted to befriend – if I did it once, she'd cling to me forever. Instead, I told her to call the fire department if she went into labor suddenly and didn't know what to do about it – they'd send paramedics over to help her out.

As I got up to leave, I asked her to call me if Howard showed up. 'And for goodness' sake, don't tell him you told me – he'll only hit you again. Just go down to the corner grocery and use their pay phone. I really need to talk to him.'

She turned pathetically forlorn eyes to me. I doubted very much if I'd ever hear from her. It would be beyond her powers to deceive her domineering husband even over so simple a matter as a phone call. I felt a pang of guilt leaving her behind, but it was swallowed by fatigue as I got to the corner of Addison and Pulaski.

I hailed a Yellow Cab there to take me crosstown to Lotty's. Five miles on city streets is a slow ride and I went to sleep in the lurching, elderly vehicle about the time we crossed Milwaukee Avenue. The movement of the taxi made me think I was back on board the *Lucella*. Bledsoe was standing next to me, holding onto the self-unloader. He kept staring at me with his compelling gray eyes, repeating, 'Vic: I wasn't on the plane. I wasn't on the plane.'

I woke up with a start as we turned onto Sheffield and the driver asked me for Lotty's apartment number. As I paid him off and made my weary way up to the second floor, my dream remained very real to me. It contained an important message about Bledsoe but I just couldn't figure out what it was.

19

PAVANE FOR A DEAD
HOCKEY PLAYER

Lotty greeted me with a most uncharacteristic gasp of relief. 'My God, Vic, it's really you! You made it back!' She hugged me fiercely.

'Lotty, what on earth is the matter? Didn't you think you'd see me again?'

She put me at arm's length, looked me up and down, kissed me again, and then gave a more Lotty-like grin. 'The boat you were on, Vic. It was on the news. The explosion and so on. Four dead, they said, one of them a woman, but they wouldn't give names until the families were notified. I was afraid, my dear, afraid you might be the only woman on board.'

By now she had ascertained my disheveled state. She hustled me into the bathroom and sat me in a steaming bath in her old-fashioned porcelain tub. She blew her nose briskly and went off to put a chicken on to simmer, then came back with two tumblers of my Scotch. Lotty rarely drank – she was clearly deeply upset.

She perched on a three-legged stool while I soaked my sore shoulder and related the highlights of my adventures.

'I can't believe Bledsoe hired Mattingly,' I concluded. 'I just don't believe my judgement of character can be so wrong. Bledsoe and his captain roused my hackles. But I liked them.' I went on to tell her the same thoughts that had tormented my four-hour ride in from the Soo. 'I guess I'll have to put my prejudices aside and look into Pole Star's insurance arrangements and their general financial health.'

'Sleep on it,' Lotty advised. 'You have a lot of different avenues to explore. In the morning one of them will look the most promising.

Maybe Phillips. He has the most definite tie to Boom Boom, after all.'

Wrapped in a large terry-cloth robe, I sat with her in the kitchen eating the chicken and feeling comfort seep into the worn spots of my mind. After dinner Lotty rubbed Myoflex into my back and arms. She gave me a muscle relaxant and I fell into a deep, peppermint-scented sleep.

The phone dragged me out of the depths some ten hours later. Lotty came in and gently touched my arm. I opened bleary eyes.

'Phone's for you, my dear. Janet somebody – used to be Boom Boom's secretary.'

I shook my head groggily and sat up to take the phone by the guest bed.

Janet's homey, middle-aged voice woke me up more thoroughly. She was upset. 'Miss Warshawski, I've been fired. Mr Phillips told me it was because they didn't have enough for me to do, with Mr Warshawski gone and all. But I think it's because I was going through those files for you. I don't think they would have fired me if I hadn't done that. I mean, there was always enough work before –'

I cut into the repetitive flow. 'When did this happen?'

'Last night. Last night I stayed behind to see if I could find out anything about Mr Phillips's paycheck, you know, like you asked me to. I thought about it, and I thought, really, now, if Mr Warshawski was killed like you say he was, and if this will help, I ought to find out. But Lois came in to see what I was doing. I guess she was all set to spy on me if I stayed late or stayed after lunch, and then she called Mr Phillips at home. Well, he wasn't home yet, of course. But she kept calling him, and about ten o'clock last night he called and told me they don't need me to come in anymore and he'll send me two weeks' salary instead of notice. And, like I said, it just doesn't seem fair.'

'No, it doesn't,' I agreed warmly. 'What did you tell her you were doing?'

'Who?'

'Lois,' I said patiently. 'When she came in and asked you what you were doing, what did you tell her?'

404

'Oh! I said I'd written a personal letter and I couldn't find it so I was looking to see if it got thrown out.'

I thought that was pretty fast thinking and said so.

She laughed a little, pleased with the compliment, but added despondently, 'She didn't believe me, because there wasn't any reason for it to be in Mr Phillips's wastebasket.'

'Well, Janet, I don't know what to say. You certainly tried your hardest. I'm extremely sorry you lost your job, and all for nothing, but if –'

'It wasn't all for nothing,' she interrupted. 'I did find his pay stub just as you thought I might.'

'Oh!' I stared at the receiver in disbelief. For once something in this cockeyed investigation had worked out the way I thought it should. 'How much does he make?'

'He gets thirty-five hundred forty-six dollars and fifteen cents every two weeks.'

I tried multiplying in my head but I was still too groggy.

'I figured it out on my calculator last night. That's ninety-two thousand a year.' She paused, wistfully. 'That's a lot of money. I was only making seventy-two hundred. And now I don't have that.'

'Look, Janet. Would you be willing to work downtown? I can get you some interviews – at the Ajax Insurance Company and a couple of other places.'

She told me she'd think about it: she'd rather find something in her neighborhood. If that didn't work out, she'd give me a call back and ask me to set up an interview for her. I thanked her profusely and we hung up.

I lay back in bed and thought. Ninety-two thousand a year was a lot of money – for me or Janet. But for Phillips? Say he had good deductions and a good tax accountant. Still, he couldn't take home more than sixty or so. His real estate tax bill was probably three thousand. A mortgage, maybe another fifteen. Dues at the Maritime Club and the monthly fees for tennis, twenty-five thousand. Tuition, et cetera, at Claremont. The boat. The Alfa. Food. Massandrea dresses for Jeannine. Maybe she bought them at the Elite Repeat shop, or used from Mrs Grafalk. Still it would take a good hundred thousand net to cover everything.

After breakfast I walked the mile between Lotty's apartment and my own down on Halsted. I was getting out of shape from lying around too much, but I wasn't sure I was up to running yet and I knew I couldn't lift my ten-pound shoulder weights.

My mailbox was bulging. I get the *Wall Street Journal* every day. Five copies were stacked with letters and a small parcel on the floor. I picked up two armfuls and climbed the three flights to my apartment. 'No place like home,' I murmured to myself, looking with a jaundiced eye at the dust, the magazines strewn around the living room, and the bed which hadn't been made for more than two weeks now. I put the mail down and gave myself over to one of my rare housewifely fits, vacuuming, dusting, hanging up clothes. Having ruined a pantsuit, a pair of jeans, a sweater, and a blouse since I left home, there was less to put away than there might have been.

Glowing with virtue, I settled down with a cup of coffee to sort through the mail. Most of it was bills, which I tossed out unopened. Why look at them just to get depressed? One envelope held a thirty-five-hundred-dollar check from Ajax to pay for a new car. I was grateful for the care of the US Postal Service, which had left that on my lobby floor for any dope addict on Halsted to find. Also, wrapped in a small box were the keys to Boom Boom's apartment with a note from Sergeant McGonnigal saying the police were through with their investigation and I could use it any time I wanted to.

I poured myself more coffee and thought about what I should do. First on the list was Mattingly. I called Pierre Bouchard and asked him where I could find Mattingly if he were in town but not at home.

He clicked his tongue against his teeth. 'That I could not tell you, Vic. I have avoided the man constantly. But I will call around and see what I can find out.'

I told him Elsie was due any day now and he clicked his tongue again. 'That man! What an excrescence he is!'

'By the way, Pierre, does Howard know how to do deep-sea diving?'

406

'Deep-sea diving?' he echoed. 'No, Vic, I am telling you, I do not know him well. I do not know his personal habits. But I will ask . . . Oh, don't hang up – I have that name for you.'

'What name?'

'Did you not call Anna before you left town? You wanted to know what man we met at Christmas, when Boom Boom met Paige Carrington?'

'Oh yes.' I'd forgotten all about that. The man who was interested in buying a few shares of the Black Hawks, the man for whom Odinflute had set up his party. 'Yes. Who was it?'

'His name is Niels Grafalk. Myron says after all he decided not to buy.'

'I see,' I said weakly. I said nothing else and after a bit Bouchard said, 'Vic? Vic? Are you still there?'

'What? Oh yes. Yes, thanks very much, Pierre . . . Let me know if you hear from Mattingly.'

Though distracted, I took my check over to Humboldt Olds where I bought an Omega, a 1981 red model with fifteen thousand miles on it, power steering and power brakes. I had to sign a finance contract for eight hundred dollars but that wouldn't prove impossible. I'd just bill Boom Boom's estate for a hefty fee when all this mess was cleaned up. If it ever was.

So Grafalk had been interested in the Black Hawks. And Paige had been present at that same party. Now whom had she known? Who took her? It was an interesting coincidence. I wondered what she would tell me if I called her.

Driving in a slight daze, I reached Boom Boom's apartment at three-thirty, parking the Olds in front of a NO PARKING sign at Chestnut and Seneca. After two weeks of neglect, which had included a burglary and a police investigation, the place looked far worse than mine had this morning. Gray dust from the fingerprint detectors covered all the papers. White chalk still marked the outline of Henry Kelvin's body next to the desk.

I poured myself a glass of Chivas. I was damned if I was going to clean up two places in one day. Instead, I made a stab at reassembling the papers in their appropriate categories. I'd hire a cleaning crew and some temporary clerks to do the rest of the work. Frankly, I was sick of the place.

I made a tour of the apartment to collect items of interest to me – Boom Boom's first and last hockey sticks, a New Guinea hut totem from the living room, and some of the pictures of him in various hockey guises from the spare-room wall. Once more the picture of me in my maroon law school robes grinned incongruously from the wall. I took it off and added it to the stack under my arms. Once the clerks had gotten the papers to the right people and the cleaners had eliminated all the greasy dirt, I'd get the condo and the rest of his possessions onto the market. With any luck, I'd never have to visit this place again. I slung the items into my trunk and drove off. No one had ticketed me – maybe my luck was beginning to turn.

Next stop: the Eudora Grain offices. I badly wanted to talk to Bledsoe about why Mattingly had left Sault Ste Marie in his airplane, but I still thought Phillips's finances were an angle worth following up.

Late Saturday afternoon was an eerie time to visit the Port of Chicago. There wasn't much activity at the elevators. The huge ships stood like sleeping giants, prepared to wake into violent activity if disturbed. I eased the Omega into the parking lot at Eudora Grain's regional office and found myself tiptoeing across the blacktop to a side door.

A small bell was set into the wall with a little sign over it reading RING FOR DELIVERIES. I rang several times and waited five minutes. No one came. If there was a night watchman, he wasn't yet on the premises. From my back pocket I pulled a house burglar's compendium of commonly used picklocks and set out methodically to open the door.

Ten minutes later I was in Phillips's office. Either he or the efficient Lois kept all the file cabinets locked. With an aggrieved sigh, I took out my picklocks again and opened all the cabinets in the room and the three in Lois's desk outside his office door. I called Lotty and told her I wouldn't be in for supper and set to work. If I'd been thinking, I would have brought some sandwiches and a thermos of coffee.

Phillips kept a strange collection of junk in his upper desk drawer – three different kinds of antacids; datebooks going back for six years, most of them without any appointments written in; nose drops; an old pair of overshoes; two broken calculators; and odd scraps of paper. These I carefully smoothed out and read. Most of them were phone messages which he'd crumpled up and tossed in the drawer. A couple from Grafalk, one from Argus. The others were all names I didn't recognize, but I wrote them down in case I ran so far out of leads that I wanted to check them.

The ledgers were in a walnut filing cabinet on the window side of the office. I pulled them out with great alacrity. They were in the form of computer printouts, issued once a month with year-to-date totals and comparisons with prior years. After a certain amount of looking, I found report A36000059-G, payments to licensed carriers. All I needed now was my list of shipping contracts and I could compare the dates and see if the totals matched.

Or so I thought. I went out to Lois's file cabinets and found the originals of the contracts Janet had photocopied for me. These I took back into Phillips's office to lay next to report A36000059-G. Only then did I discover that the ledger recorded by invoice number, not by contract date. At first I thought I could just match totals of individual orders against totals in the ledger; I pulled the Pole Star Line's as an example.

Unfortunately the carriers apparently submitted more than one job on an invoice. The invoice totals were so much greater than the individual transactions, and the number of total invoices paid so much smaller, that it seemed to me that was the only explanation.

I added and subtracted, matching the numbers up every way I could think of, but I was forced to conclude that I wasn't going to be able to tell a thing without the individual invoices. And those I could not find. Not a one. I went through the rest of Phillips's files and all through Lois's and finally through the open file cabinets out on the floor. There wasn't an invoice in the place.

Before giving up for the evening, I looked up the payroll section of the ledgers. Phillips's salary was listed there just as Janet had told me. If I'd known I was going to burgle the place I would never have let her risk getting fired by going through his garbage.

I tapped my front teeth with a pencil. If he was getting extra money from Eudora Grain, it wasn't through the payroll account. Anyway, the ledgers were printed by the computers in Eudora, Kansas – if he was monkeying around with the accounts, he'd have to do it more subtly.

I shrugged and looked at my watch. It was after nine o'clock. I was tired. I was very hungry. And my shoulder was throbbing. I'd earned a good dinner, a long bath, and a sound sleep, but there was still another errand on the day's agenda.

Back in my apartment, I threw some frozen pasta into a pot with tomatoes and basil and ran a bath. I plugged the phone into the bathroom wall and called Phillips's Lake Bluff house. He wasn't in, but his son politely asked if he could take a message.

I lifted my right leg out of the water and ran a soapy sponge over it while I considered. 'This is V. I. Warshawski,' I said, spelling it for him. 'Tell him that Mr Argus's auditors will want to know where the missing invoices are.'

The boy repeated the message back to me dubiously. 'You got it.' I gave him both my and Lotty's phone numbers and hung up.

The pasta was bubbling nicely and I took it into the bedroom with me while I got dressed – black velvet pants with a high-necked blouse and a form-fitting red and black velvet toreador jacket. High heels and very dangly earrings and I was set for an evening at the theater. Or the end of an evening at the theater. By some miracle I hadn't spilled tomato juice on the white blouse. My luck really was turning.

I got to the Windy City Balletworks just at ten-thirty. A bored young woman in a leotard and stretchy wrap-around skirt told me the performance would end in ten minutes. She gave me a program and let me go in without paying.

The tiny theater was filled and I didn't bother trying to find a seat in the dim light. I lounged against the back wall, taking off my shoes to stand in my stocking feet next to the ushers. A spirited *pas de deux* from a classical ballet was in progress. Paige was not the female dancer. Whoever it was, she seemed technically competent but lacked the special spark with which Paige infused her performance. The whole company appeared on stage for a complex finale, and the show was over.

When the lights came on, I squinted at the program to make sure Paige was, indeed, dancing tonight. Yes, *Pavane for a Dope Dealer* had been performed right before the second act of *Giselle*, which we'd just seen.

I went back out into the hallway and followed a small group down to the door leading directly to the dressing rooms. Rather than accost Paige in her shared dressing room, I sat on a folding chair outside to wait. The dancers began coming out in twos and threes, not sparing me a glance. I'd provided myself with a novel, remembering the forty-five-minute wait here the last time I'd tried talking to Paige, and flicked through the pages, looking up in vain every time the door opened.

Fifty minutes went by. Just as I was thinking she might have left at the end of the *Pavane*, she finally emerged. As usual, her exquisite good looks made me feel a little wistful. Tonight she had on a silvery fur coat, possibly fox, which made her resemble Geraldine Chaplin in the middle of the Russian winter in *Dr Zhivago*.

'Hello, Paige. I'm afraid I got here too late to see the *Pavane*. Perhaps I can make the matinee tomorrow.'

She gave a slight start and then a wary smile. 'Hello, Vic. What impertinent questions have you come to ask me? I hope they're not long, because I'm late for a dinner engagement.'

'Trying to drown your sorrows?'

She gave me an indignant look. 'Life goes on, Vic. You need to learn that.'

'So it does, Paige. I'm sorry to have to drag you into a past you're trying to forget, but I'd like to know who took you to Guy Odinflute's party.'

'Who – what?'

'Remember the Christmas party where you met Boom Boom? Niels Grafalk wanted to meet some hockey players, trying to decide whether to buy into the Black Hawks, and Odinflute gave a party for

411

him. Or have you blocked that out along with the rest of the dead past?'

Her eyes blazed suddenly dark and her cheeks turned red. Without a word, she lifted her hand to slap me in the face. I caught her by the wrist and gently lowered her hand to her side. 'Don't hit me, Paige – I learned my fighting in the streets and I wouldn't want to lose my temper and hurt you . . . Who took you to Odinflute's party?'

'None of your damned business. Now will you leave the theater before I call the guard and tell him you're molesting me? And please do not ever come back. It would make me ill to have you watch me dance.'

She moved with angry grace down the hall and out the front door. I followed in time to see her get into a dark sedan. A man was driving but I couldn't make out his face in the dim light.

I didn't feel in the humor for company, even Lotty's astringent love. I gave her a call from my apartment to tell her not to worry. She didn't, usually, but I knew she'd been pretty upset after the destruction of the *Lucella*.

In the morning I went down to the corner for the Sunday *Herald-Star* and some croissants. While the coffee dripped in my porcelain coffeepot I tried Mattingly. No one answered. I wondered if Elsie had gone to the hospital. I tried Phillips, but no one answered there either. It was almost eleven – maybe they had to put in a ritual appearance at the Lake Bluff Presbyterian Church.

I propped the paper up against the coffeepot and sat down to work my way through it. I'd once told Murray the only reason I buy the *Herald-Star* is because it has the most comics in the city. Actually, it has the best crime coverage, too. But I always read the funnies first.

I was halfway through my second cup when I came to the squib about Mattingly. I'd almost passed it over. The headline on an inner page read 'Hit-and-run Victim in Kosciuszko Park' but his name must have caught my eye and I went back and read the story through completely.

The body of a man identified as Howard Mattingly was found late last night in Kosciuszko Park. Victor Golun, 23, of North

Central Avenue, was jogging through the park at ten last evening when he found Mattingly's body concealed behind a tree on one of the jogging paths. Mattingly, 33, was a reserve wing for the Chicago Black Hawks. Police say he had been hit by a car and carried to the park to die. They estimated he had been dead at least twenty hours when Golun found the body. Mattingly is survived by his wife, Elsie, 20, by two brothers, and by his mother.

I counted back in my head. He'd died by two Saturday morning at the latest, probably been hit sometime Friday evening, maybe right after he got back from Sault Ste Marie. I knew I should call Bobby Mallory and tell him to trace Mattingly's movements from when he got off Bledsoe's plane Friday night. But I wanted to talk to Bledsoe myself first and find out why Mattingly had flown home in his plane.

Bledsoe's home phone wasn't listed in any of the Chicago or suburban directories. On an off chance I tried the Pole Star Line, but of course no one was there on Sunday.

I called Bobby Mallory to find out if anything had happened in the Henry Kelvin murder. 'I got the keys back and went down there. The place was pretty grim. You guys make an arrest yet?'

'You on their payroll or something, Vicki? That family's bugging us day in and day out. We don't solve crimes faster for that kind of hassling.'

Depends on who's doing the hassling, I thought. But I kept that comment to myself – I wanted information more than I wanted to hear Bobby scream at me. So I made a sympathetic clucking in my throat.

'I read about that hit-and-run case in Kosciuszko Park. You know, that guy Mattingly used to play with Boom Boom on the Black Hawks. I hope the Hawks have got a good employee benefits plan – the team doesn't seem to be holding up too well.'

'You know I don't like you calling up and chatting about crime with me, Vicki. And I hope you wouldn't do it just to get my goat. So it must be you've got some special interest in the case. What is it?'

'No, not that,' I said hastily. 'But I know his wife. She's a fragile woman – just a child, really, and I don't think this shock'll be too good for her. Her first baby is due any second.'

'Yeah, she had it this morning. Between you and me, she's well rid of that specimen. He was a pretty grafter, had his hand stuck in everybody's pocket. He owed gambling money, too. If he'd been a starter they'd of had him fixing games.'

'You figure one of his creditors got tired of waiting and ran him over?'

'I don't figure anything for your consumption. If I've told you once, I've told you a hundred times, quit fooling around with crime. You'll only get hurt. Leave that –'

'– to the police. They're paid to handle it.' I finished with him in chorus. 'Make it more like a million times, Bobby. Thanks. Give my love to Eileen,' I added as he hung up on me.

Next I tried Murray Ryerson. He wasn't at the *Star* but I found him at home, just staggering out of bed.

'V.I. who?' he grumbled. 'It's only eleven in the morning.'

'Wake up, sunshine. I want to talk to you.'

'Vic, if you knew how long I've waited to hear those words from you. My mother keeps telling me, "No, she's just using you, Murray. She just wants to worm crime information out of you." But deep down, I keep believing, in my secret heart, that one day my warmest passions will be reciprocated.'

'Murray, your warmest passion, next to beer, is for a hot story. I guess I reciprocate that. Why don't you come up and watch the poor old Cubbies take on the winningest team in baseball and I'll give you an exclusive on the wreck of the *Lucella*.'

'What do you know about that?' he asked sharply.

'I was there. I was an eyewitness. I watched the whole thing happen. I may even have seen the man – or woman – who planted the depth charges.'

'My God, Vic, I don't believe it. I don't believe you're calling me out of the blue with this. Who was it? Where did you see them? Was it up at the locks? Is this on the level?'

'Certainly,' I said virtuously. 'Have we got a date?'

'Let me get Mike Silchuck up there with his camera to get a shot of

414

you. Now, let's start at the beginning. Why were you on the *Lucella*?'

'Are you going to come to the game with me or not?'

'Oh, all right. But it's no joy for me to watch Atlanta massacre our faithful boys in blue.'

He agreed to meet me at the bleachers at twelve forty-five. Right before he hung up he said, 'What do you want from me, Vic? Why the elaborate setup?'

'See you at the game, Murray.' I laughed and hung up.

Before leaving for the park I tried Phillips again. Jeannine answered.

'Hello, Mrs Phillips. This is V. I. Warshawski. I'm a business associate of your husband's. May I speak to him, please?'

He wasn't in. She didn't know when he would be in. I thought she was lying. Under her hauteur she sounded scared. I tried probing a little but couldn't get a handle on it. Finally I asked her what time he'd gone out. She hung up on me.

20
UNLOADING

The Braves did clobber the Cubs. Only Keith Moreland, hitting around .345, did anything we could enjoy, knocking a ball into the hands of an eager kid around nine sitting in front of me. However, the day was sunny, if chilly, the crowd enthusiastic, and Murray and I enjoyed a few hot dogs. I let him drink the beer – I don't like the stuff.

Mike Silchuck had taken my picture a few dozen times in front of the ticket counter. Unfortunately all my scars were in places I didn't feel like flashing in the middle of Addison, so they had to be content with a look of noble courage. Murray asked me questions briskly during the first three innings, then spent the fourth phoning his exclusive into the *Herald-Star*.

In the top half of the sixth, while the Braves scored five runs, I asked Murray about Mattingly.

'He's a small-time hood, Vic. What do you want to know about him?'

'Who killed him?'

Like Mallory, he assumed immediately that Mattingly or his wife / mother / brothers were my clients. I gave him the same story I'd told Bobby.

'Besides, even though Boom Boom hated him, he felt sorry for poor little Elsie. I know he used to slip her a few bucks to stretch the housekeeping money, which I guess Mattingly doled out with a grudging fist, since he needed it for his gambling debts.'

'Why did she stay with him?' Murray asked irritably.

'Oh, Murray, grow up. Why does anyone stay with anyone? She

416

was a child, a baby. She couldn't have been eighteen when he married her, and everyone she knows is in Oklahoma . . . Well, let's not get into the psychology of marriage. Just tell me if there are any leads into his death.'

He shook his head. 'He was out of town for three or four days. Elsie doesn't know where he went or how he got there, and the police haven't dug up anyone who can help. They'll question the hockey team, of course, but as far as I can tell most of the guys felt the same way your cousin did.'

So the connection with Bledsoe was still secret. Or the connection with his airplane, at any rate. 'Was he wearing size twelve Arroyo hiking boots by any chance?'

Murray looked at me strangely. 'The footprint left in Boom Boom's apartment? I don't know – but I'll find out.'

I turned my attention to the rest of the game. My hero, Bill Buckner, struck out. Such is life. I kind of knew the feeling.

After the game Murray wandered home with me for something more substantial than hot dogs. I scrounged around in my bare larder and came up with tuna, frozen fettucine, and olives. We drank a bottle of Barolo and put crime behind us for a few hours, while I found out how much exercise my dislocated shoulder was up to.

Murray and I have been competitors on the crime scene, friends, and occasional lovers for several years. Somehow, though, the relationship never seems to develop. Maybe our rivalry over crime investigation gets in the way.

Around midnight the *Star* signaled him on his beeper and he left to deal with a Mafia shooting in River Forest. Beepers are one of the twentieth century's most useless inventions. What difference does it make if your office finds you now rather than an hour from now? Why not give yourself a break?

I asked Murray this as he pulled his T-shirt over the thick auburn curls on his chest.

'If they didn't know where to find me, the *Sun-Times* or the *Trib* would beat me to the story,' he mumbled through the cloth.

'Yeah,' I grumbled, lying back in bed. 'Americans are afraid that if

417

they unplug themselves from their electronic toys for five minutes they'll miss out on – everything. Life. Imagine no TV, no telephones, no beepers, no computers, for three minutes. You'd die. You'd be like a beached whale –'

I was working myself into a frenzy over our appalling dependency on gadgets when Murray dropped a pillow over my face. 'You talk too much, Vic.'

'This is what happened to the girl in *Looking for Mr Goodbar*.' I padded naked after him down the hall to make sure all the locks got closed behind him. 'She brings this guy home and he suffocates her with her own pillow . . . I hope you write a definitive exposé of the Chicago mob and get them run out of town.'

After Murray left I couldn't get back to sleep. We'd gone to bed early, around seven-thirty, and slept for a couple of hours. Now I felt all the loose ends of the case whirling around in my head like trails of fettucine. I didn't know where to find Bledsoe. It was too late to try the Phillipses again. Too late to call Grafalk, to find out if he had gone to that Christmas party alone. I'd already burgled the Eudora Grain offices. I'd even cleaned my apartment earlier in the day. Unless I wanted to wash dishes twice in twenty-four hours, there wasn't anything for me to do except pace.

About one-thirty the walls started to close in on me. I got dressed and took one of my mother's diamond earrings from the locked cupboard built into my closet. I went out onto Halsted, deserted in the early morning except for a few drunks, got into the Omega, and headed out to Lake Shore Drive. I rode south for several miles, past the Loop, and pulled off at Meigs Field, the small airport on Chicago's lakefront.

The blue landing lights cast no illumination in the thick dark. They seemed like meaningless dots, not part of a human network. Behind the tiny runway lapped Lake Michigan, a dark shape. I felt desolate. Not even a beeper linked me with the rest of the world.

I skirted the runway and stumbled through the weed-grown rocks down to the water's edge, shivering at the nameless menace in the black water. The water slapping at my feet seemed to call me to itself. Let me enfold you in the mysteries of my depths. All the dark things

418

you fear will become your delight. Don't think of drowning, of Boom Boom choking and fighting for air. Think of infinite rest, no responsibilities, no need for control. Just perfect rest.

The roar of an engine brought me back to myself. A two-seater plane was landing. It looked like a living creature, its lights flashing busily, wings flopping for the descent, like a noisy insect settling down for a short rest.

I stumbled back across the rocks to the little terminal. No one was in the waiting room. I went back outside and followed the two men who had just landed into an office. There a thin young man with straw-colored hair and a very pointed nose went over their flight charts with them. They were talking about some wind pattern which had caught them up around Galena and the three had an animated discussion on what might have caused it. This went on for a good ten minutes while I wandered around the room looking at different aerial photos of the city and surrounding countryside.

At last the thin young man pulled himself reluctantly from the weather map and asked if he could help me in some way.

I gave my most ingratiating smile – Lauren Bacall trying to get Sam Spade to do her dirty work for her. 'I came in on Mr Bledsoe's plane Friday night and I think I might have lost an earring.' I pulled my mother's diamond drop from my jacket pocket. 'It looks like this. The post must have come out.'

The young man frowned. 'When did you come in?'

'Friday. It would have been around five, I guess.'

'What kind of plane does Bledsoe fly?'

I gave a helpless, feminine shrug. 'I don't know. It seats about six people, I think. It's new,' I added helpfully. 'The paint's fresh and shiny –'

The young man exchanged a masculine smirk with the other two. Women are *so* stupid. He pulled a logbook out of a drawer and ran his finger down the entries. 'Bledsoe. Oh yes. A Piper Cub. Came in at five-twenty on Friday. There was only one passenger, though. The pilot didn't say anything about a woman.'

'Well, I did ask him specially not to. I didn't want a record that I'd been on the plane. But now I've lost this earring and all, I don't know what I'll do . . . Will Cappy be in this morning? Could you ask him to look for me?'

'He only comes in when Mr Bledsoe needs him to fly.'

'Well, maybe you have a number where I could reach him?'

After a certain amount of hemming and hawing, during which the other two were winking surreptitiously at each other, the young man gave me Cappy's phone number. I thanked him profusely and took off. Whatever gets the job done.

Back home I remembered the memorabilia I'd picked up at Boom Boom's apartment and took them out of the trunk. My left arm continued to heal, despite constant abuse, and the load brought on only minor twinges. With the pile of stuff balanced on my right arm, I fumbled at the door locks left-handed. The New Guinea totem started to wobble. I struggled to save it, and the pictures crashed to the floor. I swore under my breath, put everything down, unlocked the door with both hands, propped it open with my foot, and carried the things properly into the building.

I'd saved the totem, but the glass over the pictures had cracked. I put them on the coffee table and took the frames apart gingerly, knocking the glass into a waste can.

The photo of me in my graduation robes was wedged extremely tightly into the frame. Boom Boom must have put too many sheets of cardboard in to allow the back to fit properly. 'You shouldn't have bought such a cheap frame for me, Boom Boom,' I muttered to myself. I finally went into the kitchen for a couple of oven mitts. With those on, I forced the frame away from the backing, spilling glass everywhere.

Between the picture and the backing was a thickly folded stack of white paper. No wonder the photo was wedged in so tightly.

I unfolded the stack. It turned out to be two sheets of paper. One was an invoice from the Grafalk Steamship Line to the Eudora Grain Company. Terms: 10 days, 2 per cent, 30 days net, 60 days 18 per cent interest. It showed loads by vessel, date of shipment, and date of arrival. The second, written in Boom Boom's meticulous hand, listed six dates when Pole Star had lost shipments to Grafalk.

Boom Boom had also listed the bids. In four lots, Pole Star was the low bidder. I started hunting through the apartment for my bag with the contract copies in it, then remembered I had left it at Lotty's. Not even Lotty could I rouse at three in the morning just to get some papers.

I fixed myself a large Scotch and stood at the living room window drinking it. I stared down at the late-night traffic on Halsted. Boom Boom had tried to call me to tell me what he'd found out. When he couldn't get hold of me, he stuffed the papers behind my picture – not for me to find, but to keep anyone else from finding them. He'd thought he'd get back to them, and to me, so he didn't leave a message for me. A spasm of pain contracted my chest. I missed Boom Boom terribly. I wanted to cry, but no tears would come.

I finally left the window and went to bed. I didn't sleep much and what sleep I had was tormented by dreams of Boom Boom stretching his arms out from a cold, black lake while I stood helplessly by. At seven I gave up trying to rest and took a bath. I waited until eight o'clock, then called Bledsoe's pilot, Cappy. His wife answered and called him in from the backyard where he was planting petunias.

'Mr Cappy?' I said.

'Capstone. People call me Cappy.'

'I see . . . Mr Capstone, my name is Warshawski. I'm a detective and I'm looking into Howard Mattingly's death.'

'Never heard of the guy.'

'Wasn't he your passenger back from Sault Ste Marie on Friday night?'

'Nope. Not that guy.'

'Bright red hair? Scar on the left side of his face? Stocky build?'

He guessed that sounded like the same person.

'Well, we believe he was traveling under an assumed name. He turned up dead later that night. What I'm trying to find out is where he went when he left the airport.'

'Couldn't tell you that. All I know, there was a car waiting for him at Meigs. He got in it and they took off. I was filling out my log forms, didn't really notice.'

He hadn't been able to see the driver. No, he couldn't say what kind of car. It was big, not a limo, but it might have been a Caddy or an Oldsmobile.

'How did you come to take this guy home? I thought you were going to fly Mr Bledsoe down, but you left before the *Lucella* got through the lock.'

'Yeah, well, Mr Bledsoe called and told me he wasn't flying down. Told me to take this guy instead. He said his name was Oleson and that's what I put down on the log.'

'When did Bledsoe call you? He was on board ship all day Friday.'

He'd called Thursday afternoon. No, Cappy couldn't swear it was Bledsoe. Matter of fact, Bledsoe himself had just phoned with the same question. But he didn't take orders from anyone except the plane owner – so who else could it have been?

The logic of this argument somewhat escaped me. I asked him for whom else he flew, but he got huffy and said his client list was confidential.

Hanging up slowly, I wondered again if it was time to turn my information about Mattingly over to Bobby Mallory. The police could put their investigative machinery into motion and start questioning everyone who'd been at Meigs Field on Friday night until they found someone to identify that car. I looked at Boom Boom's documents on the table next to the phone. The answer to the mess lay in these papers. I'd give myself twenty-four more hours, then turn it over to Bobby.

I tried calling Pole Star. The lines were busy. I tried Eudora Grain. The receptionist told me Mr Phillips had not yet come in for the day. Was he expected? As far as she knew. I called his Lake Bluff residence. Mrs Phillips told me tightly that her husband had left for work. So he had come home last night? I asked. She hung up on me again.

I made myself coffee and toast and dressed for action: running shoes, blue jeans, a gray cotton shirt, and a denim jacket. I regretted my Smith & Wesson, lying somewhere at the bottom of the Poe Lock. Maybe when they hauled up the *Lucella* they could fish my gun out of the moldy barley and give it back to me.

Before I took off, the doorbell rang. I buzzed the caller in through the front door and went on downstairs to meet him. It turned out to be a process server – a college student – with a summons for me to attend a Court of Inquiry in Sault Ste Marie next Monday. The youth seemed relieved that I accepted it so calmly, merely stuffing it into my shoulder bag. I serve a lot of subpoenas myself – recipients range from tetchy to violent.

I stopped at the corner to buy Lotty a bunch of irises and chrysanthemums and zipped up to her apartment in the Omega. Since my little suitcase was also mushed in with fifty thousand tons of barley at Sault Ste Marie, I stuffed my belongings into a grocery bag. I put the flowers on the kitchen table with a note.

Lotty darling.

Thank you for looking after me. I'm hot on the scent. I'll bring your keys by tonight or tomorrow night.

Vic

I had to keep the keys to lock the apartment door behind me.

I sat at her kitchen table with my stack of contracts and went through them until I found one that matched the invoice I had in hand. It was for three million bushels of soybeans going from Chicago to Buffalo on July 24, 1981. The price quoted in the contract was $0.33 a bushel. The invoice billed it at $0.35. Two cents a bushel on three million bushels. Came out to sixty thousand dollars.

Grafalk had been the low bidder on this shipment. Someone else had bid $0.335 and a third carrier $0.34. Grafalk picked up the bid at $0.33 and billed it at $0.35.

Boom Boom's list of Pole Star's lost contracts proved even more startling. On the forms I'd gotten from Janet, Grafalk was listed as the low bidder. But Boom Boom's notes showed Pole Star as the low bidder. Phillips either had entered the contracts wrong or the invoices Boom Boom referred to were wrong.

It was time to get some explanations from these clowns. I was tired of being shown the old shell game every time I wanted information out of them. I stuffed all the papers back into the canvas bag and headed for the Port.

It was close to noon when I turned off I-94 at 130th Street. The friendly receptionist at Eudora Grain was answering the phone and nodded to me in recognition as I walked past her into the inner office. The sales reps were hanging up their phones, straightening their ties, getting ready for lunch. In front of Phillips's office sat Lois, her bouffant hair lacquered into place. The phone was propped under her chin and she made a pretense of looking at some papers. She was talking in the intense, muttering way people do when they're trying to pretend they're not really making personal calls.

She lifted her eyes momentarily to me as I walked up to the desk but didn't interrupt her conversation.

'Where's Phillips?' I demanded.

She murmured something into the telephone and put her hand over the mouthpiece. 'Do you have an appointment?'

I grinned at her. 'Is he in today? He doesn't seem to be at home.'

'I'm afraid he's away from the office on business. Do you want to make an appointment?'

'No, thanks,' I said. 'I'll come back.' I circled behind her and looked in Phillips's office. There weren't any signs that anyone had been there since me on Saturday night – no briefcase, no jacket, no half-smoked cigars. I didn't think he was lurking outside the window in the parking lot but I went over and peered behind the drapes.

My assault on her boss's office brought Lois, squawking, into his den. I grinned at her again. 'Sorry to interrupt your conversation. Tell your mother it won't happen again. Or is it your sister?'

She turned red and stomped back to her desk. I left, feeling pleased with myself.

I headed to the main part of the Port. Grafalk wasn't in; he didn't come down to the Port every day, the receptionist explained. I debated going to talk to Percy MacKelvy, the dispatcher, but decided I'd rather talk directly to Grafalk.

I walked over to Pole Star's little office. The office manager there was harassed but trying to be calm. As I talked to her she took one call from the Toronto *Sun* inquiring into the *Lucella*'s accident and another from K L W N Radio in Lawrence, Kansas.

424

'It's been like this all morning. I'd like to get the phone disconnected, but we need to stay in touch with our lawyers, and we do have other ships carrying freight. We don't want to miss any orders.'

'I thought the *Lucella* was the only ship you owned.'

'It's the only big one,' she explained. 'But we lease a number of others. In fact Martin got so sick of the newspapers he went down to Plymouth Iron and Steel to watch them unload coal from the *Gertrude Ruttan*. She's a seven-hundred-foot self-unloading vessel. We lease her from Triage – they're a big shipbuilding company. Sort of like Fruehauf for trucks – they don't carry much cargo in their own right, just lease the vessels.'

I asked for directions to the Plymouth yard and she obligingly gave them to me. It was another ten miles around the lake to the east. She was a very helpful young woman – even gave me a pass to get into the Plymouth plant.

We were into the middle of May and the air was still quite chilly. I wondered whether we were heading for a new ice age. It's not cold winters that cause them but cool summers when the snow doesn't melt. I buttoned my jacket up to the neck and rode with the windows rolled all the way up.

As I moved into steel territory the blue air darkened and turned red-black. I felt as though every movement closer to the mills carried me further back in time to the grimy streets of South Chicago where I grew up. The women on the streets had the same pinched, worn look as they hurried their toddlers along. A grocery store on a corner reminded me of the place at 91st and Commercial where I used to buy a hard roll on my way to school, and I stopped the car to get a snack in lieu of lunch. I almost expected old Mr Kowolsky to step up behind the counter, but instead an energetic young Mexican weighed my apple and carefully wrapped a carton of blueberry yogurt for me.

He gave me detailed directions on how to find the plant entrance, eyeing me with impartial enthusiasm while he did so. I felt slightly cheered by his guileless admiration and slowly made my way to the steelworks, eating my yogurt with my left hand while I drove with the right.

It was just two o'clock. The plant was between shift changes, so mine was the only car going past the guard station at the main entrance. A beefy young man inspected the pass they'd given me at Pole Star.

'You know where to find the *Gertrude*?'

I shook my head.

'Take the road around to the left. You'll go past the coke ovens and a slag heap. You'll be able to see the ship from there.'

I followed his directions, going by a long narrow building where fire danced inside, visible through sliding doors opened to let in the cool air. Slag formed a mountain on my left. Bits of cinder blew onto the windshield of the Omega. Peering through it at the rutted track in front of me, I continued on around the furnaces until I saw the *Gertrude* looming above me.

Great hills of coal framed the lakefront. The *Gertrude* was getting ready to dump her load onto one of them. Hard-hatted men in boiler suits had tied up the ship. As I left the car and picked my way across the pockmarked yard, I could see them turning the swivel top of the ship's self-unloader to position it over one of the smaller coal piles.

Bledsoe was on the ground talking with a man in a dirty gray boiler suit. The two weren't speaking when I came up, just looking at the activity going on above them.

Bledsoe had lost weight in the three days since I'd last seen him. It was shockingly noticeable – he must have dropped ten pounds. His tweed jacket sagged across his shoulders instead of straining as if to contain his monumental energy.

'Martin,' I said. 'Good to see you.'

He smiled with genuine pleasure. 'Vic! How'd you run me to earth?'

I explained and he introduced me to the man he was standing with, the shift foreman. As we talked, a great clanking started and coal began moving down the conveyor belt onto the heap below.

'The self-unloader is quite a machine. You ought to watch it in action,' Bledsoe said into my ear. He went back to his car and got a second hard hat out of the trunk for me. We climbed up a ladder on the port side of the ship, away from the self-unloader, and Bledsoe

426

took me over to watch coal coming up the wide figure-eight belt from the holds.

The coal came through quite fast, in large chunks. It takes about eight hours to unload the holds with a self-unloader, compared to two days using manual labor.

Bledsoe was clearly tense. He walked around, talking a bit to the crew, clenching and unclenching his fingers. He couldn't stand still. At one point he caught me watching him and said, 'I won't relax until this load is off. Every time I move a cargo from now on, I'm not going to be able to sleep until I know the ship has made it in and out of port safely.'

'What's the story on the *Lucella*?'

He grimaced. 'The Coast Guard, the Corps of Engineers, and the FBI are mounting a full-scale investigation. Trouble is, until they get her out of the lock they won't even be able to see what kind of explosive was used.'

'How long will that take?'

'A good ten months. That lock will be shut all summer and it'll take most of next year to repair the gates.'

'Can you save the ship?'

'Oh yes, I think so. Mike's been all over it with the guys from the Costain boatyard – the people who built her. They'll take her out in sections, tow her back to Toledo, and weld her back together. She should be running again by the end of next summer.'

'Who pays to repair the lock?'

'I don't know, but I'm not responsible for the damned thing blowing up. The army has to fix it. Unless the Court of Inquiry assigns liability to me. But there's no way in hell they can do that.'

We were speaking almost in shouts to be heard over the clanking of the conveyor belts and the rattling of the coal going over the side. Some of the old energy was coming back into Bledsoe's face as he talked. He was starting to elaborate on his legal position, pounding his right fist into his left palm, when we heard a piercing whistle.

The noise came to an abrupt halt. The conveyor belt stopped and with it all its attendant racket. An authoritative figure moved over to the opening into the hold and called down a demand as to the cause of the belt's stopping.

'Probably just an overload on one of the side belts,' Bledsoe muttered, looking extremely worried.

We heard a muffled shout from the hold, then a young man in a dirty blue boiler suit erupted up the ladder onto the deck. His face was greeny white under its smear of coal dust and he just made it to the side before he was sick.

'What is it?' the authoritative man yelled.

There were more cries coming from the hold. With a glance at Bledsoe, I started down the ladder the young engineer had just climbed up. Bledsoe followed close on my hands.

I jumped down the last three rungs onto the steel floor below. Six or seven hard-hatted figures were huddled over the figure-eight belt where it joined the side conveyors feeding it from the holds. I strode over and shoved them aside, Bledsoe peering around my back.

Clayton Phillips was staring up at me. His body was covered with coal. The pale brown eyes were open, the square jaw clenched. Blood had dried across his freckled cheekbones. I moved the men away and bent over to peer closely at his head. Coal had mostly filled in a large hole on the left side. It was mixed with congealed blood in a reddish-black, ghastly clot.

'It's Phillips,' Bledsoe said, his voice constricted.

'Yes. We'd better call the police. You and I have a few questions to discuss, Martin.' I turned to the group of men. 'Who's in charge down here?'

A middle-aged man with heavy jowls said he was the chief engineer.

'Make sure no one touches the body or anything else. We'll get the police over here.'

Bledsoe followed me tamely back up the ladder to the deck and off the ship. 'There's been an accident down below,' I told the Plymouth foreman. 'We're getting the police. They won't be unloading the rest of the coal for a while.' The foreman took us into a small office just around to the side of a long shed. I used the phone to call the Indiana State Police.

Bledsoe got into the Omega with me. We drove away from the yard in silence. I made my way back to the interstate and rode the few remaining miles over to the Indiana Dunes State Park. On a weekday afternoon, in early spring, the place was deserted. We climbed across the sand down to the shore. The only other people there were a bearded man and a sporty-looking woman with their golden retriever. The dog was swimming into the frothy waves after a large stick.

'You have a lot of explaining to do, Martin.'

He looked at me angrily. 'You owe me a lot of explanations. How did Phillips get into that ship? Who blew up the *Lucella*? And how come you're so quick on the spot every time disaster is about to strike Pole Star?'

'How come Mattingly flew back to Chicago on your plane?'

'Who the hell is Mattingly?'

I drew a breath. 'You don't know? Honestly?'

He shook his head.

'Then who did you send back to Chicago in your plane?'

'I didn't.' He made an exasperated gesture. 'I called Cappy as soon as I got to town and demanded the same thing of him. He insists I phoned from Thunder Bay and told him to fly this strange guy back – he said his name was Oleson. Obviously someone was impersonating me. But who and why? And since you clearly know who this guy is, *you* tell *me*.'

I looked out at the blue-green water. 'Howard Mattingly was a second-string wing for the Chicago Black Hawks. He was killed early Saturday morning – run over by a car and left to die in a park on Chicago's northwest side. He was up at the Soo on Friday. He fits the description of the guy Cappy flew back to Chicago. He exploded the depth charges on the *Lucella* – I watched him do it.'

Bledsoe turned to me and grabbed my arm in a gesture of spontaneous fury. 'Goddamn it – if you watched him do it, how come you haven't said anything to anyone? I've been talking my head off to the FBI and the Corps of Engineers for two days and you – you've been sitting on this information.'

I twisted away from his grasp and spoke coldly. 'I only realized after the fact what Mattingly had been doing. I didn't recognize him immediately. As we went down to the bottom of the lock, he picked up what looked like an outsize pair of binoculars. They must have been the radio controls for the detonators. The whole thing only dawned on me after the *Lucella* had gone sky-high . . . You may recall that you were in shock. You weren't in any position to listen to anyone say anything. I thought I'd better leave and see if I could track him down.'

'But later. Why didn't you talk to the police later?'

'Ah. That was because, when I got to the airport at Sault Ste Marie, I found Mattingly had gone back to Chicago on your airplane, presumably under your orders. That really upset me – it made a mockery out of my judgement of your character. I wanted to talk to you about it first, before I told the police.'

The dog came bounding up to us, water spraying from its red-gold hair. It was an older dog – she sniffed at Martin with a white muzzle. The woman called to her and the dog bounded off again.

'And now?' he demanded.

'And now I'd like to know how Clayton Phillips came to be on the self-unloader of a ship you were leasing.'

He pounded the beach beside him. 'You tell me, Vic. You're the smart detective. You're always turning up whenever there's a crime about to be committed on my fleet . . . Unless you've decided that a man with my record is capable of anything – capable of destroying his own dreams, capable of murder?'

I ignored his last statement.

'Phillips has been missing since yesterday morning. Where were you yesterday morning?'

His eyes were dark spots of anger in his face. 'How dare you?' he yelled.

'Martin: listen to me. The police are going to ask that and you're going to have to answer.'

He pressed his lips together and debated within himself. Finally he decided to master his temper. 'I was closeted with my Lloyd's representative up at the Soo until late yesterday. Gordon Firth – the

Ajax chairman – flew up with him in Ajax's jet and they brought me back down to Chicago about ten last night.'

'Where was the *Gertrude Ruttan*?'

'She was tied up at the Port. She steamed in Saturday afternoon and had to tie up for the weekend until they were ready to unload her. Some damned union regulation.'

So anyone who could get into the Port and get onto the ship could have put a hole in the side of Phillips's head and shoved him into a cargo hold. He'd just fall down into the load and show up with the rest of the cargo when it came out on the conveyor belt. Very neat. 'Who knew the *Gertrude Ruttan* would be there over the weekend?'

He shrugged. 'Anyone who knows anything about the ships in and out of the Port.'

'That narrows it down a lot,' I said sarcastically. 'Same thing for who fixed my car, for who killed Boom Boom. I was figuring Phillips for that job, but now he's dead too. So that leaves the other people who were around at the time. Grafalk. Bemis. Sheridan. You.'

'I was up in the Soo all day yesterday.'

'Yeah, but you could hire someone.'

'So could Niels,' he pointed out. 'You're not working for him, are you? Did he hire you to set me up?'

I shook my head.

'Who're you working for then, Warshawski?'

'My cousin.'

'Boom Boom? He's dead.'

'I know. That's why I'm working for him. We had a pact, Boom Boom and I. We took care of each other. Someone shoved him under the *Bertha Krupnik*. He left me evidence of the reason why which I found last night. Part of that evidence implicates you, Martin. I want to know why you were letting so many of your contracts with Eudora go to Grafalk.'

He shook his head. 'I looked at those contracts. There was nothing wrong with them.'

'There was nothing wrong with them, except that you were letting Grafalk pick up a number of orders when you were the low bidder. Now are you going to tell me why or am I going to have to go to Pole

Star and interrogate your staff and go through your books and repeat that boring routine?'

He sighed. 'I didn't kill your cousin, Warshawski. If anyone did, it was Grafalk. Why don't you focus on him and find out how he blew up my ship and forget these contracts?'

'Martin, you're not a dummy. Think it through. It looks like you and Grafalk were in collusion on those shipping orders. Mattingly flew back to Chicago in *your* plane and Phillips's body was found on *your* ship. If I was a cop, I wouldn't look too much further – if I had all that information.'

He made a wrenching gesture with his right arm. Frustration.

'All right. It's true,' he shouted. 'I did let Niels have some of my orders. Are you going to put me in jail for it?'

I didn't say anything.

After a brief pause he continued more calmly. 'I was trying to put financing together for the *Lucella*. Niels was getting desperate for orders. The steel slump was hurting everyone, but Grafalk was really taking it on the chin because of all those damned small ships of his. He told me he would let the story of my evil past out to the financial community if I didn't give him some of my orders.'

'Could that really have hurt you?'

He gave a wry smile. 'I didn't want to find out. I was trying to raise fifty million dollars. I couldn't see the Fort Dearborn Trust giving me a nickel if they knew I'd served two years for embezzling.'

'I see. And then what?'

'Oh, as soon as the *Lucella* was launched I told Niels to publish and be damned. As long as I'm making money no one is going to care a tinker's dam about my record. When you need money, they make you sign an acolyte's pledge before they give it to you. When you've got it – they don't care where it came from. But Niels was furious.'

'It's a mighty big jump from pressuring you over a few grain orders to blowing up your ship, though.'

He insisted stubbornly that no one else cared enough. We talked about it for half an hour or more, but he wouldn't budge. I told him finally that I'd investigate Niels as well.

The golden retriever had departed with her people by the time we got to our feet and climbed back over the sand hills to the parking lot. A few children stared at us incuriously, waiting for the grown-ups to disappear before launching their own reckless deeds.

I drove Bledsoe back to the steel mill, now heavily thronged with Indiana and Chicago police. The four o'clock shift was arriving and I dropped him at the gates. The cops might want to talk to me later, as a witness, but they'd have to find me – I had other things to do.

21

FISHING TRIP

It is easier for a camel to go through the eye of a needle than for a private investigator in blue jeans to see the chairman of a major US corporation. I reached Ajax Insurance headquarters in the south Loop a little after five – traffic had been heavy all the way into the city. I was figuring on it being late enough for me to avoid the phalanx of secretaries who pave the entrance to a CEO's office, but I'd forgotten Ajax's security system.

Guards in the marble lobby of the sixty-story skyscraper demanded an employee identification card from me. I obviously didn't have one. They wanted to know whom I was visiting – they would issue me a visitor's pass if the person I wanted to see approved my visit.

When I told them Gordon Firth, they were appalled. They had a list of the chairman's visitors. I wasn't on it, and they suspected me of being an assassin from Aetna, hired to bump off the competition.

'I'm a private investigator,' I explained, pulling the photostat of my license from my wallet to show them. 'I'm looking into a fifty-million-dollar loss Ajax sustained last week. It's true I don't have an appointment with Gordon Firth, but it's important I see him or whomever he's designating to handle this loss. It may affect Ajax's ultimate liability.'

I argued with them some more and finally persuaded them if Ajax had to pay for the *Lucella's* hull because they had kept me out of Firth's office I'd remember their names and see that the money came out of their hides.

These arguments did not get me to Firth – as I say, it's easier for a

434

camel to pass through the eye of a needle – but they did bring me to a man in their Special Risks Department who was handling the loss. His name was Jack Hogarth and he came down to the lobby for me.

He walked briskly up to the guard station to meet me, his shirtsleeves pushed up to the elbows, his tie hanging loosely around his neck. He was about thirty-five or forty, dark, slight, with humorous brown-black eyes just now circled with heavy shadows.

'V. I. Warshawski, is it?' he asked, studying my card. 'Come on up. If you've got some information on the *Lucella* you're more welcome than a heat wave in January.'

I had to trot to keep up with him on the way to the elevator. We were carried quickly to the fifty-third floor; I yawned a couple of times to clear my ears. He barely waited for the elevator to open before plunging down the hall again, through double glass doors enclosing the elevator bank, and on to a walnut and crimson suite in the southeast corner of the building.

Papers were strewn across an executive-size walnut desk. A photograph of the *Lucella* as she lay fractured in the Poe Lock covered a table at one side, and a cutaway picture of a freighter hull was taped to the wood-paneled west wall.

I stopped to look at the photograph, enlarged to about three feet by two feet, and shuddered with remembered shock. Several more hatch covers had popped loose since I last saw the ship and the surfaces pointing steeply into the lock were covered with a thick smear of wet barley.

As I studied it, a very tall man got to his feet and strolled over to stand next to me. I hadn't seen him when I first walked into the room – he'd been sitting in a corner behind the door.

'Shocking, isn't it?' he said with a pronounced English accent.

'Very. It was even more shocking when it occurred.'

'Oh, you were there, were you?'

'Yes,' I answered shortly. 'I'm V. I. Warshawski, a private investigator. And you're –?'

He was Roger Ferrant from the London firm of Scupperfield,

Plouder, the lead underwriters on the *Lucella*'s hull and cargo insurance.

'Roger is probably the most knowledgeable man in the world about Great Lakes shipping, even though he operates out of London,' Hogarth told me. He added to Ferrant, 'Miss Warshawski may know something about our ultimate liability on the *Lucella*.'

I sat down in an armchair by the window where I could see the setting sun paint Buckingham Fountain a faint pink-gold. 'I'm looking into the accident to the *Lucella* as part of a murder investigation. At the moment I have two separate crimes – the murder of a young man connected with the Eudora Grain Company, and the destruction of the *Lucella*. It's not clear to me that they intersect. However, I was on board the *Lucella* pursuing my murder investigation when she blew up, and that's given me something of a personal interest in the explosion.'

'Who's your client?' Hogarth demanded.

'It's a private individual – not someone you'd know . . . How long does it take to clear up a claim like this?'

'Years.' Ferrant and Hogarth spoke in chorus. The Englishman added, 'Honestly, Miss Warshawski, it takes a very long time.' He stumbled a bit pronouncing my name, unlike Hogarth, who got it right the first time.

'Well, who pays Bledsoe's expenses while he reassembles the *Lucella*?'

'We do,' Hogarth said. 'Ferrant here handles the hull damage. We pay for the destroyed cargo and the business interruption – the loads that Bledsoe is forgoing by having his ship lying in the bottom of the lock.'

'Do you ante up a check to cover the cost of repairing the ship?'

'No,' Ferrant said. 'We pay the bills as the shipyard submits them.'

'And your policy covers Pole Star even though it's clear that someone blew up the ship, that it didn't just crack due to bad workmanship?'

Ferrant crossed one storklike leg over the other. 'That was one of the first questions we went into. As far as we can tell, it was not

436

blown up as an act of war. There are other exclusions under the policy, but that's the main one . . . Unless Bledsoe destroyed the ship himself.'

'There'd have to be a significant financial advantage to him for doing so,' I pointed out. 'If he collected the value of the hull and could invest it while he rebuilt the ship, there might be some, but otherwise it doesn't sound like it.'

'No,' Hogarth said impatiently. 'There isn't any point to ruining a brand-new ship like the *Lucella*. Now if it were one of those old clunkers that cost more to operate than they bring in in revenues, I'd see it, but not a thousand-foot self-unloader.'

'Like Grafalk's, you mean,' I said, remembering the *Leif Ericsson* running into the side of the wharf my first day down at the Port. 'He's better off collecting the insurance money than running his ships?'

'Not necessarily,' said Hogarth uneasily. 'It'd depend on the extent of the damage. You're thinking of the *Leif Ericsson*, aren't you? He'll have to pay for the damage to the wharf. That's going to run him more than the cost of repairing the *Ericsson*'s hull.'

Bledsoe had told me he wasn't liable for the damage to the lock. I asked Hogarth about that. He made a face. 'That's another one that's going to tie the lawyers up for a decade or two. If Bledsoe was responsible for the damage to the ship, which in turn damaged the forward lock gates, he's liable. If we can find the real culprit, he's liable. That's what we'd like to do: find whoever blew up the ship so we can subrogate against him – or her.'

I looked a question.

'Subrogate – get him to repay us for whatever we pay Bledsoe. And if we don't find the real culprit, your rich Uncle Sam is going to pay for the lock. He'll probably have to anyway – no one could afford to replace that. They'll just prosecute and send whoever did it to jail for twenty years. If they can find him.' The phone rang and he answered it. The caller seemed to be his wife: he told her placatingly that he'd be out of the office in twenty minutes and please to hold dinner for him.

He turned to me with an aggrieved expression. 'I thought you

437

came by because you had some hot information on the *Lucella*. All we've been doing is answering your questions.'

I laughed. 'I don't have any information for you now. But I think I may in a day or two. You've given me some ideas I want to play around with first.' I hesitated, then decided to go ahead and tell them about Mattingly. I was on my way to the police to let them know, anyway. 'The thing is, the guy who probably set off the explosion has been murdered himself. If the police can track down who killed him, they'll probably find the person who paid him to blow up the ship. I'm sure Mattingly was killed to keep him from bragging about it. He was a disagreeable guy who liked to boast about the sleazy things he did.'

Getting the inside story on Mattingly cheered up Hogarth and Ferrant, even though it hadn't helped their investigation into ultimate liability much. They put on their suit jackets and walked out of the office with me.

'The thing is,' Ferrant said confidentially in his English accent, 'it's just cheering to know there may really be a villain out there.'

'Yeah,' I said as we came out in the deserted lobby, 'but what if you find he works for another one of your insureds?'

'You mustn't say things like that,' Ferrant said. 'You really mustn't. I feel like eating for the first time since I heard about the *Lucella* last Saturday morning. I don't want you to ruin my dinner with horrible suggestions.'

Hogarth departed for the Northwestern Station and a train to Schaumburg. Ferrant was staying in Scupperfield, Plouder's apartment in the Hancock Building. I offered him a ride up in my Omega, which was parked in an underground garage nearby.

Before starting it I checked under the hood, looked at the oil, the brake fluid, the radiator. When Ferrant asked what I was doing I explained that I'd been in an accident recently and it made me more cautious about my car. Nothing seemed to be wrong.

On the short trip up Michigan Avenue to the Hancock I asked him if Scupperfield, Plouder had also underwritten the hull damage to the *Leif Ericsson*. They had; they underwrote all of the Grafalk Line.

438

'That's how Bledsoe came to us – he knew us from working with Grafalk.'

'I see.' I asked for his opinion of Bledsoe.

'One of the smartest men in the industry today. It's not a good time to be in Great Lakes shipping, at least not for US carriers. Your government gives considerable advantages to foreign flagships they don't accord to US vessels. Furthermore, old firms like Grafalk have some special legal positions that make it hard for a newcomer to break into the business. But Bledsoe can do it if anyone can. I just hope the wreck of the *Lucella* doesn't put an end to Pole Star.'

He invited me to dine with him, but I thought I'd better get to the police with my news about Mattingly. I'd told my tale to Bledsoe, and now to the insurance people. Although I hadn't given Murray Ryerson the name of the man with binoculars I'd seen at the Soo, he was no dummy – he might easily tie it in with my interest in Mattingly. Bobby Mallory was not going to look at me kindly if he read the story first in the *Herald-Star*.

I felt uneasy as I moved my car onto Lake Shore Drive. My life had been threatened two weeks ago. Phillips was dead, possibly because of the veiled threat I'd left with his son Saturday night. Perhaps he'd panicked, threatened to reveal what he knew, and been killed for his pains. Mattingly was dead, probably to keep him from boasting in the locker room that he'd blown up a ship. Boom Boom was dead because he knew that Phillips was fiddling grain invoices. Why was I still driving around? Maybe they thought more people would be killed when the *Lucella* went up. They might have been relying on that to get rid of me and be thinking up some other accident for me now. Or maybe they just didn't believe I knew anything important.

I tried comforting myself with that idea the rest of the way home, but I had known even less when my car was sabotaged ten days ago. It occurred to me as I exited at Belmont that the deaths in this case had been staged as a species of accident: Boom Boom had fallen overboard, Mattingly had been hit by a car, Phillips crushed in a self-unloader. If my car had killed me as it was supposed to, I don't suppose anyone would have gone to great pains to find that the steering control was sabotaged.

I hadn't been able to convince the police that there might be a connection between the night watchman's death and Boom Boom's. They wanted to treat the threat on me as a routine act of vandalism. In other words, the murderer had gauged the psychology of the situation accurately. Now that I was prepared to divulge what I knew about Mattingly, how likely were the police to tie that in with Kelvin and Boom Boom? Not terribly.

I was half tempted to keep the news to myself. But the police have a good machinery for sifting through large crowds of witnesses. If they did follow up on my information, they could find out who picked Mattingly up at Meigs last Friday far more readily than I.

As I parked the car, carefully selecting a spot in front of a restaurant so that would-be attackers would face a maximum of witnesses, I decided I'd keep the story of Mattingly and the binoculars to myself. Just say that he'd flown back in Bledsoe's plane.

22
NIGHT-TIME CHISELER

When I got to my apartment, I saw I was going to have to choose a story quickly. Sergeant McGonnigal was waiting for me in an unmarked brown Dodge. He got out when he saw me walking up the steps to the front door.

'Good evening, Miss Warshawski. Would you mind coming downtown with me? Lieutenant Mallory wants to ask you some questions.'

'What about?' I asked, taking out my keys and putting them in the front door.

McGonnigal shook his head. 'I don't know – he just asked me to bring you down.'

'Lieutenant Mallory thinks I should be living in Melrose Park with a husband and six children. I suspect any questions he wants to ask me have to do with how close I am to reaching that goal. Tell him to send me a Christmas card.' Just because I'd been going to see the police voluntarily didn't mean I had to like it when they came to fetch me.

McGonnigal set his handsome mouth in a thin line. 'You're not as funny as you think you are, Miss Warshawski. Your fingerprints were found in Clayton Phillips's office. Anyone else, we'd have a warrant and bring them in as a material witness. Because Lieutenant Mallory was a friend of your father's he wants you to come of your own free will to answer some questions.'

I was going to have to start wearing gloves if I ever wanted to make it as a burglar. 'Very well. I'm coming of my own free will.' I opened the front door. 'I need to get something to eat first. Want to come up with me to make sure I don't swallow a cyanide tablet?'

McGonnigal made an angry gesture and told me he'd wait in the car. I ran quickly up the three flights to my apartment. The larder was still bare – I hadn't had time to go to the store yet. I settled for a peanut butter sandwich made with the last two pieces of bread in the refrigerator and coffee reheated from breakfast. While I ate, I took Boom Boom's documents and taped them inside a couple of old copies of *Fortune*.

I went into the bathroom and brushed my teeth and washed my face. I needed to feel fresh and alert for a conversation with Bobby. I ran lightly back down the stairs to McGonnigal's waiting car. My shoulder gave me only faint twinges. I realized gloomily that I could start jogging again in the morning.

McGonnigal had the engine running. He took off with an ostentatious squeal of rubber before I even closed the door all the way. I put on the seat belt. 'You ought to wear yours if you're going to drive like that,' I told him. 'Insurance people and police – the two groups who see the most car accidents and the two you never see with seat belts.'

McGonnigal didn't answer. In fact conversation flagged all the way downtown. I tried to interest him in the Cubs' chances with Lee Elia and Dallas Green at the helm. He didn't want to talk about it. 'I hope you're not a Yankee fan, Sergeant. If you are, you're going to have to arrest me to get me into the same car with you.'

His only response was to drive faster. I kept up a monologue on the perfidies of the Yankees until we got to Twelfth Street, forbearing to comment on the fact that he was driving too fast for normal road conditions. He parked the car two feet from the curb and swung himself out, slamming the door behind him. I followed him into the back door of the Twelfth Street station.

'By the way, Sergeant, did you ever find anyone in the Kelvin murder?'

'It's still open,' he said stiffly.

Mallory rated a tiny office in the maze making up the homicide division. The back wall was covered with a map of the city, precinct boundaries outlined in heavy black, high crime areas marked in red.

Mallory was on the phone when we came in. I went over to look at my neighborhood. We had a very high homicide rate. There were a lot of rapes there, too. Maybe I would be better off in Melrose Park with six children.

Bobby hung up the phone and picked up a stack of papers. He put on his wire-rimmed glasses and started reading reports. 'Come over here and sit down, Vicki.'

I sat on the far side of his metal desk while he continued reading. 'You were at Plymouth Steel this morning when Clayton Phillips's body was discovered.'

I didn't say anything and he said sharply, 'You were there, weren't you?'

'I thought you were making a statement, not asking a question. Of course I was there – I called the police and I didn't make any secret of who I was.'

'Don't get smart with me. What were you doing down there?'

'I put Phillips's body in the hold Sunday morning and I wanted to see people's faces when it came out on the conveyor belt.'

Bobby slapped the desk top with his open palm. 'Vicki, you're this close to going to jail as a material witness.' He held up his thumb and middle finger to indicate a very tiny distance. 'Tell me what you were doing down there.'

'I was looking for Martin Bledsoe. He owns the Pole Star Line.'

Bobby relaxed a bit. 'Why?'

'I was on board the *Lucella* when she blew up last week. That's his flagship. Someone put depth charges under her last Friday up in Sault Ste Marie and –'

'Yes, I know all about that. What did you want to see Bledsoe for?'

'My suitcase fell into the middle of the ship. I wanted to know if they recovered it.'

Mallory turned red at that. 'You don't go bothering the owner of a steamship line for that kind of crap. Cut out the horseplay and tell me the truth.'

I shook my head earnestly. 'I am telling you the truth. No one else knew anything about it, so I went to see him. You see, my Smith &

443

Wesson was in my case. That cost me three hundred dollars and I can't afford to replace it.'

I knew that would divert Bobby's attention. He does not like the idea of my carrying a gun. He knows that my dad taught me how to use one. Tony believed most shooting accidents were caused by children not knowing anything about firearms. Since he had to keep his police revolver at home sometimes, he made me learn how to clean, load, and shoot it. Nonetheless, the idea of a woman toting around a Smith & Wesson is contrary to all Bobby's notions of a proper lady's life-style. He jumped on that, demanding to know why I had the gun with me on board ship and what I was doing on the *Lucella* anyway.

That was easier ground. I reminded him of my car accident. 'You guys wanted to believe it was vandals. I thought it was someone connected with the Port. I went up to Thunder Bay to talk to the captain and the chief engineer of the *Lucella*. Since one of them might have tried to kill me, I took my gun with me.'

We talked about that for a while. I reiterated my belief that Boom Boom had been pushed under the *Bertha Krupnik*. I told him I thought Henry Kelvin, the night watchman in his building, had been killed when he surprised intruders trying to find evidence that Boom Boom had of a crime down at the Port. Bobby wouldn't be persuaded. As far as he was concerned, Boom Boom had fallen in by accident, I was the victim of vandals, and Kelvin had interrupted a routine housebreaking. At that point a stubborn decision to keep the rest of my information overtook me. If they were going to be so damned pigheaded, I would be too.

When Bobby got back to my fingerprints in Phillips's office, I evaded the issue. 'What were you guys doing fingerprinting the man's office, anyway?'

'He was killed, Vicki,' Bobby said with heavy sarcasm. 'We were printing his office and doing everything else to it to find out if he was killed there.'

'Was he?'

Mallory drew a doodle on his desk pad. 'He actually died of suffocation in the cargo holds. We don't know where he received the head wound – that would have killed him anyway if he hadn't suffocated first.'

My stomach turned over. What a terrible death. I didn't like Phillips but I hadn't wished him that kind of end. Although if he had pushed Boom Boom overboard . . . 'When do they think it happened?'

'About six Sunday morning. Give or take a few hours. Now, Vicki: I want to know what you were doing in the guy's office. And when you were doing it.'

'About six yesterday morning I went down there to talk to him about my cousin's death. When he refused to answer my questions, I became enraged and hit him over the head with that brass thing he's got sitting on the front of his desk.'

Bobby gave me such an angry stare, I felt my stomach turn over again. He called to McGonnigal, who was waiting outside the door. 'Take down everything she says. If there's one more smart remark, book her as a material witness. I'm getting sick of this.' He turned back to me. 'When were you down there?'

I looked at the fingernails on my right hand. Time for a manicure. The left was no better. 'Saturday night.'

'And what were you doing there?'

'If I'd been burglarizing the place, I'd have been smart enough to wear gloves. I wasn't. I was looking for information that might show Phillips led a life of crime.'

'Who's your client, Vicki?'

I shook my head. 'Privileged information, Bobby.'

We talked about that for a while. I still regarded Boom Boom as my client, but I was damned if I was going to tell Bobby that. Lock me up indeed.

'You can't drag a body into the Port without someone noticing you,' I remarked at one point. 'There's a police guard at the gates. Have you asked them for the names of everyone who came into the Port early Sunday?'

Mallory gave me a withering look. 'We can think of the easy ones too. We're questioning those people right now.'

'Was Niels Grafalk one of them?'

445

Bobby gave me a sharp glance. 'No. Our guy didn't see him. Why?'

I shrugged. 'Just curious.'

Bobby kept asking why I was down at Phillips's office, what information I had expected to find, and so on.

Finally I said, 'Bobby, you think Boom Boom's death was an accident. I think he was murdered. I was looking for something that would tie Eudora Grain into his death, because it happened at their elevator after he had been arguing with their man.'

Mallory made a neat pile of the papers on his desk. He took off his wire-rimmed glasses and placed them on top of it. That was a signal that the interrogation was over. 'Vicki, I know how much you loved Boom Boom. I think that's making you place too much importance on his death. We see that a lot in here, you know. Someone loses their son or wife or father in a terrible accident. They can't believe it's happened, so they say it's murder. If there's a conspiracy, it makes the death easier to handle – their loved one was important enough for someone to want to kill.

'Now, you've had a rough time lately, Vicki. Your cousin died and you almost got killed yourself in a bad accident. You go away for a few weeks, go someplace warm and lie in the sun for a while. You need to give yourself a chance to recover from all this.'

After that, naturally, I didn't tell him about Boom Boom's documents or about Mattingly flying in from the Soo on Bledsoe's plane. McGonnigal offered to take me home, but in a continuing spirit of perverseness I told him I could find the way myself. I got up stiffly – we'd been talking for over two hours. It was close to ten when I boarded the north-bound subway at Roosevelt Road. I took it as far as Clark and Division, then transferred to a number 22 bus, getting off at Belmont and Broadway. I could walk the last half mile or so home.

I was very tired. The pain had come back in my shoulder, perhaps from sitting so long in one position. I walked as rapidly as I could across Belmont to Halsted. Lincoln Avenue cuts in at an angle there, and a large triangle on the south side of the street is a scraggy vacant lot. I held my keys clenched between my fingers, watching shadows in the bushes. At the front door to my building I kept a weather eye out for anything unusual. I didn't want to be the fourth victim of this extremely efficient murderer.

Three DePaul students share the second-floor apartment. As I walked up the stairs, one of them stuck her head out the door. 'Oh, it's you,' she said. She came all the way out, followed by her two roommates, one male and one female. In an excited trio they told me someone had tried to break into my apartment about an hour before. A man had rung their doorbell. When they buzzed him in, he'd gone past their door to the third floor.

'We told him you weren't home,' one of the women said, 'but he went on up anyway. After a while we heard him kind of chiseling away at the door. So we got the bread knife and went up after him.'

'My God,' I said. 'He could have killed you. Why didn't you call the police?'

The first speaker shrugged thin shoulders in a Blue Demon T-shirt. 'There were three of us and one of him. Besides, you know what the police are like – they'd never come in time in this neighborhood.'

I asked if they could describe the intruder. He was thin and seemed wiry. He had a ski mask on, which frightened them more than the incident itself. When he saw them coming up the stairs, he dropped the chisel, pushed past them, and ran down the steps and up Halsted. They hadn't tried to chase him, for which I was grateful – I didn't need injuries to them on my conscience, too.

They gave me the chisel, an expensive Sorby tool. I thanked them profusely and invited all three up to my apartment for a nightcap. They were curious about me and came eagerly. I served them Martell in my mother's red Venetian glasses and answered their enthusiastic questions about my life as a private investigator. It seemed a small price to pay for saving my apartment, and perhaps me, from a late night intruder.

23
A HOUSE OF MOURNING

I woke up early the next morning. My would-be intruder convinced me that I didn't have much time before another accident would overtake me. My anger with Bobby continued: I didn't report the incident. After all, the police would just treat it as another routine break and entry. I would solve the crimes myself; then they'd be sorry they hadn't listened to me.

I felt decidedly unheroic as I ran slowly over to Belmont Harbor and back. I only did two miles instead of my normal five, and that left me sweating, the ache returning to my left shoulder. I took a long shower and rubbed some ligament oil into the sore muscles.

I checked the Omega over with extra care. Everything seemed to be working all right, and no one had tied a stick of dynamite to the battery cable. Even taking time for exercise and a proper breakfast, I was on the road by nine o'clock. I whistled Fauré's 'Après un rêve' under my breath as I headed for the Loop. My first stop was the Title Office at City Hall. I found an empty parking meter on Madison Street and put in a quarter. Half an hour should be enough time for what I wanted to do.

The Title Office is where you go to register ownership of buildings in Chicago. Maybe all of Cook County. Like other city offices, this was filled with patronage workers. Henry Ford could study a city office and learn something about the ultimate in division of labor. One person gave me a form to fill out. I completed it, copying Paige Carrington's Astor Street address out of Boom Boom's address book. The filled-in form went to a second clerk, who date-stamped it and gave it to a heavy black man sitting behind a cage. He, in turn, assigned the form to one of the numerous pages whose job it was to fetch out the title books and carry them to the waiting taxpayers.

I stood behind a scarred wooden counter with other title searchers, waiting for a page to bring me the relevant volume. The man who finally filled my order turned out to be surprisingly helpful – city workers usually seem to be in a secret contest for who can harass the public the most. He found the entry for me in the heavy book and showed me how to read it.

Paige occupied a floor in a converted apartment building, an old five-flat built in 1923. The entries showed that there was some kind of dwelling on that site as far back as 1854. The Harris Bank had owned the current building until 1978 when it was converted to condominiums. Jay Feldspar, a well-known Chicago land developer, had acquired it then and done the conversion. Paige's unit, number 2, was held as a trust by the Fort Dearborn Trust. Number 1123785-G.

Curiouser and curiouser. Either Paige owned the thing herself as part of a trust, or someone owned it for her. I looked at my watch. I'd already been here forty minutes; might as well take a little more time and risk a parking ticket. I wrote the trust number down on a piece of paper in my shoulder bag, thanked the attendant for his help, and went out to find a pay phone. I'd been to law school with a woman who was now an attorney on the Fort Dearborn's staff. She and I had never been friends – our aspirations were too different. We'd never been enemies, either, though. I thought I'd call her and give a tug on the old school tie.

It took more than a tug – trust documents were confidential, she could be disbarred, let alone thrown out of the bank. I finally persuaded her that I'd get the *Herald-Star* to come in and suborn the clerical staff if she didn't find the name of the person behind the trust number for me.

'You really haven't changed a bit, Vic. I remember how you bullied everyone during moot court in our senior year.'

I laughed.

'I didn't mean it as a compliment,' she said crossly, but she agreed to call me at home that night with the information.

While I was wasting dimes and adding to the risk of a ticket, I

449

checked in with my answering service. Both Ryerson and Pierre Bouchard had called.

I tried Murray first. 'Vic, if you'd lived two hundred years ago they would have burned you at the stake.'

'What are you talking about?'

'That Arroyo hiking boot. Mattingly was wearing them when he died, and we're pretty sure they're a match for the footprint the police found in Boom Boom's place. We'll have the story on the front page of the early editions. Got any other hot tips?'

'No. I was hoping you might have something for me. Talk to you later.'

Bouchard wanted to tell me that he had checked around with Mattingly's cronies on the team. He didn't think Howard knew how to dive. Oh, and Elsie had given birth to a nine-pound boy two days ago. She was calling him Howard after the worthless snake. The members of the team were pitching in to make a donation to her since Howard had died without a pension and left very little life insurance. Would I give something from Boom Boom? Pierre knew my cousin would want to be included.

Certainly, I told him, and thanked him for his diligence.

'Are you making any progress?' he asked.

'Well, Mattingly's dead. The guy who I'm sure pushed Boom Boom in the water was killed Sunday. Another few weeks like this and the only person left alive will be his murderer. I guess that's progress.'

He laughed. 'I know you will have success. Boom Boom told me many times how clever you are. But if you need some muscle, let me know. I'm a good man for a fight.'

I agreed with him wholeheartedly – I'd watched him cutting people's heads open on the ice with good-natured enthusiasm many times.

I sprinted back to my car, too late. A zealous meter maid had already filled out a parking ticket for letting the meter run out. I stuck it into my shoulder bag and inched my way across the Loop to Ontario Street, the closest entrance to the Kennedy Expressway.

The weather had finally warmed up slightly. Under a clear blue sky, trees along the expressway put out tentative, pale green leaves toward the sun. The grass was noticeably darker than it had been the week before. I started singing some Elizabethan love songs. They suited the weather and the chirping birds better than Fauré's moodiness. Off the Kennedy to the Edens, past the painfully tidy bungalows of the Northwest Side where people balanced their paychecks with anxious care, up to the industrial parks lining the middle-class suburbs of Lincolnwood and Skokie, on to the Tri-State Tollway and the rarefied northern reaches of the very rich.

'"Sweet lovers love the spring",' I sang, turning off onto route 137. Over to Green Bay Road, making the loop around the Harbor Road without a single wrong turn. I went on past the Phillips residence and parked the Omega around the southern bend in the road, away from the house. I was wearing my navy Evan Picone pantsuit, a compromise between comfort and the need to look respectable in a house of mourning.

I walked briskly back along the greensward to the Phillips house in my low-heeled loafers, my legs a little sore from the unaccustomed run this morning.

Once on the driveway, I stopped singing. That would be indecorous. Three cars were parked behind the blue Oldsmobile 88. Phillips's green Alfa. So he hadn't driven himself down to the Port Sunday morning? Or had the car been returned? I'd have to ask. A red Monte Carlo, about two years old and not kept up as well as the neighborhood demanded. And a silver Audi 5000. The sight of the Audi drove any desire to sing from my heart.

A pale teenager in Calvin Klein jeans and an Izod shirt answered the door. Her brown hair was cut short and frizzed around her head in a perm. She looked at me with an unfriendly stare. 'Well?' she said ungraciously.

'My name is V. I. Warshawski. I've come to see your mother.'

'Well, don't expect me to pronounce that.' She turned her head, still holding onto the doorknob. 'Mo-ther,' she yelled. 'Some lady's here to see you. I'm going for a bike ride.'

'Terri. You can't do that.' Jeannine's voice floated in from the back.

Terri turned her whole attention to her mother. She put her hands on her hips and shouted down the hall, 'You let Paul take the boat out. If he can take the boat out, how come I can't go for a stupid little bike ride? I'm not going to sit here and talk to you and Grandma all day long.'

'Real charming,' I commented. 'You read about that in *Cosmopolitan* or pick it up watching *Dallas*?'

She turned her angry face to me. 'Who asked you to butt in? She's back in there.' She jerked her arm down the hall and stomped out the front door.

An older woman with carefully dyed hair came out into the hallway. 'Oh dear. Did Terri go out? Are you one of Jeannine's friends? She's sitting back in here. It's awfully nice of you to stop by.' The skin around her mouth had gotten soft, but the pale eyes reminded me of her daughter. She was wearing a long-sleeved beige dress, tasteful but not in the same price range as her daughter's clothes.

I followed her past the pale blue living room into the family room at the back where I had interviewed Jeannine the week before. 'Jeannine dear, someone's come to visit you.'

Jeannine was sitting in one of the wing chairs at the windows overlooking Lake Michigan. Her face was carefully made up and it was hard to tell how she felt about her husband's death.

Across the room, feet tucked up under her on an armchair, sat Paige Carrington. She put down her teacup with a crash on a glass coffee table at her left arm. It was the first thing I'd seen her do that wasn't totally graceful.

'I thought I recognized your Audi out there,' I remarked.

'Vic!' Her voice came out in a hiss. 'I won't have it. Are you following me everywhere?'

At the same time Jeannine said, 'No, you must go away. I'm not answering any questions now. My – my husband died yesterday.'

Paige turned to her. 'Has she been after you too?'

'Yes. She was out here last week asking me a lot of questions about my life as a corporate wife. What was she talking to you about?'

452

'My private life.' Paige's honey-colored eyes flicked over me warily.

'I didn't follow you here, Paige: I came to see Mrs Phillips. I might start staking out your place, though – I'm kind of curious about who's paying those monthly assessments. Astor Place – that's got to run you seven-eight hundred a month without the mortgage.'

Paige's face turned white under her rust-toned makeup. Her eyes were dark with emotion. 'You had better be joking, Vic. If you try bothering me any further, I'll call the police.'

'I'm not bothering you at all. As I said, I came here to see Mrs Phillips . . . I need to talk to you, Mrs Phillips. Privately.'

'What about?' Jeannine was bewildered. 'I answered all your questions last week. And I really don't feel like talking to anyone right now.'

'That's right, dear,' her mother said. She turned to me. 'Why don't you leave now? My daughter's worn out. Her husband's death came as quite a shock.'

'I can imagine,' I said politely. 'I hope his life insurance was paid up.'

Jeannine gasped. Paige said, 'What a singularly tasteless remark, even from you.'

I ignored her. 'Mrs Phillips, I'm afraid I talked to you last week under false pretenses. I'm not from a survey research firm. I'm a detective, and I was trying to find out if your husband might have attempted to murder me two weeks ago.'

Her tightly clenched jaw went momentarily slack with surprise.

'My investigations have shown me that your husband had substantial sources of income beyond his salary. I'd like to talk to you privately about it. Unless you want your mother and Ms Carrington to hear.'

At that, her composure cracked. 'He promised me no one would ever know.' Tears carved two furrows in the makeup on her cheeks. Her mother hurried over with a box of tissues and fussed over her, telling her somewhat confusedly to go ahead and have a good cry.

I was still standing. 'I really think we'd better continue this

453

conversation alone. Is there another room we can go to, Mrs Phillips?'

'What are you talking about?' her mother said. 'Clayton had a very good salary at Eudora Grain. Why, when they made him an officer five years ago, he and Jeannine bought this house.'

'That's okay, Mother.' Jeannine patted the older woman's hand. 'I'd better talk to this woman.' She turned to Paige and said with sudden venom, 'I suppose *you* know all about it.'

Paige gave her triangular smile. 'I know a fair amount.' She shrugged her slim shoulders. 'But who am I to cast stones, after all?' She picked up a sweater lying on the table beside her. 'Better talk to Vic, Jeannine. If you don't, she'll only come in and burglarize the place so she can examine your bankbooks.' She drifted over to Jeannine's chair and kissed the air by her cheek. 'I'm going back to the city. I'll see you at the funeral tomorrow afternoon – unless you want me to come up before then.'

'No, that's all right, dear,' Jeannine's mother said. 'We'll manage fine.' She bustled out to the hall behind the elegant younger woman.

I looked after them, puzzled. I assumed at first that Paige must have met Jeannine at some Eudora Grain function when she was dating Boom Boom. But that last exchange made it sound like a fairly close relationship.

'How do you know Paige?' I asked.

Jeannine turned her tear-streaked face to me for the first time since I'd mentioned the invoices. 'How do I know her? She's my sister. Why wouldn't I know her?'

'Your sister!' We sounded like a couple of damned parrots. 'Sisters. I see.' Actually, I didn't see a thing. I sat down. 'Did you take her to the party where she met my cousin?'

She looked surprised. 'What party was that?'

'I don't know who gave it. Probably Guy Odinflute. He lives around here, doesn't he? Niels Grafalk was interested in buying a share in the Black Hawks. My cousin came up along with some of the other players. Paige was there and she met my cousin. I want to know who brought her.'

Jeannine swallowed a sly smile. '*That* party. No, we didn't go.'

454

'But were you invited?'

'Mr Odinflute may have asked us . . . We get asked to a lot of parties at Christmas. If you want to know who Paige went with, though, you ask her.'

I looked at her narrowly: she knew, but she wouldn't tell. I turned my attention to the money. 'Tell me about the invoices, Jeannine.'

'I don't know what you're talking about.'

'Sure you do. You just said he'd promised no one would ever know. I called about them Saturday night – left a message with your son Paul. What did your husband do next?'

She shed a few more tears but in the end it came out that she didn't know. They got back late. Paul had left the message by the kitchen phone. When Clayton saw it, he went into his study and shut the door. He made a phone call and left a few minutes later. No, not in the Alfa. Had someone picked him up? She didn't know. He was very upset and told her not to bother him. It was about one-thirty Sunday morning when he went out. That was the last time she ever saw him.

'Now tell me about the invoices, Jeannine. He was padding them, wasn't he?'

She didn't say anything.

'People would give him bids on Eudora Grain cargoes and he would log the orders at one price but bill them at another. Is that right?'

She started crying again. 'I don't know. I don't know.'

'You don't know how he worked it, but you know he was doing it. That's true, isn't it?'

'I didn't ask, as long as the bills got paid.' She was sobbing harder.

I was losing my temper. 'Did you know what your husband's salary was?'

'Of course I knew what Clayton earned.' Her tears stopped long enough for her to glare at me.

'Sure you did. And you knew ninety-two thousand, however good it looks compared to the other girls at Park Forest South High, or whatever it was, wasn't enough to pay for a boat. This house. Your designer clothes. The kid at Claremont. Those high-ticket cars. The Izod T-shirts little Terri runs around in. Dues at the Maritime Club.

455

Just out of curiosity, what does the Maritime Club run you a year? I was betting twenty-five thousand.'

'You don't understand!' She sat up and stared at me with fierce, angry eyes. 'You don't know what it's like when all the other girls have everything they want and you're making do with last year's clothes.'

This sounded like a real heartache to me. 'You're right – I don't. My high school, most of us girls had a couple of dresses we started with as sophomores and wore out the door when we graduated. Park Forest South may be a bit tonier than South Chicago – but not a lot.'

'Park Forest South! My mother moved there later. We grew up here in Lake Bluff. We had horses. My father kept a boat. We lived down the road from here. Then he lost everything. Everything. I was a junior in high school. Paige was only eight. She's too young to remember the humiliation. The way people stared in school. Mother sold the silver. She sold her own jewels. But it didn't do any good. He shot himself and we moved away. She couldn't stand the pity people like old Mrs Grafalk dished out at the country club. And I had to go to Roosevelt instead of Northwestern.'

'So you decided you were going to move back here, no matter what it took. What about your husband? He a Lake Bluffer in exile who made his way back?'

'Clayton came from Toledo. Eudora Grain brought him here when he was twenty-five. He rented an apartment in Park Forest and we met there.'

'And you thought he had possibilities, that he might go all the way for you. When did you find out that wasn't going to happen?'

'When Terri was born. We were still living in that crappy three-bedroom house.' She was screaming now. 'Terri and Ann had to share a room. I was buying all my clothes at Wieboldt's. I couldn't stand it! I couldn't stand it any more. And there was Paige. She was only eighteen, but she already knew – knew –'

'Knew what, Jeannine?'

She recovered some of her control. 'Knew how to get people to help her out,' she said quietly.

'Okay. You didn't want Paige outdressing you. So you put

pressure on your husband to come up with more money. He knew he was never going to have enough if he just struggled along on his salary. So he decided to skim something off the top before it ever hit Eudora's books. Did he fiddle with anything besides the invoices?'

'No, it was just the invoices. He could make – make – about a hundred thousand extra a year from them. He – he didn't do it with all the orders, only about ten per cent. And he paid taxes on them.'

'Paid taxes on them?' I echoed incredulously.

'Yes. We didn't want to run – run a risk with the I R S auditing us. We called it commission income. They don't know what his job's supposed to be like. They don't know whether he should be earning commissions or not.'

'And then my cousin found out. He was going through the papers, trying to see what a regional manager does to run an office like that, and he ended up comparing some invoices with the original contract orders.'

'It was terrible,' she gulped. 'He threatened to tell David Argus. It would have meant the end of – of Clayton's career. He would have been fired. We would have had to sell the house. It would have been –'

'Spare me,' I said harshly. A pulse throbbed in my right temple. 'It was a choice between the Maritime Club and my cousin's life.'

She didn't say anything. I grabbed her by the shoulders and shook her. 'Answer me, damn you! You decided my cousin had to die to keep you in your Massandrea dresses. Is that what happened? Is it?'

In my rage I had lifted her from her wing chair and was shaking her. Mrs Carrington came bustling into the room.

'What is going on here?' she fussed behind me. I was still screaming at Jeannine. Mrs Carrington grabbed my arm. 'I think you'd better go now. My daughter cannot afford any more upsets. If you don't leave, I will call the police.'

Somehow her scratchy voice penetrated and I forced my anger back. 'You're right. I'm sorry, Mrs Carrington. I'm afraid I got carried away by my work.' I turned to Jeannine. 'Just one more question before I leave you to your mourning. What was Paige's role in all this?'

'Paige?' she whispered, rubbing her shoulders where I had grabbed them. She gave the sly smile I'd seen earlier. 'Oh, Paige was supposed to keep track of what Boom Boom was up to. But you'd better talk to her. She hasn't given away my secrets. I won't give away hers.'

'That's right,' Mrs Carrington said. 'You girls should be loyal to each other. After all, you're all that you have.'

'Besides a boat and a condo on Astor Place,' I said.

24
A QUESTION OF POLICY

I was sick by the side of the road as soon as I got to the end of the drive. Terri rode up on her bicycle, a Peugeot ten-speed, I noticed as I wiped my mouth with a Kleenex. Boom Boom, you did not die in vain if you preserved a French racing bicycle for that girl.

I walked slowly down the road to the Omega and sat in it for a long time without starting the engine. My shoulder ached from grabbing Jeannine and lifting her up.

I had found out about Boom Boom's death. Or proved to myself what I had suspected for several days, at any rate. I felt a sharp pain across my diaphragm, as though someone had inserted a little needle behind it which jabbed me every time I breathed. That's what people mean when they say their hearts ache. They really mean their diaphragms. My face felt wet. I passed a hand across my eyes, expecting to find blood. I was crying.

After a while I looked at my watch. It was one o'clock. I looked at my face in the rearview mirror. It had gone very pale and my gray eyes stood out darkly in contrast. There were days when I'd looked better, but that couldn't be helped. I switched on the engine and slowly turned the car around on the narrow pavement. My arms felt leaden, so heavy I could scarcely lift them to the steering wheel. It would be nice to follow Bobby's advice and go someplace warm for a few weeks. Instead I drove up the road past the Phillips house to the Grafalks'.

The garage was behind the house to the left; I couldn't see the cars to tell if anyone was home. I climbed up the shallow wide step to the front porch and rang the bell. A minute or two passed; I was going to ring again when the thickset maid, Karen, answered. She looked at me grudgingly. She remembered my vulgar interest in Mr Grafalk's movements last week.

I gave her my card. 'Is Mrs Grafalk in, please?'

'Is she expecting you?'

'No. I'm a detective. I want to talk to her about Clayton Phillips.'

She seemed undecided about whether or not she was going to take my card back. I was too worn out from my encounter with Jeannine to put up much of a fight. As we stood there at an impasse, a high, clipped voice demanded of Karen who it was.

The maid turned around. 'It's a detective, Mrs Grafalk. She says she wants to talk to you about Mr Phillips.'

Mrs Grafalk came into the hall. Her graying black hair was styled to emphasize her high cheekbones, which she had further accentuated with a dark rouge. She was dressed to go out, in a salmon silk suit with a ballet skirt and a flared, ruched jacket. Her eyes were sharp but not unfriendly. She took the card from Karen, who positioned herself protectively between us.

'Miss Warshawski? I'm afraid I don't have much time. I'm on my way to a Ravinia planning meeting. What did you want to talk about?'

'Clayton and Jeannine Phillips.'

An expression of distaste crossed her face. 'There's not a lot I can tell you about them. Clayton is – was, I should say – a business associate of my husband's. For reasons I have never understood, Niels insisted we entertain them, even sponsor them at the Maritime Club. I tried to interest Jeannine in some of the work that I do, particularly with the poor immigrant community in Waukegan. I'm afraid it's hard to get her to think of anything but her clothes.'

She spoke rapidly, scarcely pausing for breath between sentences.

'Excuse me, Mrs Grafalk, but Mr Grafalk implied that Jeannine was a protégé of yours and that you wanted to get her into the Maritime Club.'

She raised her black, painted eyebrows and opened her eyes very wide. 'Why did Niels say that? I wonder. Clayton obliged him on some business deal and Niels sponsored him in the club to show his appreciation. I'm perfectly sure that was the way it happened. Niels keeps what he does with Grafalk Steamship to himself, so I've never known what the arrangement was – in fact I can't imagine being interested in it. I'm sorry Clayton's dead, but he was an insufferable climber and Jeannine is no better . . . Does that answer your questions? I'm afraid I must go now.' She started for the door, buttoning on a pair of pale salmon gloves. I didn't know anyone wore gloves anymore. She walked outside the door with me, moving at a good clip on needle-pointed shoes. A woman with less force of personality would have looked absurd in that outfit. Mrs Grafalk seemed elegant.

As I got into the Omega, someone drove the Bentley up for her. A thin, sandy-haired man got out, helped her into the car, and headed back to the garage behind the house.

Slowing driving back to Chicago, I thought about Mrs Grafalk's remarks. The business deal must have been connected with the Eudora shipping invoices. What if Phillips had split the difference in the bills with Grafalk? Say he got ninety thousand dollars extra over the price registered on the computer for the shipment and gave forty-five thousand to Grafalk. That didn't make sense, though. Grafalk was the biggest carrier on the lakes. What did he need with penny-ante stuff like that? If Grafalk were involved, the payoff had to be more impressive. Of course, Grafalk operated all those older ships. It cost him more to carry cargo. The amount in the invoices was probably the true price of what it cost Grafalk to carry the stuff. If that was the case, Phillips was really stealing from Eudora Grain – not just pocketing the difference between how much he logged into the contract and the ultimate invoice, but losing money for Eudora on every shipment he recorded when Grafalk was the carrier. What Grafalk got out of it was more shipments in a depressed market in which he had a hard time competing because of his older, inefficient fleet.

Suddenly I saw the whole thing. Or most of it, anyway. I felt as though the truth had been hammered in at me from the day I walked into Percy MacKelvy's office at Grafalk Steamship down at the Port. I remembered listening to him trying to place orders on the phone, and

461

my frustration while we were talking. Grafalk's reaction to Bledsoe at lunch. The times in the last two weeks I'd heard how much more efficient the thousand-footers were to operate. I even had an idea where Clayton Phillips had been murdered and how his body had been carried onto the *Gertrude Ruttan* without anyone seeing it.

A seventy-ton semi blared its horn behind me. I jumped in my seat and realized I had brought the Omega almost to a standstill in the second lane of the Kennedy. No need for anyone to arrange subtle accidents for me – I could kill myself without help. I accelerated quickly and drove on into the Loop. I needed to talk to the Lloyd's man.

It was three in the afternoon and I hadn't eaten. After leaving the car in the Grant Park underground garage, I went into the Spot, a little bar and grill behind Ajax, for a turkey sandwich. In honor of the occasion I also had a plate of french fries and a Coke. My favorite soft drink, but I usually avoid it because of the calories.

I marched across Adams to the Ajax Building, singing, '"Things go better with Coca-Cola"', under my breath. I told the guard I wanted to see Roger Ferrant – the Lloyd's man – up in the Special Risks office. After some delay – they couldn't figure out the Special Risk phone number – they got through to Ferrant. He would be happy to see me.

With my visitor's ID clipped to my lapel, I rode to the fifty-third floor. Ferrant came out of the walnut office to meet me. A shock of lanky brown hair flopped in his eyes and he was straightening his tie as he came.

'You've got some news for us, have you?' he asked eagerly.

'I'm afraid not yet. I have some more questions I didn't think to ask yesterday.'

His face fell, but he said cheerfully, 'Shouldn't expect miracles, I guess. And why should you succeed where the FBI, the US Coast Guard, and the Army Corps of Engineers have failed?' He ushered me courteously back into the office, which was more cluttered than it had been the night before. 'I'm staying in town through the formal inquiry at the Soo next Monday, then back to London. Think you'll crack the problem by then?'

He was speaking facetiously, but I said, 'I should have the answer in another twenty-four hours. I don't think you're going to like it, though.'

He saw the seriousness in my face. Whether he believed me or not, he stopped laughing and asked what he could do to help.

'Hogarth said yesterday you were the most knowledgeable person in the world on Great Lakes shipping. I want to know what's happening to it with this lock blown up.'

'Could you explain what you mean, please?'

'The accident to the lock must be having quite an impact, right? Or can ships still get through?'

'Oh – well, shipping hasn't come to a complete standstill. They closed the MacArthur and the Davis locks for several days while they cleaned debris out of them and tested them, but they can still use the Sabin Lock – that's the one in Canadian waters. Of course, the biggest ships are shut off from the upper lakes for a year – or however long it takes them to fix the Poe – the Poe was the only lock that could handle the thousand-footers.'

'And how serious is that? Does it have much of a financial impact?'

He pushed the hair out of his eyes and loosened his tie again. 'Most of the shipping is between Duluth and Thunder Bay and ports lower down. Sixty percent of the grain in North America goes out of those two ports on freighters. That's a hell of a lot of grain, you know, when you think of everything that's produced in Manitoba as well as the upper Midwest – maybe eighteen billion bushels. Then there's all that taconite in Duluth.' He pursed his lips in thought. 'The Soo locks handle more cargo every year than Panama and Suez combined, and they're only open for nine months instead of year-round like those two. So there is some financial impact.'

'The cargoes will still come out, but the smaller ships will have an advantage?' I persisted.

He smiled. 'Just until they get the Poe Lock back under operation. Actually, there's been a lot of disarray, both in the grain markets and among the Great Lakes shippers since the lock blew up. They'll settle down in a few weeks when they realize that most traffic won't be impaired.'

'Except for the carriers who've converted primarily to thousand-foot ships.'

'Yes, but there aren't too many of those. Of course, grain concerns like Eudora are scrambling to get all their cargoes onto the smaller fleets, even bypassing the 740-foot ships. Grafalk's is picking up a number of orders. They aren't jacking up their rates, though, the way some of their less scrupulous brethren are.'

'How profitable is Grafalk's, in general?'

He looked at me in surprise. 'They are the biggest carrier on the lakes.'

I smiled. 'I know – I keep being told that. But do they make money? I understand that these smaller ships are unprofitable and they make up his whole fleet.'

Ferrant shrugged. 'All we do is insure the hulls. I can't tell you how much freight they're carrying. Remember, though, profitability is relative. Grafalk may not make as much as a firm like American Marine, but that doesn't mean they're unprofitable.'

Hogarth had come in while we were talking. 'Why do you want to know, Miss Warshawski?'

'It's not just idle curiosity. You know, no one's come forward claiming responsibility for the bombing – the PLO or the FALN or the Armenians. If it wasn't a random act of terrorism, there had to be a reason for it. I'm trying to find out if that reason included switching cargo from the big freighters to small vessels like the ones in Grafalk's fleet.'

Hogarth looked annoyed. 'Not Grafalk, I assure you, Miss Warshawski. Niels Grafalk comes from a very old shipping family. He's devoted to his fleet, to his business – and he's a gentleman.'

'That's a fine testimonial,' I said. 'It does a lot of credit to your heart. But a fifty-million-dollar ship has been blown up, the North American shipping industry has been thrown into disarray, however temporary, and a lot of business interrupted. I don't know how the courts interpret such a thing, but someone is going to have to pay for that business interruption. Grafalk stands to gain a lot by this accident. I want to know what shape his business is in. If it's doing well, there's less of a motive.'

464

Ferrant looked amused. 'You certainly look for the less pleasant side of human nature . . . Jack, you have some idea of the state of the business, don't you? Just look at your records, see how much cargo coverage he's got and what his workers compensation insurance is like.'

Hogarth said mulishly that he had a meeting to get to and he thought it was a waste of time.

'Then I'll do it,' Ferrant said. 'You just show me where the files are, Jack, and I'll have a look-through for Miss Warshawski here . . . No, really, I think she's got a good point. We ought to follow up on it.'

Hogarth finally called his secretary on the intercom and asked her to bring him five years of Grafalk Steamship files. 'Just don't ever let the old boy know you did this. He's very touchy where his family name is concerned.'

Hogarth left for his next meeting and Ferrant made some phone calls while I watched the boats out on Lake Michigan. Monroe Harbor was filling up rapidly with its summer fleet of sailboats. A lot of people were taking advantage of the beautiful weather; the near horizon was filled with white sails.

After some twenty minutes a middle-aged woman in a severely tailored suit came into the office pushing a large wire cart full of files. 'These are the Grafalk Steamship files Mr Hogarth asked for,' she said, leaving the cart in the middle of the room.

Ferrant was enthusiastic. 'Now we'll see what shape the business is in. You can't tell that just from the hull insurance, which is all I do for Grafalk.'

Five years of Grafalk history was a substantial amount of paper. We had workers compensation policies, which went on for about a hundred pages a year, showing classes of employees, states covered, Longshoremen's Act exclusions, and premium audits. There was a business interruption policy for each year, cargo coverage, which was written on a per-shipment basis, and inland marine, to cover Grafalk's liability for cargo once it was unloaded from his ships.

Ferrant sorted through the mass with an experienced eye. 'You know, the cargo and the compensation are going to tell us the most.

We'll just see the value of the freight he's carrying and how many people he's employing to do it. You tot up those workers compensation policies – look at the final audited statements and that'll tell you how many people he's got sailing for him every year. I'll go through these cargo policies.'

I sat down at a round wooden table and joined him in stacking the papers covering it down on the floor. 'But I thought the whole shipping business was depressed. If he's not carrying much, how will that tell us anything besides the fact that the industry's depressed?'

'Good point, good point.' Ferrant placed a stack of workers compensation policies in front of me. 'We have some industry statistics – the average load carriers are hauling as a percentage of their available tonnage, that sort of thing. We'll just compare them. I'm afraid it's a rough approximation. The other thing, though, is that we know about what it costs a day to own one of those old clunkers. Now if it's not carrying cargo, there's still overhead – it has to be docked someplace. Unless the ship is in mothballs – which also costs something per diem – you have to have a skeleton crew on board. You need to be able to turn the beast on in a hurry and get to the place where you have a cargo waiting. So we can make a good guess at his costs and then look at these cargoes, here, and see how much he's earning.'

That seemed like a reasonable approach. I started on my part of the assignment, secretly entertained by Ferrant's enthusiasm for the project. He didn't have Hogarth's personal feeling for the insured.

The first page of the 1977 policy explained that Grafalk Steamship was a closely held corporation, principal address at 132 North La Salle Street in Chicago. The summary of the coverage on the declarations page showed Grafalk with fifteen hundred employees in eight states. These included sailors, secretaries, stevedores, longshoremen, truck drivers, and general office workers. Directors and officers were excluded from the coverage. The total premium for 1977 was four million eight hundred thousand dollars. I whistled to myself. A lot of money.

I flipped through the pages of state and class detail to the back where the audit of the premium was attached. This section was completed at the end of the year. It showed how many people had actually worked each day by class of job and how much premium Grafalk in fact owed Ajax for 1977. The reduction was substantial – down to three million dollars. Instead of three million hours of work, Grafalk's employees had put in under two million for the year ending then.

I showed this result to Ferrant. He nodded and went back to the cargo policies. I finished the compensation ones, scribbling summary results on a sheet of paper. Ferrant handed me a stack of cargo policies. He was tabulating them by date, total value of contract, and vessel used. We'd compare them later to the tonnage figures of the individual ships.

Hogarth came in as we were finishing the masses of paper. I looked at my watch. It was almost six o'clock.

'Any luck?' Hogarth asked.

Ferrant pursed his lips, his long hair falling over his eyes again. 'Well, we have to add up what we've got. Doesn't look good, though. I say, Hogarth, be a sport and give us a hand – don't look so sour. Think of this as an intellectual problem.'

Hogarth shook his head. 'Count me out. I told Madeleine I'd be home on time for once tonight and I'm already late. I'm going to catch the six thirty-five.'

He left and Ferrant and I continued our work, tedious and un-inspiring. In the end, though, it became clear that Grafalk had been using only forty of his sixty-three vessels for the last five years. In fact he'd sold three ships in the middle of 1979.

'He should have sold more,' Ferrant said gloomily.

'Maybe he tried and there wasn't a market.'

By eight-thirty we'd completed a sketchy analysis of Grafalk's finances. His ships cost about two thousand dollars a day to operate when they weren't sailing, about ten thousand dollars a day when they were. So the total expense to Grafalk each season for running the steamship company was about a hundred twenty million dollars a year. And the total value of the cargoes he was carrying came out to only a hundred million in 1977. Things were a little better in '78 and '79 but hadn't improved much the past two years.

'That answers your question all right,' Ferrant said. 'The lad is definitely losing money.' He lined up his stacks of notes. 'Odd how much cargo he's been carrying for Eudora Grain the last five years. Almost twenty percent of his total volume.'

'Odd indeed,' I said. 'Of course, Eudora's a big concern . . . Where's Grafalk been coming up with the money to cover these losses? They're pretty staggering.'

'The steamship company isn't the only thing he owns.' Ferrant was sweeping the policies back into their jackets. 'There's a profitable railway that connects the Port of Buffalo with Baltimore – he can unload there and ship by rail to oceangoing vessels in Baltimore. That does very well for him. His family owns a big block of stock in Hansen Electronic, the computer firm. You'd have to see if you could get his broker to tell you whether he's been selling off the stock to pay for this. He's into a number of other things. I think his wife has some money, too. But the steamship company has always been his first love.'

We piled the policies back into the cart and left it in the hallway for someone to take care of in the morning. I yawned and stretched and offered to buy Ferrant a drink.

25

THE OLD GIRL NETWORK

He walked with me to the Golden Glow on Jackson and Federal. It's a place for serious drinkers – no quiche and celery sticks to entice imbibers of white wine on their way to the commuter trains. Sal, the magnificent black woman who owns the place, has a mahogany horseshoe-shaped bar, relic of an old Cyrus McCormick mansion, and seven tiny booths crammed into a space wedged out between a bank and an insurance company.

I hadn't been in for several weeks and she came over to our booth herself for our order. I asked for my usual, a Johnnie Walker Black up, and Ferrant had a gin martini. I asked Sal for the use of a phone and she brought one over to the table for me.

My answering service told me Adrienne Gallagher, the woman I know at the Fort Dearborn Trust, had called. She'd left her home number and a message that I could call before ten.

A little girl answered the phone and called her mommy in a shrill voice.

'Hello, Vic. I got the information you wanted.'

'I hope they're not trying to fire you or disbar you.'

She gave a little laugh. 'No – but you owe me some free detective work. Anyway, the condominium is owned by a Niels Grafalk – Vic? Are you there? Hello?'

'Thanks, Adrienne,' I said mechanically. 'Let me know when you need the detective work.'

I hung up and dialed the Windy City Balletworks to see if they were performing tonight. A recorded voice told me that performances were held Wednesday through Saturday at

469

eight; Sundays at three. Today was Tuesday; Paige might be home.

Ferrant looked at me courteously. 'Something wrong?'

I made a gesture of distaste. 'Nothing I hadn't suspected since this morning. But it's upsetting anyway – Grafalk owns real estate along with everything else.'

'You know, Miss War – Do you have a first name? I just can't keep my tongue around your last one – Vic, you're being terribly mysterious. I take it you think Grafalk may be behind the damage to the Poe Lock, since we just spent most of the afternoon proving that he was losing money. Would you mind telling me what's going on?'

'Some other time. There's someone I need to talk to tonight. I'm sorry, I know it's rude to run out on you like this, but I must see her.'

'Where are you going?' Ferrant asked.

'To the Gold Coast.'

He announced that he was coming with me. I shrugged and headed for the door. Ferrant tried putting some money on the table, but Sal gave it back to him. 'Vic'll pay me when she's got the money,' she said.

I flagged a taxi on Dearborn. Ferrant got in beside me, again demanding to know what was going on.

'I'll tell you later,' I said. 'It's too long a story to start during a short cab ride.'

We pulled up in front of a massive pale pink brick building with white concrete corners and white-enameled shutters. It was dark now, but black wrought-iron street lamps illuminated the building's façade.

Ferrant offered to accompany me inside, but I told him this was a job I had to handle alone. He watched me as I rang the bell, set in a lighted brass box outside the front door. A house phone was nestled inside the box for communicating with the inmates. When Paige's voice came tinnily through the receiver, I pitched my voice high and told her it was Jeannine. She buzzed me in.

The stairs were carpeted in a rose-patterned blue rug. My tired feet sank gratefully into the pile. Paige was waiting for me in the doorway at the top of the stairs, wearing her white terry-cloth robe, her face

470

not made up, her hair pulled back under a towel as I'd seen her after rehearsal.

'What brings you into the city, Jeannie?' she was saying as my head came in sight. The rest of her sentence died in her throat. She stood immobile with surprise for a second too long. I reached the door as she started to slam it and pushed my way inside.

'We're going to talk, Paige. A little heart-to-heart.'

'I have nothing to say to you. Get out of here before I call the police.' Her voice came out in a harsh whisper.

'Be my guest.' I sat down in a wide armchair upholstered in rust brocade and looked around the large, light room. A Persian rug covered about two thirds of the dark parquet. Gold brocade drapes were looped back from the windows overlooking Astor Street and sheer gauze hung underneath. 'The police will be very interested in your role in Boom Boom's death. Please do call them.'

'They think it's an accident.'

'But you, dear Paige? Do you think it is?'

She turned her face away, biting her lip.

'Jeannine told me this morning your role was to keep tabs on what my cousin was up to. I thought she meant for her and Clayton. But she wasn't talking about them, was she? No, you were keeping track of him for Grafalk.'

She didn't say anything but kept staring at a picture on the west wall as if seeking inspiration from it. It looked like a very good copy of a Degas. For all I knew, it was an original. Even with the losses to the steamship line, Niels Grafalk could afford to give his lover that kind of trifle.

'How long have you been Grafalk's mistress?'

Spots of color stained her cheeks. 'What an offensive remark. I have nothing to say to you.'

'Then I'll have to do the talking. You correct me where I'm wrong. Jeannine and Clayton moved to Lake Bluff five years ago. Niels knew Clayton was fiddling around with Eudora Grain invoices. He promised not to turn him in to Argus if Clayton would start giving Grafalk a preferred position on shipping orders.'

'I don't know anything about the Grafalk Steamship Line.'

'You and your sister are so pure-minded, Paige. You don't want to know anything about where your money comes from, just that it's there to spend when you need it.'

'I scarcely know Niels Grafalk, Vic. I've met him socially at my sister's. If Clayton and he did have some kind of business arrangement, I would be the last person to know about it.'

'Oh, bullshit, Paige. Grafalk owns this condominium.'

'How do you know that?' she demanded, sitting down suddenly on a sofa near me. 'Did Jeannine tell you?'

'No, Paige. Your sister kept your secret. But property titles are a matter of public record in Chicago. I was curious about this place, since I suspect Windy City can't afford to pay you very much. Anyway, where was I? Oh yes, Grafalk got Clayton to give him preferred customer treatment. In exchange, Grafalk helped pave the way for them socially when they moved back to Lake Bluff. Got them into the Maritime Club and all that good stuff.

'Well, of course, you don't like Jeannine enjoying the good things in life alone – and vice versa. So you started hanging out with her around the Maritime Club. Now Mrs Grafalk's an interesting lady, but she's going at about a hundred knots all day long with her charities and Ravinia and the Symphony Board, and Niels saw you and thought you were just about the most beautiful little thing he'd ever laid eyes on. You saw your chance to get set up in a big way, and three years ago, when Feldspar converted this building, Niels moved you in. Right so far?'

Paige spoke in a low voice. 'You are totally insufferable, Vic. You have absolutely no understanding of this sort of thing, or the kind of life I lead.'

I interrupted her. 'Jeannine already gave me the heartbreaking details of the Carrington family's slide into poverty and the attendant humiliation. Take it as fact that I'm too vulgar to understand how shattering that must have been to the two of you. What I really want to know is where my cousin fitted into this. You told me a few weeks ago that you two were falling in love with each other. Did you think my cousin was a better prospect in the long run because he wasn't married? Not as much money, but more of it might come to you?'

'Stop it, Vic, stop it. Do you think I have no feeling at all? Do you know what I went through when I learned Boom Boom was dead? I had no choice. I had no choice!' The last sentence was uttered in a rising cadence.

'What do you mean?' I was controlling my temper with increasing difficulty. 'Of course you had choices. If you really were in love with Boom Boom, you could do without a lot of things. And he didn't exactly live in poverty, even by Lake Bluff standards.'

Her honey-colored eyes were filled with tears. She held out a hand in a beseeching gesture. 'Vic, Niels pays for everything. This place, all the furniture. My bills at Saks and I. Magnin run me a thousand dollars a month alone. He pays those without question. If I want to go to Majorca for a month in October, he pays the American Express bills. I owe him so much. It seemed like such a little thing to go out with your cousin a few times and see if he had learned anything about the invoices.'

I gripped the sides of the chair to keep from rising up and strangling her. 'Such a little thing. You never thought of Boom Boom as a person, with feelings, or the right to live, did you?'

'I liked Boom Boom, Vic. Please, you must believe me.'

'I believe nothing you say. Nothing. You dare call me insufferable!' I stopped and checked myself. 'Tell me what happened that day you went sailing. That Saturday before my cousin was murdered.'

She winced. 'You mustn't say that, Vic. It was an accident. Niels assured me it was an accident and the police believe so too.'

'Yes, well, tell me about the sailing trip. Mattingly was there, right? And Phillips. Grafalk, of course. What was the purpose? Why did you drag Boom Boom up for that?'

'Mattingly wasn't there, Vic. I keep telling you I don't know him. You accuse me of being unfeeling, but I'm not. When I told Niels that Boom Boom had – gotten close to the truth on the invoices, he wanted Clayton to get rid of him on the spot. But I told him not to.' She lifted her chin and looked at me proudly. 'We went up there to see if Niels could persuade Boom Boom to see things their way. On Saturday it looked as though he might. But the next Monday he had a terrible argument with Clayton over the matter, and Niels said it was no use trying to talk to him, in fact that we'd better do something before Boom Boom called Argus. But then – then he slipped and fell and that ended the matter. I was so relieved. I was terrified Niels might do something dreadful.'

It was my turn to be speechless. I couldn't find words that matched my horror and my anger. Finally I choked, 'You tried to bribe Boom Boom and he didn't live that way. You vermin just couldn't understand that. You gave him a chance to be corrupted and he refused to take it . . . What about the water in the holds of the *Lucella*? What did that have to do with Clayton and Niels?'

She looked blank. 'I don't know what you're talking about.'

'The *Lucella* couldn't take on a load of grain because someone had poured water into her holds. Boom Boom was going to talk to the captain about it before he called Argus . . . Never mind. What about Clayton? Were you with Niels Sunday morning when he put a big hole in the side of Clayton's head?'

She looked at me with gentle reproof. 'I don't think you should talk to me like that, Vic. You may not approve of my relations with Niels, but he is my lover.'

I gave a crack of manic laughter. 'Me not approve! Christ, Paige, you're a whole separate universe. Why should I give a damn about you and Grafalk? It's what the two of you did to my cousin that I care about. That's what makes your relationship stink.'

Paige looked at her watch. 'Yes, well, I don't agree with you. I think I pointed out to you what an obligation I'm under to Niels. He's coming over in a few minutes, too, so unless you want to meet him I'd suggest you leave.'

I got up. 'One last question, Paige darling. Was it the photocopy of Grafalk's invoice you were looking for in Boom Boom's apartment the day after the funeral? If it was, I've found it. And as for the letter Boom Boom wrote you – "Beautiful Paige" – I don't think he sent that to the Royal York in Toronto at all. He wrote you the Sunday before he died, didn't he? To tell you he didn't want to see you again. You put it in an old envelope to prove to me that you were writing each other love letters. You knew I'd look at the heading and not read the letter.' I choked on a sob and swallowed it. If I stayed any longer the last threads of my self-control would snap.

Paige watched me with dark, angry eyes as I walked across the Persian rug to the front door. For once her exquisite poise deserted her; lines appeared around her mouth and eyes and she looked older.

26
ON THE TILES

Back outside I sat on the stoop, unable to move any farther. Fatigue fogged my brain. The day had started at Jeannine's with confirmation that her husband pushed Boom Boom under the propeller of the *Bertha Krupnik*. Now came the news that her sister had gone out with Boom Boom only to spy on him for Grafalk.

What good would it do Boom Boom if I could prove Grafalk's complicity in his death, or even in destroying the *Lucella* and the Poe Lock? Revenge brings only limited satisfaction, and I didn't feel noble enough to act out of a disinterested sense of justice.

I stood up and looked around vaguely for a cab. A tall figure detached itself from the shadows and crossed the street to me.

'A satisfactory encounter?' Ferrant asked.

'You waiting around for me?' I said. 'How about finding me a cab? Speaking as a detective, I guess it was satisfactory. But, as a human being, I can't say it appealed to me much.'

'Look, how about dinner and you can tell me about it?'

'Roger, I'm too tired to eat and I don't feel like telling anyone about it.'

He trotted over to State Street and flagged a cab there. He helped me inside and followed after.

'Look, you don't have to tell me about the interview, but you'll feel better after something hot to eat and another drink.'

I finally let myself be persuaded. He'd been very cooperative about looking into Grafalk's records. If he wanted to hear the gory details of the rest of the case, why not?

We went to the Filigree, a restaurant in the Hanover House Hotel that resembles my idea of a men's club: discreet tables with maroon drapes shielding diners from one another, a fireplace with a high marble mantel, and elderly waiters who seem to ooze a vague distrust of women diners: do they really appreciate the fine old vintages they're drinking?

You go to the Filigree for steaks. Over a thick-cut T-bone and a bottle of Château St Georges (1962) I felt myself reviving.

'Earlier this evening you said you weren't really concerned about the locks or the freighters – that you were involved in this from a personal standpoint. What is that?'

I explained to Ferrant about my cousin and the problems down at Eudora Grain. 'I was just visiting the woman he was dating the three months before he died. Her name is Paige Carrington. She's a talented dancer, maybe not New York quality, but quite good. She is exquisite, the kind of woman you gawk at but who appears too perfect to touch. Anyway, it seems she's been Grafalk's mistress for a number of years. He arranged a party at which she could meet my cousin – said he wanted to buy some shares in the Hawks and asked Guy Odinflute to hold a party for him and the team. Boom Boom was always included in that kind of function and Grafalk saw to it that Paige had an invitation too.

'Well, my cousin was easily as susceptible as the next man. When Paige made a dead-set at him, he responded – probably with enthusiasm. She's that type of person. And she spent the next three or four months tracking what he was doing at Eudora Grain.

'When it became obvious that Boom Boom had discovered the extent of the problem there and was planning on blowing the whistle to Argus – Eudora's chairman – Paige's tender heart was touched: she got Grafalk and Phillips to try to buy off my cousin. Instead, they knocked him off.'

I drank some more wine and slumped back in my seat. I'd only been able to eat half the excellent steak.

I gestured with the wineglass. 'This whole business with the freighters and the locks looks like something separate altogether. I wouldn't even be interested if it didn't seem to tie in with what happened to my cousin.' I finished my wine and poured myself another glass. At this rate I was going to be mildly sozzled; after the day I'd had, it felt good. Ferrant ordered a second bottle.

'I've got a couple of problems right now. One is, although Jeannine Phillips as good as told me that her husband pushed Boom Boom off the wharf, I don't have any proof. She didn't come out and say it in so many words, and nobody witnessed the drowning. I do have some skeletal proof about what was going on at Eudora. I could send that to Argus, but all it would do is discredit Phillips. Even if they could make the tie-in with Grafalk stick, it doesn't prove anything more criminal than taking kickbacks.'

The waiter took my plate with a contemptuous glance at the unfinished steak as the wine steward opened the second bottle of St Émilion for us. Like many very thin men, Ferrant ate a great deal – he'd consumed a sixteen-ounce sirloin while we talked, along with oysters florentine, the special potatoes Filigree, and a platter of beefsteak tomatoes. He ordered chocolate cheesecake; I passed on dessert and had some more wine.

'The one thing I might be able to get Grafalk on is murdering Phillips.'

Ferrant sat up in his chair. 'Go on, Vic! Grafalk murder Phillips?'

'He was last seen alive around one o'clock Sunday morning. The police figure he was in the holds and suffocated by 8.00 a.m. at the latest. So between one in the morning and eight in the morning someone bonked him on the head and got him onto a Great Lakes freighter. The police have a guard on duty at the entrance to the Port. Not that many people enter the Port that late at night, and they have a pretty good list of who came in. I'm sure that they've been through those people's cars quite thoroughly. If one of them had driven Phillips's body into the Port, they'd have nailed him for it. But they haven't made an arrest.'

'Maybe the murderer brought him on board in a plastic bag and no blood got on his car . . . Was Grafalk at the Port that night?'

'He didn't drive down there.'

'What'd he do – fly?'

'Don't think so – a helicopter would be pretty noisy.'

'Then how did he get there?'

'Good heavens, Roger, I'm ashamed of you. You come from this island country, famous for four centuries of naval prowess. It ought to be the first thing to leap to your mind.'

His brow creased. 'By boat? You must be joking.' He thought it over. 'I suppose he could. But can you prove he did?'

'I don't know. The evidence is so circumstantial – it's going to be hard to sell people on it. For instance, you. Do you buy Grafalk as master criminal?'

He gave a half smile. 'I don't know. We proved the figures on Grafalk this afternoon. And yet – that's a big jump to stuffing someone into a freighter to die . . . What about Bledsoe?'

I shook my head. 'Bledsoe was up in the Soo and his plane was down in Chicago. Not only that, someone sent his plane back down here in such a way as to implicate him for a different murder.'

I wondered what the waiters would do if I curled up on the plush cushion and went to sleep. I yawned. 'The trouble is, if I can't convince you, when you believe the financial evidence, I know I'll never convince the cops enough to swear out a search warrant. It's a big step, going to look at a rich man's yacht. They have to be real convinced before they do something like that.'

I leaned back in the seat and closed my eyes, still holding the wineglass. 'He can't get away with it,' I muttered to myself. But it looked as though he might. Even with blowing up the *Lucella*, because nobody knew where the depth charges came from. If only I had evidence, someone who'd seen Grafalk and Phillips at his boat Sunday morning – or some bloodstains on the foredeck of Grafalk's yacht.

I opened my eyes at Ferrant. 'I need to get some proof. And the cards are not going to be stacked all his way. They just can't be. Even if he is as rich as Rockefeller.'

On this dramatic statement I got up from the table and walked with careful dignity to the front door. The maître d'hôtel also gave me a scornful glance. Not only can women not appreciate the great vintages, they swill them disgustingly and get revoltingly drunk.

'Thank you, my good man,' I said as he held the door open for me.

479

'Your contempt for women will bring you more pleasure than any paltry tip I could give you. Good night.'

In the lobby of the hotel was a pay phone. I walked over to it, carefully avoiding the Greek columns haphazardly dotting the floor, and tried to call the Great Lakes Naval Training Station. The operator and I went a few rounds before I got my meaning across and she found a number for me. The phone rang twenty times or so, but nobody answered. A grandfather clock by the front door showed that it was close to midnight.

Ferrant was standing nearby holding my handbag, which I'd left at the table.

'Who's defending the country at midnight?' I demanded as I took my bag from him. 'If nobody answers the phone, how will they ever know the Russians are attacking?'

Ferrant took my arm. 'You know, Vic, I think you should wait till morning to get your proof.'

'If I wait until morning he'll get away with it,' I protested stubbornly. 'Get me a cab!' I yelled at the doorman.

'Where are you going?' Ferrant demanded.

'Back to my car. Then out to Grafalk's boat. I'm going to get proof.'

The doorman looked at us uncertainly.

'Are you getting my cab?' I called at him. He shrugged and went outside with his whistle.

Ferrant followed me into the chilly night. He kept trying to take my arm and I kept pushing him aside. When the cab came I climbed in and told the driver to take me to my car.

'Yeah, well, where is your car?'

'In the garage,' I mumbled, and fell asleep.

27

ON BOARD THE DRAGON SHIP

When I woke up, my head pounded uncomfortably and I felt sick. Bright sunlight was coming in through a window, blinding me. That didn't make sense – I sleep with heavy drapes pulled across my windows. Someone must have broken in during the night and opened my curtains.

Holding my head with one hand, I sat up. I was on a couch in a strange room. My shoes, purse, and jacket were lying on a glass-topped coffee table next to me with a note.

> Vic
>
> I couldn't get you to wake up long enough to tell me your address, so I brought you back here to the Hancock. I hope you find your proof.
>
> R.F.

I staggered across the room and out into a carpeted hallway, looking for a bathroom. I took four aspirin from a bottle in the medicine chest and ran a hot bath in the long yellow tub. I couldn't find any washcloths on the shelves, so I soaked a heavy hand towel in the water and wrapped it around my head. After about half an hour in the water I started feeling more like me and less like a carpet after spring cleaning. I couldn't believe I'd gotten that drunk on one bottle of wine. Maybe I'd drunk two.

I wrapped myself in a dressing gown hanging on the back of the bathroom door and went on down the hallway to find a kitchen, a small but completely equipped room gleaming in white and stainless steel. A clock hung next to the refrigerator. When I saw the time I put my head next to the face to see if it was still running. Twelve-thirty. No wonder Ferrant had left me to go downtown.

Puttering around, I found an electric coffee maker and some canned coffee and brewed a pot. Drinking it black, I recalled last night's events – the meeting with Paige and dinner with Ferrant. I dimly remembered trying to call the Great Lakes Naval Training Station. The reason why came back to me. Sober, it still sounded like a good idea.

Using a white wall phone next to the stove, I tried the Station again. This time a young man answered. I told him I was a detective, which he interpreted as meaning I was with the police. Many people think that and it helps not to disillusion them.

'Niels Grafalk keeps his private yacht at the Training Station,' I said. 'I want to know if he took it out early Sunday morning.'

The young sailor switched me down to the dock, where I talked to a guard. 'Mr Grafalk handles his boat privately,' the guard told me. 'We can call around and try to find out for you.'

I told him that would be great and I would call again in an hour. I put my clothes back on. They were smelling rather stale by this time. I was short a corduroy pantsuit, jeans, and two shirts as a result of this case. Maybe it was time for new clothes. I left Ferrant's apartment, rode the elevator down to the ground, and walked across the street to Water Tower Place, where I treated myself to a new pair of jeans and a red cotton shirt with a diagonal yellow stripe at Field's. Easier than going back to my apartment at this point.

I went back down to the Loop. I hadn't been in my office since the morning I talked to Mrs Kelvin, and the floor inside the door was piled with mail. I looked through it quickly. Bills and advertisements – no solicitations from millionaires to find their missing husbands. I dumped the lot in the trash and phoned the Naval Station again.

The young sailor had exerted himself to be helpful. 'I called over to Admiral Jergensen's office, but no one there knew anything about the boat. They told me to call Mr Grafalk's chauffeur – he usually helps out when Mr Grafalk wants to sail. Anyway, he wanted to know why we were asking, so I told him the police were interested, and he said the boat hadn't been out on Saturday night.'

I thanked him weakly for his help and hung up. I simply hadn't anticipated that. Calling Grafalk. At least they had said police and not given my name, since I'd never told the sailor who I was. But if there was evidence on the boat, they'd be at pains now to get rid of it.

I debated calling Mallory but I couldn't see how I could convince him to get a search warrant. I thought about all possible arguments I might use. He still believed Boom Boom and I had been victims of separate accidents. I was never going to be able to convince him Grafalk was a murderer. Not unless I had a sample of Phillips's blood from Grafalk's yacht.

Very well, then. I would get the sample. I went to a safe built into the south wall of my office. I'm not Peter Wimsey and I don't carry a complete police lab around with me, but I do have some of the rudiments, like chemicals to test for the presence of blood. And some self-sealing plastic pouches to put samples in. I had a Timothy Custom Utility Knife in there, so I took that along. With a three-inch blade, it wasn't meant as a weapon but a tool, its razor-honed blade ideal for cutting up a piece of deck or carpet or something containing the evidence. My picklocks and a magnifying glass completed my gear.

I emptied everything out of my shoulder bag, put my driver's license and my detective I D in my pocket with some money and stuck the detective equipment in the zippered side compartment. Back to Grant Park for my car, which cost me fifteen dollars to retrieve. I wasn't sure I was going to remember all my expenses for submitting a bill to Boom Boom's estate. I needed to be more methodical in recording them.

It was after four when I reached the Edens Expressway. I kept the speedometer at sixty-five all the way to the tollway. Traffic was heavy with the first wash of north-bound executives from the city and I kept pace with the cars in the fast lane, not risking a ticket and the delays that would bring me.

At five I exited onto route 137 and headed toward the lake. Instead of turning south on Green Bay for Lake Bluff, I went on to Sheridan

Road and turned left, following the road up to the Great Lakes Naval Training Station.

A guard was on duty at the main entrance to the base. I gave my most vivacious smile, trying hard not to look like a Soviet spy. 'I'm Niels Grafalk's niece. He's expecting me to join a party down at the *Brynulf Nordemark*.'

The guard consulted a list in the booth. 'Oh. That's the private boat the admiral lets the guy keep here. Go on in.'

'I'm afraid this is my first time up here. Can you give me directions?'

'Just follow this road down to the docks. Then turn left. You can't miss it – it's the only private sailboat down there.' He gave me a permit in case anyone asked me any questions. I wished I was a Soviet spy – this would be an easy place to get into.

I followed the winding road past rows of stark barracks. Sailors were wandering around in groups of two or three. I passed a few children, too. I hadn't realized that families lived on the base.

The road led down to the docks, as the guard had said. Before I reached the water I could see the masts of the ships sticking up. Smaller than the lakes freighters, covered with turrets and radar equipment, the naval ships looked menacing, even in the golden light of a spring evening. Driving past them, I shuddered and concentrated on the road. It was pitted from the heavy vehicles that routinely used it and the Omega bounced from hole to hole past the line of training ships.

About a hundred yards farther down, in splendid isolation, sat the *Brynulf Nordemark*. She was a beautiful vessel with two masts, sails furled neatly about them. Painted white, with green trim, she was a sleekly lined boat, floating easily against the ropes that fastened her to the dock, like a swan or some other water bird, natural and graceful.

I parked the Omega on the boat's far side and walked out on the little jetty to which the *Brynulf* was tied. Pulling one of the guys slightly to bring her over to me, I grabbed the wooden railing and swung myself over onto the deck.

All of the fittings were made of teak, varnished and polished to a reflecting sheen. The tiller was set in a gleaming brass base, and the instrument panel, also teak, contained a collection of the most up-to-date gadgets – gyro compass, wind gauges, depth sounders, and other instruments I couldn't begin to understand. Grafalk's grandfather had bought the yacht, I recalled – Grafalk must have updated the equipment.

Feeling like a caricature of a detective, I pulled the magnifying glass out of my handbag and began to scrutinize the deck – on hands and knees, just like Sherlock Holmes. The tour took some time and I failed to discover anything remotely like blood on the highly polished surface. I continued the inspection along the sides. Just as I was about to give up on the deck, I spotted two short blond hairs caught in the starboard railing. Grafalk's hair was white, the chauffeur's sandy. Phillips had been a blond, and this was a good spot for his head to have banged as they dragged him off the yacht. Grunting with satisfaction, I took a pair of eyebrow tweezers from my purse, plucked out the hairs, and put them in a little plastic bag.

A small flight of stairs next to the tiller led to the cabin. I paused for a minute, hand on the wheel, to look at the dock before I went down. No one was paying any attention to me. As I started down the stairs my eye was caught by a large warehouse across the road from me. It was a corrugated Quonset hut, dingy like the other buildings on the base. Plastered with red triangles, it had a neatly lettered sign over the entrance: MUNITIONS DEPOT. HIGH EXPLOSIVES. NO SMOKING.

No guard patrolled the depot. Presumably, if you had clearance to be on the base at all, you weren't likely to rifle the munitions. Grafalk passed the dump every time he went sailing. His chauffeur probably had the tools to get past the lock on the large rolling doors. As a friend of the admiral's, Grafalk might even have gone in on some legitimate pretext. I wondered if they kept an inventory of their explosives. Would they be able to tell if enough depth charges were gone to blow up a thousand-foot ship?

I went down the short flight of stairs where a locked door led to the living quarters. It was after six and the sun was starting to set. Not much light made its way into the stairwell and I fumbled with the picklocks for several minutes before getting the door open. A hook on the wall clipped to another hook on the door to hold it open.

The one thing I'd forgotten was a flashlight. I hunted for a light and finally found a chain connected to an overhead lamp. Pulling it on, I saw I was in a small hallway, carpeted in a green that matched the boat's trim. A latched door at my right opened into a master bedroom with a king-size bed, mirrored walls, and teak fittings. A sliding wardrobe door opened on a good collection of men's and women's clothes. I looked at the women's outfits doubtfully: Paige and Mrs Grafalk were both thin and short – the wardrobe could have belonged to either.

The master bedroom had an attached bathroom with a tub and a sink fitted with gold faucets. It didn't seem too likely that Grafalk and Phillips would have fought in there.

I went back out to the hallway and found two other bedrooms, less opulent, each with sleeping for four, on the port side. A dining room with an old mahogany table bolted to the floor and a complete set of Wedgwood in a handsome breakfront was next to them on the port side of the bow. Next, in the very tip of the bow, was a well-equipped galley with a gas stove. Between the master bedroom and the galley on the starboard side was a lounge where the sailors could read or play bridge or drink during inclement weather. A shallow cupboard unlatched to reveal several decanters and a good collection of bottles. The Scotch was J & B. I was disappointed – the first sign of bad taste on Grafalk's part. Maybe Paige selected the whisky.

Unless Phillips had been knocked out on deck, my guess was he had been hit in either the lounge or the dining room. I started on the lounge as the more hopeful place. It contained a leather-covered card table and a desk, a number of chairs, a couch, and a small fireplace with an electric fire in it.

The lounge floor was covered with a thick, figured green carpet. As I surveyed the room, trying to decide where most efficiently to begin my search, I noticed that the pile in front of the little fireplace was brushed back at a different angle than the rest of the rug. That seemed promising. I skirted around the brushed area and began inspecting it with my glass. I found another blond hair. No blood, but a strong smell of cleanser, something like Top Job. The carpet was still faintly damp to my touch, although it had been three days since Phillips's death. I smelled other sections of the rug, but the odor of cleanser and the damp only came from the section in front of the fireplace.

I pulled myself to my feet. Now the problem was going to be to get the police up here for a more formal search. Their equipment could detect whether blood stuck to the rug in microscopic quantities. Maybe the thing to do was to cut off a bit of the pile and get them to examine it. If there were blood on it, they'd be more likely to want to see where the rug fragments came from. Using my Timothy Custom Knife, I cut a small section of fibers from the place where I'd found the blond hair.

As I put the fabric into a clean specimen bag, I heard a thud on the deck. I sat quite still and listened, straining my ears. The cabin was so well paneled, you couldn't hear much above you. Then another, gentle thud. Two people had boarded the boat. Navy children playing around the docks?

I stuck the specimen bag in my pocket. Holding the knife firmly, I went to the door and turned out the light. I waited inside the room, listening. Through the hallway I could hear a faint murmur of male voices. These were grown-ups, not children.

Footsteps moved overhead, toward the bow. At the stern an engine turned over and caught. The boat, which had been floating aimlessly with the water currents, started vibrating and then began moving slowly backward.

I looked around for a hiding place. There was none. The card table and the couch offered no protection. Through the porthole in the lounge's starboard wall I watched a destroyer slide by, then the gray concrete of a breakwater, and finally a small white channel marker, its light flashing green as it swung around. We were out of the channel into the open lake. Straining my ears near the door, I heard the sharp slapping noise of wind on canvas: they were raising the sails. Then more voices, and finally a footstep on the carpeted stairs.

'I hope you're not going to play hide-and-seek with me, Miss

Warshawski. I know this boat much better than you do.' It was Grafalk.

My heart pounded sickeningly. My stomach turned over. I felt short of breath and too weak to speak.

'I know you're here – we saw your car on the quay.'

I took several diaphragm breaths, slowly exhaling on a descending scale, and stepped into the hallway.

'Good evening, Mr Grafalk.' Not the world's greatest line, but the words came out without a tremor. I was pleased with myself.

'You're a very smart young woman. Knowledgeable, too. So I won't point out to you that you're trespassing on private property. It's a beautiful night for a sail, but I think we can talk more easily down here. Sandy will be able to manage the boat alone for a while now that the sails are up.'

He took my arm in a steely grip and moved me back into the lounge with him, turning the light back on with his other hand.

'Do sit down, Miss Warshawski. You know, you have my heartfelt admiration. You are a very resourceful lady, with good survival instincts. By now you should be dead several times over. And I was impressed with the reconstruction you gave Paige, quite impressed indeed.'

He was wearing evening clothes, a black suit tailored to his wide shoulders and narrow hips. He looked handsome in them, and there was an expression of suppressed excitement in his face which made him appear younger than he was.

He let go of my arm and I sat in one of the leather-covered straight-back chairs next to the card table. 'Thank you, Mr Grafalk. I'll have to remember to ask you for a reference the next time a client inquires.'

He sat down facing me. 'Ah, yes. I fear your clients will be deprived of your services soon, Miss Warshawski. A pity, since you have the brains and the skill to be of help to people. By the way, who are you working for now? Not Martin, I hope.'

'I'm working for my cousin,' I said levelly.

'How quixotic of you. Avenging the memory of the dead Boom

Boom. Paige says you don't believe he fell under the *Bertha Krupnik* by accident.'

'My parents discouraged a faith in Santa Claus at an early age. Paige never struck me as terribly naive, either – just reluctant to face facts which might upset her comfort.'

Grafalk smiled a bit. He opened the latched liquor cupboard and pulled out a decanter. 'Some Armagnac, Vic? You don't mind if I call you that, do you? Warshawski is an awkward name to keep repeating and we have a long conversation in front of us . . . Don't blame Paige, my dear Vic. She's a very special person, but she has these strong needs for material possessions that go back to her early childhood. You know the story of her father?'

'A heartrending tale,' I said dryly. 'It's amazing that she and her sister were able to go on living at all.'

He smiled again. 'Poverty is all relative. At any rate, Paige doesn't want to jeopardize her current standard of living by thinking about anything . . . too dangerous.'

'How does Mrs Grafalk feel about the situation?'

'With Paige, you mean? Claire is an admirable woman. Now that our two children are through school she's thoroughly absorbed in a variety of charities, all of which benefit profoundly by Grafalk backing. They claim the bulk of her attention and she's just as pleased to have mine diverted elsewhere. She's never been very interested in Grafalk Steamship either, unfortunately.'

'Whereas it has Paige's breathless attention? That's a little hard for me to picture, somehow.'

'You're sure you don't want any Armagnac? It's quite good, really.'

'I'll take your word for it.' My stomach warned me against putting any more alcohol on top of last night's St Émilion.

He poured himself some more. 'Paige is in a position where she has to be interested in what interests me. I don't mind knowing I've bought her attention – it's quite intense and delightful whether bought or volunteered. And I'm afraid the steamship line is the thing I care most about.'

'So much that you killed Phillips and Mattingly, got Phillips to push my cousin off the wharf, and blew up the *Lucella Wieser* to protect it? Oh yes. I forgot Henry Kelvin, the night watchman in Boom Boom's building.'

Grafalk stretched his legs out and swirled the brandy in his glass. 'Technically, Sandy did most of the damage. Sandy's my chauffeur and general factotum. He planted the depth charges on the *Lucella* – quite a diver. He was a frogman in the navy, served on my ship in World War II. When he was discharged I hired him. Anyway, technically, Sandy did the dirty work.'

'But you're an accessory. The law holds you equally responsible.'

'The law will have to find out first. Right now, they seem extremely uninterested in me.'

'When they have the evidence that Phillips received his head wound here in this lounge their interest will pick up considerably.'

'Yes, but who's going to tell them? Sandy won't. I won't. And you, I'm afraid, aren't going to be with us when we return to port. So you won't.'

He was trying to frighten me and succeeding rather well.

'Phillips called you Saturday night after he got my message, didn't he?'

'Yes. I'm afraid Clayton was cracking. He was a smart enough man in his way, but he worried about details too much. He knew if you told Argus about the invoices his career would be finished. He wanted me to do something to help him out. Unfortunately, there wasn't much I could do at that point.'

'Why'd you kill him, though? What possible harm could it do you if word got out that you'd been involved in some kickbacks in assigning cargoes? You own the controlling interest in Grafalk Steamship – your board can't force you to resign.'

'Oh, I agree. Unfortunately, even though we hadn't involved Clayton in the – uh – mishap to the *Lucella*, he knew my feelings toward Martin too well. He suspected I was responsible and threatened to divulge that to the Coast Guard if I didn't protect him with Argus.'

'So you smashed a hole in the side of his head – What'd you use? One of these andirons? – and sailed him down to the Port. Putting him on the *Gertrude Ruttan* was a macabre touch. What would you have done if Bledsoe hadn't had a ship in port?'

'Used someone else's. It just seemed more poetic to use one of Martin's. What made you think of it?'

'It wasn't that difficult, Niels. The police patrol that facility. They were questioning everyone who'd been down there between midnight and six Sunday morning, inspecting their cars, too, I'm sure. So whoever put the body in the holds had to get to the ship without going by the police. Once I realized that, it was pretty easy to see it must have come by boat. A helicopter would have attracted too much attention.'

It pricked his vanity to have his great idea treated lightly. 'We won't run those risks with you, Vic. We'll leave you a couple of miles offshore with a good strong weight to hold you down.'

I have always feared death by drowning more than any other end – the dark water sucking me down into itself. My hands were trembling slightly. I pressed them to the sides of my legs so that Grafalk couldn't see.

'It was the destruction of the *Lucella* I couldn't figure out at first. I knew you were angry with Bledsoe for leaving you, but I didn't realize how much you hated him. Also, the Eudora shipping contracts I looked at puzzled me. There were quite a number of orders last year which Pole Star gave up to Grafalk Steamship. For a while I thought you two were in collusion, but there wasn't any financial advantage to Bledsoe from the *Lucella* being blown up. Quite the contrary.

'Then he told me Monday that you'd pressured him while he was financing the *Lucella* – you knew he'd never raise the money if word got out on the street that he'd been in jail for embezzling. So you promised to keep it to yourself if he'd give you some of his shipping contracts.

'That explained the water in the holds too. Once the *Lucella* was financed, you could tell the world and be damned, as far as he cared. He started underbidding you – considerably – and you got Mattingly to bribe one of the sailors to put water in her holds. So she lost the load, and in a rather expensive way.'

491

Grafalk wasn't so relaxed now. He drew his legs up and crossed them. 'How'd you know that?' he asked sharply.

'Boom Boom saw Mattingly there. He wrote Pierre Bouchard that he'd seen Mattingly under odd circumstances. I thought it must have been up here on the *Brynulf*, but Paige told me Mattingly didn't go on that expedition. The only other really odd place for my cousin to have seen him was down at the Port. It bothered Boom Boom enough to try to get Bouchard to trace Mattingly, and he wouldn't have done that for something trivial . . . But what I really want to know, Niels, is how long Grafalk Steamship has been losing money?'

He got up with a sudden movement that knocked his brandy glass over. 'Who told you that?'

'Niels, you're like an elephant on a rampage. You're leaving a trail of broken trees behind you and you think no one else can see them. You didn't have to tell me Grafalk Steamship was the only thing you really cared about. It was obvious the first day I met you. Then your fury with Bledsoe for deserting you was totally irrational. People leave jobs every day for new jobs or to set up their own businesses. I could see you might feel hurt if you gave Bledsoe his big chance. But, my God! You acted like King Richard when one of his barons broke the oath of fealty. Bledsoe didn't work for Grafalk Steamship – he worked for you. It was a personal betrayal when he left you.'

Grafalk sat down again. He picked up his glass and poured some more Armagnac; his hand wasn't quite steady.

'Now you're a relatively smart man, and you don't need money. Not personally. There wasn't any reason for you to get sucked up in Clayton's scheme for your personal gain. But there was if your steamship company needed help.

'My first day down at the Port I heard your new dispatcher on the phone trying to get orders. He just couldn't get his bids down low enough. You're operating this antiquated fleet. When the *Leif Ericsson* ran into the wharf, Martin Bledsoe asked if that was how you were planning on getting rid of your old ships. That was when you needled him about his prison background. He reacted violently, and everyone's attention was diverted. But you *did* need to get rid of your old ships. Martin hadn't been able to persuade you to build

492

the thousand-footers, and you were stuck with these unprofitable clunkers.'

He swept the brandy decanter from the table with a violent movement and sent it flying against the starboard wall. It smashed and a shower of glass and Armagnac sprayed my back.

'I never thought they'd be profitable!' he shouted. 'They're too big. There weren't many ports that could handle them. I was sure they were a passing fad.' He clenched his fists and his face took on an angry, brooding look. 'But then I started losing orders and I just couldn't get them back. And Martin! Goddamn him to hell! I saved him from prison. I gave him his life back. And how did he thank me? By building that damned *Lucella Wieser* and flaunting her under my nose.'

'Why didn't you just build your own at that point?' I asked irritably.

He bared his teeth at me. 'I couldn't afford to. The steamship company was overleveraged by then. I'd mortgaged a lot of my other holdings and I couldn't find anyone to lend me that kind of money.

'Then I found Phillips and his pathetic wife and I saw a way at least to get some orders. But last fall your damned cousin started nosing around. I knew if he got onto the truth we were all in trouble, so I sicced Paige on him.'

'I know that part. Spare me a rerun – these sentimental stories make me gag . . . What made you blow up the *Lucella*?'

'That crack of Martin's – had I deliberately run the *Ericsson* into the wharf? At first I was wishing I could blow up my whole fleet and collect the insurance. Then I had a better idea. Get rid of the *Lucella* and close the upper lakes to the big ships at the same time. I can't keep the Poe Lock shut forever. But I've got three of those bastards stopped up at Whitefish Bay. They'll have to trundle tiddlywinks between Thunder Bay and Duluth for the next twelve months and there's no place big enough for them to dock for the winter up there.'

He laughed crazily. 'I can carry a lot of freight this summer. I should be out of the woods by next spring – I'll be able to start capitalizing some new freighters next year. And Martin should be wiped out by then.'

'I see.' I felt tired and depressed. I couldn't think of any way to stop him. I hadn't left a trail of my investigation. I hadn't even told anyone about the documents taped in my old copies of *Fortune*.

As if reading my thoughts, Grafalk added, 'Paige told me you had those invoices Boom Boom threatened Clayton with. Sandy went over there early this morning – no kids with bread knives to get in his way. He had to tear the place up a bit, but he found them. Pity you weren't there. We wondered where you were.'

The anger had subsided in Grafalk's face and the look of suppressed excitement returned. 'And now, Vic, it's your turn. I want you to come on deck with me.'

I pulled my utility knife from my back pocket. Grafalk smiled at it tolerantly. 'Don't make it difficult for yourself, Vic. I assure you, we'll kill you before you go overboard – no unpleasant drowning for you.'

My heart was beating faster, but my hands were calm. I remembered a day many years ago when Boom Boom and I had taken on a gang of South Side bullies. The excitement in Grafalk's face made him look like one of those twelve-year-old punks.

Grafalk started around the table for me. I let him follow until he was behind it and my back was to the door. I turned and ran down the hall toward the bow, slashing through my shirt sleeve with the knife as I ran. I cut the surface of my arm and blood rolled down it to my hand.

Grafalk had expected me to head for the stairs and I gained a few seconds. In the dining room I whirled and kicked the china cabinet with the Wedgwood in it. Glass shattered across the room and cups and saucers fell from their perches with the rocking of the vessel and crashed to the floor. I ran behind the table and wiped my bleeding arm on the drapes.

'What are you doing?' Grafalk bellowed.

'Leaving a trail,' I panted. I scraped the knife across the mahogany table and rubbed my blood into the scratches.

Grafalk stood momentarily transfixed as I cut chair fabric. I opened the shattered doors to the china closet and swept the rest of the Wedgwood out, ignoring glass fragments that cut my arm. Grafalk recovered himself and lunged for me. I slid a chair into his path and backed into the galley.

The gas-burning stove stood there and a mad idea seized me. I turned on a burner and a blue flame flared up. As Grafalk came through the door at me I tore a curtain from the porthole and dropped it on the burner. It caught fire immediately. I brandished it in front of me like a torch, whirled it around, and set the other galley curtains on fire.

Grafalk came at me in a diving tackle and I jumped out of the way. He fell, heavily, and I ran with my torch back to the dining room where I set the drapes on fire. Grafalk tore after me with a fire extinguisher. He started spraying at me and the curtains. The chemical stung my lungs and partially blinded me. Holding my shirt over my face, I ran back down the hall and up the stairs to the deck.

Grafalk ran at my heels, spraying the fire extinguisher. 'Stop her, Sandy. Stop her!'

The sandy-haired man looked up from the tiller. He grabbed at me and tore a piece from my new shirt. I ran to the back of the boat. It was dark now and the water was black as the *Brynulf* cut through it. Running lights from other boats winked in the distance and I screamed futilely for help.

Grafalk charged on to the deck toward me, his face a maniacal mask, fire extinguisher gripped in front of him. I took a breath and jumped overboard.

28

THE FIRE SHIP OF WODIN

The black water was very cold. It washed the chemical from my aching face and I trod water for a few seconds, coughing to clear my lungs. For a minute I panicked, thinking of the depths stretching beneath me, and I took in a mouthful of water. Sputtering, choking, I forced myself to relax, to breathe deeply.

I kicked off my running shoes, then reached into the water and pulled off my socks and shirt. The *Brynulf*, under full sail, was moving at a good clip and had gone some thirty feet past me.

I was alone in the icy water. My toes were numb and the water hurt my face. I might last twenty minutes – not enough to swim to shore. I looked over my shoulder. The yacht started to turn. Firelight flickered through the starboard portholes. A searchlight lit up the water and Grafalk quickly picked me up. I tried not to panic, to breathe naturally.

The boat continued to come toward me. Swimming on my back, I saw Grafalk at the bow, a rifle in his hand. As the *Brynulf* came alongside, I took a breath and dove under the keel. I pushed my way along underneath until I came out the back. The engine wasn't running – there were no chopping propeller blades to slice me.

Something slapped against my face as I surfaced. One of the ropes used for tying the boat was trailing in the water. I seized it and let the *Brynulf* tow me while Grafalk scanned the water with the searchlight. He turned it toward the stern. His face appeared at the side. The rifle pointed at me. I was too numb to dive.

A blinding flash came, but not from the gun. The galley fuel must have exploded. The shock knocked me loose from the rope and deflected Grafalk's arm. A bullet grazed the water near me and the yacht moved away. A hatch cover blew off and a small fireball flew at the tiller.

Bits of the yacht broke off and floated past me. I seized a spar and leaned on it, kicking doggedly. My left shoulder ached from the cold.

The *Brynulf* continued to move away from me, her sails still catching the wind while Sandy struggled with them, finally letting them go so they hung limply. The yacht then floated in a little circle about fifteen yards from me, moved by the heat of the fire.

Grafalk appeared next to Sandy. I was close enough to see his shock of bleached white hair. He was arguing with Sandy, grabbing him. They struggled in the flickering light. Sandy wrenched himself free and leaped overboard.

Grafalk shook his arms in fury. Walking to the stern, rifle in hand, he searched the water and found me. He pointed the rifle and stood there for a long minute, sighting me. I was too frozen to dive, too frozen to do anything except move my legs mechanically up and down.

Suddenly he dropped the rifle over the side and raised his right arm in a salute at me. Slowly he walked toward the flaming tiller. Another explosion came, this one jarring my numb arms. It must have stove in the side, for the yacht began to sink.

I thought I saw Wodin, who cares nothing for murder, come for this out-of-time Viking to carry him off in his dragon-ship pyre. As the *Brynulf* went down a sudden gust tore loose a flaming shard from one of the sails and sent it over my head. It lit up the black fearsome water around me. Wodin was calling me. I clung to my spar, gritting my teeth.

Strange hands pulled me from the water. The spar was locked in my fingers. I was babbling of gods and dragon ships. There was no trace of the *Brynulf*.

29

THE LONG GOOD-BYE

We sat on a stone terrace overlooking Lake Michigan. The water, pale blue under a soft summer sky, lapped gently at the sand below us. A green canvas awning protected our faces. The May day was bright and clear, although the air was cool out of the direct light of the sun. I buttoned my green serge jacket up to my chin.

Claire Grafalk inspected the brass and teak trolley. I could see a bottle of Taittinger poking over the side of a silver ice bucket. Some salmon, something that looked like a duck sliced and reassembled, and a salad were the only items I could identify without peering too greedily.

'Thank you, Karen. We can take care of ourselves.' As the stocky maid disappeared up the path toward the house, Mrs Grafalk deftly uncorked the champagne and poured it into a tulip glass.

'I don't drink myself, but I enjoy serving champagne – I hope you like this.'

I muttered something appreciative. She poured water for herself and handed me a plate, creamy bone china with her initials on it twined in a green and gold wreath. She was wearing a gray shirtwaist dress with a scarf neck and a strand of heavy pearls. Her high cheekbones were covered with the circles of rouge which were doll-like yet somehow elegant and endearing.

She perched her head, birdlike, on one side, eyeing me questioningly but not talking until I had filled my plate. I sipped the champagne and ate a little cold duck. Both were excellent.

'Now. I must hear what happened. The papers gave only the sketchiest accounts. What happened to Niels's boat?'

498

'There was an accident in the galley and the hull caught fire.' This was the answer I had given to the police and to Murray Ryerson and I wasn't going to change it now.

Mrs Grafalk shook her head vigorously. 'No, my dear. That won't do. Gordon Firth, the chairman of Ajax, came to visit me two days ago with a most extraordinary story about Niels. He had a young Englishman with him, Roger Ferrant. Mr Ferrant says you and he discovered that Niels was running Grafalk Steamship at a loss and had cause to suspect him of blowing up Martin's ship.'

I put the champagne glass down.

'And what do you want me to tell you?'

She looked at me sharply. 'The truth. I still have to deal with this matter. I am still Niels's chief heir; I shall have to dispose of the remaining assets of Grafalk Steamship somehow. Martin Bledsoe would be the ideal person to take over the company. He and I – were good friends a number of years ago and I still have a special spot for him. But I must know the whole story before I talk to him or to my lawyers.'

'I don't have any proof – just a chain of suggestions. Surely you don't want to hear a lot of unsubstantiated allegations. The police or the FBI or the Coast Guard may find proof of wrongdoing. But they may well not. Wouldn't you prefer to let the dead bury the dead?'

'Miss Warshawski. I am going to tell you something that no one besides Karen knows. I expect you to respect my privacy – but if you don't, it doesn't matter that much. Niels and I have lived as two neighbors for over a decade.' She fluttered small, ring-covered hands. 'We gradually grew apart. It happens that way, you know. Then he became more and more obsessed by Grafalk Steamship. He couldn't think about anything else. He was bitterly disappointed that our son wasn't interested in the steamship company: Peter is a cellist. Our daughter is a thoracic surgeon. When it became clear that no one of his name lived to care about Grafalk Steamship, Niels removed himself emotionally from the house.

'I have paid little attention to Niels in the last several years. Nevertheless, it became quite clear to me that he was growing more and more erratic over the past eight or nine months. I invited you up

499

here for lunch because you struck me as clever and intelligent the day we talked. I think you can tell me what Niels was doing. You were not a social acquaintance of my husband's. I don't believe you were his mistress –'

She paused to look at me sharply. I couldn't help laughing, but I shook my head.

'Yes. You don't have the look about you. Now. I want to know why you were on Niels's boat and how it came to burn up.'

I took another swallow of champagne. If anyone had the right to know, Claire Grafalk did. I told her the whole tale, beginning with Boom Boom's death and ending with the icy waters of Lake Michigan. I glanced at it, involuntarily shivering.

'And how did you get out? Someone rescued you?'

'Another sailboat came up. They were attracted by the fire. I don't remember it too clearly.'

'And the evidence of Clayton's death?'

I shook my head. 'I still have the plastic pouches with his hair and the carpet scraping. I think I keep them because they give some reality to the whole episode, not because I want to use them.'

Her head was still perched on one side. She reminded me of a robin or a sparrow – not cruel, just impersonal.

'But you don't want to prosecute?'

'I talked to Mrs Kelvin. She's the black woman whose husband was killed in Boom Boom's apartment. I figure she and I are the chief mourners – Jeannine doesn't count.' I stared unseeing out at the lake, remembering the conversation with Mrs Kelvin. I spent two days in the hospital recovering from the shock of my near drowning; she came to see me late on the second day. We talked for a long time, about Boom Boom and Henry Kelvin, and love.

'Niels and Sandy are both dead, so there's no one left to prosecute. Legal action against your husband's estate would bring no pleasure, only sully the memories of two heroic men. We have no interest left.'

She didn't say anything but nibbled with delicate energy on a petit four. I drank some more champagne. The food was excellent, but reviewing my time in Lake Michigan brought knots to my stomach.

It looked so peaceful now under the May sun, but it is not a tame lake.

'The United States Government may try to prove a case against Grafalk Steamship. It will really depend on their proving that your husband engineered theft of the depth charges and all the rest of that. With Sandy and Howard Mattingly both dead, there aren't any witnesses. And as long as he gets the *Lucella* floating again, Martin doesn't want to push it too hard. I think the investigation will go on quite a while, but they're never going to be able to fix blame for blowing up the *Lucella*. Not unless Admiral Jergensen decides to testify that your husband stole the explosives. He doesn't seem to want to right now.'

Bledsoe had been around once or twice. He figured out most of the story when he read about the accident to the *Brynulf*. I went drinking with Bledsoe one night while I told him the rest. His lovemaking matched his kissing. That had helped, but I knew the nightmares would last a long time.

Claire Grafalk looked away from me and said in a flat voice, 'Niels left Paige Carrington a condo on Astor Place.'

I drew a sharp breath. Paige was the spot that still hurt, the little needle in the diaphragm every time I thought of her. 'I was wondering how she'd be able to afford that. Of course, she still has those monthly assessments to keep up. They're not cheap.'

Mrs Grafalk still didn't look at me. 'She's in London now with Guy Odinflute.'

'Do you mind so much?' I asked gently.

Tears sparkled briefly in her bright eyes, but she gave a twisted smile. 'Do I mind? Niels has been dead to me for many years. But once – it was different. For the sake of the man I once loved, I would have liked to see her mourn.'

KILLING ORDERS

For Courtenay
All other things to their destruction draw

ACKNOWLEDGEMENTS

Thanks to Bill Tiritilli, director of research for the brokerage firm Rodman and Renshaw, for advice on law and practice in takeovers of publicly held companies.

Marilyn Martin, JD, is a public defender. Unlike V. I. Warshawski, she has not allowed the discouragements of the job to stop her from practicing it. She supplied me with information about the Illinois criminal code, probable grounds for arrest, and about Chicago's Women's Court. Any mistakes are due to my ignorance, not her information.

Kimball Wright, enraged by repeated errors regarding the Smith & Wesson in V.I.'s previous adventures, provided me with better information about the weapon.

The Reverend Albertus Magnus, OP, has often allowed me the great pleasure of visiting him and his brother Dominicans at the House of Studies in Washington. Because I know this order better than any other, I chose it as part of the setting for this story. The Priory of Albertus Magnus in Chicago is totally fictitious, as are the friars who reside there.

And many thanks, too, to James H. Lorie.

CONTENTS

1
OLD WOUNDS

My stomach muscles contracted as I locked the car door. I hadn't been to Melrose Park for ten years, but, as I walked up the narrow pavement to the house's side entrance, I felt a decade of maturity slipping from me, felt the familiar sickening, my heart thudding.

The January wind scattered dead leaves around my feet. Little snow had fallen this winter, but the air blew cold. After ringing the bell I jammed my hands deep into the pockets of my navy car coat to keep them warm. I tried to argue my nervousness away. After all, they had called me . . . begged me for help . . . The words meant nothing. I had lost an important battle by responding to the plea.

I stamped my feet to loosen the toes frozen inside thin-soled loafers and heard, at last, a rattling behind the painted blue door. It swung inward into a dimly lit vestibule. Through the screen I could just make out my cousin Albert, much heavier than he'd been ten years ago. The screen and the dark behind him softened his pout.

'Come in, Victoria. Mother is waiting for you.'

I bit back an excuse for being a quarter hour late and turned it into a neutral comment on the weather. Albert was almost bald, I noted with pleasure. He took my coat ungraciously and draped it over the banister at the foot of the narrow, uncarpeted stairs.

A deep, harsh voice called to us. 'Albert! Is that Victoria?'

'Yes, Mama,' Albert muttered.

The only light in the entryway came from a tiny round window facing the stairs. The dimness obscured the pattern in the wallpaper, but as I followed Albert down the close corridor I could see it hadn't changed: gray paper with white loops, ugly, cold. As a child, I thought the paper oozed hate. Behind Albert's wobbling thighs the old chill stuck out tendrils at me and I shivered.

I used to beg my mother, Gabriella, not to bring me to this house. Why should we go? Rosa hated her, hated me, and Gabriella always cried after the long el ride home. But she would only set her lips in a tight smile and say, 'I am obligated, *cara*. I must go.'

Albert led me into the formal parlor at the back of the house. The horsehair furniture was as familiar to me as my own apartment. In my nightmares I dreamed of being trapped in this room with its stiff furniture, the ice-blue drapes, the sad picture of Uncle Carl over the fake fireplace, and Rosa, thin, hawk-nosed, frowning, seated poker-backed in a spindle-legged chair.

Her black hair was iron-colored now, but the severe, disapproving stare was unaltered. I tried taking diaphragm breaths to calm the churning in my stomach. You're here because *she* begged *you*, I reminded myself.

She didn't stand up, didn't smile – I couldn't remember ever seeing her smile. 'It was good of you to come, Victoria.' Her tone implied it would have been better if I'd come on time. 'When one is old, one doesn't travel easily. And the last few days have made me old indeed.'

I sat down in what I hoped was the least uncomfortable chair. 'Yes,' I said noncommittally. Rosa was about seventy-five. When they performed her autopsy, they would find her bones were made of cast iron. She did not look old to me: she hadn't begun to rust yet.

'Albert. Pour some coffee for Victoria.'

Rosa's single virtue was her cooking. I took a cup of the rich Italian coffee gratefully, but ignored the tray of pastries Albert proffered – I'd get pastry cream on my black wool skirt and feel foolish as well as tense.

Albert sat uneasily on the narrow settee, eating a piece of *torta del re*, glancing surreptitiously at the floor when a crumb dropped, then at Rosa to see if she'd noticed.

'You are well, Victoria? You are happy?'

'Yes,' I said firmly. 'Both well and happy.'

'But you have not remarried?'

The last time I'd been here was with my brief husband for a strained bridal visit. 'It is possible to be happy and not married, as Albert doubtless can tell you, or as you know yourself.' The last was a cruel remark: Uncle Carl had killed himself shortly after Albert was born. I felt vindictively pleased, then guilty. Surely I was mature enough not to need that kind of satisfaction. Somehow Rosa always made me feel eight years old.

Rosa shrugged her thin shoulders disdainfully. 'No doubt you are right. Yet for me – I am to die without the joy of grandchildren.'

Albert shifted uncomfortably on the settee. It was clearly not a new complaint.

'A pity,' I said. 'I know grandchildren would be the crowning joy of a happy and virtuous life.'

Albert choked but recovered. Rosa narrowed her eyes angrily. 'You, of all people, should know why my life has not been happy.'

Despite my efforts at control, anger spilled over. 'Rosa, for some reason you think Gabriella destroyed your happiness. What mysterious grievance a girl of eighteen could have caused you I don't know. But you threw her out into the city on her own. She didn't speak English. She might have been killed. Whatever she did to you, it couldn't have been as bad as what you did to her.

'You know the only reason I'm here: Gabriella made me promise that I would help you if you needed it. It stuck in my gut and it still does. But I promised her, and here I am. So let's leave the past in peace: I won't be sarcastic if you'll stop throwing around insults about my mother. Why not just tell me what the problem is.'

Rosa tightened her lips until they almost disappeared. 'The most difficult thing I ever did in my life was to call you. And now I see I should not have done it.' She rose in one movement, like a steel crane, and left the room. I could hear the angry clip of her shoes on the uncarpeted hall and up the bare stairs. In the distance a door slammed.

I put down my coffee and looked at Albert. He had turned red with discomfort, but he seemed less amorphous with Rosa out of the room.

'How bad is her trouble?'

He wiped his fingers on a napkin and folded it tidily. 'Pretty bad,' he muttered. 'Why'd you have to make her mad?'

'It makes her mad to see me here instead of at the bottom of Lake Michigan. Every time I've talked to her since Gabriella died she's been hostile to me. If she needs help, all I want is the facts. She can save the rest for her psychiatrist. I don't get paid enough to deal with it.' I picked up my shoulder bag and stood up. At the doorway I stopped and looked at him.

'I'm not coming back to Melrose Park for another round, Albert. If you want to tell me the story I'll listen. But if I leave now, that's it; I won't respond to any more pleas for family unity from Rosa. And by the way, if you do want to hire me, I'm not working out of love for your mother.'

He stared at the ceiling, listening perhaps for guidance from above. Not heaven – just the back bedroom. We couldn't hear anything. Rosa was probably jabbing pins into a piece of clay with a lock of my hair stuck to it. I rubbed my arms involuntarily, searching for damage.

Albert shifted uneasily and stood up. 'Uh, look, uh, maybe I'd better tell you.'

'Fine. Can we go to a more comfortable room?'

'Sure. Sure.' He gave a half smile, the first I'd seen that afternoon. I followed him back down the hall to a room on the left. It was tiny, but clearly his private spot. A giant set of stereo speakers loomed from one wall; below them were some built-in shelves holding an amplifier and a large collection of tapes and records. No books except a few accounting texts. His high-school trophies. A tiny cache of bottles.

He sat in the one chair, a large leather desk chair with a hassock next to it. He slid the hassock over to me and I perched on that.

In his own place, Albert relaxed and his face took on a more decisive look. He was a CPA with his own business, I remembered. When you saw him with Rosa, you couldn't imagine him managing anything on his own, but in here it didn't seem so improbable.

He took a pipe from the desk top next to him and began the pipe smoker's interminable ritual with it. With luck I'd be gone before he actually lit it. All smoke makes me ill, and pipe smoke on top of an empty stomach – I'd been too tense for lunch – would be disastrous.

'How long have you been a detective, Victoria?'

'About ten years.' I swallowed my annoyance at being called Victoria. Not that it isn't my name. Just that if I liked using it I wouldn't go by my initials.

'And you're good at it?'

'Yes. Depending on your problem, I'm about the best you can get . . . I have a list of references if you want to call someone.'

'Yeah, I'd like a name or two before you go.' He had finished drilling out the pipe bowl. He knocked it methodically against the side of an ashtray and began packing it with tobacco. 'Mother's gotten herself involved with some counterfeit securities.'

Wild dreams of Rosa as the brains behind Chicago's Mob ran through my head. I could see six-point screamer headlines in the *Herald-Star*.

'Involved how?'

'They found some in the St Albert Priory safe.'

I sighed to myself. Albert was deliberately going to drag this out. 'She plant them there? What's she got to do with this priory?'

The moment of truth had come: Albert struck a match and began sucking on the pipe-stem. Sweet blue smoke curled up around his head and wafted toward me. I felt my stomach turn over.

'Mother's been their treasurer for the last twenty years. I thought you knew.' He paused a minute to let me feel guilty about not keeping up with the family. 'Of course they had to ask her to leave when they found the securities.'

'Does she know anything about them?'

He shrugged. He was sure she didn't. He didn't know how many there were, what companies they were drawn on, how long since

513

they'd last been examined, or who had access to them. The only thing he knew was the new prior wanted to sell them in order to make repairs on the building. Yes, they'd been in a safe.

'Her heart's broken because of the suspicion.' He saw my derisive look and said defensively, 'Just because you only see her when she's upset or angry you can't imagine she has real feelings. She's seventy-five, you know, and that job meant a lot to her. She wants her name cleared so she can go back.'

'Surely the FBI is investigating, and the SEC.'

'Yes, but they'd be just as happy to hang it on her if it made things easier for them. After all, who wants to take a priest to court? And they know she's old, she'd get off with a suspended sentence.'

I blinked a few times. 'Albert. No. You're out of touch. If she were some poor West Side black, they might railroad her. But not Rosa. She'd scare 'em too much for one thing. And the FBI – they'll want to get to the bottom of this. They're never going to believe an old woman masterminded a counterfeiting scheme.' Unless, of course, she had. I wished I could believe it, but Rosa was malicious, not dishonest.

'But that church is the only thing she really loves,' he blurted, turning crimson. 'They might believe she got carried away. People do.'

We talked about it some more, but it ended as I suppose I'd known it had to, with me pulling out two copies of my standard contract for Albert to sign. I gave him a family rate on the fee – sixteen dollars an hour instead of twenty.

He told me the new prior would be expecting my call. Boniface Carroll his name was. Albert wrote that on a piece of paper along with a rough map of how to find the priory. I frowned as I stuck it in my bag. They were taking an awful lot for granted. Then I laughed sourly at myself. Once I'd agreed to make the trek to Melrose Park they could take a lot for granted.

Back at my car I stood rubbing my head for a few minutes, hoping the cold clean air would blow the pipe fumes from my throbbing brain. I glanced back at the house. A curtain fell

514

quickly at an upstairs window. I climbed into the car somewhat cheered. To see Rosa spy furtively on me – like a small child or a thief – made me feel somehow that more of the power lay in my hands.

2

REMEMBRANCE OF THINGS PAST

I woke up sweating. The bedroom was dark and for a moment I couldn't remember where I was. Gabriella had been staring at me, her eyes huge in her wasted face, the skin translucent as it had been those last painful months of her life, pleading with me to help her. The dream had been in Italian. It took time to reorient myself to English, to adulthood, to my apartment.

The digital clock glowed faintly orange. Five-thirty. My sweat turned to a chill. I pulled the comforter up around my neck and clenched my teeth to keep them from chattering.

My mother died of cancer when I was fifteen. As the disease ate the vitality from her beautiful face, she made me promise to help Rosa if her aunt ever needed me. I had tried to argue with Gabriella: Rosa hated her, hated me – we had no obligation. But my mother insisted and I could not refuse.

My father had told me more than once how he met my mother. He was a policeman. Rosa had thrown Gabriella out on the street, an immigrant with minimal English. My mother, who always had more courage than common sense, was trying to earn a living doing the only thing she knew: singing. Unfortunately, none of the Milwaukee Avenue bars where she auditioned liked Puccini or Verdi and my father rescued her one day from a group of men who were trying to force her to strip. Neither he nor I could understand why she ever saw Rosa again. But I made her the promise she wanted.

My pulse had calmed down but I knew more sleep was out of the question. Shivering in the cold room, I padded naked to the window and pulled back the heavy curtain. The winter morning was black. Snow falling like a fine mist glowed in the streetlamp at the corner of the alley. I kept shivering, but the still morning held me entranced, the thick black air pressing at me comfortingly.

At last I let the curtain drop. I had a ten o'clock meeting in Melrose Park with the new prior of St Albert's. I might as well get going.

Even in the winter I try to run five miles a day. Although financial crime, my specialty, doesn't often lead to violence, I grew up in a rough South Side neighborhood where girls as well as boys had to be able to defend themselves. Old habits die hard, so I work out and run to stay in shape. Anyway, running is the best way I know to ward off the effects of pasta. I don't enjoy exercise, but it beats dieting.

In the winter I wear a light sweatshirt, loose pants, and a down vest. Once warmed up I donned these and ran quickly down the hall and three flights of stairs to keep my muscles loose.

Outside, I wanted to abandon the project. The cold and damp were miserable. Even though the streets were already filling with early commuters, it was hours before my usual waking time, and the sky had barely begun to lighten by the time I got back to Halsted and Belmont. I walked carefully up the stairs to my apartment. The steps were shiny with age and very slippery when wet. I had a vision of myself sliding backward on wet running shoes, cracking my skull on old marble.

A long hallway divides my apartment in half and makes it seem bigger than its four rooms. The dining room and kitchen are to the left; bedroom and living room to the right. For some reason the kitchen connects to the bathroom. I turned on water for a shower and went next door to start coffee.

Armed with coffee, I took my running clothes off and sniffed them. Smelly, but not too bad for one more morning. I dropped them over a chair back and gave myself up to a long hot shower. The stream of water drumming on my skull soothed me. I relaxed, and without realizing it, I started to sing a bit under my breath. After a while the tune drifted into my consciousness, a sad Italian folksong Gabriella used to sing. Rosa was really lying heavy on my mind – the nightmare, visions of my skull breaking, now mournful songs. I was not going to let her control me this way – that would be the ultimate defeat. I shampooed my hair vigorously and forced myself to sing Brahms. I don't like his *Lieder*, but some, like 'Meine Liebe Ist Grün' are almost painfully cheerful.

Coming out of the shower I switched to the dwarfs' song from *Snow White*. Off to work we go. My navy walking suit, I decided, to make me mature and dignified. It had a three-quarter-length double-breasted jacket and a skirt with two side pleats. A knit silk top of pale gold, almost the color of my skin, and a long scarf bright with red and navy and brushed again with the same gold. Perfect. I edged the corners of my eyes with a faint trace of blue pencil to make their gray color bluer, added a little light rouge and lipstick to match the red in the scarf. Open-toed red-leather pumps, Italian. Gabriella brought me up to believe that my feet would fall off if I wore shoes made anyplace else. Even now that a pair of Magli pumps go for a hundred forty dollars, I can't bring myself to wear Comfort-Stride.

I left the breakfast dishes in the sink with last night's supper plates and those from a few other meals. And the bed unmade. And the clothes strewn around. Perhaps I should save the money I spend on clothes and shoes and invest in a house-keeper. Or even a hypnosis program to teach me to be neat and tidy. But what the hell. Who besides me was going to see it?

3

THE ORDER OF
PREACHERS

The Eisenhower Expressway is the main escape route from Chicago to the western suburbs. Even on warm sunny days, it looks like a prison exercise yard for most of its length. Run-down houses and faceless projects line the tops of the canyons on either side of its eight lanes. El stations are planted along the median. The Eisenhower is always choked with traffic, even at three in the morning. At nine on a wet workday it was impossible.

I could feel tension tightening the cords in the back of my neck as I oozed forward. I was on an errand I did not wish to make to talk to a person I had no desire to see about the troubles of an aunt I loathed. To do so I had to spend hours stalled in traffic. And my feet were cold inside their open-toed pumps. I turned up the heat further but the little Omega didn't respond. I curled and uncurled my toes to get the blood moving but they remained obstinately frozen.

At First Avenue the traffic eased up as the offices there sucked up most of the outbound drivers. I exited north at Mannheim and meandered through the streets, trying to follow Albert's roughly sketched directions. It was five after ten when I finally found the priory entrance. Being late did nothing to improve my humor.

The Priory of St Albertus Magnus included a large block of neo-Gothic buildings set to one side of a beautiful park. The architect apparently believed he had to compensate for the beauties of nature: in the misty snow the gray stone buildings loomed as ungainly shapes.

A small lettered sign identified the nearest concrete block as the

House of Studies. As I drove past, a few men in long white robes were scuttling into it, hoods pulled over their faces so that they looked like medieval monks. They paid no attention to me.

As I crept slowly up the circular drive I saw a number of cars parked to one side. I left the Omega there and quickly ran to the nearest entrance. This was labelled simply ST ALBERT'S PRIORY.

Inside, the building had the half-eerie, half-tired atmosphere you often find in religious institutions. You can tell people spend a lot of time praying there, but perhaps they also spend too much time feeling depressed or bored. The entryway had a vaulted concrete ceiling that disappeared in the gloomy light several stories up. Marble flagstones added to the coldness.

A corridor ran at right angles to the entrance. I crossed to it, my heels echoing in the vaulted chamber, and looked doubtfully around. A scarred wooden desk had been stuck in a corner formed by the entry hall and a stairwell. A thin young man in civvies sat behind it reading *The Greater Trumps* by Charles Williams. He put it down reluctantly after I'd spoken several times. His face was extremely thin; he seemed to burn with a nervous asceticism, but perhaps he was merely hyperthyroid. At any rate, he directed me to the prior's office in a hurried whisper, not waiting to see if I followed his directions before returning to the book.

At least I was in the right building, a relief since I was now fifteen minutes late. I turned left down the corridor, passing icons and shut doors. A couple of men in white robes passed me, arguing vigorously but in subdued voices. At the end of the hall I turned right. On one side of me was a chapel and across from it, as the youth had promised, the prior's office.

The Reverend Boniface Carroll was on the phone when I came in. He smiled when he saw me and motioned me to a chair in front of his desk, but continued his conversation in a series of grunts. He was a frail man of perhaps fifty. His white woolen robe had turned faintly yellow with age. He looked very tired; as he listened to his caller he kept rubbing his eyes.

The office itself was sparsely furnished. A crucifix over one wall was the only decoration, and the wide desk was scuffed with age.

The floor was covered with institutional linoleum, only partly hidden by a threadbare carpet.

'Well, actually she's here right now, Mr Hatfield . . . No, no, I think I should talk to her.'

I raised my eyebrows at that. The only Hatfield I knew worked on fraud for the FBI. He was a competent young man, but his sense of humor left something to be desired. When our paths crossed, it was usually to our mutual irritation, since he tried to overcome my flippancy with threats of the might of the FBI.

Carroll terminated the conversation and turned to me. 'You are Miss Warshawski, aren't you?' He had a light, pleasant voice with a trace of an eastern accent.

'Yes.' I handed him one of my cards. 'Was that Derek Hatfield?'

'The FBI man. Yes, he's been out here with Ted Dartmouth from the Securities Exchange Commission. I don't know how he learned we were going to meet, but he was asking me not to talk to you.'

'Did he say why?'

'He thinks this is a matter for the FBI and the SEC. He told me an amateur such as yourself might muddy the waters, make the investigation more difficult.'

I rubbed my upper lip thoughtfully. I'd forgotten the lipstick until I saw the smear on my forefinger. Cool, Vic. If I were being logical, I'd smile politely at Father Carroll and leave; after all, I'd been cursing him, Rosa, and my mission all the way from Chicago. However, there's nothing like a little opposition to make me change my mind, especially when the opposition comes from Derek Hatfield.

'That's sort of what I said to my aunt when I talked to her yesterday. The FBI and the SEC are trained to handle this kind of investigation. But she's old and she's scared and she wants someone from the family in her corner.

'I've been a private investigator for almost ten years. I've done a lot of financial crime and I've got a good reputation – I could give you the names of some people in the city to call so you don't have to take just my word for it.'

Carroll smiled. 'Relax, Miss Warshawski. You don't have to sell me. I told your aunt I would talk to you and I feel we owe her something here, if only a conversation with you. She's worked for St Albert's very faithfully for a long time. It really hurt her when we asked her to take a leave of absence. I hated doing it, but I've made the same request to everyone with access to the safe. As soon as we get this business cleared up, she knows we want her back. She's extremely competent.'

I nodded. I could see Rosa as a competent treasurer. It flashed through my mind that she might have been less angry if she had channeled her energy into a career: She would have made a good corporate financial officer.

'I don't really know what happened,' I said to Carroll. 'Why don't you tell me the story – where the safe is, how you came to find the fakes, how much money is involved, who could have gotten at them, who knew about them – and I'll butt in when I don't understand.'

He smiled again, a shy sweet smile, and got up to show me the safe. It was in a storeroom behind his office, one of those old cast-iron models with a combination lock. It was stuck in a corner amid stacks of paper, an ancient mimeo machine, and piles of extra prayer books.

I knelt to look at it. Of course, the priory had used the same combination for years, which meant anyone who'd been there a while could have found out what it was. Neither the FBI nor the Melrose Park police had discovered any signs that the lock had been forced.

'How many people do you have here at the priory?'

'There are twenty-one students at the House of Studies and eleven priests on the teaching faculty. But then there are people like your aunt who come in and work during the day. We have a kitchen crew, for example; the brothers do all the washing up and waiting at table, but we have three women who come in to do the cooking. We have two receptionists – the young man who probably directed you to my office and a woman who handles the afternoon shift. And of course there are a lot of neighborhood people who worship with us in the chapel.' He smiled again. 'We Dominicans are preachers and scholars. We don't usually run parish churches, but a lot of people do treat this as their parish.'

I shook my head. 'You've got too many people around here to make sorting this out easy. Who actually had official access to the safe?'

'Well, Mrs Vignelli, of course.' That was Rosa. 'I do. The procurator – he handles the financial affairs. The student master. We have an audit once a year, and our accountants always examine the stocks, along with the other assets, but I don't think they know the combination to the safe.'

'Why'd you keep the things here instead of in a bank vault?'

He shrugged. 'I wondered the same thing. I was just elected last May.' The smile crept back into his eyes. 'Not a post I wanted – I'm like John Roncalli – the safe candidate who doesn't belong to any of the factions here. Anyway, I'd never been at all involved in running this – or any other – priory. I didn't know anything about it. I didn't know we kept five million dollars' worth of stock certificates on the premises. To tell you the truth, I didn't even know we owned them.'

I shuddered. Five million dollars sitting around for any casual passerby to take. The wonder was that they hadn't simply been stolen years before.

Father Carroll was explaining the history of the stocks in his gentle, efficient voice. They were all blue-chip shares – AT&T, IBM, and Standard of Indiana primarily. They had been left to the priory ten years ago by a wealthy man in Melrose Park.

The priory buildings were close to eighty years old and needed a lot of repairs. He pointed to some cracks in the plaster on the wall and I followed the line of damage to a wide brown stain on the ceiling.

'The most urgent problems are the roof and the furnace. It seemed reasonable to sell some shares and use the money to repair the plant, which is, after all, our main asset. Even though it's ugly and uncomfortable we couldn't begin to replace it today. So

I brought up the matter at chapter meeting and got an agreement. The next Monday I went into the Loop and met with a broker. He agreed to sell eighty thousand dollars' worth of shares. He took them from us then.'

That had been the last of the matter for a week. Then the broker had called back. The Fort Dearborn Trust, the company's stock-transfer agent, had examined the shares and found they were counterfeits.

'Is there a possibility the broker or the banker made an exchange?'

He shook his head unhappily. 'That's the first thing we thought of. But we had all the remaining certificates looked at. They're all fakes.'

We sat silently for a bit. What a dispiriting prospect.

'When was the last time the shares were authenticated?' I asked at last.

'I don't know. I called the accountants, but all they do is verify that the shares are there. According to the FBI man, these certificates are extremely good forgeries. They were found out only because the serial numbers had not been used by the issuing companies. They'd fool any ordinary observer.'

I sighed. I probably should talk to the former prior, and to the student master and procurator. I asked Carroll about them. His predecessor was in Pakistan for a year, running a Dominican school there. But the student master and procurator were both in the building and would be at lunch.

'You're welcome to join us if you like. Ordinarily the refectory in a convent is cloistered – that means only friars can use the room,' he explained in answer to my puzzled look. 'And yes. We friars call this a convent. Or a friary. Anyway, we've lifted the cloister here at the school so that the young men can eat with their families when they come to visit . . . The food isn't very interesting, but it's an easier way to meet Pelly and Jablonski than trying to track them down afterward.' He pulled back a yellowed sleeve to reveal a thin wrist with a heavy leather watchband on it. 'It's almost noon. People will be gathering outside the refectory now.'

I looked at my own watch. It was almost twenty of twelve.

Duty had driven me to worse things than undistinguished cuisine. I accepted. The prior locked the storeroom carefully behind him. 'Another example of locking the barn door,' he said. 'There was no lock on that storeroom until we discovered the fake securities.'

We joined a throng of white-robed men walking down the corridor past Carroll's office. Most of them said hello to him, eyeing me covertly. At the end of the hall were two swinging doors. Through their glass top halves I could see the refectory, looking like a high-school gym converted to a lunch room: long deal tables, metal folding chairs, no linens, hospital-green walls.

Carroll took me by the arm and led me through the huddle to a pudgy middle-aged man whose head emerged from a fringe of gray hair, like a soft-boiled egg from an egg cup. 'Stephen, I'd like you to meet Miss Warshawski. She's Rosa Vignelli's niece, but she's also a private investigator. She's looking into our crime as an *amica familiae*.' He turned to me. 'This is Father Jablonski, who's been the student master for seven years . . . Stephen, why don't you dig up Augustine and introduce him to Miss Warshawski. She needs to talk to him, too.'

I was about to murmur a social inanity when Carroll turned to the crowd and said something in Latin. They answered and he rattled off what I assumed was a blessing; everyone crossed himself.

Lunch was definitely uninteresting: bowls of Campbell's tomato soup, which I loathe, and toasted cheese sandwiches. I put pickles and onions inside my sandwich and accepted coffee from an eager young Dominican.

Jablonski introduced me to Augustine Pelly, the procurator, and to some half dozen other men at our table. These were all 'brothers', not 'fathers'. Since they tended to look alike in their fresh white robes I promptly forgot their names.

'Miss Warshawski thinks she can succeed where the FBI and the SEC are baffled,' Jablonski said jovially, his nasal midwestern accent blaring above the dining room cacophony.

Pelly gave me a measuring look, then smiled. He was almost as thin as Father Carroll, and very tanned, which surprised me – where did a monk go sunbathing in mid-winter? His blue eyes were sharp and alert in his dark face. 'I'm sorry, Miss Warshawski – I know Stephen well enough to tell he's joking, but I'm afraid I don't get the joke.'

'I'm a private investigator,' I explained.

Pelly raised his eyebrows. 'And you're going to look into our missing securities?'

I shook my head. 'I don't really have the resources to match the FBI on that type of thing. But I'm also Rosa Vignelli's niece; she wants someone from the family on her side in the investigation. A lot of people have had access to that safe over the years; I'm here to remind Derek Hatfield of that if he starts breathing down Rosa's neck too hard.'

Pelly smiled again. 'Mrs Vignelli doesn't strike one as the type of woman to need protection.'

I grinned back at him. 'She certainly doesn't, Father Pelly. But I keep reminding myself that Rosa's been ageing just like any other human being. At any rate, she seems a little frightened, especially that she won't be able to work here anymore.' I ate some of my sandwich. Kraft American. Next to Stilton and Brie my favorite cheese.

Jablonski said, 'I hope she knows that Augustine and I are also forbidden access to the priory's finances until this matter is cleared up. She's not being singled out in any way that we aren't.'

'Maybe one of you could call her,' I suggested. 'That might make her feel better . . . I'm sure you know her well enough to realize she's not a woman with a lot of friends. She's centered a good part of her life around this church.'

'Yes,' Pelly agreed. 'I didn't realize she had any family besides her son. She's never mentioned you, Miss Warshawski. Nor that she had any Polish relatives.'

'Her brother's daughter was my mother, who married a Chicago policeman named Warshawski. I've never understood the laws of kinship too well. Does that mean that she has Polish relatives because I'm half Polish? You don't think I'm posing as Rosa's niece just to get inside the priory, do you?'

Jablonski gave his sardonic smile. 'Now that the securities are gone, there's nothing worth worming your way into the priory for. Unless you have some secret fetish for friars.'

I laughed, but Pelly said seriously, 'I assume the prior looked into your credentials.'

'There wasn't any reason for him to; he wasn't hiring me. I do have a copy of my PI license on me, but I don't carry any identification that proves I'm Rosa Vignelli's niece. You could call her, of course.'

Pelly held up a hand. 'I'm not doubting you. I'm just concerned for the priory. We're getting some publicity which none of us relishes and which is really detrimental to the studies of these young men.' He indicated the intently eavesdropping young brothers at our table. One of them blushed in embarrassment. 'I really don't want anyone, even if she's the pope's niece, stirring things up here further.'

'I can understand that. But I can also see Rosa's point – it's just too convenient to have her on the outside of the priory taking the fall. She doesn't have a big organization with lots of political connections behind her. You do.'

Pelly gave me a freezing stare. 'I won't attempt to untangle that one, Miss Warshawski. You obviously are referring to the popular myth about the political power of the Catholic Church, the direct line from the Vatican that was going to control John Kennedy, that sort of thing. It's beneath discussion.'

'I think we could have a pretty lively discussion about it,' I objected. 'We could talk about the politics of abortion, for example. How local pastors try to influence their congregations to vote for anti-choice candidates regardless of how terrible their qualifications may be otherwise. Or maybe you'd like to discuss the relations between Archbishop Farber and Police Superintendent Bellamy. Or even between him and the mayor.'

Jablonski turned to me. 'I think pastors would be gravely lax in their moral duty if they didn't try to oppose abortion in any way possible, even urging their parishioners to vote for pro-life candidates.'

I felt the blood rush to my head, but smiled. 'We're never going to agree on whether abortion is a moral issue or a private matter between a woman and her physician. But one thing is clear – it is a highly political issue. There are a lot of people scrutinizing the Catholic Church's involvement in this area.

'Now the tax code spells out pretty specifically how clear of politics you have to stay to keep your tax-exempt status. So when bishops and priests are using their offices to push political candidates, they're walking a pretty thin line on tax-exempt status. So far, no tax-court judge has been willing to take on the Catholic Church – which in itself argues some hefty clout.'

Pelly turned an angry crimson under his tan. 'I don't think you have the least idea what you're talking about, Miss Warshawski. Maybe you could keep your remarks to the specific points that the prior asked you to discuss.'

'Fine,' I said. 'Let's concentrate on the priory here. Is there anyone who would have reason to take close to five million dollars?'

'No one,' Pelly said shortly. 'We take vows of poverty.'

One of the brothers offered me more coffee. It was so thin as to be almost undrinkable, but I accepted it absently. 'You got the shares ten years ago. Since then, almost anyone with access to the priory could have taken the money. Discounting random strangers walking in off the street, that means someone connected with this place. What kind of turnover do you have among your monks?'

'They're actually called friars,' Jablonski interjected. 'Monks stay in one place; friars roam around. What do you mean by turnover? Every year students leave – some have been ordained, others find the conventual life doesn't suit them for some reason. And there's a lot of movement among the priests, too. People who taught at other Dominican institutions come here, or vice versa. Father Pelly here just returned from six months in Ciudad Isabella. He was a student in Panama and likes to spend a certain amount of time down there.'

That explained his suntan, then. 'We can probably eliminate people who move on to other Dominican seats. But what about any young men who've left the order in the last decade? Could you find out if any of them claimed coming into an inheritance?'

Pelly shrugged disdainfully. 'I suppose so, but I would be most reluctant to do so. When Stephen said young men find the monastic life doesn't suit them, it's not usually because of lack of luxury. We do a careful screening of our applicants before we allow them to become novices. I think we'd turn up the type who would steal.'

Father Carroll joined us at that point. The refectory was clearing. Knots of men stood talking in the doorway, some staring at me. The prior turned to the brothers lingering at our table. 'Don't you have exams next week? Perhaps you should be studying.'

They got up a little shamefacedly and Carroll sat in one of the empty seats. 'Are you making any progress?'

Pelly frowned. 'We've progressed past some wild accusations about the Church in general to a concentrated attack on young men who have left the order in the last decade. Not exactly what I'd expect from a Catholic girl.'

I held up a hand. 'Not me, Father Pelly. I'm not a girl and I'm not a Catholic . . . We're really at a standstill. I'll have to talk to Derek Hatfield and see if he'll share the FBI's ideas with me. What you need to find is someone with a secret bank account. Perhaps one of your brothers, possibly my aunt. Although if she stole the money, it certainly wasn't to use on herself. She lives very frugally. Perhaps, though, she's a fanatic about some cause I don't know anything about and stole to support it. Which might be true of any of you as well.'

Rosa as a secret Torquemada appealed to me but there wasn't any real evidence of it. It was hard to imagine her feeling positive enough about anyone or anything to love it, let alone steal for it.

'As the procurator, Father Pelly, perhaps you know whether the shares were ever authenticated. If this wasn't done when you got them, it's possible they came to you as forgeries.'

Pelly shook his head. 'It never occurred to us. I don't know if we're too unworldly to handle assets, but it doesn't seem like the kind of thing anyone does.'

'Probably not,' I agreed. I asked him and Jablonski some more questions, but neither was very helpful. Pelly still seemed miffed with me over the Church and politics. Since I'd compounded my sin by not being a Catholic girl, his answers were fairly frosty. Even Jablonski commented on it.

'Why are you on such a high horse with Miss Warshawski, Gus? So she's not a Catholic. Neither is eighty-five percent of the world's population. That should make us more charitable, not less.'

Pelly turned his cold stare on him, and Carroll remarked, 'Let's save group criticism for chapter, Stephen.'

Pelly said, 'I'm sorry if I seem rude, Miss Warshawski. But this business is very worrying, especially because I was the procurator for eight years. And I'm afraid my experiences in Central America make me sensitive to criticisms about the Church and politics.'

I blinked a few times. 'Sensitive how?'

Carroll intervened again. 'Two of our priests were shot in El Salvador last spring; the government suspected they were harboring rebels.'

I didn't say anything. Whether the Church was working for the poor, as in El Salvador, or supporting the government, as in Spain, it was still, in my book, up to its neck in politics. But it didn't seem polite to pursue the argument.

Jablonski thought otherwise. 'Rubbish, Gus, and you know it. You're only upset because you and the government don't see eye to eye. But if your friends have their way, you know very well that the Friary of San Tomás will have some very powerful allies.' He turned to me. 'That's the trouble with people like you and Gus, Miss Warshawski – when the Church is on your side, whether it's fighting racism or poverty, it's just being sensitive, not political. When it goes against your position, then it's political and up to no good.'

Carroll said, 'I think we're all getting a long way from Miss Warshawski's real business in coming out here. Stephen, I know we Dominicans are supposed to be preachers, but it violates some rules of hospitality to preach at a guest over lunch, even so meager a lunch as this.'

He stood up and the rest of us got up also. As we walked from the refectory, Jablonski said, 'No hard feelings, Miss Warshawski.

I like a good fighter. Sorry if I offended you in your role as a guest.'

To my surprise I found myself smiling at him. 'No hard feelings, Father. I'm afraid I got a little carried away myself.'

He shook hands with me briskly and walked down the hall in the opposite direction from Carroll, who said, 'Good. I'm glad you and Stephen found some common ground. He's a good man, just a little aggressive sometimes.'

Pelly frowned. 'Aggressive! He's completely without –' He suddenly remembered to save group criticism for chapter and broke off. 'Sorry, Prior. Maybe I should go back to San Tomás – that's where my mind seems to be these days.'

4
RETURN ENGAGEMENT

It was close to three when I threaded my way to my office in the South Loop. It's in the Pulteney Building, which is of the right vintage to be a national historic landmark. I sometimes think it might even qualify if it ever acquired a management interested in looking after it. Buildings around there don't fare well. They're too close to the city lockup, the slums, the peepshows and the cheap bars, so they attract clients like me: detectives on shoestring budgets, bail bondsmen, inept secretarial services.

I put the car into a lot on Adams and walked the block north to the Pulteney. The snow, or rain, or whatever it was had stopped. While the skies were still sullen, the pavement was almost dry and my beloved Magli pumps were free from further insults.

Someone had left a bourbon bottle in the lobby. I picked it up and carried it with me to throw out in my office. My long-awaited oil-tanker billionaire might show up and be put off by empty whiskey bottles in the lobby. Especially if he saw the brand.

The elevator, working for a change, clanked lugubriously down from the sixteenth floor. I stuck the bottle under one arm and slid open an ancient brass grille with the other. If I never worked out I'd stay in shape just by coming to the office every day – between running the elevator, repairing the toilet in the ladies' room on the seventh floor, and walking up and down the stairs between my fourth-floor office and the bathroom.

The elevator grudgingly stopped at the fourth floor. My office was at the east end of the corridor, the end where low rents sank even further because of the noise of the Dan Ryan el running directly underneath it. A train was clattering by as I unlocked the door.

I spend so little time in my office that I've never put much into furnishing it. The old wooden desk I'd bought at a police auction. That was it, except for two straight-backed chairs for clients, my chair, and an army-green filing cabinet. My one concession to grace was an engraving of the Uffizi over the filing cabinet.

I picked up a week's accumulation of mail from the floor and started opening it while I called my answering service. Two messages. I didn't need to get in touch with Hatfield; he'd called me and would see me in his office at nine the next morning.

I looked at a bill from a stationery company. Two hundred dollars for letterhead and envelopes? I put it in the trash and dialed the F B I. Hatfield wasn't in, of course. I got his secretary. 'Yes, please tell Derek I won't be free tomorrow morning but three tomorrow afternoon will be fine.' She put me on hold while she checked his calendar. I continued through the mail. The Society of Young Women Business Executives urged me to join. Among their many benefits was a group life and health insurance plan. Derek's secretary came back on the line and we dickered, compromising on two-thirty.

My second message was more of a surprise and much more welcome. Roger Ferrant had called. He was an Englishman, a re-insurance broker whom I'd met the previous spring. His London firm had underwritten a ship that blew up in the Great Lakes. I was investigating the disaster; his firm was protecting its fifty-million-dollar investment. We hadn't seen each other since a night when I'd fallen asleep – to put it politely – across from him at a posh steakhouse.

I reached him at his firm's apartment in the Hancock Building. 'Roger! What are you doing in Chicago?'

'Hello, Vic. Scupperfield, Plouder sent me over here for a few weeks. Can we have dinner?'

'Is this my second chance? Or did you like my act the first time so well you want an encore?'

He laughed. 'Neither. How about it? Are you free this week anytime?'

I told him I was free that very night and agreed to meet him at the Hancock Building for a drink at seven-thirty. I hung up in much better spirits — I deserved a reward for messing around in Rosa's affairs.

I quickly sorted through the rest of my mail. None of it needed answering. One envelope actually contained a check for three hundred fifty dollars. Way to pick your clients, Vic, I cheered silently. Before leaving, I typed out a few bills on the old Olivetti that had been my mother's. She subscribed firmly to the belief that IBM had stolen both the Executive and Selectric designs from Olivetti and would have been ashamed of me if I'd owned one of the Itsy-Bitsy Machine Company's models.

I quickly finished the bills, stuffed them in envelopes, turned out the lights, and locked up. Outside the street was jammed with rush-hour crowds. I jostled and darted my way through them with the ease of long experience and retrieved the Omega for another long slow drive through stop-and-go traffic.

I bore the delays meekly, swooping off the Kennedy at Belmont and detouring around to my bank with the check before going home. In a sudden burst of energy I washed the dishes before changing clothes. I kept on the yellow silk top, found a pair of black velvet slacks in the closet, and put on a black-and-orange scarf. Eye-catching but not vulgar.

Ferrant seemed to think so, too. He greeted me enthusiastically in the Scupperfield, Plouder apartment at the Hancock. 'I remembered you were tough and funny, Vic, but I'd forgotten how attractive you are.'

If you like thin men, which I do, Ferrant looked good himself. He had on well-tailored casual slacks with tiny pleats at the waist, and a dark green sweater over a pale yellow shirt. His dark hair, which had been carefully combed when he opened the door, fell into his eyes when I returned his hug. He pushed it back with a characteristic gesture.

I asked what brought him to Chicago.

'Business with Ajax, of course.' He led me into the living room, a modernistically furnished square overlooking the lake. A large orange couch with a glass-and-chrome coffee table in front of it was flanked by chrome chairs with black fabric seats. I winced slightly.

'Hideous, isn't it?' he said cheerfully. 'If I have to stay in Chicago more than a month, I'm going to make them let me get my own apartment. Or at least my own furniture . . . Do you drink anything besides Château St Georges? We have a complete liquor cabinet.'

He swept open a blond-and-glass cabinet in one corner to display an impressive array of bottles. I laughed: I'd drunk two bottles of Château St Georges when we went to dinner together last May. 'Johnny Walker Black if they have it.' He rummaged through the cupboard, found a half-used bottle, and poured each of us a modest drink.

'They must hate you in London to send you to Chicago in January. And if you have to stay through February you'll know you're really on their hit list.'

He grimaced. 'I've been here before in winter. It must explain why you American girls are so tough. Are they as hardboiled as you in the South?'

'Worse,' I assured him. 'They're tougher but they hide it under this veneer of soft manners, so you don't know you've been hit until you start coming to.'

I sat at one end of the orange couch; he pulled up one of the chrome chairs close to me and leaned storklike over his drink, his hair falling into his eyes again. He explained that Scupperfield, Plouder, his London firm, owned three percent of Ajax. 'We're not the largest stockholder, but we're an important one. So we keep a finger in the Ajax pie. We send our young fellows here for training and take some Ajax people and teach them the London market. Believe it or not, I was a young fellow once myself.' Like many people in English insurance, Ferrant had started to work right after high school, or what we think of as high school. So at thirty-seven he had close to twenty years of experience in the topsy-turvy reinsurance business.

'I'm telling you that so you won't be so startled to hear I'm now a corporate officer *pro tem.*' He grinned. 'A lot of people at Ajax feel their noses bent because I'm so young, but by the time they have my experience, they'll be six or eight years older.'

Aaron Carter, the head of Ajax's reinsurance division, had died suddenly last month of a heart attack. His most likely successor had left in September to join a rival company. 'I'm just filling in until they can find someone with the right qualifications. They need a good manager, but they must find someone who knows the London market upside down.'

He asked me what I was working on. I had a few routine cases going, but nothing interesting, so I told him about my aunt Rosa and the counterfeit securities. 'I'd love to see her put away for securities fraud, but I'm afraid she's just an innocent bystander.' On second thought, no one who ever met Rosa would think of her as innocent. Crime-free might be a better adjective.

I declined a second scotch, and we put on our coats to go into the winter night. A strong wind was blowing across the lake, driving away the clouds but dropping the temperature down to the teens. We held hands and half ran into its face to an Italian restaurant four blocks away on Seneca.

Despite its location in the convention district, the Caffè Firenze had a cheerful unpretentious interior. 'I didn't know you were part Italian when I made the reservation, or I might have hesitated,' Ferrant said as we turned our coats over to a plump young girl. 'Do you know this place? Is the food authentic?'

'I've never heard of it, but I don't eat in this part of town too often. As long as they make their own pasta we should be fine.'

I followed the *maître d'* to a booth against the far wall. Firenze avoided the red-checked cloth and Chianti bottles so many Italian restaurants display in Chicago. The polished wood table had linen placemats on it and a flower stuck in a Tuscan pottery vase.

We ordered a bottle of Ruffino and some *pasticcini di spinaci*, enchanting the waiter by speaking Italian. It turned out Ferrant

536

had visited the country numerous times and spoke Italian passably well. He asked if I'd ever seen my mother's family there.

I shook my head. 'My mother's from Florence, but her family was half Jewish – her mother came from a family of scholars in Pitigliano. They scattered widely at the outbreak of the war – my mother came here, her brother went to Africa, and the cousins went every which way. My grandmother died during the war. Gabriella went back once in 1955 to see her father, but it was depressing. He was the only member of her immediate family left in Florence and she said he couldn't deal with the war or the changes it brought; he kept pretending it was 1936 and the family still together. I think he's still alive but –' I made a gesture of distaste. 'My dad wrote him when my mother died and we got back a very unsettling letter inviting us to hear her sing. I've never felt like dealing with him.'

'Was your mother a singer, then?'

'She'd trained as one. She'd hoped to sing opera. Then, when she had to flee the country, she couldn't afford to continue her lessons. She taught instead. She taught me. She hoped I'd pick it up and have her career for her. But I don't have a big enough voice. And I don't really like opera all that well.'

Ferrant said apologetically that he always had tickets for the Royal Opera and enjoyed it thoroughly.

I laughed. 'I enjoy the staging and the sheer – virtuosity, I guess it is – of putting an opera together. It's very strenuous work, you know. But the singing is too violent. I prefer *Lieder*. My mother always saved enough money from the music lessons to take the two of us to a couple of Lyric Opera performances every fall. Then in the summer my dad would take me to see the Cubs four or five times. The Lyric Opera is better than the Chicago Cubs, but I have to admit I've always gotten more pleasure from baseball.'

We ordered dinner – fried artichoke and *pollo in galantina* for me, veal kidneys for Ferrant. The talk moved from baseball to cricket, which Ferrant played, to his own childhood in Highgate, and finally to his career in Scupperfield, Plouder.

As I was finishing my second cup of espresso, he asked me idly if I followed the stock market at all.

I shook my head. 'I don't have anything to invest. Why?'

He shrugged. 'I've only been here a week, but I noticed in *The Wall Street Journal* that Ajax's volume seems quite heavy compared to the other stock-insurance companies, and the price seems to be going up.'

'Great. Looks like your firm picked a winner.'

He signaled for the check. 'We're not doing anything spectacular in the way of earnings. Not buying any companies or selling off any properties. What else makes a share price go up?'

'Sometimes institutional investors take a whimsical fancy to a stock. Insurance companies fared better during the last depression or recession or whatever than most businesses. Ajax is one of the biggest – maybe the funds and the other big investors are just playing it safe . . . If you want, I could give you the name of a broker I know; she might have some other information.'

'Maybe so.'

We collected our coats and headed back into the wind. It was blowing harder, but fried artichokes and half a bottle of wine made it seem less penetrating. Ferrant invited me up for a brandy.

He turned the lamp by the bar on a low switch. We could see the bottles but the garish furniture was mercifully muted. I stood at the window looking down at the lake. Ice reflected the streetlights on Lake Shore Drive. By squinting I could make out the promontories farther south, which held Navy Pier and McCormick Place. In the clear winter air the South Works twelve miles away glowed red. I used to live there in an ill-built wooden row house, made distinctive by my mother's artistry.

Ferrant put his left arm around me and handed me a snifter of Martell with the right. I leaned back against him, then turned and put both arms around him, carefully holding the snifter away from his sweater. It felt like cashmere and might not take kindly to brandy. He was thin but wiry, not just an opera-loving beanpole. He slid his hand under my silk top and stroked my back, then began fumbling for the bra strap.

'It opens in front.' I was having a hard time maintaining my balance and the snifter at the same time, so I put the brandy down on the window ledge behind me. Ferrant had found the front hook. I fumbled with the buttons on his pleated trousers. Making love standing up is not as easy as they make it look in the movies. We slid down onto the thick orange carpet together.

5
FRUSTRATION

We finished the brandy and the rest of the night in a king-sized bed with a blond Scandinavian headboard. When we woke up well after eight the next morning, Ferrant and I smiled at each other with sleepy pleasure. He looked fresh and vulnerable with his dark hair hanging down in his dark blue eyes; I put an arm around him and kissed him.

He kissed me back enthusiastically, then sat up. 'America is a country of terrible contrasts. They give you these wonderful outsize beds, which I'd give a month's pay for back home, then they expect you to hop out of them in the middle of the night to be at work. In London I wouldn't dream of being in the City before nine-thirty at the earliest, but here my whole staff has already been at the office for half an hour. I'd better get going.'

I lay back in bed and watched him go through the male dressing ritual, which ended when he had encased his neck meekly in a gray-and-burgundy choker. He tossed me a blue paisley robe and I got up to drink a cup of coffee with him, pleased with my foresight in changing my meeting with Hatfield to the afternoon.

After Ferrant left, muttering curses against the American work ethic, I phoned my answering service. My cousin Albert had called three times, once late last night and twice this morning. The second time he'd left his office number. My pleasure in the morning began to evaporate. I put on last night's clothes, frowning at myself in the wide mirrors that served as closet doors. An outfit that looks sexy at night tends to appear tawdry in the morning. I was going to have to change for my meeting with Hatfield; I might as well go home and do it before calling Albert.

I paid dearly for parking the Omega at the Hancock Building for fourteen hours. That did nothing to cheer me up, and I earned a whistle and a yell from the traffic cop at Oak Street for swinging around the turning traffic onto the Lake Shore Drive underpass. I sobered up then. My father had drummed into my head at an early age the stupidity of venting anger with a moving car. He was a policeman and had taken guns and cars very seriously – he spent too much time with the wreckage of those who used such lethal weapons in anger.

I stopped for a breakfast falafel sandwich at a storefront Lebanese restaurant at Halsted and Wrightwood and ate it at the red lights the rest of the way up Halsted. The decimation of Lebanon was showing up in Chicago as a series of restaurants and little shops, just as the destruction of Vietnam had been visible here a decade earlier. If you never read the news but ate out a lot you should be able to tell who was getting beaten up around the world.

From North Avenue to Fullerton, Halsted is part of the recently renovated North Side, where young professionals pay two hundred fifty thousand or more for chic brick townhouses. Four blocks farther north, at Diversey, the rich have not yet stuck out rehabilitation tentacles. Most of the buildings, like mine, are comfortably run-down. One advantage is the cheap rents; the other is space to park on the street.

I stopped the Omega in front of my building and went inside to change back into the navy walking suit for my meeting with Hatfield. By then I had delayed calling Albert long enough. I took a cup of coffee into the living room and sat in the overstuffed armchair while I phoned. I studied my toes through my nylons. Maybe I'd paint the nails red. I can't stand nail polish on my fingers, but it might be sexy on my toes.

A woman answered Albert's work number. His secret lover, I thought: Rosa assumes she's his secretary, but he secretly buys her perfume and zabaglione. I asked for Albert; she said in a nasal, uneducated voice that 'Mr Vignelli' was in conference and would I leave a message.

'This is V. I. Warshawski,' I said. 'He wants to talk to me. Tell him this is the only time I'll be available today.'

She put me on hold. I drank coffee and started an article in *Fortune* on chicanery at CitiCorp. I was delighted. I've never forgiven them for taking two years to answer a billing complaint. I was just getting into illegal currency manipulation when Albert came on the line, sounding more petulant than usual.

'Where have *you* been?'

I raised my eyebrows at the mouthpiece. 'At an all-night sex and dope orgy. The sex was terrible but the coke was really great. Want to come next time?'

'I might have known you'd just laugh instead of taking Mama's problems seriously.'

'I'm not laughing, Albert. If you read the paper, you know how hard it is to get good coke these days. But tell me, has Rosa's problem taken a turn for the worse? Just to show you I mean well, I won't even charge you for my time waiting on hold.'

I could visualize his fat round face puckered up in a full-scale pout as he breathed heavily into my ear. At last he said angrily, 'You went to St Albert's Priory yesterday, didn't you?'

I assented.

'What did you find out?'

'That this is going to be incredibly tough to sort out. Our best hope is that the securities had already been faked before the priory got them. I'm meeting with the FBI this afternoon and I'm going to see if they're looking into that.'

'Well, Mama has changed her mind. She doesn't want you to investigate this after all.'

I sat frozen for a few seconds while anger came to a focus inside my head. 'What the hell do you mean, Albert? I'm not a vacuum cleaner that you switch on and off at will. You don't start me on an investigation, then call up two days later to say you've changed your mind.'

I could hear paper rustling in the background, then Albert said smugly, 'Your contract doesn't say that. It just says "Termination of the case may be requested by either party, whether the requested results are obtained or not. Regardless of the state of the investigation, and regardless of whether either party disagrees with the results, the fee and expenses incurred to the time of termination shall be paid." If you send me a bill, Victoria, I'll pay promptly.'

I could smell my brain burning. 'Albert. When Rosa called me on Sunday she made it sound as though her suicide would be on my head if I didn't come out and help her. What's happened since then? She find a detective she likes better? Or did Carroll call and promise her her job back if she'd get me out of the investigation?'

He said aloofly, 'She told me last night she felt she was acting in a very unchristian way by getting so worried about this. She knows her name will be cleared; if it's not, she'll bear it like a Christian.'

'How noble,' I said sarcastically. 'Rosa as a bitter martyr is a pose I know well. But the woman of sorrows is a new departure.'

'Really, Victoria. You're acting like an ambulance chaser. Just send me a bill.'

At least I had the dubious satisfaction of hanging up first. I sat fuming, cursing Rosa in Italian, then in English. Just like her to jack me around! Get me out to Melrose Park by screaming about Gabriella and my duty to my dead mother, if not to my live aunt, send me off on a wild-goose chase, then call the whole thing off. I was strongly tempted to phone her and tell her once and for all exactly what I thought of her, omitting no detail, however slight. I even looked her number up in my address book and started dialing before I realized the futility of such an act. Rosa was seventy-five. She was not going to change. If I couldn't accept that, then I was doomed to be a victim of her manipulation forever.

I sat for a while with *Fortune* open in my lap, staring across the room at the gray day outside. Last night's strong wind had blown clouds in front of it across the lake. What was Rosa's real reason for wanting the investigation to stop? She was cold, angry, vindictive –

a dozen disagreeable adjectives. But not a schemer. She wouldn't call a hated niece after a ten-year hiatus just to run me through hoops.

I looked up St Albert's Priory in the phone book and called Carroll. The call went through a switchboard. I could see the ascetic young man at the reception desk reluctantly putting down his Charles Williams to answer the phone on the sixth ring, picking up the book again before switching the call through. I waited several minutes for the prior. At last Carroll's educated, gentle voice came on the line.

'This is V. I. Warshawski, Father Carroll.'

He apologized for keeping me waiting; he'd been going over the household accounts with the head cook and the receptionist had paged the kitchen last.

'No problem,' I said. 'I wondered if you'd spoken with my aunt since I saw you yesterday.'

'With Mrs Vignelli? No. Why?'

'She's decided suddenly that she doesn't want any investigation into the counterfeit securities, at least not on her behalf. She seems to think that worrying about them is very unchristian. I wondered if someone at the priory had been counseling her.'

'Unchristian? What a curious idea. I don't know; I suppose it would be if she got absorbed by this problem to the exclusion of other more fundamental matters. But it's very human to worry about a fraud that might harm your reputation. And if you think of being Christian as a way to be more fully human, it would be a mistake to make someone feel guilty for having natural human feelings.'

I blinked a few times. 'So you didn't tell my aunt to drop the investigation?'

He gave a soft laugh. 'You didn't want me to build a watch; you just wanted the time. No, I haven't talked to your aunt. But it sounds as though I should.'

'And did anyone else at the priory? Talk to her, I mean.'

Not as far as he knew, but he'd ask around and get back to me. He wanted to know if I had learned anything useful yet. I told him

544

I'd be talking to Hatfield that afternoon, and we hung up with mutual promises to stay in touch.

I puttered around the apartment, hanging up clothes and putting a week's accumulation of newspapers into a stack on the back porch where my landlord's grandson would collect them for recycling. I made myself a salad with cubes of cheddar cheese in it and ate it while flicking aimlessly through yesterday's *Wall Street Journal*. At twelve-thirty I went down for the mail.

When you thought about it seriously, Rosa was an old lady. She probably had imagined she could make her problem disappear by scowling at it, the way she'd made all her problems, including her husband, Carl, disappear. She thought if she called me and ordered me to take care of it, it would go away. When the reality came a little closer after she'd talked with me, she decided it just wasn't worth the energy it would take to fight it. My problem was that I was so wound up in all the old enmities that I suspected everything she did was motivated by hatred and a need for revenge.

Ferrant called at one, partly for some light chat, and partly because of questions about Ajax's stock. 'One of my responsibilities seems to be our investment division. So I got a call today from a chap named Barrett in New York. He called himself the Ajax specialist at the New York Stock Exchange. I know reinsurance, not the US stock market, or even the London stock market, so I had some trouble keeping up with him. But you remember I told you last night our stock seemed really active? Barrett called to tell me that. Called to let me know he was getting a lot of orders from a small group of Chicago brokers who had never traded in Ajax before. Nothing wrong with them, you understand, but he thought I should know about it.'

'And?'

'Now I know about it. But I'm not sure what, if anything, I should do. So I'd like to meet that friend you mentioned – the one who's the broker.'

Agnes Paciorek and I had met at the University of Chicago when I was in law school and she was a math whiz turned MBA. We actually met at sessions of University Women United. She was a maverick in the gray-tailored world of MBAs and we'd remained good friends.

I gave Roger her number. After hanging up I looked up Ajax in The *Wall Street Journal*. Their range for the year went from 281¼ to 55½ and they were currently trading at their high. Aetna and Cigna, the two largest stock-insurance carriers, had similar bottom prices, but their highs were about ten points below Ajax. Yesterday they'd each had a volume of about three hundred thousand, compared to Ajax's which was almost a million. Interesting.

I thought about calling Agnes myself, but it was getting close to time for me to leave to meet Hatfield. I wrapped a mohair scarf around my neck, pulled on some driving gloves, and went back out into the wind. Two o'clock is a good time to drive into the Loop. The traffic is light. I made it to the Federal Building on Dearborn and Adams in good time, left the Omega in a self-park garage across the street and walked in under the orange legs of the three-story Calder designed for Chicago's Federal Building. We pride ourselves in Chicago on our outdoor sculptures by famous artists. My favorite is the bronze wind chimes in front of the Standard Oil Building, but I have a secret fondness for Chagall's mosaics in front of the First National Bank. My artist friends tell me they are banal.

It was exactly two-thirty when I reached the FBI offices on the eighteenth floor. The receptionist phoned my name in to Hatfield, but he had to keep me waiting ten minutes just to impress me with how heavily Chicago's crime rested on his shoulders. I busied myself with a report for a client whose brother-in-law had been pilfering supplies, apparently out of bitterness from some long-standing family feud. When Hatfield finally stuck his head around the corner from the hall, I affected not to hear him until the second time he called my name. I looked up then and smiled and said I would be just a minute and carefully finished writing a sentence.

'Hello, Derek,' I said. 'How's crime?'

For some reason this jolly greeting always makes him grimace, which is probably why I always use it. His face has the bland handsomeness required by the FBI. He's around six feet tall with a square build. I could see him doing a hundred sit-ups and push-ups every morning with methodical uncomplaining discipline, always turning down the second martini, picking up only college girls to make sure someone with a modicum of brains would breathe in his ear how smart and how brave he was. He was dressed today in a gray-plaid suit – muted gray on slightly paler gray with the discreetest of blue stripes woven in – a white shirt whose starch could probably hold up my brassiere for a week, and a blue tie.

'I don't have a lot of time, Warshawski.' He shot back a starched cuff and looked at his watch. Probably a Rolex.

'I'm flattered, then, that you wanted to make some of it available to me.' I followed him down the hall to an office in the southwestern corner. Hatfield was head of white-collar crime for the Chicago Region, obviously a substantial position judging by the furniture – all wood veneer – and the location.

'That's a nice view of the metropolitan lockup,' I said, looking out at the triangular building. 'It must be a great inspiration for you.'

'We don't send anyone there.'

'Not even for overnight holding? What about Joey Lombardo and Allen Dorfmann? I thought that's where they were staying while they were on trial.'

'Could you cut it out? I don't know anything about Dorfmann or Lombardo. I want to talk to you about the securities at St Albert's.'

'Great.' I sat down in an uncomfortable chair covered in tan Naugahyde and put a look of bright interest on my face. 'One of the things that occurred to me yesterday was that the certificates might have been forged before they were passed on to St Albert's. What do you know about the donor and his executors? Also, it is possible some ex-Dominican with a grudge could have been behind it. Do you have a trail on people who left the order in the last ten years?'

'I'm not interested in discussing the case with you, Warshawski. We're very well able to think of leads and follow them up. We have an excellent record here in the bureau. This forgery is a federal offense and I must request you to back out of it.'

I leaned forward in my chair. 'Derek, I'm not only willing but eager for you to solve this crime. It will take a cast of thousands to sort it out. You have that. I don't. I'm just here to make sure that a seventy-five-year-old woman doesn't get crushed by the crowd. And I'd like to know what you've turned up on the possibilities I just mentioned to you.'

'We're following all leads.'

We argued it back and forth for several more minutes, but he was adamant and I left empty-handed. I stopped in the plaza at a pay phone next to the praying mantis and dialed the *Herald-Star*. Murray Ryerson, their chief crime reporter, was in. He and I have been friends, sometimes lovers, and easy rivals on the crime scene for years.

'Hi, Murray. It's V. I. Is three o'clock too early for a drink?'

'That's no question for the crime desk. I'll connect you with our etiquette specialist.' He paused. 'a.m. or p.m.?'

'Now, wiseass. I'll buy.'

'Gosh, Vic, you must be desperate. Can't do it now, but how about meeting at the Golden Glow in an hour?'

I agreed and hung up. The Golden Glow is my favorite bar in Chicago; I introduced Murray to it a number of years ago. It's tucked away in the DuSable Building, an 1890s skyscraper on Federal, and has the original mahogany bar that Cyrus McCormick and Judge Gary probably used to lean over.

I went to my office to check mail and messages and at four walked back up the street to the bar. Sal, the magnificent black bartender who could teach the Chicago police a thing or two about crowd control, greeted me with a smile and a majestic wave. She wore her hair in an Afro today and had on gold hoop earrings that hung to her shoulder. A shiny blue evening gown showed her splendid cleavage and five-foot-eleven frame to advantage. She brought a double Black Label to my corner booth and chatted for a few minutes before getting back to the swelling group of early commuters.

Murray came in a few minutes later, his red hair more disheveled than usual from the January wind. He had on a sheepskin coat and western boots: the urban cowboy. I said as much by way of greeting

548

while a waitress took his order for beer; Sal only looks after her regular customers personally.

We talked about the poor showing the Black Hawks were making, and about the Greylord trial, and whether Mayor Washington would ever subdue Eddie Vrdolyak. 'If Washington didn't have Vrdolyak he'd have to invent him,' Murray said. 'He's the perfect excuse for Washington not being able to accomplish anything.'

The waitress came over. I declined a refill and asked for a glass of water.

Murray ordered a second Beck's. 'So what gives, V. I.? I won't say it always spells trouble when you call up out of the blue, but it usually means I end up being used.'

'Murray, I bet you a week of my pay that you've gotten more stories out of me than I have gotten clients out of you.'

'A week of your pay wouldn't keep me in beer. What's up?'

'Did you pick up a story last week about some forged securities in Melrose Park? Out in a Dominican priory there?'

'Dominican priory?' Murray echoed. 'Since when have you started hanging around churches?'

'It's a family obligation,' I said with dignity. 'You may not know it, but I'm half Italian, and we Italians stick together, through thick and thin. You know, the secret romance of the Mafia and all that. When one member of the family is in trouble, the others rally around.'

Murray wasn't impressed. 'You going to knock off somebody in the priory for the sake of your family honor?'

'No, but I might take out Derek Hatfield in the cause.'

Murray supported me enthusiastically. Hatfield was as uncooperative with the press as he was with private investigators.

Murray had missed the story of the faked certificates.

'Maybe it wasn't on the wires. The feds can be pretty secretive about these things – especially Derek. Think this prior would make a good interview? Maybe I'll send out one of my babies to talk to him.'

I suggested he send someone to interview Rosa, and gave him the list of possibilities I'd offered Hatfield. Murray would work

549

those into the story. He'd probably get someone to dig up the name of the original donor and get some public exposure on his heirs. That would force Hatfield to do something – either eliminate them as being involved or publicly announce how old the dud certificates were. 'Them that eat cakes that the Parsee man bakes make dreadful mistakes,' I muttered to myself.

'What was that?' Murray said sharply. 'Are you setting me up to do your dirty work for you, Warshawski?'

I gave him a look that I hoped implied limpid innocence. 'Murray! How you talk. I just want to make sure the FBI doesn't railroad my poor frail old aunt.' I signaled to Sal that we were ready to leave; she runs a tab that she sends me once a month, the only bill I ever pay on time.

Murray and I moved up north for seafood at the Red Tide. For eight dollars you can get a terrific whole Dungeness crab, which you eat sitting at a bar in a dark basement about half the size of my living room. Afterward I dropped Murray at the Fullerton el stop and went on home alone. I'm past the age where bed-hopping has much appeal.

6

UNCLE STEFAN'S PROFESSION

Snow was falling the next morning as I made my five-mile run to Belmont Harbor and back. The ice-filled water was perfectly still. Across the breakwater I could see the lake motionless, too. Not peaceful, but sullenly quiet, its angry gods held tightly by bands of cold.

A Salvation Army volunteer was stamping his feet and calling cheery greetings to commuters at the corner of Belmont and Sheridan. He gave me a smiling 'God bless you' as I jogged past. Must be nice to have everything so simple and peaceful. What would he do with an Aunt Rosa? Was there any smile broad enough to make her smile back?

I stopped at a little bakery on Broadway for a cup of cappuccino and a croissant. As I ate at one of the spindly legged tables, I pondered my next actions. I'd met with Hatfield yesterday more out of bravado than anything else – it brought me some sort of perverse pleasure to irritate his well-pressed Brooks Brothers façade. But he wasn't going to do anything for me. I didn't have the resources to pry into the Dominicans. Anyway, even if Murray Ryerson turned something up, what would I do about it if Rosa didn't want me investigating? Wasn't my obligation finished with her abrupt command to stop?

I realized that I was carrying on this internal monologue as an argument with Gabriella, who didn't seem pleased with me for bugging out so early. 'Goddamn it, Gabriella,' I swore silently. 'Why did you make me give you that crazy promise? She hated you. Why do I have to do anything for her?'

If my mother were alive she would shrivel me on the spot for swearing at her. And then turn fierce intelligent eyes on me: so Rosa fired you? Did you go to work only because she hired you?

I slowly finished my cappuccino and went back out into a minor blizzard. Strictly speaking, Rosa had not fired me. Albert had called to say she didn't want me on the job any longer. But was that Albert or Rosa speaking? I should at least get that much clear before deciding what else to do. Which meant another trip to Melrose Park. Not today – the roads would be impossible with the snow: traffic creeping, people falling into ditches. But tomorrow would be Saturday. Even if the weather continued bad there wouldn't be much traffic.

At home I peeled off layers of shirts and leggings and soaked in a hot tub for a while. Being self-employed, I can hold my review of operations and management anywhere. This means time spent thinking in the bath is time spent working. Unfortunately, my accountant doesn't agree that this makes my water bill and bath salts tax deductible.

My theory of detection resembles Julia Child's approach to cooking: grab a lot of ingredients from the shelves, put them in a pot and stir, and see what happens. I'd stirred at the priory, and at the FBI. Maybe it was time to let things simmer a bit and see if the smell of cooking gave me any new ideas.

I put on a wool crêpe-de-Chine pantsuit with a high-necked red-striped blouse and low-heeled black boots. That should be warm enough to walk in if I got stuck in the snow someplace. Wrapping my big mohair scarf around my head and neck, I went back into the storm, adding the Omega to the queue of slowly moving, sliding cars trying to get onto Lake Shore Drive at Belmont.

I crept downtown, barely able to see the cars immediately next to me, and slithered off at Jackson. Leaving the Omega next to a snowdrift behind the Art Institute, I trudged the six blocks to the Pulteney Building, which looked worse than usual in the winter weather. Tenants had tracked snow and mud into the lobby. Tom Czarnik, the angry old man who calls himself the building superintendent, refuses to mop the floor on stormy mornings. His theory is that it will just get nasty again at lunch, so why bother? I should applaud a man whose housekeeping views coincide so closely with mine, but I cursed him under my breath as my boots slid in the lobby slush. The elevator wasn't working today either, so I stomped up four flights of stairs to my office.

After turning on the lights and picking up the mail from the floor, I phoned Agnes Paciorek at her broker's office. On hold while she sold a million shares of AT&T, I looked through bills and pleas for charity. Nothing that wouldn't wait until next month. At last her brisk deep voice came on the line.

'Agnes. It's V. I. Warshawski.'

We exchanged pleasantries for a few minutes, then I explained who Roger Ferrant was and said I'd given him her number.

'I know. He called yesterday afternoon. We're meeting for lunch at the Mercantile Club. Are you downtown? Want to join us?'

'Sure. Great. You find anything unusual?'

'Depends on your definition. Brokers don't think buying and selling stock is unusual but you might. I've got to run. See you at one.'

The Mercantile Club sits on top of the old Bletchley Iron Building down in the financial district. It's a businessmen's club, which reluctantly opened its doors to women when Mrs Gray became president of the University of Chicago, since most of the trustees' meetings were held there. Having admitted one woman they found others sneaking through in her wake. The food is excellent and the service impeccable, although some of the old waiters refuse to work tables with women guests.

Ferrant was already sitting by the fire in the reading room where the *maître d'* sent me to wait for Agnes. He looked elegant in navy-blue tailoring and stood up with a warm smile when he saw me come into the room.

'Agnes invited me to gate-crash; I hope you don't object.'

'By no means. You look very smart today. How are your forgeries coming?'

I told him about my useless interview with Hatfield. 'And the Dominicans don't know anything, either. At least not about forgery. I need to start at the other end – who could have created them to begin with?'

Agnes came up behind me. 'Created what?' She turned to Ferrant and introduced herself, a short, compact dynamo in a brown-plaid suit whose perfect stitching probably required an eight-hundred-dollar investment. Half a day's work for Agnes.

She shepherded us into the dining room where the *maître d'* greeted her by name and seated us by a window. We looked down at the South Branch of the Chicago River and ordered drinks. I seldom drink whiskey in the middle of the day and asked for oloroso sherry. Ferrant ordered a beer, while Agnes had Perrier with lime – the exchanges didn't close for almost two hours and she believes sober brokers trade better.

Once we were settled she repeated her initial question. I told her about the forgery. 'As far as I know, the Fort Dearborn Trust discovered it because the serial numbers hadn't been issued yet. The FBI is being stuffy and close-mouthed, but I know the forgery was pretty high quality – good enough to pass a superficial test by the auditors, anyway. I'd like to talk to someone who knows something about forging – try to find out who'd have the skill to create that good a product.'

Agnes cocked a thick eyebrow. 'Are you asking me? I just sell 'em; I don't print 'em. Roger's problem is the type of thing I'm equipped to handle. Maybe.' She turned to Ferrant. 'Why don't you tell me what you know at this point?'

He shrugged thin shoulders. 'I told you on the phone about the call from our specialist in New York, Andy Barrett. Maybe you can start by telling me what a specialist is. He doesn't work for Ajax, I take it.'

'No. Specialists are members of the New York Stock Exchange – but they're not brokers for the public. Usually they're members of a firm who get a franchise from the Exchange to be specialists – people who manage buy-and-sell orders so business keeps flowing. Barrett makes markets in your stock. Someone wants to sell a thousand shares of Ajax. They call me. I don't go down to the floor of the Chicago Exchange waving 'em around until a buyer happens

554

along – I phone our broker in New York and he goes to Barrett's post on the floor. Barrett buys the shares and makes a match with someone who's looking for a thousand shares. If too many people are unloading Ajax at once and no one wants to buy it, he buys on his own account – he's got an ethical obligation to make markets. Once in a great while, if the market gets completely haywire, he'll ask the Exchange to halt trading in the stock until things shake out.'

She paused to give us time to order, Dover sole for me, rare steaks for her and Roger. She lit a cigarette and began punctuating her comments with stabs of smoke.

'From what I gather, something of the opposite kind has been going on with Ajax the last few weeks. There's been a tremendous amount of buying. About seven times the normal volume, enough that the price is starting to go up. Not a lot – insurance companies aren't glamor investments, so you can have heavy action without too much notice being taken. Did Barrett give you the names of the brokers placing the orders?'

'Yes. They didn't mean anything to me. He's sending a list in the mail . . . I wondered, if it wouldn't be too great an imposition, Miss Paciorek, whether you'd look at the names when I get them. See if they tell you anything. Also, what should I do?'

To my annoyance, Agnes lit a second cigarette. 'No, no imposition. And please call me Agnes. Miss Paciorek sounds too much like the North Shore . . . I guess what we're assuming, to put the evil thought into blunt words, is that someone may be trying a covert takeover bid. If that's true, they can't have got too far – anyone with five percent or more of the stock has to file with the S E C and explain what's he doing with it. Or she.' She grinned at me.

'How much stock would someone need to take over Ajax?' I asked. The food arrived, and Agnes mercifully stubbed out her cigarette.

'Depends. Who besides your firm owns sizable chunks?'

Ferrant shook his head. 'I don't really know. Gordon Firth, the chairman. Some of the directors. We own three percent and

Edelweiss, the Swiss reinsurers, holds four percent. I think they're the largest owners. Firth maybe owns two. Some of the other directors may have one or two percent.'

'So your present management owns around fifteen percent. Someone could carry a lot of weight with sixteen percent. Not guaranteed, but that would be a good place to start, especially if your management wasn't aware it was happening.'

I did some mental arithmetic. Fifty million shares outstanding. Sixteen percent would be eight million. 'You'd need about five hundred million for a takeover, then.'

She thought for a minute. 'That's about right. But keep in mind that you don't need to come up with that much capital. Once you've bought a large block you can leverage the rest – put your existing shares up as collateral for a loan to buy more shares. Then you leverage those and keep going. Before you know it, you've bought yourself a company. That's oversimplified, of course, but that's the basic idea.'

We ate in silence for a minute; then Ferrant said, 'What can I do to find out for sure?'

Agnes pursed her square face as she thought about it. 'You could call the SEC and ask for a formal investigation. Then you'd be sure of getting the names of the people who are really doing the buying. That's an extreme step though. Once they're called in they're going to scrutinize every transaction and every broker. You'd want to talk to your board before you did that – some of your directors might not relish having all their stock transactions revealed to the piercing light of day.'

'Well, short of that?'

'Every brokerage firm has what we call a compliance officer. Once you get the list of firms from Barrett, you can try calling them and find out on whose behalf they're trading. There's no reason for them to tell you, though – and nothing illegal about trying to buy a company.'

The waiters hovered around our table. Dessert? Coffee? Ferrant absentmindedly selected a piece of apple pie. 'Do you think they'd talk to you, Miss – Agnes? The compliance officers, I mean. As I told Vic, I'm way out of depth with this stock-market stuff. Even if you coached me in what to ask, I wouldn't know if the answers I was getting were right.'

Agnes put three lumps of sugar in her coffee and stirred vigorously. 'It would be unusual. Let me see the list of brokers before I let you know one way or another. What you could do is call Barrett and ask him to send you a list of the names the shares were registered in when he sold them. If I know anyone really well – either the brokers or the customers – I could probably call them.'

She looked at her watch. 'I've got to get back to the office.' She signaled for a waiter and signed the bill. 'You two stay though.'

Ferrant shook his head. 'I'd better call London. It's after eight there – my managing director should be home.'

I left with them. The snow had stopped. The sky was clear and the temperature falling. One of the bank thermometers showed eleven degrees. I walked with Roger as far as Ajax. As we said goodbye he invited me to go to a movie with him Saturday night. I accepted, then went on down Wabash to my office to finish the report on pilfered supplies.

During the slow drive home that night I pondered how to find someone who knew about forging securities. Forgers were engravers gone wrong. And I did know one engraver. At least I knew someone who knew an engraver.

Dr Charlotte Herschel, Lotty to me, had been born in Vienna, grew up in London where she ultimately received her doctor of medicine degree from London University – and lived about a mile from me on Sheffield Avenue. Her father's brother Stefan, an engraver, had immigrated to Chicago in the twenties. When Lotty decided to come to the States in 1959, she picked Chicago partly because her uncle Stefan lived here. I had never met him – she saw little of him, just saying it made her feel more rooted to have a relative in the area.

My friendship with Lotty goes back a long way, to my student days at the University of Chicago when she was one of the physicians working with an abortion underground I was involved in. She knew Agnes Paciorek from that time, too.

557

I stopped at a Treasure Island on Broadway for groceries and wine. It was six-thirty when I got home and phoned Lotty. She had just come in herself from a long day at the clinic she runs on Sheffield near her apartment. She greeted my offer of dinner enthusiastically and said she would be over after a hot bath.

I cleaned up the worst ravages in my living room and kitchen. Lotty never criticizes my housekeeping, but she is scrupulously tidy herself and it didn't seem fair to drag her out for a brain-picking session on such a cold night, then have her spend it in squalor.

Chicken, garlic, mushrooms, and onions sautéed in olive oil, then flamed with brandy made an easy attractive stew. A cup of Ruffino finished the dish. By the time I had water hot for *fettucine*, the doorbell rang.

Lotty came up the stairs briskly and greeted me with a hug. 'A lifesaver that you called, my dear. It was a long, very depressing day: a child dead of meningitis because the mother would not bring her in. She hung an amulet around her neck and thought it would bring down a fever of forty-one degrees. There are three sisters; we put them in St Vincent's for observation, but my God!'

I held her for a minute before we went into the apartment, asking if she wanted a drink. Lotty reminded me that alcohol is poison. For extreme situations she believes brandy is permissible, but she did not consider today's woes extreme. I poured myself a glass of Ruffino and put on water for her coffee.

We ate by candlelight in the dining room while Lotty unburdened herself. By the time we had finished the salad, she felt more relaxed and asked me what I was working on.

I told her about Rosa and the Dominicans and Albert's phoning me to tell me the whole thing was off.

The candlelight was reflected in her black eyes as she narrowed them at me. 'And what are you trying to prove by continuing?'

'It was Albert who phoned. Rosa may not agree,' I said defensively.

'Yes. Your aunt dislikes you. She's decided – for whatever reason – to discontinue the effort to protect herself. So what are you doing? Proving that you are tougher, or smarter, or just plain better than she is?'

I thought it over. Lotty is sometimes about as pleasant as a can opener, but she braces me. I know myself better when I talk to Lotty.

'You know, I don't spend a lot of time thinking about Rosa. It's not as though she's an obsession; she doesn't control my head that much. But I feel very protective of my mother. Rosa hurt her and that makes me angry. If I can show Rosa she was wrong to stop the investigation, that I can solve this problem despite failure by the FBI and the SEC, I'll have proof that she was wrong about everything. And she'll have to believe it.' I laughed and finished my glass of wine. 'She won't, of course. My rational self knows that. But my feeling self thinks otherwise.'

Lotty nodded. 'Perfectly logical. Does your rational self have any way of solving this problem?'

'There are lots of things the FBI can do that I can't because they have so much manpower. But one thing I could look into is who actually did the forgeries. Let Derek concentrate on who planted them and which ex-Dominicans are living in luxury.

'I don't know any forgers. But it occurred to me that a forger is really a species of engraver. And I wondered about your uncle Stefan.'

Lotty had been watching me with an expression of shrewd amusement. Now her face changed suddenly. Her mouth set and her black eyes narrowed. 'Is this an inspired guess? Or have you spent your spare time investigating me?'

I looked at her in bewilderment.

'You wondered why you never met my uncle Stefan? Although he is my only relative living in Chicago?'

'No,' I said doggedly. 'I never thought about it for a minute. You've never met my aunt Rosa. Even if she weren't a virago, you'd probably never have met her – friends seldom have much in common with relatives.'

She continued to stare searchingly at me. I felt very hurt but could think of nothing to say that would bridge the gulf of Lotty's suspicious silence. The last time I had felt this way was the night I realized the man I had married and thought I loved was as foreign to me as Yasser Arafat. Could a friendship evaporate in the same mist as a marriage?

My throat felt tight, but I forced myself to talk. 'Lotty. You've known me for close to twenty years and I've never done anything behind your back. If you think I've started now . . .' That sentence wasn't going in the right direction. 'There's something you don't want me to know about your uncle. You don't have to tell me. Carry it to the grave with you. But don't act as though everything you know about me suddenly has no foundation.' A light bulb went on over my head. 'Oh, no. Don't tell me your uncle really is a forger?'

The set look held in Lotty's face for a few seconds, then cracked into a wry smile. 'You are right, Vic. About my uncle. And about you and me. I'm truly sorry, my dear. I won't try to make excuses – there are none. But Stefan . . . When the war ended, I found there was left of my family only my brother and the distant cousins who had taken us in during the war. Hugo – my brother – and I spent what time and money we had searching for relatives. And we found Papa's brother Stefan. When Hugo decided to move to Montreal, I came to Chicago – I had an opportunity for a surgical residency at Northwestern, too good a chance to turn down.' She made a throwaway gesture with her left hand. 'So I set out to find Uncle Stefan. And discovered him in a federal prison at Fort Leavenworth. Currency was his specialty, although he had a social conscience: he was also forging passports for sale to the many Europeans trying to come to America at the time.'

She grinned at me, the old Lotty grin. I leaned across the table and squeezed her hand. She returned the pressure, but went on talking. Detectives and doctors both know the value of talking. 'I went to see him. He's likable. Like my father, but without the moral foundation. And I let him stay with me for six months when he was released – 1959 that was; I was his only family, too.

'He got a job, doing custom work for a jeweler – after all, he wasn't a robber, so they weren't afraid he'd lift the sterling. As far as I know, he's never stepped over the edge again. But naturally I haven't asked.'

'Naturally not. Well, I will try to find a different engraver.'

Lotty smiled again. 'Oh, no. Why not call him? He's eighty-two, but he still has all his wits and some besides. He might be the one person who could help you.'

She would talk to him the next day and arrange a time when I could have tea with him. We had coffee and pears in the living room and played Scrabble. As usual, Lotty won.

7
CHRISTIAN CHARITY

The air was clear and cold the next morning and a bright winter sun cast a strong glare back from the drifts lining the roads. Halsted had not been plowed, at least not north of Belmont, and the Omega jumped skittishly from rut to rut on the way to the Kennedy Expressway and Melrose Park.

I put on sunglasses and turned on WFMT. Satie. Unbearable. I turned it off again and started singing myself – nothing very noble, just the theme from *Big John and Sparky*. 'If you go down to the woods today you'd better not go alone.'

It was a little after ten when I turned north on Mannheim and made my way to Rosa's. In Melrose Park, even the side streets had been carefully cleaned. Maybe there was something to be said for suburban living after all. The path leading to her side door had been shoveled neatly, not just a path half a person wide like my building super believed in. There was even something to be said for living with Albert. Which just went to show.

Albert came to the door. The light was behind me and I could see his petulant face through the thick screen. He was surprised and angry. 'What are you doing here?'

'Albert. If Rosa has stressed it once, she's stressed a hundred times the importance of families sticking together. I'm sure she'd be shocked to hear you greet me so ungraciously.'

'Mama doesn't want to talk to you. I thought I made that clear the other day.'

I pulled the screen door open. 'Nope. You made it clear you didn't want *me* talking to *her*. That's by no means the same thing.'

Albert probably outweighs me by eighty pounds, which may be why he thought it would be easy to push me back out the door. I twisted his left arm up behind him and circled around past him. I hadn't felt so good in weeks.

Rosa's harsh voice wafted down the dim hall from the kitchen, demanding to know who was at the door and why Albert didn't shut it. Didn't he know what they were paying to heat this house?

I followed the voice, Albert walking sulkily behind me. 'It's me, Rosa,' I said, walking into the kitchen. 'I thought we ought to have a little talk about theology.'

Rosa was chopping vegetables, presumably for soup, since a shinbone was browning in oil on the stove. The kitchen still had its old 1930s sink. The stove and refrigerator were old, too, small white appliances set against unpainted walls. Rosa put the paring knife down on the counter with a snap, turned full face, and hissed angrily, 'I have no wish to talk to you, Victoria!'

I pulled a kitchen chair around and sat backward on it, leaning my chin on its back. 'Not good enough, Rosa. I'm not a television that you turn on and off at whim. A week ago you called me and played a tremolo passage on the family violin and dragged me out here against my will. On Thursday, suddenly your morals or ethics got the better of you. You looked at the lilies of the field and decided that it was wrong to have me toiling and spinning over your innocence.' I looked at her earnestly. 'Rosa, it sounds beautiful. It just doesn't sound like you.'

She drew her thin mouth into a tight line. 'How should you know? You were never even baptized. I would not expect you to know how a Christian behaves.'

'Well, you could be right. The modern world offers few opportunities to see one in action. But you don't understand. You tugged hard on my emotions to get me out here. It's going to be even harder to get rid of me. If you had picked a private investigator out of the Yellow Pages, one who had no connection with you, it would be different. But you insisted on me and it's me you've got.'

Rosa sat down. Her eyes blazed fiercely. 'I have changed my mind. That is my right. You should not do anything more.'

'I want to know something, Rosa. Was this your own idea? Or did someone else suggest it to you?'

Her eyes darted around the kitchen before she spoke. 'Naturally I discussed it with Albert.'

'Naturally. Your right-hand man and *confidant*. But who else?'

'No one!'

'No, Rosa. That little pause and the look around the room says the opposite. It wasn't Father Carroll, unless he lied to me on Thursday. Who was it?'

She said nothing.

'Who are you protecting, Rosa? Is it someone who knows about these forgeries?'

Still silence.

'I see. You know, the other day I was trying to figure an approach that I was better equipped to handle than the FBI. I came up with one, but you've just offered me a better. I'll get some surveillance on you and find out just who you talk to.'

The hate in her face made me recoil physically. 'So! What I should have expected from the daughter of a whore!'

Without thinking I leaned forward and slapped her on the mouth.

Slyness joined the hate in her face, but she was too proud to rub her mouth where I'd hit it. 'You would not love her so much if you knew the truth.'

'Thanks, Rosa. I'll be back next week for another lesson in Christian conduct.'

Albert had stood silently in the kitchen doorway throughout our altercation. He walked me to the outer door. The smell of burning olive oil followed us down the hall. 'You really should knock it off, Victoria. She's pretty worried.'

'Why do you stick up for her, Albert? She treats you like a retarded four-year-old. Stop being such a goddamned Mama's boy. Go get yourself a girlfriend. Get your own apartment. No one's going to marry you while you're living with her.'

He mumbled something inaudible and slammed the door behind me. I got into the car and sat heaving for several minutes. How

564

dared she! She had not only insulted my mother, she had manipulated me into hitting her. I couldn't believe I'd done it. I felt sick from rage and self-disgust. But the last thing I would ever do was apologize to the old witch.

On that defiant note, I put the car into gear and headed for the priory. Father Carroll was hearing confessions and would be busy for an hour. I could wait if I wanted. I declined, leaving a message that I would call later in the weekend, and headed back to the city.

I was in no mood to do anything but fight. Back at the apartment I got out my December expenses but couldn't keep my mind on them. Finally I gathered all my stale clothes and took them down to the washing machine in the basement. I changed the sheets and vacuumed and still felt terrible. At last I gave work up as a bad idea, dug my ice skates out of the closet, and drove over to the park at Montrose Harbor. They flood an outdoor rink there and I joined a crowd of children and skated with more energy than skill for over an hour. Afterward I treated myself to a late, light lunch at the Dortmunder Restaurant in the basement of the Chesterton Hotel.

It was close to three when I got home again, tired but with the anger washed out of me. The phone was ringing as I started undoing the upper of the two locks on my door. My fingers were stiff with cold; I heard the phone ring eleven times but by the time I got the bottom lock open and sprinted across the hall to the living room, the caller had hung up.

I was meeting Roger Ferrant for a movie and dinner at six. A short nap and a long bath would restore me and even leave a little time to work on my bills.

Lotty called at four, just as I had the taps running, to ask if I wanted to go with her to Uncle Stefan's tomorrow at three-thirty. We arranged for me to pick her up at three. I was lying well submerged and slightly comatose when the phone began to ring again. At first I let it go. Then, thinking it might be Ferrant calling to change plans, I leaped from the tub, trailing a cloud of Chanel bubbles behind me. But the phone had stopped again when I reached it.

Cursing the perversity of fate, I decided I had put off work long enough, got a robe and slippers, and started in earnest. By five I had my year-end statement almost complete and December's bills ready to mail to clients, and I went to change with a feeling of awesome virtue. I put on a full peasant skirt which hit me mid-calf, knee-high red cavalier boots, and a full-sleeved white blouse. Ferrant and I were meeting at the Sullivan for the six o'clock showing of *Terms of Endearment*.

He was waiting for me when I got there, a courtesy I appreciated, and kissed me enthusiastically. I declined popcorn and Coke and we spent an agreeable two hours with half our attention on Shirley MacLaine and half on each other's bodies, making sure that various parts abandoned on Thursday morning were still where they belonged. The movie over, we agreed to complete the survey at my apartment before eating dinner.

We walked lazily up the stairs together arm in arm. I had just gotten the bottom lock unfastened when the phone started to ring again. This time I reached it by the fourth ring.

'Miss Warshawski?'

The voice was strange, a neutral voice, no accent, a hard-to-define pitch.

'Yes?'

'I'm glad to find you home at last. You're investigating the forged securities at St Albert's, aren't you?'

'Who is this?' I demanded sharply.

'A friend, Miss Warshawski. You might almost call me an *amicus curiae*.' He gave a ghostly, self-satisfied laugh. 'Don't go on, Miss Warshawski. You have such beautiful gray eyes. I would hate to see them after someone poured acid on them.' The line went dead.

I stood holding the phone, staring at it in disbelief. Ferrant came over to me.

'What is it, Vic?'

I put the receiver down carefully. 'If you value your life, stay away from the moor at night.' I tried for a light note, but my voice sounded weak even to me. Roger started to put an arm around me,

566

but I shook it off gently. 'I need to think this out on my own for a minute. There's liquor and wine in the cupboard built into the dining-room wall. Why don't you fix us something?'

He went off to find drinks and I sat and looked at the phone some more. Detectives get a large volume of anonymous phone calls and letters and you'd be a quick candidate for a straitjacket if you took them very seriously. But the menace in this man's voice had been very credible. Acid in the eyes. I shivered.

I'd stirred a lot of pots and now one of them was boiling. But which one? Could poor, shriveled Aunt Rosa have gone demented and hired someone to threaten me? The idea made me laugh a little to myself and helped restore some mental balance. If not Rosa, though, it had to be the priory. And that was just as laughable. Hatfield would like to see me out of the case, but this wasn't his kind of maneuver.

Roger came in with a couple of glasses of Burgundy. 'You're white, Vic. Who was that on the phone?'

I shook my head. 'I wish I knew. His voice was so – so careful. Without accent. Like distilled water. Someone wants me away from the forgeries bad enough to threaten to pour acid on me.'

He was shocked. 'Vic! You must call the police. This is horrible.' He put an arm around me. This time I didn't push him away.

'The police can't do anything, Roger. If I called and told them – do you have any idea of the number of crank calls that are made in this city in any one day?'

'But they could send someone around to keep an eye on you.'

'Sure. If they didn't have eight hundred murders to investigate. And ten thousand armed robberies. And a few thousand rapes. The police can't look after me just because someone wants to make crank phone calls.'

He was troubled and asked if I wanted to move in with him until things quieted down.

'Thanks, Roger. I appreciate the offer very much. But now I have someone worried enough to do something. If I stay here, I may just catch him doing it.'

We'd both lost our interest in lovemaking. We finished the

wine and I made us a *frittata*. Roger spent the night. I lay awake
until after three, listening to his quiet, even breathing, trying
to place that accentless voice, wondering who I knew who threw
acid.

8
AT THE OLD FORGE

Sunday morning I drove the mile to Lotty's through a succession of residential one-way streets, turning often, waiting on the blind side of intersections. No one was following me. Whoever had called last night wasn't that interested. Yet.

Lotty was waiting for me in her building entryway. She looked like a little elf: five feet of compact energy wrapped in a bright green loden jacket and some kind of outlandish crimson hat. Her uncle lived in Skokie, so I went north to Irving Park Road and over to the Kennedy, the main expressway north.

As we drove past the grimy factories lining the expressway, a few snowflakes began dancing on the windshield. The cloud cover remained high, so we didn't seem to be in for a heavy storm. Turning right on the Edens fork to the northeast suburbs, I abruptly told Lotty about the phone call I'd had last night.

'It's one thing for me to risk my life just to prove a point, but it's not fair to drag you and your uncle into it as well. The odds are it was just an angry call. But if not – you need to know the risk ahead of time. And make your own decision.'

We were approaching the Dempster interchange. Lotty told me to exit east and drive to Crawford Avenue. It wasn't until I'd followed her directions and we were moving past the imposing homes on Crawford that she answered. 'I can't see that you're asking us to risk anything. You may have a problem, and it may be exacerbated by your talking to my uncle. But as long as he and I don't tell anyone you've been to see him, I don't think it'll matter. If he thinks of anything you can use – well, I would not permit you in my operating room telling me what was and what was not too great a risk. And I won't do that with you, either.'

We parked in front of a quiet apartment building. Lotty's uncle met us in the doorway of his apartment. He carried his eighty-two years well, looking a bit like Laurence Olivier in *Marathon Man*. He had Lotty's bright black eyes. They twinkled as he kissed her. He half bowed, shaking hands with me.

'So. Two beautiful ladies decide to cheer up an old man's Sunday afternoon. Come in, come in.' He spoke heavily accented English, unlike Lotty, who had learned it as a girl.

We followed him into a sitting room crammed with furniture and books. He ushered me ceremoniously to a stuffed chintz armchair. He and Lotty sat on a horsehair settee at a right angle to it. In front of them, on a mahogany table, was a coffee service. The silver glowed with the soft patina of age, and the coffee pot and serving pieces were decorated with fantastic creatures. I leaned forward to look at it more closely. There were griffins and centaurs, nymphs and unicorns.

Uncle Stefan beamed with pleasure at my interest. 'It was made in Vienna in the early eighteenth century, when coffee was first becoming the most popular drink there.' He poured cups for Lotty and me, offered me thick cream, and lifted a silver cover by its nymph-handle to reveal a plate of pastries so rich they bordered on erotic.

'Now you are not one of those ladies who eats nothing for fear of ruining her beautiful figure, are you? Good. American girls are too thin, aren't they, Lottchen? You should prescribe *Sacher torte* for all your patients.'

He continued speaking about the healthful properties of chocolate for several minutes. I drank a cup of the excellent coffee and ate a piece of hazelnut cake and wondered how to change the subject gently. However, after pouring more coffee and urging more cakes on me, he abruptly took the plunge himself.

'Lotty says you wish to talk about engraving.'

'Yes, sir.' I told him briefly about Aunt Rosa's problems. I own a hundred shares of Acorn, a young computer company, given me

570

in payment for an industrial espionage case I'd handled for them. I pulled the certificate out of my handbag and passed it to Uncle Stefan.

'I think most shares are printed on the same kind of paper. I'm wondering how difficult it would be to forge something like this well enough to fool someone who was used to looking at them.'

He took it silently and walked over to a desk that stood in front of a window. It, too, was an antique, with ornately carved legs and a green leather top. He pulled a magnifying glass from a narrow drawer in the middle, turned on a bright desk lamp, and scrutinized the certificate for more than a quarter of an hour.

'It would be difficult,' he pronounced at last. 'Perhaps not quite as difficult as forging paper money successfully.' He beckoned me over to the desk; Lotty came, too, peering over his other shoulder. He began pointing out features of the certificate to me: The paper stock, to begin with, was a heavy-grade parchment, not easy to obtain. 'And it has a characteristic weave. To fool an expert, you would need to make sure of this weave. They make the paper like this on purpose, you see, just to make the poor forger's life more difficult.' He turned to grin wickedly at Lotty, who frowned in annoyance.

'Then you have the logo of the issuing company, and several signatures, each with a stamp over it. It is the stamp that is most difficult; that is almost impossible to replicate without smearing the ink of the signature. Have you seen those fake shares of your aunt's? Do you know what they did wrong?'

I shook my head. 'All I know is that the serial numbers were ones that the issuing companies had never used. I don't know about these other features.'

He snapped off the desk lamp and handed me back the certificate. 'It's a pity you haven't seen them. Also, if you knew how the forger intended to use them, that would tell you how good, how – convincing – they had to be.'

'I've thought about that. The only real use for a phony share would be as collateral. They're always examined closely by the banks at the time of sale.

'In this case, though, some real stocks were stolen. So the thief just needed to convince some priests and their auditors that they still had their assets. That way it wouldn't be like an ordinary theft where you'd know just when the stuff was taken and who had had access to it since you last saw it.'

'Well, I'm sorry I can tell you nothing else, young lady. But surely you will have another piece of cake before you go.'

I sat back down and took a piece of apricot-almond torte. My arteries were screaming in protest as I ate a bite. 'Actually, sir, there is something else you might know. The forgeries could have been done anytime in the last ten years. But suppose, for the sake of argument, they were made relatively recently. How could I find out who did them? Assuming he – or she – worked in the Chicago area?'

He was gravely silent for a long minute. Then he spoke quietly. 'Lottchen has told you about my past, how I created twenty-dollar bills. Masterpieces, really,' he said with a return of his more jovial manner. 'Considering I made all my own equipment.

'There are really two breeds of forger, Miss Warshawski. Independent artisans like me. And those who work for an organization. Now here you have someone who has done the work at another person's request. Unless you believe that the same person who created the new stole and disposed of the old. Really, what you want is not the – the master engraver, but his client. Am I not right?'

I nodded.

'Well, I cannot help you with finding this engraver. We independent artisans tend not to – to make public our handiwork and I am not part of a network of forgers. But perhaps I could help you find the client.'

'How?' Lotty asked before I could.

'By making up such a piece and letting it be known that I have one for sale.'

I thought about it. 'It might work. But you'd be running a terrible risk. Even with my most persuasive intervention, it would be hard to convince the feds that your motives were pure. And remember that the people who ordered these things might be violent – I've already had a threatening phone call. If they found out you were doublecrossing them, their justice would be even harder to take than a stint at Fort Leavenworth.'

Uncle Stefan leaned over and clasped one of my hands. 'Young lady, I am an old man. Although I enjoy life, my fear of death has passed. And such an occupation would be rejuvenating for me.'

Lotty interrupted with some vigorous arguments of her own. Their discussion got quite heated and moved into German, until Lotty said disgustedly in English, 'On your grave we will put a marker reading "He died stubborn."'

After that, Uncle Stefan and I discussed practical details. He would need to keep my Acorn certificate and get some others. He would find any supplies he needed and send me the bills. To be on the safe side, in case my anonymous caller really meant business, he wouldn't phone me. If he needed to talk to me, he'd run an ad in the *Herald-Star*. Unfortunately, he couldn't promise very speedy results.

'You must resign yourself to weeks, perhaps many weeks, not days, my dear Miss Warshawski.'

Lotty and I left amid mutual protestations of goodwill – at least between Uncle Stefan and me. Lotty was a little frosty. As we got into the car she said, 'I suppose I could call you in to consult on geriatric cases. You could think of criminal enterprises that would bring adventure and the flush of youth back to people worried about making ends meet on Social Security.'

I drove over to Route 41, the old highway connecting Chicago and the North Shore. Nowadays it offered a quiet, pretty drive past stately homes and the lake. 'I'm sorry, Lotty. I didn't go there with anything more than the hope that your uncle might know who's who in Chicago forging. Personally, I think his idea is a long shot. If he can do the job and make some contacts, how likely is it he'll come up with the right people? But it's a clever idea, and better than anything I can think of. Anyway, I'd certainly rather have a charming criminal as my only Chicago relative than an honest bitch; if you're too upset, I'll trade you Rosa for Stefan.'

573

Lotty laughed at that and we made the drive back to Chicago peaceably, stopping on the far North Side for a Thai dinner. I dropped Lotty at her apartment and went on home to call my answering service. A Father Carroll had phoned, and so, too, had Murray Ryerson from the *Star*.

I tried the priory first. 'They told me you were by here yesterday, Miss Warshawski. I'm sorry I couldn't see you then. I don't know if you've heard, but we had some rather extraordinary news this morning: We found the original certificates.'

I stood momentarily stunned. 'That *is* extraordinary,' I finally said. 'Where did they turn up?'

'They were on the altar this morning when we began celebrating mass.' Since well over a hundred people had legitimate business in the priory chapel on Sunday mornings, no one could possibly say who might or might not have gone there early and returned the stolen goods. Yes, the FBI had sent someone out to take possession, but Hatfield had called at three to say that these shares were genuine. The FBI was keeping them awhile to run lab tests on them. And Carroll didn't know now if they'd ever get them back.

Out of curiosity I asked if Rosa had been to mass that morning. Yes, and looking grimly at anyone who tried to talk to her, Carroll assured me. Her son stayed away, but he usually did. As we started to hang up, he remembered my question about whether anyone at the priory had talked to Rosa about pulling out of the investigation. He had asked the fathers whom Rosa would most likely listen to and none of them had talked to her.

I called Murray next. He wasn't as full of the returned certificates as I expected. More recent news occupied his attention.

'I talked to Hatfield twenty minutes ago. You know what an arrogant, uncommunicative bastard he is. Well, I couldn't get shit out of him about the returned stocks and I asked every question in my arsenal and more besides. I got him in a corner finally and he as good as admitted the FBI is dropping the investigation. Putting it on the back burner, he said, cliché hack that he is. But that means dropping it.'

'Well, if the real things have turned up, they don't need to worry so much.'

'Yeah, and I believe in the Easter bunny. Come on, Vic!'

'Okay, wordly-wise newspaperman. Who's applying the screws? The FBI isn't scared of anyone except maybe J. Edgar's ghost. If you think someone's backing them off, who is it?'

'Vic, you don't believe that any more than I do. No organization is exempt from pressure if you know where the right nerves are. If you know something you're not telling I'll – I'll –' he broke off unable to think of an effective threat. 'And another thing. What was that crap you gave me about your poor frail old aunt? I sent one of my babies out to talk to her yesterday afternoon and some fat goon who claimed he was the son practically broke my gal's foot in the door. Then the Vignelli woman joined him in the hall and treated her to some high-level swearing on newspapers in general and the *Star* in particular.'

I laughed softly. 'Okay, Rosa! Two points for our side.'

'Goddamn it, Vic, why'd you sic me onto her?'

'I don't know,' I said irritably. 'To see if she'd be as nasty to anyone else as she is to me? To see if you could learn something she wouldn't tell me? I don't know. I'm sorry your poor little protégée had her feelings hurt, but she's going to have to learn to take it if she plans to survive in your game.' I started to tell Murray that I, too, had been warned off the investigation, then held back. Maybe someone had brushed back the FBI. And maybe that someone had called me as well. If the FBI respected them, so should I. I bade Murray an absentminded good-night and hung up.

9
FINAL TRADE

The snow held off overnight. I got up late to do my virtuous five miles, running north and west through the neighborhood. I didn't think anyone was watching me, but if they were, it was sensible to vary my route.

A little later I followed the same procedure in my car, looping the Omega north and west through the side streets, then hitting the Kennedy from the west at Lawrence. I seemed to be clean. Thirty miles south on the expressway, past the city limits, is the town of Hazel Crest. You cannot buy handguns in Chicago, but a number of suburbs do a flourishing legal business in them. At Riley's, on 161st Street, I showed them my private investigator's license and my certificate that proved I'd passed the state's exam for private security officers. These enabled me to waive the three-day waiting period and also to register the gun in Chicago; private citizens can't register handguns here unless they bought them before 1979.

I spent the rest of the day finishing up a few outstanding problems – serving a subpoena to a bank vice-president hiding unconvincingly in Rosemont, and showing a small jewelry store how to install a security system.

And I kept wondering who was backing off first Rosa and then the FBI. It wouldn't help to park in front of Rosa's and watch her. What I really needed was a tap on her phone. And that was beyond my resources.

I tried thinking about it from the other end. Who had I talked to? That was easy: the prior, the procurator, and the student master.

I'd also told Ferrant and Agnes what I was doing. None of these five seemed a likely candidate for threatening either me or the FBI.

Of course, Jablonski could be that type of antiabortion fanatic who thinks it's a worse sin to have an abortion than to kill someone who promotes freedom of choice, but he hadn't struck me as particularly crazy. Despite Pelly's protests, the Catholic Church does carry a lot of clout in Chicago. But even if it could pressure the FBI out of the investigation, why would it want to? Anyway, a priory in Melrose Park was on the fringes of the Church power structure. And why would they steal their own stock certificates? Even assuming they were in touch with forgers the whole idea was too far out. I went back to my original theory – my phone call had come from a crank, and the FBI was backing out because it was understaffed and overworked.

Nothing happened to make me change my mind during the next several days. I wondered vaguely how Uncle Stefan was doing. If it weren't for the fact that there really had been a forgery, I would have put the whole thing out of my mind.

On Wednesday I had to go to Elgin to testify in a case being tried in the state appeals court there. I stopped in Melrose Park on my way back to town, partly to see Carroll, partly to see if a visit to the priory might tickle my threatening caller back to life. If it didn't, it would prove nothing. But if I heard from him again, it might show he was watching the priory.

It was four-thirty when I reached St Albert's, and the friars were filing into the chapel for vespers and evening mass. Father Carroll came out of his office as I stood hesitating and gave me a welcoming smile, inviting me to join them for evening prayer.

I followed him into the chapel. Two rows of raised stalls faced each other in the middle of the room. I went with him to the back row on the left side. The seats were divided by arms raised between them. I sat down and slid back in the seat. Father Carroll gave me a service book and quietly pointed out the lessons and prayers they would be using, then knelt to pray.

In the winter twilight, I felt as though I had slipped back five or six centuries in time. The brothers in their white robes, the candlelight flickering on the simple wooden altar to my left, the few people coming in from the outside to worship in the public space divided from the main chapel by a carved wooden screen – all evoked the medieval Church. I was the discordant note in my black wool suit, my high heels, my makeup.

Father Carroll led the service, singing in a clear, well-trained voice. The whole service was sung antiphonally between the two banks of stalls. It's true, as Rosa said, that I'm no Christian, but I found the service satisfying.

Afterward, Carroll invited me back to his office for tea. Almost all tea tastes like stewed alfalfa to me, but I politely drank a cup of the pale green brew and asked him if he'd heard anything more from the FBI.

'They tested the shares for fingerprints and a lot of other things – I don't know what. They thought there might be dust or something on them that would show where the things had been stored. I guess they didn't find anything, so they're going to bring them back tomorrow.' He grinned mischievously. 'I'm making them give me an armed escort over to the Bank of Melrose Park. We're getting those things into a bank vault.'

He asked me to stay for dinner, which was being served in five minutes. Memories of Kraft American cheese restrained me. On an impulse I invited him to eat with me in Melrose Park. The town has a couple of excellent Italian restaurants. Somewhat surprised, he accepted.

'I'll just change out of my robe.' He smiled again. 'The young brothers like to go out in them in public – they like people to look at them and know they're seeing a foreign breed. But we older men lose our taste for showing off.'

He returned in ten minutes in a plaid shirt, black slacks, and a black jacket. We had a pleasant meal at one of the little restaurants on North Avenue. We talked about singing; I complimented him on his voice and learned he'd been a student at the American Conservatory before entering the priesthood. He asked me about my work and I tried to think of some interesting cases.

'I guess the payoff is you get to be your own boss. And you have the satisfaction of solving problems, even if they're only little problems most of the time. I was just out in Elgin today, testifying at the state court there. It brought back my early days with the Chicago public defender's office. Either we had to defend maniacs who ought to have been behind bars for the good of the world at large, or we had poor chumps who were caught in the system and couldn't buy their way out. You'd leave court every day feeling as though you'd just helped worsen the situation. As a detective, if I can get at the truth of a problem, I feel as though I've made some contribution.'

'I see. Not a glamorous occupation, but it sounds very worthwhile . . . I'd never heard Mrs Vignelli mention you. Until she called last week, I didn't know she had any family besides her son. Are there other relatives?'

I shook my head. 'My mother was her only Chicago relative – my grandfather and she were brother and sister. There may be some family on my uncle Carl's side. He died years before I was born. Shot himself, actually – very sad for Rosa.' I fiddled with the stem on my wineglass, tempted to ask him if he knew what lay behind Rosa's dark insinuations about Gabriella. But even if he knew, he probably wouldn't tell me. And it seemed vulgar to bring up the family enmity in public.

After I took him back to the priory I swung onto the Eisenhower back to Chicago. A little light snow had begun falling. It was a few minutes before ten; I turned on WBBM, Chicago's news station, to catch news and a weather forecast.

I listened vaguely to reports of failed peace initiatives in Lebanon, continued high unemployment, poor retail sales in December despite Christmas shopping. Then Alan Swanson's crisp voice continued:

Tonight's top local story is the violent death of a Chicago stockbroker. Cleaning woman Martha Gonzales found the body of broker Agnes Paciorek in one of the conference rooms in the offices of Feldstein, Holtz and Woods, where Miss Paciorek worked. She had been shot twice in the head. Police have not ruled out suicide as a cause of death. CBS news correspondent Mark Weintraub is with Sergeant McGonnigal at the Fort Dearborn Tower offices of Feldstein, Holtz and Woods.'

Swanson switched over to Weintraub. I almost swerved into a ditch at Cicero Avenue. My hands were shaking and I pulled the car over to the side. I turned off the engine. Semis roared past, rattling the little Omega. The car cooled, and my feet began growing numb inside their pumps. 'Two shots in the head and the police still haven't ruled out suicide,' I muttered. My voice jarred me back to myself; I turned the motor on and headed back into the city at a sober pace.

WBBM played the story at ten-minute intervals, with few new details. The bullets were from a twenty-two-caliber pistol. The police finally decided to eliminate suicide since no gun was found by the body. Miss Paciorek's purse had been recovered from a locked drawer in her desk. I heard Sergeant McGonnigal saying in a voice made scratchy by static that someone must have intended to rob her, then killed her in rage because she didn't have a purse.

On impulse I drove north to Addison and stopped in front of Lotty's apartment. It was almost eleven: no lights showed. Lotty gets her sleep when she can – her practice involves a lot of night emergencies. My trouble would keep.

Back at my own apartment, I changed from my suit into a quilted robe and sat down in the living room with a glass of Black Label whiskey. Agnes and I went back a long way together, back to the Golden Age of the sixties, when we thought love and energy would end racism and sexism. She'd come from a wealthy family, her father a heart surgeon at one of the big suburban hospitals. They'd fought her about her friends, her life-style, her ambitions, and she'd won every battle. Relations with her mother became more and more strained. I would have to call Mrs Paciorek, who disliked me since I represented everything she didn't want Agnes to be. I'd have to hear how they always knew this would happen, working downtown where the niggers are. I drank another glass of whiskey.

I'd forgotten all about laying some bait for my anonymous phone caller until the telephone interrupted my maudlin mood. I jumped slightly and looked at my watch: eleven-thirty. I picked up a Dictaphone from my desk and turned it to 'Record' before picking up the receiver.

It was Roger Ferrant, feeling troubled about Agnes's death. He'd seen it on the ten o'clock news and tried calling me then. We commiserated a bit; then he said hesitantly, 'I feel responsible for her death.'

The whiskey was fogging my brain slightly. 'What'd you do — send a punk up to the sixtieth floor of the Fort Dearborn Tower?' I switched off the Dictaphone and sat down.

'Vic, I don't need your tough-girl act. I feel responsible because she was staying late working on this possible Ajax takeover. It wasn't something she had time for during the day. If I hadn't called her —'

'If you hadn't called her, she would have been there late working on another project,' I interrupted him coldly. 'Agnes often finished her day late — the lady worked hard. And if it comes to that, you wouldn't have called her if I hadn't given you her number, so if anyone's responsible, it's me.' I took another swallow of whiskey. 'And I won't believe that.'

We hung up. I finished my third glass of scotch and put the bottle away in the built-in cupboard in the dining room, draped my robe over a chair back, and climbed naked into bed. Just as I turned out the bedside light, something Ferrant had said rang a bell with me. I called him back on the bedside phone.

'It's me, Vic. How did you know Agnes was working late on your project tonight?'

'I talked to her this afternoon. She said she was going to stay late and talk to some of her broker pals; she didn't have time to get to it during the day.'

'In person or on the phone?'

'Huh? Oh, I don't know.' He thought about it. 'I can't remember exactly what she said. But it left me with the impression that she was planning to see someone in person.'

'You should talk to the police, Roger.' I hung up and fell asleep almost immediately.

10

MIXED GRILL

No matter how often I wake up with a headache, I never remember
it the next time I'm putting away five or six ounces of whiskey.
Thursday morning a dry mouth and pounding head and heart woke
me at five-thirty. I looked disgustedly at myself in the bathroom
mirror. 'You're getting old, V.I., and unattractive. When your face
has cracks in it the morning after five ounces of scotch, it's time
to stop drinking.'

I squeezed some fresh orange juice and drank it in one long
swallow, took four aspirins, and went back to bed. The ringing
phone woke me again at eight-thirty. A neutral young male voice
said he was connected with Lieutenant Robert Mallory of the
Chicago police department and would I be able to come downtown
that morning and talk to the lieutenant.

'It's always a pleasure for me to talk to Lieutenant Mallory,' I
replied formally, if somewhat thickly, through the miasma of sleep.
'Perhaps you could tell me what this is about.'

The neutral young man didn't know, but if I was free at nine-
thirty, the lieutenant would see me then.

My next call was to the *Herald-Star*. Murray Ryerson hadn't
yet come in for the day. I called his apartment, and felt vindictive
pleasure at getting him out of bed. 'Murray, what do you know
about Agnes Paciorek?'

He was furious. 'I can't believe you got me out of bed to ask me
that. Go buy the fucking morning edition.' He slammed the phone
down.

Angry myself, I dialed again. 'Listen, Ryerson. Agnes Paciorek was one of my oldest friends. She got shot last night. Now Bobby Mallory wants to talk to me. I'm sure he's not calling for deep background on University Women United, or Clergy and Laity Concerned About Vietnam. What was in her office that makes him want to see me?'

'Hang on a second.' He put the receiver down; I could hear his feet padding away down the hall, then water running and a woman's voice saying something indistinguishable. I ran into the kitchen and put a small pot of water on the stove, ground beans for one cup of coffee, and brought cup, water, and filter back to my bedside phone – all before Murray returned.

'I hope you can hold off Jessica or whatever her name is for a few seconds.'

'Don't be catty, Vic. It isn't attractive.' I heard springs creaking, then a muffled 'ouch' from Murray.

'Right,' I said dryly. 'Now tell me about Agnes.'

Paper rustled, springs creaked again, and Murray's smothered voice whispered, 'Knock it off, Alice.' Then he put the mouthpiece in front of his lips again and began reading from his notes.

'Agnes Paciorek was shot at about eight last night. Two twenty-two bullets in the brain. Office doors not locked – cleaning women lock behind when they finish sixtieth floor, usually at eleven o'clock. Martha Gonzales cleans floors fifty-seven through sixty, got to floor at her usual time, nine-fifteen, saw nothing unusual on premises, got to conference room at nine-thirty, saw body, called police. No personal attack – no signs of rape or struggle. Police presume attacker took her completely by surprise or possibly someone she knew . . . That's the lot. You're someone she knew. They probably just want to know where you were at eight last night. By the way, since you're on the phone, where were you?'

'In a bar, waiting for a report from my hired gun.' I hung up and looked sourly around the room. The orange juice and aspirin had dissipated the headache, but I felt rotten. I wasn't going to have time for running if I had to be in Mallory's office by nine-thirty, and a long, slow run was what I needed to get the poisons out of my system. I didn't even have time for a long bath, so I steamed myself under the shower for ten minutes, put on the crêpe-de-Chine pant-suit, this time with a man-tailored shirt of pale lemon, and ran down the stairs two at a time to my car.

If the Warshawski family has a motto, which I doubt, it's 'Never skip a meal,' perhaps in Old Church Slavonic, wreathed around a dinner plate with knife and fork rampant. At any rate, I stopped at a bakery on Halsted for coffee and a ham croissant and headed for Lake Shore Drive and the Loop. The croissant was stale, and the ham might have been rancid, but I plowed into it bravely. Bobby's little chats can go on for hours. I wanted to fortify myself.

Lieutenant Mallory had joined the police the same year as my dad. But my father, his better in brains, never had a lot of ambition, certainly not enough to buck the prejudice against Polish cops in an all-Irish world. So Mallory had risen and Tony had stayed on the beat, but the two remained good friends. That's why Mallory hates talking to me about crime. He thinks Tony Warshawski's daughter should be making a better world by producing happy healthy babies, not by catching desperadoes.

I pulled into the visitors' parking lot at the Eleventh Street station at nine-twenty-three. I sat in the car to relax for a few minutes, finish my coffee, clear my mind of all thoughts. For once, I had no guilty secrets. It should be a straightforward conversation.

At nine-thirty I made my way past the high wooden admissions desk where pimps were lining up to redeem last night's haul of hookers, and went down the hallway to Mallory's office. The place smelled a lot like St Albert's Priory. Must be the linoleum floors. Or maybe all the people in uniform.

Mallory was on the phone when I got to the cubicle he calls an office. His shirt sleeves were rolled up and the muscular arm that waved me in strained the white fabric. Before entering, I helped myself to coffee from a pot in the corner of the hall, then sat in an uncomfortable folding chair across the desk while he finished his call. Mallory's face betrays his moods. He turns red and blustery on days when I'm on the periphery of some crime; relaxed and genial means he's thinking of me as his old buddy Tony's daughter.

Today he looked at me gravely as he hung up the phone. Trouble. I took a swallow of coffee and waited.

He flicked a switch on the intercom on his desk and waited silently while someone answered his summons. A young black officer, resembling Neil Washington from *Hill Street Blues*, came in shortly with a steno pad in one hand and a cup of coffee for Mallory in the other. Mallory introduced him as Officer Tarkinton.

'Miss Warshawski is a private investigator,' Mallory informed Tarkinton, spelling the name for him. 'Officer Tarkinton is going to keep a record of our conversation.'

The formality and the display of officialdom were supposed to intimidate. I drank some more coffee, puzzled.

'Were you a friend of Agnes Marie Paciorek?'

'Bobby, you're making me feel like I ought to have my attorney here. What's going on?'

'Just answer the questions. We'll get to the reasons quickly enough.'

'My relations with Agnes aren't a secret. You can get the details from anyone who knows both of us. Unless you tell me what's behind this, I'm not answering any questions.'

'When did you first meet Agnes Paciorek?'

I drank some more coffee and said nothing.

'You and Paciorek are described as sharing an alternative life-style. This same witness says you are responsible for introducing the dead woman to unconventional behavior. Do you want to comment on that?'

I felt my temper rising and controlled it with an effort. It's a typical police tactic in this type of interrogation – get the witness mad enough to start mouthing off. And who knows what self-constructed pitfalls you'll wander into? I used to see it all the time in the public defender's office. I counted to ten in Italian and waited.

Mallory clenched his fist tightly around the edge of his metal desk. 'You and Paciorek were lesbians, weren't you?' Suddenly his control broke and he smashed his fist on the desk top. 'When Tony was dying you were up at the University of Chicago screwing around like a pervert, weren't you? It wasn't enough that you demonstrated against the war and got involved with that filthy abortion underground. Don't think we couldn't have pulled you in on that. We could have, a hundred times over. But everyone wanted to protect Tony. You were the most important thing in the world to him, and all the time – Jesus Christ, Victoria. When I talked to Mrs Paciorek this morning, I wanted to puke.'

'Are you charging me with something, Bobby?'

He sat smoldering.

'Because if you're not, I'm leaving.' I got up, putting an empty Styrofoam cup on the corner of his desk, and started out the door.

'No you don't, young lady. Not until we get this straightened out.'

'There's nothing to straighten out,' I said coldly. 'First of all, under the Illinois criminal code, lesbianism between consenting adults is not an indictable offense. Therefore it is none of your goddamned business whether or not Ms Paciorek and I were lovers. Second, my relations with her are totally unconnected with your murder investigation. Unless you can demonstrate some kind of connection, I have absolutely nothing to say to you.'

We locked gazes for an angry minute. Then Bobby, his face still set in hurt hard lines, asked Officer Tarkinton to leave. When we were alone he said in a tight voice, 'I should have gotten someone else to handle the interrogation. But goddamn it, Vicki . . .'

His voice trailed off. I was still angry, but I felt grudging sympathy for him. 'You know, Bobby, what hurts me is that you talk to Mrs Paciorek, whom you never met before in your life, and believe a shopping list of calumny from her without even asking me, and you've known me since I was born.'

'Okay, talk. I'm asking. Talk to me about the Paciorek girl.'

I picked up the Styrofoam cup and looked inside. It was still empty. 'Agnes and I met when we were both students in the college. I was prelaw and she was a math major who ultimately decided to get an MBA. I'm not going to try to describe to you what it felt like in those days – you don't have much sympathy for the causes that consumed us. I think sometimes that I'll never feel so – so alive again.'

A wave of bittersweet memory swept over me and I closed my eyes tightly to keep tears at bay. 'Then the dream started falling apart. We had Watergate and drugs and the deteriorating economy, and racism and sexual discrimination continued despite our enthusiasm. So we all settled down to deal with reality and earn a living. You know my story. I guess my ideals died the hardest. It's often that way with the children of immigrants. We need to buy the dream so bad we sometimes can't wake up.

'Well, Agnes's story was a little different. You met the parents. First of all, her father is a successful cardiac surgeon, pulls in a good half million a year at a conservative guess. But more important, her mother is one of the Savages. You know, old Catholic money. Convent of the Sacred Heart for prep school, then the deb balls and all the other stuff. I don't know exactly how the very rich live, just differently from you and me.

'Anyway, Agnes was born fighting it. She fought it through twelve years at Sacred Heart, and came to the U of C against their harshest opposition. She borrowed the money because they wouldn't pay to send her to a Jewish commie school. So it wasn't too surprising that she got swept up in all the causes of the sixties. And for both of us, feminism was the most important, because it was central to us.'

I was talking more to myself than to Bobby; I wasn't sure how much he could really hear of what I was saying.

'Well, after Tony died, Agnes used to invite me up to Lake Forest for Christmas and I got to know the Pacioreks. And Mrs Paciorek decided to hang all Agnes's weird behavior on me. It took her off the hook, you see – she wasn't a failure as a parent. Agnes, who figured as sweet and impressionable in this scenario, had fallen under my evil influence.

'Well, buy that or not as you choose, but keep in mind that sweet impressionable people don't build up the kind of brokerage business Agnes did.

'Anyway, Agnes and I were good friends at the University. And we stayed good friends. And in its way that was a small miracle. When our rap group followed the national trend and split between radical lesbians and, well, straights, she became a lesbian and I didn't. But we remained very good friends – an achievement for that era, when politics divided marriages and friends alike. It seems pointless now, but it was very real then.'

Like a lot of my friends, I'd resented suddenly being labeled straight because of my sexual preferences. After all, we'd been fighting the straights – the prowar, antiabortion, racist world. Now overnight we were straights, too? It all seems senseless now. The older I get, the less politics means to me. The only thing that seems to matter is friendship. And Agnes and I had been good friends for a long time. I could feel tears behind my eyes and squeezed them tightly again. When I looked up at Bobby he was frowning at the desk top, drawing circles on it with the back of a ballpoint pen.

'Well, I've told you my story, Bobby. Now explain why you needed to hear it.'

He continued to stare at the desk. 'Where were you last night?'

My temper began rising again. 'Goddamn it, if you want to charge me with murder, come out and do it. I'm not accounting for my movements otherwise.'

'From the way the body looked, we believe she was seeing some-one she expected, not a chance intruder.' He pulled a leather-covered date book from the middle desk drawer. He flipped it open and tossed it to me. For Wednesday, January 18, Agnes had written: 'V.I.W.,' heavily underscored, followed by several exclamation points.

'Looks like a date, doesn't it.' I tossed the book back to him. 'Have you established that I'm her only acquaintance with those initials?'

'There aren't too many people in the metropolitan area with those initials.'

'So the current theory reads that she and I were lovers and we had a falling-out? Now she's been living with Phyllis Lording for three years and I've been involved with God-knows-who-all since we left school, besides being married once – oh, yeah, I guess the theory would say I divorced Dick to keep Agnes happy. But despite all that, suddenly we decided to have a grand lovers' quarrel and because I'm trained in self-defense and carry a gun at times, I won by putting a couple of bullets through her head. You said hearing about me from Mrs Paciorek made you want to puke; frankly, Bobby, listening to what goes on in the alleged minds of the police makes me feel like I've wandered into a really low-grade porn shop. Talk about puking . . . Anything else you want to know?' I stood up again.

'Well, you tell me why she wanted to see you. And were you there last night?'

I stayed on my feet. 'You should have started with your last question. I was in Melrose Park last night with the Reverend Boniface Carroll, OP, Prior of St Albert's Dominican Priory, from about four-thirty to about ten. And I don't know why Agnes wanted to talk to me – assuming I'm the one she wanted to talk to. Try Vincent Ignatius Williams.'

'Who's he?' Bobby demanded, startled.

'I don't know. But his initials are V.I.W.' I turned and left, ignoring Bobby's voice as it came bellowing down the corridor after me. I was furious; my hands were shaking with rage. I stood by the door of the Omega taking in deep gulps of icy air, slowly expelling it, trying to calm myself.

Finally I climbed into the car. The dashboard clock read eleven. I headed the Omega north into the Loop, parking at a public lot not too far from the Pulteney. From there I walked three blocks to Ajax's headquarters.

Their glass-and-steel skyscraper occupies sixty of the ugliest stories in Chicago. Located at the northwestern corner of Michigan and Adams, it overwhelms the Art Institute opposite. I've often wondered why the Blairs and the McCormicks allowed a monster like Ajax so near their favorite charity.

Uniformed security guards patrol Ajax's gray lobby. Their job is to keep miscreants like me from attacking officers like Roger Ferrant. Even after they'd checked with him and found he was willing to see me, they made me fill out a form for a visitor's pass. By that time my temper was so brittle that I scribbled a note under my signature promising not to mug any of their executives in the hallway.

Ferrant's office lay on the lake side of the fifty-eighth floor, which proved the importance of his temporary position.

An angular secretary in a large antechamber informed me that Mr Ferrant was engaged and would see me shortly. Her desk, facing the open door, kept her from seeing Lake Michigan. I wondered if that was her own idea, or if Ajax management didn't think secretaries could be trusted to work if they saw the outside world.

I sat in a large, green-covered plush armchair and flicked through the morning's *Wall Street Journal* while I waited. The headline in 'Heard on the Street' caught my eye. The *Journal* had picked up the rumor of a potential takeover for Ajax. The Tisch brothers and other likely insurance-company owners had been interviewed, but all of them professed total ignorance. Ajax chairman Gordon Firth was quoted as saying:

Naturally we're watching the share price with interest, but no one has approached our shareholders with a friendly offer.

And that seemed to be all they knew in New York.

At a quarter to twelve the door to the inner office opened. A group of middle-aged men, mostly overweight, came out talking in a subdued hubbub. Ferrant followed, straightening his tie with one hand and pushing his hair out of his eyes with the other. He smiled, but his thin face was troubled.

'Have you eaten? Good. We'll go to the executive dining room on sixty.'

I told him that was fine and waited while he put on his suit jacket. We rode in silence to the top of the building.

In the executive dining and meeting rooms, Ajax compensated for the stark unfriendliness of the lobby. Brocade drapes were looped back over gauze hangings at the windows. Walls were paneled in dark wood, possibly mahogany, and the recessed lighting picked up strategically placed bits of modern sculpture and painting.

Ferrant had his own table near a window, with plenty of space between him and any eavesdropping neighbors. As soon as we were seated, a black-uniformed waiter popped out of the ground to waft luncheon menus in front of us and ask for our drink orders. Last night's scotch was adding to the discomfort of my morning with Mallory. I ordered orange juice. I flipped indifferently through the menu. When the waiter came back with our drinks, I found I didn't have any appetite.

'Nothing for me now.'

Ferrant looked at his watch and said apologetically that he was on a short timetable and would have to eat.

Once the waiter was gone, I said abruptly, 'I spent the morning with the police. They think Agnes was expecting someone last night. You said the same thing. Did she tell you anything – anything at all that would help identify the one she was waiting for?'

'Barrett sent me the names of brokers here in Chicago who've been trading in Ajax. It came in Monday's mail and I met Agnes for lunch on Tuesday and gave it to her then, along with the list of those the shares had been registered to. She said she knew a partner in one of the firms pretty well and would call him. But she didn't tell me who.'

'Did you keep a copy of the names?'

He shook his head. 'I've kicked myself a hundred times over for that. But I don't have the American photocopy habit. I always thought it was stupid, generated mounds of useless paper. Now I'm changing my mind. I can get Barrett to send me another copy, but I won't get it today.'

I drummed my fingers on the table. Useless to be irritated about that. 'Maybe her secretary can dig it up for me . . . When she talked to you yesterday, did she mention my name at all?'

He shook his head. 'Should she have?'

'She had my initials in her date book. With Agnes, that means – meant – a reminder to herself. She didn't write down her appointments; she relied on her secretary to keep track of them. So my initials meant she wanted to talk to me.' I'd been too angry with

Mallory to explain that to him, too angry, as well, to tell him about Ferrant and Ajax.

'The police came up with an extraterrestrial theory about Agnes and me being lovers and my shooting her out of spite or revenge or something. It didn't make me too confiding. But I can't help wondering . . . You saw the story in this morning's *Journal*?'

He nodded.

'Well, here you've got a possible takeover bid. None of the principals – if there are any – step into the open. Agnes starts prying. She wants to talk to me, but before she does that she ends up dead.'

He looked startled. 'You don't really think her death has anything to do with Ajax, do you?'

The waiter brought him a club sandwich and he began eating automatically. 'It really troubles me to think my questions might have sent that poor girl to her death. You pooh-poohed me last night for feeling responsible. Christ! I feel ten times as responsible now.' He put his sandwich down and leaned across the table. 'Vic, no company takeover is more valuable than a person's life. Leave it be. If there is a connection – if you stir up the same people – I just couldn't bear it. It's bad enough to feel responsible for Agnes. I scarcely knew her. But I just don't want to worry about that with you, too.'

You can't touch someone in the executive dining room; every corporate officer I ever met was a born-again gossip. Word would spread through all sixty floors by nightfall that Roger Ferrant had brought his girlfriend to lunch and held hands with her.

'Thanks, Roger. Agnes and I – we're grown women. We make our own mistakes. No one else has to take responsibility for them. I'm always careful. I think you owe taking care of yourself to the friends who love you, and I don't want to cause my friends any grief . . . I'm not sure I believe in immortality or heaven or any of those things. But I do believe, with Roger Fox, that we all have to listen to the voice within us, and how easily you can look at yourself in the mirror depends on whether you obey that voice or not. Everyone's voice gives different counsel, but you can only interpret the one you hear.'

He finished his drink before answering. 'Well, Vic, add me to the list of friends who don't want to grieve over you.' He got up abruptly and headed for the exit, leaving his sandwich half eaten on the table.

11
ACID TEST

The Fort Dearborn Trust, Chicago's largest bank, has buildings on each of the four corners of Monroe and LaSalle. The Tower, their most recent construction, is a seventy-five-story building on the southwest side of the intersection. Its curved, aqua-tinted glass sides represent the newest trend in Chicago architecture. The elevator banks are built around a small jungle. I skirted trees and creeping vines until I found the elevators to the sixtieth floor, where Feldstein, Holtz and Woods, the firm in which Agnes had been a partner, occupied the north half. I'd first been there when the firm moved in three years ago. Agnes had just been made a partner and Phyllis Lording and I were helping her hang pictures in her enormous new office.

Phyllis taught English at the University of Illinois-Chicago Circle. I'd called her from the Ajax dining room before coming over to the Fort Dearborn Tower. It was a painful conversation, Phyllis trying unsuccessfully not to cry. Mrs Paciorek was refusing to tell her anything about the funeral arrangements.

'If you're not married, you don't have any rights when your lover dies,' she said bitterly.

I promised to come see her that evening and asked if Agnes had said anything, either about Ajax or why she wanted to see me.

'She told me she'd had lunch with you last Friday, you and some Englishman . . . I know she said he'd brought up an interesting problem . . . I just can't remember anything else now.'

If Phyllis didn't know, Agnes's secretary might. I hadn't bothered phoning ahead to Feldstein, Holtz and Woods, and I arrived on a scene of extraordinary chaos. The inside of a brokerage firm always looks like a hurricane's just been through; brokers carve perilous perches for themselves inside mountains of documents – prospectuses, research reports, annual reports. The wonder is that they ever work through enough paper to know anything about the companies they trade in.

A murder investigation superimposed on this fire hazard was unbearable, even for someone with my housekeeping standards. Gray dusting powder covered the few surfaces not crowded with paper. Desks and terminals were jammed into the already overflowing space so work could go on while police cordoned off parts of the floor they thought might yield clues.

As I walked through the open area towards Agnes's office, a young patrolman stopped me, demanding my business. 'I have an account here. I'm going to see my broker.' He tried to stop me with further questions, but someone barked an order at him from the other side of the room and he turned his back on me.

Agnes's office was roped off, even though the murder had taken place on the other side of the floor. A couple of detectives were going through every piece of paper. I figured they might finish by Easter.

Alicia Vargas, Agnes's young secretary, was huddled miserably in a corner with three word-processor operators; the police had commandeered her rosewood desk as well. She saw me coming and jumped to her feet.

'Miss Warshawski! You heard the news. This is terrible, terrible. Who would do a thing like that?'

The word-processor operators all sat with their hands in their laps, green cursors blinking importunately on blank screens in front of them. 'Could we go someplace to talk?' I asked, jerking my head toward the eavesdroppers.

She collected her purse and jacket and followed me at once. We rode the elevator back down to the coffee shop tucked into one corner of the lobby jungle. My appetite had come back. I ordered corned beef on rye – extra calories to make up for skipping lunch at the executive dining room.

Miss Vargas's plump brown face was swollen from crying. Agnes had picked her out of the typing pool five years ago when Miss Vargas was eighteen and on her first job. When Agnes was made partner, Miss Vargas became her personal secretary. The tears marked genuine grief, but probably also concern for her uncertain future. I asked her whether any of the senior partners had talked to her about her job.

She shook her head sadly. 'I will have to talk to Mr Holtz, I know. They will not think of it until then. I am supposed to be working for Mr Hampton and Mr Janville' — two of the junior partners — 'until things are straightened out.' She scowled fiercely, keeping back further tears. 'If I must go back to the pool, or working for many men, I – I, well I will have to find a job elsewhere.'

Privately I thought that was the best thing for her to do, but being in a state of shock is not the best time to plan. I set my energies instead to calming her down and asking her about Agnes's interest in the putative Ajax takeover.

She didn't know anything about Ajax. And the brokers' names given Agnes by Ferrant? She shook her head. If they hadn't come in the mail, she wouldn't have seen them in the normal course of things. I sighed in exasperation. I'd have to get Roger to ask Barrett for a duplicate list if it didn't turn up in the office.

I explained the situation to Miss Vargas. 'There's a strong possibility that one of the people on the list might have been coming to see Agnes last night. If so, that would be the last person to see her alive. It might even be the murderer. I can get another copy of the list, but it'll take time. If you can look through her papers and find it, it'd be a help. I'm not sure what will identify it. It should be on letterhead from Andy Barrett, the Ajax specialist. May even be part of a letter to Roger Ferrant.'

She agreed readily enough to look for the list, although she didn't hold out much hope of finding it in the mass of papers in Agnes's office.

I settled the bill and we went back to the disaster area. The police pounced on Miss Vargas suspiciously: Where had she been? They needed to go over some material with her. She looked at me help-lessly; I told her I'd wait.

While she talked to the police I nosed out Feldstein, Holtz's research director, Frank Bugatti. He was a young, hard-hitting MBA. I told him I'd been a client of Miss Paciorek. She'd been looking into insurance stocks for me.

'I hate to seem like a vulture – I know she's only been dead a few hours. But I saw in this morning's paper that someone might be trying to take over Ajax. If that's true, the price should keep going up, shouldn't it? Maybe this is a good time to get into the stock. I was thinking of ten thousand shares. Agnes was going to check with you and see what you know about it.'

At today's prices, a customer buying ten thousand shares had a good half million to throw around. Bugatti treated me with com-mensurate respect. He took me into an office made tiny by piles of paper and told me all he knew about a potential Ajax takeover: nothing. After twenty minutes of discoursing on the insurance industry and other irrelevancies, he offered to introduce me to one of the other partners who would be glad to do business with me. I told him I needed some time to adjust to the shock of Miss Paciorek's death, but thanked him profusely for his help.

Miss Vargas was back at her makeshift desk when I returned to the floor. She shook her head worriedly when I appeared. 'I find no list of the kind you're looking for. At least not on top of her desk. I'll keep looking if the police let me back in her office' – she made a contemptuous face – 'but maybe you should get the names elsewhere if you can.'

I agreed and called Roger from her phone. He was in a meeting. I told the secretary this was more important than any meeting he could be in and finally bullied her into bringing him to the phone. 'I won't keep you, Roger, but I'd like another copy of those names you gave Agnes. Can you call Barrett and ask him to express mail them to you? Or to me? I could get them on Saturday if he sent them out tomorrow morning.'

'Of course! I should have thought of that myself. I'll call him right now.'

Miss Vargas was still staring at me hopefully. I thanked her for her help and told her I'd be in touch. When I walked past Agnes's roped-off office I saw the detectives still toiling away at papers. It made me glad to be a private investigator.

That was about the only thing I was glad about all day. It was four o'clock and snowing when I left the Dearborn Tower. By the time I picked up the Omega the traffic had congealed; early commuters trying to escape expressway traffic had immobilized the Loop.

I wished I hadn't agreed to stop in on Phyllis Lording. I'd started the day exhausted; by the time I'd left Mallory's office at eleven I was ready for bed.

As it turned out, I wasn't sorry I went. Phyllis needed help dealing with Mrs Paciorek. I was one of her few friends who knew Agnes's mother and we talked long and sensibly about the best way to treat neurotics.

Phyllis was a quiet, thin woman several years older than Agnes and me. 'It's not that I feel possessive about Agnes. I know she loved me – I don't need to own her dead body. But I have to go to the funeral. It's the only way to make her death real.'

I understood the truth of that and promised to get the details from the police if Mrs Paciorek wouldn't reveal them to me.

Phyllis's apartment was on Chestnut and the Drive, a very posh neighborhood just north of the Loop overlooking Lake Michigan. Phyllis also felt depressed because she knew she couldn't afford to keep the place on her salary as a professor. I sympathized with her, but I was pretty sure Agnes had left her a substantial bequest. She'd asked me to lunch one day last summer shortly after she'd redone her will. I wondered idly if the Pacioreks would try to overturn it.

It was close to seven when I finally left, turning down Phyllis's offer of supper. I had been too overloaded with people for one day. I needed to be alone. Besides, Phyllis believed eating was just a duty you owed your body to keep it alive. She maintained hers with cottage cheese, spinach, and an occasional boiled egg. I needed comfort food tonight.

I drove slowly north. The thickly falling snow coagulated the traffic even after rush hour. All food starting with *p* is comfort food, I thought: pasta, potato chips, pretzels, peanut butter, pastrami, pizza, pastry . . . By the time I reached the Belmont exit I had quite a list and had calmed the top layer of frazzle off my mind.

I needed to call Lotty, I realized. By now she would have heard the news about Agnes and would want to discuss it. Remembering Lotty made me think of her uncle Stefan and the counterfeit securities. That reminded me in turn of my anonymous phone caller. Alone in the snowy night his cultured voice, weirdly devoid of any regional accent, seemed full of menace. As I parked the Omega and headed into my apartment building, I felt frail and very lonely.

The stairwell lights were out. This was not unusual – our building super was lazy at best, drunk at worst. When his grandson didn't come round, a light often went unchanged until one of the tenants gave up in exasperation and took care of it.

Normally, I would have made my way up the stairs in the dark but the night ghosts were too much for me. I went back to the car and pulled a flashlight from the glove compartment. My new gun was inside the apartment, where it could do me the least good. But the flashlight was heavy. It would double as a weapon if necessary.

Once in the building I followed a trail of wet footprints to the second floor, where a group of De Paul students lived. The melted snow ended there. Obviously I'd let my nerves get the better of me, a bad habit for a detective.

I started up the last flight at a good clip, playing the light across the worn shiny stairs. At the half landing to the third floor, I saw a small patch of wet dirt. I froze. If someone had come up with wet feet and wiped the stairs behind him, he might have left just such a small, streaky spot.

I flicked off the light and wrapped my muffler around my neck and face with one arm. Ran up the stairs fast, stooping low. As I neared the top I smelled wet wool. I flung myself at it, keeping my head tucked down on my chest. I met a body half again as big as mine. We fell over in a heap, with him on the bottom. Using the flashlight I smashed where I thought his jaw should be. It connected with bone. He gave a muffled shriek and tore himself away. I pulled back and started to kick when I sensed his arm coming up toward my face. I ducked and fell over in a rolling ball, felt liquid on the back of my neck underneath the muffler. Heard him tearing down the stairs, half slipping.

I was on my feet starting to follow when the back of my neck began burning as though I'd been stung by fifty wasps. I pulled out my keys and got into the apartment as quickly as I could. Double-bolting the door behind me, I ran to the bathroom shedding clothes. I kicked off my boots but didn't bother with my stockings or trousers and leaped into the tub. Turning the shower on full force, I washed myself for five minutes before taking a breath.

Soaking wet and shivering I climbed out of the tub on shaking legs. The mohair scarf had large round holes in it. The collar of the crêpe-de-Chine jacket had dissolved. I twisted around to look at my back in the mirror. A thin ring of red showed where the skin had been partially eaten through. A long fat finger of red went down my spine. Acid burn.

I was shaking all over now. Shock, half my mind thought clinically. I forced myself out of wet slacks and pantyhose and wrapped up in a large towel that irritated my neck horribly. Tea is good for shock, I thought vaguely, but I hate tea; there wasn't any in my house. Hot milk – that would do, hot milk with lots of honey. I was shaking so badly I spilled most of it on the floor trying to get it into a pan, and then had a hard time getting the burner lighted. I stumbled to the bedroom, pulled the quilt from the bed, and wrapped up in it. Back in the kitchen I managed to get most of the milk into a mug. I had to hold the cup close to my body to keep from spilling it all over me. I sat on the kitchen floor draped in blanketing and gulped down the scalding liquid. After a while the shakes eased. I was cold, my muscles were cramped and aching, but the worst was over.

I got stiffly to my feet and walked on leaden legs back to the bedroom. As best I could I rubbed Vaseline onto the burn on my back, then got dressed again. I piled on layers of heavy clothes and still felt chilly. I turned on the radiator and squatted in front of it as it banged and hissed its way to heat.

When the phone rang I jumped; my heart pounded wildly. I stood over it fearfully, my hands shaking slightly. On the sixth ring I finally answered it. It was Lotty.

'Lotty!' I gasped.

She had called because of Agnes, but demanded at once to know what the trouble was. She insisted on coming over, brusquely brushing aside my feeble protests that the attacker might still be lurking outside.

'Not on a night like this. And not if you broke his jaw.'

She was at the door twenty minutes later. 'So, *Liebchen*. You've been in the wars again.' I clung to her for a few minutes. She stroked my hair and murmured in German and I finally began to warm up. When she saw that I'd stopped shivering she had me take off my layers of swaddling. Her strong fingers moved very gently along my neck and upper spine, cleaning off the Vaseline and applying a proper dressing.

'So, my dear. Not very serious. The shock was the worst part. And you didn't drink, did you? Good. Worst possible thing for shock. Hot milk and honey? Very good. Not like you to be so sensible.'

Talking all the while she went out to the kitchen with me, cleaned the milk from the floor and stove, and set about making soup. She put on lentils with carrots and onions and the rich smell filled the kitchen and began reviving me.

When the phone rang again, I was ready for it. I let it ring three times, then picked it up, my recorder switched on. It was my smooth-voiced friend. 'How are your eyes, Miss Warshawski? Or Vic, I should say – I feel I know you well.'

'How is your friend?'

'Oh, Walter will survive. But we're worried about you, Vic. You might not survive the next time, you know. Now be a good girl and stay away from Rosa and St Albert's. You'll feel so much better in the long run.' He hung up.

602

I played the tape back for Lotty. She looked at me soberly. 'You don't recognize the voice?'

I shook my head. 'Someone knows I was at the priory yesterday, though. And that can only mean one thing: One of the Dominicans has to be involved.'

'Why, though?'

'I'm being warned off the priory,' I said impatiently. 'Only they know I was there.' A terrible thought struck me and I began shivering again. 'Only they, and Roger Ferrant.'

12
FUNERAL RITES

Lotty insisted on spending the night. She left early in the morning for her clinic, begging me to be careful. But not to drop the investigation. 'You're a Jill-the-Giant-Killer,' she said, her black eyes worried. 'You are always taking on things that are too big for you, and maybe one day you will take on one big thing too many. But that is your way. If you weren't living so, you would have a long unhappy life. Your choice is for the satisfied life, and we will hope it, too, is a long one.'

Somehow these words did not cheer me up.

After Lotty left, I went down to the basement where each tenant has a padlocked area. With aching shoulders I pulled out boxes of old papers and knelt on the damp floor sorting through them. At last I found what I wanted — a ten-year-old address book.

Dr and Mrs Thomas Paciorek lived on Arbor Drive in Lake Forest. Fortunately their unlisted phone number hadn't changed since 1974. I told the person who answered that I would speak to either Dr or Mrs Paciorek, but was relieved to get Agnes's father. Although he'd always struck me as a cold, self-absorbed man, he'd never shared his wife's personal animosity toward me. He believed his daughter's problems stemmed from her own innate willfulness.

'This is V. I. Warshawski, Dr Paciorek. I'm very sorry about Agnes. I'd like to come to her funeral. Can you tell me when it will be?'

'We're not making a public occasion of it, Victoria. The publicity around her death has been bad enough without turning her funeral into a media event.' He paused. 'My wife thinks you might know something about who killed her. Do you?'

'If I did, you can be sure I would tell the police, Dr Paciorek. I'm afraid I don't. I can understand why you don't want a lot of people or newspapers around, but Agnes and I were good friends. It matters a lot to me to pay my last respects to her.'

He hemmed and hawed, but finally told me the funeral would be Saturday at Our Lady of the Rosary in Lake Forest. I thanked him with more politeness than I felt and called Phyllis Lording to let her know. We arranged to go together in case the Knights of Columbus were posted at the church door to keep out undesirables.

I didn't like the way I was feeling. Noises in my apartment were making me jump, and at eleven, when the phone rang, I had to force myself to pick it up. It was Ferrant, in a subdued mood. He asked if I knew where Agnes's funeral was being held, and if I thought her parents would mind his coming.

'Probably,' I said. 'They don't want me there and I was one of her oldest friends. But come anyway.' I told him the time and place and how to find it. When he asked if he could accompany me, I told him about Phyllis. 'She probably isn't up to meeting strangers at Agnes's funeral.'

He invited me to dinner, but I turned that down, too. I didn't really believe Roger would hire someone to throw acid at me. But still . . . I had eaten dinner with him the same day I'd made my first trip to the priory. It was the next day that Rosa decided to back out of the case. I wanted to ask him, but it sounded too much like Thomas Paciorek asking me on my honor as a Girl Scout if I'd helped kill his daughter.

I was scared, and I didn't like it. It was making me distrust my friends. I didn't know where to start looking for an acid thrower. I didn't want to be alone, but didn't know Roger well enough to be with him.

At noon, as I walked skittishly down Halsted to get a sandwich, an idea occurred to me that might solve both my immediate problems. I phoned Murray from the sandwich shop.

'I need to talk to you,' I said abruptly when he came to the phone. 'I need your help.'

He must have sensed my mood, because he didn't offer any of his usual wisecracks, agreeing to meet me at the Golden Glow at five.

At four-thirty I changed into a navy wool pantsuit, and stuck a toothbrush, the gun, and a change of underwear in my handbag. I checked all the locks, and left by the back stairs. A look around the building told me my fears were unwarranted; no one was lying in wait for me. I also checked the Omega carefully before getting in and starting it. Today at least I was not going to be blown to bits.

I got stuck in traffic on the Drive and was late to the Golden Glow. Murray was waiting for me with the early edition of the *Herald-Star* and a beer.

'Hello, V. I. What's up?'

'Murray, who do you know who throws acid on people he doesn't like?'

'No one. My friends don't do that kind of thing.'

'Not a joke, Murray. Does it ring a bell?'

'Who do you know had acid thrown at them?'

'Me.' I turned around and showed him the back of my neck where Lotty had dressed the burn. 'He was trying for my eyes but I was expecting it and turned away in time. The thrower's name is probably Walter, but the man who got him to throw it – that's who I want.'

I told him about the threats, and the fight, and described the voice of the man who had called. 'Murray, I'm scared. I don't scare easily, but – Jesus Christ! the thought of some maniac out there trying to blind me! I'd rather take a bullet in the head.'

He nodded soberly. 'You're stepping on the feet of someone with bunions, V. I., but I don't know whose. Acid.' He shook his head. 'I'd be sort of tempted to say Rodolpho Fratelli, but the voice doesn't sound right – he's got that heavy, grating voice. You can't miss it.'

Fratelli was a high-ranking member of the Pasquale family. 'Maybe someone who works for him?' I asked.

606

He shrugged. 'I'll get someone to look into it. Can I do a story on your attack?'

I thought about it. 'You know, I haven't been to the police. I guess I'm too angry with Bobby Mallory.' I sketched my interview with him for Murray. 'But maybe it will make my anonymous caller a little more cautious if he sees there's a big universe out there keeping an eye open for him . . . The other thing is – I'm kind of embarrassed to ask this, but the truth is, I'm not up to a night alone. Can I crash with you?'

Murray looked at me for a few seconds, then laughed. 'You know, Vic, it's worth the earful I'll get canceling my date just to hear you plead for help. You're too fucking tough all the time.'

'Thanks, Murray. Glad to make your day.' I wasn't liking myself too well when he went off to the telephone. I wondered what column this went under: taking prudent precautions, or being chicken?

We went to dinner at the Officers' Mess, a romantic Indian restaurant on Halsted, and then dancing at Bluebeard's. As we were climbing into bed at one, Murray told me he'd sicced a couple of reporters on digging up information about acid throwers.

I got up early Saturday and left Murray still asleep – I needed to change for Agnes's funeral. All was still quiet at my apartment, and I began to think I was letting fear get far too much the better of me.

Changing into the navy walking suit, this time with a pale gray blouse and navy pumps, I took off to collect Lotty and Phyllis. It was only ten degrees out, and the sky was overcast again. I was shivering with cold by the time I got back into the car – I needed to replace my mohair shawl.

Lotty was waiting in her doorway dressed in black wool, for once dignified enough to be a doctor. She didn't say much on the drive down to Chestnut Street. When we got to the condo, she got out to fetch Phyllis, who didn't look as if she'd slept or eaten in the two days since I'd seen her last. The skin on her pale, fine-boned face was drawn so tightly I thought it might crack, and she had bluish shadows under her eyes. She was wearing a white wool suit with a pale yellow sweater. I had a vague idea that those were mourning colors in the Orient. Phyllis is a very literary person and she would pay tribute to a dead lover with some kind of mourning that only another scholar would understand.

She smiled at me nervously as we headed back north toward Lake Forest. 'They don't know I'm coming, do they?' she asked.

'No.'

Lotty took exception to that. Why was I acting in a secretive way, which could only precipitate a scene when Mrs Paciorek realized who Phyllis was.

'She's not going to do that. Graduates of Sacred Heart and St Mary's don't have scenes at their daughters' funerals. And she won't take it out on Phyllis – she'll know I was the real culprit. Besides, if I'd told her ahead of time who I was bringing she might have instructed the bouncer not to seat us.'

'Bouncer?' Phyllis asked.

'I guess they call them ushers in churches.' That made Phyllis laugh and we made the rest of the drive considerably more at ease.

Our Lady of the Rosary was an imposing limestone block on top of a hill overlooking Sheridan Road. I slid the Omega into a parking lot at its foot, finding a niche between an enormous black Cadillac and an outsize Mark IV. I wasn't sure I'd ever find my car again in this sea of limos.

As we climbed a steep flight of stairs to the church's main entrance, I wondered how the elderly and infirm made it to mass. Perhaps Lake Forest Catholics were never bed- or wheelchair-ridden, but wafted directly to heaven at the first sign of disability.

Agnes's brother Phil was one of the ushers. When he saw me his face lit up and he came over to kiss me. 'V. I.! I'm so glad you made it. Mother told me you weren't coming.'

I gave him a quick hug and introduced him to Lotty and Phyllis. He escorted us to seats near the front of the church. Agnes's coffin rested on a stand in front of the steps leading up to the altar. As people came in they knelt in front of the coffin for a few seconds. To my surprise, Phyllis did so before joining us in the pew. She knelt for a long time and finally crossed herself and rose as the organ began playing a voluntary. I hadn't realized she was a Catholic.

One of the ushers, a middle-aged man with a red face and white hair, escorted Mrs Paciorek to her place in the front row. She was wearing black, with a long black mantilla pinned to her head. She looked much as I remembered her: handsome and angry. Her glance at the coffin as she entered her pew seemed to say: 'I told you so.'

I felt a tap on my shoulder and looked up to see Ferrant, elegant in a morning coat. I wondered idly if he'd packed mourning clothes just on the chance of there being a funeral in Chicago and moved over to make room for him.

The organ played Fauré for perhaps five minutes before the procession entered. It was huge and impressive. First came acolytes, one swinging a censer, one carrying a large crucifix. Then the junior clergy. Then a magnificent figure in cope and miter, carrying a crosier – the cardinal archbishop of Chicago, Jerome Farber. And behind him, the celebrant, also in cope and miter. A bishop, but not one I recognized. Not that I know many bishops by sight – Farber is in the papers fairly regularly.

I realized after the ceremony had begun that one of the junior priests was Augustine Pelly, the Dominican procurator. That was odd – how did he know the Pacioreks?

The requiem mass itself was chanted in Latin, with Farber and the strange bishop doing a very creditable job. I wondered how Agnes would have felt about this beautiful, if archaic, ritual. She was so modern in so many ways. Yet the magnificence might have appealed to her.

I made no attempt to follow the flow of the service through risings and kneelings. Nor did Lotty and Roger. Phyllis, however, participated completely, and when the bell sounded for communion I wasn't surprised that she edged her way past us and joined the queue at the altar.

As we were leaving the church, Phil Paciorek stopped me. He was about ten years younger than Agnes and me and had had a mild crush on me in the days when I used to frequent the Lake Forest house. 'We're having something to eat at the house. I'd like it if you and your friends came along.'

I looked a question at Lotty, who shrugged as if to say it would be a mistake either way, so I accepted. I wanted to find out what Pelly was doing here.

I hadn't been to the Paciorek house since my second year in law school. I sort of remembered it as being near the lake, but made several wrong turns before finding Arbor Road. The house looked like a Frank Lloyd Wright building with a genetic malfunction – it had kept reproducing wings and layers in all directions until someone gave it chemotherapy and stopped the process.

We left the car among a long line of others on Arbor Road and went into one of the boxes that seemed to contain the front door. When I used to visit there, Agnes and I had always come in from the side door where the garage and stables were.

We found ourselves in a black-and-white marbled foyer where a maid took Lotty's coat and directed us to the reception. The bizarre design of the house meant going up and down several short marble staircases that led nowhere, until we had made two right turns, which took us to the conservatory. This room had been inspired by the library at Blenheim Palace. Almost as big, it contained a pipe organ as well as bookstacks and some potted trees. I wasn't sure why they called it a conservatory instead of a music room or a library.

Phil spotted us at the door and came over to greet us. He was finishing a combined MD-Ph.D. program at the University of Chicago. 'Dad thinks I'm crazy,' he grinned. 'I'm going into neuro-biology as a researcher, instead of neurosurgery where the money is. I think Cecelia is the only one of his children who has turned out satisfactorily.' Cecelia, the second daughter after Agnes, was standing near the organ with Father Pelly and the strange bishop. At thirty she already looked like Mrs Paciorek, including an imposing bosom under her expensive black suit.

I left Phil talking to Phyllis and skirted my way through the crowd to the organ. Cecelia refused to shake hands and said, 'Mother told us you weren't coming.' This was the same thing Phil had said when I met him at the church, except that he was pleased and Cecelia was angry.

'I haven't talked to her, Cecelia. I spoke with your dad yesterday and he invited me.'

'She said she phoned you.'

I shook my head. Since she wasn't going to introduce me, I said to the strange bishop, 'I'm V. I. Warshawski, one of Agnes's old school friends. Father Pelly and I have met out at the Friary of Albertus Magnus.' I half held out my hand, but dropped it when the bishop made no corresponding gesture. He was a lean, gray-haired man of perhaps fifty, sporting a purple episcopal shirt with a gold chain draped across it.

Pelly said, 'This is the Right Reverend Xavier O'Faolin.'

I whistled mentally. Xavier O'Faolin was a Vatican functionary, in charge of the Vatican's financial affairs. He'd been in the papers quite a bit last summer when the scandal broke over the Banco Ambrosiano and Roberto Calvi's tangled problems. The Bank of Italy believed O'Faolin might have had a hand in Ambrosiano's vanishing assets. The bishop was half Spanish, half Irish, from some Central American country, I thought. Heavy friends, Mrs Paciorek had.

'And you were both old friends of Agnes's?' I asked a bit maliciously.

Pelly hesitated, waiting for O'Faolin to say something. When the bishop didn't speak, Pelly said austerely, 'The bishop and I are friends of Mrs Paciorek's. We met in Panama when her husband was stationed there.'

The army had put Dr Paciorek through medical school; he'd done his stint for them in the Canal Zone. Agnes had been born there and spoke Spanish quite well. I'd forgotten that. Paciorek had come a long way from a man too poor to pay his own tuition.

'So she takes an interest in your Dominican school in Ciudad Isabella?' It was an idle question, but Pelly's face was suddenly suffused with emotion. I wondered what the problem was – did he think I was trying to revive the Church-in-politics argument at a funeral?

He struggled visibly with his feelings and at last said stiffly, 'Mrs Paciorek is interested in a wide range of charities. Her family is famous for its support of Catholic schools and missions.'

611

'Yes, indeed.' The archbishop finally spoke, his English so heavily accented as to be almost incomprehensible. 'Yes, we owe much to the goodwill of such good Christian ladies as Mrs Paciorek.'

Cecelia was biting her lips nervously. Perhaps she, too, was afraid of what I might say or do. 'Please leave now, Victoria, before Mother realizes you're here. She's had enough shocks because of Agnes.'

'Your father and brother invited me, Ceil. I'm not gate-crashing.'

I pushed my way through a mink and sable farm glistening with diamonds to the other side of the room where I'd last seen Dr Paciorek. About halfway there I decided the best route lay on the outside of the room through the corridor made by the potted plants. Skirting sideways against the main flow of traffic, I made my way to the edge. A few small knots of people were standing beyond the trees, talking and smoking desultorily. I recognized an old school friend of Agnes from Sacred Heart, lacquered hard and encrusted with diamonds. I stopped and exchanged stilted pleasantries.

As Regina paused to light a fresh cigarette, I heard a man speaking on the other side of the orange tree we stood under. 'I fully support Jim's policy in Interior. We had dinner last week in Washington and he was explaining what a burden these diehard liberals are making of his life.'

Someone else responded in the same vein. Then a third man said, 'But surely there are adequate measures for dealing with such opposition.' Not an unusual conversation for a right-wing bastion of wealth, but it was the third speaker's voice that held me riveted. I was certain I'd heard it on the phone two nights ago.

Regina was telling me about her second daughter, now in eighth grade at Sacred Heart, and how clever and beautiful she was. 'That's wonderful, Regina. So nice to see you again.'

I circled the orange tree. A large group stood there, including the red-faced man who'd been ushering at the church, and O'Faolin. Mrs Paciorek, whom I hadn't seen earlier, was standing in the middle, facing me. In her late fifties, she was still an attractive woman. When I knew her, she followed a rigorous exercise regimen, drank little, and didn't smoke. But years of anger had taken their toll on her face. Under the beautifully coiffed dark hair it was pinched and lined. When she saw me, the furrows in her forehead deepened.

'Victoria! I specifically asked you not to come. What are you doing here?'

'What are you talking about? Dr Paciorek asked me to the service, and Philip invited me to come here afterward.'

'When Thomas told me yesterday that you were coming I phoned you three times. Each time I told the person who answered to make sure you knew you were not welcome at my daughter's funeral. Now don't pretend you don't know what I'm talking about.'

I shook my head. 'Sorry, Mrs Paciorek. You spoke with my answering service. I was too busy to phone in for messages. And even if I'd gotten your orders, I would still have come: I loved Agnes too much to stay away from her funeral.'

'Loved her!' Her voice was thick with anger. 'How dare you make filthy innuendos in this house.'

'Love? Filthy innuendos?' I echoed, then laughed. 'Oh. You're still stuck on the notion that Agnes and I were lovers. No, no. Just good friends.'

At my laughter her face suffused with crimson. I was afraid she might have a stroke on the spot. The red-faced white-haired man stepped forward and took my arm. 'My sister made it clear you're not wanted here. I think it's time you left.' His heavy voice was not that of my threatening caller.

'Sure,' I said. 'I'll just find Dr Paciorek and say goodbye to him.' He tried to propel me toward the door but I shook his hand loose with more vigor than grace. I left him rubbing it and paused in the crowd behind Mrs Paciorek, straining for the smooth, accentless voice of my caller. I couldn't find it. At last I gave up, found Dr Paciorek, made some routine condolences, and collected Phyllis and Lotty.

13
LATE TRADES

Ferrant dropped by late in the afternoon with a copy of Barrett's list. He was grave and formal and declined an offer of a drink. He didn't stay long, just looked over the brokers with me, told me none of those registered as buying the stock were Ajax customers, and left.

None of the firms listed was familiar to me, nor were the names of the stock registrants. In fact, most of the registrants were the brokers themselves. Barrett's cover letter to Roger explained that this was typically the case right after a stock changed hands — it generally took a month or so for the actual owner's name to be filed.

One company appeared several times: Wood-Sage, Inc. Its address was 120 S. LaSalle. Three of the brokers also had addresses there, a fact that seemed more interesting than it really was. When I looked it up on my detailed map of the Loop, I discovered that it was the Midwest Stock Exchange.

There wasn't much I could do with the list until Monday, so I put it in a drawer and concentrated on the NFL Pro Bowl. I sent out for a pizza for supper and spent the night restlessly, the Smith & Wesson loaded next to my bed.

Sunday's *Herald-Star* had a nice little story about my acid burn on the front page of *Chicago Beat*. They'd used a picture taken last spring at Wrigley Field, a bright eye-catching shot. Readers who made it to Section III couldn't avoid seeing me. The personal ads included numerous thanksgivings to St Jude, several lovers seeking reconciliations, but no message from Uncle Stefan.

Monday morning, I stuck my gun in a shoulder holster under a loose tweed jacket and drove the Omega into the Loop to begin a day at the brokerage houses. At the offices of Bearden & Lyman, Members of the New York Stock Exchange, I told the receptionist I had six hundred thousand dollars to invest and wanted to see a broker. Stuart Bearden came out to meet me personally. He was a dapper man in his middle forties, wearing a charcoal pinstripe suit and a David Niven mustache.

He led me through a maze of cubicles where earnest young people sat with phones in one hand, typing on their computer terminals with the other, to his own office in the far corner of the floor. He brought me coffee and treated me with the deference half a million dollars commands. I liked it. I'd have to tell more people I was rich.

Calling myself Carla Baines, I explained to Stuart that Agnes Paciorek had been my broker. I was getting ready to place an order for several thousand shares of Ajax when she'd warned me away from the stock. Now that she was dead I was looking for a new broker. What did Bearden & Lyman know about Ajax? Would they agree with Ms Paciorek's advice?

Bearden didn't blink or blench on hearing Agnes's name. Instead, he told me what a tragedy her death was; what a tragedy, too, that you couldn't feel safe working in your own office at night. He then punched away at his computer and told me the stock was trading at 54⅜. 'It's been going up the last few weeks. Maybe Agnes had some inside news that the stock is cresting. Are you still interested?'

'I'm not in any hurry to invest. I guess I should make up my mind about Ajax in the next day or so, though. Do you think you could scout around and let me know if you hear anything?'

He looked at me closely. 'If you've been thinking about this move for some time, you must know there's a lot of talk about a covert takeover bid. If that's the situation, the price will probably continue to go up until the rumor is confirmed one way or another. If you're going to buy, you should do it now.'

I spread my hands. 'That's why I don't understand Ms Paciorek's advice. That's why I came here – to see if you knew why she'd warn me *not* to buy.'

Bearden called his research director. The two had a short conversation. 'Our staff hasn't heard anything to counter-indicate a buy order. I'd be very happy to take it for you this morning.'

I thanked him but said I needed to do some more research before I made a decision. He gave me his card and asked me to let him know in a day or two.

Bearden & Lyman was on the fourteenth floor of the Stock Exchange. I rode the elevator down eleven floors to my next quarry: Gill, Turner & Rotenfeld.

By noon, having talked myself dry in three different brokerage offices, I beat a discouraged retreat to the Berghoff for lunch. Ordinarily I don't like beer, but their homemade dark draft is an exception. A stein and a plate of sauerbraten helped recoup my strength for the afternoon. Everyone had given me essentially the same information I'd gotten from Stuart Bearden. They knew the rumors about Ajax and they urged me to buy. None of them showed any dismay on hearing either Agnes's name or my interest in Ajax. I wondered if I'd taken the wrong approach. Maybe I should have used my own name. Maybe I was barking up an empty tree. Perhaps a late-night burglar, intent on computer terminals, had found Agnes and shot her.

I continued to prove that a woman with six hundred thousand dollars to invest gets red-carpet treatment. I'd talked to no one but senior partners all morning and Tilford & Sutton was no exception: Preston Tilford would see me personally.

Like the firms I'd visited that morning, this one was medium-sized. The names of twenty or so partners were on the outer door. A receptionist directed me down a short hallway and through the trading room where a score of frantic young brokers manned phones and terminals. I picked my way through the familiar stacks of debris to Tilford's office in the far corner.

His secretary, a pleasant, curly-haired woman in her late forties, told me to go in. Tilford was nervous, his finger-nails bitten down to the quick. This was not necessarily a sign of guilty knowledge, at least not guilty knowledge about Agnes – most of the brokers I'd seen today were high-strung. It must be nerve-racking following all that money up and down.

He doodled incessantly as I pitched my tale to him. 'Ajax, hmm?' he said when I'd finished. 'I don't know. I have – had a lot of respect for Agnes's judgment. It so happens we're not recommending anyone to buy now, either, Ms, uh, Baines. Our feeling is that these takeover rumors have been carefully placed by someone trying to manipulate the stock. The bottom could crash out at any time. Now, if you're looking for a growth stock, I have several here that I could recommend for you.'

He pulled a stack of prospectuses from a desk drawer and shuffled through them with the speed of a professional card dealer. I left with two hot prospects tucked into my bag and a promise to call again soon. On my way to number seven, I called my answering service and told them to take messages if anyone phoned asking for Carla Baines.

At four-thirty, I'd finished with Barrett's list. Except for Preston Tilford, everyone had recommended buying Ajax. He was also the only one who discounted the takeover rumors. That didn't prove anything one way or another about him. It might mean only that he was a shrewder broker than the rest – after all, only one man in one brokerage firm had recommended against buying Baldwin when its stock was soaring, and he was the only one out of the entire universe of security analysts who had been correct. Still, Tilford's recommendation against Ajax was the sole unusual incident of the day. So that was where I had to start.

Back home I changed out of my business clothes into jeans and a sweater. Pulled on my low-heeled boots. Before charging into action, I called the University of Chicago and undertook the laborious process of tracking down Phil Paciorek. Someone finally referred me to a lab where he was working late.

'Phil, it's V.I. There was someone at your house yesterday whose name I'd like to know. Trouble is, I don't know what he looks like, only how his voice sounds.' I described the voice as best I could.

'That could be a lot of different people,' he said dubiously.

'No accent at all,' I repeated. 'Probably a tenor. You know, most people have some kind of regional accent. He doesn't. No midwestern nasal, no drawl, no extra Boston *r*s.'

'Sorry, V.I. Doesn't ring a bell. If something occurs to me, I'll call you, but that's too vague.'

I gave him my phone number and hung up. Gloves, pea jacket, picklocks and I was set. Cramming a peanut butter sandwich into my coat pocket, I clattered down the stairs into the cold January night. Back at the Stock Exchange, a security guard in the hall asked me to sign in. He didn't want any identification so I put down the first name that came to me: Derek Hatfield. I rode to the fifteenth floor, got off, checked the stairwell doors to see that they weren't the kind that lock behind you, and settled down there to wait.

At nine o'clock a security guard came up the stairs from the floor below. I slid back into the hallway and found a ladies' room before he got to the floor. At eleven, the floor lights went out. The cleaning women, calling to each other in Spanish, were packing up for the night.

After they left, I waited another half hour in case anyone had forgotten anything. Finally leaving the stairwell, I walked down the hall to the offices of Tilford & Sutton, my boots clopping softly on the marble floor. I'd brought a flashlight, but fire-exit lights gave enough illumination.

At the outer door I shone my flashlight around the edges to make sure there was no alarm. Offices in a building with internal security guards usually don't have separate alarms, but it's better to be safe than sorry. Pulling my detective's vade mecum from my pocket, I tried a series of picklocks until I found one that worked.

No windows opened onto the outer office. It was completely dark, except for the green cursors flashing urgent messages on blank computer screens. I shivered involuntarily and ran a hand across the burn spot on the back of my neck.

Using my light as little as possible, I picked my way past desks and mounds of papers to Preston Tilford's office. I wasn't sure how often the security guards visited each floor and didn't want to risk

618

showing a light. Tilford's door was locked, too, and took a few minutes of fumbling in the dark. I'd learned to pick locks from one of my more endearing clients in the public defender's office, but had never achieved the quickness of a true professional.

Tilford's door was solid wood, so I didn't have to worry about light shining through a panel as I did with the outer door. Closing it softly, I flipped a switch and took my bearings. One desk, two filing cabinets. Try everything first to see what's locked and look in the locked drawers.

I worked as quickly as I could, keeping my gloves on, not really sure what I was trying to find. The locked file cabinet contained files for Tilford's private customers. I picked a couple at random for close scrutiny. As far as I could tell, they were all in order. Not knowing what should be in a customer statement made it hard to know what to look for — high debit balances, maybe. But Tilford's customers seemed to keep on top of their accounts. I handled the pages carefully, leaving them in their original order, and refiled them neatly. I looked at the names one by one to see if any of his customers sounded familiar. Other than a handful of well-known Chicago business names I didn't see any I knew personally until I came to the Ps. Catherine Paciorek, Agnes's mother, was one of Preston's clients.

My heart beating a little faster, I pulled out her file. It, too, was in order. Only a small amount of the fabled Savage fortune amassed by Agnes's grandfather was handled at Tilford & Sutton. I noticed that Mrs Paciorek had purchased two thousand shares of Ajax on December 2. That made me raise my eyebrows a little. Hers was a blue-chip portfolio with few transactions. In fact, Ajax was the only company she'd traded in 1983. Worth pursuing further?

I could find no other clients trading in Ajax stock. Yet Tilford had registered many more than Catherine Paciorek's two thousand shares. I frowned and turned to the desk.

This was carefully built, of dark mahogany, and the lock in the middle drawer was tough. I ended up scratching the surface as I fumbled with the picklocks. I stared at it in dismay, but it was too late now to worry.

Tilford kept an unusual collection in his private space: besides a half-empty bottle of Chivas, which wasn't too surprising, he had a fine collection of hard-core porn. It was the kind of stuff that makes you feel we should work toward Shaw's idea of a disembodied mind. I grimaced, flipping through the whole stack to make sure nothing more interesting was interleafed.

After that, I figured Tilford owed me a drink and helped myself to some of the Chivas. In the bottom drawer I uncovered file folders of more clients, perhaps his ultrapersonal, super-secret accounts. There were nine or ten of these, including an organization called Corpus Christi. I dimly remembered reading something about it recently in the *Wall Street Journal*. It was a Roman Catholic lay group, made up primarily of wealthy people. The current pope liked it because it was conservative on such important points as abortion and the importance of clerical authority, and it supported right-wing governments with close Church ties. The pope liked the group so much, according to the *Journal*, that he'd appointed some Spanish bishop as its leader and had him – the Spaniard – reporting directly to him – the pope. This miffed the archbishop of Madrid because these lay groups were supposed to report to their local bishops. Only Corpus Christi had a lot of money and the pope's Polish missions took a lot of money, and no one was saying anything directly, but the *Journal* did some discreet reading between the ledger lines.

I flipped through the file, looking at transactions for the Corpus Christi account. It had started in a small way the previous March. Then it began an active trading program, which ran to several million dollars by late December. But no record existed of what it was trading in. I wanted it to be Ajax.

Tilford & Sutton was supposed to have taken largish positions in Ajax, according to Barrett. Yet the two thousand shares Mrs Paciorek bought in December were the only trace of Ajax activity I'd seen in the office. Where were copies of Corpus Christi's statement showing what it was actually buying and selling? And why wasn't it in the file, as was the case with the other customers? Tilford's office didn't include a safe. Using my flashlight as little as possible,

I surveyed the other offices. A large modern safe stood in a supply room, its door to be opened by someone who knew which eighteen numbers to punch on the electronic lock. Not me. If Corpus Christi's records were in there, they were in there for good.

The bells at the nearby Methodist Temple chimed the hour: two o'clock. I took the Corpus Christi and Mrs Paciorek files out to the main room and hunted around for a photocopier. A large Xerox machine stood in the corner. It took a while to warm up. Using my flashlight surreptitiously, I copied the contents of the two files. To separate the pages I had to take off my gloves. I stuffed them in my back pocket.

I had just finished when the night watchman came by and looked in through the glass panel. Like a total imbecile, I had left Tilford's office door ajar. As the watchman fumbled with his keys, I hit the off button and looked around desperately for a hiding place. The machine had a paper cupboard built in underneath. My five-feet-eight frame fit badly, but I squeezed in and pulled the door as nearly shut as I could.

The watchman turned on the overhead lights. Through a crack in the door I watched him go into Tilford's office. He spent long enough in there to decide the place had been burglarized. His voice crackled dimly as he used his walkie-talkie to call for reinforcements. He made a circuit of the outer room, shining his flashlight in corners and closets. Apparently he thought the Xerox machine held nothing but its own innards: he walked past it, stopped directly in front of me, then returned to the inner office.

Hoping he would stay there until help arrived, I gently shoved the door open. Silently easing my cramped body onto the floor, I crawled on hands and knees to the near wall where a window overlooked a fire escape. I slid the window open as quietly as possible and climbed out into the January night.

The fire escape was covered with ice. I almost ended my career forever as I skidded across its narrow iron platform, saving myself with a grab at the burning-cold railing. I'd been holding both the originals and photocopies of Tilford's documents, as well as my flashlight. These flew across the ice as I seized the guardrail. Cursing to myself, I crawled precariously across the platform retrieving documents, stuffing them into my jeans waistband with numbed fingers. I pulled the gloves from my back pocket and put them on while skidding my way down as quickly as possible to the floor below.

The window was locked. I hesitated only seconds, then kicked it in. Brushing glass fragments away with my sweatshirted arm, I soon had a hole big enough to climb through.

I landed on top of a desk covered with files. These scattered in my wake. I kept bumping into desks and cabinets as I tried running to the far door. How could people get to their desks in the morning with so much clutter blocking their paths? I cracked the outer door, heard nothing, and made my way down the hall. I was about to open the stairwell door when I heard feet pounding on the other side.

Turning back down the hall, I tried every door. Miraculously one opened under my hand. I stepped inside onto something squishy and was hit in the nose by someone with a stick. Fighting back, I found myself wrestling a large mop.

Outside I could hear the voices of two patrolmen agreeing in low murmurs about which parts of the floor to guard. Trying to move quietly, I edged my way to the wall of the supply closet and ran into a coatrack. Clothes were hanging from it: the regulation smocks of the cleaning women. I fumbled in the dark, pulled my jeans off, stuck my documents inside the waistband of my tights, and pulled on the nearest smock. It came barely to my knees, and was miles too large in the shoulders, but it covered me.

Hoping I was not covered with paper, glass shards, or blood, and praying that these patrolmen had not dandled me on their knees thirty years ago, I swung open the closet door.

The policemen were about twenty feet from me, their backs turned. 'You!' I screamed, donning Gabriella's thick accent. They swirled around. 'What goes on here, eh? I am calling manager!' I started off in righteous indignation to the elevator.

They were on me in an instant. 'Who are you?'

'Me? I am Gabriella Sforzina. I work here. I belong. But you?

622

What you doing here, anyway?' I started shouting in Italian, trusting none of them knew the words to 'Madamina' from *Don Giovanni*.

They looked at each other uncertainly. 'Take it easy, lady. Take it easy.' The speaker was in his late forties, not far from pension time, not wanting any trouble. 'Someone broke into one of the offices upstairs. We think he left by the fire escape. You haven't seen anyone on this floor, have you?'

'What?' I shrieked, adding in Italian, 'Why do I pay taxes, eh, that's what I want to know – for bums like you to let burglars in while I'm working? So I can be raped and murdered?' I obligingly translated into English for them.

The younger one said, 'Uh, look, lady. Why don't you just go on home.' He scribbled a note on a pad and ripped off the sheet for me. 'Just give that to the sergeant at the door downstairs and he'll let you out.'

It was only then that I realized my gloves were lying with my jeans on the floor of the supply closet.

14
FIERY AUNTS,
MOURNING MOTHERS

Lotty was not amused. 'You sound just like the CIA,' she snapped, when I stopped by the clinic to tell her my adventure. 'Breaking into people's offices, stealing their files.'

'I'm not stealing the files,' I said virtuously. 'I wrapped them up and mailed them back first thing this morning. What troubles me from a moral standpoint is the jacket and gloves I left there – technically their loss is a business expense. Yet will the IRS turn me in if I itemize? I should call my accountant.'

'Do that,' she retorted. Her Viennese accent was evident, as always when Lotty was angry. 'Now leave. I'm busy and have no wish to talk to you in such a mood.'

The break-in had made the late editions. Police speculated that the watchman interrupted the thief before he took anything of value, since nothing of value was missing. My prints are on file at the Eleventh Street station, so I hoped none showed up that I couldn't reasonably account for as part of my business visit to Tilford's office.

What would they make of Derek Hatfield's name on the Stock Exchange's sign-in register, I wondered. I had to figure out some way of finding out if they questioned Hatfield about it.

Whistling through my teeth, I started the Omega and headed out to Melrose Park. Despite Lotty's ill humor I was pleased with myself. Typical criminal failing – you carry off a coup, then have to brag about it. Sooner or later one of your bragees tells the police.

Snow was beginning to fall as I turned onto Mannheim Road. Small dry spitballs, Arctic snow, no good for snowmen. I was wearing long underwear under my navy pantsuit and hoped that would be enough protection against a minus twenty-eight wind chill. Some time today I'd have to find an Army-Navy Surplus and get another pea jacket.

The Priory of Albertus Magnus loomed coldly through the driving pellets. I parked the car out of the wind as far as possible and fought my way to the priory entrance. The wind sliced through suit and underwear and left me gasping for air.

Inside the high-vaulted, stale hallway the sudden silence was palpable. I rubbed my arms and stamped my feet and warmed myself before asking the anemic ascetic at the reception desk to find Father Carroll for me. I hoped I was too early for evening prayers and too late for classes or confessions.

About five minutes later, as the building's essential chill began making me shiver, Father Carroll himself came down the hall. He was moving quickly, yet not hurrying, a man in control of his life and so at peace.

'Miss Warshawski. How nice to see you. Have you come about your aunt? She's back today, as she probably told you.'

I blinked a few times. 'Back? Back here, you mean? No, she hadn't told me. I came . . . I came to see if you could give me any information about a Catholic lay organization called Corpus Christi.'

'Hmm.' Father Carroll took my arm. 'You're shivering – let's get to my office and have a cup of tea. You can have a nice chat with your aunt. Father Pelly and Father Jablonski are there, too.'

I followed him meekly down the hall. Jablonski, Pelly, and Rosa were sitting at a deal table in Pelly's outer office, drinking tea. Rosa's steel-colored hair was as stiffly waved as though made, in fact, from cast iron. She wore a plain black dress with a silver cross at the throat. She was listening attentively to Pelly as Carroll and I came in. At the sight of me her face changed. 'Victoria! What are you doing here?'

The hostility was so obvious that Carroll looked astounded. Rosa must have noticed this, but her hatred was too fierce for her to care about externals; she continued to glare at me, her thin bosom heaving. I walked around the table to her and kissed the air by her cheek. 'Hello, Rosa. Father Carroll says they've brought you back – as the treasurer, I hope? How splendid. I know Albert must be ecstatic, too.'

She looked at me malevolently. 'I know well I cannot make you be quiet, or stop you harassing me. But perhaps in the presence of these holy fathers you will at least not strike me.'

'I don't know, Rosa. Depends on what the Holy Spirit prompts you to say to me. Don't bet on anything, though.'

I turned to Carroll. 'I'm Rosa's brother's only surviving grand-daughter. When she sees me, it always chokes her up like this . . . Could I trouble you for that cup of tea?'

Glad of something to do to cover the tension, Carroll bustled with an electric kettle behind me. When he handed me a cup I asked, 'Does this mean you've found who was responsible for the forgeries?'

He shook his head, his pale brown eyes troubled. 'No. Father Pelly persuaded me, though, that Mrs Vignelli really could not have been involved. We know how valuable her work is, and how much it means to her – it seemed unnecessarily cruel to make her sit at home for months or years.'

Pelly put in, 'Actually, we're not sure they will ever clear the matter up. The FBI seems to have lost interest. Do you know anything about it?' He looked questioningly at me.

I shrugged. 'I get all my news from the daily papers. I haven't seen anything in there about the FBI dropping the investigation. What has Hatfield said to you?'

Carroll answered, 'Mr Hatfield hasn't told us anything. But since the real stocks turned up, they don't seem to be as interested in the investigation.'

'Could be. Derek doesn't talk too much to me.' I sipped some of the pale green tea. It was warming; that was the best that could be said for it. 'I really came out here for a different reason. A friend of mine was shot last week. Saturday I learned Father Pelly was a friend of hers, too. Perhaps the rest of you knew her – Agnes Paciorek?'

Carroll shook his head. 'Of course, we've all been praying for her this week. But Augustine was the only person out here who knew her personally. I don't think we can tell you much about her.'

'I didn't come about her. Or not directly about her. She was shot while tracking down some information for an Englishman I introduced her to. That would make me feel responsible even if we hadn't been good friends. I think she was looking at something connected with a Catholic lay organization called Corpus Christi. I wanted to know if you could tell me anything about it.'

Carroll smiled gently. 'I've heard of it, but I couldn't tell you much about it. They like to operate secretly — so even if were a member I couldn't tell you anything.'

Rosa said venomously, 'And why do you want to know, Victoria? To sling mud at the Church?'

'More mud? Sorry, Rosa. Just because I'm not a Catholic doesn't mean I go around persecuting the Church.'

'No? Then why do you involve yourself in protest meetings on abortion? I saw you at that demonstration last year outside the diocesan offices.'

'Rosa! Don't tell me you were out there with the fetus worshippers! Were you the old woman who spat at a girl in a wheelchair?'

Rosa's teacup clattered from the deal table to the uncarpeted linoleum floor. The institutional mug was too heavy to break, but tea spilled everywhere. She leaped to her feet, ignoring the tea dripping down the front of her black dress. '*Figlia di puttana!*' she shouted. 'Mind your own business. Leave the business of good Catholics alone.'

Carroll looked shocked, whether from the unexpected outburst or because he understood Italian I couldn't tell. He took Rosa's arm. 'Mrs Vignelli. You're letting yourself get overexcited. Maybe the strain of this terrible suspicion has been too much for you. I'm going to call your son and ask him to come pick you up.'

He told Jablonski to get some towels and sat Rosa down in the room's one armchair. Pelly squatted on the floor next to her. He

627

smiled chidingly. 'Mrs Vignelli. The Church admires and supports those who support her, but even ardor can be a sin if not held in check and used properly. A good Catholic welcomes all questions about the Church and the faith. Even if you suspect your niece of scoffing at you and your faith, treat her with charity. If you turn the other cheek long enough, that's how you'll win her. If you abuse her, you'll only drive her away.'

Rosa folded thin lips into an invisible line. 'You're right, Father. I spoke without thinking. You will forgive me, Victoria: I am old and small things affect me too much.'

The charade of piety made me faintly ill. I smiled sardonically and told her that was fine; I could make allowances for her enfeebled state.

A young brother came in with an armful of towels. Rosa took these from him and cleaned herself, floor, and table with her usual angry efficiency. She smiled bleakly at Father Carroll. 'Now. If you will let me use the phone I will call my son.'

Pelly and Carroll ushered her into the inner office; I sat in one of the folding chairs at the table. Jablonski was eyeing me with lively curiosity.

'Do you usually rub your aunt the wrong way?'

I smiled. 'She's old. Little things get to her.'

'She's extremely difficult to work with,' he said abruptly. 'We've lost a lot of part-time people over the years because of her – no one can do anything perfectly enough for her. For some reason she listens to Gus, but he's the only one who can make her see reason. She even snaps at Boniface, and you have to be pretty thin-skinned not to get along with him.'

'Why keep her then? What's all the anxiety to bring her back?'

'She's one of those indispensable battle-axes,' he grimaced.

'She knows our books, she works hard, she's efficient – and we pay her very little. We'd never get anyone with her skill or dedication for what we can afford to give her.'

I grinned to myself: served Rosa right for all her anti-feminist attacks to be the victim of wage discrimination herself.

She came out with Pelly, backbone as straight as ever, ignoring me pointedly as she said goodbye to Jablonski. She was going to wait for Albert in the entrance hall, she announced. Pelly took her elbow solicitously and escorted her out the door. The only man who could get along with Rosa. What a distinction. For a fleeting moment I wondered what her life had been like when Uncle Carl was alive.

Carroll came back into the outer office a few seconds later. He sat down and looked at me for a while without talking. I wished I hadn't let myself get caught up in Rosa's anger.

When he spoke, it wasn't about my aunt. 'Do you want to tell me why you're asking about Corpus Christi and Agnes Paciorek?'

I chose my words carefully. 'The Ajax Insurance Company is one of the country's largest property-casualty insurers. One of their officers came to me a couple of weeks ago concerned that a covert takeover bid might be in the offing. I talked to Agnes about it – as a broker she had ready access to trading news.

'The night she died, she called the man from Ajax to tell him she was meeting with someone who might have information about the stock. At the least, that person was the last who saw her alive. Since he – or she – hasn't come forward, it might even be the person who killed her.'

Now came the tricky part. 'The only clue I have is some notes she scribbled. Some of the words made it clear she was thinking about Ajax when she wrote them. Corpus Christi appeared on that list. It wasn't a memo or anything like that – just the cryptic comments you make when you're writing while you think. I have to start someplace, so I'm starting with these notes.'

Carroll said, 'I really can't tell you much about the organization. Its members guard their privacy zealously. They take literally the injunction about doing your good works in secret. They also take quasi-monastic vows, those of poverty and obedience. They have some kind of structure with the equivalent of an abbot in all the locations where they have members, and their obedience is to the abbot, who may or may not be a priest. He usually is. Even so, he'd be a secret member, carrying out his parish duties as his regular work.'

'How can they take vows of poverty? Do they live in communes, or monasteries?'

He shook his head. 'But they give all their money to Corpus Christi, whether it's their salary or inheritance or stock-market earnings or whatever. Then the order gives it back to them according to their level of need, and also the kind of life-style they need to maintain. Say you were a corporate lawyer. They'd probably let you have a hundred thousand dollars a year. You see, they don't want any questions about why your living standard is so much lower than that of your fellow lawyers.'

Pelly came back into the room at that point. 'Lawyers, Prior?'

'I was trying to explain to Miss Warshawski how Corpus Christi works. I don't really know too much about it. Do you, Gus?'

'Just what you hear around. Why do you want to know?'

I told him what I'd told Carroll.

'I'd like to see those notes,' Pelly said. 'Maybe they'd give me some idea what the connection was in her mind.'

'I don't have them with me. But the next time I come out I'll bring them.' If I remembered to put something down on paper.

It was nearly four-thirty when I got back to the Eisenhower and the snow was coming down as furiously as ever. It was dark now, too, and nearly impossible to see the road. Traffic moved at about five miles an hour. Every now and then, I'd pass some poor soul who'd slid off the side completely.

As I neared the Belmont exit, I debated whether to go home and leave my next errand for an easier day. Two angry ladies in one afternoon was a little hard on the system. But the sooner I talked to Catherine Paciorek the sooner I'd get her out of my life.

I continued north. It was seven by the time I reached the Half Day Road exit.

Away from the expressway arteries the roads were unplowed. I almost got stuck a few times on Sheridan Road, and came to a complete halt just after turning onto Arbor. I got out and looked thoughtfully at the car. No one in the Paciorek house was likely to give me a push. 'You'd better be moving by the time I come back,' I warned the Omega, and set off to do the last half mile on foot.

I moved as quickly as possible through the deep snow, glad of earmuffs and gloves, but wishing desperately for a coat. I let myself into the garage and rang the bell at the side entrance. The garage was heated and I rubbed my hands and feet in the warmth while I waited.

Barbara Paciorek, Agnes's youngest sister, answered the door. She had been about six when I last saw her. A teenager now, she looked so much like Agnes had when I first met her that a small shock of nostalgia ran through me.

'Vic!' she exclaimed. 'Did you drive all the way up from Chicago in this terrible weather? Is Mother expecting you? Come on in and get warm.' She led me in through the back hallway, past the enormous kitchen where the cook was hard at work on dinner. 'Daddy's stuck at the hospital — can't get home until they plow the side roads, so we're going to eat in about half an hour. Can you stay?'

'Sure, if your mother wants me.'

I followed her across vaguely remembered hallways until we reached the front part of the house. Barbara led me into what the Pacioreks called the family room. Much smaller than the conservatory, perhaps only twenty or thirty feet across, the room held a piano and an enormous fireplace. Mrs Paciorek was doing needlepoint in front of the fire.

'Look who's dropped in, Mother,' Barbara announced as though she was bringing a pleasant surprise.

Mrs Paciorek looked up. A frown creased her handsome forehead. 'Victoria. I won't pretend I'm happy to see you; I'm not. But there is something I wanted to discuss with you and this saves me the trouble of phoning. Barbara! Leave, please.'

The girl looked surprised and hurt at her mother's hospitality. I said, 'Barbara, there's something you could do for me if you'd be good enough. While your mother and I are talking, could you find a filling station with a tow truck? My Omega is stuck about a half mile down the road. If you call now, they should have a truck free by the time I leave.'

I sat in a chair near the fire across from Mrs Paciorek. She put her needlepoint aside with a tidy anger reminiscent of Rosa. 'Victoria, you corrupted and destroyed the life of my oldest child. Is it any wonder that you are not welcome in this house?'

'Catherine, that is pig swill, and you know it.'

Her face turned red. Before she could speak, I regretted my rudeness – today was my day for tangling with angry women.

'Agnes was a fine person,' I said gently. 'You should be proud of her. And proud of her success. Very few people achieve what she did, and almost no women. She was smart and she had guts. She got a lot of that from you. Be proud – feel pleased. Grieve for her.'

Like Rosa, she had lived with her anger too long to want to give it up. 'I won't flatter you by arguing with you, Victoria. It was enough for Agnes to know I believed in something for her to believe the opposite. Abortion. The war in Vietnam. Worst of all, the Church. I thought I had seen my family name degraded in every possible way. I didn't realize how much I could have forgiven until she announced in public that she was a homosexual.'

I opened my eyes very wide. 'In public! She actually announced it right in the middle of LaSalle Street? Out where every taxi driver in Chicago could hear her?'

'I know you think you're being very funny. But she might as well have screamed it in the middle of LaSalle Street. Everyone knew about it. And she was proud of it. Proud of it! Archbishop Farber even agreed to talk to her, to make her understand the degradation she was subjecting her body to. Her own family as well. And she laughed at him. Called him names. The kinds of things *you* would think of. I could tell you had led her into that, just as you led her into all her other horrible activities. And then – to bring that – that creature, that vile thing to my daughter's funeral.'

'Just out of curiosity, Catherine, what did Agnes call Archbishop Farber?'

Her face turned alarmingly red again. 'It's that kind of thing. That kind of attitude. You have no respect for people.'

I shook my head. 'Wrong. I have a lot of respect for people. I respected Agnes and Phyllis for example. I don't know why Agnes chose lesbian relations. But she loved Phyllis Lording, and Phyllis loved her, and they lived very happily together. If five percent of married couples brought each other that much satisfaction the divorce rate wouldn't be what it is . . . Phyllis is an interesting woman. She's a substantial scholar; if you read her book *Sappho Underground* you might get some understanding of what she and Agnes were all about in their life together.'

'How can you sit there and talk about this – perversion and dare compare it with the sacrament of marriage?'

I rubbed my face. The fire was making me a little lightheaded and sleepy. 'We're never going to agree about this. Maybe we should just agree not to discuss it anymore. For some reason, it brings you solace to be furious at Agnes's way of living, and it brings you further pleasure to blame it on me. I guess I don't really care that much – if you want to be that blind about your daughter's character and personality and how she made her choices, that's your problem. Your views don't affect the truth. And they only make one person miserable: you. Maybe Barbara some. Perhaps Dr Paciorek. But you're the main sufferer.'

'Why did you bring her to the funeral?'

I sighed. 'Not to piss you off, believe it or not. Phyllis loved Agnes. She needed to see her funeral. She needed that ritual . . . Why am I talking? You're not listening to what I'm saying, anyway. You just want to fuel your rage. But I didn't come all the way out here in a snowstorm just to talk about Phyllis Lording, although I enjoyed that. I need to ask you about your stock transactions. Specifically, how you came to buy two thousand shares of Ajax last month.'

'Ajax? What are you talking about?'

'The Ajax Insurance Company. You bought two thousand shares on December second. Why?'

Her face had turned pale; the skin looked papery in the firelight. It seemed to me a cardiac surgeon would talk to his wife about the strain her wild mood changes put on her heart. But they say you notice least about the ones you're closest to.

Her iron control came through for her. 'I don't expect you to understand what it's like to have a lot of money. I don't know what two thousand shares of Ajax are worth –'

'Almost a hundred twenty thousand at today's prices,' I put in helpfully.

'Yes. Well, that's a fraction of the fortune my father left in my care. It's very possible my accountants thought it was a good year-end investment. For transactions that small they wouldn't bother to consult me.'

I smiled appreciatively. 'I can understand that. What about Corpus Christi? You're an influential Catholic. What can you tell me about them?'

'Please leave now, Victoria. I'm tired and it's time for my dinner.'

'Are you a member, Catherine?'

'Don't call me Catherine. Mrs Paciorek is appropriate.'

'And I would prefer you to call me Miss Warshawski . . . Are you a member of Corpus Christi, Mrs Paciorek?'

'I never heard of it.'

There didn't seem to be anything left to discuss at that point. I started to leave, then thought of something else and stopped in the doorway. 'What about the Wood-Sage corporation? Know anything about it?'

Maybe it was just the firelight, but her eyes seemed to glitter strangely. 'Leave!' she hissed.

Barbara was waiting for me at the end of the hallway where it angled off toward the back of the house. 'Your car's in the garage, Vic.'

I smiled at her gratefully. How could she have grown up so sane and cheerful with such a mother? 'How much do I owe you? Twenty-five?'

She shook her head. 'Nothing. I – I'm sorry Mother's so rude to you.'

'So you're making up for it by towing my car?' I took out my billfold. 'You don't have to do that, Barbara. What your mother says to me doesn't affect how I feel about you.' I pushed the money into her hand.

She smiled with embarrassment. 'It was only twenty.'

I took the extra five back.

'Do you mind if I ask you something? Were you and Agnes, like Mother keeps saying –' she broke off, blushing furiously.

'Were your sister and I lovers? No. And while I love many women dearly, I've never had women lovers. It makes your mother happier, though, to think that Agnes couldn't make her own decisions.'

'I see. I hope you're not angry, that you don't mind . . .'

'Nope. Don't worry about it. Phone me sometime if you want to talk about your sister. She was a good lady. Or give Phyllis Lording a call. She'd appreciate it very much.'

15
THE FIRE NEXT TIME

It was so late when I got home that I didn't check with my answering service until the next morning. They told me then that Roger had called several times, and Murray Ryerson had also left a message. I tried Murray first.

'I think I found your friend Walter. A man calling himself Wallace Smith was treated last Thursday at St Vincent's for a broken jaw. He paid cash for the visit, which astounded the staff because he was there overnight and the bill came to more than a thousand dollars. Still, you know what they say – the best medical care today costs no more than the cheapest nuclear submarine.'

'His address a fake?'

'I'm afraid so. Turned out to be a vacant lot in New Town. But we got a good description from the night nurse in the emergency room. Big surly guy with black curly hair, bald in front. No beard. I gave it to my gofer at the police. He said it sounded like Walter Novick. He's a stevedore and usually uses a knife. Might explain why he didn't do so well with acid.'

I didn't say anything and Murray added penitently, 'Sorry. Not funny, I guess. Anyway, he's a freelance, but he's done a lot of work for Annunzio Pasquale.'

I felt an unaccustomed surge of fear. Annunzio Pasquale. Local mob figure. Murder, torture, you name it: yours for the asking. What could I possibly have done to arouse the interest of such a man?

'You there, Vic?'

'Yes. For a few more hours, anyway. Send irises to my funeral; I've never cared much for lilies.'

'Sure, kid. You be careful who you open doors to. Look both ways before you cross Halsted . . . Maybe I'll run a little story on this – might make the mean streets a bit safer for you.'

'Thanks, Murray,' I said mechanically, and hung up. Pasquale. It had to be the forgeries. Had to be. If you wanted to create money and push it into circulation, who's the first person you'd hire? A Mafia man. Ditto for securities.

I don't frighten easily. But I'm not the Avenger – I can't take on organized crime with my own bare hands. If Pasquale really was involved with the forgeries I'd graciously concede the round. Except for one thing. My life had been threatened gratuitously. Not just my life – my eyesight, my livelihood. If I gave in to that, I'd never have a moment's peace with myself again.

I frowned at a stack of newspapers on the coffee table. There might be a way. If I could talk to Pasquale. Explain where our interests diverged. Explain that the matter of the securities would blow up in his face and just to leave that alone. I'd turn the other cheek if he would withdraw his protection from Novick.

I wondered how I could best get this message to the don. An ad in the *Herald-Star* would do the trick, but might bring the law down on me hard and heavy, too. Hatfield would love to be able to hold me on an obstructing federal justice charge.

I called a woman I know in the DA's office. 'Maggie – V. I. Warshawski. I need a favor.'

'I'm on my way to court, V. I. Can it wait?'

'This won't take long – I just want to know some of Don Pasquale's fronts – restaurants, laundries, anyplace I might be able to get discreetly in touch with him.'

A long silence at the other end. 'You're not so hard up you'd work for him, are you?'

'No way, Maggie – I don't think I could stand up in court to an interrogation by you.'

Another pause, then she said, 'I guess I'm happier not knowing why you want to know. I'll call you when I'm free – maybe about three this afternoon.'

I wandered restlessly around the apartment. I was sure it wasn't Pasquale who'd been on the phone to me. I'd seen him in the Federal Building once or twice, heard him speak in a thick Italian accent. Besides, say Pasquale was ultimately responsible for the forged stocks, responsible for creating them, he couldn't be the one who got them into the priory safe. Maybe he lived in Melrose Park, maybe he went to church at the priory. Even so, he'd have to have bought off a lot of people there to get at the safe. Boniface Carroll or Augustine Pelly as front men for the Mafia? Ludicrous.

Of course, there was always Rosa. I snorted with laughter at the image of Rosa as a Mafia moll. She'd keep Annunzio in line good and proper – yes, no pasta for you tonight, Annunzio, unless you burn my niece with acid.

I suddenly thought of my cousin Albert. I hadn't even included him in the picture before; he was so much in Rosa's shadow. But . . . he was a CPA and the mob could always use good CPAs. And here he was, fat, forty, unmarried, dominated by this truly awful mother. Maybe that would rouse some antisocial spirit in him – it would in me. What if Rosa had called me without his knowing it? Then afterward he talked her into sending me away. For some bizarre reason he had stolen St Albert's stocks and replaced them with counterfeits, but when the investigation heated up he replaced them. He could have gotten the combination to the safe at any time from Rosa.

I continued to work up a case against Albert while cooking curried eggs with peas and tomatoes for lunch. I didn't know my cousin very well. Almost anything could go on behind that bloated, amorphous exterior.

Roger Ferrant called again while I was halfway through the curried eggs. I greeted him cheerfully.

'Vic. You're sounding more like yourself again. I want to talk to you.'

'Sure. Have you learned something new about your Ajax takeover?'

638

'No, but there's something else I want to discuss with you. Can we have dinner tonight?'

On an impulse, still preoccupied with Albert, I not only agreed but even offered to cook. After hanging up I cursed myself – that meant cleaning up the damned kitchen.

Feeling slightly aggrieved, I scrubbed out a collection of stale pots and plates. Made the bed. Trudged through unshoveled sidewalks to the grocery, where I bought a pot roast and cooked it like beef Bourguignon, with onions, mushrooms, salt pork, and of course, Burgundy. To show Roger I didn't suspect him anymore – or at least not at the moment – I decided to serve dinner wine in the red Venetian glasses my mother had brought from Italy. She had originally carried out eight, carefully wrapped in her underwear, but one of them broke several years ago when my apartment was ransacked. I now keep them in a locked cupboard in the back of my clothes closet.

When Maggie called at four-thirty, I realized one side benefit of heavy housework – it definitely keeps your mind off your troubles. I'd been too busy to think about Don Pasquale all afternoon.

Her voice on the phone brought the clutch of fear back to my stomach.

'I just took a brief glance through his files. One of his favorite meeting places is Torfino's in Elmwood Park.'

I thanked her with as much heartiness as I could muster.

'Don't,' she said soberly. 'I don't think I'm doing you any favor telling you this. All I'm doing is speeding you on your way. I know you'd find it out for yourself – one of your newspaper pals would be glad to send you to your funeral just to generate a snappy story.' She hesitated. 'You were always a maverick when you were on the public defender's roster – I hated appearing against you because I never knew what outrageous defense you might rig up. I know you're a good investigator, and I know you have a lot of pride. If you're onto something that leads to Pasquale, call the police, call the FBI. They've got the resources to handle the Mob, and even they're fighting a losing battle.'

'Thanks, Maggie,' I said weakly. 'I appreciate the advice. I really do. I'll think about it.'

639

I got the number of Torfino's restaurant. When I called and asked for Don Pasquale, the voice at the other end said brusquely he'd never heard of such a man and hung up.

I dialed again. When the same voice answered, I said, 'Don't hang up. If you should ever happen to meet Don Pasquale, I'd like to give him a message.'

'Yes?' Grudgingly.

'This is V. I. Warshawski. I'd like a chance to talk to him.' I spelled my last name slowly, giving him my phone number, and hung up.

By now my stomach was jumping in earnest. I wasn't sure I'd be able to handle either Roger or dinner, let alone a combination of the two. To relax, I went into the living room and picked out scales on my mother's old piano. Deep diaphragm breaths. Now, scales on a descending 'Ah.' I worked vigorously for forty-five minutes, starting to feel some resonance in my head as I loosened up. I really should practice regularly. Along with the red glasses, my voice was my legacy from Gabriella.

I felt better. When Roger arrived at seven with a bottle of Taittinger's and a bunch of white spider mums, I was able to greet him cheerfully and return his polite kiss. He followed me to the kitchen while I finished cooking. I wished now I hadn't cleaned up this morning. The place was such a mess I'd have to wash up again tomorrow.

'I lost track of you at Agnes's funeral,' I told him. 'You missed a good old scene with some of her relatives.'

'Just as well. I'm not much of a scene person.'

I dressed a salad and handed it to him and pulled the roast from the oven. We went into the dining room. Roger uncorked the champagne while I dished out the dinner. We ate without talking for a while, Roger staring at his place. At last I said, 'You said there was something you wanted to discuss – not anything very pleasant, I take it.'

He looked up at that. 'I told you I'm not interested in scenes. And I'm afraid what I want to discuss has the makings of a row.'

I set down my wineglass. 'I hope you're not going to try to talk me into laying off my investigation. That would lead to a first-class fight.'

'No. I can't say I'm crazy about it. It's the way you do it, that's all. You've closed me out of any discussion about that – or anything you're doing. I know we haven't spent that much time together so maybe I don't have the right to have expectations about you, but you've been damned cold and unfriendly the last few days. Since Agnes was shot, in fact, you've been really bitchy.'

'I see . . . I seem to have stirred up some people who are a lot bigger than me. I'm afraid, and I don't like that. I don't know who I can trust, and that makes it hard to be open and friendly with people, even good friends.'

His face twitched angrily. 'What the hell have I done to deserve that?'

I shrugged. 'Nothing. But I don't know you that well, Roger, and I don't know who you talk to. Listen. I guess I am being bitchy – I don't blame you for getting mad. I got involved in a problem that was puzzling but didn't seem too dangerous – my aunt's thing with the fake stock shares – and the next thing I knew someone tried pouring acid in my eyes.' He looked shocked. 'Yes. Right on this very landing. Someone who wants me away from the priory.

'I don't really think that's you. But I don't know where it's coming from, and that makes me draw away from people. I know it's bitchy, or I'm bitchy, but I can't help it. And then Agnes's being shot . . . I do feel kind of responsible, because she was working on your problem, and I sent you to her. Even if her being shot doesn't have anything to do with Ajax, which maybe it doesn't, I still feel responsible. She was working late, and probably meeting someone involved in the takeover. I know that's not very clear, but do you understand?'

He rubbed a hand through his long forelock. 'But, Vic, why couldn't you say any of this to me? Why did you just draw back?'

'I don't know. It's how I operate. I can't explain it. It's why I'm a private eye, not a cop or a fed.'

'Well, could you at least tell me about the acid?'

'You were here the night I got the first threatening phone call. Well, they tried making good on it last week. I anticipated the attack and broke the guy's jaw and took the acid on my neck instead of my face. Still, it was very – well, shocking. I thought I heard the man who made the phone call talking at Agnes's funeral. But when I tried to find him, I couldn't.' I described the voice and asked Roger if he remembered meeting anyone like that.

'His voice . . . it was like someone who didn't grow up speaking English and is disguising an accent. Or someone whose natural accent would be a strong drawl or something regional that he's trying to cover.'

Roger shook his head. 'I can't differentiate American accents too well, anyway . . . But, Vic, why couldn't you tell me this? You didn't really think I was responsible for it, did you?'

'No. Not really, of course. I just have to solve my own problems. I don't plan to turn into a clinging female who runs to a man every time something doesn't work out right.'

'Do you think you could find some middle way between those two extremes? Like maybe talking your problems over with someone and still solving them yourself?'

I grinned at him. 'Nominating yourself, Roger?'

'It's a possibility, yes.'

'I'll think about it.' I drank some more champagne. He asked me what I was doing about Ajax. I didn't think I should spread my midnight adventure at Tilford & Sutton too far – a story like that is very repeatable. So I just said I'd done a little digging. 'I came across the name of a holding company, Wood-Sage. I don't know that they're involved in your problem, but the context was a bit unusual. Do you think you could talk to your specialist and see if he's heard of them? Or to some of your corporate investment staff?'

Roger half bowed across the table. 'Oh, wow! Legman for V. I. Warshawski. What's the male equivalent of a gangster's moll?'

I laughed. 'I don't know. I'll get you fitted out with a machine gun so you can do it in the best Chicago style.'

Roger reached a long arm across the table and squeezed my free hand. 'I'd like that. Something to tell them about in the box at

Lloyd's . . . Just don't shut me out, V. I. Or at least tell me why you're doing it. Otherwise I start imagining I'm being rejected and get complexes and other Freudian things.'

'Fair enough.' I disengaged my hand and moved around the table to his chair. I don't blame men for loving long hair on women; there was something erotic and soothing about running my fingers through the long mop that kept falling into Ferrant's eyes.

Over the years I've noticed that men hate secrets or ambiguities. Sometimes I even feel like pampering them about it. I kissed Roger and loosened his tie, and after a few minutes' uncomfortable squirming on the chair, led him into the bedroom.

We spent several agreeable hours there and fell asleep around ten o'clock. If we hadn't gone to bed so early, my deepest sleep wouldn't have been over by three-thirty. I might have been sleeping too heavily for the smoke to wake me.

I sat up in bed, irritated, momentarily thinking I was back with my husband, one of whose less endearing habits was smoking in bed. However, the acrid smell in no way resembled a cigarette.

'Roger!' I shook him as I started scrambling around in the dark for a pair of pants. 'Roger! Wake up. The place is on fire!'

I must have left a burner on in the kitchen, I thought, and headed toward it with some vague determination to extinguish the blaze myself.

The kitchen was in flames. That's what they say in the newspapers. Now I knew what they meant. Living flames enveloped the walls and snaked long orange tongues along the floor toward the dining room. They crackled and sang and sent out ribbons of smoke. Party ribbons, wrapping the floor and the hallway.

Roger was behind me. 'No way, V. I.!' he shouted above the crackling. He grabbed my shoulder and pulled me toward the front door. I seized the knob to turn it and drew back, scorched. Felt the panels. They were hot. I shook my head, trying to keep panic at bay. 'It's on fire, too!' I screamed. 'Fire escape in the bedroom. Let's go!'

Back down the hall, now purple and white with smoke. No air. Crawl on the ground. On the ground past the dining room. Past the remains of the feast. Past my mother's red Venetian glasses, wrapped with care and taken from Italy and the Fascists to the precarious South Side of Chicago. I dashed into the dining room and felt for them through the smog, knocking over plates, the rest of the champagne, finding the glasses while Roger yelled in anguish from the doorway.

Into the bedroom, wrapping ourselves in blankets. Shutting the bedroom door so opening the window wouldn't feed the hungry flames, the flames that devoured the air. Roger was having trouble with the window. It hadn't been opened in years and the locks were painted shut. He fumbled for agonizing seconds while the room grew hotter and finally smashed the glass with a blanketed arm. I followed him through the glass shards out into the January night.

We stood for a moment gulping in air, clinging to each other. Roger had found his pants and was pulling them on. He had bundled up all the clothes he could find at the side of the bed and we sorted out the leavings. I had my jeans on. No shirt. No shoes. One of my wool socks and a pair of bedroom slippers had come up in the bundle. The freezing iron cut into my feet and seemed to burn them. The slippers were moth-eaten, but the leather was lined with old rabbit fur and cut out the worst of the cold. I wrapped my naked top in a blanket and started down the slippery, snow-covered steps, clutching the glasses in one hand and the icy railing in the other.

Roger, wearing untied shoes, trousers, and a shirt, came hard on my heels. His teeth were chattering. 'Take my shirt, Vic.'

'Keep it,' I called over my shoulder. 'You're cold enough as it is. I've got the blanket . . . We need to wake up the kids in the second-floor apartment. Your legs are so long, you can probably hang over the edge of the ladder and reach the ground – it ends at the second floor. If you'll take my mother's goblets and carry them down, I'll break in and get the students.'

He started to argue, chivalry and all that, but saw there wasn't time. I wasn't going to lose those glasses and that was that. Grabbing the snow-covered rung at the end of the escape with his bare hands, he swung over the edge. He was about four feet from the ground. He dropped off and stretched up a long arm for the goblets. I hooked my legs over one of the rungs and leaned over. Our fingertips just met.

'I'm giving you three minutes in there, Vic. Then I'm coming after you.'

I nodded gravely and went to the bedroom window on the second story. While I pounded and roused two terrified youths from a mattress on the floor, half my mind was working out a puzzle. Fire at the front door, fire in the kitchen. I might have started a kitchen fire by mistake, but not one at the front door. So why was the bottom half of the building not on fire while the top half was?

The students – a boy and a girl in the bedroom, another girl on a mattress in the living room – were confused and wanted to pack their course notes. I ordered them roughly just to get dressed and move. I took a sweatshirt from a stack of clothes in the bedroom and put it on and bullied and harassed them out the window and down the fire escape.

The fire engines were pulling up as we half slid, half jumped, into the snow below. For once I was grateful to our building super for not shoveling better – the snow made a terrific cushion.

I found Roger in front of the building with my first-floor neighbors, an old Japanese couple named Takamoku. He'd gone in for them through a ground-floor window. The fire engines were drawing an excited crowd. What fun! A midnight fire. In the flashing red lights of the engines and the blue of the police cars, I watched avid faces gloating while my little stake in life burned.

Roger handed me my mother's wineglasses and I cradled them, shivering, while he put an arm around me. I thought of the other five, locked in my bedroom, in the heat and flames. 'Oh, Gabriella,' I muttered, 'I'm so sorry.'

16
NO ONE IS LUCKY FOREVER

The paramedics hustled us off to St Vincent's hospital in a couple of ambulances. A young intern, curly-haired and exhausted, went through some medical rituals. No one was badly hurt, although Ferrant and I both were surprised to find burns and cuts on our hands – we'd been too keyed up during our getaway to notice.

The Takamokus were badly shocked by the fire. They had lived quietly in Chicago after being interned during World War II, and the destruction of their tiny island of security was a harsh blow. The intern decided to admit them for a day or two until their daughter could fly from Los Angeles to make housing arrangements for them.

The students were excited, almost unbearably so. They couldn't stop talking and yelling. Nervous reaction, but difficult to bear. When the authorities came in at six to question us, they kept shouting and interrupting each other in their eagerness to tell their tale.

Dominic Assuevo was with the fire department's arson unit. He was a bull-shaped man – square head, short thick neck, body tapering down to surprisingly narrow hips. Perhaps an ex-boxer or ex-football player. With him were a uniformed fireman and Bobby Mallory.

I'd been sitting in a torpor, anguished at the wreck of my apartment, unwilling to think. Or move. Looking at Bobby, I knew I'd need to pull my wits together. I took a deep breath. It almost didn't seem worth the effort.

The weary intern gave exhausted consent for the police to question us – except for the Takamokus, who had already been wafted into the hospital's interior. We moved into a tiny office near the emergency room, the hospital security-staff room, obligingly vacated by two drowsing security guards. The eight of us made a tight fit, the investigators and one of the students standing, the rest in the room's few chairs.

Mallory looked at me in disgust and said, 'If you knew what you looked like, Warshawski. Half naked and your boyfriend no better. I never thought I'd see the day I'd be glad Tony was dead, but I'm thankful he can't see you now.'

His words acted like a tonic. The dying war horse staggers to its feet when it hears a bugle. Police accusations usually rouse me.

'Thank you, Bobby. I appreciate your concern.'

Assuevo intervened quickly. 'I want the full story on what happened tonight. How you became aware of the fire, what you were doing.'

'I was asleep,' I explained. 'The smoke woke me up. Mr Ferrant was with me; we realized the kitchen was on fire, tried the front door and found it was on fire, too. We got out by the fire escape – I roused these kids, he got Mr and Mrs Takamoku. That's all I know.'

Roger confirmed my story. We both vowed that the people we'd gotten up had been sound asleep at the time. Could they have been faking it? Assuevo wanted to know.

Ferrant shrugged. 'They could have been, but they seemed pretty deep in sleep to me. I wasn't concerned about that kind of thing, Mr Assuevo. Just to get them up and out.'

After thrashing that out, Assuevo went on to explore our feelings about the landlord – did any of us bear a grudge, what kind of problems had we had with the apartment, how had the landlord responded. To my relief, even the overwrought students sensed where those questions were going.

'He was a landlord,' one of the girls said, the thin, long-haired one who'd been in the living room. The other two chimed in their agreement. 'You know, the place was clean and the rent was cheap. We didn't care about anything else.'

After a few more minutes of that, Assuevo murmured with Bobby near the door. He came back and told the students they could leave.

'Why don't you go, too?' I said to Roger. 'It's time you were getting down to Ajax, isn't it?'

Ferrant gripped my shoulder. 'Don't be an ass, V.I. I'll call my secretary in a bit – it's only seven o'clock. We'll see this out together.'

'Thank you, Mr Ferrant,' Assuevo said swiftly. 'Since you were in the apartment at the time of the fire, we would have to ask you to stay, anyway.'

Bobby said, 'Why don't you explain how you two know each other and why?'

I looked coldly at Mallory. 'I can see where this is headed, and I don't like it one bit. If you are going to imply in any way that either Mr Ferrant or I knew anything about the fire, we are going to insist on charges being brought before we answer any questions. And my attorney will have to be present.'

Roger scratched his chin. 'I'll answer any questions that'll help solve this problem – I assume everyone agrees the apartment was set on fire by an arsonist – but if you're charging me with breaking any laws, I'd better call the British consul.'

'Oh, get off your high horse, both of you. I just want to know what you were doing tonight.'

I grinned at him. 'No, you don't, Bobby: it'd make you blush.'

Assuevo stepped in again. 'Someone tried to kill you, Ms Warshawski. They broke the lock on the front door to get into the building. They poured kerosene on your apartment door and set fire to it. You want my opinion, you're lucky to be alive. Now the lieutenant and I gotta make sure, Ms Warshawski, that there aren't some bad guys' – his eyebrows punctuated the remark to let me know that 'bad guys' was facetious – 'out there who are trying for you personally. Maybe it's just someone with a grudge against the landlord, and he goes after you as a sideline. But maybe it's against you, okay? And so maybe Mr Ferrant here' – sketching a gesture at Roger – 'is assigned to make sure you stay in the apartment tonight. So don't be such an angry lady. The lieutenant and I, we're just doing our job. Trying to protect you. Unless maybe you set the fire yourself, huh?'

I looked at Roger. He pushed the hair out of his eyes and tried straightening a nonexistent tie before speaking. 'I can see you have to look into that, Mr Assuevo. I've done my share of fire-claim investigations and I assure you, I know you have to explore every possibility. While you're doing that, though, maybe we can try to find out who actually set that fire.' He turned to me. 'Miss Warshawski, you don't think it could be the same person who threw –'

'No,' I interrupted him firmly, before he could complete the sentence. 'Not at all.'

'Then who? If it was personally directed – no, not the people who shot Agnes?' Roger looked at Mallory. 'You know, Miss Paciorek was murdered recently while looking into a takeover attempt for me. Now Miss Warshawski's trying to pick up that investigation. This is something you really need to look into.'

Roger, you goon, I thought. Did that just occur to you? Mallory and Assuevo were talking in unison. 'Threw what?' Bobby was demanding, while Assuevo said, 'Who's Miss Paciorek?'

When they quieted down, I said to Bobby, 'Do you want to explain Agnes Paciorek to Mr Assuevo, Lieutenant?'

'Don't ride me, Warshawski,' he warned. 'We've had our discussion on that. If you or Mr Ferrant has some hard evidence to show she was killed because she was looking into those Ajax buyers, give it to me and I'll follow it to the end. But what you've told me so far doesn't add up to more than the kind of guilt we always find with friends and relations – she was killed because I didn't do this or that or because I asked her to stay late or whatever. You have anything to add to that, Mr Ferrant?'

Roger shook his head. 'But she told me she was staying late to talk to someone about the sales.'

Bobby sighed with exaggerated patience. 'That's just what I mean. You're the college-educated one, Vicki. You explain to him about logic and moving from one argument to the other. She was working late on Ajax and she got shot. Where's the connection?'

'Ah,' Assuevo said. 'That stockbroker who was killed. My sister's husband's niece is a cousin of her secretary . . . Do you think there's a connection with the fire, Ms Warshawski?'

I shrugged. 'Tell me something about the arson. Does it have a signature you recognize?'

'It could be the work of any professional. Quick, clean, minimum fuel, no prints – not that we expect prints in the middle of January. No evidence left behind. It was *organized*, Ms Warshawski. Organized. So we want to know who is organizing against you. Maybe the enemies of Ms Paciorek?'

Mallory looked at me thoughtfully. 'I know you, Vicki. You're just arrogant enough to go stirring that pot without telling me. What have you found?'

'It's not arrogance, Bobby. You made some really disgusting accusations the morning after Agnes died. I figure I don't owe you one thing. Not one name, not one idea.'

His round face turned red. 'You don't talk to me that way, young lady. If you obstruct the police in the performance of their duties, you can be arrested. Now what have you found out?'

'Nothing. I know who the Chicago brokers were for the big blocks of Ajax sales the last six-seven weeks. You can get those from Mr Ferrant here. That's what I know.'

His eyes narrowed. 'You know the firm of Tilford and Sutton?'

'Stockbrokers? Yeah, they're on Mr Ferrant's list.'

'You ever been to their offices?'

'I don't have anything to invest.'

'You wouldn't have been there two nights ago, would you, *investigating* their Ajax sales?'

'At night? Stockbrokers do business during the day. Even I know that . . .'

'Yeah, clown. Someone broke into their offices. I want to know if it was you.'

'There were eight or nine brokers on Mr Ferrant's list. Were they all broken into?'

He smashed his fist on the table to avoid swearing. 'It was you, wasn't it?'

'Why, Bobby? You keep telling me there's nothing to investigate there. So why would I break in to investigate something that doesn't exist?'

'Because you're pigheaded, arrogant, spoiled. I always told Tony and Gabriella they should have more children – they spoiled you rotten.'

'Well, too late to cry about that now . . . Look, I've had a rough night. I want to find some place to crash and then try to get my life going again. Can I go back to the apartment and see if any of my clothes are salvageable?'

Assuevo shook his head. 'We got a lot more to discuss here, Ms Warshawski. I need to know what you're working on.'

'Oh, yeah,' Bobby put in. 'Ferrant here started to ask if it was the same person who threw something, and you cut him off. Who threw what?'

'Oh, some kids on Halsted threw a rock at the car the other night – random urban violence. I don't think they'd set fire to my apartment just because they missed the car.'

'You chase them?' Assuevo demanded. 'You hurt them in some way?'

'Forget it,' Bobby told him. 'It didn't happen. She doesn't chase kids. She thinks she's Paladin or the Lone Ranger. She's stirred up something big enough to hire a professional torch, and now she's going to be a heroine and not say anything about it.' He looked at me, his gray eyes serious, his mouth set in a tight line. 'You know, Tony Warshawski was one of my best friends. Anything happens to you, his and Gabriella's ghosts will haunt me the rest of my life. But no one can talk to you. Since Gabriella died, there isn't a person on this planet can get you to do something you don't want to do.'

I didn't say anything. There wasn't anything I could say.

'C'mon, Dominic. Let's go. I'm putting a tail on Joan of Arc here; that's the best we can do right now.'

After he left, the exhaustion swept over me again. I felt that if I didn't leave now I'd pass out in the chair. Still wrapped in the blanket, I forced myself to my feet, accepting Roger's helping hand gratefully. In the hallway, Assuevo lingered a moment to talk to me. 'Ms Warshawski. If you know *anything* about this arson attempt, and do not tell us, you are liable for criminal prosecution.' He stabbed my chest with his finger as he talked. I was too tired even to become angry. I stood holding my glasses and watched him trot to catch up with Bobby.

Roger put an arm around me. 'You're all done in, old girl. Come back to the Hancock with me and take a hot bath.'

As we reached the outer door, he felt in his pockets. 'I left my wallet on your dresser. No money for a cab. You have any?'

I shook my head. He ran across the parking lot to where Bobby and Assuevo were climbing into Bobby's police car. I staggered drunkenly after him. Roger demanded a lift back to my apartment so he could try to rummage for some money. And possibly some clothes.

The ride back down Halsted was strained and quiet. When we got to the charred remains of my building, Assuevo said, 'I just want you to be very clear that that building may not be safe. Any accidents, you're on your own.'

'Thanks,' I said wearily. 'You guys are a big help.'

Roger and I picked our way across ice mountains formed by the frozen jets of water from the fire trucks. It was like walking through a nightmare – everything was familiar, yet distorted. The front door, broken open by the firefighters, hung crazily on its hinges. The stairs were almost impassable, covered with ice and grime and bits of walls that had fallen in.

At the second-floor landing, we decided to separate. The stairs and floor might take the weight of one person, but not two. Locked in my stubborn desire to cling to my mother's two surviving wineglasses, I allowed Roger to go ahead and stood holding them, shivering in my slippers, wrapped in the blanket.

He picked his way cautiously up to the third floor. I could hear him going into my apartment, heard the occasional thud of a brick or piece of wood falling, but no crashes or loud cries. After a few minutes he came back to the hallway. 'I think you can come up, Vic.'

I clutched the wall with one hand and stepped around the ice. The last few stairs I had to do on hands and knees, moving the glasses up a step, then myself, and so to the landing.

The front of my apartment had essentially been destroyed. Standing in the hall, you could look directly into the living room through holes in the walls. The area around the front door had been incinerated, but by stepping through a hole in the living-room wall you could stand on supporting beams.

Such furniture as I owned was destroyed. Blackened by fire and soaked with water, it was irrecoverable. I tried picking out a note on the piano and got a deadened twang. I bit my lip and resolutely moved past it toward the bedroom. Because bedroom and dining room were on either side of the main hall and the main path of the fire, the damage there was less. I'd never sleep in that bed again, but it was possible, by sorting carefully, to find some wearable clothes. I pulled on a pair of boots, donned a smoke-filled sweater, and rummaged for an outfit that would carry me through the morning.

Roger helped me pack what seemed restorable into two suitcases, prying open their frozen locks.

'What we don't take now I might as well kiss goodbye – the neighborhood will be poking through the remains before too long.'

I waited until we were ready to leave before looking in the cupboard at the back of my closet. I was too afraid of what I'd find. Fingers shaking, I pried the door off its sagging hinges. The glasses were wrapped carefully in pieces of old sheet. I unrolled these slowly. The first one I picked had a jagged piece broken from it. I bit my lower lip again to keep it in order and unwrapped the other four. They seemed to be all right. I held them up to the dim morning light and twirled them. No cracks or bubbles.

Roger had been standing silently. Now he picked his way across the debris. 'All well?'

'One's broken. Maybe someone could glue it, though – it's just one big piece.' The only other valuables in the cupboard were Gabriella's diamond drop earrings and a necklace. I put these in my pocket, rewrapped the glasses and placed them in one suitcase, and put on the shoulder holster with my Smith & Wesson in it. I couldn't think of anything else I desperately needed to keep. Unlike Peter Wimsey, I collect no first editions. Such kitchen gadgets as I owned could be replaced without too much grief.

As I started lugging the suitcases to the hole in the living-room wall, the phone rang. Roger and I looked at each other, startled. It never occurred to us that Ma Bell could keep the wires humming after a fire. I managed to find the living-room extension buried under some plaster.

'Yes?'

'Miss Warshawski?' It was my smooth-voiced friend. 'You were lucky, Miss Warshawski. But no one is lucky forever.'

17
THE FALLEN KNIGHT

We drove down to the Hancock in the Omega. I let Roger out with my baggage and went to find street parking. By the time I staggered back to his apartment I knew I wasn't going to be able to do anything until I got some sleep. Pasquale, Rosa, Albert, and Ajax whirled muzzily through my brain, but walking was so difficult that thinking was impossible.

Roger let me in and gave me a set of keys. He had showered. His face was gray with fatigue, but he didn't think he could take the day off with so many rumors flying around about the takeover – management was meeting daily, mapping strategy.

He held me tightly for a few minutes. 'I didn't say much at the hospital because I was afraid I might ruin your story. But please, Vic, please don't run off into anything stupid today. I like you better in one piece.'

I hugged him briefly. 'All I care about right now is getting some sleep. Don't worry about me, Roger. Thanks for the place to stay.'

I was too tired to bathe, too tired to undress. I just managed to pull my boots off before falling into bed.

It was past four when I woke again, stiff and foggy but ready to start moving again. I realized with distaste that I stank and my clothes stank, too. A small utility room next to the bathroom held a washing machine. I piled in jeans, underwear, and everything in the suitcases that didn't require dry cleaning. A long soak in the bathtub and I felt somewhat more human.

As I waited for my jeans to dry I called my answering service.

No message from Don Pasquale, but Phil Paciorek had phoned and left his on-call number. I tried it, but he apparently was handling some emergency surgery. I gave Ferrant's number to the hospital and tried Torfino's restaurant again. The same gritty voice I'd talked to the day before continued to disclaim all knowledge of Don Pasquale.

The early evening editions had arrived in the downstairs lobby. I stopped in the coffee shop to read them over a cappuccino and a cheese sandwich. The fire had made the *Herald-Star*'s front page – ARSON ON THE NORTH SIDE – in the lower left corner. Interview with the De Paul students. Interview with the Taka-mokus' worried daughter. Then, in a separate paragraph with its own subhead: 'V. I. Warshawski, whose apartment was the focal point of the fire, has been investigating a problem involving forged securities at the Priory of Albertus Magnus in Melrose Park. Ms Warshawski, the victim of an acid-throwing mugger two weeks ago, was not available for comment on a connection between her investigation and the fire.'

I ground my teeth. Thanks a bunch, Murray. The *Herald-Star* had already run the acid story, but now the police were bound to read it and see the connection. I drank some more cappuccino, then flipped to the personal section of the classifieds. A small message was waiting for me: 'The oak has sprouted.' Uncle Stefan and I had agreed on this since he'd been working with my certificates of Acorn stock. I had last looked at the personals on Sunday; today was Thursday. How long had the ad been running?

Roger was home when I got back to the apartment. He told me apologetically that he was all done in; could I manage dinner alone while he went to bed?

'No problem. I slept all day.' I helped him into bed and gave him a backrub. He was asleep by the time I left the room.

I pulled on long underwear and as many sweatshirts as I could manage, then walked back to Lake Shore Drive to retrieve my car. A wind blowing across the lake cut through my pullovers and long underwear. Tomorrow I'd definitely stop at Army-Navy Surplus for a new pea jacket.

I wondered about the tail Bobby claimed he was going to slap on me. No one had followed me to my car. Looking in the rearview mirror, I didn't see any waiting cars. And no one would loiter on the street in this wind. I decided it must have been bravado – or someone had countermanded Bobby.

The Omega started only after severe grumbling. We sat and shivered together, the car refusing to produce any heat. A five-minute warm-up finally persuaded the transmission to groan into gear.

While side streets were still piled with snow, Lake Shore Drive was clear. After a few turgid blocks, the car moved north briskly. At Montrose the heater finally kicked grudgingly into life. At the Evanston border I had stopped shivering and was able to pay more attention to traffic and road conditions.

The night was clear; on Dempster the heavy rush-hour traffic was moving well. I spun off onto Crawford Avenue and made it to Uncle Stefan's a few minutes before seven. Before leaving the car, I jammed the Smith & Wesson into the front of my jeans where the butt dug into my abdomen – the pullovers made a shoulder holster impractical.

Whistling through my teeth, I rang Uncle Stefan's bell. No answer. I shivered in the entryway a few minutes, and rang again. It hadn't occurred to me that he wouldn't be home. I could wait in the car, but the heater wasn't very efficient. I rang the other bells until someone buzzed me in – one in every building, letting the muggers and buggers in.

Uncle Stefan's apartment was on the fourth floor. On my way up, I passed a pretty young woman coming down with a baby and a stroller. She looked at me curiously. 'Are you going to visit Mr Herschel? I've been wondering whether I should look in on him – I'm Ruth Silverstein – I live across the hall. When I take Mark for a walk at four, he usually comes out to give us cookies. I didn't see him this afternoon.'

'He could have gone out.'

I could see her flush in the stairway light. 'I'm home alone with the baby, so maybe I pay more attention to my neighbors than I should. I usually hear him leave – he walks with a cane, you know, and it makes a particular kind of noise on the stairs.'

'Thanks, Mrs Silverstein.' I trotted up the last flight of stairs, frowning. Uncle Stefan was in good health, but eighty-two years old. Did I have any right to break in on him? Did I have a duty to do so? What would Lotty say?

I pounded loudly on the heavy apartment door. Put an ear to the panel and heard nothing. No, a faint buzz of noise. The TV or radio. Shit.

I went back down the stairs two at a time, propped open the outer door with a glove, and jogged across the slippery sidewalk to the Omega. My picklocks were in the glove compartment.

As I dashed back into the building, I watched Mrs Silverstein and Mark disappear into a small grocery store up the block. I might have ten minutes to get the door open.

The trick about prying open other people's doors is to relax and go by feel. Uncle Stefan had two locks, a deadbolt and a regular Yale. I worked the deadbolt first. It clicked and I realized with dismay that it had been open when I started on it; I'd just double-locked the door. Trying to breathe loosely I chivvied it the other way. It had just slid back when I heard Mrs Silverstein come into the building. At least, judging from the sounds, that's who it was; someone talking briskly to a baby about the nice chicken Daddy would have when he got back from his late meeting. The stroller bumped its way to the fourth-floor landing. The lower lock clicked back and I was inside.

I picked my way past an Imari umbrella stand into the ornately decorated living room. In the light of a brass lamp I could see Uncle Stefan lying across the leather desk, its green dyed red-brown by a large congealing pool of blood. 'Oh, Christ!' I muttered. While I felt the old man's wrist, all I could think of was how furious Lotty would be. Unbelievably, a faint pulse still fluttered. I leaped over chairs and footstools and pounded on the Silverstein door. Mrs Silverstein opened it at once – she'd just come home, coat still on, baby still in stroller.

'Get an ambulance as fast as you can – he's seriously injured.'

She nodded matter-of-factly and bustled into the interior of her apartment. I went back to Uncle Stefan. Grabbing blankets from a tidy bed in a room off the kitchen, wrapping him, lowering him gently on the floor, raising his feet onto an intricately cut leather footstool, and then waiting. Waiting.

Mrs Silverstein had sensibly asked for paramedics. When they heard about shock and blood loss, they set up a couple of drips – plasma and glucose. They were taking him to Ben Gurion Memorial Hospital, they told me, adding that they would make a police report and could I wait in the apartment, please.

As soon as they were gone, I phoned Lotty.

'Where are you?' she demanded. 'I read about the fire and tried phoning you.'

'Yes, well, that can wait. It's Uncle Stefan. He's been seriously wounded. I don't know if he'll live. They're taking him to Ben Gurion.'

A long silence at the other end, then Lotty said very quietly, 'Wounded? Shot?'

'Stabbed, I think. He lost a lot of blood, but they missed the heart. It had clotted by the time I found him.'

'And that was when?'

'About ten minutes ago . . . I waited to call until I knew what hospital he'd be going to.'

'I see. We'll talk later.'

She hung up, leaving me staring at the phone. I prowled around the living room, waiting for the police, trying not to touch anything. As the minutes passed, my patience ran out. I found a pair of gloves in a drawer in the tidy bedroom. They were several sizes too large, but they kept me from leaving prints on the papers on the desk. I couldn't find any stock certificates at all – not forged, not my Acorn shares.

The room, while crowded with furniture, held few real hiding places. A quick search revealed nothing. Suddenly it occurred to me that if Uncle Stefan had made a forged stock certificate, he'd have to have tools lying around, tools the police would be just as happy not seeing. I sped up my search and found parchment, blocks, and tools in the oven. I bundled them up into a paper bag and went to find Mrs Silverstein.

She came to the door, cheeks red, hair frizzled from heat; she must have been cooking. 'Sorry to bother you again. I've got to wait here for the police and I'll probably have to go to the station with them. Mr Herschel's niece will be by later for some things. Would you mind if I told her to ring your bell and pick this bag up from you?'

She was happy to help. 'How is he? What happened?'

I shook my head. 'I don't know. The paramedics didn't say anything. But his pulse was steady, even though it was weak. We'll hope for the best.'

She invited me in for a drink but I thought it best not to give the police any ideas connecting the two of us and waited for them across the way. Two middle-aged men finally arrived, both in uniform. They came in with guns drawn. When they saw me, they told me to put my hands on the wall and not to move.

'I'm the person who called you. I'm just as surprised by all this as you are.'

'We'll ask the questions, honey.' The speaker had a paunch that obscured his gunbelt. He patted me down clumsily, but found the Smith & Wesson without any trouble. 'You got a license for this, girlie?'

'Yup,' I said.

'Let's see it.'

'Mind if I take my hands off the wall? Hampers any movements.'

'Don't be a wiseass. Get the license and get it fast.' This was the second cop, leaner, with a pockmarked face.

My purse was on the floor near the door – I'd dropped it without thinking when I saw Uncle Stefan and hadn't bothered to pick it up. I pulled out my billfold and took out my PI license and my permit for the gun.

The stout cop looked them over. 'Oh, a private eye. What are you doing here in Skokie, girlie?'

I shook my head. I hate suburban police. 'The bagels in Chicago aren't as good as the ones they make out here.'

Fat cop rolled his eyes. 'We picked up Joan Rivers, Stu . . . Listen, Joan. This ain't Chicago. We want to put you away, we can, won't worry us none. Now just tell us what you were doing here.'

'Waiting for you guys. Clearly a mistake.'

The lean cop slapped my face. I knew better than to react – up here resisting arrest could stick and I'd lose my license. 'Come on, girlie. My partner asked you a question. You going to answer it?'

'You guys want to charge me? If so, I'll call my lawyer. If not, no questions.'

The two looked at each other. 'Better call your lawyer, girlie. And we'll be hanging onto the gun. Not really a lady's weapon.'

18

IN THE SLAMMER

The DA was mad at me. That didn't bother me too much. Mallory was furious — he'd read about the acid in the *Herald-Star*. I was used to Mallory's rage. When Roger learned I'd spent the night in a Skokie lockup, his worry turned to frustrated anger. I thought I could handle that. But Lotty. Lotty wouldn't speak to me. That hurt.

It had been a confused night. Pockmark and Fatso booked me around nine-thirty. I called my lawyer, Freeman Carter, who wasn't home. His thirteen-year-old daughter answered. She sounded like a poised and competent child, but there wasn't any way of telling when she'd remember to give her father the message.

After that we settled down for some serious questioning. I decided not to say anything, since I really didn't have much of a story I wanted to tell. I couldn't tell the truth, and with the mood Lotty was in, she'd be bound to screw up any embroidery I came up with.

Pockmark and Fatso gave way to some senior cops fairly early in the evening. It must have been around midnight when Charles Nicholson came in from the DA's office. I knew Charles. He was a figure in the Cook County court system. He liked to think he was an heir of Clarence Darrow, and resembled him superficially, at least as far as shaggy hair and a substantial stomach went. Charles was the kind of guy who liked to catch his subordinates making personal phone calls on county time. We'd never been what you might call close.

'Well, well, Warshawski. Feels like old times. You, me, a few differences, and a table between us.'

'Hello, Charlie,' I said calmly. 'It does seem like old times. Even down to your shirt not quite meeting at the sixth button.'

He looked down at his stomach and tried pulling the straining fabric together, then looked at me furiously. 'Still your old flippant self, I see – even on a murder-one charge.'

'If it's murder one, they changed the booking without telling me,' I said irritably. 'And that violates my Miranda rights. Better read the charge slip and double-check it.'

'No, no,' he said in his mayonnaise voice. 'You're right – just a manner of speaking. Obstruction was and is the charge. Let's talk about what you were doing in the old man's apartment, Warshawski.'

I shook my head. 'Not until I have legal advice – in my opinion anything I say on that topic may incriminate me, and since I don't have specific knowledge of the crime, there isn't anything I can do to forward the police investigation.' That was the last sentence I uttered for some time.

Charlie tried a lot of different tactics – insults, camaraderie, high-flown theories about the crime to invite my comments. I started doing some squad exercises – raise the right leg, hold for a count of five, lower, raise the left. Counting gave me a way to ignore Charlie, and the exercises rattled him. I'd gotten to seventy-five with each leg when he gave up.

Things changed at two-thirty when Bobby Mallory came in. 'We're taking you downtown,' he informed me. 'I have had it up to here' – he indicated his neck – 'with your smartass dancing around. Telling the truth when you feel like it. How dared you – how *dared* you give that acid story to Ryerson and not tell us this morning? We talked to your friend Ferrant a few hours ago. I'm not so dumb I didn't notice you cutting him off this morning when he started to ask if these were the same people who threw something. Acid. You should be in Cook County Psychiatric. And before the night's over, you're either going to spill what you know or we're going to send you there and make it stick.'

663

That was just talk, and Bobby knew it. Half of him was furious with me for concealing evidence, and half was plain mad because I was Tony's daughter and might have gotten myself killed or blinded.

I stood up. 'Okay. You got it. Although Murray ran the acid story when it happened. Just get me out of the suburbs and away from Charlie and I'll talk.'

'And the truth, Warshawski. You cover up anything, *anything*, and we'll have you in jail. I don't care if I run you in for dope possession.'

'I don't do dope, Bobby. They find any in my place, it's planted. Anyway, I don't have a place.'

His round face turned red. 'I'm not taking it, Warshawski. You're two sentences away from Cook County. No smartassing, no lies. Got it?'

'Got it.'

Bobby got the Skokie people to drop charges and took me away. Technically I wasn't under arrest and didn't have to go with him. I also wasn't under any illusions.

The driver was a likeable young man who seemed willing to chat. I asked him whether he thought the Cubs were going to let Rick Sutcliffe go. One blistering remark from Bobby shut him up, however, so I discoursed alone on the topic. 'My feeling is, Sutcliffe turned that team around after the All-Star break. So he wants five, six million. It's worth it for another crack at the World Series.'

When we got to Eleventh Street, Bobby hustled me into an interrogation room. Detective Finchley, a young black cop who'd been in uniform when I first met him, joined us and took notes.

Bobby sent for coffee, shut the door, and sat behind his cluttered desk.

'No more about Sutcliffe and Gary Matthews. Just the facts.'

I gave him the facts. I told him about Rosa and the securities, and the threatening phone calls. I told him about the attack in the hallway and how Murray thought it might be Walter Novick. And I told him about the phone call this morning when I went back for my clothes. 'No one is lucky forever.'

664

'And what about Stefan Herschel? What were you doing there the day he was stabbed?'

'Just chance. Is he all right?'

'No way, Warshawski. I'm asking the questions tonight. What were you doing at his place?'

'He's an uncle of a friend of mine. You know Dr Herschel . . . He's an interesting old man and he gets lonely; he wanted me to have tea with him.'

'Tea? So you let yourself in?'

'The door was open when I got there – that worried me.'

'I'll bet. The girl across the hall says the door was shut and that worried her.'

'Not standing open – just not locked.'

Bobby held up my collection of picklocks. 'You wouldn't have used these, by any chance?'

I shook my head. 'Don't know how to use them – they're a souvenir from one of my clients when I was a public defender.'

'And you carry them around for sentiment after what – eight years as a PI? Come on, let's have it.'

'You got it, Bobby. You got the acid, you got Novick, you got Rosa. Talk to Derek Hatfield, why don't you. I'd be real curious who was backing the FBI off those securities.'

'I'm talking to you. And speaking of Hatfield, you wouldn't know why his name was on the register at the Stock Exchange, would you, the night someone broke into Tilford and Sutton's office?'

'You ask Hatfield what he was doing there?'

'He says he wasn't.'

I shrugged. 'The feds never tell you anything. You know that.'

'Well, neither do you, and you've got less excuse to hold back. Why were you visiting Stefan Herschel?'

'He invited me.'

'Yeah. Your apartment burned down last night, so today you've been feeling chipper, you'll just go to tea in Skokie. *Damn* it, Vicki, *level with me.*' Mallory was truly upset. He doesn't hold with swearing around women. Finchley looked worried. I was worried, too, but I just couldn't blow the whistle on Stefan Herschel. The old man had got himself killed, or close to it, on account of the forgery. I didn't want to get him arrested, too.

At five, Bobby charged me with concealing evidence of a crime. I was printed, photographed, and taken to the holding cells at Twenty-sixth and California with some rather disgruntled prostitutes. Most wore high-heeled boots and very short skirts – jail must at least have been a warmer place on a January night than Rush and Oak. There was a little hostility at first as they tried to make sure I wasn't working any of their territories.

'Sorry, ladies – I'm just here on a murder charge.' Yeah, my old man, I explained. Yeah, the bastard beat me. But the last straw was when he tried to burn me. I showed them my arms where the fire had scorched the skin.

Lots of sympathetic clucking. 'Oh, honey, you did right . . . Man touch me that way, I stick him.' 'Oh, yeah, 'member when Freddie tried to cut me, I throw boil' water on him.'

They quickly forgot me as each tried to outdo the other with tales of male violence and bravado in handling it. The stories made my skin crawl. At eight though, when the Freddies and Slims and JJs showed up to collect them, they acted glad enough to see them. Home is where they have to take you in, I guess.

Freeman Carter came for me at nine. He's the partner in Crawford, Meade – my ex-husband's high-prestige firm – who does their criminal stuff. It's a constant thorn to Dick – my ex – that Freeman does my legal work. But not only is he good, in a smooth, WASPy way, he likes me.

'Hi, Freeman. The other pimps got their hookers out an hour ago. I guess I'm not very valuable merchandise.'

'Hi, Vic. If you had a mirror you'd see why your street value has plummeted. You're going to have a hearing in Women's Court at eleven. Just a formality, and they'll release you on an I-bond.' An I-bond, as in I-solemnly-swear-to-come-back-for-the-trial, is given to people the court knows as responsible citizens. Like me. Freeman lent me a comb and I made myself as presentable as possible.

We went down the hall to a small meeting room. Freeman looked as elegant as ever, his pale blond hair cut close to his head, smooth-shaven, his perfectly tailored navy suit fitted to his lean body. If I looked only half as grubby as I felt, I must be pretty disgusting. Freeman glanced at his watch. 'Want to talk? They booked you because they felt you were withholding on Stefan Herschel.'

'I was,' I admitted. 'How is he?'

'I called the hospital on my way over here. He's in intensive care, but seems to have stabilized.'

'I see.' I felt a lot better already. 'You know he had a forgery rap back in the fifties? Well, I'm afraid someone knifed him because he was playing boy detective on some stock forgeries. But I can't tell Bobby Mallory until I've talked to the old man. I just don't want to get him in trouble with the police and the feds.'

Freeman made a sour face. 'If I were your pimp, I'd beat you with a clothes hanger. Since I'm just your lawyer, could I urge you to tell Mallory all you know? He's a good cop. He's not going to railroad an eighty-year-old man.'

'He might not, but Derek Hatfield would in thirty seconds. Less. And once the feds move in, there isn't shit Bobby or I – or even you – can do.'

Freeman remained unconvinced as I told him about the forgeries and Uncle Stefan's role in them, but he swept me through the hearing with aplomb. He kissed me goodbye afterward when he dropped me at the Roosevelt Road el stop. 'And that is proof of devotion, Vic. You are badly in need of a bath.'

I rode the el to Howard Street, caught the Skokie Swift, and walked the ten blocks from the station to my car. A bath, a nap, Roger, Lotty, and Uncle Stefan. Those were priorities in reverse order, but I needed to get clean before I could face talking to anyone else.

The priorities got reversed a bit – Roger was waiting for me when I got back to the Hancock. He was on the phone, apparently with Ajax. I sketched a wave and headed for the bathroom. He came in ten minutes later as I was lying in the tub. Trying to lie in the tub. It was one of those nasty modern affairs where your knees come up to your chin. My apartment had a wonderful thirties bath, long enough for a tall person to lie down in it.

Roger closed the toilet and sat on it. 'The police woke me at one this morning to ask me about your acid burn. I told them everything I knew, which was damned little. I had no idea where you were, what you were doing, what danger you might be in. I begged you yesterday morning not to do anything stupid. But when I wake up at one in the morning and you're not here, no note – goddamn it, why did you do this?'

I sat up in the tub. 'I had an eventful evening. Saved an old man's life, then spent five hours in a Skokie jail and four in a Chicago one. I got one phone call and I needed it for my lawyer. Since he wasn't home, only his kid, I couldn't send messages to my friends and relations.'

'But damn it, Vic, you know I'm worried sick about you and this whole business' – he waved an arm, indicating frustration and incoherence. 'Why the hell didn't you leave me a note?'

I shook my head. 'I didn't think I was going to be gone long. Gosh, Roger, if I'd known what I was going to find, I would have written you a novel.'

'That's not the point. You know it's not. We talked about this last night, or two nights ago, whenever the hell your place burned down. You can't just slide off and leave everyone else gasping for air.'

I was starting to get angry, too. 'You don't own me, Ferrant. And if my staying here makes you think you do, I'll leave at once. I'm a detective. I'm paid to detect things. If I told everyone and his dog Rover what I was up to, not only would my clients lose all confidence in me, I'd be sandbagged everywhere I went. You told the cops everything you knew. If you'd known everything I know, a poor old man would be under arrest right now as well as in intensive care.'

Roger looked at me bleakly, his face pale. 'Maybe you should leave, Vic. I don't have the stamina for any more nights like this. But let me tell you one thing, Wonder Woman: if you'd shared what you were doing with me, I wouldn't have had to tell the cops

– I'd have known that you didn't need their particular help. I told them not to sandbag you but to protect you.'

Anger was tightening my vocal cords. 'No one protects me, Roger. I don't live in that kind of universe. I wouldn't screw around with some business deal you were cutting just because there are a lot of dangerous and unscrupulous people dealing in your world. You want to talk to me about your work, I'll listen and try to make suggestions if you want them. But I won't try to protect you.' I got out of the tub. 'Well, give me the same respect. Just because the people I deal with play with fire instead of money doesn't mean I need or want protection. If I did, how do you think I'd have survived all these years?'

I was clenching and unclenching my fists, trying to keep rage under control. Protection. The middle-class dream. My father protecting Gabriella in a Milwaukee Avenue bar. My mother giving him loyalty and channeling her fierce creative passions into a South Chicago tenement in gratitude.

Roger picked up a towel and began soberly drying my back. He wrapped it around my shoulders and gave me a hug. I tried to relax, but couldn't. 'Vic. I have to go screw around in some business deals . . . You're right – I glory in knowing I can come out on top in a real scrum. If you sailed in and dislocated someone's thorax, or whatever you do, I'd be furious . . . I don't think I own you. But the remoter you get, the more I need something to grab hold of.'

'I see.' I turned around. 'I still think it would be easier on both of us if I found another place to stay. But I'll – I'll try to keep in better touch.' I stood on my toes and kissed him gently.

The phone rang. I went to the dryer where I'd left my clothes and pulled out fresh jeans and another shirt while Roger picked up the bathroom extension. 'For you, Vic.'

I took it in the bedroom. Roger said he was leaving and hung up. The caller was Phil Paciorek. 'You still want your man with the non-accent? There's an archdiocesan dinner tonight at the Hanover House Hotel – Farber's giving a party for O'Faolin. Because Mother shells out a million or so to the Church every year, we're invited.

Most of the people at the funeral will be there. Want to be my date?'

An archdiocesan dinner. Thrills. That meant a dress and nylons. Which meant a trip to the shops, as anything even remotely suitable for the Hanover House was still lying smokefilled in my suitcase. Since Phil wouldn't be able to leave the hospital until seven, he asked if I'd mind meeting him at the hotel – he'd be there as close to seven-thirty as possible. 'And I've called the archdiocese – if I'm not there, just give your name to the woman at the reception desk.'

After that I tried taking a nap, but I couldn't sleep. Lotty, Uncle Stefan, Don Pasquale were churning around in the foreground of my brain. Along with Rosa and Albert and Agnes.

At noon I gave up on rest and tried calling Lotty. Carol Alvarado, the nurse at Lotty's North Side clinic, answered the phone. She went to find the doctor, but came back with the message that she was too busy to talk to me right now.

I walked across the street to Water Tower and found a severely tailored crimson wool crêpe dress on sale at Lord & Taylor. In front, it had a scalloped neck; in back the neckline dropped to a V closing just above my bra strap. I could wear my mother's diamond drops with it and be the belle of the ball.

Back at the Hancock I tried Lotty again. She was still too busy to talk. I got the morning paper and looked through the classifieds for furnished apartments. After an hour of calling, I found a place on Racine and Montrose that offered two-month leases. I packed the suitcase again, mushing laundered clothes together with the smoke-stained ones, then left a long note to Roger, explaining where I was moving and what I was doing for dinner and could we please stay in touch, and tried Lotty one last time. Still too busy.

The Bellerophon had seen better days, but it was well cared for. For two fifty a month, I had possession of a sitting room with a Murphy bed, a comfortable armchair, a small TV, and a respectable table. The kitchen included a minuscule refrigerator and two gas burners, no oven, while the bathroom had a real tub in it. Good enough. The room had phone jacks. If the neighborhood vandals hadn't walked off with my phones, I ought to be able to get service switched through. I gave Mrs Climzak a check for the first month's rent and left.

My old apartment looked forlorn in the winter sunlight – Manderley burned out – broken glass in the windows, the Takamokus' print curtains sagging on their rods. I climbed past the debris on the stairs through the hole in the living-room wall. The piano was still there – too big to move – but the sofa and coffee table were gone. Charred copies of *Forbes* and the *Wall Street Journal* were scattered around the room. The living-room phone had been ripped out of the wall. In the dining room, someone had swiped all the liquor. Naturally. Most of the plates were gone. Thank God I'd never had enough money for Crown Derby.

My bedroom extension was still there, buried under a pile of loose plaster. I unplugged it from the wall and left. Stopped at the Lincoln Park Post Office to arrange forwarding for my mail and pick up what they'd held for me since the fire. Then, gritting my teeth, I drove north on Sheffield to Lotty's storefront clinic.

The waiting room was full of women and small children. A din combined of Spanish, Korean, and Lebanese shrieks made the small space seem even tinier. Babies crawled on the floor with sturdy wooden blocks in their fists.

Lotty's receptionist was a sixty-year-old woman who'd raised seven children of her own. Her chief skills were keeping order in the waiting room and making sure that people were seen in order either of appearance or emergency. She never lost her temper, but she knew her clientele like a good bartender and kept order the same way.

'Miss Warshawski. Nice to see you. We have a pretty full house today – lots of winter colds and flu. Is Dr Herschel expecting you?'

Mrs Coltrain would not call anyone by her first name. After years of coaxing, Lotty and I had given up. 'No, Mrs Coltrain. I stopped by to see how her uncle was doing, to find out if I can visit him.'

Mrs Coltrain disappeared into the back of the clinic. She came back with Carol Alvarado a few minutes later. Carol told me Lotty was with a patient but would see me for a few minutes if I'd go into her office.

Lotty's office, like the waiting room, was furnished to set worried mothers and frightened children at ease. She didn't need a desk, she said – after all, Mrs Coltrain kept all the files in file cabinets. Instead, a few comfortable chairs, pictures, a thick carpet, and the ever-present building blocks made the room a cheerful place. Today I didn't find it relaxing.

Lotty made me wait half an hour. I thumbed through the *Journal of Surgical Obstetrics*. I drummed my fingers on the table next to my chair, did leg lifts and a few other stretches.

At four, Lotty came in quietly. Above her white lab coat her face was set in uncompromising lines. 'I am almost too angry to speak to you, Vic. Fortunately, my uncle has survived. And I know he owes his life to you. But he almost owes his death to you, too.'

I was too tired for another fight today. I ran my hands through my hair, trying to stimulate my brain. 'Lotty, you don't have to work to make me feel guilty: I do. I should never have involved him in such a crazy, dangerous business. All I can say is, I've taken my share of the knocks. If I'd known what was coming, I would have done my utmost to keep him from being attacked.' I laughed mirthlessly. 'A few hours ago I had a blazing fight with Roger Ferrant – he wants to protect me from arsonists and suchlike. Now you're fighting me because I didn't protect your uncle.'

Lotty didn't smile. 'He wants to talk to you. I tried to forbid this – he doesn't need any more excitement or strain. But it seems to be more stress to keep him from you than otherwise. The police want to question him and he's refusing until he's seen you.'

'Lotty, he's an old man, but he's a sane man. He makes his own choices. Don't you think some of your anger comes from that? And from helping me involve him? I do my best with my clients, but I know I can't help all of them, not a hundred percent.'

'Dr Metzinger is in charge of his case. I'll call and let him know you'll be out – when?'

I gave up the argument and looked at my watch. I could just make it and dress for dinner if I went now. 'In half an hour.'

She nodded and left.

figure up the stairs and moved along corridors as quietly... [cut off]
waiter had arrived to collect it... been in for half an hour...
his friend and left.

19

DINNER DATE

Ben Gurion Hospital lay close to the Edens. Visible from the expressway, it was easy to get to. It was barely five o'clock when I got out of the car in the hospital parking lot, even after stopping to buy a pea jacket at an Amvets Store. It's always struck me as the ultimate insult to pay to park at hospitals; they incarcerate your friends and relations in rooms that cost six or seven hundred dollars a day, then put a little sting in by charging a few extra bucks to visit them. I pocketed the lot ticket with ill humor and stomped into the lobby. A woman at the information desk called the evening nurse in Intensive Care, then told me I was expected, to go on up.

Five o'clock is a quiet time in a hospital. Surgery and therapies are over for the day; the evening visitors haven't started arriving yet. I followed red arrows painted on deserted hallways up two flights of stairs to the intensive-care unit.

A policeman sat outside the door to the unit. He was there to protect Uncle Stefan, the night nurse explained. Would I mind showing identification and letting him pat me down. I thoroughly approved the caution. At the back of my mind was the fear that whoever had stabbed the old man might return to finish the job.

The policeman satisfied, medical hygiene had to be accommodated. I put on a sterile mask and disposable gown. In the changing-room mirror I looked like a stranger: gray eyes heavy with fatigue, hair wind-tangled, the mask disguising my personality. I hoped it wouldn't terrify a weak old man.

When I came out, Dr Metzinger was waiting for me. He was a

674

balding man in his late forties. He wore Gucci loafers and had a heavy gold bracelet on his left wrist. Got to spend the money somehow, I guess.

'Mr Herschel has insisted so hard on talking to you we thought it best for you to see him,' he said in a low voice, as though Uncle Stefan might hear and be disturbed. 'I want you to be very careful, though. He's lost a lot of blood, been through a very severe trauma. I don't want you to say anything that might cause a relapse.'

I couldn't afford to antagonize anyone else today. I just nodded and told him I understood. He opened the door to the intensive-care unit and ushered me through. I felt as though I were being conducted into the presence of royalty. Uncle Stefan had been isolated from the rest of the unit in a private room. When I realized Metzinger was following me into it I stopped. 'I have a feeling what Mr Herschel has to say is confidential, Doctor. If you want to keep an eye on him, can you do it through the door?'

He didn't like that at all and insisted on coming in with me. Short of breaking his arm, which was a tempting idea, there wasn't much I could do to stop him.

The sight of Uncle Stefan lying small in a bed, attached to machines, to a couple of drips, to oxygen, made my stomach turn over. He was asleep; he looked closer to death than he had in the apartment last night.

Dr Metzinger shook him lightly by the shoulder. He opened his guileless brown eyes, recognized me after a few bewildered seconds, and beamed feebly. 'Miss Warshawski. My dear young lady. How I have been longing to see you. Lotty has told me how you saved my life. Come here, eh, and let me kiss you – never mind these terrible machines.'

I knelt down next to the bed and hugged him. Metzinger told me sharply not to touch him – the whole point of the gown and gauze was to keep germs out. I got to my feet.

Uncle Stefan looked at the doctor. 'So, Doctor. You are my good protector, eh? You keep the germs away and get me healthy quickly. Now, though, I have a few private words for Miss Warshawski only. So could I trouble you to leave?'

I studiously avoided Metzinger's face as he withdrew with a certain amount of ill grace. 'You can have fifteen minutes. Remember, Miss Warshawski – you're not to touch the patient.'

'No, Dr Metzinger. I won't.' When the doctor had closed the door with an offended snap I pulled a chair to the side of the bed.

'Uncle Stefan – I mean, Mr Herschel – I'm so sorry I let you get involved in this. Lotty is furious, and I don't blame her – it was thoughtless. I could beat myself.'

The wicked grin that made him look like Lotty came. 'Please – call me Uncle Stefan. I like it. And do not beat your beautiful body, my dear new niece – Victoria, is it not? I told you to begin with that I am not afraid of death. And so I am not. You gave me a beautiful adventure, which I do not at all regret. Do not be sad or angry. But be careful. That is why I had to see you. The man who attacked me is very, very dangerous.'

'What happened? I didn't see your ad until yesterday afternoon – I've had sort of a wild week myself. But you made a stock certificate?'

He chuckled wearily. 'Yes, a very fine one, if I say so. For IBM. A good, solid company. One hundred shares common stock. So. Last Wednesday I finished him, no them. Sorry, with this injury my English goes a bit.' He stopped and breathed heavily for a minute. I wished I could hold his hand. Surely a little contact would do him more good than isolation and sterility.

His papery eyelids fluttered open again. 'Then I call a man I know. Who it is, maybe best you do not hear, my dear niece. And he calls a man, and so on. And on Wednesday afternoon one week later, I get a call. Someone is interested. A buyer, and he will be there Thursday afternoon. I rush to get an ad in the paper.

'So, in the afternoon a man shows up. I know at once he is not a boss. The manner is that of an underling. Maybe you call him a legman.'

'Legman. Yes. What did he look like?'

'A thug.' Uncle Stefan produced the slang word proudly. 'He is maybe forty. Heavy – not fat, you know. He looks Croatian, that thick jowl, thick eyebrows. He is as tall as you, but not as beautiful. Maybe a hundred pounds heavier.'

He stopped again to breathe, and closed his eyes briefly. I glanced surreptitiously at my watch. Only five more minutes. I didn't try to hurry him; that would only make him lose his train of thought.

'Well, you were not there, and I, I had to play the clever detective. So I tell him I know about the priory forgeries, and I want a piece of that particular business. But I have to know who pays. Who the boss is. So we get into a – a fight. He takes my IBM stock. He takes your Acorn stock. He says, "You know too much for your own good, old man!" and pulls out the knife, which I see. I have acid at my side, acid for my etching, you understand. This I throw at him, so when he stabs me, his hand is not quite true.'

I laughed. 'Wonderful. When you've recovered maybe you'd like to join my detective agency. I've never wanted a partner before, but you'd bring class to the operation.'

The mischievous smile appeared briefly, weakly; he shut his eyes again. 'It's a deal, dear Victoria,' he said. I had to strain to catch the words.

Dr Metzinger bustled in. 'You'll have to leave now, Miss Warshawski.'

I got up. 'When the police talk to you, give them a description of the man. Not anything else. Random burglar after your silver, perhaps. And put in a good word for me with Lotty – she's ready to flay me.'

The lids fluttered open and his brown eyes twinkled weakly. 'Lotty was always a headstrong, unmanageable child. When she was six –'

Dr Metzinger interrupted him. 'You're going to rest now. You can tell Miss Warshawski later.'

'Oh, very well. Just ask her about her pony and the castle at Kleinsee,' he called as Metzinger hustled me out of the room.

The policeman stopped me in the hallway. 'I need a full report on your conversation.'

'For what? Your memoirs?'

677

The policeman grabbed my arm. 'My orders are, if anyone talks to him, I have to find out what he said.'

I jerked my arm down and away. 'Very well. He told me he was sitting home on Thursday afternoon when a man came up the stairs. He let him in. Mr Herschel's an old man, lonely, wants visitors more than he wants to suspect people. He's got a lot of valuable stuff in that apartment and it probably isn't too much of a secret. Anyway, they got into a tussle of sorts – as much as a thug can be said to tussle with an eighty-year-old man. He had some jewelry cleaner in his desk, acid of some kind, threw it at him and got a knife in his side. I think he can give you a description of sorts.'

'Why did he want to see you?' Metzinger demanded.

I wanted to get home more than I wanted to fight. 'I'm a friend of his niece, Dr Herschel. He knows me through her, knows I'm a private detective. An old man like that would rather talk to someone he knows about his troubles than get caught in the impersonal police machinery.'

The policeman insisted on my writing down what I had just told him and signing it before he let me go. 'And your phone number. We need a number where we can reach you.' That reminded me – I hadn't gotten to the phone company. I gave him my office number and left.

Traffic on the Edens was thick by the time I reached it. It would be a parking lot where it joined the Kennedy. I exited on Peterson and headed south on side streets to Montrose. It was six-fifteen when I got to the Bellerophon. Setting my alarm for seven, I pulled the Murphy bed out of the wall and fell across it into a dreamless sleep.

When the alarm rang, it took me a long time to wake up. At first I thought it was morning in my old place on Halsted. I switched off the ringing and started to go back to sleep. It dawned on me, however, that the bedside table was missing. I'd had to reach over the side of the bed to the floor to turn off the clock. This woke me enough to remember where I was and why I had to get up.

I staggered into the bathroom, took a cold shower, and dressed in the new crimson outfit with more haste than grace. I dumped makeup from my suitcase into my purse, pulled on nylons and boots, stuck my Magli pumps under my arm, and headed for the car. I had a choice of the navy pea jacket or something filled with smoke, and chose the pea jacket – I'd just be checking it, after all.

I was only twenty minutes late to the Hanover House, and happened to arrive at the same time as Phil. He was too well behaved to look askance at my outfit. Kissing me lightly on the cheek, he tucked my arm into his and escorted me into the hotel. He took boots and coat from me to check. The perfect gentleman.

I'd put my makeup on at traffic lights and run a comb through my hair before leaving the car. Remembering the great Beau Brummell, who said that only the insecure primp once they've reached the party, I resisted the temptation to study myself in the floor-length mirrors covering the lobby walls.

Dinner was served in the Trident Salon on the fourth floor. Smaller than the Grand Ballroom, it seated two hundred people who had paid a hundred dollars each for the privilege of dining with the archbishop. A gaunt woman in black collected tickets at the entrance to the salon. She greeted Phil by name, her thin, sour face coming close to pleasure at seeing him.

'I guess it's Dr Paciorek, now isn't it? I know how proud your parents must be of you. And is this the lucky young lady?'

Phil blushed, suddenly looking very young indeed. 'No, no, Sonia . . . Which table for us?'

We were seated at table five, in the front of the room. Dr and Mrs Paciorek were at the head table, along with O'Faolin, Farber, and other well-to-do Catholics. Cecelia and her husband, Morris, were at our table. She was wearing a black evening gown that emphasized her twenty extra pounds and the soft flab in her triceps.

'Hello, Cecelia. Hi, Morris, good to see you,' I said cheerfully. Cecelia looked at me coldly, but Morris stood up to shake hands with me. An innocuous metals broker, he didn't share the family feud against Agnes and her friends.

For a hundred dollars, we got a tomato-based seafood chowder. The others at our table had already started eating; waiters brought

Phil and me servings while I studied the program next to my plate. Funds raised by the dinner would support the Vatican, whose assets had been depleted by the recent recessionary spiral and the fall of the lira. Archbishop O'Faolin, head of the Vatican Finance Committee, was here to thank us in person for our generosity. After dinner and speeches by Farber and O'Faolin, and by Mrs Catherine Paciorek, who had graciously organized the dinner, there would be an informal reception with cash bar in the George IV Salon next to our dining room.

The overweight man on my left took a second roll from the basket in front of him but forbore to offer me any: hoard the supplies. I asked him what kind of business he was in and he responded briefly, 'Insurance,' before popping half the roll into his mouth.

'Splendid,' I said heartily. 'Brokerage? Company?'

His wife, a thin, twittery woman with a wreath of diamonds around her neck, leaned across him. 'Harold is head of Burhop and Calends' Chicago office.'

'How fascinating!' I exclaimed. Burhop and Calends was a large national brokerage house, second in size behind Marsh and McLennan. 'It so happens I'm working for Ajax Insurance right now. What do you think the impact would be on the industry if an outside interest acquired them?'

'Wouldn't affect the industry at all,' he muttered, pouring a pint of Thousand Island dressing over the salad he'd just received.

Phil nudged my arm. 'Vic you don't have to do a suburban Girl Scout impersonation just because I asked you to dinner. Tell me what you've been doing, instead.'

I told him about my fire. He grimaced. 'I've been on call almost all week. Haven't seen a paper. I sometimes think the world could blow up and the only way I'd know would be by the casualties coming into ER.'

'But you like what you do?'

His face lit up, 'I love it. Especially the research end. I've been working with epileptics during surgery to try to map neuron activity.' He was still young enough to give an uneducated audience

680

the full force of his technical knowledge. I followed as best I could, more entertained by his enthusiasm than by what he was actually saying. How you get a verbal response from people whose brains are being operated on carried us through some decent halibut steak, which Phil ignored as he drew a diagram in pen on his cloth napkin.

Cecelia tried to catch his eye several times; she felt tales of blood and surgery were not suited to the dinner table, although most of the guests were discussing their own operations, along with their children or what kind of snow-removal equipment they owned.

When the waiters removed the dessert plates, including Phil's uneaten profiteroles, the room quieted so that his was the only voice that carried. 'That's what they really mean by a physiological map,' he said earnestly. A ripple of laughter made him blush and break off in midsentence. It also drew the head table's attention to him.

Mrs Paciorek had been too busy entertaining Archbishop O'Faolin to look at her children during dinner. Since eating had been well under way when we arrived, she probably never noticed Phil and me at all. Now his exposition and the laughter made her turn slightly so that she could identify the source. She saw him, then me. She froze, her well-bred mask slipping slightly. She glanced sharply at Cecelia, who made a helpless gesture.

Mrs Paciorek nudged Archbishop O'Faolin and whispered to him. He, too, turned to stare at our table, which was only fifteen feet or so away. Then he whispered back to Mrs Paciorek, who nodded firmly. Instructions to get the Swiss Guard to throw me out?

Phil was furiously stirring cream into his coffee. He was also still young enough to mind very much being laughed at. Under the noise of scraping chairs, as people rose for Cardinal Farber's post-dinner benediction, I patted his arm comfortingly and said, 'Remember: the only real social sin is to care what other people think of you.'

Farber gave a brisk blessing for the meal we had just enjoyed, and went on to talk about how the Kingdom of Heaven could only be tended on earth with the help of earthly things, that God had given us an earthly creation to care for, and that the work of the temporal church could only be carried out with material goods. He felt especially blessed in being the archbishop of Chicago, not just the world's largest archdiocese but also the most generous and loving. He was gratified at the response Chicago had made to the urgent needs of the Vatican, and here to thank us in person was the Most Reverend Xavier O'Faolin, archbishop of Ciudad Isabella and head of the Vatican Finance Committee.

Well pleased with his praise, the crowd clapped enthusiastically. O'Faolin stepped to the podium at a raised stand in front of the room, commended his words to God in Latin, and began to speak. Once again the Spanish accent was so thick as to be nearly incomprehensible. People strained to listen, then squirmed, and finally began murmured private conversations.

Phil shook his head. 'I don't know what's wrong with him tonight,' he said. 'The old boy usually speaks perfect English. Mother must have knocked him off balance.'

I wondered again at the whispered exchange between her and O'Faolin. Since it was impossible to follow the Panamanian archbishop I let my mind wander. Applause roused me from a doze, and I shook my head to try to wake up again completely.

Phil commented sarcastically on my sleeping, then said, 'Now comes the fun part. You go around the reception detecting to see if you can find your mysterious caller, and I'll watch.'

'Great. Maybe you can incorporate it into an article on search-and-sort routines in the brain.'

As we got up to follow the throng into the George IV Salon, Mrs Paciorek pushed herself against the tide of traffic and came up to us. 'What are you doing here?' she demanded of me abruptly.

Phil pulled my hand through his arm. 'She's my dinner date, Mother. I didn't think I could face the Plattens and Carrutherses without some moral support.'

She stood fulminating, her color changed dangerously, but she had the sense to know she couldn't order me out of the hotel. At last she turned to Cecelia and Morris. 'Try to keep her away from Archbishop Farber. He doesn't need to be insulted,' she tossed over her shoulder.

Phil made a sour face. 'Sorry about that, V. I. Want me to stay at your side? I don't want anyone else to be rude to you.'

I was amused and touched. 'Not necessary, my friend. If they're too rude, I'll break their necks or something and you can patch them up and come out looking like a hero.'

Phil went to get me a brandy, while I started counterclockwise around the room, stopping at small knots of people, introducing myself, chatting enough to get everyone to say a few words, and moving on. About halfway up the left side, I ran into Father Pelly with Cecelia and some strangers.

'Father Pelly! Nice to see you.'

He smiled austerely. 'Miss Warshawski. I hardly thought of you as a supporter of the archdiocese.'

I grinned appreciatively. 'You thought correctly. Young Phil Paciorek brought me. How about yourself? I hardly thought the priory could afford this type of entertainment.'

'We can't. Xavier O'Faolin invited me — we used to work together, and I was his secretary when he was sent to the Vatican ten years ago.'

'And you keep in close touch. That's nice. He visit the priory while he's in town?' I asked idly.

'Actually, he'll stay with us for three days before he flies back to Rome.'

'That's nice,' I repeated. Faced with Cecelia's withering glare, I moved on. Phil caught up with me as I was nearing the knot around O'Faolin.

'Nothing like an evening with the old gang to make you feel you're in kindergarten,' he said. 'Every third person remembers when I broke the windows at the church with my catapult.'

He introduced me to various people as I slowly worked my way up to O'Faolin. Someone was shaking hands with him and leaving just as I reached the group, so Phil and I were able to slip in next to him.

'Archbishop, this is Ms Warshawski. Perhaps you remember her from my sister's funeral.'

The great man favored me with a stately nod. He wore his

episcopal purple shirt under a black suit of exquisite wool. His eyes were green, from his Irish father. I hadn't noticed them before. 'Perhaps the archbishop would prefer to converse in Italian,' I said, addressing him formally in that language.

'You speak Italian?' Like his English, his Italian accent was tinged with Spanish, but not so distortingly. Something about his voice sounded familiar. I wondered if he'd been on television or radio while he was in Chicago and asked him that.

'NBC was good enough to do a small interview. People think of the Vatican as a very wealthy organization, so it is hard for us to bring our story of poverty and begging to the people. They were kind enough to help.'

I nodded. Chicago's NBC station gave a lot of support to Catholic figures and causes. 'Yes. The Vatican finances have been much in the papers here. Particularly after the unfortunate death of Signor Calvi last summer.' Was it my imagination, or did he flinch a bit? 'Has your work with the Vatican Finance Committee involved you at all with the Banco Ambrosiano?'

'Signor Calvi was a most loyal Catholic. Unfortunately, his ardor caused him to overstep the bounds of propriety.' He had switched back to his heavily accented English. Although I made one or two more attempts at conversation, the interview was clearly over.

Phil and I moved off to sit on a small couch. I needed to rest my feet before tackling the other side of the room. 'What was that about Calvi and the Banco Ambrosiano?' he asked. 'My Spanish is just good enough that I could follow some of the Italian . . . You must have miffed him, though, for his English to go bad again like that.'

'Possibly. He certainly didn't want to talk about Ambrosiano.'

We sat in silence for a few minutes. I gathered my wits for an assault on the rest of the party. Suddenly, behind me, I heard the Voice again. 'Thank you so much, Mrs Addington. His Holiness will be joining me in prayer for all of you generous Chicago Catholics.'

I leaped to my feet, spilling brandy down the front of the new crimson dress.

Phil stood up in alarm. 'What is it, Vic?'

'That's the man who's been calling me. Who is that?'

'Who?'

'Didn't you hear someone just promising the pope's prayers? Who said that?'

Phil was bewildered. 'That was Archbishop O'Faolin. Has he been calling you?'

'Never mind. No wonder you were so surprised by his accent, though.' The voice of a man whose English has been carefully taught to avoid an accent. Irish or Spanish or both. I rejoined the group around the archbishop.

He stopped in midsentence when he saw me.

'Never mind,' I said. 'You don't have to put the thick Spanish back on again. I know who you are. What I don't understand is your connection with the Mafia.'

I found I was shaking so badly I could hardly stand. This was the man who wanted to blind me. I had just enough control not to jump him on the spot.

'You're confusing me with someone else, young woman.' O'Faolin spoke coldly, but in his normal voice. The rest of the group around him stood like Stonehenge. Mrs Paciorek swooped up from nowhere.

'Dear Archbishop,' she said. 'Cardinal Farber is ready to leave.'

'Ah, yes. I'll come at once. I must thank him for his most generous hospitality.'

As he got ready to leave I said coldly, 'Just remember, Archbishop: no one is lucky forever.'

Phil helped me back to the couch. 'Vic, what's wrong? What has O'Faolin done to you? Surely you don't know him?'

I shook my head. 'I thought I did. He's probably right, though. I must be confusing him with someone else.' I knew I wasn't, though. You do not forget the voice of someone who wants to pour acid in your eyes.

Phil offered to drive me home, to get more brandy, to do anything and everything. I smiled at him gratefully. 'I'm okay. Just, with the fire at my place and everything, I haven't had much sleep. I'll

685

sit here for a while and then drive back to my apartment.' Or whatever the Bellerophon was.

Phil sat next to me. He held my hand and talked about general things. He was a very likeable young man. I pondered again how Mrs Paciorek could have produced three such attractive children as Agnes, Phil, and Barbara. 'Cecelia's your mother's only success,' I said abruptly.

He smiled. 'You only see Mother at her worst. She's a fine person in a lot of ways. All the good she does, for example. She inherited that huge Savage fortune, and instead of turning into a Gloria Vanderbilt or Barbara Post, she's used it almost exclusively for charity. She set up trusts for us kids, enough to keep us from want – mine paid my medical-school tuition, for example. But most of it goes to different charities. Especially to the Church.'

'Corpus Christi, perhaps?'

He looked at me sharply. 'How do you know about that?'

'Oh,' I said vaguely. 'Even members of secret societies talk. Your mother must be pretty active in it.'

He shook his head. 'We're not supposed to talk about it. She explained it to each of us when we turned twenty-one, so we'd know why there wasn't going to be much of an estate to inherit. Barbara doesn't know yet. We don't even discuss it among ourselves, although Cecelia's a member.'

'But you're not?'

He smiled ruefully. 'I'm not like Agnes – haven't lost my faith and turned my back on the Church. It's just, with Mother so active, I've had too much opportunity to see the venality of the organization. It doesn't surprise me – after all, priests and bishops are human, and they get their share of temptation. But I don't want them managing my money for me.'

'Yes, I can see that. Someone like O'Faolin, for example, getting a chance to play ducks and drakes with the faithful's money. Is he part of Corpus Christi?'

Phil shrugged.

'But Father Pelly is,' I said with calm certainty.

'Yeah, Pelly's a good guy. He's hot-tempered, but he's a fanatic like Mother. I don't think anyone could accuse him of working for his own self-interest.'

The room was starting to shimmer in front of me. Too much knowledge, rage, and fatigue made me feel as if I might faint.

With Farber's and O'Faolin's departure the room was thinning rapidly of people. I got up. 'I need to get home.'

Phil reiterated his willingness to drive me. 'You don't look in any shape to be on the road, Vic . . . I see too many head and neck injuries in the Emergency Room – let me drive you.'

I declined firmly. 'The air will wake me up. I always wear my seat belt, and I'm a careful driver.' I had too much to sort out. I needed to be alone.

Phil retrieved my boots and coat for me and helped me into them with anxious courtesy. He walked me to the entrance of the lot where I was parked and insisted on paying the ticket. I was touched by his good manners and didn't try to override him. 'Do me a favor,' he said, as I turned to go into the garage. 'Call me when you get in. I'm catching a train to the South Side – should be at my place in an hour. I'd just like to know you got home safely.'

'Sure, Phil,' I called, and turned in to the garage.

The Omega was parked on the third level. I rode the elevator up, keeping a cautious eye out for prowlers. Elevators are nasty places at night.

As I bent to unlock the car door, someone grabbed my arm. I whirled and kicked as hard as I could. My booted foot rammed his shin and he gave a yelp of pain and fell back.

'You're covered, Warshawski. Don't try to fight.' The voice came from the shadows beyond my car. Light glinted on metal. I remembered in dismay that the farts in the Skokie police had my gun. But a fight is no time for regrets.

'Okay, I'm covered,' I agreed levelly. I let my Magli pumps slide to the ground and judged distances. He'd have a hard time killing me in the dark, but he could probably hit me.

'I could have killed you as you unlocked your car,' the man with the gun pointed out, as if reading my thoughts. He had a heavy, gravelly voice. 'I'm not here to shoot you. Don Pasquale wants to talk to you. My partner will forgive you for kicking him – he shouldn't have tried to grab you. We were told you were a good street fighter.'

'Thank you,' I said gravely. 'My car or yours?'

'Ours. We're going to blindfold you for the drive.'

I picked up my shoes and let the man take me to a Cadillac limousine waiting on the far side of the floor with its motor running. There was no point in fighting. They wrapped a large black silk scarf around my eyes. I felt like Julius Schmeese waiting for the firing squad.

Gravel Voice sat in the back with me, his gun held lightly against my side. 'You can put that away,' I told him tiredly. 'I'm not going to jump you.'

The metal withdrew. I leaned back in the well-sprung plush seat and dozed. I must have fallen asleep in earnest; Gravel Voice had to shake me awake when the car stopped. 'We take the blindfold off when you're inside.' He guided me quickly but not roughly along a stone path and up a flight of stairs, exchanged greetings with a guard at the entrance, and led me down a carpeted hallway. Gravel knocked at a door. A faint voice told him to come in.

'Wait here,' he ordered.

I leaned against the wall and waited. In a few moments the door opened. 'Come in,' Gravel told me.

I followed his voice and smelled cigar smoke and a fire. Gravel untied the scarf. I blinked a few times, adjusting to the light. I was in a large room, decorated in crimson – carpet, drapes, and chairs all done in matching velvets and wools. The effect was opulent, but not unbearable.

In an armchair by a large fireplace sat Don Pasquale. I recognized him at once from his courtroom appearances, although he appeared older and frailer now. He might be seventy or more. He was thin, with gray hair and a pair of horn-rimmed glasses. He wore a red-velvet smoking jacket and held an enormous cigar in his left hand.

'So, Miss Warshawski, you want to speak to me.'

I stepped up to the fire and took an armchair facing his. I felt a bit like Dorothy in Oz, finally getting to meet the talking head.

'You are a very courageous young lady, Miss Warshawski.' The voice was old, but heavy, like parchment. 'No man has ever fallen asleep while being driven to see me.'

'You've worn me out, Don Pasquale. Your people burned down my apartment. Walter Novick tried to blind me. Someone stabbed poor Mr Herschel. I'm short on sleep now, and I take it where I can.'

He nodded. 'Very sensible . . . Someone told me you speak Italian. Can we converse in that language, please.'

'*Certo*,' I said. 'I have an aunt, an old woman. Rosa Vignelli. Two weeks ago she phoned me in deep distress. The safe at the Priory of Albertus Magnus, for which she was responsible, was found to contain forged stock certificates.' I'd learned most of my Italian before I was fifteen, when Gabriella died. I had to scramble for some of the words, particularly a way to describe forgery. Don Pasquale provided a phrase.

'Thank you, Don Pasquale. Now owing to the Fascists and their friends the Nazis, my aunt has very little family left. In fact, only her son and I remain. So she turned to me for help. Naturally.'

Don Pasquale nodded gravely. In an Italian family, you turn first to one another for help. Even if the family is Rosa and me.

'Soon after that, someone telephoned me. He threatened me with acid, and told me to stay away from the priory. And eventually, in fact, someone did throw acid on me. Walter Novick.'

I picked my next words with utmost care. 'Now naturally, I am curious about those forged securities. But to be truthful, if they are going to be investigated and the facts about them discovered, it will be the FBI that does it. I don't have the money or the staff to do that kind of work.' I watched Pasquale's face. Its expression of polite attention didn't change.

'My main concern is for my aunt, even though she is a disagreeable old woman. I made a promise to my mother, you see, a promise as she was dying. But when someone attacks me, then my honor is involved, too.' I hoped I wasn't overdoing it.

Don Pasquale looked at his cigar, measuring the ash. He puffed on it a few times and carefully knocked the ash into a bronze cube at his left hand. 'Yes, Miss Warshawski. I sympathize with your tale. But still – how does it involve me?'

'Walter Novick has . . . boasted . . . of being under your protection. Now I am not certain, but I believe it was he who tried to stab Stefan Herschel two days ago. Because this man is old, and because he was helping me, I am obligated to seek out his assassin. That is two counts against Walter Novick.

'If it were clear to everyone that he is not under your protection, I could deal with him with a clear conscience just on the grounds of his stabbing Mr Herschel. I would forget the attack on me. And I would lose all interest in the securities – unless my aunt's name became involved in them again.'

Pasquale gave a little smile. 'You are one woman working alone. You are very brave, but you are still alone. With what do you propose to bargain?'

'The FBI has lost interest in the case. But if it knew in which direction to look, its interest might be aroused again.'

'If you never left this house, the FBI would never know.' The parchment voice was gentle, but I felt the hairs prickle along the back of my neck.

I looked at my hands. They appeared remarkably small and fragile. 'It's a gamble, Don Pasquale,' I finally said. 'I know now who called to threaten me. If your interests are tied to his, then it's hopeless. One of these times, someone will kill me. I won't always make it out of the burning apartment, or be able to break my attacker's jaw. I will fight to the end, but the end will be clearly discernible to everyone.

'But if you and my caller are – business acquaintances only – then the story is a little altered. You're right – I have nothing to bargain with. The *Herald-Star*, the Chicago police, even the FBI, all these would vigorously investigate my death. Or even a tale of forgery if I told it. But how many indictments have you avoided in the past?' I shrugged.

'I appeal only to your sense of honor, your sense of family, to understand why I've done what I've done, and why I want what I want.' To the myth of the Mafia, I thought. To the myth of honor.

But many of them liked to believe it. My only hope was that Pasquale's view of himself mattered to him.

The ash on the cigar grew long again before he spoke. 'Ernesto will drive you home now, Miss Warshawski. You will hear from me in a few days.'

Gravel Voice, or Ernesto, had stood silently by the door while we talked. Now he came to me with the blindfold. 'Unnecessary, Ernesto,' Pasquale said. 'If Miss Warshawski decides to tell all she knows, she will be unable to say it.'

Once again the goosepimples stood out on my neck. I curled my toes inside my boots to control the shaking in my legs. Trying hard to keep my voice level, I bade the don good-night.

I told Ernesto to take me to the Bellerophon. By now Phil Paciorek was right. I was in no condition to drive a car. The strain of talking to Pasquale, on top of the other stresses of the day, had pushed me over the edge of fatigue. So what if driving me home showed Ernesto where I lived. If Pasquale wanted to find me, this would only cut a day or two off his time.

I slept all the way back. When I got to the Bellerophon, I staggered up the stairs to the fourth floor, kicked off my boots, dropped the new dress on the floor, and fell into bed.

20
GOING TO THE
CLEANERS

It was past eleven when I woke up again. I lay in bed for a while, reveling in the sense of rest, trying to reconstruct a dream I'd had in the middle of my sleep. Gabriella had come to me, not wasted as in the final days of her illness, but full of life. She knew I was in danger and wanted to wrap me in a white sheet to save me.

I had an urgent feeling that the dream held a clue to my problem or how to solve it, but I couldn't grab hold of it. I had very little time, and needed whatever prodding my subconscious could give me. Don Pasquale had said I would hear from him in a few days. That meant I might have forty-eight hours to straighten matters out to the point that any action of his against me would be superfluous.

I got out of bed and took a quick shower. The burns on my arms were healing well. Physically I was in condition to run again, but I couldn't bring myself to put on my sweats and go into the cold. The fire in my apartment had upset me more than I would admit to Roger. I wanted some security, and running through winter streets didn't feel like a way to get it.

I pulled the clothes out of my suitcase. The laundered ones still smelled of smoke. I put them away in the closet that housed the Murphy bed. My mother's wineglasses I set on the little dining table. That done, I'd moved in.

I bundled up the remaining clothes to take to a dry cleaner and went downstairs. Mrs Climzak, the manager, saw me and called to me as I was walking out the door. She was a thin, anxious woman who always seemed to be gulping for air.

She came out from behind the lobby counter and hurried over

to me with a brown paper bag. 'Someone left these for you this morning,' she gasped.

I took the bag dubiously, fearing the worst. Inside were my red Magli pumps, forgotten in Don Pasquale's limousine last night. No message. But at least it was a friendly gesture.

After so much breathless protesting that I could have walked the four flights up to my room and back, Mrs Climzak agreed to keep them downstairs for me until I returned. She came running up behind me as I was going to the door to add, 'And if you're taking those to a dry cleaner, there's a good one around the corner on Racine.'

The woman at the cleaner's informed me triumphantly that it would cost me extra to get the smoke out. She made a great show of inspecting each garment, clucking her teeth over it, and writing it down on a slip with the laboriousness of a traffic cop writing a ticket. At last, impatient, I grabbed up the clothes and left.

A second cleaner, sharing a dingy storefront with a tailor several blocks down, was more obliging. The woman at the counter accepted the smoky clothes without comment and wrote up the ticket quickly. She directed me to a lunch counter that served homemade soup and stuffed cabbage. Not the ideal choice for the day's first meal, but the piping hot, fresh barley soup was delicious.

Using their pay phone to check in with my answering service, I learned Phil Paciorek had called several times. I'd forgotten all about him. Murray Ryerson. Detective Finchley.

I called Illinois Bell and explained my situation. They agreed to switch my number over to the Bellerophon. Also to charge me for the stolen phone. I called Freeman Carter and said I'd seen Uncle Stefan and would make a statement to the police if they would drop charges. He agreed to look into it. I called Phil and left a message with the hospital that I would get back to him. I saved Murray and the police for later.

Once downtown I retrieved my car and headed for the Pulteney Building. The mail piled in front of my office door was horrendous. Sorting through it quickly for checks and letters, I tossed the rest. No bills until my life had stabilized a bit. I looked around me affectionately. Bare, but mine. Maybe I could move in a mattress and a little sink and stove and live here for a while.

The desk top was covered with a film of grime. Whatever pollution the el exudes had filtered under the window. I filled an old coffee cup at the hall drinking fountain and scrubbed the desk with some Kleenex. Good enough.

Using one of the envelopes I'd just pitched, I made out a 'To Do' list:

1. Inspect Mrs Paciorek's private finances & papers
2. Ditto for O'Faolin
3. Ditto for Pelly
4. Find out if Walter Novick had stabbed Uncle Stefan
5. If yes, bag him

I couldn't figure out what to do with the first three items. But it should be easy enough to take care of four. Five might follow. I called Murray at the *Herald-Star*.

'V.I. – you ain't dead yet,' he greeted me.

'Not for lack of trying,' I answered. 'I need some photographs.'

'Wonderful. The Art Institute has some on sale. I tried calling you last night. We'd like to do a story about Stefan Herschel and your arrest.'

'Why talk to me? Just make it up. Like your story of a couple of days ago.'

'Trade you photographs for a story. Who do you want?'

'Walter Novick.'

'You figure he stabbed Herschel?'

'I just want to know what he looks like in case he comes after me again.'

'All right, all right. I'll have your pictures at the Golden Glow around four. And you give me half an hour.'

'Just remember you're not Bobby Mallory,' I said irritably. 'I don't have to tell you anything.'

'What I hear, you don't tell Mallory much either.' He hung up.

I looked at my watch. Two o'clock. Time enough to think of a way to get at the papers I wanted to see. I could disguise myself as an itinerant member of Corpus Christi and go knocking on Mrs Paciorek's door. Then, while she was praying intensely, I could find her safe, crack the combination and . . .

And . . . *I could disguise myself.* Not for Mrs Paciorek, but for the priory. If O'Faolin was out there, I could take care of him and Pelly in one trip. If the disguise worked. It sounded like a lunatic idea. But I couldn't think of anything better.

As you go along Jackson Street to the river, you pass a number of fabric shops. At Hofmanstahls, on the corner of Jackson and Wells, I found a bolt of soft white wool. When they asked how much I needed I had no idea. I sketched the garment and we settled on ten yards. At eight dollars a yard, not exactly a bargain. They didn't have belts and it took close to an hour of wandering around leather stores and men's shops to find the heavy black strap I needed. A religious-goods store near Union Station provided the other accessories.

As I walked back across the slushy streets toward the Golden Glow, I passed a seedy print shop. On an impulse I went in. They had some photographs of old Chicago gangsters. I took a collection of six to mix in with the shots of Novick that Murray was bringing me.

It was almost four – there wasn't time to get to the little tailor on Montrose before meeting Murray. But if I didn't make it there today, it would have to wait till Monday and that was too late. Murray would have to come with me and talk in the car.

He obliged with ill grace. When I came in he was happily absorbed in his second beer, had taken off his boots, and was warming his socks on a small fender next to the horseshoe mahogany bar. While he bitterly pulled on his wet boots I picked up a manila folder from the bar in front of him. In it were two shots of Novick, neither in sharp focus, but clear enough to identify him. Both were courtroom shots taken when Novick had been arrested for attempted manslaughter and armed robbery. He'd never been convicted. Pasquale's friends seldom were.

I was relieved at not recognizing Novick's face. I'd been half afraid that he might have been the man I'd kicked last night – if he was that close to Pasquale there was no chance the don would turn him loose.

I led Murray down the street to my car at a good clip.

'Damn it, V.I., slow down. I've been working all day and just drank a beer.'

'You want your story, come and get it, Ryerson.'

He climbed into the passenger seat, grumbling that the car was too small for him. I put the Omega in gear and headed for Lake Shore Drive.

'So how come you were visiting Stefan Herschel the day he got knifed?'

'What's he say about it?'

'Damned hospital won't let us in to talk to him. That's why I'm stuck asking you, and I know what that means – half a story. My gofer at the police station told me you'd been booked. For concealing evidence of a crime. What crime?'

'That's just Lieutenant Mallory's flamboyant imagination. He didn't like my being at Mr Herschel's apartment and saving his life. He had to charge me with something.'

Murray demanded to know what I was doing there. I gave him my standard story – about Uncle Stefan being a lonely old man and my just happening to drop in. 'Now when I saw him at the hospital –'

'You've talked to him!' Murray's shout made the little car's windows rattle. 'What did he say? Are you going there now? Did Novick stab him?'

'No, I'm not going there now. I don't know if Novick stabbed him. The police story right now is that this was random housebreaking. Since Novick runs with the Mob I don't see him as a housebreaker unless he does his own thing on the side. I don't know.' I explained about the silver collection, and how eager Uncle Stefan was to shower people with tortes and hot chocolate. 'If someone rang the bell, he'd just assume it was the neighborhood kids and let them in. Maybe it was the neighborhood kids. Poor old goon.'

I had an inspiration. 'You know, you should talk to his neighbor – Mrs Silverstein. She saw a lot of him. I bet she could give you some good tips.'

Murray made a few notes. 'Still, I don't trust you, V.I. It's just too damned pat, you being there.'

I shrugged and pulled up in front of the cleaners. 'That's the story. Take it or leave it.'

'We had to drive all this way so you could get to the cleaners? That's your emergency? You'd better be planning on getting me back to the Loop.'

'Some emergencies are more obscure than others.'

I took my parcel of fabric and went into the little store. The tailoring part of the shop was a jumbled array of old spools of thread, a Singer that must have dated to the turn of the century, and scraps and snippets of cloth. The man huddled crosslegged on a chair in the corner, hunched over a length of brown suiting, might have gone back to 1900 as well.

Although he jerked a sideways glance at me, he continued to sew. When he'd finished whatever he was doing, he folded the fabric tidily, put it on a heaped table to his left, and looked at me. 'Yes?' He spoke with a heavy accent.

'Could you sew something for me without a pattern?'

'Oh, yes, young lady. No question about it. When I was a young man, I cut for Marshall Field, for Charles Stevens. Those were the days before you were born, when they made clothes right there in the store. I cut all day long, and made, with no patterns. What is it you want?'

I showed him my sketch and pulled the wool from its brown wrapping. He studied the picture for a moment, and then me. 'Oh, that would be no problem. No problem at all.'

'And – could I have it by Monday?'

'Monday? Oh, the young lady is in a hurry.' He waved an arm in the direction of several heaps of cloth. 'Look at all these orders. They thought in advance. They bring their work in many weeks ahead of you. *Monday*, my dear young lady!'

I sat down on a footstool and negotiated in earnest. At last he agreed to do it for double his normal fee, payable in advance. 'Forty dollars. I cannot do it for a penny less.'

I tried to appear incredulous, as if I thought I was being gouged. The fabric alone had cost double that. Finally I pulled two twenties from my wallet. He told me to stop in at noon on Monday. 'But next time, no rushes.'

Murray had left a note under my windshield wiper, informing me that he'd caught a cab downtown and that I owed him sixteen dollars. I tossed the paper in the trashcan and headed for Skokie.

Uncle Stefan had been moved to a regular room that afternoon. That meant I didn't have to go through a routine with nurses and Metzinger just to see him. However, the police guard had also been removed – if his attackers were ordinary B & E men, he wasn't in any danger, according to the cops. I bit my lip. Caught by my own story, damn it. Unless I told the truth about the forgeries and the Mob, there was no way to convince the police that Uncle Stefan needed protection.

The old man was delighted to see me. Lotty had been by in the morning, but no one else was visiting him. I pulled out the photographs and showed them to him. He nodded calmly. 'Just like *Hill Street Blues*. Do I recognize the mug shots?'

He selected Novick from the pile without hesitation.

'Oh, yes. That face is not easy to forget. Even though this picture is not totally clear, I have no doubt, no question. That is the man with the knife.'

I stayed and talked with him for a while, turning over in the back of my mind various possibilities for his protection. If I just gave Novick's picture to the police . . . but if Pasquale wasn't willing to let him go, then he'd get both me and Uncle Stefan without any compunction or difficulty.

I abruptly interrupted a reminiscence of Fort Leavenworth. 'Excuse me. I can't leave you here without a guard. And while I can stay until the end of visiting hours tonight, it's just too easy for someone to get in and out of a hospital. If I call a security service I trust and get someone over here, will you tell Dr Metzinger it's your idea? He may think you're a paranoid old man, but he won't turn your guard out the way he will if I put it to him.'

Uncle Stefan was disposed to be heroic and fought the idea, until I told him the same hoods were gunning for me: 'If they kill me, and you're dead, there isn't a soul on earth who can go to the police for me. And our detective agency will vanish.' Put as an appeal to his chivalry, the idea was palatable.

The service I used was called All Night – All Right. In a way, its employees were as amateurish as their name. Three enormous brothers and two of their friends made up the entire staff, and they only took jobs that appealed to them. No North Shore weddings, for example. I'd used them once when I had a load of rare coins I was returning to an Afghani refugee.

Jim Streeter answered the phone. When I explained the situation to him, he agreed to send someone up in a couple of hours. 'The boys are out moving someone's furniture' – one of their sidelines. 'When they get back I'll send Tom up.'

Uncle Stefan obediently rang for the night nurse and explained his fears to her. She was inclined to be sarcastic, but I murmured a few words about hospital safety and malpractice suits and she said she would tell 'Doctor'.

Uncle Stefan nodded approvingly at me. 'You are a very tough young lady. Ah, if only I had known you thirty years ago, the FBI never would have caught me.'

A gift shop in the lobby yielded a pack of cards. We played gin until Tom Streeter showed up at eight-thirty. He was a big quiet, gentle man. Seeing him, I knew I'd stopped one hole. At least temporarily.

I kissed Uncle Stefan goodnight and left the hospital, checking carefully at each doorway, mixing with a large family group leaving the building. I inspected my car before opening the door. As near as I could tell, no one had wired it with dynamite.

Driving down the Edens, what puzzled me was the connection between O'Faolin and the forgeries. He hires Novick from Pasquale. How does he know Pasquale? How would a Panamanian archbishop know a Chicago mobster? Anyway, he hires Novick from Pasquale to back me off the forgeries. But why? The only connection I could think of was his long-term friendship with Pelly. But that made Pelly responsible for the forgeries and that still didn't make sense. The answer had to be at the friary and I had to get through Sunday somehow before I could find it.

Back at the Bellerophon, I plugged my phone into the wall. It seemed to work. My answering service told me Ferrant had tried phoning me as well as Detective Finchley.

I tried Roger first. He sounded subdued. 'There's been a disturbing development in this takeover attempt. Or maybe it's a relief. Someone has stepped forward and filed five percent ownership with the SEC.' He'd been closeted with the Ajax board all day discussing it. One of the other managing partners from Scupperfield, Plouder would be flying in tomorrow. Roger wanted to have dinner with me and get my ideas, if any.

I agreed to meet him. If nothing else, it would give me something to think about until Monday.

While I ran water in the bathtub I made my other call. Detective Finchley had left for the day, but Mallory was still at work. 'Your lawyer says you're ready to make a statement about Stefan Herschel,' he growled.

I offered to see him first thing Monday morning. 'What did Detective Finchley want?'

I could get my gun back, Bobby said grudgingly. They'd gotten the Skokie police to send it down to them. They were confiscating the picklocks, though. It hurt Bobby physically to tell me about the gun. He didn't want me carrying it, he didn't want me in the detective business, he wanted me in Bridgeport or Melrose Park with six children and, presumably, a husband.

21
DEADLINE

Roger poked moodily at his steak. 'By the way, thanks for the note you left yesterday. How was the archbishop?'

'There were two. One was fulsome, the other ugly. Tell me about this filing.'

I had met him at the Filigree and been moved by his total exhaustion. We had drinks in the bar before dinner, Roger so worn that he hadn't felt like talking. Now he rubbed his forehead tiredly.

'I am baffled. Totally and utterly baffled. I've been dealing with it all day, and I still can't understand it . . . It's like this. If you own five percent or more of a company's stock, you have to file with the SEC and tell them what you mean to do with your holding. You know you asked me a week or so ago about a Wood-Sage company? Well, they're the ones who made the filing.

'Now they did it late yesterday, just so they wouldn't have to answer a lot of questions or be in the *Journal* or anything. But of course, our lawyers got all the material. Such as it was. Wood-Sage isn't a corporation that *does* anything apparently. They're just a group of people who buy and sell stocks for their mutual benefit, figuring if they pool their investments they can do better than they would alone. It's not that unusual. And they're claiming they only bought so many Ajax shares because they think the company's a good buy. The trouble is, we can't get any kind of line on who owns Wood-Sage.' He ran his fingers through his long hair and pushed his plate away, much of the steak uneaten.

'The disclosure to the SEC should include the owners, shouldn't it?' I asked.

He shrugged. 'The owners are the shareholders. There is a board of directors, but it seems to be made up of brokers, including Tilford and Sutton.'

'The buyers must include their customers, then.' I thought back to my burglary of their offices. 'I don't have a list of all their customers. And I don't know what it would tell you, anyway. The one strange thing about them is they do business for Corpus Christi. Corpus Christi bought several million dollars of stock last fall. It might have given them to Wood-Sage.'

Roger had never heard of Corpus Christi.

'Not surprising – it's a group that tries to stay secret.' I told him what I'd read about them in the *Journal*. 'Because they do everything in secret, maybe they don't publicize their ownership of a company like Wood-Sage . . . Catherine Paciorek is a member – her son let that fall inadvertently . . .'

Roger fiddled with the stem of his wineglass. 'There's something I want to ask you,' he finally said abruptly. 'It's hard for me, because we've gotten into difficulties about your detective work and my reaction to it. But I'd like to hire you, for Scupperfield, Plouder. I'd like you to try to find out who's behind Wood-Sage. Now this business with Corpus Christi and Mrs Paciorek – it gives you an inside edge on the investigation.'

'Roger, the SEC and the FBI have the kind of resources you need for that sort of investigation. I don't. By Tuesday or Wednesday they'll have the information. It'll be in the public domain.'

'Maybe. But that may be too late. We're doing what we can – sending mailings to shareholders urging them to support current management. Our lawyers are working madly. But no one's getting results.' He leaned across the table earnestly and took my hand. 'Look. It's a lot to ask. I realize that. But you know Mrs Paciorek. Can't you talk to her – find out if Corpus Christi is involved in this Wood-Sage thing at all?'

'Roger, the lady doesn't talk to me. I don't even know what I could do to get her to see me.'

He looked at me soberly. 'I'm not asking you to do me a favor. I'll hire you. Whatever your normal fee is, Scupperfield, Plouder will double it. I just cannot run the risk of omitting a course of action that might help. If we knew who the owners were, if we knew why they were trying to buy the company, it could make a big difference to our being able to hold on to Ajax.'

I thought of the three dollars in my wallet, the new furniture I was going to have to buy, the fee to the Streeter brothers for protecting Uncle Stefan. And then my shoulders sank. It was my fault Uncle Stefan was lying in the hospital needing protection. After a couple of weeks of working on the forgeries, I had done nothing but lose my apartment and my life's possessions. Lotty, my refuge, wouldn't speak to me. I had never felt so discouraged or incapable in all my years as an investigator. I tried, awkwardly, to explain some of my feelings.

Roger squeezed my hand. 'I understand how you feel.' He grinned briefly. 'I was the young hotshot coming over to manage the Ajax operation, show them how to do the job. Now our management are fighting for our lives. I know it's not my fault — but I feel futile and embarrassed that I can't do anything about it.'

I made a wry face, but returned his handshake. 'So we'll bolster each other's failing vanity? I suppose . . . But next week you've got to go to the FBI and the SEC. Set up a meeting for me with them. They won't talk to me otherwise. Just as long as you know it's a most unlikely project, I'll try to think of a way to get Catherine Paciorek to talk to me.'

He smiled gratefully. 'You don't know what a relief this is to me, Vic. Just the idea that someone I can trust absolutely will be involved. Can you come in Monday and meet the board? The lawyers can give you a full picture on what they know — three hours to say nothing, maybe.'

'Monday's full. Tuesday?' He agreed. Eight a.m. I blenched slightly but wrote the time into my date book.

We left the Filigree at nine and went to a movie. I called the hospital from the theater to check on Uncle Stefan. All was well there. I wished someone cared enough for my safety to hire some huge bodyguards to protect me. Of course, a hard-boiled detective is never scared. So what I was feeling couldn't be fear. Perhaps nervous excitement at the treats in store for me. Even so, when Roger asked me, tentatively, if I wanted to go back to the Hancock with him, I assented without hesitation.

By morning the *Herald-Star* and the *Tribune* had both picked up the Wood-Sage story in their Sunday business sections. No one on the Ajax board had been available for comment. Pat Kollar, the *Herald-Star*'s financial analyst, explained why someone would want to acquire an insurance company. There wasn't much else to say about Wood-Sage.

Roger read the papers gloomily. He left at two to meet his partner's plane. 'He'll have the *Financial Times* and the *Guardian* with him and I'll get the *New York Times* on my way to the car. That way we can have a real wake surrounded by all the bad news at once . . . Want to stay to meet him?'

I shook my head. Godfrey Anstey would be sleeping in the apartment's second bedroom. Two's company but three's embarrassing.

After Roger left, I stayed for a few minutes to call my answering service. Phyllis Lording had phoned several times around noon. Somewhat surprised, I dialed the Chestnut Street apartment.

Phyllis's high, rather squeaky voice sounded more flustered than usual. 'Oh, hi, Vic. Is that you? Do you have any time this afternoon, by any chance?'

'What's up?'

She gave a nervous laugh. 'Probably nothing. Only it's hard to explain over the phone.'

I shrugged and agreed to walk over. When she met me at the door, she appeared thinner than ever. Her chestnut hair was pulled carelessly from her face, pinned on her head. Her swanlike neck seemed pitifully slender beneath the mass of hair, the fine planes in her face standing out sharply. In an oversize shirt and tight jeans she looked unbearably fragile.

She led me into the living room where the day's papers were spread out on the floor. Like Agnes, she was a heavy smoker, and a blue haze hung in the air. I sneezed involuntarily.

She offered me coffee from an electric percolator sitting on the

704

floor near the overflowing ashtray. When I saw how brackish it was I asked for milk.

'You can check in the refrigerator,' she said doubtfully, 'but I don't think I have any.'

The huge refrigerator held nothing except a few condiments and a bottle of beer. I went back to the living room. 'Phyllis! What are you eating?'

She lit a cigarette. 'I'm just not hungry, Vic. At first I kept trying to make myself meals, but I'd get sick if I ate anything. Now I'm just not hungry.'

I squatted down on the floor next to her and put a hand on her arm. 'Not good, Phyl. It's not a way to memorialize Agnes.'

She blinked a few times through the smoke. 'I just feel so alone, Vic. Agnes and I didn't have many friends in common – the people I know are all at the university and her friends were brokers and investors. Her family won't talk to me . . .' Her voice trailed off and she hunched her thin shoulders.

'Agnes's youngest sister would like very much to talk to you. Why don't you give her a call? She was twenty years younger than Agnes and didn't know her too well, but she liked and admired her. She's too young to know how to phone you without embarrassment after the way her mother's acted.'

She didn't say anything for a few minutes. Then she gave her intense smiled and a brief nod. 'Okay. I'll call her.'

'And start eating something?'

She nodded again. 'I'll try, Vic.'

We talked about her courses for a bit. I wondered if she could get someone to take them for her for a week while she went south for some sunshine; she said she'd think about it. After a while, she got around to the reason behind her phone call.

'Agnes and I shared a subscription to the *New York Times*.' She smiled painfully and lit another cigarette – her fifth since I'd arrived forty minutes earlier. 'She always went straight to the business section while I hit the book reviews. She . . . she teased me about it. I don't have much of a sense of humor; Agnes did, and it always got under my skin a bit . . . Since she died, I've, I've' – she bit her lips and looked away, trying to hide tears trickling down the inner corners of her face – 'I've started reading the business section. It's . . . it's a way to feel I'm still in touch with her.'

The last sentence came out in a whisper and I had to strain to hear her. 'I don't think that's foolish, Phyl. I have a feeling if it had been you who died, Agnes would plunge into Proust with the same spirit.'

She turned to look at me again. 'You were closer to Agnes in some ways than I could ever be. You and she are a lot alike. It's funny. I loved her, desperately, but I didn't understand her very well . . . I was always a little jealous of you because you understood her.'

I nodded. 'Agnes and I were good friends for a long time. I've had times when I was jealous of your closeness with her.'

She put her cigarette out and seemed to relax; her shoulders fell back from their hunched position. 'That's very generous of you, Vic. Thanks . . . Anyway, in the *Times* this morning I saw a story about a takeover bid for Ajax. You know, the big insurance company downtown.'

'I know. Agnes was looking at that before she died and I've been scratching around at it, too.'

'Alicia Vargas – Agnes's secretary – sent me all her personal papers. Things she'd kept notes on, anything that was handwritten and didn't relate to company business. I went through them all. Her latest notebook especially. She kept them – like Jonathan Edwards – or Proust.'

She stood up and went to the coffee table where I could see some spiral college notebooks among stacks of *Harper's* and the *New York Review of Books*. I'd assumed they belonged to Phyllis.

She took the top one and riffled through it quickly, then folded it back to show me the page. Agnes's sprawling hand was difficult to read. She'd written in '1/12', followed by 'R. F., Ajax'. That wasn't too difficult to follow – she'd first talked to Ferrant about Ajax on January 12. Other cryptic entries that week apparently referred to various things she was thinking about or working on. One was a note to go to Phyllis's poetry reading, for example.

Then, on the eighteenth, the day she died, was a heavily scored entry: '$12 million, C-C for Wood-Sage'.

Phyllis was looking at me intently. 'You see, Wood-Sage didn't mean anything to me by itself. But after I read the paper this morning . . . And the C-C. Agnes told me about Corpus Christi. I couldn't help but think . . .'

'Neither can I. Where the hell did she get that information?'

Phyllis shrugged. 'She knew a lot of brokers and lawyers.'

'Can I use your phone?' I asked Phyllis abruptly.

She led me to a porcelain-gold replica of the early telephones; I dialed the Paciorek number. Barbara answered. She was glad to talk to me; she'd be really happy to hear from Phyllis; and yes, her mother was home. She came back a few minutes later to say in considerable confusion that Mrs Paciorek refused to talk to me.

'Tell her I just called to let her know that Corpus Christi's ownership of Wood-Sage will be in the *Herald-Star* next week.'

'Corpus Christi?' she repeated doubtfully.

'You got it.'

Five minutes passed. I read the *Times* story on Ajax — more words to say less than had been in the Chicago papers. I scanned more verbiage on the AT&T divestiture. I looked at help wanted ads. Maybe I could find a better line of work. 'Seasoned professional not afraid of challenges.' That meant someone to work hard for low pay. What do you season professionals with, anyway?

Finally Mrs Paciorek came on the line. 'Barbara gave me some garbled message.' Her voice was tight.

'It's like this, Mrs Paciorek: The SEC knows, of course, that Wood-Sage has bought a five-percent position in Ajax. What they don't know is that most of the money was put up by Corpus Christi. And that most of Corpus Christi's money comes from you, the Savage fortune you turned over to them. Securities law is not my specialty, but if Corpus Christi is putting up the money for Wood-Sage to buy Ajax stock, the SEC is not going to be happy that it wasn't mentioned in your filing.'

'I don't know what you're talking about.'

'You've got to work on your answers. When the papers get hold of you, they're not going to believe that for one minute.'

'If something called Corpus Christi is buying Ajax stock, I know nothing about it.'

'That's marginally better,' I conceded. 'The problem is, when Agnes – your daughter, you know – died, she left behind some notes showing a connection between Corpus Christi and Wood-Sage. If I turn the FBI's attention to your lawyers, I'm sure it would be able to get the name of the broker who handles the Corpus Christi portfolio. That is presumably where Agnes got her information. In addition, on a smaller scale, it will be interested in the block transfers Preston Tilford handled.'

There was silence at the other end while Mrs Paciorek marshaled her defenses. I shouldn't have expected to force such a controlled woman into blurting out anything indiscreet. At last she said, 'My attorneys will doubtless know how to handle any investigation, however harassing. That isn't my concern.'

'We'll see about that. But the police may want to ask you some questions, too. They may want to know to what lengths you would go to keep Agnes from publishing Corpus Christi's attempted takeover of Ajax.'

After a long pause, she replied, 'Victoria, you are obviously hysterical. If you think you know something about the death of my daughter, perhaps I will see you.'

I started to say something, then thought better of it. The woman was going to talk to me – what more did I need right now? She wasn't free today, but she could see me at her home tomorrow night at eight.

With my nerves in their current jangled state, I didn't feel like going back to the Bellerophon. I explained the fire and my predicament to Phyllis, who instantly offered me her spare bedroom. She drove with me to visit Uncle Stefan, now feeling well enough to be bored in the hospital. To my relief, the doctors wanted to hold him a few more days – once he got home he would be impossible to keep an eye on.

Robert Streeter, the youngest brother, was with him when we

arrived. Apparently someone had tried to get into the room around midnight. Jim, then on duty, sensibly didn't try to chase him since that would have left the room unguarded. By the time he'd roused hospital security, the intruder was long gone.

I shook my head helplessly. One more problem I couldn't handle. Lotty arrived as we were leaving. At the sight of Phyllis, her heavy black brows went up. 'So! Vic is roping you into her masquerade as well?'

'Lotty! You and I need to talk,' I said sharply.

She gave me a measuring look. 'Yes. I think that would be a good thing . . . Are these thugs with Stefan your idea or his?'

'Call me when you've climbed off your cross!' I snapped and walked away.

Phyllis was too polite to ask about the incident. We didn't speak much, but had a pleasant meal at a little restaurant on Irving Park Road before heading back to Chestnut Street.

Cigarette smoke had permeated the bedclothes in the guest room. The smell, combined with my nervous tension, made sleep difficult. At three, I got up to read, and found Phyllis sitting in the living room with a biography of Margaret Fuller. We talked companionably for several hours. After that I slept until Phyllis stopped in to say good-bye before going to her eight-thirty class. She invited me to come back at night. Despite the stale air, I accepted gratefully.

I thought I might be safer with a rental car than my own, which was by now well known to any hoodlum in Chicago trying to find me. On my way over to the police station I stopped at a rental agency and got a Toyota whose steering must have been used by the US weightlifting team while they trained for the Olympics. They told me they didn't have anything else that size and to take it or leave it. Snarling, I took it – I didn't have time to shop for cars.

Lieutenant Mallory wasn't in when I got to Roosevelt Road. I gave my statement to Detective Finchley. Not having Bobby's history with me, he accepted what I had to say and returned the Smith & Wesson. Freeman Carter, who accompanied me, told me we'd have a formal hearing in the morning, but that my character was once more unblemished – not even a moving violation in the last three years.

It was afternoon when I reached my ancient tailor on Montrose. He had finished the robe for me; it fit perfectly, right hem length, right sleeve length. I thanked him profusely, but he responded with more harsh words on young ladies who couldn't plan ahead – he'd had to work all day Sunday for me.

I had to make a stop at the Bellerophon to pick up the rest of my disguise. Mrs Climzak came out breathlessly from behind the counter with my shoes. She'd never have taken them if she'd known she'd have to be responsible for them for two days. If I was going to turn out to be the thoughtless type of tenant, she didn't know if they could keep me. And certainly not if I entertained men in the middle of the night.

I was turning to go upstairs, but this seemed like a specific, not a generic accusation. 'What men in the middle of the night?'

'Oh, don't try to act so innocent, Miss Warshawski. The neighbors heard him and called the night clerk. He got the police and your friend left. Don't pretend you don't remember that.'

I left her midsentence and galloped up the stairs to the fourth floor. I hadn't had time to make a mess of my shabby little room. Someone else had done it for me. Fortunately, there wasn't too much to toss around – no books, except a Gideon Bible. No food. Just my clothes, the Murphy bed mattress, and the pots and pans in the kitchen. I held my breath while I inspected the Venetian glasses. Whoever had been here wasn't totally vindictive: they stood unharmed on the little card table.

'Oh, *damn*!' I shouted. 'Leave me alone!' I shuffled things together as best I could, but didn't really have time to clean up. Didn't feel like cleaning up, come to that. What I felt like was taking to my bed for a week. Except I didn't have a bed anymore, not my own anyway.

I lugged the heavy mattress back onto the bed and lay on it. The cracks in the ceiling made a fine mesh. They resembled my own incoherent thoughts. I stared at them morosely for a quarter of an hour before forcing myself to abandon self-pity and start thinking.

The likeliest reason someone was searching my room was to find the evidence I'd told Catherine Paciorek about yesterday. No wonder she hadn't wanted to see me last night. She was getting someone to find me and find whatever document Agnes had left behind. Very well. That would make it easier to get her to talk when I saw her tonight.

I put Catherine and the ransacking to one side. Now that I was thinking again, I could cope. Changing into jeans and boots, I put the robe into a paper bag with the rest of my disguise, digging the component pieces out of the mess in the room.

My shoulder holster was wedged under the chest of drawers in the closet. It took close to half an hour to find. I looked nervously at my watch, not sure what my deadline was, but fearing that time was running very short indeed. I still had to stop for some bullets, but that delay was essential. I wasn't going to the bathroom unarmed until this mess was straightened out.

22
WANDERING FRIAR

A store in Lincolnwood sold me three dozen bullets for twenty-five dollars. Despite what the gun haters may think, it, isn't cheap killing people. Not only is it not cheap, it's time-consuming. It was nearly three. I didn't have time for lunch if I wanted to get to the priory on schedule. Stopping at a corner grocery I picked up an apple and ate it as I drove.

A bright winter sun reflected against the snow, breaking into diamonds of glinting, blinding color. My dark glasses, I suddenly remembered, had been in a dresser drawer in the old apartment. No doubt they were a lump of plastic now. I shielded my eyes as best I could with the visor and my left hand.

Once in Melrose Park, I toured the streets looking for a park. Pulling in from the roadway, I took off my pea jacket and pulled the white wool robe on over jeans and shirt. The black leather belt tightened the gown at the middle. The rosary I attached to the right side of the belt. It wasn't exactly the real thing, but in dim light I ought to be able to pass for a Dominican friar.

By the time I got back to the priory and parked behind the main building it was almost four-thirty, time for evening prayers and mass. I waited until four-thirty-five, and went into the main hallway.

The ascetic youth sat hunched over a devotional work. He glanced up at me briefly. When I headed for the stairs instead of the chapel, he said, 'You're late for vespers, Brother,' but went back to his reading.

My heart was pounding as I reached the wide landing where the marble staircase turned back on itself up into the private upper reaches of the friary. The area was cloistered, not open to the public, male or female, and I couldn't suppress a feeling of dread, as though I were committing some kind of sacrilege.

I'd been expecting a long, open ward like a nineteenth-century hospital. Instead, I came on a quiet corridor with doors opening onto it, rather like a hotel. The doors were shut, but not locked. Next to each, making my task infinitely easier, were little placards with the monks' names printed in a neat scroll. Each man had a room to himself.

I squinted at each in turn until I came to one that had no name on it. Cautiously, I knocked, then opened the door. The room contained only a bare single bed and a crucifix. At the far end of the hall, I came to a second nameless room, which I opened in turn. This was O'Faolin's temporary quarters.

Besides the bed and crucifix, the room held a small dresser and a little table with a drawer in the middle. O'Faolin's Panamanian passport and his airline ticket were in the drawer. He was on a ten p.m. Alitalia flight on Wednesday. Forty-eight hours to – to what?

The dresser was filled with stacks of beautiful linen, hand-tailored shirts, and a fine collection of silk socks. The Vatican's poverty didn't force her employees to live in squalor.

Finally, under the bed, I found a locked attaché case. I mourned my picklocks. Using the barrel of the Smith & Wesson, I smashed the hinges. I hated doing anything so blatant, but time was short.

The case was stacked with papers, most in Italian, some in Spanish. I looked at my watch. Five o'clock. Thirty minutes more. I shuffled through the stack. A number of papers with the Vatican seal – the keys to the kingdom – dealt with O'Faolin's fund-raising tour of the States. However, Ajax's name caught my eye and I looked slowly through the papers until I found three or four referring to the insurance company. I don't read Italian as fast as I do English, but these seemed to be technical documents from a financial house, detailing the assets, outstanding debt, number of shares of common stock, and names and expiration dates of the terms of the current board of directors.

The most interesting document in the collection was clipped to the inside cover of Ajax's 1983 annual report. It was a letter, in Spanish, to O'Faolin from someone named Raúl Díaz Figueredo. The letterhead, embossed with an intricate logo, and Figueredo's name as *Presidente*, was for the Italo-Panama Import-Export Company. Spanish is enough like Italian that I could work out the gist: after reviewing many US financial institutions, Figueredo wished to bring Ajax to O'Faolin's attention, the easiest object – target? – for a plan of acquisition. The Banco Ambrosiano assets resided happily – no, safely – in Panamanian and Bahamian banks. Yet for these assets to be – fecund? no, productive – as His Excellency wisely understands, they must be usable in public works.

I sat back on my heels and looked soberly at the document. Here was evidence of what lay behind the Ajax takeover. And the connection with Wood-Sage and Corpus Christi? I looked nervously at my watch. Time enough to sort that out later. I slipped the letter from the paper clip, folded it, and put it in my jeans pocket under the robe. Stacking the papers together as neatly as I could, I put them back in the attaché case and slid the case under the bed.

The hallway was still deserted. I had one more stop. Given the Figueredo letter, it was worth the significant risk of being caught.

Father Pelly's room was at the other end of the hall, near the stairs. I cocked an ear. No voices below. The service must still be in progress. I pushed open his door.

As spartan as the other rooms, Pelly's nonetheless had the personal stamp of a place that's been inhabited for a long time by one person. Some family photographs stood on the little deal table, and a bookcase was filled several layers deep.

I found what I was looking for in the bottom drawer of the dresser. A list of Chicago area members of Corpus Christi with their addresses and phone numbers. I went through it quickly, keeping one nervous ear strained for voices. If worse came to worst, I might be able to leave from the window. It was narrow, but we were only on the second floor and I thought I could squeeze through.

Cecelia Paciorek Gleason was listed, and Catherine Paciorek of course. And near the bottom of the list, Rosa Vignelli. Don Pasquale was not a member. One secret society was enough for the man, I supposed.

As I stuck the list in the drawer and got up to leave, I heard voices in the hallway outside, and then a hand on the door. It was too late to try the window. I looked around desperately and slid under the bed, the rosary making a faint clicking noise as I pulled my robes in around me.

My heart was pounding so hard that my body vibrated. I took deep, silent breaths, trying to still the movement. Black shoes appeared near my left eye. Then Pelly kicked them off and climbed onto the bed. The mattress and springs were old and not in the best of shape. The springs sagging under his weight almost touched my nose.

We lay like that for a good quarter of an hour, me stifling a sneeze prompted by the cold steel, Pelly breathing gently. Someone knocked at the door. Pelly sat up. 'Come in.'

'Gus. Someone's been in my room and broken into my attaché case.'

O'Faolin. I'd know his voice anywhere for the rest of my life. Silence. Then Pelly: 'When did you last look at it?'

'This morning. I needed to write a letter to an address I had in there. It's hard to believe one of your brothers would do a thing like this. But who? It couldn't possibly be Warshawski.'

No indeed.

Pelly asked him sharply if anything was missing.

'Not as far as I can tell. And there wasn't anything that would prove anything, anyway . . . Except for a letter Figueredo wrote me.'

'If Warshawski broke in –' Pelly began.

'If Warshawski broke in, it doesn't really matter,' O'Faolin interrupted. 'She isn't going to be a problem after tonight. But if she shows the letter to someone in the meantime, I'll have to start all over again. I should never have left you on your own to handle this business. Forging those securities was a lunatic idea, and

715

now . . .' He broke off. 'No point rehashing all that. Let's just see if the letter's missing.'

He turned abruptly and left. Pelly pulled his shoes back on and followed him. I got up quickly. Pulled the hood well around my face and cracked the door to watch Pelly disappear into O'Faolin's room. Then, trying to remain calm, I went down the stairs with my head tucked into my chin. A couple of brothers greeted me *en route*, and I mumbled in response. At the bottom, Carroll said good evening. I mumbled and took off for the front door. Carroll said sharply, 'Brother!' Then to someone else, 'Who is that? I don't recognize him.'

Outside, I hitched up my habit and ran to the back of the building, started the Toyota, and drove it bumpily down the drive back to Melrose Park. There I quickly divested myself of the robe at a dry cleaner, telling them it was for Augustine Pelly.

In the car I sat laughing for a few minutes, then soberly considered what I'd found and what it meant. The letter from Figueredo seemed to imply that they wanted to acquire Ajax in order to launder Banco Ambrosiano money. Bizarre. Or maybe not. A bank, or an insurance company, made a highly respectable cover for moving questionable capital into circulation. If you could do it so the multitude of auditors didn't notice . . . I thought of Michael Sindona and the Franklin National Bank. Some people thought the Vatican had been involved in that escapade. With the Banco Ambrosiano, the connection was documented, if not understood: the Vatican was part owner of Ambrosiano's Panamanian subsidiaries. So was it strange that the head of the Vatican's Finance Committee would take an interest in the disposition of the Ambrosiano assets?

O'Faolin was an old friend of Kitty Paciorek. Mrs Paciorek's sizeable fortune was tied up with Corpus Christi. Ergo . . . She was expecting me in a couple of hours. I had some evidence, evidence she wanted badly enough to get someone to search the Bellerophon. But did it link her to the Wood-Sage/Corpus Christi connection strongly enough to make her talk? I didn't think so.

Thoughts of Mrs Paciorek reminded me of O'Faolin's last

716

remark: I wasn't going to be a problem after tonight. The queasiness, which seemed to be more and more a permanent resident, returned to my stomach. He might have meant they'd have Ajax sewn up by tonight. But I didn't think so. It seemed more likely that Walter Novick would be waiting for me in Lake Forest. Mrs Paciorek presumably had no scruples about doing such a favor for her old friend, although she probably wouldn't have me killed while her husband and Barbara were watching. What would she try? An ambush on the grounds?

Between Melrose and Elmwood Park, North Avenue forms a continuous strip of fast-food restaurants, factories, used-car lots, and cheap, small shopping malls. I selected one of these at random and found a public phone. Mrs Paciorek answered. Using the nasal twang of the South Side, I asked for Barbara. She was spending the night with friends, Mrs Paciorek said, demanding in a sharp voice to know who was calling. 'Lucy van Pelt,' I answered, hanging up. I couldn't think of a way to find out where the doctor and the servants were.

A Jewel/Osco had a public photocopier, which yielded a greasy gray copy of Figueredo's letter to O'Faolin. I bought a packet of cheap envelopes and a stamp from a stamp machine and mailed the original to my office. I thought for a minute, then scribbled a note to Murray on one of the envelopes, telling him to look at my office mail if I turned into a Chicago floatfish. Folded in three, it fit into another envelope, which I mailed to the *Herald-Star*. As for Lotty and Roger, what I wanted to tell them was too complicated to fit onto an envelope.

By now it was close to seven, too late for me to have a proper sit-down meal. The apple I'd had at three had been my only meal since breakfast, though, and I needed something to brace me for a possible fight at Mrs Paciorek's. I bought a large Hershey bar with almonds at the Jewel and stopped at Wendy's for a taco salad. Not the ideal thing to eat in a moving car, I realized as I joined the traffic on the tollway, and the salad dribbled down the front of my shirt. If Mrs Paciorek was planning to sic German shepherds on me they'd know where I was by the chili.

As I exited onto Half Day Road, I went over what I knew of the Paciorek estate. If an ambush was attempted, it would be laid either by the front door or at the garage entrance. In back of the house were the remains of a wood. Agnes and I had sometimes taken sandwiches out there to eat sitting on logs by a stream feeding Lake Michigan.

The property ended a half mile or so back of the house at a bluff overlooking the lake. In the summer, in broad daylight, it might be possible to climb that bluff, but not on a winter's night with waves roaring underneath. I'd have to come at the house from the side, across neighboring lots, and hope for the best.

I left the Toyota on a side street next to Arbor Road. Lake Forest was dark. There were no street lights, and I had no flashlight. Fortunately the night was relatively clear – a snowstorm would have made the job impossible.

Hunching down in my navy-surplus pea jacket, I made my way quietly past the house on the corner. Once in the backyard, the snow muffled any sound of my feet; it also made walking laborious. As I reached the fence dividing the yard from its neighbor, a dog started barking to my left. Soon it sounded as though all the dogs in suburbia were yapping at me. I climbed over the fence and moved east, away from the baying, hoping to get deep enough to hit the Paciorek house from behind.

The third lot was comparable in size to the Pacioreks'. As I moved into the wooded area, the dogs finally quieted down. Now I could hear the sullen roar of Lake Michigan in front of me. The regular, angry slapping of wave against cliff made me shiver violently with a cold deeper than that of freezing toes and ears.

Totally disoriented in the dark, I kept bumping into trees, stumbling over rotting logs, falling into unexpected holes. Suddenly I skidded down a small bank and landed with a jolt on my butt on some rocky ice. After picking myself up and slipping again, I realized I must be at the stream. If I walked away from the roaring lake, I should, with luck, be at the back of the Paciorek house.

In a few minutes I had fought my way clear of the trees. The house loomed as a blacker hole in the dark in front of me. Agnes and I had usually come out through the kitchen, which was on the far left along with rooms for the servants. No lights shone there now. If the servants were in, they were not giving any sign of it. In front of me were French windows leading into the conservatory-library-organ room.

My fingers were thick with cold. It took agonizing minutes to unbutton the pea jacket and take it off. I held it over the glass next to the window latch. With a numb hand, I pulled the Smith & Wesson clumsily from its holster, tapped the jacket lightly but firmly with the butt, and felt the glass give underneath. I paused for a minute. No alarms sounded. Holding my breath, I gently knocked glass away from the frame, stuck an arm through the opening, and unlatched the window.

Once inside the house I found a radiator. Pulling off boots and gloves, I warmed my frozen extremities. Ate the rest of the Hershey bar. Squinted at phosphorescent hands on my watch – past nine o'clock. Mrs Paciorek must be getting impatient.

After a quarter of an hour, I felt recovered enough to meet my hostess. Pulling the damp boots back on my toes was unpleasant, but the cold revived my mind, slightly torpid from the hike and the warmth.

Once outside the conservatory I could see lights coming from the front of the house. I followed them through long marble passages until I came to the family room where I'd talked to Mrs Paciorek a couple of weeks ago. As I'd hoped, she was sitting there in front of the fire, the needlepoint project in her lap but her hands still. Standing at an angle in the hall, I watched her. Her handsome angry face was strained. She was waiting for the sound that would tell her I had been shot.

23
LAKE FOREST PARTY

I'd been holding the Smith & Wesson in one hand, but she was clearly alone. I put the gun back in the holster and walked into the room.

'Good evening, Catherine. None of the servants seemed to be here, so I let myself in.'

She stared at me, frozen. For a moment I wondered if she really were having a stroke. Then she found her voice. 'What are you doing here?'

I sat down facing her in front of the fire. 'You invited me, remember? I tried getting here at eight, but I got lost in the dark – sorry to be so late.'

'Who? – how? –' she broke off and looked suspiciously at the hallway.

'Let me help you out,' I said kindly. 'You want to know how I got past Walter Novick – or whoever you have waiting for me out front, don't you?'

'I don't know what you're talking about,' she said fiercely.

'Then we'll go and find out!' I stood up again. Walking behind her, I grabbed her under the armpits and pulled her to her feet. She wasn't much heavier than I and had no fighting skills whatsoever. She tried struggling with me, but it wasn't an equal contest. I frog-marched her to the front door.

'Now. You are going to call whoever is out there to come in. My right hand is now holding my Smith and Wesson revolver, which is loaded and ready to shoot.'

She opened the door angrily. Casting me a look of loathing, she went to the shallow porch. Two figures broke away from the shadows near the driveway and came toward her. 'Leave!' she yelled. 'Leave! She came in through the back.'

The two men stood still for a minute. I aimed the gun at the one nearer my right hand. 'Drop your weapons,' I shouted. 'Drop your weapons and come into the light.'

At my voice they both shot at us. I pushed Mrs Paciorek into the snow and fired. The man on the right staggered, tripped, sprawled in the snow. The other fled. I heard a car door slam and the sound of tires trying to grab hold.

'You'd better come with me, Catherine, while we see what kind of shape he's in. I don't trust you alone in there with a phone.'

She didn't say anything as I dragged her pump-clad feet through the snow. When we came to the sprawled figure, he pointed a gun at us. 'Don't shoot again, you lunatic,' I cried. 'You'll hit your employer!'

When he didn't put the gun down, I let go of Mrs Paciorek and jumped on his arm. The gun went off, but the bullet sailed harmlessly into the night. I kicked the weapon from his hand and knelt to look at him.

In the lights marking the driveway I made out his heavy Slavic jawline. 'Walter Novick!' I hissed. I couldn't keep my voice quite steady. 'We can't keep meeting in the dark like this.'

As nearly as I could tell, I'd hit his right leg just above the knee. It should have been a bad enough wound to keep him from moving, but he was strong and he was scared. He tried scrabbling away from me in the snow. I grabbed his right arm and yanked it up behind him.

Mrs Paciorek turned on her heel and headed for the front door. 'Catherine!' I yelled. 'Better call an ambulance for your friend. I'm not sure O'Faolin can get reinforcements out here in time to shoot me if you phone him first anyway.'

She must have heard me, but gave no sign. A few seconds later the front door slammed shut behind her. Novick was cursing loudly if unimaginatively, his voice slightly muffled by the wiring holding his jaw together. I didn't want to leave him, but I didn't want Mrs

Paciorek summoning help, either. Gathering the hit man by the armpits, I started dragging him toward the house. He screamed with pain as his right leg bumped along the ground.

I dropped him and knelt again, this time looking him in the face. 'We need to talk, Walter,' I panted. 'I'm not leaving you here on the chance you can make it to the road for your buddy to find you. Not that he's likely to – he's probably in DuPage County by now.'

He tried to hit me, but the cold and blood loss were getting to him. The blow landed ineffectually on my shoulder.

'Your working days are over, Walter. Even if they patch that leg up, you're going to spend a long, long time in Joliet. So we'll talk. When you feel at a loss for words, I'll help you out.'

'I don't have anything to say,' he gasped hoarsely. 'They haven't made – a – charge stick yet. They won't – won't do it now.'

'Wrong, Walter. Stefan Herschel is going to be your downfall. You're slipping. You didn't kill him. He's alive. He's already ID'd you from your photo.'

He managed a contemptuous shrug. 'My – my friends – will prove – he's wrong.'

Fury, compounded of fatigue, of Lotty's accusations, of the attempt on my eyes, rose in me. I shook him, enough to jar the injured leg, and was glad when he yelped.

'Your friends!' I shouted at him. 'Don Pasquale, you mean. The don didn't send you here, did he? Did he?' When Novick didn't say anything, I picked him up by the shoulders and started dragging him toward the house again.

'Stop!' he yelled. 'No. No, it wasn't the don. It – it was someone else.'

I leaned over him in the snow. 'Who, Novick?'

'I don't know.'

I grabbed his armpits. 'All right!' he screamed. 'Put me down. I don't know his name. He's – he's someone who called me.'

'Have you ever met him in person?'

In the floodlights, I saw him nod weakly. A middle-aged man. He had met him once. The day he stabbed Uncle Stefan. This man had come with him to the apartment. No, Uncle Stefan might not have seen him – he'd waited in the hall until after the stabbing. Then gone in to collect the forged stocks. He was fifty-five or sixty. Green eyes. Gray hair. But the voice Novick especially remembered – a voice you'd recognize in hell, he called it.

O'Faolin. I sat back on my heels and looked at the hit man. Sour bile filled my mouth. I swallowed a handful of snow, gagged, swallowed again, trying to force down the desire to kill Novick where he lay.

'Walter, you're a lucky man. Pasquale doesn't give a damn whether you live or die. Neither do I. But you're going to live. Isn't that nice? And if you swear in court that the man who ordered you out here tonight was behind the stabbing of Stefan Herschel, I'll see you get a good plea bargain. We'll forget the acid. We'll even forget the fire. How about it?'

'The don won't forget me.' This was in a thread of a voice. I had to stick my ear close to his revolting face to hear it.

'Yes, he will, Walter. He can't afford to be tied to the forgeries. He can't afford the FBI and the SEC subpoenaing his accounts. He isn't going to know you.'

He still didn't say anything. I pulled the Smith & Wesson from my jeans belt. 'If I shoot your left kneecap, you'll never be able to prove it didn't happen when you attacked me at the door.'

'You wouldn't,' he gasped.

He was probably right; my stomach was churning as it was. What kind of person kneels in the snow threatening to destroy the leg of an injured man? Not anyone I wanted to know. I pulled the hammer back with a loud click and pointed the gun at his left leg.

'No,' he cried. 'No, don't. I'll do it. Whatever you say. But you get me a doctor. Get me a doctor.' He was sobbing pitifully. Toughest man in the Mafia.

I put the gun away. 'Good boy, Walter. You won't regret it. Now, just a few more questions and we'll get you an ambulance – Kitty Paciorek seems to have forgotten you.'

Novick eagerly told the little he knew. He'd never seen Mrs Paciorek before. The Man with the Voice had called yesterday and told him to get out here at seven tonight, to make sure no one saw him, to shoot me as I walked up to the house from my car. Yes, it was the Man with the Voice who hired him to throw acid at me.

'How did he know you, Walter? How did he know to get in touch with you?'

He didn't know. 'The don must have given him my number. That's all I can figure. He told the don he needed a good man and the don gave him my number.'

'You are a good man, Walter. Pasquale must be proud of you. You came for me three times and all you got out of it was a broken jaw and a smashed up leg . . . I'm going to get you an ambulance. You'd best be praying your godfather forgets all about you, because from what I hear he doesn't like failures too much.'

I covered him with my coat and headed for the front door. As I reached the steps a car pulled into the driveway. Not an ambulance. I froze, then jumped from the shallow porch to shelter in some evergreens running from the house to the garage. The same place, I saw from the trampled snow, where Novick had waited for me.

The garage doors opened electronically; the car pulled in and stopped. I peered around the edge of a tree. A dark blue Mercedes. Dr Paciorek. How much did he know about tonight's escapade? Now was as good a time as any to find out. I stepped into the garage.

He looked up in surprise as he locked the car door. 'Victoria! What are you doing here?'

'I came out to see your wife – I had some papers of Agnes's she wanted to see. Someone was lying in wait out front here and took a shot at her. I've hit him in the leg and I need to get an ambulance for him.'

He looked at me suspiciously. 'Victoria. This isn't your idea of a joke, is it?'

'Come and see for yourself.' He followed me to the front. Novick was dragging himself toward the road as fast as he could, a feeble activity that had moved him ten feet or so. 'You!' Paciorek yelled. 'Stop!'

Novick continued to move. We trotted over to him. Dr Paciorek handed me the briefcase he was carrying and knelt to look at the hit man. Novick tried to fight with him, but Paciorek didn't need my help to hold him down. After a few minutes' feeling of the leg, during which Novick cursed more loudly than ever, Paciorek said briefly, 'The bone is broken but there isn't much else the matter except cold. I'll get an ambulance and call the police. You don't mind staying with him, do you?'

I was starting to shiver. 'I guess not. Can you lend me your coat? I gave him mine.'

He gave me a surprised glance, then took off his cashmere coat and draped it around my shoulders. After the doctor's bulky body vanished into the house, I squatted down next to Novick. 'Before you pass out, let's get our stories straight.' By the time the Lake Forest police arrived, we had agreed that he'd gotten lost and come to the door looking for help. Mrs Paciorek, terrified, had screamed. That brought me to the scene with my gun out. Walter had taken fright at that and fired at me. I shot him. Not very believable, but I was damned sure Mrs Paciorek wouldn't contradict it.

The sirens sounded in the distance. Novick had fainted finally, and I stood back to let the officials take over. I was dizzy and close to fainting myself. Fatigue. Nausea at the depths of my own rage. How like a mobster I had behaved – torture, threats. I don't believe the end justifies the means. I'd just been plain raving angry.

As wave on wave of policemen interviewed me, I kept dozing off, waking up, keeping my wits together enough to tell the same story each time, then dozing again. It was one o'clock when they finished and left.

Dr Paciorek had refused to let his wife talk. I don't know what she told him, but he sent her to bed; the locals didn't argue that decision. Not with that much money behind it.

Dr Paciorek had let the police use his study as an interrogation room. After they left, he came in and sat in the leather swivel chair behind his desk. I was sprawled in a leather armchair, three parts asleep.

'Would you like a drink?'

I rubbed my eyes and sat up a little straighter. 'Brandy would be nice.'

He reached into a cabinet behind the desk for a bottle of Cordon Bleu and poured two hefty servings.

'What were you doing here tonight?' he asked abruptly.

'Mrs Paciorek wanted to see me. She asked me to come out around eight.'

'She says you showed up unexpectedly.' His tone wasn't accusatory. 'Monday nights are when the Lake County Medical Society gets together. I usually don't go. Catherine asked me to leave her alone tonight because she was having a meeting with a religious group she belongs to; she knows that isn't of much interest to me. She says you showed up threatening her and brought that man along with you; that she was struggling with you when your gun went off and hit him.'

'Where did her religious friends go?'

'She says they had left before you showed up.'

'Do you know much about this Corpus Christi outfit she belongs to?'

He stared at his brandy for a while, then finished it with one swallow and poured himself another shot. I held out my snifter; he filled it recklessly.

'Corpus Christi?' he finally said. 'When I married Catherine, her family accused me of being a fortune hunter. She was an only child and that estate was worth close to fifty million. I didn't care much about the money. Some, but not much. I met her in Panama – her father was the ambassador; I was working off my loan from Uncle Sam. She was very idealistic, was doing a lot of work in the poor community there. Xavier O'Faolin was a priest in one of those shantytowns. He interested her in Corpus Christi. I met her because I was trying to keep dysentery and a lot of other unpleasant stuff under control in that shantytown. A hopeless battle, really.'

He swallowed some more brandy. 'Then we came back to Chicago. Her father built this house. When he died we moved in. Catherine turned most of the Savage fortune over to Corpus Christi. I started becoming successful as a heart surgeon. O'Faolin moved on to the Vatican.

'Catherine was genuinely idealistic, but O'Faolin is a charlatan. He knew how to look good and do well at the same time. It was John the Twenty-third who brought him to the Vatican – thought of him as a real people's priest. After John died, O'Faolin headed quickly to where the money and power were.'

We drank quietly for several minutes. Few things go down as easily as Cordon Bleu.

'I should have spent more time at home.' He gave a mirthless smile. 'The plaint of the suburban father. At first Catherine was pleased to see me at the hospital twenty hours a day – after all, it proved I shared her lofty ideals. But after a while, she burned out on suburban living. She should have had her own career. But it didn't go with her ideals of Catholic motherhood. By the time I saw how angry she'd become, Agnes was in college and it was too late for me to do anything. I spent the time with Phil and Barbara I should have spent with Agnes and Cecelia, but I couldn't help Catherine.'

He held the bottle up to his desk lamp. 'Enough for two more.' He divided it between us and tossed the bottle into a leather wastebasket at his feet.

'I know she blamed you for Agnes's – life-style. I need to know. Was she so angry with you that she'd try to get someone to shoot you?'

It had taken him a quarter bottle of good brandy to get that out. 'No,' I said. 'Not that simple, I'm afraid. I have some evidence showing that Corpus Christi is trying to take over a local insurance company. Mrs Paciorek is most anxious that that information not become public. I'm afraid I had reasons for thinking someone might be waiting for me out front, so I broke in through a window in your conservatory. The police didn't search the back of the house or they would never have left.'

'I see.' He looked suddenly old and shrunken in his tailored navy suit. 'What are you going to do about it?'

'I'm going to have to let the FBI and the SEC know about Corpus Christi's involvement. I don't plan to tell them about tonight's ambush, if that's any consolation.' Nor could I bring myself to tell him about Agnes's note. If she'd been killed because of her investigation into the Ajax takeover, then in some way or other, her mother bore responsibility for her death. Dr Paciorek didn't need to hear that tonight.

He stared bitterly at the desk top for a long time. When he looked up, he was almost surprised to see me sitting there. Wherever he'd been was a long way away. 'Thanks, Victoria. You've been more generous than I had a right to expect.'

I finished my own brandy, embarrassed. 'Don't thank me. However this ends, it's going to be bad for you and your children. While I'm really most interested in Xavier O'Faolin, your wife is heavily involved in Corpus Christi. Their money is being used in an attempt to take over Ajax insurance. When the facts come out, she's going to be right up front on the firing line.'

'But wouldn't it be possible to show she was just O'Faolin's dupe?' He smiled bitterly. 'Which she has been, since she first met him in Panama.'

I looked at him with genuine pity. 'Dr Paciorek, let me tell you the situation as I understand it. The Banco Ambrosiano is missing over a billion dollars, which disappeared into unknown Panamanian companies. Based on a letter from a Panamanian named Figueredo to Archbishop O'Faolin, it looks as though O'Faolin knows where that money is. He's in sort of a bind. As long as he doesn't use it, no one will know where it is. Once he starts to move it, the game is up.

'O'Faolin's no dummy. If he can get some large financial institution, like an insurance company, under his control, he can launder the money and use it however he wants. Michael Sindona tried that on behalf of the Mob with the Franklin National Bank, only he was stupid enough to strip the bank's assets. So he's languishing now in a federal prison.

'Corpus Christi in Chicago has a huge endowment, thanks to Mrs Paciorek. O'Faolin is a member and recruited your wife. Very well. Let them put together a dummy corporation, call it Wood-Sage, and use that to acquire Ajax stock. Once the connection comes out between Corpus Christi and the Ajax takeover – and it will;

728

the SEC is investigating like crazy – your wife's involvement will be front-page news. Especially here in Chicago.'

'But that's not criminal,' the doctor pointed out.

I frowned unhappily. At last I said, 'Look. I didn't want to tell you this. Particularly not tonight, when you've had such a shock. But there's Agnes's death, you see.'

'Yes?' His voice was harsh.

'She was looking into the takeover for one of the Ajax officers . . . She found out about the Corpus Christi involvement. She was killed that night while waiting to meet with someone to discuss it.'

His white, stricken face was like an open wound in the room. I could think of nothing to say to ease that pain. At last he looked up and gave a ghastly smile. 'Yes. I can see. Even if Xavier is the main culprit, Catherine can't avoid her own responsibility for her daughter's death. No wonder she's been so . . .' His voice trailed off.

I got up. 'I wish I could think of some comfort for you. I can't. But if you want my help, please call me. My answering service takes messages twenty-four hours a day.' I put my card on the desk in front of him and left.

I was bone-weary and stiff. I'd have gladly lain down in front of the family-room fire and passed out, but I willed my aching body down the front stairs to the street. Going by road, it was only a five-minute walk to my car instead of the half hour it had taken me cross-country.

My watch said three when I moved the stiff Toyota back onto the tollway. I found a motel at the first southbound exit, checked in, and fell asleep without bothering to undress.

24
BAITING THE TRAP

It was past noon when I woke again. Every muscle ached. I'd remembered to put the Smith & Wesson aside before going to sleep, but not the holster. My left side was sore from where the leather had pressed into my breast all night. My clothes stank. I'd fought Walter Novick in this shirt, put in a heavy stint of cross-country hiking, and slept in it. The smell bore acute witness to these activities.

I longed for a bath, but not if it meant redonning my repellent apparel. I picked up the Toyota and maneuvered its clumsy steering down the expressway to the Bellerophon. Mrs Climzak gave me a darkling glance from behind the counter but forbore any criticism, so I gathered no one had tried burglarizing my apartment in the night.

It was only after a long soak in the stained porcelain tub that I realized how hungry I was. Dry, reclothed, I stiffly descended the four flights of stairs.

What would the don's reaction be to losing Novick? Would he be gunning for me, or would he realize Novick wasn't salvageable and cut his losses? Only the Shadow knew. Just in case Pasquale was pissed, I braved Mrs Climzak's breathy protests and went past the front desk to explore the Bellerophon's nether regions. The lobby's back entrance led to a hallway where her apartment was situated. Her mules flopping, she scampered behind me like an angry hen. 'Miss Warshawski! Miss Warshawski! What are you doing back here? Get out. Get out before I call my husband. Before I call the police!'

Her apartment door opened and the fabled Mr Climzak appeared, in a T-shirt and baggy trousers. A day's growth of beard helped hide his drink-reddened cheeks. He didn't look as though he could throw me out, but he might be alert enough to call the police.

'Just looking for the back door,' I told him brightly, continuing down the passage.

As I undid the dead bolt, Mrs Climzak hissed, 'This is the last straw. You will have to find other lodgings.'

I looked at her before going outside. 'I hope so, Mrs Climzak. I certainly hope so.'

No hail of machine-gun bullets strafed me in the alley. Nor were any suspicious-looking cars hovering on the street. I found a Polish restaurant and ate heartily, if not healthily, of cabbage soup, chicken, dumplings, and apple tart.

I felt decidedly more human. Over a second cup of coffee, an idea began glimmering at the back of my brain. Preposterous. It would need Murray's cooperation. And Uncle Stefan's.

Illinois Bell, poverty-stricken by the AT&T dismemberment, had raised the price of pay phone calls to a quarter. After fishing for change, I reached Murray at the desk of the *Herald-Star*. If I gave him a big, huge story would he sit on it until it came to an end?

'Ain't you dead yet, Warshawski? What am I supposed to do in exchange for this big huge story?'

'Run a couple of lines on the front page of the evening and morning editions.'

'I'm not the editor – I don't control what goes on the front page. Or even page sixty-two of the middle section.'

'Murray! I'm shocked. You told me you were an important newspaperman. Can it be you lied? Can it be I have to go to the *Tribune* and talk to Lipinski?'

Grumbling, he agreed to meet me at the Golden Glow around five p.m. The schoolroom clock over the counter said two-thirty. Time to check things out with Uncle Stefan.

Another quarter to my answering service reminded me I hadn't told Phyllis I wouldn't be back to her place last night. Or Roger that I'd miss his board meeting. And Bobby wanted to see me to talk about Walter Novick. 'Not your jurisdiction,' I muttered.

'What was that?' the operator said.

'Nothing. Any other calls?'

Dr Paciorek wanted to talk to me. He'd left his paging number at the hospital for me. Frowning, I put another quarter in the machine. Twenty-five cents gets you three tries. Clicked from operator to operator at the hospital, I finally connected with Dr Paciorek.

'Victoria! I was afraid you wouldn't get my message.' His normally controlled voice was rough and human. 'Could you come back to the house tonight? I know it's a lot to ask. O'Faolin's coming out – I'm going to settle this matter.'

I rubbed my eyes with my free hand. Would this upset my other plans? Dr Paciorek breathed anxiously in my ear while I considered. Maybe I could put a little advance pressure on the archbishop. 'I guess so. Can't make it before eight, though.'

'Fine. Fine. Thanks very much, Victoria.'

'Don't thank me for anything, Dr Paciorek. This story is not going to have a happy ending.'

A long silence, then 'I realize that' and he hung up.

Jim Streeter met me at Uncle Stefan's door. 'The doctors say the old man can be released tomorrow. He's been trying to reach his niece. I guess she's planning on taking him home with her. What do you want us to do?'

Of course he would be going home with Lotty, I thought in irritation. 'I'd better talk to him.'

Uncle Stefan was delighted to see me, delighted to be going home. 'And why are you frowning, my little niece? Aren't you pleased for me?'

'Oh, certainly. Yes, I'm very pleased. How are you feeling?'

'Fine. Chipper. Yes, chipper.' He beamed proudly at producing this colloquial word. 'Every day I go for physical therapy and every day I am stronger, walk farther. All I need now is chocolate.'

I grinned and sat on the bed. 'I have a favor to ask of you. Please say no if you don't want to do it, because there's some danger involved. Not a lot, but some.'

He cocked a lively eye at me and demanded details.

'Instead of going to Lotty's, would you come home with me? I need you to pretend you're dead for twenty-four hours, then arise from the grave with a flourish.'

'Lotty will be *wutend*.' He beamed.

'No doubt, if that means what I think it does. Console yourself with the thought that it's me she wants to murder.'

He patted my hand comfortingly. 'Lotty is a headstrong girl. Don't worry about her.'

'You didn't see a second man in your apartment the day you were stabbed, did you?'

He shook his head. 'Just the – the thug.'

'Would you be willing to say that you saw him? He was there, you see. Just hovering outside until your thug had stabbed you.'

'If you say he was there, my dear niece, I believe you.'

25

KNIGHT TAKES BISHOP

Murray grudgingly agreed to run the story. 'I'll have to tell Gil the whole tale,' he warned me. Gil was the front page editor.

I explained the entire situation to him – Ajax, the Banco Ambrosiano, Corpus Christi.

Murray finished his beer and signaled to the waitress for another. Sal was busy behind the bar with commuting drinkers. 'You know, it's probably O'Faolin who backed away the FBI from the case.'

I nodded. 'That's what I think. Between Mrs Paciorek and him, there's enough money and power to strangle a dozen investigations. I'd like to get Derek out to the priory with me tomorrow, but he doesn't listen to me at the best of times. Neither does Bobby. And today wasn't the best of times.'

I'd spent a frustrating afternoon on the phone. I'd had a long talk with Bobby, in which he read me the riot act for not fingering Novick earlier. He refused to listen to my story. Refused to send men out to the priory to question the archbishop or Pelly. And was aghast at the accusation against Mrs Paciorek. Bobby was a salt-of-the-earth Catholic; he wasn't taking on a prince of the Church. Nor yet a princess.

Derek Hatfield was even less cooperative. A suggestion that he at least block O'Faolin's departure for forty-eight hours was met with frosty contempt. As so often happened in my encounters with Derek, I ended the discussion with a rude remark. That is, I made a rude remark and he hung up. Same thing, really.

A conversation with Freeman Carter, my lawyer, was more fruit-

734

ful. He was just as skeptical as Bobby and Derek, but at least he worked for me and promised to get some names – in exchange for a hundred and a quarter an hour.

'I'll be at the priory,' Murray promised.

'No disrespect, but I'd like a dozen men with guns.'

'Just remember, Miss Warshawski: The pen is mightier than the pencil,' Murray said portentously.

I laughed reluctantly.

'We'll tape it,' Murray promised. 'And I'll have someone there with a camera.'

'It'll have to do . . . And you'll take Uncle Stefan home with you?'

Murray grimaced. 'Only if you pay for the funeral when Lotty finds out what I've done.' He'd met Lotty enough times to know what her temper was like.

I looked at my watch and excused myself. It was close to six, the time I was to call back Freeman at his club before he left for a dinner meeting.

Sal let me use the phone in the cube she calls an office, a windowless room directly behind the bar with one-way glass overlooking the floor. Freeman was brisk, but brief. He gave me two names, Mrs Paciorek's attorney and her broker. And yes, the broker had handled a twelve-million-dollar transaction for Corpus Christi to buy Ajax shares.

I whistled to myself as Freeman hung up. Worth a hundred twenty-five dollars. I looked at my watch again. Time for one more call, this time to Ferrant, still at his Ajax office.

He sounded more tired than ever. 'I talked to the board today and tried urging them to find my permanent replacement. They need someone managing the insurance operations, or those will go to hell and there won't be anything left to take over. All my energy is going into meetings with legal eagles and financial wizards and I don't have time to do the only thing I do well – broker insurance deals.'

'Roger, I think I may have a way out of the problem for you. I don't want to tell you what it is, because you'd have to tell your partner and your board. It may not work, but if a lot of people know about it, it definitely won't work.'

Roger turned this over. When he spoke again, his voice had more energy than I'd heard for some time. 'Yes. You're right. So I won't press you . . . Could I see you tonight? Dinner maybe?'

'A very late dinner – say ten o'clock?'

That suited his schedule; he would be closeted with eagles and wizards for several hours yet. 'Can I tell them we may have a break coming our way?'

'As long as you don't tell them who you heard it from.'

When I got back to the table, Murray had left a brief note torn from his steno notebook informing me he was off to talk to Gil to try to make the last edition.

The one advantage the rented Toyota had over my little Omega was that its heater worked. January was sliding into February without any noticeable change in the weather. The thermometer had dropped below freezing New Year's Eve and hadn't climbed above it since. As I slid out of the underground garage and turned onto Lake Shore Drive, the car was already warm enough that I could take off my coat.

Exiting at Half Day Road, I wondered how safe it was to drive right up to the Pacioreks' front door. What if Dr Paciorek agreed with O'Faolin that I should be bumped off? It might save his wife's reputation. What if O'Faolin knocked him out with a crucifix and shot me?

The doctor met me at the door, his face grave and pinched. He looked as though he hadn't slept since I left him the night before. 'Catherine and Xavier are in the family room. They don't know you're here – I didn't think Xavier would stay if he knew you were coming.'

'Probably not.' I followed him down the familiar hallway into the familiar, hot living room.

Mrs Paciorek sat, as usual, by the fire. O'Faolin had pulled a straight-backed chair up to the couch on which she sat. As Dr Paciorek and I came in, they looked toward the door and let out simultaneous gasps.

O'Faolin was on his feet and coming toward the door. Paciorek put out an arm, strong through years of sawing people open, and propelled him back into the room.

'We need to talk.' His voice had recovered its firmness. 'You and Catherine haven't been saying anything to the point; I thought Victoria could help us out.'

O'Faolin gave me a look that made my stomach jump. Hatred and destruction. I tried to force down my own fury at the sight of him – the man who tried to get me blinded, who burned my apartment. Now was not the time to try to strangle him, but the urge was strong.

'Good evening, Archbishop. Good evening, Mrs Paciorek.' I was pleased to hear my voice come out without a quaver. 'Let's talk about Ajax and Corpus Christi and Agnes.'

O'Faolin had himself back under control. 'Topics about which I know very little, Miss Warshawski.'

The accentless voice was supercilious. 'Xavier, I hope you have a confessor with a lot of pull.'

He narrowed his eyes slightly, whether at my use of his first name or at the accusation I couldn't know.

'How dare you talk to the archbishop like that?' Mrs Paciorek spat out.

'You know me, Catherine: brave enough to try anything. It all comes with practice, really.'

Dr Paciorek held up his hands pleadingly. 'Now that you've all insulted each other, could we get down to some real conversation? Victoria, you talked last night about the link between Corpus Christi and Ajax. What evidence do you have?'

I fished in my purse for the greasy photocopy of Rául Díaz Figueredo's letter to O'Faolin. 'I guess what I really have is O'Faolin's involvement in the Ajax takeover. You read Spanish, don't you?'

The doctor nodded silently and I handed the photocopy across to him. He read it carefully, several times, then showed it to O'Faolin.

'So it *was* you!' he hissed.

I shrugged. 'I don't know what was me, but I do know this letter shows you being advised that Ajax was the best, if not easiest takeover target. You've got a billion dollars in Banco Ambrosiano assets sitting in Panama banks. You can't use them – if you withdraw the money and start spending it, the Bank of Italy is going to come down on you like lions on an early Christian.

'So you remembered Michael Sindona and the Franklin National Bank and realized what you needed was a US financial institution to launder money through. And an insurance company is better than a bank in lots of ways because you can play all these games with loss reserves and your life-company assets and nobody will really be able to tell. Figueredo got someone to check out the available stock companies. My guess is Ajax looked good because it's in Chicago. The money boys are myopic when something happens outside New York City – it'll take them longer to notice what's going on. With me so far?'

Catherine had gone quite pale. Her mouth was set in a thin line. O'Faolin, however, was at ease, smiling contemptuously. 'It's a beautiful theory. But if a friend of mine points out that Ajax is a good takeover target, that is not illegal. And if I am taking it over, that, too, is not illegal, although where I would get such money is a good question. But so far as I know, I am not taking it over.'

He sank back in his chair, legs stretched out, ankles crossed.

'Alas for the venality of the human condition.' I tried a contemptuous smile myself, but suavity is not my long suit. 'My attorney, Freeman Carter, spoke with yours this afternoon, Mrs Paciorek. Freeman belongs to the same club as Fuller Gibson and Fuller didn't mind telling him who handles the brokerage business for the Paciorek Trust. And then it wasn't too difficult getting verification of the note Agnes left for me: Corpus Christi used twelve million to buy Ajax shares in the name of the Wood-Sage Corporation.'

No one said anything for a minute. Mrs Paciorek made a strangled little noise and fainted, falling over on the couch. Paciorek went to her side while O'Faolin got up and strolled toward the door. I stood in the doorway, blocking his path. He was half a foot taller than I and maybe forty pounds heavier, but I was twenty years younger.

He tried to shove me aside with his left arm. Since his weight was forward on that side, I grabbed the arm and pulled, sending him sprawling on his face into the hall. This small piece of violence unleashed the fury I'd been holding barely in check. Panting slightly, I waited for him to climb to his feet.

He got up, backing warily away from me. I laughed slightly. 'Not scared are you, Xavier?' I curled my right fingers at the second joint, and came in with my left elbow to his diaphragm. He landed an inexpert blow on my shoulder, while I used my crooked fingers to push at his eyes. Holding the back of his head with my left hand I pushed up with the right while he shoved at me and kicked. Not a fighter.

'I might blind you. I might kill you. If you fight, you up the pressure.'

I felt an arm on my left shoulder, pulling, and shrugged it away, but it pulled more insistently. I came away, gasping for air, red rage swirling through my head. 'Let go of me! Let go of me!'

'Victoria!' It was Dr Paciorek. I felt a stinging on my face, realized he'd slapped me, and came slowly back to the marble hallway.

'He tried to blind me,' I panted. 'He tried to burn me to death. He probably killed Agnes. You should have let me kill him.'

O'Faolin was white except for his eyes – the skin around them was scarlet from the pressure of my fingers. He straightened his clerical collar. 'She's mad, Thomas. Call the police.'

Paciorek let go of my arm and I leaned against the wall. As reality returned, I remembered the other part of my plan. 'Oh, yes. Stefan Herschel died tonight. That's another crime that this prince of peace is responsible for.'

Paciorek frowned. 'Who is Stefan Herschel?'

'He was an old man, a master engraver, who tried to interest Xavier here in buying a forged stock certificate. Xavier stole the certificate, but not before his buddy Walter Novick had stabbed the man. Walter is the man who was lying shot on your lawn last night. He gets around.'

'Is this true?' Paciorek demanded.

'This woman is a lunatic, Thomas. How can you believe what she says? The old man is dead, apparently, so how can you verify your story? All of this is hearsay, anyway: an old man dead; Corpus Christi buying Ajax shares; Figueredo writing about Ajax's investment potential – how does that implicate me in a crime?'

Paciorek was pale. 'Whether you are implicated or not, Catherine is. Thanks to you, it's her money that funds Corpus Christi here in Chicago. And it's that money that's being used to buy Ajax stock. And now, maybe because she was looking into that, my oldest daughter is dead. O'Faolin, I hold you responsible. You got Catherine involved in all this.'

'For years you have insisted I was Catherine's evil genius, her Rasputin.' O'Faolin was haughty. 'So it is no surprise to me that you blame me now.'

He turned on his heel and left. Neither Paciorek nor I moved to stop him. Paciorek looked wearier than ever. 'How much of that is true?'

'How much of what?' I said irritably. 'Is Corpus Christi behind Wood-Sage? Yes, that's true. And Wood-Sage behind the Ajax takeover bid? Yes, they filed Friday with the SEC. And Agnes killed because of looking into it? Never will be proved. Probable.'

'I need a drink,' he muttered. 'Months go by and I have one glass of wine. Here I am drinking two days in a row.' He led me through the labyrinth to his study.

'How's Catherine?'

'Catherine?' The name seemed to surprise him. 'Oh, Catherine. She's all right. Just shock. She doesn't need me, in any event.' He looked in his liquor cupboard. 'We finished the brandy last night, didn't we? I have some whiskey. You drink Chivas?'

'You have Black Label?'

He pawed through the little cupboard. No Black Label. I accepted a Chivas and sat in the leather armchair.

'What about the old man? The engraver?'

I shrugged. 'He's dead. That makes O'Faolin an accessory, if Novick can make the identification stick. Trouble is, it won't be in time. He'll be on that plane to Rome tomorrow at ten. As long as he never comes back to Chicago, he'll be home free.'

'And the Ajax takeover?' He finished the whiskey in a gulp and poured another. He offered the bottle to me, but I shook my head – I didn't want to be drunk for the drive back to Chicago.

'I think I can stop that.'

'How?'

I shook my head. 'It's a small piece of SEC law. So small that Xavier probably never noticed it.'

'I see.' He finished his second drink and poured himself a third. There wasn't any point in watching him get drunk. At the door I turned for a moment to look at him. He was staring into the bottom of the glass, but he sensed my departure. Without looking up, he said, 'You say Agnes's death will never be proved. But how sure are you?'

'There's no evidence,' I said helplessly.

He put the glass down with a snap. 'Don't. When someone has a fatal heart condition, I tell them. I tell them these things are never certain and that gutsy people and lucky people beat the odds. But without a scan I know what's happening. As one professional to another, how sure are you about Agnes's death?'

I met his brown eyes and saw with a twinge that tears swam in them. 'As one professional to another – very certain.'

'I see. That's all I wanted to know. Thank you for coming up tonight, Victoria.'

I didn't like to leave him in this state. He ignored my outstretched arm, picked up a journal lying on a corner of the desk, and studied it intently. I didn't tell him it was upside down.

26
LOADING THE GUN

Roger met me at Grillon's, an old Chicago tradition where waiters leave you alone instead of popping up every five minutes to ask if everything is to your satisfaction. They rolled a huge joint of beef up to the table and cut off rare slices for us. Stilton, flown in from Melton Mowbray just for the restaurant, went well with a '64 port. Despite my worries and the ugly scene I'd been through with O'Faolin, I felt good.

Roger was buoyant. 'You've given me something to look forward to, V. I. I told the board that I had a private-inquiry agent looking into the matter and that he thought he had a way out. They were most keen, but since I didn't have any information, I couldn't give them any.'

I smiled tiredly and clasped his hand. It was midnight when we finished the port and the waiter brought our check. Roger asked hesitantly if he could come home with me. I shook my head regretfully.

'Not that I wouldn't like it – the company would be most welcome. But it's not much of a place and right now what's there is a shambles. Someone was pawing through it looking for a document and I just don't feel like sharing the mess.'

'Is that the way an American girl tells someone to go to hell?'

I leaned across the table and kissed him. 'When I tell you to go to hell, you won't have any doubts at all that that's what you heard . . . I guess what I'm telling you is that I'm homeless and don't like it. I feel disoriented and I need to be alone with it.'

He nodded soberly. 'People on my staff are always telling me,

'I can deal with that.' I guess that's an Americanism. Anyway, I can deal with that.'

When he offered to drive me, I gratefully accepted, abandoning the Toyota in the underground garage. If it wasn't still there in the morning, no big loss.

It was after one-thirty when he deposited me in front of the Bellerophon. Courteously waiting until I was safely inside, he waved and drove off.

Mrs Climzak had sat up for me. As soon as I came in the door she came huffing over, her face resembling an angry peony.

'You're going to have to leave, Miss Warshawski, or whatever your name really is.'

'I want to, Mrs Climzak. I don't like the Bellerophon any better than it likes me. But we'll both have to stick it out until the end of the week.'

'This isn't funny!' She stamped her foot. I was afraid some of the petals might start falling off. 'You have disrupted your apartment. You have strange men in at all hours of the night.'

'Not disrupted, Mrs Climzak. You mean there's been an irruption in the apartment. I don't think you disrupt apartments, only meetings.'

'Don't try to change the subject. Now, tonight, two men burst in and almost frightened my husband to death.'

'What did they do – show him a job application?'

'You get out of here by eight tomorrow morning. And take those men with you.'

'What men?' I started to say, then realized what she was talking about. My heart began beating faster. I wished I hadn't drunk so much at dinner, but the Smith & Wesson gently pushing into my side brought some comfort. 'They're still in the apartment? You didn't call the police?'

'Why should I?' she said in thin triumph. 'I figured they were *your* problem, not mine.'

'Thanks, Mrs Climzak. Don't call the mayor's office for your good-citizen medal – they'll call you.'

Pushing my way past her I went behind the lobby desk, picked up the phone and dialed my room. She was squawking and pulling at my arm but I ignored her – I'd beaten up an archbishop today. An old lady wasn't going to trouble me any.

After fifteen rings, a gravelly voice I knew well answered. 'Ernesto. It's V. I. Warshawski. You going to shoot me if I come up to my room?'

'Where are you, Warshawski? We've been waiting here since eight o'clock.'

'Sorry. I got carried away by religion.'

He asked again where I was and told me to wait for him in the lobby. When I'd hung up, Mrs Climzak was shrieking that she was going to get her husband to call the cops if I touched that phone again.

I leaned over and kissed her. 'Would you really? There are a couple of gangsters waiting to cart me off. If you call the cops, you might be in time to rescue me.'

She gazed at me in horror and dashed off to the nether regions. Ernesto, looking the picture of a corporate executive, came through the stairwell door, a seedy, thin man in an ill-fitting chauffeur's uniform at his heels.

Surely, if they meant to shoot me, they would have hidden outside and not broadcast their faces to the world like this. Surely. Yet my hands didn't believe me. They started sweating and I was afraid they might be trembling so I stuck them into my pockets.

'Your room's a mess, Warshawski.'

'If I'd known you were coming, I would've cleaned up.'

He ignored the sarcasm. 'Someone's been searching it. Sloppy job. You know that?'

I told him I knew it and followed him into the cold night. The limousine was parked around the corner. Ernesto and I sat in the backseat, me not blindfolded this time. I lay against the comfortable upholstery, but couldn't sleep. This has to work, I told myself. Has to. This can't be a summons to shoot me in revenge for wounding Walter Novick. For that they'd just gun me down on the street.

Jumbled with these thoughts was O'Faolin's contemptuous face as he left me tonight, Paciorek's despair. And somewhere in the

744

city, a furious Lotty, hearing that Uncle Stefan was going home with Murray, was going to play the tethered goat for me.

On North Avenue we turned into the parking lot of an enormous restaurant. No wonder they hadn't blindfolded me – nothing secret about this place. A huge neon sign with a champagne glass bubbling over perched on top of the marquee. Underneath it, flashing lights proclaimed this as Torfino's Restaurant, Italian food and wine.

When the limousine pulled up in front of the entrance, a doorman sprang from nowhere to open the car for Ernesto and me. The driver took off, whispering hoarsely the first sound I'd heard from him. 'Call when you're ready.'

I followed Ernesto through the restaurant, empty of customers, to a hallway behind the kitchen. Spare linoleum and green, grease-spattered walls gave it a common institutional look. A bored young man stood guard at a closed door. He moved to one side as Ernesto approached. Behind the door lay a private office where the don sat talking on a phone, gently smoking a large cigar. He nodded at Ernesto and waved a hand at me, signaling me to come in.

Like the don's library, this office was decorated in red. Here the effect was cheap. The curtains were rayon, the seat covers vinyl, the desk a mere box on four legs.

Pasquale hung up and asked Ernesto what had taken him so long. In Italian Ernesto explained my long absence. 'Further, someone else is interested in Signorina Warshawski. Her room has been carelessly searched.'

'And who would that be, Miss Warshawski?' Pasquale asked with grave courtesy.

I blinked a few times, trying to readjust myself to the imaginary world of honor. 'I thought you might know, Don Pasquale. I assumed it was done by your henchman, Walter Novick, at the request of Mrs Paciorek.'

The don looked at his cigar, measuring the ash, then turned to Ernesto. 'Do we know a Walter Novick, Ernesto?'

Ernesto gave a disdainful shrug. 'He has run a few errands for you, Don. He is the type who likes to grab at the coattails of the powerful.'

Pasquale nodded regally. 'I regret that Novick gave the appearance of being under my protection. As Ernesto said, he had illusions above his abilities. These illusions led him to use my name in a compromising way.' Again he examined the ash. Still not ripe. 'This Novick is acquainted with many petty criminals. A man like that frequently engages in foolish or dangerous exploits with such criminals in order to impress a man such as myself.' He gave a world-weary shrug. I knew, and he knew that such exploits were the acts of the childish, but – what would you? The ash now proved ready for a gentle tapping.

'Among these criminals were some forgers. Novick conceived an act of staggering folly: to engage these forgers to make fake stock certificates and put them in the safe of a religious house.'

He paused to invite my comment on this staggering folly. 'How, Don, did these forgers know for which companies and in which denominations to make the fakes?'

Pasquale hunched a shoulder impatiently. 'Priests are guileless men. They talk indiscreetly. Someone no doubt overheard them. Such things have happened before.'

'You would have no objection to my bringing this tale to Derek Hatfield?'

He smiled blandly. 'None whatsoever. Although it is merely hearsay – I can see no benefit to my talking to Hatfield myself.'

'And you wouldn't know the names of these forgers, would you?'

'Regrettably, no, my dear Miss Warshawski.'

'And you wouldn't know why these forgers used the priory, would you?'

'One presumes, Miss Warshawski, because it was easy for them. It is not of great interest to me.'

I could feel sweat prickling on the palms of my hands. My mouth was dry. This was my chance; I just hoped Pasquale, student of human terror that he was, couldn't detect my nervousness. 'Unfortunately, Don, you may have to take an interest.'

Pasquale didn't change position, nor did he alter his look of polite attention. But his expression somehow froze and the eyes glittered in a way that made cold sweat break out on my forehead. His voice, when he spoke, chilled my marrow. 'Is that a threat, Miss Warshawski?'

Out of the corner of one eye, I could see Ernesto, who'd been slouching in a vinyl chair, come to attention. 'Not a threat, Don Pasquale. Just for your information. Novick's in the hospital, and he's going to talk. And Archbishop O'Faolin's going to say it was all your idea about the forgeries, and attacking me, and all that stuff. He isn't going to know anything about it.'

Pasquale had relaxed slightly. I was breathing more easily. Ernesto sank back in his chair and started looking at his pocket diary.

'As you may know, Don, the SEC will not allow anyone with known Mafia connections to own an insurance company or a bank. So O'Faolin is going to back away from Novick as fast as he can. He'll leave on a ten o'clock flight tomorrow night and let you handle the situation as best you can.'

The don nodded with a return of his grave courtesy. 'As always, your comments are fascinating, Miss Warshawski. If I knew this O'Faolin' – he spread his hands deprecatingly. 'Meanwhile, I am desolated by the discomfort Walter Novick has brought into your life.' He looked at Ernesto; a red-leather checkbook materialized. The don wrote in it. 'Would twenty-five thousand cover the loss to your apartment?'

I swallowed a few times. Twenty-five thousand would get me a co-op, replace my mother's piano, or enable me to spend the rest of the winter in the Caribbean. What did I want with such things, however? 'Your generosity is fabled, Don Pasquale. Yet I have done nothing to deserve it.'

He persisted, politely. Keeping my eyes on a poor reproduction of Garibaldi over the pressed-wood desk, I steadfastly resisted. Pasquale finally gave me a measuring look and told Ernesto to see that I got home safely.

27
LUCK OF THE ARCHBISHOP

At four-thirty in early February the sky is already turning dark. Inside the Chapel of Our Lady of the Rosary, the candles created warming circles of light. Behind an ornately carved wooden screen, separating the friars' choir stalls from the secular mob, the room was dim. I could barely make out Uncle Stefan's features, but knew he was there from the comforting clasp of his hand. Murray was at my left. Beyond him was Cordelia Hull, one of his staff photographers.

As Father Carroll began to chant the introit in his high clear tenor, my depression deepened. I shouldn't be here. After making a complete fool of myself in as many ways as possible, I should have retired to the Bellerophon and pulled the covers over my head for a month.

The day had started badly. Lotty, enraged at the four-paragraph story in the *Herald-Star* announcing her uncle's sudden relapse and death, was not mollified by his decision to go home with Murray. According to Murray, the argument had been brief. Uncle Stefan chuckling and calling Lotty a hotheaded girl did not amuse her and she had switched to German to give vent to her fury. Uncle Stefan told her she was interfering where it was none of her business whereat she tore off in her green Datsun to find me. I didn't have the advantage of knowing Lotty as a headstrong little girl willfully riding her pony up the castle steps at Kleinsee. Besides, her accusations were too close to my nerve centers. Egotistical. So single-minded I would sacrifice Uncle Stefan trying to solve a problem that had the FBI and the SEC baffled.

'But, Lotty. I put my own body on the line, too. That arson at my apartment –'

She contemptuously swept away my protest. Hadn't the police asked for full information? Hadn't I withheld it in my usual arrogant way? And now I wanted someone to weep because I was suffering the consequences?

When I tried to suggest to Uncle Stefan – and Murray – that we drop the project and retire quietly, Murray had been angry in his turn: not after all he'd been through to sell Gil on the project. If I was too lily-livered all of a sudden to follow through on this, he wasn't. He'd take Uncle Stefan to the priory himself and I could go sulk in my tent and enjoy it alone.

Uncle Stefan took me to one side. 'Really, Victoria. By now you should know better than to pay the least heed to Lotty when she is in such a tantrum. If you are letting her overset you it is only because you are very tired.' He patted my hand and insisted that Murray go to a bakery and buy some chocolate cake. 'And none of that Sara Lee or Davidson cake. I mean a real bakery, young man. There must be one in your area.'

So Murray returned with a hazelnut chocolate cake and whipped cream. Uncle Stefan cut me a large slice, poured cream over it, and stood watching me eat it with anxious benevolence. 'So, *Nichtchen*, now you are feeling better, right?'

I wasn't, not really. Somehow I couldn't re-create the terror I'd felt earlier dealing with O'Faolin. All I could think of was Father Carroll's probable reaction to my antics in his chapel. But at three-thirty I'd followed Uncle Stefan into the backseat of Murray's Pontiac Fiero.

We reached the chapel early and were able to get seats in the front row behind the wooden screen. I was assuming that Rosa, hard at work on priory finances, would attend the service, but I didn't want to run the risk of her recognizing me, even in the gloomy half light, by turning around and peering.

Around us people joined in the service, knowing which chants permitted group singing, which ones were solo performances. The four of us sat quietly.

When the offertory announced the beginning of the mass, my heart started beating faster. Shame, fear, anticipation all crowded together. Next to me Uncle Stefan continued to breathe calmly while my palms turned wet and my breath came in short, gasping chunks.

Through the rood screen I could see the priests forming a large semicircle around the altar. Pelly and O'Faolin stood side by side, Pelly small, intent, O'Faolin tall and self-assured, the chief executive officer at an office picnic. O'Faolin wore a black cassock instead of the white Dominican robe. He was not part of the order.

We let the congregation file past us to receive communion. When Rosa's ramrod back and cast-iron hair marched by, I gently nudged Uncle Stefan. We stood up together and joined the procession.

Some half dozen priests were passing out wafers. At the altar the procession split as people quietly went to the man with the fewest communicants in front of him. Uncle Stefan and I moved behind Rosa to Archbishop O'Faolin.

The archbishop wasn't looking at people's faces. He had performed this ritual so many times that his mind was far from the benevolent superiority of his face. Rosa turned to go back to her seat. She saw me blocking her path and gave an audible gasp. It brought O'Faolin abruptly to the present. His startled gaze went from me to Uncle Stefan. The engraver grabbed my sleeve and said loudly.

'Victoria! This man helped to stab me.'

The archbishop dropped the ciborium. 'You!' he hissed. His eyes glittered. 'You're dead. So help me God, you're dead.'

A camera flashed. Cordelia Hull on the job. Murray, grinning, held up his microphone. 'Any more comments for posterity, Archbishop?'

By now the mass had come to a complete halt. One of the more level-headed young brothers had leaped to retrieve the spilled communion wafers from the floor before they were stepped on. The few remaining communicants stood gaping. Carroll was at my side.

'What is the meaning of this, Miss Warshawski? This is a church, not a gladiators' arena. Clear these newspaper people so we can finish the mass. Then I'd like to see you in my office.'

'Certainly, Prior.' My face felt red but I spoke calmly. 'I'd appreciate it if you'd bring Father Pelly along, too. And Rosa will be there.' My aunt, rooted at my side, now tried to make for the door. I held her thin wiry arm in a grasp tight enough to make her wince. 'We're going to talk, Rosa. So don't try to leave.'

O'Faolin started justifying himself to Carroll. 'She's mad, Prior. She's dug up some old man to hurl accusations at me. She thinks I tried to kill her and she's been persecuting me ever since I came out to the priory.'

'That's a lie,' Uncle Stefan piped up. 'Whether this man is an archbishop I couldn't say. But that he stole my stocks and watched a hoodlum try to kill me, that I know. Listen to him now!'

The prior held up his arms. 'Enough!' I hadn't known the gentle voice could carry so much authority. 'We're here to worship the Lord. These accusations make a mockery of the Lord's Supper. Archbishop, you will have your turn to speak. Later.'

He called the congregation to order, and gave a pithy homily on how the devil could be at our side to tempt us even at the very gates of heaven, and had everyone join in a group confession. Still holding on to Rosa, I moved away from the center of the chapel to one side. As the congregation prayed, I watched O'Faolin head toward the exit behind the altar. Pelly, standing near him, looked wretched. If he left now with O'Faolin, he made a public statement of complicity. If he stayed behind, the archbishop would never forgive him. His choices flitted across his intense, mobile face with the clarity of a stock quotation on an electronic ticker. At length, his cheeks flushed with misery, he joined his brothers in the final prayers and filed silently with them from the chapel.

As soon as Carroll was out of sight, the congregation burst into loud commentary. Above the clatter I listened for a different sound. It didn't come.

Rosa started muttering invectives at me in a loud undertone.

'Not here, Auntie dear. Save it for the prior's study.' With Stefan and Murray on my heels, I guided my aunt firmly through the gaping, chattering crowd to the hallway door. Cordelia stayed behind to get a few group photos.

Pelly was sitting with Carroll and Jablonski. Rosa started to say something when she saw him, but he shook his head and she shut up. Power in the word. If we were all still alive at the end of the session, I might try to hire him as her keeper.

As soon as we were seated, Carroll demanded to know who Murray and Uncle Stefan were. He told Murray that he could stay only on condition that none of the conversation was either recorded or reported. Murray shrugged. 'Then there isn't much point in my staying.'

Carroll was adamant. Murray acquiesced.

'I tried to get Xavier to join us but he is getting ready to go to the airport and refuses to say anything. I want an orderly explanation from the rest of you. Starting with Miss Warshawski.'

I took a deep breath. Rosa said, 'Don't listen to her, Father. She is nothing but a spite-filled –'

'You will have your turn, Mrs Vignelli.' Carroll spoke with such cold authority that Rosa surprised herself by shutting up.

'This tale has its roots some thirty-five years ago in Panama,' I told Carroll. 'At that time, Xavier O'Faolin was a priest working in the Barrio. He was a member of Corpus Christi and a man of deep ambition. Catherine Savage, a young idealistic woman with a vast fortune, joined Corpus Christi under his persuasion and turned most of her money into a trust for the use of Corpus Christi.

'She met and married Thomas Paciorek, a young doctor in the service. She spent four more years in Panama and developed a lasting interest in a seminary where Dominicans could continue the work she and O'Faolin had undertaken among the poor.'

As I got well into my story, I finally started relaxing. My voice came out without a tremor and my breathing returned to normal. I kept a wary eye on Rosa.

'Toward the end of her stint in Panama, a young man came to the Priory of San Tomás who shared her passion and her idealism. Not to spin out the obvious, it was Augustine Pelly. He, too, joined Corpus Christi. He, too, fell under Xavier O'Faolin's influence.

When O'Faolin's ambition and acuity got him a coveted promotion to Rome, Pelly followed and served as his secretary for several years – not a typical venue for a Dominican friar.

'When he rejoined his brothers, this time in Chicago, he met Mrs Vignelli, another ardent, if very angry, soul. She, too, joined Corpus Christi. It gave some meaning to an otherwise bitter life.'

Rosa made an angry gesture. 'And if it is bitter, whose fault is that?'

'We'll get to that in a moment,' I said coldly. 'The next important incident in this tale took place about three years ago when Roberto Calvi, prompted by his own internal devils, set up some Panamanian subsidiaries for the Banco Ambrosiano, using over a billion dollars in bank assets. When he died, that money had completely disappeared. We probably will never know what he meant to use it for. But we do know where much of it is now.'

As I sketched the transactions between Figueredo and O'Faolin and the effort to take over Ajax, I continued to strain for sounds in the background. I stole a look at my watch. Six o'clock. Surely . . .

'That brings me to the forgeries, Prior. That they played a role in the takeover, I feel certain. For it was to stop my investigation that O'Faolin dug up a petty hoodlum named Walter Novick. He got him to throw acid at me and to burn my apartment building down. Indeed, it was sheer luck that kept seven people from being murdered by his mania to stop my investigation into the forgeries.

'What puzzles me is Rosa's role and that played by her son, Albert. I can only think that Rosa didn't know the forgeries had been put in the safe by Corpus Christi until *after* she called me in to investigate. Suddenly, and with uncharacteristic humility, she tried to get me out of the case. She wouldn't discuss it. She mouthed pieties. Yet initially she was so fearful of an FBI frame-up that she forced me to listen to repeated insults in order to clear her blameless character.'

Rosa could contain herself no longer. 'Insults! Why should I ask you for help? What have I not suffered at the hands of that whore who called herself your mother!'

'Rosa.' This was Pelly. 'Rosa. Calm yourself. You do the Church no favor with these accusations.'

Rosa was beyond his influence. The demon that had rocked her sanity two weeks ago was too close to her now. 'I took her in. Oh, how I was betrayed. Sweet Gabriella. Beautiful Gabriella. Talented Gabriella.' Her face contorted in an angry mimicry. 'Oh, yes. The darling of the family. Do you know what your precious Gabriella did? Did she ever have the courage to tell you? Not she, filthy whore.

'She came to me. I took her in from the goodness of my heart. I was forty and my belly was swollen with child. What did I want with a baby? I hated men. Hated their foul hands touching me in the night. I, who kept myself pure and childless, destroyed by the lusts of your uncle. Carrying my shame for all the world to see.

'Did she pity me? Not she! While I worked my fingers to the bone for her, she seduced my husband. If I would divorce him, he would take my child. He would support me. Only let him live with his sweet, talented Gabriella.'

Spit was flecking her lips. We all sat, unable to think of anything that might stop the flow.

'So I threw her into the street. Who would not have? I made her promise to disappear and leave no word. Yes, she had that much shame. And what did Carl do? He shot himself. Shot himself because of a whore from the streets. Left me alone with Albert. That whore, that shameless one!'

She was screaming louder and louder, repeating herself now. I stumbled into the hallway to find a washroom. As I staggered along, catching the bile in my hands, I felt Carroll's arm around me, guiding me to a tiny dark room with a sink. I couldn't talk, couldn't think. Heaving, gasping for air, choking up images of Gabriella. Her beautiful, haunted face. How could she think my father and I would not forgive her?

Carroll wiped my face with cold towels. Gradually the terrible shuddering stopped. Leading me to a small room, he sat me on a sofa. He disappeared for a few minutes, then returned with a cup of green tea. I gulped it gratefully.

'I need to finish this conversation,' he said. 'I need to find out why Augustine did what he did. For it must have been he who put the forged certificates in the safe. Your aunt is fundamentally a pitiable creature. Can you be strong enough to keep that in mind and help me end this story as fast as possible?'

'Oh, yes.' My voice was hoarse from gagging. 'Yes.' My weariness amazed me. If I could forget this day . . . And the sooner it ended the sooner it would go away. I dragged myself up again, shook off Carroll's supportive arm. Followed him back into the study.

Pelly, Murray, and Stefan were still there. From the prior's closed inner office Rosa's screams came in a mind-shattering stream.

Uncle Stefan, pale and shaking, rushed to my side and began murmuring various soothing things at me in German. I thought I heard the word chocolate and smiled in spite of myself.

Murray said to Carroll, 'Jablonski is in there with her. He's called for an ambulance.'

'Just as well.' Carroll moved the rest of us back to the small room where he'd given me tea. Pelly could scarcely walk. His normally sunburned face was pale and his lips kept moving meaninglessly. Rosa's demented outburst had shaken the remains of his self-confidence. The story he told Carroll confirmed my analysis.

They needed money to acquire Ajax. Mrs Paciorek was supplying as much as she could, but it wasn't enough. Besides, they didn't want to get the SEC involved too early by having all the purchases come from one source.

Pelly knew about the five million in blue-chip shares in the priory safe. He wrote to O'Faolin, saying he would be glad to use them, but didn't want to arouse suspicions by their disappearing. Several months later, the forgeries arrived in the mail. Who created them he didn't know, but presumably it was done under O'Faolin's direction. Pelly substituted them for the real ones in the safe. After all, the shares hadn't been used in a decade or more. The chances were good that the Ajax purchase would long since have become history when the deception was discovered.

Unfortunately, he was out of town when the chapter voted to

sell the shares so they could build a new roof. When he returned from his annual retreat in Panama, it was to find the priory in an uproar and Rosa fired from her position as treasurer. He called Rosa and told her to dismiss me, that Corpus Christi knew all about the forgeries and would protect her.

'Xavier came to Chicago a few days later,' he muttered miserably, unable to look at either me or Carroll. 'He – he took over things at once. He was most annoyed with me for letting so much publicity escape over the forgeries, especially because he said the amount was trivial compared to what we needed. He was annoyed, too, that – that Warshawski here was still poking around in the situation. He told me he'd take over, that he would see – see that she stopped. I just assumed she was a Catholic – Warshawski, you know – that she would be persuaded by an archbishop. I didn't know about the acid. Or the arson. Not until much later, anyway.'

'The FBI investigation,' I croaked hoarsely. 'How did O'Faolin put the brakes on that?'

Pelly smiled wretchedly. 'He and Jerome Farber were good friends. And Mrs Paciorek, of course. Among them, they have a lot of influence in Chicago.'

No one spoke. Beyond the heavy silence, we could hear the sirens of Rosa's ambulance.

Carroll's face, strained and grief-stricken, rebuked any comment. 'Augustine. We'll talk later. Go to your room now and meditate. You will have to talk to the FBI. After that, I don't know.'

As Pelly wrapped himself in what dignity he could, I heard the sound I had been waiting for. A dull roar, an explosion muffled by distance and stone walls.

Murray looked at me sharply. 'What was that?'

He and Carroll got to their feet and looked uncertainly at the door. I stayed where I was. A few minutes later, a young brother, red-haired and panting, hurled himself into the room. The front of his white habit was streaked with ash.

'Prior!' he gasped. 'Prior! I'm sorry to interrupt. But you'd better come. Down at the gates. Quickly!'

Murray followed the prior from the room. A story he could use.

I didn't know what had happened to Cordelia Hull and her camera, but no doubt she was close at hand.

Uncle Stefan looked at me doubtfully. 'Should we go, Victoria?'

I shook my head. 'Not unless you have a taste for bomb sites. Someone just set off a radio bomb in O'Faolin's car.' I hoped to God he was on his own, that no brother was with him. Yes, Archbishop. No one is lucky forever.

28
THE MYTH OF IPHIGENIA

Ferrant left for England the day of the first real thaw. He had stayed long enough to install a proper vice-president of special risks at Ajax. Long enough to help me furnish my new apartment.

His check for stopping the takeover was the largest fee I'd ever collected. It easily paid for a Steinway grand to replace Gabriella's old upright. It didn't cover the cost of a co-op. But a few days after O'Faolin's death, an envelope containing twenty-five crisp thousand-dollar bills arrived in my office mail. No note, no return address. It seemed churlish to try to trace it. Anyway, I'd always wanted to own my own home. Roger helped me find a co-op on Racine near Lincoln, in a clean, quiet little building with four other units and a well-cared-for lobby.

For nearly a week after the bombing I spent most of my time in the Federal Building. Talking to the FBI, talking to the SEC. When I wasn't there, I was with Mallory. His pride was badly wounded. He wanted to assuage it by getting my license revoked, but my lawyer easily put a stop to that. What hurt Bobby the most was a letter he got from Dr Paciorek. A suicide note, really, pouring out guilt and grief over the doctor's wife and daughter. They found Catherine's body in front of the family room fire. His was in the study. Murray told me more about it than I wanted to know.

After that, I didn't have anything to do except sleep and eat and furnish the new place. I didn't like to think too much. About Rosa, or my mother, or the ugliness I'd found in myself that night with Walter Novick in the snow. Roger helped keep the thoughts at bay. At least during the day. He couldn't do much about my dreams.

After dropping him at the airport, I felt empty and lonely. And scared. Roger had kept some demons away. Now I'd have to deal with them. Maybe I'd do it someplace else, though. Take Uncle Stefan up on his offer to go to the Bahamas for a week. Or fly to Arizona and watch the Cubs go through spring training.

I sat in front of the apartment for a while, playing with the keys in the ignition. Across the street the door of a dark green Datsun opened. The car seemed familiar, with its creased fender and scratched paint. Lotty crossed the street and stood in front of the Omega, looking unlike herself, looking for once as small as a five-foot-tall person should. I climbed out of the Omega and locked the door.

'May we talk, Vic?'

I nodded without speaking and led her into the building. She didn't say anything else until we were inside my apartment. I hung her coat on a hook in the small entryway and ushered her into the living room where a comfortable chaos was already starting to build on the new furniture.

'Stefan told me Roger was leaving today. I wanted to wait for him to go before I sought you out . . . I have a lot to say to you. A lot to unsay, also. Can you – will you' – her clever, ugly face contorted in a surprising spasm. She steadied herself and started again. 'You have been the daughter I never had, V. I. As well as one of the best friends a woman could ever desire. And I abused you. I want your forgiveness. I want to – not to go back to where we were. We can't. I want to continue our friendship from here . . . Let me explain – not justify – explain . . . I've never talked about my family and the war. It's too close to the bone.

'My parents shipped my brother, Hugo, and me to London in 1938. They were to follow but never made it out of Vienna. Hugo and I spent the whole war wondering, waiting. Later we learned they had died in Buchenwald in 1941. My grandmother, all my uncles and cousins. Of that whole large happy family at Kleinsee only Hugo and I remained.

'Stefan – Stefan is a lovable rogue. If he were as hateful as your aunt, though, I would still need to protect him. He and Hugo and

759

I are all that remain of that idyllic time. When he was stabbed – I went mad, a little. I couldn't admit that he chose his fate. I couldn't admit that he had a right to do so. I blamed you. And it was very wrong of me.'

My throat was tight and the first few times I tried speaking the words came out in a whispered choke. 'Lotty. Lotty, I've been through hell and beyond this winter. I have been so alone. Do you know the torment I have been through? Agnes died because I involved her in my machinations. Dr Paciorek. Did you see what happened? He killed his wife and shot himself. And all because I chose to be narrow-minded, pigheaded, bullying my way down a road the FBI and the SEC couldn't travel.'

Lotty flinched. 'Vic. Don't torment me by throwing my angry words back at me. I've been in that hell this winter, too. But mine was worse. I created misery for my dearest friend. Stefan – Stefan told me about the scene at the priory. About Rosa and Gabriella. Oh, my dear. How much I knew you needed me, and how I tortured myself for knowing I had only myself to thank that I couldn't go to you.'

'Do you know what my middle name is, Lotty?' I burst out. 'Do you know the myth of Iphigenia? How Agamemnon sacrificed her to get a fair wind to sail for Troy? Since that terrible day at the priory, I can't stop dreaming about it. Only in my dreams it's Gabriella. She keeps laying me on the pyre and setting the torch to it and weeping for me. Oh, Lotty! Why didn't she tell me? Why did she make me give her that terrible promise? Why did she do it?'

And suddenly the grief for Gabriella, the grief for myself over-whelmed me and I started to weep. The tears of many years of silence would not stop. Lotty was at my side holding me. 'Yes, my darling, yes, cry, yes, that's right. They named you well, Victoria Iphigenia. For don't you know that in Greek legend Iphigenia is also Artemis the huntress?'

READ MORE IN PENGUIN

In every corner of the world, on every subject under the sun, Penguin represents quality and variety – the very best in publishing today.

For complete information about books available from Penguin – including Puffins, Penguin Classics and Arkana – and how to order them, write to us at the appropriate address below. Please note that for copyright reasons the selection of books varies from country to country.

In the United Kingdom: Please write to *Dept. EP, Penguin Books Ltd, Bath Road, Harmondsworth, West Drayton, Middlesex UB7 ODA*

In the United States: Please write to *Consumer Sales, Penguin USA, P.O. Box 999, Dept. 17109, Bergenfield, New Jersey 07621-0120.* VISA and MasterCard holders call 1-800-253-6476 to order Penguin titles

In Canada: Please write to *Penguin Books Canada Ltd, 10 Alcorn Avenue, Suite 300, Toronto, Ontario M4V 3B2*

In Australia: Please write to *Penguin Books Australia Ltd, P.O. Box 257, Ringwood, Victoria 3134*

In New Zealand: Please write to *Penguin Books (NZ) Ltd, Private Bag 102902, North Shore Mail Centre, Auckland 10*

In India: Please write to *Penguin Books India Pvt Ltd, 706 Eros Apartments, 56 Nehru Place, New Delhi 110 019*

In the Netherlands: Please write to *Penguin Books Netherlands bv, Postbus 3507, NL-1001 AH Amsterdam*

In Germany: Please write to *Penguin Books Deutschland GmbH, Metzlerstrasse 26, 60594 Frankfurt am Main*

In Spain: Please write to *Penguin Books S. A., Bravo Murillo 19, 1° B, 28015 Madrid*

In Italy: Please write to *Penguin Italia s.r.l., Via Felice Casati 20, I–20124 Milano*

In France: Please write to *Penguin France S. A., 17 rue Lejeune, F–31000 Toulouse*

In Japan: Please write to *Penguin Books Japan, Ishikiribashi Building, 2–5–4, Suido, Bunkyo-ku, Tokyo 112*

In South Africa: Please write to *Longman Penguin Southern Africa (Pty) Ltd, Private Bag X08, Bertsham 2013*

BY THE SAME AUTHOR

Tunnel Vision

Vic Warshawski is in a professional and financial mess. What she needs is a lucrative case. What she doesn't need are the woes of a homeless family, a love-sick teenage computer-hack – and a dead body slumped over her desk . . .

'One of Paretsky's very best . . . a story of nonstop immediacy and action, peopled with vivid and often tragically affecting characters . . . (she) remains unique among the women writing about women' – *Los Angeles Times*

Guardian Angel

Mitch Kruger, lonely, drifting, with a great gift for the drink, has taken up temporary residence with Vic's downstairs neighbour, Mr Contreras. Mitch claims that he has found the gold at the end of the rainbow and that some information he has about Diamond Head – the company that once employed him and Mr Contreras – will make him a rich man.

Then Mitch's body turns up in the morgue. He was already dead when he fell in the canal. Vic doesn't believe in coincidences . . .

also published:

Toxic Shock   **Bitter Medicine**

Bitter Medicine *read by Christine Lahti and* Guardian Angel *read by Jane Kaczmarek, are also available as Penguin Audiobooks.*

forthcoming:

V.I. for Short

In these nine irresistible, entertaining stories, Vic uses all of her skills, her judgement, her intuition – and sometimes her Smith & Wesson – to get the better of her adversaries. Like the person who will go to any lengths to see a young tennis champion keep on winning. Or the client who wants to find her sister – and her priceless cat.

'The only writer who is the natural inheritor of Damon Runyan's language plus Chandler's suspense is Paretsky' – *Independent*